Pendragon's Banner

Also by Helen Hollick

The Kingmaking – Book One of Pendragon's Banner

Pendragon's Banner

Being the second part of a trilogy

HELEN HOLLICK

St. Martin's Press ☈ New York

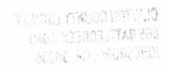

PENDRAGON'S BANNER. Copyright © 1995 by Helen Hollick.
All rights reserved. Printed in the United States of America.
No part of this book may be used or reproduced in any
manner whatsoever without written permission except in
the case of brief quotations embodied in critical articles or
reviews. For information, address St. Martin's Press, 175
Fifth Avenue, New York, N.Y. 10010.

Library of Congress Cataloging-in-Publication Data

Hollick, Helen.
   Pendragon's banner / Helen Hollick.
        p.   cm. —(Pendragon's banner ; bk. 2)
      ISBN 0-312-14699-X
      1. Arthur, King—Fiction.   2. Great Britain—
History—to 1066—Fiction.   3. Britons—Kings and
rulers—Fiction.   4. Arthurian romances—Adaptations.
I. Title.   II. Series: Hollick, Helen. Pendragon's banner ;
bk. 2.
   PR6058.O4464P46   1996
   823'.914—dc20   96-27963
                                              CIP

First published in Great Britain by William Heinemann Ltd

First U.S. Edition: December 1996

10 9 8 7 6 5 4 3 2 1

To my dearest, and most cherished Ron. My husband and friend.
I am so lucky –
I have you, you've only got me!

Acknowledgements

The research into the background facts of *Pendragon's Banner* has been interesting, rewarding – and time consuming! I am indebted to so many: the efficient and welcoming staff at Higham Hill Public Library, Walthamstow; Charles Evans-Gunther and Fred and Marilyn Stedman-Jones for their encouragement and support.

At Heinemann my sincere thanks go to Lynne Drew, my Editor, for her enthusiasm, experience and patience, and to Mic Cheetham, my agent. I don't know what I'd do without them.

Thank you to my special friends, Hazel and Derek Cope, Mal Phillips and Sharon Penman – writing is a solitary occupation, true friends are especially needed. Also, a thank you to Richard Cope for his knowledge of birds; Sue and Geoff Williams for showing me the very beautiful area of Wales near Valle Crucis Abbey; Joan Bryant, and her late husband Bill, who taught me so much about horses; and Doris Hawkins and Joan Allen, both lovely ladies – it is often the little things that help the most! To my Mum, Iris Turner and sister Margaret Clark, thank you for being there. My only regret is that my Dad is not alive to share the pleasures of success.

Finally, and most important, I thank my husband Ron and daughter Kathy. Kathy has never complained at my involvement in my work, nor minded the long journeys to visit remote sites for research. Only occasionally does she grumble that I monopolise the computer! Ron has supported me, financially and emotionally, through all these difficult years of writing. I am proud to have him as a husband, and to him I dedicate *Pendragon's Banner*, with all my love.

Britain circa AD462

Pronunciation

a basic guide to the rough pronunciation of some of the Welsh names

Amlawdd	am-low-th
Amr	am-err
Aesc	aysk
Bedwyr	bed-weir
Cei	keye
Enniuan	ay-nee-yon
Gwenhwyfar	gwen-hoo-ee-var
Gwydre	gwed-ray
Hueil	hee-aisle
Icel	ikel
Ider	ee-der
Llacheu	(h) lak-eye
Meriaun	may-ree-on
Morgaine	morg-eye-neh
Morgause	mor-guy-seh
Rhica	rhee-ka

Places

Abus	River Humber
Alclud	Dumbarton
Aquae Sulis	Bath
Bodotria	Firth of Forth
Caer Arfon	Caernarvon
Caer Cadan	Cadbury Castle, Somerset
Caer Gloui	Gloucester
Caer Luel	Carlisle
Calleva	Silchester
Cilurnum	Chesters (Hadrian's Wall)
Deva	Chester
Dalriada	Area around Dumbarton
Din Eidyn	Edinburgh
Dun Pelidr	Traprain Law
Durnovaria	Dorchester
Durovernum	Canterbury (Canti Byrig)
Eboracum	York
The Great River	River Tweed
Gwy	River Wye
Hafren	River Severn
Lindinis	Ilchester
Lindum Colonia	Lincoln
Mount of Frogs	Brent Knoll, Somerset
Pengwern	Bury Walls, Shropshire

Place of Ravens	Dinas Bran
Summer Land	Somerset
Tava	Firth of Tay
Treanta	River Trent
Trimontium	Eildon near Melrose
Venta Bulgarium	Winchester (Winifred's Castre)
Vercovicium	Houseteads Fort, Hadrian's Wall
Viroconium	Wroxeter
Winta Ingas Hem	Winteringham
Yns Witrin	Glastonbury Tor
Yr Wyddfa	Mount Snowdon

FAMILY TREE

Circa AD 462

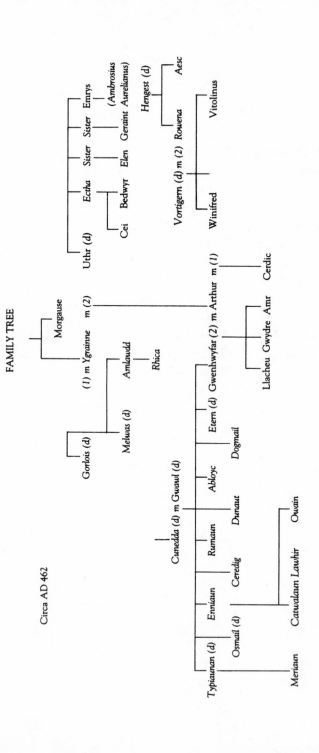

PART ONE

The Sewing

October 459

§ I

With an exhausted grunt of effort Arthur, the Pendragon, raised his sword and with a deep intake of breath, brought it down through the full force of weight and momentum into the skull of an Anglican thegn. Another battle. Arthur was four and twenty years of age, had been proclaimed Supreme King over Greater and Less Britain three years past by the army of the British – and had been fighting to keep the royal torque secure around his neck ever since.

The man crumpled, instantly dead. Arthur wrenched his blade from shattered bone and tissue with a sucking squelch, a sickening sound, one he would never grow used to. Oh, the harpers told of the glories of battle, the victory, the brave daring and skill – but they never told of the stench that assaulted your nostrils, bringing choking vomit to your throat. Nor of the screams that scalded your ears, nor the blood that clung foul and sticky and slippery to hands and fingers, or spattered face and clothing.

He turned, anxious, aware that a cavalryman was vulnerable on the ground. His stallion was somewhere to the left, a hindleg injured. The horses. Hah! No harper, no matter how skilled, could ever describe the sound of a horse screaming its death agony. There was no glory in battle, only the great relief that you were still alive when it was all over.

Sword ready to strike again, Arthur found with a jolt of surprise that there was no one before him, no one to fight. Eyebrows raised, breathless, he watched the final scenes of fighting with the dispassionate indifference of an uninvolved spectator. No more slopping and wading through these muddied, sucking water-meadows; the Angli were finished, beaten. The rebellion, this snatching of British land that was not theirs for the taking, was over.

The Anglican leader, Icel, had wanted to be more than a petty chieftain over a scatter of huddled, backwater settlements, and that

5

wanting had plunged deep – deep enough for him to unite the English warbands. Fighting against the British had been sporadic at first, skirmishes, night raids and isolated killings. Arthur had not been King, then, when Icel began making a nuisance of himself, but when the Pendragon bested Hengest the Saxon, away down to the south of Londinium, the army of Britain acclaimed him as Supreme. And Icel sent word across the sea for his kinsmen to come with the next spring, to come and fight this new-made king of the British who rode at the head of an élite cavalry force; to come and fight, for surely the victory over such a war-lord would be worth the winning! The thing had grumbled on through the roll of seasons ever since.

Those Anglicans able to run or walk or crawl were escaping, running away to die or survive within the safe, enveloping darkness of fast-coming evening. It was over, after all these long, weary months, over. Until the next uprush of the Saex-kind tried for the taking of more land, or some upstart son of a British chieftain fancied for himself the command of supreme rule.

With slow-expelled breath, the Pendragon lowered his sword and unbuckled the straps of his helmet, let them dangle free, his face stinging from the release of the tight, chaffing leather. He was tired. By the Bull of Mithras, was he tired! Arthur stabbed his sword-blade into the churned grass and sank to his knees. His fingers clasped the sword's pommel as he dropped his forehead to rest on his hands, conscious suddenly of the great weariness in his arms and legs and across his neck and shoulders. It had been a long day, a long season. He was bone tired of fighting and this stink of death. He had a wife, two sons born, another child on the way; he needed to be with them, to be establishing a secure stronghold fit for a king and his queen; to be making laws and passing judgements – raising his sons to follow after him. A king needed sons. Llacheu would reach his fourth birthday next month . . . Arthur had hardly seen his growing; the occasional few days, a passing week. He needed Gwenhwyfar, but she was to the north, more than a day's ride at Lindum Colonia, uncomfortable in her bulk of child-bearing. Love of Mithras, let it be a third son!

Movement. Arthur opened his eyes but did not lift his head. Two booted feet appeared in his lowered line of vision, the leather was scratched and spotted with the staining of blood. He would recognise those fine-made boots anywhere, the intricate patterning around the heel, the paler inlet of doe-hide. He looked up with a spreading grin of triumph into his cousin and second-in-command's face. Cei, wiping sweat and the spatter of other men's blood from his cheeks, grinned back, his teeth gleaming white behind the darkness of his stubble-bearded face. For a while and a while the two men stood, grinning at each other like inane moon-calves.

'That is it then,' Arthur said, climbing slowly to his feet and pulling his sword from the ground. It felt heavy to his hand now, now that the fighting was done. 'Happen we can think about going home to our women and families.'

Cei shrugged a non-committal answer. If God was willing they could go home soon. When the dead were buried and the wounded tended. When the submissions were concluded, hostages taken and the King's supremacy over these Saex scum endorsed. When the grumbling and muttering from the British, discontent with Arthur's objectives, were silenced. Aye, happen then, they could.

Arthur bent to wipe his blade against the tunic of a dead Anglian lying face down in the blood-puddled, muddied grass. He gazed at the man's back a moment, with his foot turned over the body. A boy, not a man, with only the faint shadow of hair wisping chin and upper lip. A boy who had listened to the harper's tales of battle and had felt his heart quicken for the excitement and honour. A boy, who knew nothing of the reality of this god-damned mess! Sons were needed to fight with their fathers. And to die alongside them. The harpers ought sing of that! Sing of the cruelty of losing a beloved son; the pain of wounds that were beyond healing. Arthur sighed. So many sons and fathers dead. So much spilt blood.

He pulled the spear that had killed the boy from the body. Said with regret, 'We ought to live together in peace, Cei. Angli, Jute and Saxon in peace aside us British. Surely there is enough land for us all to build our dwelling places, enough grass to graze our cattle?'

He bent to close the boy's staring, frightened eyes. 'Why must strength be shown by the blade of a sword? Why not through discussion and wise talk?'

A voice answered from behind, the accent guttural, the words formed in hesitant Latin. 'Because you and I were born to different ideas and beliefs, my Lord King. Differences breed mistrust and suspicions, which spread like weeds in a neglected cornfield. Fear – and greed – grows unchecked until eventually it rots into swollen lies and black untruths. Overspills onto a battlefield.'

Arthur remained squatting over the dead boy, wiped his hand across his face, fingers firm against nose, across cheeks, down to the stubble on his chin. Wiped away this seeping mood of bleak depression. He jerked upright, turning with the same movement to clap his hand to the newcomer's shoulder, announced with a smile as broad as a furrowing sow's belly, 'But you and I, Winta of the Humbrenses, you and I think different!'

The answering smile was as friendly, as astute. 'If we did not my Lord, then would I fight beneath your Dragon against English kinsmen?'

Sliding his arm full around the man's shoulders, Arthur began to steer the tall, fair-haired man towards the northern end of the battlefield, to where, beyond a clump of wind-moulded trees, the British had set their camp. To where soon, the prisoners would be herded and forced to kneel before a British king.

'Some of us,' Arthur said, walking with long strides, keeping Winta close by the grip of his hand on the man's arm, 'have found enough sight and wisdom to see beyond the differences, to learn of them with interest and intelligence. Some of us,' he patted the man's shoulder for good measure, 'are astute enough to go into the fields and hoe the weeds. We, my friend, prefer to see the gold of ripening corn.'

Arthur halted, beckoned his cousin to walk at his other side. 'Some weeds though, can be cultivated, used for good purpose. Can they not, Cei?'

Cei was scowling slightly, saying nothing. To his mind all weeds ought to be pulled up and burnt. He shrugged non-committally. He disliked – no – mistrusted Winta, a petty lord over a scattering of Saex settlements along the southern shore of the Abus river. Weeds were weeds, whatever their brilliance of flower or healing use. Angli? Jute? Ally, enemy?

Saex were Saex, whatever their given title and declared promises!

§ II

Although the water was not as warm as she would have liked, Gwenhwyfar elected to stay a while longer in the main pool of Lindum's only remaining bath-house. Enid was already out, wrapping a linen towel around her body before seeing to Llacheu. The boy was crying, standing beside the nurse, his little face scrunched up, pathetically unhappy; he wanted to stay in longer too, wanted to stay in the water with his mam. Enid though, was a no-nonsense young woman, more than capable of dealing with recalcitrant children. Briskly, efficiently, she swept a towel around the boy and scooping him under her arm, bore him away to the changing room, his protesting wail trailing in their wake.

Gwenhwyfar laughed to herself, swam a few strokes from the pool edge, then turned on her back, arms outstretched, head back, her copper-gold hair floating about her like the tresses of legendary sea-maids. She had the place to herself at this fresh hour of the morning, a trick she had learned early on in her stay in this unhospitable, dilapidated Roman town. Her belly rippled, the child within moving, the great bulge of late pregnancy standing like a whale-hump from the water; she felt like a whale too, a beached, blubber-weighted whale. Voices were approaching, the patter of bare feet on tiled flooring, laughter, the rise and fall of female gossip. One voice in particular stood out, speaking in tidy, correct Latin, with a nasal twang and a laugh like a sow's grunt. Swimming to the steps, the luxury of solitude receding, Gwenhwyfar ascended, draped rough woven linen towelling about her shoulders and marched through the approaching group of women, ignoring their sudden cessation of

9

chatter and disapproving looks, aware that one of them would make comment. 'Bathing naked in your condition, Madam, is indecent. There should be modesty at all times in a public place.' The Governor's matronly wife wore a thigh-length tunic, her hair bound tight about her head. The other women were dressed similarly, or wore breast-bands and loin cloths. The woman, a self-opinionated bore, wrinkled her nose, disgusted, at the swell of Gwenhwyfar's belly and breasts.

Several scathing retorts flooded Gwenhwyfar's mind but she swallowed them. As Queen she could do something to silence the more offensive remarks, but Arthur had expressed an explicit plea:

'I leave you in Lindum to play the part of diplomacy. Where the Queen is, they are reminded of the King. And I don't want them reminded of the wrong things.'

'I have to be civil to them then?'

'Very civil.'

'Even to the Governor's wife?'

'Especially to the Governor's wife.'

Damn the Governor's wife – and damn Arthur! It was all right for him, he had stayed but one night and then ridden off with his men, the proud cavalry of the Artoriani. Gwenhwyfar had no choice in the matter. The coming babe forced her to stay in this decaying town with its crumbling, grumbling citizens. And so today she remarked pleasantly, and with her hand on her bulge, 'Yet pregnancy is such a wondrous miracle. Should we hide the generous blessings of God?' She managed to hide a broadening smile of triumph as she pushed through the group of women and made her way to the changing rooms, where Llacheu was still fitfully wailing.

Vigorous, angrily, she towelled herself dry, rubbed her hair, shaking it, fluffing the curls with her fingers. Dressed, she suggested to Llacheu, who had ceased his crying now that she was also out of the pool, that they stop at the bath-house shop to purchase a pastry before going back to the Governor's palace. It was the last place she truly wanted to go – but then she wanted to go nowhere in this damned town. The lad crowed his delight and swarmed into her arms for an extravagant cuddle. Ah, what did those foul women matter, when she had her sons with her? And Arthur would be back soon. She hoped.

Until the tenth hour, the bath-house was for women to use, the morning was gathering stride, and more customers were entering. Most at least nodded a courteous greeting to their King's wife, a few gazed past her, but none would dare be as outwardly rude as the Governor's wife. This growing ripple of hostility towards Gwenhwyfar was permeating through Lindum as powerfully as the stench that rose from the disintegrating main sewer. Narrow-eyed glares, a refusal to meet Gwenhwyfar's eyes, men and women who crossed the roads to the far pavement rather than meet her; that she was not welcome – within the public bath-house, in this town – had been made more than plain since the day of her arrival. That Arthur was mistrusted to the point of dislike, as evident. And these as yet unspoken feelings were maturing and swelling like a water-bloated corpse.

The entrance to the baths had lost the opulence of its former glory. The colonnades were cracking, the once vivid mosaic flooring faded and with pieces, large patches in places, missing. Few people noticed. The whole town was in a like state. Houses falling down, shops empty and shuttered, weeds growing through the cracked pavements and roads. Gwenhwyfar bought Llacheu his pastry, and one for herself and Enid. They were hungry, having left their rooms in the palace before breaking their fast.

They walked obliquely across the square from the baths, Gwenhwyfar stopped, as was her habit, to admire the statue at the centre. It was bronze, life-size, of a rider sitting proud astride a prancing horse. The white marble inlaid eyes had gone, and the inscription was too faded to read – Gwenhwyfar had made enquiries, but no one knew who the rider was. A Caesar certainly, for he wore a circlet of laurel around his head and looked a noble man, very wise. Too perfectly beautiful to be real. Arthur was more rugged, with his long, straight nose, dark eyes and slight-curled hair that often looked as if it needed a comb tugged through it. The horse, though, was glorious, a well-bred animal of desert stock, its quality made obvious by the arched neck, concave face, small pricked ears and high-arched tail. Gwenhwyfar could almost imagine the horse leaping from the marble plinth and galloping off, across the square and out, under the north gate . . . ah, but she would like to gallop, escape with him! Where would they go? South, to join Arthur? Or west to the land of her birth? To Gwynedd, where the mountains would be green, cloud-wraithed and beautiful? There was nowhere of her own to go, no home, no settled Hall or stronghold. Arthur had not had the time to find a good place, to build, to establish himself. Always, there was fighting, this incessant fighting!

Llacheu wanted to pat the horse, Enid lifted him. The square was filling now, traders setting up their stalls for the day, shops opening their shutters, the smell of cooking from the inns strong in the air. People were starting their day, hurrying about their tasks, shopping, business. A group of boys swaggered past, calling loudly to each other, their slates tucked beneath their arms on their way to the school-tutor.

Gwenhwyfar sighed, indicated they must rejoin her bodyguard, who had waited patiently in the early-morning pale-fringed sunshine for their lady. She hated Lindum Colonia. And, on occasion, hated Arthur for leaving her here. She reached up to touch the bronze muzzle of the horse, and caught her breath as something whistled past her ear, struck the statue with a resounding thwack and fell to the ground. She moved away, without fuss indicated her men ought to draw nearer. With dignity she left the square and made her way back to the safe confines of the palace.

Enid knew there was something wrong, but then Enid knew her mistress well, and had also heard the thrown stone, had seen it fall and settle there on the worn paving.

§ III

'Council will not like it.'

'I do not ask for, nor want, Council's opinion.'

Cei sighed; three years as King, and already Arthur and his Council were squabbling like dogs after the same bone.

12

'There are those,' Cei tried again, 'who say that to spend more than a week discussing treaties of alliance with a defeated enemy is not good judgement.'

Arthur, mending a broken bridle strap, made no answering comment. The hail that had sputtered on and off all day drummed a tattoo on the roofing of the leather tent and bounced like tossed pebbles on the worn, hollowed patch of mud-packed turf by the open entrance flap.

Watching the pea-sized balls of ice a moment, Cei stared, fascinated as the ground turned white – then the sudden-come storm ceased. The wind whipped up the dark clouds and sent them scurrying from a dazzling blue sky. Beyond the tent, everything dripped and gleamed, the white ice melted into fairy-sized diamond-drops. 'For Hengest,' Cei continued as if he had not ceased talking, 'Council could see reason behind the giving of territory. Wrong or right, he had been originally invited here to fight on our side by Vortigern – God rot his mouldering soul.'

'I did not give,' Arthur interrupted. 'I rent Hengest those Cantii lands, rent for a large payment of taxation. He rules under my gaze and is ultimately answerable to me. As Icel shall be, when he edges around to seeing reason.'

'Pah!' Cei swarmed to his feet, toppling his stool backward. 'Reason? It is already reasonable that he still has his head and balls, it is already reasonable that those who follow him are alive, not dangling at the end of ropes!'

Quietly, Arthur finished the mending of the strap, fixed it back to the bridle. 'So I have Icel executed? And then one day, one day very soon, these Anglian settlers will find for themselves another cock-proud young princeling to follow and we will then need to fight them.' He stood, hung the bridle on a nail jutting from the tent pole, faced his cousin and second-in-command with outspread hands. 'I have shadow-chased this Anglian leader from the Treanta river to the coast, from the Fosse Way down to the forests. If I grant a legitimate holding of land then Icel is beholden to me. And whenever a new cub decides he wants more than a ploughed field to crow over, he will first have to square that wanting with Icel, not with me.'

Pouting, Cei answered with, 'Too much is being given to these damn Saex. The Council of Britain do not like it.' His thoughts added *Neither do I*.

Arthur grinned, irritatingly friendly, knowing full well those unspoken thoughts. 'Ah, but then I am the King; a king is expected to do things that are not liked.' His grin broadened. 'A prerequisite of the position. The ability to annoy.'

Cei grunted. 'Oh aye, you have a talent for rubbing people the wrong way. Always have done, even as a child.'

Arthur laughed to hide the bitter memory of his unpleasant childhood. The difference between being a boy and a man was acute. As a child, thought to be the bastard brat of a serving girl, Arthur had nothing to call his own save a battered gold ring, a dream and a hope of better things to come. Ill-treated, shunned and tormented by all adults except the man who later proved to be his true father, childhood had been miserable and corrupted by fear. He accepted, now that he was grown, that Uthr Pendragon had to keep his only son hidden from Vortigern's ugly malice. Accepted that, but not the cruelties his real mother had deliberately turned her eyes from. Cei's idle comment hurt. He had tried to please, tried to do right, but still received cuffs and kicks, was still called bastard. Well, it was his turn now to do the kicking, and if men called him a bastard, it was for the other meaning of the word.

He poured wine for himself and Cei, said nothing more of the subject. Cei had always been the jealous one. Understandably. The one thing that had made life tolerable for Arthur as a child was the interest Uthr had shown in him – he had not known why, then. Why Uthr himself taught a bastard-born to use shield and spear and sword. Why Uthr himself had taught a supposed serving girl's brat how to ride a horse and plan for battle. Why Uthr had loved a fatherless whore's cub above the older boy, Cei, his brother's son. He handed the goblet to his cousin. 'I intend to squeeze everything I can from Icel. Gold, leather, grain. Hostages. He will find submission hard.'

Righting the stool, Cei seated himself again. 'What if he does not agree to your demands, eh? He might not.'

Arthur sat also, pushing his booted feet nearer the fluctuating warmth of the brazier. Two nights until Samhain, the night the dead walked. He would rather be tucked within the warmth of Gwenhwyfar's bed at Lindum by then. Icel was a proud man, would welcome death; even the threat of the living death of blinding and male mutilation would not daunt him. There would have to be something more, some promise of what Arthur would do if the Anglian did not offer total submission. The Pendragon had once made such a thing clear to Hengest, and then not so long since, to Winta of the Humbrenses. *'Your people and your family shall pay for defeat. The men will lose their hands and eyes, the women and children will be taken into slavery, used as whores. Until natural death releases them, they will face great misery and suffering. Your settlements will be burnt, and your cattle slaughtered. Not you. You will be taken to a fortress far away. You will be guarded, but you will have light and warmth and the best food; a comfortable bed, even a woman to share that bed with. On fine days you will be allowed to ride and hunt, you will be treated as an honoured guest with no privilege spared, save that of your freedom to leave. And while you live in this luxury, you can think of your wife and your children. Of their distress and pain'.*

Winta had seen the sense in not trying his luck against this British lord who meant every word he said, for Winta was not full of greed and wanting as Hengest had been, and was older and wiser than the young cox-comb Icel. He valued too highly all that could be lost were victory not to come his way, and so had not even tried for the winning of it. By joining with the Pendragon his reward had proved great and welcome. Winta was already a wealthy man, and by uniting with the British, trade that was already flourishing, would increase – double, treble. Soon he would be able to extend his held land, amicably, with Arthur's consent and permission, for Winta was wily enough to realise that there was more than one way to obtain a title of king.

Arthur's servant came to light the lamps. Soon it would be time for the officers to gather again around the fire, laid in the space beyond this tent, between the sacred place where the standards of the Turmae and the Pendragon's own banner stood. Time to have

Icel brought before them, and watch his eyes as the King declared his final word.

Arthur leant sidewards and reached for the wine, refilled his goblet, passed the jug across to Cei. 'Icel's wife and children?' he asked, although he knew the answer.

'Are held two mile from here.'

'Have them fetched up after dark has fallen. Bring them in, bound and chained.'

Cei scowled displeasure. 'The youngest is a girl child of four summers. Even her?'

The Pendragon sipped his wine. Four summers, the age of his own son. He shrugged. War was a bloody, distasteful business. 'Especially her.' He regarded Cei with the expression that was a part of Arthur as much as his long nose and golden torque – one eyebrow raised, the other eye half closed; a look of warning. He would be obeyed. ' 'Tis you who says I must obtain results. I cannot afford to be squeamish, Cei. Have men who are not of the Christian faith bring them, who will not balk should I need to order Icel's family stripped and passed around the tents this night.' He raised one finger, stopped the comment rising on Cei's lips. 'And again, aye, the youngest as well. Icel must bow to me. Or pay the price.'

November 459

§ IV

Removing her foot from the cradle's rocker, Gwenhwyfar laid aside her distaff, mindful of the unspun wool. It was cheap, coarse stuff, full of snags; of little use for weaving anything of quality – it would suffice for the coming baby. Beyond the unshuttered windows daylight was fading into a murky evening. Night seemed to fall slowly here above the fenlands, descending ponderous like a flock of uncertain wild geese, circling and circling those vast, empty skies before finally plucking courage to land. She sighed, long and slow, and walked to the window, easing the ache in her back. A boring, dull, landscape spreading beyond the enclosing walls of Lindum. Empty marshland, empty sky. Empty houses and empty-minded people.

She pulled her shawl tighter around her shoulders. Arthur had been gone so long! Moving back to the cradle where her second son slept, she wrapped her arms around herself and rocked it absently with her foot. Gwydre was getting too big for a cradle, would need to move to a bed when the new babe came. Glancing again out of the window, she watched a heron flap lazily against the backdrop of blue-grey, rain-spattered sky. The year before, and for years before that, she had accompanied the Artoriani, making herself useful among the wounded, for wherever there was fighting there would always be the wounded. This year she was here in this town, an unwilling and unwelcome guest.

Lindum Colonia stood, a defiant bastion of Roman culture, caught between the people of the Humbrenses to the north, and persistent harassing from the Anglians of the south-east. There had been sporadic fighting between British and Saxon in and around this marshy corner of Britain for years – even before Rome had pulled out her Legions to fight her own death struggle. Skirmishes and ambushes, farmsteadings and villas looted and burnt, men

19

slaughtered, women and children taken as slaves. Atrocities committed and suffered on both sides.

Arthur had been forced to prove himself against these Saex – aye, and the British – that he was, and would remain, supreme. Prove that he was a worthwhile king. Gwenhwyfar stayed with her husband until the sickness and discomfort of this pregnancy became over-much to bear, then, reluctant, Arthur had brought her away from his army to leave her here in Lindum.

From her second-floor window she could see two of the narrow, cobbled streets, and a small part of an intersecting third. Dark, gloomy places at the best of times, sinister at the moment, with the onset of this half-light of evening. There were people down there, angry people, milling around the palace walls, filling those dark, narrow streets with their ugly shouting and malicious presence. A mob hammering on the gates, demanding their grievance be heard. Where in the Bull's name was Arthur!

It was against him they jeered, cursing his name and yelling disgusting ways to bring about his end. The mistrust of the previous uneasy days had overspilled into rage and derision, fuelled by fear. For rumours had come, brought by traders from the south, mischief-makers. There had been a battle they said, a great battle, for they had seen the churned battlefield and the mounds of the dead. They knew nothing more, save that Icel was returning to his home-steading, gloating that he now had land to call his own. And what of Arthur, Lindum asked. Where was he? Why had no official word come to confirm or deny the tale? There could only be one reason why; a reason Gwenhwyfar would not, could not contemplate.

She thought back to the day Arthur had departed, that sun-bright August morning, through the north gate, escorted by his personal guard with their padded tunics white-brilliant beneath their scarlet-red, woollen cloaks. A bustling eastern sea-wind had spilled through the gaping mouth of the tubular, red and gold Dragon, causing it to leap and writhe as if it were alive. Gwenhwyfar had watched them leave from the defence wall walkway, watched as her husband rode away, weeks ago, to fight. She sighed. Ah, but it seemed years!

Word had come ten days past that Icel had summoned his men together, and the two armies had met. Ten days, with no more word, save rumours fanning like wind-whipped fire across dry grass, and the mood in Lindum growing as ugly as those rumours. Arthur had lost, they said, the Pendragon had failed to turn Icel's army. Yet there had come no confirmation of British failure and death. Where in all the gods' names was he? Gwenhwyfar again eased the incredible ache in her back, bending her spine to stretch the discomfort. The babe had his legs pressed there, so Enid told her. What did she know about the birthing of babes? She was a child's nursemaid, and a maiden still!

The two boys, Gwenhwyfar had carried easily – disregarding those first few weeks of intermittent nausea, but with this pregnancy, the sickness had barely stopped. She felt dizzy, her hands and feet were puffed and swollen – she wanted another son, but, by the Goddess of Wisdom, not this constant illness.

A while since, the shouting of the mob had grown louder, turned to a hideous belling, a keening for the blood of death. It was becoming quite dark now. Walking from lamp to lamp, Gwenhwyfar lit the wicks, lit too, the beeswax candles. She would have light in her room for light chased away the threatening shadows of fear, and tonight was Samhain, the night when the dead returned. She had no reason to fear the dead, her brother, her father, they would be welcome visitors, but if Arthur were indeed slain by Icel . . . !

She closed the woodworm-riddled shutters, hiding the night and muffling the noise of the angry town. Her hand flew to her throat as beyond the door a man's heavy tread approached, iron-trimmed boots scraping on the flagstones, stopping outside. It was not unexpected. They had come for her. She took Gwydre up from his sleep, stood facing the door, a hundred thoughts whirling. What of her sons? Would the hate and the fear that Lindum showed for Arthur's policy of ceding territory to the Saex spill over to her sons? Would the resentment lead to the killing of the Pendragon's children also? She held the boy over her shoulder, her free hand drawing her dagger. Had they slaughtered Llacheu already? Mithras, knowing this rising mood, she ought to have had his supper sent up here, not let him go to the kitchens. She had not thought! Had assumed the crowd would be contained beyond the palace walls, assumed the Governor would not give in to their demands, that she was safe . . .

The latch began to move upward. Gwenhwyfar took firmer hold of the dagger – kill her they might, but not without their own shed blood! The door opened, creaking on its rusting hinges. A man, stubble-bearded face smeared with dust, clothes grimed and muddied, entered the room, his sword coming into his hand as he stepped across the threshold.

§ V

Her head swam. Gwenhwyfar stumbled to her knees, catching her son tighter to her shoulder, struggling for breath. Someone took the child, who wailed loud protest, then arms were around her, strong, protective arms clad in what had once been a white tunic, his red cloak flung back.

'Cymraes?' Arthur stroked her hair with agitated concern, cradled his wife to him. 'What is wrong? Does the birthing come?'

Laughing, crying, both at once, Gwenhwyfar shook her head and clung to her husband. She wiped aside scudding tears, looked up with a smile into his anxious dark eyes, laughed at her own foolishness. 'I thought they had come to kill me!'

Arthur grinned astonished amusement. He brought Gwenhwyfar to her feet, set her on the couch and passed Gwydre, wailing louder, back to her. 'When you so often defy me to go your own sweet way, then aye, I feel like wringing your pretty neck.' His fingers moved around her throat, lightly touching the soft, unblemished skin. He bent to kiss the throbbing pulse. 'But having ridden hard for several hours in a bitter wind, absent all these weeks bringing Icel firm to the leash, then na, I can think of no reason to do away with you.' He held her close a long while, savouring her warmth and the scent of woman and baby, easing her violent trembling. Unusual for Gwenhwyfar to take such fright, but understandable, given her condition.

A discreet knocking at the door was followed by the raucous bellow of an annoyed child. Llacheu burst in with Enid trotting behind, apologising profusely for the intrusion. The boy ran to his father, arms outstretched. Releasing his wife, Arthur turned to scoop his son into his arms, Llacheu instantly hurling questions like shot arrows. 'Have you been in battle? Did you kill many Saex? Tell me, Da!'

Arthur held the lad high, at arm's length. 'Is this my son? Na, this lad is too tall!'

'I am, Da, I am!'

'Na. Llacheu was knee-high to a hound when I last saw him. You are almost a man grown!'

The boy swelled with pride at his father's attention and teasing. 'Mam's teached me to sword fight!'

Bending over the cradle to resettle Gwydre, Gwenhwyfar corrected, ' "Teaching", lad. I have been teaching you to sword fight.'

The excited boy ignored her. 'Shall I show you, Da?' He squirmed out of his arms and ran to fetch his little wooden sword.

Laughing, Arthur strolled across the room and retrieved his own sword and scabbard that he had dropped in his haste to run to Gwenhwyfar's aid. He placed it on a table and seated himself on the couch. Stretching his aching thighs and back he watched his son busy burrowing among the childhood clutter sprawled over the floor. From beneath a bundle of wool, Llacheu pulled out his toy, sending his mother's distaff clattering across the floor.

'Oh Llacheu!' she scolded. 'Look what you have done!' Gwydre was passed to Enid as Gwenhwyfar strode acros the room to retrieve her spoilt wool, to pick with dismay at the knots and tangles. 'It took me ages to work that!' she wailed.

Arthur ruffled the boy's hair. 'Were you aware that your mam is more at ease sword fighting than spinning?'

With wide, innocent eyes the lad answered, 'The Governor's wife said a lady need not know how to use a man's sword. Mam laughed at her and said even a gutter whore knows how to use such a delight to her advantage.' As he innocently repeated the adult conversation, the boy gave a few ineffectual swipes with his toy. He looked up at his grinning father, said seriously, 'I am not sure what Mam meant, but I liked it because it annoyed the horrid woman.'

Gwenhwyfar's cheeks had reddened at her son's repetition of her play on words – lewd words which she had assumed he would not overhear, let alone remember! Arthur roared his delight, briefly hugging his son to him as he winked at her. 'You'll discover what your mam meant when you are a man grown and in full use of your own weapon!'

Llacheu parried and thrust with the wooden toy. 'Will I have a sword as wondrous as yours one day, Da?'

Arthur laughed the louder; Gwenhwyfar, attempting with not much success to keep her stern composure, stepped forward and took the toy from her son, chastising her husband with her eyes to remain quiet. 'If you mean Caliburn,' she said to Llacheu, 'I expect that particular sword will be yours when your da has no further need of it.' She caught Arthur's eye, burst into laughter herself. Neither had need to make verbal reference to the other meaning, but the mutual thought of pleasurable love-making after these months apart sped swift and unspoken between husband and wife.

Gwydre, disturbed so roughly from his sleep, was still sobbing. Gwenhwyfar asked Enid to take him to his wet-nurse for feeding, and then to see about Llacheu's bed-time. With their going, the chamber fell into hushed quiet. Gwenhwyfar began to tidy Llacheu's scattered toys, a sewn ball, a carved boat, told as she worked of the unsettled alarm within the city. 'How did you fare, riding in? The shouting seemed most hostile.'

Arthur stood and encircled her bulk with his arms, kissed her with a passion that revealed how he had missed her. 'Everything is settled,' he said. 'The Governor of Lindum is a prize ass. He could no more stem malicious rumours than he could return Britain to Roman rule.' He drew away, eyed her bulge and patted the swelling with pride, then seating himself, began to tug off his left boot.

24

Gwenhwyfar kicked a scatter of wooden building bricks beneath the couch, and as an afterthought kicked the spoilt wool to join them. She squatted, pulled at Arthur's other boot. 'The resentment against you here frightens me.'

Arthur scratched at the itch of his beard. He needed to shave. 'Would that statement have any connection with the dagger that greeted my return?'

She tried to make light of the thing, waved her hands casually and shrugged. Retrieving the boot Arthur had tossed aside, she stood it with its pair to the side of the couch. 'I finally told a few plain truths this afternoon, that is all. The Governor's wife did not much like the hearing of them.'

'For that, you think murder at the opening of a door!' Arthur lay back, rested his hands behind his head and closed his eyes. It was good to be in the warm and dry. Good to feel a couch beneath your backside. He snorted at a passing thought, why did horsehair not feel as comfortable when it was still on the horse?

Gwenhwyfar had made no answer. He opened one eye and saw her squatting still on the floor. He reached a hand forward, stroked the smoothness of her cheek.

'Has it been that bad for you here, Cymraes?'

She took his hand in her own, held it against her skin, her own eyes closing against threatening tears. It had been that bad.

'Ah, beloved.' Arthur leant forward, placed a kiss on her forehead. 'It took longer than I thought, Icel is a strong and determined man.' He again lay back. 'It took a time to convince him I am the stronger, and more determined.'

Gwenhwyfar picked up her fallen distaff, regarded the spoilt wool a moment before ripping it from the wooden haft. She poked it with the rest beneath the couch, said, 'You have ceded him territory. As you did with Hengest?'

'Aye. And for the same valid reasons.'

She flared. 'Valid reasons? Valid reasons! You spend all these months fighting Icel, losing men, good men, to his spears, and then after gaining the victory you calmly give him the land he's been after!' She was walking about the room, hands animated, the distaff waving as she moved. 'Valid reason or no, Arthur, it makes no sense to me, nor,' she pointed the distaff in the direction of the window, 'nor to the people out there. They too are frightened, and fear breeds anger.'

Arthur was watching her from where he lay. How often had he listened to the same conversation? With Cei, with his officers. Not half an hour past with Lindum's Governor.

'I give, Cymraes. There is a difference between giving to a man to rule over as your subject, and him taking it by force to rule as his own lord. I give on my terms. Not theirs. Mine.'

'Huh.'

'There's no "huh" about it.' He swung his legs to the floor, leant forward, one arm leaning across his thigh. 'They will come anyway, the Saex. Far better for the inevitable outcome to be on my saying.'

For a moment she remained silent, letting the sudden eddy of anger flow from her. Calmer, for she knew him to be right, she said as he resettled himself to lie back on the couch, 'I think there are those in this town who plan to kill you. I thought they were to make their start on the boys and myself.' She wiped aside an unexpected tear. 'Foolish of me, but . . .'

Arthur tugged his fingers through the tangle of his collar-length dark-brown hair, scratched at an itch to the nape of his neck. A haircut would not fall amiss. 'Not so foolish. Half the country have such plans to make an end of me.'

'You know?'

Eyes shut, 'Of course I know.'

Gwenhwyfar still had the distaff in her hand. She lunged at Arthur, thwacked his shoulder with it.

'Ow!' He opened his eyes, sat up. 'What was that for!'

'For taking over-many risks with your life, my life and the life of our sons!' She hit him again, harder. He laughed, grabbed at her weapon and holding it tight, pulled her closer.

'You were safe enough.' He gave a sudden tug at the distaff, toppling her off balance. 'They have not yet plucked enough courage to defy their King, or his wife.'

Gwenhwyfar fell across him, swiped him with her hand.

'However,' he glanced about the room, 'I cannot say the same for myself, cannot guarantee your safety now.' He kissed her, his tongue probing her mouth, hands fumbling for the pins holding her shift.

Attempting to squirm from his embrace, Gwenhwyfar brushed her free hand over her huge figure. She wanted him so much, so very much, but said, 'We cannot, not with this babe.' Diverting the subject she asked, 'Have you eaten? We dined some hours since but I suspect I can fetch something . . .'

Keeping firm hold of her, Arthur pulled her closer and nibbled her earlobe. 'Not for weeks.'

She smiled. 'I meant food, you fool! Have you eaten food?'

He narrowed his eyes, an idiotic grin smirking his expression. 'A banquet of flesh will suffice.'

Ignoring his expressive leer, Gwenhwyfar began to unfasten the lacings of his riding gear, her nose wrinkling with distaste at the smell of stale sweat. 'You stink more of horse than the horse does!'

'That is unquenched desire that you smell!'

'I cannot cleanse you with this babe so large inside me.'

'Not so,' Arthur muttered, fondling her enlarged breasts. He chuckled as he thought of his son's innocent repetition of Gwenhwyfar's words. 'There are other ways of using a sword aside from thrusting straight in with the point.' They laughed together, Gwenhwyfar's arms coiling around Arthur as he kissed her again. She had a passing thought as he stripped away the last garment of her clothing and began gently caressing her swollen body; they ought to bolt the door. But then, who would be fool enough to disturb the King and his wife after they had been so long apart?

§ VI

The lamps in the bed chamber were burning low, several had gutted out. Gwenhwyfar lay asleep, her head on Arthur's chest, her copper-gold hair, spread in a tangle over her face and his

27

shoulder. She twitched occasionally as some dream infringed on sleep. Once, she murmured something.

Arthur was awake, unable to sleep. He moved his arm, released a long sigh, puffing his cheeks with expelled air. The victory was his, Icel was undeniably beaten. But there would always be another Icel somewhere, other aspiring young men who would make a try for something more. At least there would be no more fighting in this flat, inhospitably windy part of Britain, not for a long while.

He watched Gwenhwyfar breathing. Watched the steady rise and fall of her pregnancy-swollen breasts and the relaxed peace on her face. She was one and twenty, and he had loved her – known her – for the past nine years. With his finger he dabbed at the tip of her nose. She twitched, dreamily batted away the irritation with a limp hand.

'Gwenhwyfar. I need to talk.'

'Mm? Not now.' She shifted position. Slept.

'Gwen.'

'In . . .' yawn, '. . . the morning.'

'It cannot wait till morning, Cymraes.'

Gwenhwyfar groaned, opened her eyes. She wriggled from his arms and rolled out of the bed. 'You toad. Was it necessary to wake me?'

Padding across the semi-darkened room, she squatted over the chamber pot. 'It's not so much this bulk I have to carry, nor the pummelling against my ribs and spine as he stretches and kicks inside that makes me so loathe pregnancy,' she shivered and scuttled back to the warmth of bed, 'but this damn need to pee so frequently!'

'Gwenhwyfar?'

She had been settling down to sleep again, opened her eyes suspicious. 'I like it not when you say "Gwenhwyfar" like that.'

Arthur toyed with a strand of her hair. 'I have an offer of permanent alliance that I cannot refuse.'

She regarded him steadily. His fringe, falling away from a natural side parting, flopped forward over his eye. Gwenhwyfar brushed it back, slid her hand around his neck. The slight curl to his hair was the more noticeable here at the back where the length, when he was dressed, rested against his tunic neck-band.

28

There were the beginnings of shadowed lines to the corners of his eyes, light, like a little bird's delicate track. His face was thin, the cheek-bones quite prominent aside his chin and long, straight nose. He looked tired.

In those dark eyes Gwenhwyfar saw uncertainty and doubt. Arthur excelled at keeping his thoughts close, his features passive and unreadable. To Gwenhwyfar alone he occasionally dropped the guarded mask; trusting her enough to allow the show of reality.

He was four and twenty and he carried a weight of worries and problems that would have cowed a man twice his age.

'Have you slept?' she asked.

He shook his head.

Gwenhwyfar hesitated, thinking. She knew she was not going to like this offer, whatever it was. She ought to say something encouraging but this was like picking at the end of a loose thread. You knew that to pull at it would unravel more and more of the weave, that it ought to be left alone or sewed secure, but the irresistible urge was there, your fingers just had to pick at it.

She said lightly, 'Who from?'

Arthur pulled a strand of her hair through his fingers, watched its subtle change of colour in the feeble light.

'An English rival to Icel. He has a flourishing settlement along the Humbrenses river.' He scratched at his nose. 'He joined battle with me, has made offer to secure a lasting alliance.'

Gwenhwyfar shifted weight from her elbow, lay down on her back. 'This leader of Saxons, is he a man of importance?' There, another few hand-spans of thread unravelled.

'English, these are English people, Gwen.'

Gwenhwyfar shrugged, unimpressed. 'Saex, Angli, English, whatever. They are all foreigners and murdering sea-raiders.'

'Na, Cymraes,' Arthur plumped the pillow behind him, settled his back into it. 'Not all of them, and aye, Winta is important. He wants lasting peace between us.'

The thread was unravelling faster, the weave disappearing before her eyes. Gwenhwyfar ought to leave this conversation, go back to sleep, but the thread slid so easily between her fingers. 'What!

29

Peace? Is the Pendragon turning complaisant now that he has the royal torque for a while longer, safe around his throat?' Words spoken behind a weight of scorn.

Arthur sat forward hugging his knees, hurting. 'I have enough of that kind of talk from Cei and my uncle Emrys.'

'Happen because Cei and Emrys and I have reason to talk so.' It was unreasonable for her to say that, but at this early hour of the morning and with great need to sleep, she was not feeling at all reasonable.

For answer, he slammed the mattress with his fist, spoke through clenched teeth. 'Why is it that people moan and wail and protest when I say we must fight – yet when I offer a sure way of avoiding the fighting, those same people complain I am becoming simple-minded! Can I not please anyone?'

The weave was completely unthreaded now. Gwenhwyfar sat up, moved a little away from him, her body straight, expression glaring. 'You intend to set Winta as another Saex, client king.' She spread her hands before her, emphatic and angry. 'You gave Hengest the Cantii territory, and now Icel has his own portion of land instead of losing his head. Arthur, no more! The Council out there,' she flagged a hand in the direction of the closed door, 'your Governors and Elders are plotting to be rid of you because you are systematically parcelling out this country into barbarian rule. You have been King almost three years, and now seem determined to give your kingdom away. Our son's inheritance? Hah, there'll be nothing left!'

Arthur grasped her waving arms, fingers digging into her flesh. His straight brows descended into a deep frown. 'I thought I would be able to talk to you about this! Thought you, at least, would understand what I am trying to do!' Disgusted, he threw her from him and swung his legs off the bed. He sat a while breathing heavily, the surge of anger thumping in his chest.

Bringing his fingers over his eyes, and slowly down his cheeks, Arthur let his caught breath ease. With his face cupped between his hands said, 'I fought to win supreme command and I intend to keep it. But I cannot hold these desolate coastal lands, Gwenhwyfar. For all my fine, brave Artoriani, I cannot. I have not the men or the finance. Where do I find men constantly to patrol the run of rivers and the miles of sea-shore? Where do I, at the same moment, find other men to fight? Hengest, Icel, Winta – the many, many others of their kind – can call on ships to cross the sea to come and join them. Keel after keel of prime, young fighting men. What have I got? A few Turmae of loyal men, a handful of scattered militia who mostly do not know a pitchfork from a spear blade, and a pig-brained Council who harp on how it was in the old days of Rome!' His shoulders slumped, head drooped. He laced his fingers, swivelled the heavy dragon-shaped ring on his left index finger. 'Some of these English, men like Icel, are arrogant bastards who respect no word outside that of a war-cry. A few, a very few, are like Winta, older and wiser men who can see the sense in avoiding the spilling of men's blood – British or English – if the opportunity is given.'

He brought one leg over the other, rested an elbow on his knee, spoke with a mixture of resignation and anger. 'Bogs and quagmires trap my horses. Mud clings, tires, dispirits even the stoutest heart. I came over close to losing to Icel.' He looked at her, held her eyes with his own. 'Another few weeks, Cymraes, and we would have been finished. I won because Fortuna smiled on me and Mithras, the soldiers' god, took pity. I do not favour courting their combined benevolence again.' Was he getting through to her? Surely she understood? Surely! 'Without amicable agreement, Winta will fight for what he wants, as did the others. Must I, then, fight him next? For what? A marsh running aside a muddy river that only he wants and that he will take in the end anyway?'

Gwenhwyfar tossed her head. 'That is fine, brave war-lord talk!'

'It's sensible talk.'

'Huh!' Gwenhwyfar folded her arms, glowering.

'It makes sense to make agreement without bloodshed.'

'Give in to him, you mean!'

'No!' Arthur hurled himself from the bed, took a few quick paces, his fists clenching and unclenching. 'I am not giving in! I am settling the inevitable on my terms. In a year, two, three, it could well be on his.' He stabbed a finger at her, emphatic. 'And that advantage, woman, I do not intend to give him!' Briefly closing his eyes, Arthur ran a hand through his hair, rumpling it even further. Softer-toned added, 'By giving Winta the right to rule over his people in my name, I get what I want.'

Gwenhwyfar's answer was still laced with sarcasm. 'What is that? You need the loyalty of your Council and Governors; you also need the blessing of our Christian church. Can some Saex barbarian give you that?' She was shouting, kneeling up on the bed, her fists clenched.

Arthur shouted back at her. 'I must keep control of my kingdom! By treating with Winta, I ensure the crossing over the Abus river and the road up into Eboracum remains open to me. With the gold and silver I receive from Winta, I can pay my men. The cattle, sheep and swine that he will give to me will feed my men. For the privilege of being Lord under me, Winta will give cloth and weapons to clothe and arm my men! Damn it,' Arthur's nostrils flared, 'he will even give me the *men*, should I demand them!' He stepped towards Gwenhwyfar, stood over the bed, his arms resting to either side of her rigid body. He dropped the exclamation from his voice. 'This will be the third wolf I invite near the fold – but the fold has strong walls and a solid gate. Fighting cannot be the only way. I have not yet enough loyal men behind me to fight for peace between English and British. Fighting takes time and men's lives. Negotiation takes courage and wisdom.' He chewed his lip; how to explain further? 'I am clinging to this title of king by a thread. I do not have the power of men and gold behind to let me snap my fingers in defiance at those who oppose me. Do you not see?' He searched her expression, let her go, sat on the edge of the bed with his back to her. 'Na, you do not. To keep my kingdom, Cymraes, I am going to have to, one day, fight our own British men. I need to know my back will not be exposed to the danger of the English.'

His shoulders slumped, his chin tucked into his chest. 'All right? What do I do then? Tell me.'

As swiftly as it had risen, Gwenhwyfar's anger passed. What he said was true. They had not the men to justify fighting over land that few, save peasant folk and Saex, wanted. From behind, she slid her arms around him, snuggled as close as her bulk would permit. He was usually so sure, so firm-footed. Why the uncertainty this night? He obviously needed to discuss his worries; why had she let him down with her petty bickering? She laid her head on his back. A jagged scar, white against pink skin, snaked from his right shoulder to his spine. Her eyes closed. What she really wanted was to go back to sleep. She said, 'I love you. I have more reason than any to wish for peace.' She let out a slow breath. 'But Arthur, you could never settle for a life without battle, without a sword in your hand and the sound of war in your ears. The Morrigan, the Goddess of War, holds you too fast to her breast. It is my fear that I shall lose you to her one day.'

He sat silent.

'I scorn your talk of peace,' she continued, 'because always will there be a battle, somewhere, to be fought.'

He shuffled round on his buttocks and tipped her face up to his with one finger. Mithras, how he loved this woman! 'The Morrigan may send her ravens flapping about my head, but by her triple guise of beauty, hag, or carrion bird, my heart beats glad that I have you as wife.' Arthur brushed her cheek with his thumb, a tinge of self-consciousness touching his beard-shadowed cheeks. It was not often he found the courage to speak these deep-held feelings of love.

'I need allies, and peace among the English. I need to show Winta, and through him other Saex settlers, that we can live as friends, that we can each achieve what we desire without the need to kill. Winta is a good man and, I believe, a trustworthy one.' Taking her hand, his eyes implored her to back his reasoning as he admitted the last truth. 'He intends, eventually, to call himself King of the Lindissi, the people of Lindum.'

Her finger, that had sensuously been stroking his back, stilled. 'Lindum will not much like that.'

Arthur slid a sarcastic smile across his face. 'Is there anything the people of Lindum do like?' He turned to her, serious again, his hands going around her broad figure. 'Ah Gwen, so many are against me. They see no further than the end of their noses.' He chuckled, touched his finger to the side of his own nose that was a little over-large and prominent, though not out of proportion to the firmness of his other features. 'Mine is large enough, but I can see past it! I am doing right.' The burst of enthusiasm faltered. He lay back across the bed, eyes closed. 'I think I do right.'

For a moment, they were silent. Gwenhwyfar settled herself under the bed-fur, huddling into the slight warmth that remained where she had lain before. 'What of Lindum?' she asked companionably, the anger quite gone. She cared nothing for the future of this withered town, in fact, took a delight in what would be greeted with horror by these arrogant, obnoxious people.

'Trade will prosper and inter-marriages will become commonplace. It is already happening where the Saex have been settled for many years. What was British is becoming English.'

'And that does not bother you?'

Arthur climbed into bed, wriggled down under the furs as his wife had done. He jammed his cold feet against her for warmth. Gwenhwyfar squealed and kicked them away. When they stopped laughing, he said, 'It bothers me. But it bothers me more that if I do not do this thing in a sensible and practical way, then all that is British may become swamped and destroyed. Better to fight for the little and win, than the whole and lose.'

Gwenhwyfar caressed his cheek. 'Do not doubt yourself, husband. You do the right.'

Arthur beamed a sudden grin. He sat up, grabbed her hands. 'Then you will ride north with me on the morrow, to meet with Winta?'

'What!' Gwenhwyfar jolted upright.

'He holds a feast to celebrate – some long-standing feud prompts the excess of victory. I have been invited, you also. Llacheu will love it! Winta has several sons, one his age.'

'But I am pregnant! The babe will be born any day now!' Gwenhwyfar put a hand on her bulging abdomen, could not believe she was hearing this nonsense. 'You have been back a few hours and now you are riding off again? Oh, Arthur!'

Not hearing her, Arthur rubbed his hands together, bubbling excitement chasing away his tiredness. 'It would set a future seal on this alliance were my third son to be born at Winta's hearth.'

'No!' Gwenhwyfar spoke with such venom that Arthur drew back.

'No?' Astonished.

'No. I will not give birth in some squalid, Saex hovel!'

'Winta's Hall is finer than some of our crumbling Roman buildings.'

Emphatic. 'No.'

Arthur shrugged, left the bed and began searching for discarded clothing, started to dress. Would he never understand women? 'That's your final word?'

'That's my final word.'

'I will take Llacheu – and Gwydre.'

'Take them.'

'Winta hopes to welcome my Lady.'

'Then he will be disappointed.'

Arthur laced the last fastening of his tunic, ambled towards the door. 'I will see what food is in the kitchen, my stomach growls like a wounded bear. Why are you being so obstinate?'

'Why are you being so inconsiderate?'

He paused, said with his back to her, 'Winta and I are justifiably suspicious of each other's intentions. To show good faith I told him you will ride with me. No man intending war would bring his pregnant wife.' He had the door open. 'You will come with me Gwenhwyfar. That is my final word.' He walked out.

Gwenhwyfar hurled a pillow, its stuffing bursting through the linen as it thudded against the closing door, scattering a cloud of goose feathers.

'Bastard!' she screamed. 'Tyrant! Saex-loving cur! I will not come! I will not!'

§ VII

Midday was not much lighter than evening, with persistent drizzle turning to sleet. Gwenhwyfar tucked a bearskin tighter around her body; for what seemed the hundredth time she attempted to refasten the leather curtaining of the swaying litter. Her numbed fingers fought with the lacings; a gust of wind snarled through the opening and tore the thing from her. 'Damn it!' she cursed. The litter jolted, forcing her to cling wildly to the side. She heaved herself back among the cushions, turning her back to the flapping curtain and icy swirl of sleet beyond. A pain was niggling within her. She shut her eyes. 'Let this not be the babe coming. Not yet!' She felt sick, her head ached and her bladder needed emptying again.

Hooves drew alongside. Arthur leaned from the saddle and peered in. 'Mithras! Are you all right? You look like death!'

'Thank you very much!' Gwenhwyfar's response was as barbed as the weather. 'Since you are so concerned, husband, I assure you I feel ten times worse than I look!'

'Do you want to halt a while?' Arthur had to shout, his speech blown away by the wind.

'Aye, I want to stop. I want to climb out of this wallowing bier. I want to be in the warm and dry, back within the safe confine of my rooms at Lindum!' She was screeching at him.

Cheerily. 'Not far now.'

Through gritted teeth. 'If you say that once more, I will slap you.'

Arthur grinned. 'In all truth, 'tis not far. But we will stop.' He spurred his horse forward, shouting orders.

The litter lurched to a halt, a slave came to help her mistress from the conveyance. Out here the wind stung, assaulting the brain like a battering-ram. It tore Gwenhwyfar's wrap from her head, whipping her hair free of pins and combs. She stumbled from the road, crouched, uncaring that there was no shelter to provide privacy. A pain shuddered through her.

At this moment, she also cared little that she might give birth here in this frozen, lifeless wasteland. She adjusted her clothing and struggled against the wind back to the litter.

'Lady?' Always so formal, Cei. Always speaking in neat, precise Latin. 'Is something amiss? The child . . . ?' He whirled to Arthur. 'I said this was foolishness!'

Others were gathering around; Arthur himself swinging down from his horse, striding towards her. 'Gwenhwyfar?'

She gave in to fatigue and despair. 'I cannot, will not, climb back

36

into that . . .' she snapped her fingers at the litter, 'that, contraption.' Her legs buckled and she slid to the ground, sat there hunched and exhausted, wishing she were dead. 'I can go no further.' She sobbed then, her scalding tears rolling down her cheeks to drip onto her cold, chafed hands.

There came a lull in the wind, an eerie stillness hovered above the winter-blasted landscape. The escort, sitting astride impatient mounts, glanced nervously at each other. Snow was coming.

Squatting beside his wife, Arthur rubbed her icy fingers in his rough hands. 'You cannot give up here, Cymraes. Not in front of the men.'

'I can. I have.' The pain from the cold in her fingers and toes was unbearable, that other pain, low in her abdomen, unpleasantly insistent.

'We have only two or three more miles. There will be warmth and comfort soon and women to help you.'

'I had all that in Lindum.'

'This is not like you, Gwen. You are strong-willed and determined, a fighter. You do not usually give in so easily.' Arthur put cheery encouragement into his voice, deliberately hiding the worry. They could not linger out here on this road. The weather was closing in, they must press on.

Gwenhwyfar knew it as much as he, but did not care. Cared for nothing except the pain that was growing in her belly and the cold that was eating into her. 'I do not *usually* have to travel in a sick-making litter, in the depth of winter with a babe about to be born!' Her voice was rising, her nerve nearing breaking point. If only she knew what lay ahead! She might have to birth the child in a hut which amounted to little less than a pigsty, with uncouth barbarians looking on. None would speak Latin, let alone the British tongue. What food did they eat, what customs did they follow? How did they regard childbirth? What if she bore a daughter, would they laugh at Arthur for being presented with a girl? He probably had not thought of that possibility; damn it, had not thought of anything!

The few Saex Gwenhwyfar had met had been among the British people. Never had she gone among the English. She knew next to nothing of their domestic life. They were a savage race who it was said, drank the blood of their children in sacrifice, the men were brutes and the women drunken whores. Arthur did not fear them, but he was a man in a man's world, not a woman fearful of approaching childbirth.

Arthur chewed his lip, looked out over the bleak terrain. There was a dark shadow away over to the west. He hoped it was rain, but knew it would be snow. The wind had risen again and was tearing like a cast spear across the flat land, moaning like a banshee spirit come to announce death. 'Will you ride with me on Hasta?' he asked.

Gwenhwyfar nodded dumbly, unsure whether horseback would be better or worse than the litter. He lifted her, helped her awkward weight across his horse's withers, mounted behind her.

Another mile and the first flakes of snow began to swirl, falling quickly, blinding eyes and agitating horses who side-stepped and snorted, trying to turn their tails against the stinging whiteness. Arthur grimly kept Hasta to a steady walk, his hand tight on the rein, the animal dancing beneath the unaccustomed double weight. Once, Hasta's hooves slipped on a patch of ice, his hindlegs skidding. Arthur cursed as he heard Gwenhwyfar, leaning heavily against him, groan. He let the reins slacken for the horse to find his own balance.

The ride was a nightmare. Arthur cursed himself; the idea had been a good one, an unparalleled gesture of friendship with the people of the Humbrenses. What use gestures if he killed his wife in carrying them out? Even above the wind, he could hear Llacheu wailing from the second litter, and Gwydre's accompanying screaming. The children had slept for most this day's journey, but they were now cold and hungry. Would they never reach Winta's settlement!

Cei, riding to his left, pointed suddenly, peering through the swirling whiteness. 'There, smoke! Look, Winta Ingas Ham.'

'Thank the gods! Gwen,' Arthur spoke soft in her ear. 'Cymraes, we are here.'

Gwenhwyfar did not answer. She burrowed her head deeper into his wolf-skin cloak. His arms tight about her waist, Arthur felt her body shudder.

'Cymraes? You are not afraid?'

She nodded, desperately fighting back more tears. 'I know nothing of them as people, Arthur. Nothing.'

'You do. You know that Winta wishes to make lasting peace and that his people are ordinary people. As ordinary as you or I.'

'Na, I do not know that!' Gwenhwyfar lifted her head, tears brimming. 'I have heard things about them, terrible things.'

'And you believe them?' Arthur tossed back his head and laughed. 'Were you not told as a child that the demons would come for you if you were bad? You believed as a child, but saw reason when you grew. It's only ignorance that breeds fear, Cymraes. We fear the English because we know nothing of their ways or their gods. Because their customs and laws are different from ours we assume they are mindless, uncivilised men and women. Not so long since, I thought that too. Now I know the truth. I assure you, they are not monsters.'

Arthur did not hear her mumbled answer, for the wooden palisade surrounding the village was looming ahead. The watch had seen their approach and the gate was opening, the English running to meet them, waving, smiling, calling enthusiastic greeting.

'I would to all the gods I could believe you, husband,' Gwenhwyfar muttered, wincing as a spasm of pain arched through her. She did not look up, did not want to see as they rode through the gate. She recognised the sound of it thudding shut, heard and sensed the swell of people pressing close. Her eyes were shut, she kept them shut. It seemed safer that way.

Winta himself strode through the settling snow to greet Arthur, his arms extended, his bearded face beaming pleasure. At his side walked a tall woman, her head covered with a linen veil in the fashion of the English.

Arthur's smile was broad. He urged Hasta into a trot the last few strides, lent down to clasp Winta's outstretched hand, their combined grasp firm and strong with friendship. 'Greetings, my Lord Winta! I come in peace!'

'All Hail to you, my Lord King, I welcome you in peace!'

Gwenhwyfar risked opening her eyes, saw through tear-blurred vision a tumble of wattle-built houses and a large gathering of fair-skinned people. A sound, half scream half moan, left her. She clutched her belly with one hand, fumbled for Arthur's strong arm with the other.

'Gwenhwyfar!' Arthur cradled his wife, realised the wetness on her face was not only snow and tears; her panting breath was not alone from fear and tiredness. 'Mithras! The child comes!'

Winta's wife hurried forward, took one brief look at Gwenhwyfar's contorted face, and with a few explicit words sent slaves scurrying to prepare for an imminent birth.

Arthur leapt from Hasta, lifted Gwenhwyfar down and the Englishwoman swept her from him. Gwenhwyfar no longer cared, nothing mattered, nothing, except this god-awful pain. She felt as though she were being torn in two, one wave crashing after the other, leaving her gasping and sweating.

Other Englishwomen flurried round, shepherding her to a small, rectangular hut, one of many clustered around a central-built Hall that soared grandly upward to meet the low press of snow-thick cloud. Vaguely, Gwenhwyfar realised the great Hall looked little different from that at her childhood home of Caer Arfon. The carvings were different, English spirits, English gods and fancies, and perhaps the roof sloped more steeply, but little else.

A central hearth-fire burnt cheerfully inside their destined chamber, beeswax candles providing plentiful light. Furs and hides hung among bright woven tapestries, masking the plainness of the daub-plastered walls and muffling any draughts; a deep carpet of herb-strewn reeds covered the floor. Chattering, tutting concern, the women removed Gwenhwyfar's heavy cloak and her sodden boots and dress, rubbed life into her chilled feet and hands and dried her wet, wind-matted hair. They covered her shivering body with a warm, soft quilt, stuffed with goose down. Someone spooned a few sips of broth past her lips. It warmed her from the inside, tasted good. She would have liked more, but a birthing chair appeared and someone, Gwenhwyfar knew not who but thought it could have been Winta's wife, inspected the birth canal.

Strange voices in a strange tongue floated between the searing

40

redness of labour pains. Then Winta's wife was leaning over her, stroking her damp hair, holding her hand. She was smiling, her voice soft, speaking perfect, cultured Latin.

'The child comes quickly. Have you had the birth pains long?'

Gwenhwyfar nodded, managed to gasp. 'Aye, but not as severe.'

The gather of women had left, and aside from her own panting breath, the room had fallen quiet. The flames, bursting out their brilliance of warmth and light, hissed and cracked in the hearth, flaring and sparking occasionally as the one remaining woman, aside from Winta's wife, added wood as needed. The wind snarled beyond the doors and walls, angered that it could not get inside to destroy this comfort with its iced breath. The door fur lifted and Enid, herself dried, warmed and fed, entered quickly, ducking in with a blast of winter weather, shutting it out again by the closing of the door.

As she removed her cloak and outdoor boots, exchanging them for doe-hide house shoes, Winta's wife wiped the sweat from Gwenhwyfar's forehead, said, 'Here is your own woman come to help us, my dear. All is ready to welcome the child.'

Releasing a shaking breath, Gwenhwyfar risked a glance at the tall, well-dressed woman squatting before her. 'I know not your name, but I thank you,' she attempted a smile, 'for your kindness.'

'I am Hild. This is Eadburg.' She gestured to the other woman who was busying herself near the fire. 'She is much skilled with the matters of birthing. Your husband was wrong to bring you.'

Gwenhwyfar grimaced as another contraction came and passed. They were coming stronger now, more rapid. The English are good people, Arthur had said. She stretched her hand, took Hild's fast in it. 'Na, he was right. He's always right.' Another deep breath to control the tearing inside her body. 'My sons,' she panted as it faded, 'where are they?'

'Housed with my own childer.'

And Enid was there, taking Gwenhwyfar's hand, smiling re-assurance. 'I have seen them well settled, my Lady. Llacheu is filling his belly with a third helping of chicken broth and Gwydre already is sleeping.'

41

Satisfied that all else was well, Gwenhwyfar was content to allow the room to recede into distant sound; her baby was coming and nothing would end the pain of the birth force, save his safe arrival.

A time later, how long Gwenhwyfar was unaware – a moment, a lifetime – someone was speaking to her, calm but insistent. She was to ease her breathing, the female voice said, to pant. 'Hold back, my dear, if you push now you will tear.'

A flurry of movement, shadows leaping high on the wall with the sudden flare of the fire. Gwenhwyfar's hands flailed, no one stood beside her, she felt suddenly alone, frightened. 'Do not leave me!' she screamed. Someone grasped her hand, held it, firm, strong fingers entwined in her own. Hild.

'We are here. There is naught to fear.' A pause, talking in the Saex tongue, then a squeeze of pressure from Hild on her hand. Excited, elated. 'I see the head, dark hair! Push now, push with all your strength.'

'I have not enough strength.'

'You have!'

Gwenhwyfar felt arms encircle her from behind, a body with the suppleness of a willow and the strength of an oak, brace against her own. She arched her back against the Englishwoman and together, they brought the child safe into the world. Her body felt as though it were being ripped apart but she ignored the pain, one more, one more effort and it would all be over.

The pain went, suddenly, abruptly. Relieved, joyous laughter from the two Englishwomen and Enid mingled with a baby's thin wail of protest. Hild left Gwenhwyfar, took up the child from Eadburg and placed it, a wet, wrinkled, angry little thing, at his mother's breast. For a moment Gwenhwyfar hesitated, sweat dripping from her face down her chin to soak her soiled gown.

Uncertain, Hild remained motionless, the babe in her arms. She glanced with a question at Enid.

'You have a fine son,' Enid said at Gwenhwyfar's side, 'who has his da's bellowing temper.' That small, passing moment of confusion lifted, Gwenhwyfar smiled, took the new life from Hild's arms and gathered him to her, the pain and fear all forgotten.

'What name do you have for him?' Hild asked.

Gwenhwyfar looked up at the Englishwoman, frowned. 'It is for the father to acknowledge and name his son after the birthing, not for the mother to choose.'

Hild turned away to deal with the expelling of the afterbirth. 'For us,' she said, 'we share in the deciding before the birth, there is a name ready for the gods to know so that they might straightway welcome the new son or daughter to the hearth-place.' She shook her head. What strange customs these British followed!

Arthur entered quietly, surprising a young slave dozing before the fire. She leapt to her feet, her eyes wide and fearful. It occurred to him that it was not just his own kind who were lacking in trust; these English held the same feelings for the British. He held his hands before him, palms down, fingers spread, and emphasised his smile. He knew a few words of her own language. Pointing to himself then to her, said, 'Freond, ja? Friend?'

She smiled understanding, amused at his poor pronunciation. She nodded. 'Freond.'

Arthur held the door covering aside, gestured for her to leave. She shook her head, pointed from herself to a sleeping fur in one corner. Arthur let the skin fall, motioned her towards her bed, understanding she had orders to stay.

He crossed then to his wife, sat gently on the edge of the wooden box-bed. Gwenhwyfar stirred, looked up at him.

'We have a third son,' she said.

'I know. I have seen him, remember? I lifted him and named him Amr.'

'It seems an age ago, a dream world. Strange, now it is over, I barely remember the pain, only the pleasure of holding our son.' She took his hand, welcoming his presence. 'Hild says it is like that for most women.' She sighed, relaxed her bruised body into the warmth of the bed, drowsing back into sleep. 'I like her.'

Arthur laughed, bent forward to kiss her mouth. 'Of course you do. I said you would.'

April 460

§ VIII

Winifred delighted in showing her handsome built Hall and flourishing farmsteading to visitors, no matter who they were; men or women of the Church, traders, harpers. English, British, or foreigners from Hibernia, Gaul, and beyond. All were welcome at Winifred's hearth, and word had spread fast along the sea-lanes and traveller's tracks of where good wine and a warm belly could be obtained for the price of telling the news on the wind. Visitors were rare at first, when Arthur had divorced her and so cruelly set her aside, dumped her here, two miles down-river from the mouldering Roman town of Venta Bulgarium. But Winifred was a woman who would not be casually discarded on the midden heap and left to rot. Her pride was too important, and the son she had borne Arthur, even more so.

She was three and twenty, not the beauty her mother had been, but a handsome enough woman. Her flaxen-blonde hair remained covered beneath the veil all Christian holy women wore and her dress was black, with only a dangling gold crucifix and girdle keys for decoration. Plain dress could not hide the vivid blue of her eyes, eyes which had snared Arthur, once, seven years past when she had decided to have him as her husband.

Princess she had been then, only daughter of the King Vortigern and his English Queen Rowena, child of Hengest. No one called her princess now, for Winifred insisted on her other title, the one taken up when Arthur had placed a marriage band on her finger and spoken the vows of God's Holy Law with her. Lady Pendragon.

Signalling the next course to be served, Winifred fluttered an alluring smile at the man seated next to her at the high table. Below, along the length of trestle tables set in rows down the Hall, sat the men and women of her steading and the men of her guest. He was no noble, high-born or Church official, but Wulfric the Trader was none the less important to Winifred. He plied his trade from all ports along the Saxon shore, across to Gaul and Less Britain, Juteland, Saxony and up as far as the North Way, exchanging brocades and silks and herbs and spices; corn, ale and wine; crafted jewellery, pottery, hunting dogs, animal skins, slaves. He was welcome too, in the British places. Towns such as Eboracum and Caer Gloui; towns where the gossip buzzed and blossomed. Gossip of the King, Arthur. Winifred liked to know of him, where he was going, where he had been, for she refused to accept the divorce he had petitioned on her. Cerdic, her son by Arthur, would be the next Pendragon, not Gwenhwyfar's brats. And to ensure it, she needed to know everything of Arthur and his Gwynedd-born slut. For knowledge was power.

She served pork to Wulfric, offered him the roasted skin, crisp and succulent to chew on. The trader beamed his pleasure, laughed as he drank her health with her finest ale. Later, in the privacy of Winifred's splendidly furnished chamber, they would get to the serious business, the agreement and settling of payment for the cloth and goods that she had selected. Winifred always paid well, often in excess, for it was not only the fineries she was buying. The talk over private shared wine and haggling was the real purchase.

So Wulfric drank the lady's health and laughed with her, and when the feasting was ended, followed her from the Hall through the door at the rear, to tell her what he had gleaned of the Pendragon. Of the alliance with the Humbrenses and the granting of land to Icel; that the King's Council were discussing ways – legal and not so legal – to oppose and be rid of him, and that trouble was brewing above the Wall. But then, there would be, with that witch-woman flourishing word that she was to be called queen. Of her, he would not talk. To speak of that one was bad luck, Morgause was not a name to cross an honest trader's lips. Wulfric touched his amulet, the Thor's hammer at his throat, as her image spurred into his mind. A woman, so it was said, more beautiful than even a goddess. And more deadly than a snake!

The Pendragon would have to ride north to settle the pretensions of Morgause and her weakling husband, of that there was no doubt.

48

It was said that Arthur had sent messengers to summon Lot south to explain his wife's treasonous actions and the messengers had been returned in a wooden chest. Parts of them, their heads and privates. Of that, Wulfric would not speak either, let Winifred discover it from one of her British tale-tellers! If the Pendragon was planning to ride north and deal personally with the witch, then it was his concern, not a Saex sea-trader's. He drank more wine, took the gold Winifred offered and stowed it safe in his waist pouch. But he would have to tell her of the other thing, no way could he not, for already it was becoming common knowledge, now that the winter snows were clearing. He had been enjoying his stay, the welcome and hospitality much to his liking, but he would be lucky to escape the room before the wine jugs smashed over his head and against the walls when he told the Lady Pendragon of a third son born to the Queen.

§ IX

Gwenhwyfar could not decide which to choose, the pale ivory silk, or the gold-thread brocade. Both were lovely – expensive – but highest quality dictated highest price. Hild was known for her purchasing of such luxury stuff and the traders and seafarers made trips often up the river to Winta's settlement with their wares, knowing they would be welcomed and leave with their purses full.

Enid was fingering a heavy plaid weave with her free hand, her other hand supporting the baby, Amr, draped sound in sleep over her shoulder, his fat fists dangling down her back, face snuggled into her neck. 'This would make a fine winter's cloak,' she said with a wistful sigh of longing.

Gwenhwyfar was in a generous mood; the easy contentment of these English people had purged her weariness and anxieties. She laughed. 'Have it then, as my gift.' She draped the silk about her upper torso, relishing its sensuous feel beneath her fingers, asked 'What think you? Shall I have this or,' she reached for the brocade, 'this?'

Wulfric, delighted at the extent of sales this trip, but trying desperately to mask any excessive pleasure, ambled towards Gwenhwyfar from around the far side of the spread of jumbled bolts of material. 'That is an exceptional silk, my lady,' he crooned, 'and alas, 'tis the last I have, for I sold most of it at an earlier place of call.'

Gwenhwyfar was only half listening; traders always made much of their sales banter. He would be telling her next how much the previous lady had paid for the cloth and how lucky Gwenhwyfar was to have this last at the cheaper price. Traders were the same the world over, she supposed, whether they were British, Roman, English or whatever! Only he did not, said instead, as he took a step closer to fashion the hang of silk more attractively about her. 'It sits well against your hair colouring, Lady, better than with the lady from Venta Bulgarium.'

She looked sharply up at him, her green eyes sparking a quick flash of anger, for he had not spoken without deliberation. 'The lady of Venta would not be pleased to hear you say so,' she responded scathingly.

Wulfric chuckled. 'Ah, but she is not likely to hear my words is she? You most certainly will not tell her.' He laughed again, took the silk and began folding it, careful of its delicate fineness. He had more to say, Gwenhwyfar could see, from the way his eye slipped to hers, and from the way he kept near, not moving aside even though two of Hild's ladies had made their choosing over what to buy.

'She bid me,' Wulfric murmured as he passed the folded silk to the Queen, 'to convey her greeting to you. She wishes you and your sons all health.'

Winifred. Arthur's cursed, first wife, Winifred. Gwenhwyfar's eyes narrowed and she ignored the proffered cloth, held the trader's glinting eyes with her own hard stare. That half-breed, two-faced, lying, murdering, Saex bitch! Winifred, who refused to accept Arthur's divorce from her. Who insisted her own born son was to be the Pendragon's heir.

Scornful, Gwenhwyfar asked, 'And what would Lady Winifred be doing with the buying of such fine silk?' She flicked the stuff contemptuously with her fingers, 'I thought she wore the drab of a Holy Woman.'

Wulfric shrugged, set the silk on the table among the other materials, replied, 'I know very little of Christian women, my Lady. What they wear beneath those black garments is their business.'

There came a movement at the door to Hild's women-filled bower and a slave scuttled in, bringing with her a rise of noise from Winta's Hall where the men would be deepening into their drink and gaming. She bobbed a hasty reverence, nodding apology at the interruption towards Hild. 'Begging pardon Lady, there's been fighting in the Hall, both the young cubs are battle-bloodied.'

Hild exchanged a hasty glance with Gwenhwyfar, whose hand had gone to her mouth. Boys! How easily lured they were to quarrelling and fighting!

Hild had four sons. At four and one half years, the same age as Gwenhwyfar's Llacheu, Oswin felt himself to be pig in the middle of his brothers, two older and one younger. When Llacheu came to his father's village, Oswin's life perceptibly improved, for he had a litter cub to run with now, someone to romp with in the fresh-laid bedding of the cow-byre, a friend to join in the tickling of the huge fish languishing in the steading's fish pools. And Llacheu was fiercer than any hound bred in Winta's kennels! Llacheu was a wolfling, the son of the Pendragon and afraid of nothing, not even the eldest brother Eadric, who was eight. For that, Oswin loved Llacheu.

Now, as evening fell and the Englishmen feasted, the two friends tumbled with the hounds at the far end of the Hall, squabbling with the dogs for a few choice bones to chew on, though both boy and hound had already been fed. Llacheu cuffed a brindled dog aside and sucked the marrow from the bone in his hand.

The women were long gone to Hild's bower, leaving the men to their drinking. The boys could creep nearer the hearth now and listen to the stories and riddles. Last night a riddle had been asked that sent everyone into roars of laughter. Llacheu had not understood why it was so funny and had asked Enid the meaning of it this morning, earning for himself a smack to the ear and a rebuke about listening to adult talk. He thought again on the words he had repeated. *'He had his way and both of them were shaking, the man worked hard, his capable servant was useful at times, but strong as he was he always tired sooner than she did, exhausted by the task.'* Why Enid had gone so red and embarrassed Llacheu had no idea. The answer had been 'churning butter', what was so amusing or wrong about that? Perhaps he had missed some vital clue in the riddle's asking. He hoped they would repeat it tonight, he would listen more carefully if they did.

Da would have explained it of course, but Da had been gone several weeks, riding with his men down to the South to settle some disagreement with the Council. He had been in a foul temper for the few days before his going, something had annoyed him concerning Uncle Emrys. Llacheu did not much like Uncle Emrys, a man who made Da angry and Mam unhappy.

Oswin caught Llacheu's attention and together they wriggled across the rush-covered floor towards the central hearth. The eating tables had been cleared and men sat about in groups, talking and playing board games or burnishing weapons, mending leather harness or war-gear. They were all drinking; the mead flowed free in Winta's generous Hall.

They managed to work their way unnoticed behind a group of men playing *taefl*, and sat with their toes stretched to the warmth of the fire. Oswin was about to say something to Llacheu when there came a thump on his shoulders that sent him sprawling. He jumped up, words of protest on his lips, fell silent as his older brother's hand came out to cuff him round the head. 'You're in my place, squirt. Clear off.'

Oswin bit his lip, hiding his fear and hurt. He plucked at his friend's sleeve, intending to scuttle away, but Llacheu sitting obstinate among the rushes said, 'We got here first. This is our place.'

Eadric's eyes narrowed, his self-importance weighted with the security of his position as eldest. He saw no reason to sit in a draught when two piss-brained kids were hogging the warmth! Not used to being answered back, he hurled an insult, jabbing at Llacheu's shoulder with his finger as he spoke. 'Who do you think you're talking to? You wealas bastard!' He made to strike the boy – and found himself toppling backwards.

Llacheu's head-butt winded the older boy, the move coming so unexpected. Climbing again to his feet he began casually to brush off the reeds sticking to his woollen bracae, and almost within the same movement, lunged to grab at Llacheu's hair. Dragging the younger lad to his knees, his other hand slapped at his face. Bravely, though there was a difference in age and height, Llacheu fought back. He was the eldest son of the Pendragon, and no Saex whelp was going to insult the *next* Pendragon by calling him a fatherless foreigner!

Pummelling and kicking, his fists striking at chest and belly, feet at shins and toes, Llacheu hurtled all his strength behind his fury, and Oswin suddenly found a courage he did not know he possessed. Yelling furiously, he leapt on Eadric's back, his feet kicking, one hand holding his hair, the other punching at his head and body. Two against one; Eadric tried to shake them off, tripped, the three of them crashed down into the men, the playing pieces of their board game were scattered in all directions and the mead cups knocked over.

Cursing, the adults wiped at the drink spilt down their tunics. One grabbed at Eadric others at Llacheu and Oswin, hauled them apart, shaking them, bellowing their anger at the disturbance. Eadric's nose was spouting blood, Llacheu and Oswin each sported a blackening eye. A hush descended, men stepped aside, the boys looked up. Winta stood before them.

'I like not such squabbling at my hearth!' he bellowed, pulling the boys, one by one, to stand in a row before him. 'What is this about?' He regarded his eldest, received no answer. With his eyes, asked Oswin. Nothing. To Llacheu said. 'I am waiting for explanation.'

Fingers gripping his nose, trying to stem the blood, Eadric thought, *Go on, tell him, wealas boy. Tell tales.*

Llacheu felt no fear of Winta. The Saex man, for all his authority, had a kindly face and gentle nature towards his family.

Aside, Llacheu had several times braved his own father's fury. Nothing could outstrip that! He took a small while to consider an answer that would convey the truth but not land any of them in further trouble. He decided on: 'We were about boy's business, sir. Nothing more.'

Winta suppressed his spurt of laughter. 'Boy's business eh? Is it so important that you must spoil the peace of my Hall?'

Again Llacheu considered. 'Sometimes,' he said, his head bending back to look direct into the tall man's eyes, 'matters are better settled straight way. Otherwise the thing festers and becomes out of hand.' He had heard his da say that. It had sounded good. And obviously worked, for Winta was turning away, saying, 'Even so, Pendragon Boy, I would rather you did your settling beyond my Hall.'

Men were laughing, moving aside to retrieve their gaming pieces or pour more mead, the incident forgotten.

One hand still to his nose, Eadric extended the other to Llacheu, his grin broad behind the shielding fingers. He was impressed, said simply, 'Pax?'

Llacheu hesitated. 'If it be pax with Oswin also?'

Eadric exchanged glances with his young brother, who rubbed at the soreness of his pulled hair. 'If you've been teaching him to fight so rough, then aye, pax it had better be.'

Llacheu grinned, a smile as broad as a full moon, lifted his fingers to touch his eye. 'We'd best go find our mothers. Ask them to patch us up, I suppose.'

The blood still dripping from his nose, Eadric reluctantly agreed. In single file they trooped through the Hall, made way past the laughing men to the women's place. They felt no shame – after all, it was for the women to tend a warrior's brave gotten wounds.

Later, when the trader had packed away his wares and the women had all dispersed to their own hearth places, Gwenhwyfar herself settled Llacheu into his bed, leaving Enid to tend Gwydre and Amr. The fighting had frightened her more than she cared to admit, coming perhaps too close to the reminder of Winifred and her son's existence.

'You must not make enemies, Llacheu.' She stroked his hair back, that same irritating flop across the forehead that Arthur had also. 'You will find enough need to fight without making cause of your own.'

Llacheu chewed his lip. He knew his mam did not like fighting, knew she hated his da going away. And there was something more that troubled her, though he did not know what it was.

'I have not made an enemy of Eadric though, have I? It ended with us being friends.'

Gwenhwyfar smiled, tucked the sleeping-fur tighter around him. 'This time aye, but another time, such tactics may not reap a beneficial reward.' She blew out the lamp, made for her own bed.

She undressed slowly, carefully folding each garment as she took them off. *The lady at Venta wishes you and your sons all health!* Winifred would never send such a greeting, not in innocent friendship. What scheming was she plotting now or was this just a chance to stab a reminder of her presence?

Gwenhwyfar scuttled into her bed for it was cold this evening, the heat of summer not yet upon them. She laughed to herself as she wriggled beneath the furs. So, Winifred was not quite the shriven woman of God that she took such public care to make herself out to be! Other confessed holy women, Gwenhwyfar knew, wore hair tunics beneath their outer robes, or wrapped themselves tight in swaddling bands to hide their sinful female bodies from God's disapproving sight. Not Winifred! Fine silk for under-garments and nightwear? Hah! Then the tears came through the insincere amusement. Winifred and her son. Llacheu was not more than four and one half years and from them, he had death hanging over his head. Winifred would never allow Llacheu to take place above her own Cerdic, not without a fight.

If Arthur were here he would have chided her worrying, but he was not, and for all the happy ease that Winta's settlement created on the surface, beneath the every-day facade Gwenhwyfar wanted, so desperately wanted, a place, a home, of their own. A place where they could be happy and together. Where she, and her sons, could be safe from Winifred's poisoned darts.

§ X

Arthur disliked Aquae Sulis a fraction more than Lindum Colonia. Gwenhwyfar detested the place, which is why he had left her and the boys with Winta. Sulis was by comparison with Lindum and Eboracum in the North, a flourishing and thriving town. Trade fluctuated with the seasons, as it always had, and the buildings were in need of repair, but not to the extent of those towns on the eastern side of the country. Their decay had always been blamed on the disruption caused by the Saex. Aquae Sulis's grey cloak of dejection was being blamed on Arthur. For Mithras sake! How was it his fault the cobbles near the old Minerva Bath-House were sinking, only one year after they had been laid?

They complained of this and that, these citizens of Sulis – or Lindum or Eboracum, the moans and grumbles were the same wherever he went – whined that the quality of goods were not as they were, corn was overpriced, skilled labour difficult to come by, the roads were full of pot-holes, defence walls zigzagged with gaping cracks . . . What was it they wanted from him? Peace? Prosperity? He was riding his backside raw trying for that, yet still they bellyached!

With darkness falling and the steady drizzle of rain that had lasted for three days now, people had gone early to their homes; the shopkeepers were beginning to put up their shutters for the night. Arthur walked alone, his cloak hunched around his shoulders, head ducked against the rain. By the Bull, even the weather was bloody miserable in this town! Lamplight from a corner tavern spilt onto the rain-gleaming cobbles, Arthur glanced in as he passed; he would not say no to a drink. For a moment he was tempted, scrunched his cloak tighter and walked on. He was late already and Emrys would be in enough of a sour mood. Damn it! What would another half hour late matter?

He ordered wine from the surly-looking bartender, smiled at the girl cleaning the day's used tankards and dishes in the alcove to one side of the bar and sat at one of the four tables, his back to the three men seated at another. They had fallen silent as he entered, glowering at him with the natural suspicion of regular customers regarding a stranger. The man brought a terracotta flask shaped like a fox, and a pewter tankard, set them down with a thud that sloshed a drip of red wine from the spout, the fox's open mouth. Amicably, Arthur thanked him, tossed a small battered bronze coin. Coins were becoming rare too. Another fault of his apparently, although coinage had been rapidly declining since before his birth – Vortigern had been hard pressed to keep an adequate number in circulation. Aye, he would like to have a strong enough economy to mint new coins – he would *like* to do many things. He sipped the wine, poor quality but he had tasted worse, and contemplated some of those things. Mostly things that he could envisage doing to those pompous asses of his Council.

Hierarchical worthies of the Church and towns and estates of Britain. Older, wiser men (so they informed him), established politicians who saw themselves as self-appointed guardians of public morality, law and order. Their way was the only way, they knew better and no four-and-twenty-year-old, whoever his father had been and however talented on a battlefield, was going to tread on their toes or change the order of things. Except Arthur thought differently. He had his path laid firm and was going to follow it, Council or no Council. The meeting had gone badly this afternoon, ending with several of the older men walking out and leaving Arthur in a blazing temper. He poured more wine. He had no liking for this additional summons to see Emrys – Uncle he might be, but to dictate to the King . . . Arthur sighed and drank the wine. That was it with family of course, the law of order changed dramatically where relations were concerned. He would meet with Emrys, if only to tell him where he and the Council could shove their bureaucratic ideas.

The girl had come out to wipe down the tables, she was a young thing, ten and five, six? A slave undoubtedly; she had the appearance of a captured bird, thin cheeks, eyes that saw far away, probably to the Northern hills, for she had the look of the North about her.

Idly Arthur read the scratchings on the plaster wall in front of him, an exchanged feud of words. *'Priscus loves Julia Claudia but she says he is as useful as a worn lavatory sponge.'* Arthur chuckled at the indignant response. *'Cadwallon is jealous because I am better looking, know how to do it and have better equipment to do it with!'*

The other men, well into their ale, had forgotten his presence, had not realised who he was, beyond a cavalry officer. It took several sentences before Arthur realised they were talking of Winifred, his Winifred, his ex-wife.

'Are you going to Venta then?'

'Aye, she's offering good gold for skilled carpenters. Lashing out a fortune on this church and monastery that she's having built.'

'Aye well, she's currying favour with the Church isn't she? Getting her feet well under the table.'

Arthur stole a glance over his shoulder. The smallest of the three, a stocky little man with a drooping moustache and scarred face, was leaning back, tapping the side of his nose. 'And we all know why, of course.'

The others leant forward, expressions questioning. The Moustache paused for effect, took a swig of ale. 'She wants her son recognised as the Pendragon's heir. She's already hand-in-glove with Emrys Ambrosius you know.'

Another of the men chuckled, 'They say as how she wants him in her bed.' There was derisive laughter, jeers. 'Na 'tis true, I heard it from Lord Emrys's men only yesterday! They were here, in this very tavern!' He smacked the wooden table with his palm, causing the flagon and tankards to jump.

The girl smiled shyly at Arthur as she began cleaning his table. He lifted the wine flask for her. Pretty eyes. Dark blue. 'We're closing soon, sir.' Unmistakably from the North.

'You want to keep your ears open, Mab, if you're going along to Venta. She pays highly for gossip of the Pendragon!'

The third man, a burly type with only one eye and well full of drink, caught hold of the slave girl, as she passed. She struggled, pushing at him with her hands. 'Aye, the pair of them, her and Emrys keep sharp on our King, waitin' their chance to hack off his essentials and take the royal torque for their own.' He attempted to kiss the girl.

Their shadows leapt along the wall, she trying to fend off the man as he fumbled beneath her bodice, the other two laughing, cheering him on. Sobbing, she begged him to let her go, raising more laughter. He had her breast now, was moving lower with his other hand to lift her skirt.

'Is this tavern licensed as a whore-house then?'

The three men seated at their table turned to look at Arthur. The one with his hand half-way up the girl's leg laughed. 'Happen not, but this one's fair game I'd wager.'

Arthur had taken intense dislike to the three, the one with the moustache in particular. 'I thought it was supposed to be the Saex who were the bastards who raped British women.' He set down his tankard, slid one leg over the bench, sat half facing the men, one eye half closed, the other eyebrow slightly raised. His hand rested, casually, on his sword. 'I suggest you let her go.'

The man held his grin, but the voice was harsh, threatening. 'And I suggest you shut your mouth or I'll shut it for you. Permanently.' He thrust his hand higher up the girl's thigh, and Arthur was standing, his sword out and at the man's throat.

'Let her go.' It crossed Arthur's mind, as he stood there with the tip of his sword pricking a trickle of bright blood along the man's craggy-skinned throat, that he was behaving absurdly. The girl was in a tavern, what was she to expect? Except she was a slave, had no choice in the matter, and somehow, after all that bellyaching and demanding from his Council, freedom of choice seemed suddenly very important. 'Let her go.'

Arthur was aware of the other two men reaching for their daggers, and a disturbance at the open doorway; the tramp of feet, the smell and sound of men, the chink of armour and the grate of a sword as it was drawn from its scabbard. The Pendragon stood his ground, his sword pressing upon Moustache's windpipe, he would kill this one first, then tend to these newcomers behind him.

But he did not have to. 'Officers of the Watch! Put up your weapon!'

Lazily, the sword not moving, Arthur turned his cool, piercing eyes to the nearest officer in the doorway. Calmly, he ordered,

'Arrest this man and have him flogged for insulting and threatening behaviour.'

The officer laughed, raised his own sword – and Arthur's blade whistled, sliced through his cheek. The second officer gasped, plunged forward, shoving his bleeding comrade aside. 'Jesu Christ, it's the Pendragon!'

Even the man with the moustache became still, mouth gaping. Arthur bent down, picked up the rag that the girl had been using for cleaning the tables, and wiped his sword blade before sheathing the weapon. He drained his wine, took the girl's arm and started to leave the tavern. Almost as an afterthought he turned back, said with a malicious smile, 'When you see her, tell Lady Winifred of this. She'll be interested to hear of my Northern slave.' He nodded to the two Watch officers, flipped three coins to the barman, hovering behind them. 'For the girl. She's mine now.' And left.

June 460

§ XI

Arthur had gone north, essentially to see to Lot and his wife, Morgaeuse, also to buy horses. Those he had purchased he had sent south to begin their training.

Straightening from feeling the colt's forelegs for signs of lameness, Gwenhwyfar retained her impassive expression. Horse traders were known for their hard bargaining and dishonesty. These colts were poor, half-starved, pathetic creatures. Except for this bay – he had breeding in him, beneath the matted coat and staring ribs. Gwenhwyfar chewed her lip, shook her head as she critically walked around the animal. 'They'll need feeding up before they're of any use to the Artoriani.'

'It's a long way down from beyond the Wall, Lady. Horses lose weight on a long trek.' The trader spread his hands, rolled his eyes slightly, stating the obvious.

Gwenhwyfar ran her hand along from the bay's withers to his rump. Weight loss would occur with an excessive, persistent pace, but not to this extent. These horses had been pushed hard and ill kept, long before being brought south to Winta Ingas Ham. 'Been backed has he, this one?' she asked.

Patiently, the trader spread his arms wider. 'He's only two! Of course not!'

Gwenhwyfar had heard enough. Who did this imbecile think he was? When Arthur bought horses he purchased healthy, worthwhile stock, not creatures such as this mangy bunch fit only for sausage-meat. 'You,' she said, coming around the colt and poking the man hard in the chest, 'are a cheat and a liar.' She shoved him again, thrusting him backwards two paces. 'These are not the horses the Pendragon would have seen.' She raised her hand to stop the contradictory protest. 'My husband buys and breeds the best.' She thrust her face closer to the man's. 'These are most certainly not the best.'

A crowd of English onlookers had gathered to watch and offer advice on the horses with the children of the settlement worming their way to the front. Llacheu beamed pride as his mother effectively put this Northern scum in his place. 'There is one good horse among thirty decrepit nags. One. Not backed? Has carried no rider or saddle?' Gwenhwyfar gripped hold of the startled man's arm, dragged him forward, pointed to the white patches of hair on the bay's withers and back. 'Saddle sores! How can a two-year-old be riddled with saddle sores if he has not been backed?'

Angrily she pushed the man from her, deliberately hard. 'Go back to the Northern whore who spawned you, these are not the horses my husband asked to be brought south.' She drew her dagger. 'Cheat the king would you? You dog-turd, get from my sight!'

The man backed away, slipped on the wet, muddied grass of the river bank, scrabbled for footing and fell, tumbling into the water. Plunging after him, Gwenhwyfar caught hold of him. 'Get on your own horse, now, and ride away before I slit your throat for the cheat you are.' She gripped the collar of his tunic, thrust him up the bank, where several of the English, laughing their approval, caught his arms, unceremoniously helped him to his horse and began to lead it across the fording place that was only accessible during low tide.

'Cheat is it?' he yelled, squirming around to raise his fist at the woman standing, arms folded, on the bank behind him. 'What of my other horses, send them with me or pay me for them!'

'I would wager someone has already paid you a high price for the horses you were supposed to have brought.'

'Damn you, woman! This is an insult!'

Winta had come from his Hall, interested at the rise of laughter and jeering, had caught the last heated exchange. He strode to the edge of the ford. 'Insult is it?' he roared. 'And what of the insult to my Lady Pendragon and to the king? Be off with you! Regard the fact that you still have your head as adequate payment!'

Along the bank, a younger man, dressed in the same style of woollen bracae and tunic as the horse trader, hurriedly kissed the girl he was with goodbye, and ran for his horse. Scrabbling into the saddle, he kicked the mare to a canter, urging her into the mud-coloured water, raced to catch up with his father.

Gwenhwyfar regarded the girl he had been talking to. Nessa, the slave Arthur had brought from Aquae Sulis. She patted the bay colt thoughtfully. Fed with corn, handled gently and given the chance of a long summer's rest, the horse's vitality and sleekness would return. Some of the others would pull through too, but Arthur needed horses that could begin their training now. Good, well-bred horses that could take the pace needed of a war-horse.

'Turn these animals out to pasture,' Gwenhwyfar ordered, 'we will give them a few days to rest, then see which are worth the keeping.' She beckoned Nessa to her. Like the horses, the girl had been thin and neglected, lice-ridden and frightened. Good food and kindness paid well for humans also.

'*Did you bed with her?*' Gwenhwyfar had asked Arthur, that first night when he had returned, still nursing his anger at Emrys and the Council. They were lying together after the sharing of love, and Gwenhwyfar had regretted the question for fear of being answered with a lie, or the truth. 'No,' he had said, and she had believed him. Almost.

'You seem to know that young man,' Gwenhwyfar said to Nessa. 'Like them, you are from the north-west are you not?'

Nessa bobbed a reverence to her mistress. It had all been so different here, so calm and unhurried, people, even her mistress, treating her kindly. She was not for men to use as they pleased, nor to be dealt harsh words or blows.

'Aye, Lady, I come from the west coast, near Alclud. Those two,' she nodded at the men, 'often passed through our village with their horses.' She looked wistfully after them, and Gwenhwyfar could see there was more than two departing riders in her mind.

'You think of the north?' she said, 'your home?' Gwenhwyfar knew what it was to long for the place of your birth, your family and friends. 'There was a while when I was in exile. They were kind to me in Less Britain, but it was not my home.' She touched the girl's arm. 'Would you be riding with those two were you free to go with them?'

Nessa shrugged her shoulders, turned away, so that her back was to the riders. 'But I am not free. I was taken three years past by Scotti sea-raiders, and sold into slavery. When I became ill I was sold again to work as a slut in a stinking hovel of a tavern. The men used me and I hated it, hated their touch and their bawdy laughter. And then I was bought by a king. For what reason, I know not.'

He had spoken the truth then, for Nessa's honesty was too plain spoken. She had expected to be Arthur's whore, was puzzled that she had not been so used. They were almost across the river now, those two men, the first horse struggling, dripping and blowing, up the far bank. Gwenhwyfar asked, 'If I were to grant your freedom, Nessa – I could ask Lord Winta to witness it – would you wish to go home?'

Tempted, Nessa smiled, shook her head. 'Return to what? Even there I was no more than a slave. You treat me with more respect than my own mother did.' She smiled, raised her shoulders, let them drop, decision made. 'I would stay.'

The horse trader had halted on the far side, was shaking his fist in a tormented rage. Absently, to the wind and the rise of birds that were shifting before the flooding tide, Gwenhwyfar stated, 'I would like to know what happened to the original horses that Arthur bought. Where were they exchanged for this mange-bitten bunch I wonder?'

'Oh I know that,' Nessa said, flapping her hand as if it were common knowledge. 'Nechtan told me. Showing off! He was always one for that. They were sold to Morgause, the woman who thinks herself Queen of the North.'

§ XII

Possessive, and with swollen pride, Lot kissed his wife goodbye. She was the most beautiful woman alive and he, Lot, had her as his own! He patted her belly, the bulge that was the baby. 'Take care of my son, he will be here by the time I return.' He said it wistfully, for he did not want to go west across the hills to meet with Arthur at

Alclud. He was afraid of the Pendragon, but someone had to respond to his demanding summons, and Morgause could not go, not so near her time. Nor could he seem so weak as to prefer to see the birth of his son over meeting with the man who styled himself Supreme King.

'Our daughter,' Morgause chided, pinning his cloak a little tighter around his shoulders. 'I have told you, I carry a girl-child.'

Patiently, Lot agreed with her. They had held this disagreement throughout the pregnancy; he supposed women knew about these things more than men, but he so wanted a son! Daily he prayed to whatever god was listening that his wife would be wrong, that she would bear him a boy. He kissed her again, prepared to mount. It was not easy having an acclaimed priestess to the Great Mother as your woman; so many other things seemed to take precedence over the natural everyday things of being husband and wife.

This obsession of hers for irritating Arthur for one. If she had not acted quite so angrily when those messengers had come early this spring . . . ah, but the thing had been done, and now Arthur himself had come up above the Wall, and had sent four whole Turmae to fetch Lot to explain why Morgause had murdered two of his Artoriani. Over one hundred of those fine-mounted, disciplined Cavalry. There was no way to refuse, he had to go.

'*What do I do? What do I say?*' Lot had panicked when he realised he would have to face Arthur alone. Morgause was so much better at these things, she always knew what words to use and how to use them to best effect.

'*Humble yourself before him, beg of him – anything. Tell him his men disrespected my honour. There should be no punishment for a man who was justifiably protecting his wife from rape.*' It was a lie of course, and Lot was not so good at lying. She could not have let those messengers of Arthur's live, not let them go back tattling that Ebba son of Drust of the Picti was welcome at her hearth – and in her bed, but even Lot had not the knowing of that! Happen she ought have had them quietly dealt with. Curse that whore-son Pendragon, she had lost her temper, had ordered them slain and sent back without thinking twice of the consequences.

She returned Lot's goodbye kiss, a fond farewell before the gathered people of the settlement. With the Mother's blessing, Arthur would be angry enough at Lot to hack off his stupid head and save her the eventual doing of it!

Her plans were going well, were taking shape after all these years of convincing talk, bribes in the right places and granting favours where they would be most effective. But they were not yet ready, she and Ebba, not full ready to unite the northern British men with the Picti nation and rise against this upstart king from the South, not yet. Soon. When she had this daughter, a child of the Mother Goddess to present to the Picti; when Ebba persuaded them that it was right to unite the new way of a son following a father with the old of following down through a female line. When his mother, the woman who controlled the Picti, finally gave in to old age and joined her husband who had died last year. When Ebba married with Morgause's soon to be born daughter . . . when all that happened, the North would see this Pendragon boy beaten to his knees!

Morgause waved to her husband as he rode, reluctantly, out through the gates of Dun Pelidr, her loving smile so believably genuine. The Picti held the queen to be highest in their esteem, it was for her to chose the man who was to be her husband and their king. Drust had been a powerful man, he had almost outmanoeuvred the old hag into becoming supreme over her, almost, but not quite. Unfortunate that between them they had only produced the one living son, Ebba. The Picti would need a new woman as their queen. And Morgause so wanted to be the most powerful of all queens! Soon, ah, soon!

When the Picti accepted this new babe as the child of the Mother Goddess, when they took her to be their next queen and agreed for Ebba to be her consort, Morgause would, naturally, travel north with the baby – and take her daughter's place with the chosen king until the bride became of an age to be a wife.

Morgause laid her hand on the bulge, that false, loving smile becoming a gloat of scheming reaching fruition. The baby would never reach maturity. Morgause would see to that.

·

With the pain so unbearable, Morgause remembered why she so rarely allowed her womb to conceive, names of the gods, was this suffering worth it? She screamed as another labour pain tore through her body, cursed with vivid embellishment all she would do to the next man who touched her – and the babe was born. The two women attending lifted the mewling child, put it to Morgause's breast, twittering and cooing their inane pleasure.

Morgause wrinkled her nose, the thing was bloodied and wet, looked like a puckered, withered old apple core. She turned it over, screeched her revulsion and threw it from her, the baby tumbled, yelling its fury and pain, to the floor, one of the women darted to help it, froze as Morgause spat orders to leave it be.

'But my lady, your son . . .'

'I needed to birth a girl-child, not a disgusting brat. Dispose of it. And you,' she flicked her fingers, long, slender fingers with fine-kept nails, at the other woman. 'There is a purse of gold in that chest. Get you out into the settlement and buy me a girl-born child. Not too old, I want no one to suspect.' Both women scuttled from the room, the one clutching the child, the other the gold. Both would do as they were bid, for none dared disobey Morgause.

Sweating, her body aching, Morgause hauled herself from the birthing stool. Her head swam, her eyes blurred. She staggered to the bed, lay down, her breath coming in gasps. A boy! By all the mockery of the gods, she had birthed a damned, whoring boy!

October 460

§ XIII

The trees were wearing their autumn finery, bright red and orange, gold and bronze. Winter was beyond the horizon, waiting to come in. The year had passed at Winta's settlement among the laughter of joy and the occasional sorrow; a year of telling tales around the night-fires, of sharing dreams and hopes, all interwined with the free-given exchange of knowledge and friendship. A year that had travelled too swiftly for Gwenhwyfar. The weeks and months had scuttled by like clouds running before a fresh-paced wind. Arthur had come and gone about his business, controlling the kingdom through a mixture of diplomacy and force, spending time with her and the boys. But as the nights grew longer and a touch of white was beginning to rim the grass at dawn, Arthur returned to say they had to leave. Llacheu sobbed, and Gwenhwyfar found it hard not to weep with him. To leave new friends was hard enough, but to return to Lindum . . . ah, the prospect was dismal. They needed to find their own place, a stronghold, a King's Hall, but where was the time, the opportunity, to find and build such a place?

Seated on the rise of high ground, like a brooding eagle perched on its eerie, Lindum Colonia dominated the sparse sweep of marshland. From a distance, and in the dim light of a grey, overcast day, the cracked walls and broken gateways were indistinguishable, a pall of hearth-fire and cooking smoke balanced above the walls. Gwenhwyfar felt a niggle of doubt about returning into this decaying Roman town. Rome? The province of Britain had been abandoned to fend for herself, for the great power that had for four hundred years dominated an Empire was dying; but in Britain, a few influential men still clung obstinately to the security of Rome's tattered skirts, refusing to believe that a way of life was over, finished, and a new about to begin.

Walking their horses towards the nearing walls, Gwenhwyfar was reminded of a trader's ship she had seen as a girl. Coming over-fast towards the shore it had been swept aside by the run of the current and a rising storm wind. With a rending crash it had hit the rocks, and sunk below an angry sea that cared not a handful of white-tossed foam for the splintering of wood and the cries of drowning men. Rome was like that ship, proud and gold-laden one moment, struggling and gasping against the darkness of death the next. Rome's rule over Britain was in the past. The English, men like Winta and Icel and Hengest, were part of the new, the growing and the living. Was that why they were so hated by the British, these English? The British were a people who could only clutch in despair at torn spars and empty air, cry for help that would not come. The dying, envious of the new-born, the alive?

Gwenhwyfar feeling a small surge of hope, smiled, leant across the narrow gap between the horses to take Arthur's hand in her own, glad to be one of those alive and looking to a bright future not mouldering behind crumbling walls wishing for a life that was gone.

At the dark arch of the northern gateway, she looked behind. A year ago she had hated the emptiness that was broken only by scattered, wind-twisted stumped trees, whistling reeds and singing marsh-grass. The dizzying void of sky had filled her with dread, Gwenhwyfar was mountain bred, her father had been Lord of the high reaches of Gwynedd, Lord over sky-touching mountains that swept fierce down to the sea. For Gwenhwyfar, flat land was hostile, but Hild had changed her, had shown the patterns of the sky, its moods, tempers and unending beauty; shown Gwenhwyfar to appreciate that vault of blue or grey or moonlit silver. As a girl, the mountains had sung to her, shown her the change of season and weather. Now Gwenhwyfar knew the sky, too, could sing. She took one last look at that sky before her mare trotted beneath the arch.

Was it this confine of Lindum that troubled her? The cracks in the aqueduct were longer than she remembered, the rubble accumulating at the base of the walls higher, and the discarded refuse littering the stinking, narrow streets deeper. The children had a lean look about their faces, and the hollows in the cheeks of men and women were more pronounced. Lindum, like the Empire of Rome, was dying. But Winta's Humbrenses people brought new prospects for these townsfolk: mutual trade was picking up, a better life was on the horizon. For that, the people were grateful – how different from a year ago when the mob had shouted and chanted through the streets! As Arthur entered beneath the gates and rode with his wife, sons, and a handful of men, the cheering and shouted blessings rang clear with enthusiasm and pride.

The official welcome was less jubilant. The Governor of Lindum awaited them on the bird-dropping-plastered steps of his shabby basilica. His wife, with her perpetual scowling expression, stood dignified at his side. Several members of Council were grouped behind them, their frowns as prominent as the cracks along the basilica walls. Ordinary people forgot the anger and doubts with the onset of peace, but not these men of politics. Men of power were not so fickle minded. Resentment cemented distrust.

Jostling forward, the people lining the streets strained to touch Arthur's legs and arms, their hands stretching out to clasp his, to touch him, to take some of his luck, his wonder. Arthur had brought them peace, and peace brought trade and prosperity. There was still far to go, but at least the path was there, opened, and set before them. Young women tossed fading rose petals over him and his lady, autumn-coloured leaves were strewn before the horses' hooves. Someone took Hasta's reins, lead the stallion in triumph up towards the basilica steps – the ordinary people had no care for this squabble of politics or the shuffle for supremacy; saw only the now and the here. Trade and peace was their demand and the Pendragon had fulfilled their asking. They forgot that a year past they were baying for his blood. That would stay forgotten, unless it suited them to remember.

Before he dismounted, Arthur surveyed the swathe of faces crowding the forum. He lifted his hand, spoke with words strong enough to reach those further back. 'To the north and east and south, the Saex-kind bow their heads to me, the Pendragon. You, are their overlords. To you they must look to trade for their metals and grain and pottery. To you, they look for the sharing of a comfortable life, and you guide the reins of that life!' Cheering, whistling, much laughter. For now, Arthur fared well among these ordinary people of Lindum.

Coming down the steps, the Governor welcomed the King with traditional words, putting scant feeling behind them. His customary embrace after Arthur dismounted was stiff, wooden, when Gwenhwyfar also dismounted he turned away, a deliberate insult. She busied herself with passing Llacheu into Enid's care. So, that was how the wind blew! Had she expected ought else?

Arthur and his Queen advanced up the steps. The Pendragon's personal bodyguard had made formation, their spears crashing across their shields in salute; silver and bronze buckles of their leather and chain-linked parade armour glinting in the afternoon sunlight.

Waiting on the top step, slightly to one side, stood Emrys, youngest brother to Arthur's dead father Uthr. As different from that proud war-lord as cheese is from chalk. He stood sullen-faced, his arms folded within the long sleeves of his Christian monk-like robe. His stern eyes glared disapprovingly down the length of his nose. Gwenhwyfar had once remarked to Arthur that on the day when God had created smiles, Emrys had been elsewhere.

'Council is in a sour mood,' Emrys announced as he coolly greeted his nephew.

Arthur shrugged one shoulder, indifferent. 'When are they not?'

The returned frown on Emrys's face deepened. 'Can you never regard anything as serious, boy? The Council has convened to discuss your decision of . . .'

Arthur cut the older man short. 'I hold supreme authority. Whether Council agrees with my decisions or not is of little consequence.' He turned to thread Gwenhwyfar's arm through his own before entering the public building.

'I oft-times wonder,' he whispered to her, 'whose side my uncle is on.'

Feigning astonishment, she answered, 'Emrys? On the side of truth and justice.'

Arthur grinned, squeezed her hand as they passed through the doorway into the dull gloom of the basilica's interior. 'Ah. Not on mine then.'

Tossing her braided hair, Gwenhwyfar laughed with him, the sound trickling behind, out into the bright autumn sunshine.

Inside, they were met by a half-hearted hail of reluctant greeting. The vaulted entrance hall was filled with men, most doggedly wearing the formal white toga, the status symbol of a free Roman citizen. A stark reminder of where the majority still laid their loyalty.

His own face wearing a bright smile that cleverly masked his annoyance, Arthur surveyed the nearest expressions. He had not wanted to come, but even a king must occasionally bear witness before a summoning of the Council of All Britain. Unfortunately.

He raised his hand, broadened his placid smile. 'Peace be upon you, my most learned and wise men!'

A few muttered, polite responses. Someone stepped forward; Patricius, the recently appointed Archbishop of Southern Britain. 'We expected you yester eve,' he said curt, accusingly.

'Did you?' Arthur's hand moved casually to his sword, his fingers toying with its familiar feel. 'It is most pleasing that you grieve at missing my company for twenty and four hours!'

From away to the left came a ripple of deep laughter, two men pushed their way through the crowd. Gwenhwyfer squealed, and darting past Arthur, ran to meet them, her arms outstretched. She was hugging each of the men in turn, her joy at seeing them immense. 'My brothers! Ceredig and Enniaun!' She took a step backwards, her hands resting lightly on Ceredig's arm, her eyes roaming, pleased, over the both of them. 'How well you both look!'

Arthur, smiling broad welcome, embraced the two men with strong affection, clasping Enniaun's large hand in his own. He said, 'For reasons best not recalled, it has been a long while since Gwynedd last joined with the Council of Britain. It is good that you have come.' He slapped his hand on the man's shoulder, 'Most good. Welcome, my Lord Enniaun, welcome!'

From the time before Enniaun had become Lord, when his father, Cunedda had been the Lion Lord of Gwynedd, representatives from that mountainous corner had been deliberately absent from Council. Vortigern had been King then, not Arthur, and it had been the King's own nephew who had butchered Cunedda's youngest son and violated Gwenhwyfar, his only daughter. It had been a bad time of darkness and bloodshed, and because of it, Gwynedd had taken herself away from the destruction of Britain and claimed independence. Enniaun called himself prince, though many others of his thinking were claiming the right to title of king, as it had been in the Old Ways, before the coming of Rome. Ah, the differences between the men who had grown fat from the authority of Rome, and those who had found that her dominance left them lean and trodden under heel!

A voice from somewhere near the back of the crowd carried an insult 'So the wasps gather around the rotting fruit!'

Embarrassed silence. Men shuffled, dared not look at the next man or at Arthur. Enniaun broke the acute discomfort by suddenly laughing, his great voice booming up to the vaulted ceiling and hanging there a moment before echoing along the walls. He hugged his sister, grinned at Arthur, and said clearly, 'I would rather say bees! Worker bees constant to their hive!'

A few ripples of laughter, mostly false.

Lindum's Governor hastily motioned slaves forward to serve refreshment. Fine wine, pastries and fruits. The awkward moment of tension passed, people relaxed, began to eat and drink.

The Governor dabbed sweat from his forehead. He did not welcome Arthur, wished him gone – wished him dead – but it would not do to have the Supreme King and the great Council of Britain at each other's throats and brawling within the entrance hall to his basilica.

Time enough for that in its rightful place; on the morrow, within the confine of the Council Chamber; when they intended to curb the arrogance of the royal whelp.

§ XIV

Arthur slept poorly that night, tossing and turning beside Gwenhwyfar, mumbling through restless dreams. Some time during the long hours before dawn, Gwenhwyfar slid yawning from the bed to pour a generous goblet of wine for each of them.

'Sorry, Cymraes,' Arthur apologised as he took the offered drink. 'I am unused to sleeping within doors, the noises of night filtering through my tent is preferable to the heavy silence of stone walls.' A thing from childhood, not easily shaken, this fear of confinement, but for all that, this was an excuse.

'It has never bothered you before,' she replied, sliding back into bed beside him. Her feet had become chilled even during the short while she had been out from under the warmth of the furs. She sipped her wine, the warmth of its rich redness trickling down her throat and into her belly. 'Does the calling of this Council worry you so much?' she asked.

Arthur took several gulps of his wine before swinging his legs from the bed, letting his bare feet dangle. He played with the goblet a moment, finished the contents, then with sudden irritation flung it across the room to clang against the stone walls and land, dented, on the floor, where it bounced twice and rolled beneath a stool.

Gwenhwyfar remained still, sipped her drink. 'Since we left Winta's village you have favoured a public image of good humour. The pretence does not fool me, husband.'

He half turned to her with a sheepish smile. 'Am I so easily read?'

Gwenhwyfar placed her goblet on the floor and, wriggling across the bed, took his face between her palms and kissed his lips. 'I know what you are thinking as surely as I know my own thoughts. I hurt when you hurt, laugh when you laugh. That is part of loving the man who is as important as the sun, moon, earth and sky to me.'

'Unfortunately,' he said, returning her kiss, 'you are not my Council.'

She laughed, playfully ruffled his untidy hair. 'Glad I am then, that I am not!' She eased her legs more comfortably. 'Mithras, you look forward to meeting with your Council with as much enthusiasm as you would give to entering a plague-infested slave-pen!'

He saw her point, and laughing with her, swept her close to him, burying his head among her tumbled mass of copper-gold hair. Muffled, his voice said, 'I almost wept for joy when I saw your two brothers. Gwynedd in her independence has grown strong. She is a power to be reckoned with.'

Gwenhwyfar rubbed her hand down his back, her fingers kneading at the tense muscles in his shoulders. 'I wrote to Enniaun asking him for support,' she confessed into the dim light of the night-lit chamber. She faltered. Hard to decide between Arthur's great need and the horror and blackness of the past. Those times, as Arthur had said, were best not recalled, but too, must never be forgotten. Etern had been her beloved brother. From early childhood they had run together. Even now, after the passing of years she could not wholly believe his cruel murder, expected one day to see him walk with his jaunty swagger through a door, or hear his favourite whistled tune.

With a noticeable catch of sad memory, Gwenhwyfar said, 'It is time that the wounds were healed.' She forced a lighter note. 'I thought allies for you would not come amiss given the black mood of your Council.'

Arthur kissed her again in gratitude, once, gently, on the forehead, then stood, plunging forward with frustrated energy, slapping the wall with his palm. 'I ought to disband Council, do away with them, rule alone with no piddling little fat men trailing their whines and grumbles between my feet!'

Reaching again for her drink, Gwenhwyfar paused, her eyes widening. 'Could you do that?'

He stretched, reaching towards the low ceiling, muscles bulging and rippling along arms, naked back and shoulders. He yawned, admitted, 'I doubt it.'

'Yet there are some in Council you trust. Loyal friends, such as the Governor of Viroconium. Emrys . . .'

Arthur snorted. 'Do the words friend and Emrys belong together in the same sentence?'

She acknowledged his half-serious jest with a quick smile and inclination of her head. 'He is your uncle.'

'He was my father's brother, but still he did not support Uthr against the tyrant, Vortigern. Brothers, or fathers and sons, have killed for less disagreement than I and Emrys have regarding the ending of Roman authority.'

Gwenhwyfar frowned. 'Yet he is loyal to you?'

Arthur puffed his cheeks, sat beside her, rubbed the cold from his arms with his hands. 'Emrys believes in Rome – Rome as it is remembered, not as it is now. He claims I am hastening the fragmentation of the Province with my setting up of client kingdoms and tribal territories. We are caretakers, he says, we ought to be holding Britain in trust until the Emperor is free to return.' He placed one hand on her shoulder, touched and enjoyed the smoothness of her skin a moment, let his fingers drift across her neck, lie above the beat of her pulse. 'He would not back my father because Uthr was stirring war and he would not take part in a squabble concerning the parcelling out of goods unlawfully taken.' His fingers rambled lower, touched the swell of his wife's breast. 'Though for all his difference of opinion, Emrys has one quality. Never will he go back on an oath – and as appointed Governor of Caer Gloui, he has sworn allegiance to me. Whatever Council argue, I expect Uncle Emrys to stand firm for me.' His lips kissed where his fingers had lain. It sounded convincing enough when spoken, but was it truth? If Council intended to replace him with one of their own choosing . . . Would they choose Emrys? He spoke another thought aloud, his lips hovering above a second caress. 'Trust Emrys as a friend? Na, Gwenhwyfar, never that.'

He moved from her, searched with his eyes for his goblet, went to retrieve it and fetched a jar of wine. His back to the bed, he said, 'Until the day I can turn Hasta loose to graze peacefully in the summer sun, I need to put faith in Mithras's protection, and pray that men like Emrys see sense above personal belief.' He drained the goblet, placed it with exaggerated care on the table next to the wine jug. He lifted his arms, stretched, and let them fall with a slap to his bare thighs. He turned to face Gwenhwyfar. 'I have little faith in prayer, my Cymraes.'

Returning to the bed, he flopped down, lay on his back with hands flung behind his head. 'Why can they not see that if they were to leave defence and security to me, then I would be only too happy to leave alone their irritating little domestic worries? A king is as strong as his army – and although our numbers are not great, I command the best. The best ever.'

'They feel threatened, Arthur. Frightened. They see you as a mighty and powerful man who could crush them at the drop of your hand. Some of those men in Council saw Vortigern rise from poverty to supreme authority – those who did not see it with their own eyes, heard from the lips of their fathers. They saw hideous things happening with Vortigern's blessings – and they fear that worse may come with yours. Look what happened when Vortigern hired Hengest to fight for him! The bloodshed and enmity that followed! They see you doing the same. You show trust in the Saex, giving more to them than to the British. They see the Saex are your friends – as they were friends and kindred to Vortigern. Hengest's daughter was Vortigern's wife, their daughter once your wife. I also strongly doubted the wisdom of treating with them.'

He turned his head to her. 'Ah, but you were prepared to listen to me, to go see the results of a treaty for yourself.'

Gwenhwyfar conceded a smile, laid herself on top of her husband, her body moulding to his. 'Not at first. I protested loud, as I recall, at being forced to go among them.'

His sword- and rein-calloused hands stroked the softness of her back, running over the curve of her buttocks. 'Changed your mind though, didn't you?'

She answered, contrite, 'They are men and women who wish to grow their crops and raise their children in peace.'

Wickedly teasing he replied, 'That's not what you said as we rode north one year since. "Heathen, uncouth savages" you called them.'

'Aye well, there are many things they do differently from us.'

'Many things they do the same.' He was stroking the flesh along the inside of her thigh, his fingers inching intimately higher. 'For one thing, they make love the same way.' He twisted suddenly, brought her around beneath him, their mutual wanting making them both eager.

'Blood of the Bull!' she panted after, as they lay sweating in the aftermath. 'Are you likely to have many a sleepless night during this Council gathering?'

He grinned. 'You complain?'

'Na. Just preparing myself!'

§ XV

Weak autumn sunlight filtered through the cracked and broken glass of the high basilica windows; distorted shadows lengthening as the sun descended towards early evening. The most important and influential men of Britain were assembled in this room, a few sitting relaxed and half amused; the majority mistrustful and suspicious of the King's intentions. Men like Emrys – southern landowners, and the hierarchy of the Christian Church, headed by Archbishop Patricius. Governors, Elders; influential and wealthy merchant and tradesmen – men who relied on the patronage of those landowners and the Church. Most of them disliked the Pendragon. There was no denying that he was a good commander, but he was too blunt and intransigent, he trod on too many toes and threatened too many positions of power. Plain bloody-minded. Arthur was an army-created king who rode roughshod over civil matters, often ignored the judgements of Council and in his blatant pagan following of the soldier's god, Mithras, disregarded the holy sanctity of the true, Christian God. The people loved him well enough, farmers, peasants and common tradesmen. What did uneducated commoners know of the intricacies of government?

Britain, meaning wealthy, southern Britain, these powerful assembled men declared, was heading like a bolting horse into anarchy. Lawlessness and corruption was slithering along the crumbling streets, winding through unharvested fields and taking root in the very heart of the land. Disorder, they announced, was causing chaos and confusion. And the Pendragon, they added for good measure, far from setting seal to just and legal government was opening the gates of destruction wider.

A few men gave Arthur their support. Men from his own Dumnonia and the Summer Land; Enniaun from Gwynedd, and some other Northern lords. The old tribal areas welcomed his strong, military authority, for their lands ranged across the rugged and poorer acres of Britain, encompassing the rough grazing of the moorlands, the marshes, the hills and the hostile borders of the dark and fearful forests. Many of them were taking up the title of king, for the tribes had never quite forgotten or abandoned their Old Ways. Four hundred years of Roman dominance had not entirely despatched their traditions and beliefs – subtly altered them and intertwined them within Roman law and custom perhaps, the one shape-changing into the other, but never totally taking over. The British had long memories, and steadfast ambition. Especially where personal gain was concerned.

Outside this handful of allied lords, there were a few whom Arthur fiercely, and impotently, opposed. Dissident men, one-time heel-hounds to the king Vortigern, now several years cold in his grave, but with an irritatingly enduring influence. Men like Amlawdd. Vortigern had granted him land and a title. He had rejected any association with the Council of All Britain and was an agitating thorn in Arthur's flesh. A troublemaker, waiting for a future cauldron of dissent to come to the boil. But he was not strong enough to go openly against Arthur nor yet had he enough courage – or foolishness – to give the Pendragon the excuse he needed to give open challenge and make a fight of it.

Arthur was seated apart from Council, his chair raised on a stepped dais. Several things he would change, intended to change, when opportunity presented itself. This ridiculous seating arrangement for instance. A typical formation in the Roman style, columns of stools set facing each other across the long, narrow council chamber. Men needed to swivel or stand to see others along the rows, no chance to study expression or manner, a hindrance to close-watching a man's eye and thought. Arthur would prefer to sit in the tribal way, gathered circular, where each could clearly see the other around the central hearth-fire. Equal met, equal spoken, equal heard.

But it could not come yet, these un-Roman ideas of his. Arthur sighed, shifted his backside against the hardness of his seat. He draped a leg over the arm, sitting askew, undignified, noted the frowns of disapproval at his informality.

A discussion had been in progress this half hour concerning a raising of the tithe on goose fat. Arthur stifled a yawn. As a boy he had been attacked by a gander, a hideously vicious brute that had proved as tough in the pot as in life. He had never much liked geese after that.

Nor did he have much of a liking for these pompous little men talking so passionately about this trivial thing as if it were a life-or-death crisis. Self-important bureaucrats, seeing themselves as the protectors of the Roman Province of Britain, standing nobly firm until Rome came again to sort the chaos and restore peace and prosperity. How easily men forget!

Rome had bled Britain almost dry of gold, tin, corn and young men. With trade collapsing into ruins and the country sinking to its knees, Rome had demanded higher and higher taxes – then callously abandoned the people, leaving Britain floundering. Were it not for the still rippling repercussions of Rome's greed, Arthur would have no difficulty raising and paying a hundred times the men and horses he needed to sweep the Saex from these shores, could send them scurrying back to whence they came in one, well-planned campaign. Yet these myopic hypocrites seated here in this crumbling bastion of Roman influence refused to see through their own created fog of misremembered delusion. The golden age of Rome? Rot! Tarnished centuries of corruption and greed more like!

Decision at last reached and the vote taken. The consents had it. Arthur hid a wry smile behind his shielding hand. He must remember to inform Gwenhwyfar about the increase of her goose-fat entitlement. She would be delighted!

Archbishop Patricius stood, adjusted the fall of his robe, waited for a hush among the scuffle of shifting positions and coughing that had erupted at the conclusion of voting. He had a look about him that raised Arthur's interest. This was it then, the serious business.

Being deliberately provoking, Arthur laid his left leg across the first. Sitting sideways in his chair, he hooked an elbow to the chair-back and waited for the Voice of the Church to speak.

Patricius looked directly at the King, his intense blue eyes unwavering, stance determined. 'Land is being casually parcelled out to the heathen Saex. Our land, our sacred British land. Where the Lord Jesu himself once walked as a child, now barbarian savages seep the soil with the blood of our fellow countrymen.' Nodding heads, a tapping of agreeing hands on knees and thighs. Patricius took a pace nearer to Arthur, with a flourish, produced a thin scroll of parchment from the folds of his robe. 'I have a list of the land lost to us. A shameful, despicable, sad, sorry list.' He unrolled it, dangled the lines of neat handwriting before his captivated audience a moment before turning it to read aloud. 'Cantii. Given to that foul butcher Hengest, as his own Saxon kingdom. British land in the region of Londinium has become the dark and God-rejected East Saex and Middle Saex . . .'

Arthur noisily cleared his throat, interrupted. 'Those last two areas were settled under Rome's Governorship.' He spread his hand. 'They are third- even fourth-generation settled, peaceful English.' He smiled at the Archbishop. 'Take up the giving of that land with Rome; as you well know, it's nothing to do with me.'

For Patricius, that small detail was immaterial. He read on. 'To the south of here the marshes, Anglia, are given to Icel,' he pronounced the English names as if they had a putrid taste, his nose and mouth wrinkling. 'And I hear from Lindum's good Governor that the area you gave these poxed Humbrenses has been named Mercia, Land Of The Border!' He slapped the parchment, disgusted, with the back of his fingers, the harsh sound echoing against the damp stone walls. 'Why a Saex title? Why do we not insist on Latin or British?' His sneer deepened.

Muttered agreement, even from a few tribal lords loyal to Arthur.

Patricius was a gifted speaker, a man respected, if not liked. He rolled his small piece of parchment, stowed it again within the folds of his robe, then pausing for effect, lifted his hands in prayer to intone, 'Oh Lord our God, they have burned with fire your sanctuary on the ground, they have polluted the dwelling place of your name!' He turned suddenly and strode towards Arthur, hand outstretched, bejewelled finger pointing. 'It must stop, this wanton giving away of British land. *You* must be stopped.'

Arthur's eyebrow lifted a little higher. He shifted position but made no answer as the Archbishop swept forward to stand two strides before him. One or two councillors were on their feet, echoing his last words.

'We will have no more of it!' The Archbishop's cry clawed up into the vaulted roof, rattled among the worn, stone supports. 'Too late now to save land that has been given to the wicked demons who have raped and tortured, too late to save those British souls condemned into slavery and a life without God's light. Too late to—'

Unable to sit quiet any longer, Arthur protested, 'Your precious southern land is not under threat.' He swung his legs down, leant forward. 'On the contrary, these agreed borders ensure the protection of your massed wealth, of your holy churches and rich estates.' Arthur smiled, a wry smile that held no warmth or amusement. 'While I am King you are well enough protected. Although I cannot guarantee the lasting of these treaties after my death or,' he paused, looked along the rows of glowering men, 'departure.' He gazed a long moment at the Archbishop, then came slowly to his feet, unfolding himself from the hard, cramped chair.

The Pendragon wore cavalry dress of leather and light mail over a white linen tunic. Across his shoulders, a scarlet-red cloak fastened by a silver and ruby cloak pin, its crafted head, the size of a man's clenched fist. White and red, the colours significant of the Artoriani. Resting at his throat the royal torque. It had been his father's once, this gold, jewel-eyed, coiled dragon. The tyrant king Vortigern had personally lifted it from the bloodied, hacked neck of Uthr's severed head. Some small, pleasurable revenge had come to Arthur the day he retrieved the thing from Vortigern's treasury.

He was a tall man, Arthur, his body muscular and lithe; with his prominent nose and keen, penetrating eyes, he gave the impression of a stalking lion. Determination mixed with stubbornness. He pushed past the Archbishop, walked the length of the long, narrow council chamber, surveying each man with his unnerving gaze. At the far end, he turned, leant against the wall and folded his arms.

'I have given away nothing. I permit the English to live on our land for harsh and exacting payment. Taxes, I might add, that balance the amount I would need ask from you were I not collecting it elsewhere. Nor have I abandoned anyone into Saex slavery. All had equal chance to leave when the treaties were agreed. The farmers elected to stay – as freeborn beneath the Saex. Farmers, I have found, take small heed to who are their overlords, they tend to stay loyal to their orchards, flocks and herds.' His wry smile appeared again. 'The Church fled Durovernum, as I recall, hitched their cassocks and ran, bleating and mewling for safety.' He laughed, pushed himself from the wall and strode back up the aisle. 'So much for faith and trust in the Lord?' He reached the Archbishop. 'So much for spreading the word of God to those who have not yet embraced Him.'

Patricius blustered a moment before blurting out, 'Are you suggesting we should soil our robes by preaching the Blessed Word to those, those . . .'

Arthur finished for him, 'Pagans?' As he brushed past, heading for his seat, he paused, said wickedly in Patricius's ear, 'Yet you try often enough with me, Archbishop.' He leapt up the two steps, sat, added, 'But then, you are not overkeen on soiling your hands on me either, are you?' Several men, Arthur's supporters, laughed. Others growled and grumbled.

That flutter of tension created by the Archbishop had eased, defused by Arthur's wry humour. Patricius needed to create credence again, to master the upper hand. He did not fear Arthur for Patricius was a man who saw only his own path of ambition. 'We,' he spread his hand towards the Council, 'will have an end. No more land to be given casually to the Saex.' Arthur sighed, held his tongue. 'No more petty lords taking up these preposterous titles.'

Enniaun rose, signalled the need to speak. 'We take our independent titles, my Lord Archbishop, because were it left to Council, our swords would become rusty, our shields cracked and our spears blunted. Some of us need to defend our lands against the heathen – we do so unhampered by the humming and hawing of a Council that is, without doubt, only interested in the welfare of the South.'

Several men applauded – Northern men. Ceredig added, 'Arthur sees that we have free rein to defend our own, while giving us the extra security of knowing his men will come to our aid if asked.'

'Will you so aid us, Archbishop, the next time the Scotti raiders from Hibernia take sail and invade my Gwynedd coasts?' Enniaun asked.

'I cannot, will not, say aye to your suggestion, Archbishop.' Arthur spoke pleasantly, mildly, pronouncing the words clear and precise in Latin, as if he were patiently explaining some peculiarity of life to a small, unintelligent boy. 'The Northern lords have the right to take what title they wish, providing they pay homage unquestioned to me. The Northern lords, Archbishop, have need to keep their weapons burnished, their spears sharp.'

Someone from the far end maliciously called, 'Even Lot?' Several men laughed.

Arthur glowered, snapped a response. 'Aye, even Lot.' To Patricius he growled, 'The first request I agree to. No more land for the English.'

The Archbishop bowed, returned with measured dignity to his seat. Councillors were nodding, a few applauding, most smiling. They had achieved part victory.

Patricius made himself comfortable, folding and patting his heavy clerical robes into place. He twiddled the garnet of his curial ring, appeared intent on its dazzle, said as if it were no important matter, a mere, informal, addition, 'Vortigern dispensed with the four Roman administrative divisions of Britain. We have made decision to restore them, in an altered form of two divisions.' He folded his hands on his lap, looked up, along the row at Arthur. 'Britannia Secunda, the South, will be ours to hold. The North, Britannia Prima, save for Eboracum and Lindum, is yours to do with as you will.' Magnanimously, he added. 'You may of course retain your own lands of Dumnonia and the Summer Land; they will not be part of our administrative area.'

Arthur resisted the urge to come to his feet, to join those angered tribal lords in their immediate, loud response of rage. His first reaction was red anger, the second, raw indignation. The third stone-hard hatred. They had thought this thing through then, the ringleaders, thought it through and made a decision. *We*, Patricius has said. Who were *we*?

The outrage from the Northern lords was thunderous. All men were on their feet, bunching around the Archbishop, outnumbered by his supporters, shouting the objections down. It was Enniaun, Lord of Gwynedd who loudest voiced their opinion. 'Britain cannot be thus divided. Such an act will weaken our borders tenfold. The Saex, the Picti, raiders from Hibernia, will be the stronger if we tear our own strengths apart – even Vortigern saw that! Under the Pendragon we are firmly united in our defence, for it is him and his Artoriani and our unity our enemies fear.'

Agreeing, a group detached themselves, marched towards Arthur in appeal, Ceredig among them, demanding the Archbishop's immediate retraction. Arthur sat forward, his elbow resting on the chair arm, his face stone, inwardly seething. Above the uproar he bellowed, 'And just who, Archbishop, is to be your principal governor?'

One man had remained seated, impassive to the running emotion. The voices were calming, each man looking at the other, whispering, questioning, 'Who?'

Emrys rose to his feet, heads turning as he moved through the crush of men, stepping around Enniaun, moving past the Archbishop, walking along the aisle, walking towards the King's dais. A tall, stately-looking man. Emrys ap Constantine, a dignified, proud man, one of the few who retained the right of wearing the purple-edged toga. Uncle Emrys, always so serious, youngest brother to Uthr Pendragon; Emrys, a true, unflinching Roman. One of the most powerful civilians in authority below Arthur. Who could, if circumstance dictated, and the army consented, make valid claim for supreme king. Except Emrys passionately believed in the Empire, and for him that title was not legal. Was not Roman.

Into the hushed silence he announced simply, without need to raise his voice, 'I am.'

There must have been only a chosen few aware of the decision, for there came too many gasps, too many astonished faces into the heartbeat pause that followed. Only the prime influential men stayed smug, satisfied.

Arthur was shaken. It was cool in this high, slightly damp, stone-clad room, but he felt a trickle of sweat slither down his back and armpits. Those great, high arches seemed to be closing in, pressing forward, the room was cloying, choking. A childhood thing, this fear of enclosed spaces. His throat was dry, his skin clammy, but he mastered the swirling sensations, controlled the feelings of nausea and panic. Said, his voice steady, 'As *Comes Britanniarum*? Or do you intend for the higher title of *Dux*?' Tagged on sarcastically, 'You cannot, of course use the title "king".'

Emrys either missed, or chose to ignore, the dry humour. 'I am not challenging your personal preference, nephew, nor am I challenging your right to rule your own lands. All I take is Britannia Secunda.'

Someone else, a noted landowner from the wealthy area around Aquae Sulis, called in a derisive voice. 'The lands that your friends, the Saex, leave you, anyway!'

Arthur barely heard the remark. The sound of rushing water was gushing in his ears, the room spinning in a whirlpool of dizzying confusion and fear. He must master this! Must not appear beyond control! With effort he signalled for a slave to bring him wine, took the goblet and sipped slowly, directing his full attention to the tall, austere man standing a few yards before him. This Roman traitor to the Pendragon name.

The wine was watered, but strong enough to chase the unsteadiness far enough for Arthur to take a breath and fight it full off. The brief crisis of panic was subsiding, retreating. He took a last sip of wine, gave the goblet back to the slave, stretched, clasping his hands behind his neck. His fingers rested a moment on the great dragon-head shape of his torque, felt its smooth reassurance of power that was his. He stood, stepped from the dais. Abreast of Emrys, he stopped, regarded the man eye to eye. They were of similar height, build, though Arthur was the more muscular.

For a while and a while, Arthur stood there, holding his uncle's gaze, no sign of his rapidly calculating thoughts reaching his bland expression, then, with decision made, he nodded once, a minimal movement. 'Then it is yours, Uncle, aside from the path of the Ridge Way. That will remain mine to use as and when I need. Your boundaries shall be within a triangle between Calleva, Aquae Sulis and the Hafren.'

Emrys answered, unmoved by the chill in his nephew's tone, 'A square, Pendragon, north and west as you say, but to the east I shall have from Venta Bulgarium.'

Arthur's jaw clenched, his hawk-brown eyes darkened, his nails drove into the palm of his right hand, mastering the urge to loose his temper, ram his fist into this whore-son's teeth. His father's brother had, until this moment, been nothing more than a nagging irritant, a slight disappointment, but the rules were of a sudden changed. Emrys had become a serious threat. The opposition. An enemy.

Arthur spoke with quiet menace. 'Venta. Why Venta?'

For answer Emrys spread his hands, smiled. 'Why not?'

The Archbishop Patricius had joined Emrys, other men falling back as the three stood, squaring up to each other, defiance and anger rippling between them like flickering lightning. 'I am taking up residence within Venta's new-built Holy House.'

Arthur's eyes went from the Archbishop to his uncle, back to this pompous man of God. They were in this together then, the three of them, Patricius, Emrys, and . . Winifred. He forced a casual laugh; not for all his blood would he let them see how this had unnerved him. 'Venta, where the bitch I once bedded as wife reigns as the whore queen she is. Have it. Have her.'

The Archbishop protested, stepping nearer to Arthur, himself becoming angered. 'My Lady is a good, holy woman. Your true wife, and mother of your only legitimate son . . .'

Arthur sprang across the small gap between them, his hand coming out as fast as a snake's bite to grasp the Archbishop by the throat. Into his face he hissed, 'I know what my ex-wife is. A scheming bitch who will try anything to put her son in place of my first-born.' The Archbishop's hands were clawing at Arthur's, his throat gurgling and choking, face reddening. Emrys's hands came up, began to pull at the Pendragon, Enniaun, on the other side, persuading him to let the clergyman go. Arthur heard neither, but released the man anyway, swinging round to snarl, 'Remember this, Uncle, Winifred is a Saex whore and the daughter of a bastard tyrant.' He walked the length of the room, flung the door wide, turned to salute Council. 'Remember that when she demands more than that poxed little town.' He swung around on his heel, left, as the last glow of evening sunshine streaked in patterns of red and gold across the grimed and cracked marble floor. From outside, a thrush sang its evening chorus. The air hung heavy with the scent of damp earth and rain.

December 460

§ XVI

Lot enjoyed playing with his daughter, a bonny little bairn, with dimpled cheeks and laughing-bright eyes. She was dark of skin, hair and eye, different from his own fair colouring – and Morgause's sun-gold hair and pale, smooth skin. It was like that with some children, Morgause had said, they take after the grandsire. Her father, she told him, had hair as black as night and skin as brown as a nut shell. Lot had no way of knowing that his wife held no qualms about lying.

Dancing his daughter on his knee, the proud father gurgled and chuckled with her; she was growing so fast! The smell of roasting meat wafted through from the Hall. Lot looked up as the child's wet-nurse entered. He sighed, time for Gathering, and time for his dear-heart to suckle for her milk and be settled for the night.

He stood, and giving the babe a last hug, passed her to the waiting woman. She smelt deliciously of mother's milk and babies, a warm, comforting smell. Morgause would never smell of children. She had not even allowed the child to suckle her first milk, it would ruin the shape of her breasts, she said. Lot supposed she was right. In everything else she was. Even that she was to bear a girl-child. Again Lot sighed, more pronouncedly. He had so wanted a son. Guilt at this thought, meaning he did not love his daughter, plunged into him; feverishly he kissed the lass's head, watched proudly as she guzzled the woman's milk. Fine, large breasts, milk-swollen and round.

Hurriedly, embarrassed at his thought, Lot swung from the room to welcome the men of his guard and people of the settlement whose turn it was to dine in his Hall. He wanted a woman, wanted Morgause! But she was away, up at the Picti settlement on the banks of the Tava, sealing the agreement of marriage between their young daughter and the son of Drust with Ebba's Council.

'Come back before the snows fall, my beloved!' Lot had pleaded and Morgause had laughed, and kissed him goodbye and promised that she would. But she had not, and now the snow lay thick with more to fall. She would not be home before the thaw. Which could be weeks away yet.

Morgause curled, contended and warm, in Ebba's arms before the hearth-fire, wrapped in wolf-skins, lying on a thick bearskin rug. Ebba was so good at love-making. Almost as good as the only other man who had been worth bedding with. Uthr Pendragon; ah now he had been a man! Not the snivelling little whelk Lot had turned out to be. Why in the Mother's name had she saddled herself with him?

Ebba moved in his sleep, nuzzling closer into the softness of her naked skin. Why? Because marriage to Lot had been convenient, and had, at the time, offered the greatest potential. No matter that he was as useless as a broken spear shaft. There were others who could fill her needs.

There were no lamps lit, and beyond the firm-shut door the wind howled like a hungry wolf-pack. It was probably snowing again. Let it! Let it snow and snow! She could not leave here until the snow thawed, and she did not want to leave, not yet.

When she did, it would be to begin the slow spreading of the word of a war-hosting. Not yet, happen not until a summer and a winter passed, but the men would gather, men of Lot's Northern British and Ebba's Eastern Picti. If they were lucky, the other tribes of the Picti would join them also – and then they would head south, down across the Wall. And meet with Arthur and his damned Artoriani and wipe them – him – from the world!

She lay, watching the movement of the flames while Ebba slept. Witch-woman many called her, a title she fostered, for it brought fear into the hearts of those who served her, and fear brought loyalty. None would disobey Morgause. Not Lot, for the imbecile loved her and feared to lose her; not Ebba, for he wanted her as his own, and feared he might not get her, but that was a different fear. The peasants and farmers feared her for her knowledge and her power . . . even the King, Arthur, feared her. Hah, although he tried to hide it!

Her smile was lazy, smug. Witch-woman? It look little to make simple people believe in the nonsense of magic. A knowledge of healing herbs – aye and their destructive uses – a knowing how to write in a neat, straight hand, to read without moving your lips or speaking the words aloud; how to recognise the signs of the weather, or how a man thought by the movement of his eyes and hands. How to ensure you conceived no baby, or to change a boy into a girl! She laughed quietly to herself. Easily done. All it had needed was two cups of poisoned wine, a purse of gold and a day later, a side of pork as poisoned as the wine. The wine had been for the birthing women. They died quickly, quietly, no fuss, no suspicion. The pork? Meat was so often contaminated. She had lingered, the mother of the girl Lot thought to be his own, but even if she had talked, she had not known of who had wanted her daughter, or why.

And that left Arthur to be dealt with.

March 461

§ XVII

Winifred regarded her brother with a mixture of hatred and jealousy. Eight years old, arrived here only a few weeks past, and already the darling of the monks. Even the Archbishop, coming from the far end of the cloister, thought Vitolinus to be a model noviciate. She forced a bright smile for Patricius, said as he approached, 'My brother seems happy enough here at our holy place, I am glad.'

'Greetings, my Lady,' the Archbishop puffed, slightly short of breath through hurrying. She had arrived unannounced, unexpected. As she had an irritating tendency to do. 'You are well recovered from your slight illness?' He smiled pleasantly as Winifred nodded assent. 'Good, good.' He looked across at the boy, sitting on the sun-warmed grass among a group of youngsters his own age, occupied with stylus and wax tablet, busy chattering, occasionally laughing. 'Vitolinus has settled well, a most willing and eager young boy. I have high hopes for him, he has the potential of making a fine abbot.'

Winifred began walking, turning her back on the boy, ambling in the direction from whence the Archbishop had just come. 'Or an Archbishop?' she said.

'Who knows?' Patricius answered with light laughter. 'Perhaps he will turn missionary and take the word of God to your Jute kin.'

Winifred declined an answer, waited for the man to open the door into his rooms. This first was a small but practical chamber, with stool, table, stone-flagged floor, a single brazier – unlit. A public room that reflected the plainness of religious life. The Archbishop escorted Winifred through another door, beyond which were his personal rooms, larger, more richly furnished, made more comfortable. Few were permitted the honour of entering through here.

Winifred seated herself on a couch, accepted the offer of wine. 'I no longer associate with my mother's barbarian kin, Archbishop, as you well know. Her father, Hengest, has been nothing to me these several years past. It was my wish for my young brother to come here, into a House of God to annul any lingering blood-taint of heathenism.' And to be able to keep close eye on him; and to be permanently rid of him, should the opportunity arise, she thought to herself.

The Archbishop inclined his head in apology, well aware that the Lady Winifred intended her brother to grow to manhood safely cloistered among a religious community. Safe, where he would pose no threat against her son. There was enough rivalry for the future between Cerdic and his half-brothers by that Gwynedd woman, without the added complications of Vitolinus's prospects. He said, half to himself, 'The Pendragon was not pleased, I understand, to learn that the Comes Britanniarum had transferred responsibility of the boy from his own care into ours.'

Relaxing slightly, that flicker of hostility passing, Winifred replied, 'My husband approves of nothing even remotely connected with his uncle, or with me, Archbishop. Had the Pendragon foreseen events, he would never have given the lad into his uncle's house in the first place – but then, at the time, they were not the enemies they now are.' She smiled, she so enjoyed Arthur's mistakes! 'Of course, were the King to have his way, I, my son and my brother would have been hanged by now. His uncle too.'

Patricius was shocked by her matter-of-factness, she saw it in his face, said, 'Arthur is a harsh man, a soldier living in a soldier's world. There is little nicety about him.' She smiled to herself, remembering their years as man and wife, 'Even in the bedroom the Pendragon could be brutal. I have the scars to prove it.' She waved any answer aside, added, deliberately shocking the Archbishop further, 'For the most part, I enjoyed it that way.'

She finished her wine, rose, smoothing the creases from her black gown. 'Now, to business. How is the building of my new church coming along?'

Relieved at the turn of conversation, the Archbishop too stood, with his hand indicated they should leave the room. 'Come, I will show you, it is all but completed. Your generous funding has enabled us to erect a fine place, more magnificent than any chapel yet built. I feel that we may even be justified in giving it a grander title, for chapel or church it is not enough. Cathedral would be more fitting.'

Winifred walked before him, back out into the sunlight, pleased with herself. Her prolific cultivation of the Archbishop and alliance with Emrys, was proving worthwhile, expensive, but worthwhile. Cerdic would be King – or *Comes*, or whatever – after Arthur. The manner of the title mattered not, only the position, the power. She could not yet influence the army, but Council and the Church was another matter entirely. They had already achieved one victory over Arthur by claiming the wealthiest portion of Britain for their own. And, subtly directed by her innocently casual suggestions, they could soon consider laying claim to even more. Winifred glowed within herself – plotting Arthur's downfall was so satisfying!

Vitolinus was still sitting on the grass in the centre of the quadrangle, surrounded by laughing boys. His looks were that of their mother, nothing at all of Vortigern their father. Winifred had a sudden, distinct image of him as a baby, yowling in his mother's arms as they struggled to survive the flood waters of Caer Gloui. Arthur had come for them, the three of them, Winifred, the boy and their mother, Rowena, come to make an end of them. But Fate had intervened, spilling the rain-swollen river Hafren over its banks, allowing their escape. Bloodied from Arthur's own hand smashing into her face, shaken, scared, Winifred had run with her mother, dodging the falling walls, wading into the cold, swirling water, plunging, half swimming, through the pouring torrent to high ground; breath sobbing, skirts sodden, death running close as a shadow. Rowena had reached firm ground first, clambered to safety. Had turned to her daughter, struggling to follow – and kicked her back into the muddied waters. When Winifred emerged, gasping, near-drowned, Rowena had gone, fled, with her son.

Vitolinus glanced up, saw her watching, answered her haughty gaze with a returned stare of loathing. The Pendragon had taken him as hostage from Hengest as part of the agreed treaty for the Cantii lands. He hated his grandsire for that betrayal, as much as he hated his sister. The one trading him for land, the other wanting him dead or safe out the way. Well, he could wait, play their game, until he came to manhood. Then they would see what he, Vitolinus, had in mind for himself.

He smoothed the wax on the tablet resting on his lap with the flat end of his stylus. Drew another obscene picture for the boys to crow over. This one was of the Archbishop copulating with his po-faced sister, Winifred.

May 461

§ XVIII

Llacheu was fascinated by the ancient stones before him, and a little wary. He squatted, peered into the gloomy chamber formed beneath the giant capstone, hesitant actually to crawl under. What if there was a body beneath there? Or worse.

A blackbird shrilled in the copse of trees away to the left; Hasta, Arthur's stallion, was eating grass, the steady tear and chomp a reassuring, everyday sound. The horse snorted, raised his head to shake away the irritation of flies, the leather and metal of his harness rattling and shaking in the flurry of movement.

The earth smelt warm and damp, a wholesome, pleasant smell of grass and earth and steaming stone. There had been heavy rain these last days, but today the sun was shining, radiating a promise of summer heat. The world was washed and refreshed, smelt clean and new.

Overhearing superstitious whispers about this old burial place, Llacheu had pestered to see it. At first glance, the stones seemed nothing more than a tumbled heap of flat rocks, but men from a time long past had laboured hard to bring them up onto these hills above the Gwy river.

'There are no bones,' the boy announced, withdrawing his head from the shadows beneath the capstone, disappointed but relieved.

Arthur laughed, and ruffling the boy's hair, bent low to peer into the diffused light of what had once been a covered chamber, resting his arm on the two-hand-span thickness of the single slab which had formed the roof. 'These stones were the framework, supports for the weight of earth forming a covering mound.'

'Like the timber frame of a house?'

'Aye. Any bones would have gone the same way as the earth and turves. Rain, wind and time have taken them.'

'Why use stones? Why not timber?'

Arthur straightened, began inspecting the construction. The one great flat capstone, longer than the height of a man, rested on uprights a few feet high. Surrounding banks of earth, grassed and covered with scattered wild flowers, were all that remained of what had been the outer walls of the burial chamber.

He answered Llacheu's question tentatively. 'Timber does not last, it rots and decays. Stone like this is strong and it takes a mighty force to destroy it. Certain – special stone – is sacred to some. The Old People erected circles of stone for their gods and burial places such as this. One day I'll show you and your brothers the Great Henge. Tall, tall stones,' he indicated with his hands a height way above his head, 'higher than a man on horseback. Each with a topped lintel stone, many believe it was built with the magic of the Druid kind.' Added, 'I was proclaimed Pendragon by your grandsire beside a sacred stone.'

'Was that when you became King?'

'Na, I was only a lad myself then, but the title of Pendragon gave me the right to become King. As my father had hoped to have been.'

'Uthr?'

Arther nodded.

'Your Uncle Emrys is his brother.'

Again Arthur nodded, but said, 'Ambrosius. We must call the wretched man by his adopted Roman name now. Ambrosius Aurelianus, not Emrys.'

Llacheu was only half listening, was peering again beneath the great capstone. 'It seems a curious thing to bury someone in this way. Far easier to dig a deep hole like we do.'

'I don't think they buried everyone like this. Someone of importance was laid here. A king? Winta of the Humbrenses once told me that the high kings of his people are sometimes laid in a ship with their armour and weapons and food, then the whole thing is covered over into a great mound to be seen and remembered by all. Hard work aye, but is not such a man worth the effort? An easily dug hole in the ground is soon forgotten.'

'The person buried here has been forgotten.'

'The person but not his burial place. Men are still feared to come here after dark, still make the sign for protection as they pass. The belief and the people are forgotten – forgotten even long before the Caesars came, but enough remains to remind us that once, others walked and loved, lived and died.' Arthur seated himself on the grass mound, picked a flower, began absent-mindedly shredding its petals. 'Remember that flint arrowhead you found? And the stone axehead?'

Llacheu nodded, they were treasures indeed. He felt for the pouch at his neck, unfastened it and tipped the contents into his palm, showed the arrowhead solemnly to his father. 'I carry it with me always, as my luck charm.'

Arthur took the thing from his son, examined it closely, said with straight expression, 'You don't haul the axehead around with you as well then?'

Llacheu laughed. 'It is in the bottom of my clothes chest! I made Mam swear never to touch it.'

Overhead, a lark was singing, fit to burst his feathers. On and on went his song of joy, singing and singing – and then sudden quiet as he dropped down to his mate, nesting somewhere among the sun-warmed, wind-whispered grass.

'I wonder if this was made by the same people who built the Henge?' Arthur mused. 'I do not believe it was all fashioned by magic. It is my experience that mortal blood and sweat form a large part of hard labour.' He gave the charm back to his son, watched him slip it safely away.

A fox trotted from the copse, disappeared among the low bushes to reappear further down the slope, heading at an easy lope down into the valley. Arthur watched him go, the chestnut red of his glossy summer coat against the brilliant green of new-grown grass. It was almost like being atop the world up here. Not as high as Gwenhwyfar's mountains of Gwynedd, of course, but the stillness, the sense of being alone created the illusion. The only man – and boy – in the world. A sudden fancy, a sudden weird feeling of nothingness. They were already dead, he and Llacheu, were spirits taking a last look at the sloping hills and the winding valley before passing into the other world, the world beyond this. Over there, way

111

away, beyond that bank of darkening cloud, lay the sea, and beyond that . . .

'I think,' said Llacheu, breaking his father's thoughts, 'that I would rather be beneath these stones than buried in the earth. It would not seem much different from going to sleep in a cave would it? The darkness of cold earth is a bit frightening.'

Arthur drew his son to him, held him close. 'Any death is frightening.'

Llacheu looked up quickly into his father's face. 'Even to you?'

'Even to me.' Death. This place stank of it.

The sun had gone, evening clouds were rolling back to claim the sky. The air felt chill. 'A lad your age need not worry about death. You have years of life stretching before you.' Arthur shivered. A spirit stalking over his future grave? He stood, said with forced jollity, 'Your mam will be wondering where we are – and my belly tells me it is time for eating!' He whistled to Hasta and hoisted the boy into the saddle, made to mount himself and checked. Grinning, he looked up at his son and without word walked forward, clicking his tongue for the stallion to follow. Llacheu sat proud and straight, realising the honour his father was granting him by letting him ride alone.

Watching his son's riding ability with a discreetly critical eye, Arthur thought how well Gwenhwyfar had taught the lad. He sat a horse naturally, with no fear, hand contact on the rein gentle but firm, grip from thigh and calf relaxed. The saddle was too large of course, the four horns not fitting across the thighs or into the buttocks firmly enough for security, but still, the boy had a good seat. The ground began to drop away, the hill descending steeply down into the valley. Llacheu adjusted his balance, leaning back, shifting his weight, his body swaying with the movements of the horse as Hasta picked his way down the grassed slope. Arthur smiled, pleased. A good horseman, his son.

Walking in silence, Arthur allowed his thoughts to wander. Who had been buried in that lonely, high place? Then, would he one day end up in some equally lonely grave or would he be left unburied on the battlefield, left for carrion to strip flesh from bone? He peered back at the stones, no longer visible, hidden by the crest of the hill. Those of the past might be forgotten, but their passing lingered on in superstitious fear. Or was it the inevitability of death that brought the fear?

The stallion's forefoot slid on the wet grass, Arthur put out his hand to take hold the reins, turned in the same movement to hold the boy's leg, relaxed, let go his grip. The lad was fine, his natural balance going with the unexpected movement.

'You ride well,' Arthur said with pride. 'You are almost six years now are you not?'

Llacheu nodded.

'You will be wanting a pony of your own soon then.'

'Mam said she would ask Uncle Enniaun to find one for me when we get to Gwynedd.'

'Did she.' The reply was blunt, curt.

Llacheu bit his lip. Last night his parents had argued again about going north to Gwynedd. He had lain in the family tent opposite Arthur's place of command pretending to be asleep, listening to the harsh quarrel. Mam wanted to see her family, to go where there would be a welcome and peace. Da insisted on going south.

'So you want to go north also?' Arthur said stiffly.

The boy was unsure how to answer. 'I want a mount of my own and, although they do not breed so many now, Gwynedd still breeds the best.' He stroked Hasta's silken neck. The stallion had been bred in the pastures of Gwynedd's rich valleys, bred from the descendants of Roman-imported Arabian stock. Hasta and his kind were beautiful, short springing stride, arched neck, bold-eyed and brave-hearted. He desperately wanted a horse like Hasta for his own.

'So, if your mam decided to go you would accompany her?' Arthur knew it was an unfair question, but he did not retract it. Life was unfair, Llacheu had to learn that lesson sooner or later.

His son toyed with Hasta's mane, winding the long white strands between his fingers. 'If you would take me with you, then I would stay with you. But you always say I am too young so I suppose I will have to stay with Mam and go where she goes. And I do want my horse.'

Arthur laughed, his tension dissipating. Good enough answer. He squeezed his son's knee. 'One day soon, boy, you will not be so young. Then you may ride with me.' He winked. 'Happen you ought to have a pony first though. I'll see what I can do.'

Llacheu grinned, then risked a question. 'Why do you not want to go to Gwynedd?'

Walking at Hasta's head, Arthur was silent a long while.

The lad felt his lip trembling. Why had he asked? He had spoilt everything.

When Arthur did answer, his voice was not laced with anger as the boy had expected, but full with sadness. 'Gwynedd is the one place where I do not, yet, have to watch my back for a dagger plunging in the dark.'

The boy was puzzled by this. 'But then, why are we not there?'

Arthur put his shoulder into Hasta's chest, halting the animal. He stood looking up at his son, his hand on the boy's knee. 'I must be seen, must make my voice heard, my presence known, must try and repair the damage which has been done.' He sighed. How to explain to a child? 'There are many influential men, followers of Emrys – Ambrosius – who dislike me, dislike what I am trying to do. If they can, they will stop me. They have already made a start of it by attempting to divide Britain, but while I command the Artoriani I am a force to be reckoned with. Should I ever lose the loyalty and respect of my men, Llacheu, I am lost, we all are.' He squeezed his son's knee. 'Should I expect my men to stand in the front line while I sit on my backside in comfort and safety?'

Llacheu stared at his boots. They were muddy, he would have to clean them when they got back. He said in a quiet voice, 'I do not like it when you argue with Mam.'

'By being in as many places as possible, I am showing defiance to those men who are against me.' Arthur took hold of the bridle, walked Hasta on, said to the sky, 'I do not like arguing either lad, neither does your mam. It is a thing we seem to do of late.'

Darkness had come by the time they reached camp, and a fine drizzle had begun to fall. Gwenhwyfar said nothing as Arthur ducked into the tent, delivered the boy and immediately ducked out again.

'Was it interesting?' she asked as she helped remove the boy's wet clothing, began to rub him dry and warm. He talked almost without pause through mouthfuls of steaming broth, Gwenhwyfar listening, asking the occasional question. Her eyebrows rose when he said, 'Da has promised me a horse. I hope I can have one like Hasta.'

Tactfully, 'Hasta is a stallion. A gelding for you, and something a bit smaller?'

Llacheu pouted slightly. Brightened. 'The same colour?'

Gwenhwyfar laughed. 'I expect that can be managed.'

By full dark, the boy was abed and asleep, curled with his two brothers, Gwydre four and Amr now almost two. Gwenhwyfar stood holding the tent flap open, staring at the night and the rain. It was not cold and the rain had scented the earth, grass and trees, the air was fresh and pleasant. Lamps glowed from inside other tents, the sound of men laughing or preparing for sleep drifting across to her ears. Arthur's tent over the way was well lit. Laughter came from there also.

She sighed. The past months had been filled by petty squabbles over silly, meaningless things. They never seemed to talk these days, to laugh. Or to love.

She let the flap fall, wandered to her own bed, sat on the edge unfastening the pins and braiding of her hair. Was it her fault, this conflict between Arthur and his uncle? She removed her tunic, sat for a while in her under-shift. His frustration and anger had to have an outlet, a vent, but it was so hard taking these constant blows. Arthur was not one to let things drop, to leave water unstirred. The argument that had sent him storming from Lindum had spread ripple upon ripple, creating waves that slapped angrily against the shore, and, as each season had passed risen into a darker storm.

He led a mounted force that could, if he so commanded, bring any man opposing him to his knees. His allies welcomed the strategy of his mercenary force. His enemies did not, but for all their opposition, Arthur remained Supreme King over all but this new-named Britannia Secunda. His men patrolled the borders of the English territories. His men were quartered in the shore forts along the south coast, effectively dissuading any newcomers. Arthur's men, allied with Gwynedd, held the peace in the unsettled North. Arthur himself controlled most of the Summer Land and Dumnonia. And Arthur's men had dug and built the great earthwork to separate his land from Ambrosius's, built it to stride east from Aquae Sulis before bending south towards Venta. They had thrown up the earth banks and erected the wooden palisade along the top, patrolled the walkways or sat by night in the mile-apart wooden watch towers. The Artoriani kept Ambrosius Aurelianus, Emrys, and his cronies firmly encased within a prison of their own making. From his guarded and patrolled borders, Arthur controlled what came out of and into Britannia Secunda.

Only the wild hills beyond the Roman Wall lay beyond his full control or influence. The rest, even Britannia Secunda, was, one way or another, his. But the price to retain it was becoming high. Almost too high.

Gwenhwyfar exhaled a long, weary breath. She was sick of living in a tent, of moving from place to place, camp to camp. They still had nowhere to call their own, no safe, peaceful, protected place where there was no argument or conflict, no need constantly to watch over your shoulder or fear a moving shadow. Nowhere that did not permeate the threat of death stalking at your heels. The argument at Lindum had ended all hope of settling somewhere.

Movement at the entrance flap. Gwenhwyfar's head lifted, startled. Arthur stood there, looking tired and careworn, like a man defeated. Wearing a smile, Gwenhwyfar went to stand a few paces before him. 'Llacheu enjoyed his afternoon. He learnt much.'

'A boy any man would be proud to call son. You look lovely.'

Gwenhwyfar felt her cheeks blush. 'Do you still think so?'

'Aye.' He reached forward, brought her to him but did not kiss her. His fingers played with her hair a moment, then he said, 'You know why I cannot go to Gwynedd.'

She released a slow breath. 'I know why.'

Arthur released her, swung away. Leaning against the tent pole he rested his head against his arm. 'Then why argue?'

'I am aware of your reasons, Arthur, but knowing does not make me like them. You keep us with you to prove a point, to prove to

Ambrosius that you are not afraid of what he might do. Well, I am afraid! I fear for my sons and I fear for you. It is almost as if we are on the run, as though we are criminals living outside the law. You pretend otherwise – but is that not the truth of it? Were you to stay overlong in one place somewhere else might have the courage to rise up against you, go with your uncle. We move from camp to camp, ride north, south, east and west making your presence felt, reminding the people and your uncle and the Church that you are still the Supreme King.' She wanted to go to him, touch him, hold him, but did not. This whole situation was running over-fast, like a river in winter flood. If the rise of water did not recede soon, the bank would burst. 'I want you as a husband, as a father, not as a king. I want you to say damn the lot of them and ride away from it all. To come back to me and your sons.'

'You want too much, Cymraes.'

'I want you. Is that too much?'

He looked round at her, eyes pleading. 'Do not ask me to choose.'

Gwenhwyfar slumped on the bed, her hands falling limp into her lap. 'Let us – the children, go. Let us go to Gwynedd a while. We have trailed in the wake of the army too long – Amr knows barely anything except life on the march. We are sick of it, Arthur, heart sick of it.'

He fingered a gold buckle at his waist, intent on tracing the ornate pattern. 'You once wanted to be always with me, were once angry because I forbade you to ride with me. I was equally angry because you defied me.' He looked up, straight at her. 'Have things changed so much between us?'

A tear slid down her cheek, splashed unnoticed onto her hand. 'I was young then, Arthur, now I am tired. Tired of this bickering between you and Ambrosius and the Church.' Gwenhwyfar shut her eyes briefly, before saying with a sob, 'And I am so tired of Winifred's presence always behind me.'

Her look, when she turned to him was exhaustion, pleading for a respite. 'I will fight Winifred until the day I draw last breath. For the sake of my sons.' She had to shrug. 'Though she fights for the same reason. Her own son is no doubt as precious to her.' Gwenhwyfar ran her hands through her hair, the soft glow from the single lamp dancing gold among the strands of copper. 'I sometimes feel though, Arthur, that it would be best to leave it all; to go quietly with my three born sons and let Winifred have what she wants.' She looked up at him. 'At least that way I need not always have the fear of her son killing mine some day.'

He was shaking his head. 'Na, love. Even were we to give Winifred my royal torque this very night, she would still see to it that Llacheu, any of the boys, were not around to threaten Cerdic's claim.'

Gwenhwyfar took a long, slow breath, said, 'So you keep us with you for that reason also, to show Winifred what? That you do not trust me out of your sight or that we are a loving, happy family?' She stood, the movement portraying her defiance. 'Hardly that, Arthur, are we?'

He took a deep breath, held it for a moment before exhaling. Although he returned her gaze, there was no emotion in his face, only a blank nothingness, shielding the feelings of panic and fear that were hurtling around his head and hammering chest. His voice was quite steady when he asked, 'If I let you go to Gwynedd, how long would you stay?'

Gwenhwyfar lifted a shoulder, let it fall.

He smiled, some of the hurt showing with it. 'As long as that?' He made to leave. 'I can not let you go, Cymraes.' He ducked through the entrance, was gone. She could not see his own tears, or read the thoughts. *You may never come back to me.*

Gwenhwyfar leapt to her feet, ran. He was already walking away, she followed, pulling at his tunic, but he did not turn, just kept on walking. The rain was a fine drizzle, drenching her under-shift, moulding the thin material to her body, plastering her hair to head, neck and face. 'Arthur, please stay with me. Talk to me.'

Into the rain-swirled darkness he answered, 'You want me to stay, yet you want to leave me. Make up your mind, Gwenhwfyar.'

Anger flashed in her eyes, swirling patterns of tawny gold against darkening green. ' 'Tis you who must decide, not I.' She whirled, re-entered the tent. For a moment she thought he was going to come after her. As the seconds passed, realised he was not.

The boys' nurse, Enid, lay beside them. Disturbed by the flurried movement she raised her head, expression questioning. Gwenhwyfar motioned her back to sleep, began stripping off the saturated clothing, found a dry garment and something to rub her hair.

The sound of rain pattering on the leather of the tent was insistent, irritating, a relentless beat repeated over and over. She did not want to leave Arthur, but she could not stay much longer bound within this wretched quarrel for pre-eminence that he was waging with his uncle. Is this what it was to be King? To make camp, break camp. March and march again?

If it was, she had had a bellyful of it.

§ XIX

Arthur did not return immediately to his tent. He went to the horses, a pretence of checking Cei's chestnut. The horse had stumbled earlier in the day, cutting its knee. He peered at the cut, satisfied to see that the minor wound was already beginning to scab over. Further down the line of picketed horses, Hasta was dozing, one hindleg tipped, head down, ears flopping. He came alert with a soft whicker as Arthur reached to make a fuss of him.

Gwenhwyfar had bred the stallion from her own mare, had trained him to carry saddle and man, accept a bridle and bit. Arthur, in turn, had taught him to step over wounded or dead bodies, ignore the smell and carnage of the battlefield, stand unflinching if his rider were to fall . . . a good war-horse was worth more than any gold or jewels or finery, for a good war-horse could save your life. Arthur gently pulled the animal's ears, stripping the wet hair between his fingers. You knew where you were with horses. There was an old story, one of the Caesars had made his horse a Senator because he did not trust or like the men of his Senate. Arthur patted Hasta's neck. If Caligula had to deal with men like his own Council, then well could he believe such a story! 'Shall I make you a Councillor, my lad? Would that ease all this disagreement? Could you make those who owe me, pay their debts?'

Arthur's sigh was bound with regrets and bitterness. He was in a web of tangled demands that he could not extricate himself from. Leave it all Gwenhwyfar said, go to Gwynedd and let them all get on with it! Give up being King, give up what he had fought for, believed in, all these years? Is this what it meant to be King? To be continuously quarrelling, stamping and snarling? To feel you had not one loyal friend, not one person to trust implicity?

His fingers moved to the velvet-soft pinkness of Hasta's muzzle, the horse's breath huffing warm on his cold, wet skin. The animal began to contentedly lick Arthur's palm, relishing the slight taste of salt.

He had not expected it to be like this; as a raw lad when he aimed for the taking of Vortigern's royal torque, he had exalted only in the dreams of leading a force of superb drilled men, of winning battles and bathing in the light of achievement and glory. It had not occurred to Arthur that other men might not share his vision, might not be content to follow in his shadow, nodding and smiling agreement at all he planned to do. The tedium of reality seldom sits amicable with the shine of hopeful, youthful, expectation.

Uthr had tried for the claiming of the same dreams – had he thought of what, by necessity, came in between the planning and fighting of battles, the thrill of campaign? Would the great Uthr, had he become King, have failed as miserably at the everyday routine of Kingship as his son seemed to be failing?

'Ah, my father,' Arthur said with a deep sigh of regret, 'You taught me how to fight but gave me no instruction on how to govern.' He patted Hasta's neck, told the horse, 'Fathers, tutors, all those who instruct your childhood with a myriad of information, neglect to give counsel on how to hold a woman's love.' He turned away. The one thing he needed to know: how to keep his Cymraes from leaving him. And there was no one to ask, save his horse. What was he to do? Take himself off into the hills, and do what? Become a farmer, a horse breeder?

She did not want that either, but he could not expect her to trail

120

much longer in the wake of the Artoriani on these endless rounds of tax collecting and loyalty gathering. They were all full to the back teeth with it. There was so much more he ought to be doing – finding a stronghold of his own, securing the sea-coasts from Saex and Hibernian raiders, watching the latest movement of Morgause and her weakling husband. Instead he had to ensure and ensure again, the loyalty of petty lords and chieftains to the west and east and south and north of Ambrosius's claimed land. Men who gave their pledge of alliance to his face and sent their young men to Ambrosius behind his back.

Laying his forehead against Hasta's neck. Arthur closed his eyes. He was tired of it, tired of this wasting of time when there was so much of importance to be done. Happen Gwenhwyfar was right. Give it all to Ambrosius, let him deal with the dissidents who refused to send men to train for the local militias, let him demand the due payments of cattle and grain. Except some of them would willingly give it. Men of the Church for instance. That was why the Artoriani were here, camped beside the swollen waters of the Gwy river; because an abbot refused to pay taxes to the King. Three days they had been here, their tents sprawling across the meadows that ran between river and monastery walls, their camp fires built high, the men deliberately rowdy.

The Pendragon's envoy had been refused entry to the monastery grounds, the gate remaining firmly shut even to Arthur's personal demands of admittance. Having subsequently to shout up at high, stone-built walls while standing in a swathing curtain of rain to a defiant abbot had made Arthur look and feel slightly ridiculous.

But then, this morning, the second, and as Arthur had implicitly pointed out, last, attempt had altered the situation. The rain had ceased leaving a blue-washed sky, draped in great puff clouds that had trailed languid shadows across a sun-steaming valley. The abbot had realised that the Pendragon was not going to go away, realised too, that the King was not bluffing, that he thought his terms to be reasonable enough. You are built on my land. You pay me, or I burn down your monastery. The thirty head of red-and-white cattle were to be delivered on the morrow.

121

He would have to let Gwenhwyfar go. Why was he keeping her with him? For his sons to see the failure he was becoming? To lose even this last tentative strand of his wife's love, because of these endless, mire-bound, squabbles? He pattered Hasta's neck, walked away, his cloak and shoulders hunched. But if he let her go, he would lose the woman who made him feel ten feet tall and capable of doing anything.

The guard on watch called a good-night, Arthur returned the salute. As well it was raining; lonely tears could not be seen in the rain.

§ XX

The river Gwy was high. Fed by rain-swollen tributaries, it lapped over low-lying banks, swamping tracts of grass and reeds. A fallen tree, with tendril branches and half its trunk covered by swirling water, became an inviting place for the children to play.

Llacheu leant forward, clinging perilously to the exposed part of the trunk. With the tip of his tongue poking between his lips in concentration, he prodded a stick into the debris caught between the submerged branches, raised a triumphant cheer as the current swirled away dead leaves, twigs and the sodden body of a fledgling bird. On the bank, his feet squelching, Gwydre threw stones into the racing torrent, making a challenge of aiming each further than the last. Amr, four months short of his second birthday, stamped his sandals in the mud, delighting in the delicious sucking noise and the cool squelch of mud oozing between his toes.

It had been a warm, pleasant day. Arthur was in a good mood; the cattle had been delivered and the abbot had sent a letter of apology. Words spoken in public would have been preferable, but Arthur realised those occasions when it was best not to push Fortuna's help over-far. Tomorrow, the tents would be taken down and they would move on.

The sun was setting. Pink sky, behind heavily shadowed trees ranked in solemn row along the opposite bank, their reflections casting black and distorted, onto liquid-gold water. Summer sounds; a chorus of evening song birds, unobserved little animals rustling their way through concealed grass tunnels, the rushing gurgle of flood water and the distant noise of camp. Men laughing, a dog barking, a horse neighing. Somewhere close, two men practising with their swords, heavy grunts and the clash of metal on shield. A sudden triumphant shout as one went down. A contented, warm, summer's evening with time to relax tense muscles and ease the mind away from the brash business of the day. A quiet evening for the passing of quiet pleasures.

Arthur felt happier with himself, in good humour. He threaded fresh bait to his line, cast. The fish were biting well.

At dawn, three Turmae of Artoriani had ridden around to the rear of the monastery. Whether Arthur's men would have fire-arrowed the hotch-potch of scattered buildings if the abbot had gone back on his word was another matter. It was a bluff the good abbot was not prepared to call; the gates opened, the beef cattle were driven out. The matter was settled.

Arthur hastened to his feet, jerked his line from the water, landing a fat perch. Llacheu, having grown bored with freeing debris, darted forward to catch the wriggling fish.

'Learn where and when to fish, my son.' Arthur winked at the lad. 'The trick is to dangle the right bait.' He watched with approval as the boy brought a stone down on the fish's head, killing it.

Llacheu nodded, understanding his father was giving him a lesson in more than fishing.

Rebaiting the line, Arthur eyed Amr squatting close to the water's edge. To his mind, he would rather face the agony of a slow death in the world than the alive-death of confinement within a Holy order. 'Come away from the water, lad, it runs over-swift. Llacheu, keep a weather eye on your youngest brother, huh?'

The eldest boy sighed. Loving his two brothers dearly, he would not see harm come to either of them, but the burden of responsibility fell as a heavy weight on his shoulders at times. Amr yelled protest as Llacheu, a little too roughly, dragged him away from danger. The pig-squealing disapproval changing abruptly to a chuckle of pleasure on finding himself dumped near an ooze of thick, virgin mud. He jumped into it, slipped, lost his balance and sat down heavily.

Llacheu laughed, his second brother Gwydre, and their da joining in. Amr flung back his head and screeched a thin, high, wail of displeasure, his pride wounded and bottom uncomfortable.

'Mithras! Look at the state of the boy!' Arthur said, laughing. 'We'll need to clean him up before heading back to camp. Your mam will flay my hide if she sees him like this.' Making an effort to suppress his amusement, Arthur crossed to the child and lifted him, whirling him round until the boy's tears became chuckles of pleasure, then set him down on his feet higher up the bank.

'I'll catch one more fish for our supper, then we will go.'

A kingfisher plopped into the water on the far bank. Arthur watched fascinated as the bright-coloured bird flashed down, re-emerging with a writhing silver fish in its beak. Rainbow-coloured water trailed behind as it fought with sodden wings for flight, the extended rays from sinking sunlight changing each cascading droplet to a shower of glistening jewels. The line pulled. Arthur sat at attention, began to ease the thing in. 'I have something big!' he shouted, standing now, struggling to hold the jerking rod in his hands.

Llacheu danced beside his father, yelling with delight. Gwydre joined them, the excitement contagious.

'Pull it in!'

'It's a pike!'

'Na, a river monster!'

Arthur braced his legs, fighting to land the huge fish thrashing for its freedom in the churning water, he loosened the line a moment, began winding it in slowly, give and take, gently, gently . . . suddenly the line broke. Arthur overbalanced and toppled backwards, falling into soft mud where he lay winded, arms and legs spread. His two sons rocked with laughter.

'Now you are as mucky as Amr!'

'You'll have to wash as well!'

Up-river, a cry. A splash. The laughter ceased abruptly.

'It was a monster.' Gwydre whispered, fearful, clutching at his brother's arm 'He's angry with you, Da, for catching him.'

Arthur was on his feet walking along the bank, frowning, then movement, panic. Whirling to Llacheu, he pushed the boy fiercely in the direction of camp, shouting, 'Run boy, get help. You're brother's fallen in the river!' As he spoke, he was pulling off his sword belt, his boots, flinging them aside.

Amr was clutching wildly at a branch of the half-submerged tree. White-faced, eyes terrified, mouth open in a long, soundless, scream.

Arthur plunged into the water, the coldness hitting his stomach, taking his breath. He caught hold of the trunk as the current grasped his legs, trying to pull them from under him. With added rainfull the fast-flowing river was a torrent of swirling eddies and undercurrents, strong enough to sweep away a man. Not daring to let go his tenuous hold, Arthur eased himself forward, forcing himself to move cautiously, fighting the clamour of racing fear for his son.

He reached the end of the trunk, fought his way through the tangle of branches, unaware that he was talking, calling reassurance, encouraging Amr to hang on, hold on, Da was coming. But whether it was the branch snapping, the river's persistent drag or the boy's lack of strength – happen all three – Amr's hold gave way.

Arthur shouted something, he knew not what, as the boy was taken by the flow and disappeared beneath the surface. Arthur plunged, struggled to keep his footing and went down himself. Black, choking water engulfed him. He struggled, thrusting with his legs and arms towards the light. He broke the surface gasping for air, coughing and spitting water from his mouth.

A few yards down-river he saw the boy. A frightened face, a chubby hand reaching frantically for his father.

Arthur struck out, driving his arms through resisting water, trying and trying again to swim across the current but the river lifted his body and surged away with it, taking him too far downstream. Again and again Arthur desperately attempted to reach the boy but the river swept him aside. He saw Amr disappear, saw for one last time the small hand clutching helplessly at life. He tried to turn, tried to swim up against the flow, found himself going under, down and down. His limbs ached, breath rattled in his chest, hammering drums pounded between his ears. Easier to give in. Easier to cease fighting, to let the river have him.

Somehow, he clawed his way to the surface, death gurgling in his lungs. He was distantly aware of shouting, of a rope whistling through the air, landing an arm's length beyond him. Arthur snatched it, his hands clutching gratefully, fiercely, his body falling limp as men on the bank hauled in the line.

On the bank, numbed and shivering, Arthur crouched on hands and knees, vomiting. Someone was speaking. Cei.

'You did all you could Arthur.'

'Na.' He coughed. 'Na, not enough.'

Others, white-faced and stunned, crowded close and silent, words inadequate. Arthur clutched at Cei, hauled himself upright. His legs were trembling; body and hands shaking violently. 'Mithras God, Cei. My son.'

'Let me through! Let me by!' Gwenhwyfar struggled through the knot of gathered men. Close behind her, panting, eyes wide with fear, Llacheu.

'Where is my son?' she was screaming. Her hair fell loose from its binding pins, billowed about her frightened face. Her glazed eyes darted, questioning. Men fell back, tight of throat, as she approached Arthur.

'What have you done with my son?' Her fists pounded his chest, the words breaking into a shrill cry as she shouted, 'Where is Amr?' Her hands clutched at his tunic, the material ripping beneath the gold buckle fastening. Arthur took the blows, not feeling them, not noticing them, feeling only a blank emptiness.

'I could not reach him,' he said, his own voice quavering. 'The river took him from me.'

Gwenhwyfar stared at her husband, her hands falling still by her side. 'Why are you standing here?' she asked tonelessly. 'Why are you not searching for him?'

She dodged suddenly around Arthur. Scrabbling along the bank, heedless of brambles tearing at her skirts and thick mud sucking at her boots. She scanned the sweep of river, frantically calling her son's name.

Her foot slipped. She tried to steady herself, but the ground was treacherous and she slid with a cry into the water. Instantly, hands were on her, trying to haul her to safety but she turned on the helpers, snarling defiance, pushing them away. Clinging to reeds and low branches she struggled forward, half swimming, half wading; her breath sobbing. Arthur dropped into the water beside her, the end of the rope knotted secure around his waist. He reached his arms to Gwenhwyfar, pulling her to him. 'We are searching, Cymraes, we will find him. Cei has already sent men downstream but it is growing dark, there is little we can do till morning.'

'My son is in the river!' she screamed. 'We must find him!' Distraught, her fingers plucked at Arthur's restraining hands, trying to break away from him. She kicked out, but her wet skirts were wrapped around her legs, her footing gave way and she tumbled backwards dragging Arthur with her. As water swirled over their heads the rope tightened, saving them both from being swept away. Arthur staggered, gained firm ground. Anxious men on the bank hauled at the rope, willing hands gripping them, bringing them to safety. Blindly Gwenhwyfar hit out, catching Arthur's face. One of her rings scored a deep line across his cheek.

'Amr!' she cried, struggling to be free of Arthur's hold. 'Amr, where are you?'

'Mithras Gwen, he is gone. He's dead.' As the words stumbled from his lips, Arthur shook and shook her.

'No,' she gasped, 'no!'

'I saw him go under. He is dead.'

Gwenhwyfar fell silent, utterly silent. The sun had set. The rose-pink sky was now a darkening blue; one or two brighter stars were twinkling faintly.

Arthur's hands relaxed, released their harsh grip. 'He went under, Cymraes. Did not come up again.'

Gwenhwyfar wrenched herself from him and stumbled a few paces away, to stand, staring at the blackening water.

With a dismissive wave of his hand, Arther sent the men away, asking Cei to take Llacheu and Gwydre. Both boys were ashen-faced. Gwydre had his fist stuffed in his mouth. Arthur knew he ought to say something to them, some words of comfort. But what? He had no idea what to say.

He stepped behind Gwenhwyfar, took her in his arms bringing her around to face him, meaning to hold her, to give what little comfort he could to her. She stiffened.

'Let go of me,' she hissed, tearing herself from him, whirling away.

He stood, arms held low, spread wide, palms uppermost. Bewilderment and pain creased his face.

She seated herself on a fallen log, sat with her arms clenched around herself, rocking her body gently backwards and forwards. Sat staring silently at the rush of river.

Arthur was shivering. The cold of the water and aftermath of reaction trembling through his body. There came a soft step at his side.

Cei placed a blanket around his cousin's shoulders, gave another into his hand and nodded towards the hunched figure of Gwenhwyfar.

'You are both sodden, Arthur, come up to the fire. The men have stacked it well, they have a good blaze.'

Arthur's numbed fingers curled around the corners of his blanket, holding the thing tight to him. He handed the second back to Cei. 'She will have nothing to do with me. See if you can persuade her to come away.' He began to trudge wearily up the short incline through the trees, his body aching, jarring with bruises and fatigue. Within a few moments Cei, empty handed, joined him, matching his pace to Arthur's.

'She will not come. I have wrapped her up as well as I can. Happen Enid can talk sense into her.'

§ XXI

At first light men stirred, began the morning routine with hushed, despondent whispers. Many forwent breakfast, their stomachs not up to facing food. These were battle-hardened men, but death in the heat of battle was one thing, the cruel taking of an innocent child another entirely. They searched, poking and prying into submerged overgrowth, tearing away tangled branches and roots; tugging at clogged debris. The river had dropped during the night, the flood waters dispersing as quickly as they had risen. Much of the bank lay sodden and flattened, a stink of mud and rotting vegetation.

Llacheu had not slept. He had gone to bed chilled and grieving, not knowing where his mother was, nor Enid. Nessa was useless for she could not stop her sobbing and aside, she had Gwydre to care for. He had tried to see his father but the sentry had turned the boy away saying, kindly meant, 'Your father needs be alone lad, go to bed.'

Come morning he had wanted to help search the river, but had not been allowed, and so he sat cross-legged before his father's tent waiting for them to come back, the thoughts in his heard turning deeper and darker with each passing hour. When they finally returned they were carrying Amr, wrapped in a soldier's red cloak. Llacheu stumbled to his feet, watched his father lay the dead boy carefully on the ground before the banners and standards of the Artoriani.

Llacheu had seen Gwenhwyfar cry before. She would cry over many things; the wonder of a new-born lamb or foal, a beautiful view, a sad tale told around the night fire. She was like that, responsive to emotion, and Llacheu loved her for it because he shared those sensitive feelings, understood the way a lump could rise in the throat and tears come unbidden to the eyes. At these times he often slid his hand in hers, shared the heart-pleasure that brought the tears. She cried also after arguments with Arthur. This was a different cry, one Llacheu hated. Her tears would come at night when she thought the boys were asleep. Llacheu would ache to go to her when he heard those tears of misery, but dared not. She did not want him to know she cried, so he would not know. It was a hard pretence for him to keep.

The shock came when he saw his father cry.

Frightened, he watched Arthur weep, longing to speak to his da, to ask for answers to confused questions. When he finally gathered the courage to approach he was too late. Llacheu whispered 'Da?' but his father did not hear, for he was turning away, going down the slope between the trees towards the river, to fetch Gwenhwyfar.

She had sat there all night among the damp and rising night mist, the morning dew and swell of sunrise and bird song, refusing to move. Enid, snuffling her choked tears, had wrapped the blanket around her mistress, kindled a fire and kept vigil with her. Now, seeing Arthur approach, Enid scuttled away, a fresh flood of grief exploding from her.

Arthur stood for some while watching his wife's unnatural stillness. These months had been wretched, for her and for him, their almost constant arguing coming from a frustration that gritted in both their stomachs. He approached and squatted at her side, took her chilled fingers in his hand. Her face was still, a statue's cold, impersonal face. Running his tongue over dry lips, Arthur swallowed, found he was rubbing her icy fingers with his own, found he did not want to say aloud the words that were within him. They were too final, too much of admitting truth. He swallowed again, forced himself to speak. 'We have found him.'

Her eyes flickered once to him, then back again to the river, no other movement. The water flowed, birds sang, a breeze ruffled through the trees. One of the red-and-white cattle lowed from somewhere behind.

'It looks so peaceful,' she said, 'this river. It slips tranquilly past on its journey from mountain to sea, winding a path between the trees, through fields and farms. It goes on for ever, in and out of seasons, heat and cold, night and day. A pleasant place to be, by a river.' Her eyes, haunted, met with his. 'A fox came in the night to drink. He looked at me for a long while. Others were watching too, the spirit people and faerie folk. I felt their eyes on me.

Staring.' She stood, the blanket slithering unnoticed to the ground. 'I know not what they wanted. They just watched. They never said anything.'

Arthur had known Gwenhwyfar from when she was a leggy girl with tousled hair and darting eyes, turning from child to woman. He had loved her then. Loved her now. He had shared her life and love, joys and sadness, yet she was still a mystery to him. There was a surface knowing, solid and recognisable, dependable – yet how much lay hidden, submerged below? He so wanted to comfort her, to share their grief together, but he knew not how. Knew not what to say or do, for he was hurting as much. The pain was so intense, so hard-bound that he thought if he spoke he would break, shatter into a thousand pieces, and scream until there was no breath left in him to scream again. Without speaking, he took her hand and led her up the rise of ground, through the green weep of willow trees to where they had made their camp.

Llacheu hung back, not knowing what to expect in his mother. Tears certainly, puffed eyes, red, sore cheeks. But her iron remoteness, as she drew level with the group standing bare-headed around the bundle laid on the ground, was unexpected. She knelt, an anguished sound escaping her lips as she reached forward and lifted back the covering. 'I thought you would find him alive. I thought you would bring me back my son!'

The tears broke as she lifted the dead boy, cradling his cold, water-blown body to her breast, her hands stroking his matted hair. They watched her a while, then Arthur knelt opposite her, laid his hand over hers. 'We must bury him, Cymraes.'

'I will not put him in the dark. He hates being alone in the dark.'

Arthur's fingers made to touch the boy's cheek, but like a whiplash her hand struck out, thrusting him aside, her voice a hiss. 'Do not touch him!'

Arthur jerked his hand back. The hatred that swelled in her dark-green eyes hit him like an axe blow.

'He was in your care,' she snarled. 'You let him fall in the river, you let him drown.'

The accusation was too much for Llacheu. He darted forward,

grasping his mother's arm, a sob breaking as he cried, 'No, Mam, it was not Da's fault. I was supposed to be watching Amr. I forgot about him when Da caught the fish. It was all my fault!'

She did not intend to be callous, but grief can gust like a great wind, ruthlessly sweeping aside all in its path. Gwenhwyfar tossed Llacheu's hand off her arm, casting him from her and he fell forward onto his knee, biting his lip to stem the cry of pain as a stone cut into the flesh.

Arthur bounded forward, gathered the boy to him. 'Take your anger out on me, woman, not your son!' he shouted.

'Amr is my son. My son is dead.'

Patience receding within his own turmoil, Arthur spat back, 'He was my son also! And you have two other sons – and a husband.'

'A husband!' She looked up, hysterical laughter choking in her throat. 'A husband? Where? I had one once, long ago, but he has gone. He spends his time chasing shadows and childhood dreams! He is too busy keeping a royal torque around his neck to notice his family, to see that the love we had is turning black and sour.'

Setting Llacheu aside, Arthur hauled Gwenhwyfar to her feet. 'I will not argue with you, Gwen,' he said, resolute. 'Not here, not now, not before the men.'

Gwenhwyfar threw back her head and laughed, a weird sound that touched on madness. 'Never in front of your men. You prefer their company above mine, don't you? Why is that, Arthur? Why?' She sneered into his face. 'Because they love you more than I do? They would lay down their weapons and die for you. I would not.'

Arthur attempted to propel her in the direction of his tent. 'We will talk about this in private.'

She threw his hands off her. 'We will not! I have nothing to hide. I am not the one who murdered Amr.'

Arthur's hand met her face, slapping her cheek. She crumpled as Llacheu clawed at his father, tears spattering down his face.

'Don't, Da, don't hit her! She did not mean it!'

Arthur stood taut, his hands and teeth clenched, body rigid. Slowly the tension eased and he dropped to his knees. He rumpled Llacheu's hair and lifted his unconscious wife in his arms. 'I know, son. I know she did not. Neither did I.'

None of the men believed that careless flung accusation. It was an accident, a tragic accident. Yet, words were whispered through camp and idle gossip spread from mouth to ear; for unguarded chatter has a habit of swelling beyond recognisable shape.

Arthur laid Gwenhwyfar on his own bed, sent someone scurrying for Enid. Already the flesh along the cheek-bone was darkening. He reached for his son, held the shivering boy close. Llacheu's arms encircled his father, the tears flowing, words muffled. 'It was all my fault, Da. All my fault.'

Instantly Arthur was crouching, his hands firm, strong and secure, grasping the lad's shoulders. 'It was not, it was nobody's fault. It was a thing that happens. If someone must take blame then your mam is right, it rests on my shoulders.'

Llacheu shook his head, wiped mucus from his nose with the back of his hand. 'You told me to watch over him. I didn't, and now he is dead.'

'Ah, my son.' Arthur enfolded the boy, hugging him close. What more could he say to reassure the boy?

'Mam will never forgive me,' Llacheu said in a small, trembling voice.

'There is naught to forgive.'

Enid, flustered and swollen-eyed from crying, bustled into the tent. Arthur lifted Llacheu into his arms as though he were still a very small child and ducked out, leaving with, 'Take care of her, Enid, I go to bury my son.'

Arthur went alone, save for the body of Amr and the companionship of his eldest son, Llacheu. He carried the wrapped bundle in his arms, Llacheu riding silent upon Hasta, the horse plodding amiably at Arthur's heels. They climbed the hill to the ancient burial place, to the sanctity of the Stones. Without exchanging words, father and son dug and scraped a cavity beneath the great capstone and laid the husk that was yesterday a laughing child beneath its ancient weight. They covered the red cloak that wrapped the body with soil and rocks and left, walking back to camp as quietly as they had come.

By sun-up the next day, the camp was empty. Charred circles marked the fires, flattened discoloured grass the tent pitches. To the north, the ground was churned with the passing of many hooves. And away on the ridge of a hill, the body of a small boy lay silent and cold among the shuffling spirits of the ancient people.

March 462

§ XXII

Ambrosius Aurelianus was ill. He had never been a particularly healthy man, and this winter's damp was taking its toll. A series of purges had cleared his stomach and bowels but still, after these weeks, most of whatever he ate refused to stay down. The pains in his stomach had eased, that was something to thank God for.

He huddled his cloak tighter around his shoulders, wished the brazier gave a little more heat against the persistent draught that howled beneath the doors and between the shutters. The holy place at Venta Bulgarium might be new-built but it was damned cold! He ought to have left for warmer Aquae Sulis, but he was too ill to travel. Unscrolling the parchment in his hand, he read the pleading for help a second time. What could he do to assist Eboracum? Could he mount his horse and lead an army against the raiding Northmen? – he could not even stand without the room spinning and his stomach heaving! In a burst of impotent rage he flung the parchment from him, sending it skipping and bouncing across the stone-flagged floor. Eboracum had sent this urgent, desperate word and Ambrosius could do nothing! The militia of Britannia Secunda had refused to go. Damn it, refused to go!

The door opened, a cloying waft of perfume, the rustling sound of a woman's garments, boots tapping on the floor. Winifred fluttered in. 'Oh, my Lord, do I find you still not well?' She flustered around, tucking a second fur over Ambrosius's legs, ordering a slave to make up the brazier, fetch warmed wine. 'There is a most tall, and extremely dirty, young man waiting outside. Do I have him sent away?' Winifred managed to make the question into an order.

Ambrosius grunted. Another reason he ought to be gone from here. Lady Winifred intruded, unannounced, too often. She had financed the building of his holy community and therefore saw it as her own. Riding to worship in the grand and imposing church every day, she was a God-cursed nuisance! Politely he refused wine, expressed that he would be needing to see that young man again.

Shrugging indifference, Winifred bent to retrieve the scrolled parchment from the floor, unrolled it, read before Ambrosius could protest. Shocked, she put a hand to her throat. 'Those poor people of Eboracum! We must rouse the militia, send them northward immediately . . .'

Ambrosius interrupted. 'They will not go. They say the North is not their concern.'

'Not even Eboracum? And with the Archbishop there for a meeting of the synod?'

'Not even for Eboracum or Patricius.' Ambrosius rubbed the cold of his fingers with his other hand. Especially not for Patricius, an odious, pompous and greedy man who managed to offend everyone, from Ambrosius himself down to the poorest trader. He survived because he was Archbishop, were he any other man a dagger would have been found in his back long since.

Winifred stamped her foot. 'This is treason!'

'Alas, it is not. It is not for the militia to march beyond our boundaries. There is only one who commands men who will go anywhere at any time without thought or question.'

Sinking to a stool, Winifred's expression was clearly shocked. 'But my Lord Ambrosius, there are many wealthy men of the church at Eboracum.'

Ambrosius had to admit the truth. 'It is my belief that the Northmen attacked knowing it, guessing these comfort-loving men would travel with their worldly goods.' He snorted. 'Rich pickings, a synod of the Christian Church!'

For once, Winifred was at a loss for words. Eboracum meant nothing to her, it was just another decaying town meeting its death. Patricius would be a loss, for he was a useful man to have on her side, a man easily bought by the right weight of a purse. But the synod was to discuss the appointment of an abbess for Venta Bulgarium . . . she had sent three chests of generous gifts north to assure her appointment! She stood and kicked the stool across the room. Three chests! Three! Her future, gone to that foul-minded woman of the north – oh aye she knew it would have gone to Morgause, curse her, may the gods blacken her teeth and womb! Curse the woman!

Faintly amused, Ambrosius watched Winifred stalking, angrily, about the room, her lips tight pressed, brows drawn. He knew she had been hoping for the revered position as abbess, a position that would have generated her much power and wealth – as if she did not possess enough of both already. Ah, the pity about Eboracum, but there was, he thought with a wry smile, at least the one compensation!

She stopped her walking, whirled to face him. 'What are we to do? We cannot let the North get away with such an outrage!'

'There is only one thing I can do.' It was easier to say than he had imagined, and having said it, felt a weight lift from him and the constant feel of sickness ease from his stomach. For all his belief in Rome, he had known these last weeks that it was not working, this dividing of the country. The Pendragon, for all his many faults, was after all, a brilliant commander.

§ XXIII

Balancing on a tilted chair, legs resting on a table top and crossed at the ankles, Arthur read the words seemingly hastily scrawled on the wax tablet just delivered into his hand by the officer of the Watch. He scanned the message a second time. 'Hah!' His single bark of laughter caused Cei to glance up from the quartermaster's list he was diligently checking. Arthur handed him the tablet. 'Read that!'

Cei read. 'God in Heaven, Arthur, this is hard to believe!'

Arthur let the chair drop abruptly to its four legs, rose casually from his seat and walked behind Cei to peer over the man's shoulder. 'What part? Hard to believe Lot of the North has at last made himself ready to raid south, or that Ambrosius is begging for my help?'

Carefully, Cei placed the communication onto a precariously balanced pile of similar tablets, sat a moment, massaging his stubbled chin. A grin. 'Both I think!'

Arthur laughed again, and leaning on Cei's shoulder, reached across the mess of unread petitions and complaints on the table for the wine flask, topped Cei's goblet and cocked his eyes at the hound pup busy chewing something beneath the table. He bent to retrieve what had once been a perfectly good boot before the dog's teeth had been at it, studied the torn leather a moment and tossed it back to the pup. He might as well have it, the boot was of no more use. Sauntering to his chair, Arthur sat, poured himself another drink. 'Do I answer my uncle, or ignore him?'

Cei propelled himself upward from his stool, faced his cousin and commander with anger. Excited at the sudden movement the pup, Cabal, leapt from beneath the table, began bouncing about the tent barking and growling, the boot forgotten. 'Ignore it? Ignore it!' Cei's arms whirled, adding emphasis to his anger. 'A whore's son has been let in at the back door while you and your uncle have been piddling away time and energy snarling at each other here in the South! Eboracum has been attacked, and you say ignore it? Jesu wept, Arthur!'

Holding up his hands in submission, his grin as broad as an ancient oak tree Arthur let his balanced chair drop to stability. 'Whoa my friend, curb your horse! I was jesting!' He clicked his fingers at the young dog, diverting his playfulness back to the quieter chewing of the boot. 'I would not miss this opportunity to crow I told you so.'

Cei scowled and backed down. Reseating himself he picked up Ambrosius's plea for help once again and stabbed a finger at the second paragraph. 'This, I grant, is a turnabout.'

Leaning across the table, Arthur plucked the thing from Cei's hand and read aloud, ' "*I humbly beseech you to advance with all due expedition, to give aid and revenge to the deaths and ravaging of our Roman Town of Eboracum against the plundering heathen Lot, self-styled King of Caledonia.*" Humbly,' Arthur snorted with delight. 'I think I like that word.' He flipped the tablet closed, set it down on the table. 'Turnabout? Ambrosius Aurelianus asking for my help? Mithras, Cei, it's a bloody miracle!' His wicked grin spread wider. 'Reckon your Christian God is on my side after all?'

Cei grunted. 'If He is, you will no doubt take advantage – but will you then acknowledge Him?'

Arthur randomly selected a scrolled parchment, playfully tapped his friend's shoulder with it. 'Not today, Cei. No attempts to convert me to Christianity this day please! My uncle has come to his senses and realised I command the most powerful force in Britain. I am too busy for all that knee bending and dutiful praying.'

Cei returned to checking his list. 'Just as well the Lord does not share your views.'

Arthur was up again, striding to the open tent flap, not listening. He issued a brief order for his uncle's messenger to be brought in and turned back to Cei. 'Put that list down, man, we have a war trail brewing.'

Cei answered without raising his eyes. 'Whether in barracks or on campaign men must eat – and this list of supplies falls widely short of what is desired. Look at this!' He waved the parchment at Arthur who stretched forward for it. Cei stood, moved to his side, pointed to two separate entries. 'Look, here and here, corn and flour –mouldy, all of it mildewed and rotten. Call that tribute? I call it insult!'

Arthur chewed his lower lip, screwed his eyes to study the figures and comments written fastidiously in the quartermaster's tidy, but small, print. 'When was it delivered?'

'Yesterday evening.'

Arthur erupted into a burst of expletive anger, ending with, 'Damn it, Cei, what does it take to convince these people that I mean business?'

Cei opened his arms wide, palms uppermost. 'A raiding party from beyond the Wall?' He chuckled. 'It almost makes me think this attack by Lot was at your instigation. Deliberately let the bees swarm, then passively march in to re-hive them?'

Arthur was prising the wax stopper from a fresh flagon of wine and laughed. 'I am innocent! Mind, it's worth remembering. I could use it against Amlawdd over on the west coast. He's always trying to aim some dirty trick at me.'

Cabal, his master's attention no longer on him, sauntered to the nearest tent pole, cocked his leg and then settled himself before the glowing brazier, turning around three or four times before curling into a ball instantly to sleep.

Catching movement beyond the tent, Arthur turned. A tall lad stooped through the entrance and stood nervously before him, twiddling his woollen cap. The King studied him a moment, then asked, 'Do you come from Ambrosius Aurelianus? Are you of his men? You do not bear his insignia.'

The lad shook his head, 'Oh, na, my lord, I'm from Eboracum.' His eyes, darting nervously around Arthur's spacious tent, were red-rimmed against a hollow, ashen face. Of muscular build and tall height, he slumped now, shoulders sagging, feet dragging with the leaden weight of fatigue. Arthur judged him to be little more than ten and seven summers.

'You have ridden hard?' Arthur asked, concerned.

'Aye, my Lord,' the lad answered, swallowed hard, found a sudden interest in the iron buckle of his baldric. 'Things were right bad when we left Eboracum.'

Arthur lifted an eyebrow. 'We?'

The lad flung up his head, showing more than tiredness behind those grey, nervous eyes.

'We?' Arthur questioned again. He found he had to look up to this young man who towered two hand-spans in height above him – though Arthur himself was tall.

The young soldier cleared his throat. 'They gave us the best horses – three of us made a bolt for it. Only I got through. The Northmen took the others.' His fingers were still toying with the buckle. 'I've heard tell of what they do to prisoners.' He desperately wanted Arthur to deny those rumours of horrific tortures. One of the two had been his younger brother. But the Pendragon remained silent. There was no point in denying a truth; instead, the king turned to pour wine, offered a brimming goblet; quality vintage, not the watered stuff of the ranks. The lad accepted it eagerly and gulped the liquid down. It felt like fire in his throat and belly, gave him some small amount of strength and courage.

'Go easy on that,' Arthur said with a smile. 'What's your name, boy?'

142

'Ider, Sir.'

'So, Lot has attacked Eboracum. Tell me what happened. Take your time.'

Ider hesitated, gathering his thoughts. Where to begin? 'There were thousands of them, Sir, come up out of the dawn with the fog. Swarming all round the town, like a disturbed nest of ants.' He spoke quickly, hands and arms animated, brow furrowed.

'Have you seen action afore, lad?' Cei asked. Ider swivelled around to face him.

'I was in battle last summer.' He answered too quickly, too boldly. Meeting Cei's direct, questioning gaze he faltered and glanced at the floor, looked up again, a weak grin forming. 'Well, a skirmish.'

Arthur laughed. 'Even the smallest skirmish can make you to piss your bracae!'

Ider grinned, found himself liking the Pendragon. There was much derisive talk of Arthur in Eboracum. Ider found himself glad that he had refused to believe it. A grin flushed across his grimed face. 'I'm not certain whether I was more scared of those bastard Northmen, or of having to come in here to talk with you!'

Arthur peered at Ider through his usual expression of half-shut eye and raised eyebrow. 'You still scared of me then, boy?'

Embarrassed, Ider made no answer. 'The tales you hear are, for the most part rumours spread by my enemies,' Arthur explained. 'And some of them I foster to suit my purpose.' He said no more, what would this raw lad understand of the power struggle between himself, the Church and Ambrosius?

'So what happened?' Cei prompted the silence.

Ider answered that one eagerly enough. 'Several families from outlying settlements fled into town saying there were raiders coming down from beyond the Wall.' He snorted contemptuously. 'Those Northern bastards have raided many times. Steal a few head of cattle, take some women; burn folk's homes and fields then slither back to the midden they come from.' He shrugged, and warming to his tale, plunged on. 'A few of them approached close to Eboracum last summer, but the militia was called up and me and the lads swung out to meet them.'

He paused. Putting it like that made it sound as if the thing was boldly organised, a well-disciplined troop ready for action. Not the shambles it had been in reality. 'We fought as well we could,' he lied. 'We killed most of them.' Well, one or two. 'I caught one bastard a blow to the jaw that sent it clean through the back of his skull.' That was not quite true either. He had struck blindly out and sent someone sprawling backwards into a dung-pat. Briefly, it bothered Ider that Arthur would see through the gross exaggeration – but the truth was not glorious enough. How could he tell the poxed reality to this man? Ider always made everything bigger than it was, the habit a part of him. 'They ran, those that could run. Couldn't face up to us!' Now that was nearer fact. The raiders had run, but only because the heavens had opened in a drenching thunderstorm and scared the wits out of both sides. 'Eboracum had no more trouble until now.' That last was truth at least.

Ider rubbed his neck. His body was stiff and sore from days of riding at a fast pace. He trundled on with his report. 'A week or so back, we saw the smoke, black smoke on the horizon, curling up into the sky. Raids are a part of living so close to the Wall. Most folk insist on keeping to their farms, know that risk and accept it.'

'So what happened that was different this year?' Arthur prodded carefully for information, aware that the lad's exaggeration was a deception to hide the stark fear. Arthur had noted how his hands were trembling.

'Those folk fleeing into Eboracum – Saex folk as well as British – spoke of a great army approaching down over the northern moors. That bastard whore-son Lot. He has joined with the blue-painted people.'

Arthur raised his eyes from the intent scrutiny of Ider, squinted at Cei. The Picti? With Lot? Slowly he sucked in his breath, released it as slowly. How in the Bull's name had Morgause managed that? Cei's returned look was as meaningful. Why in all the names of the gods had they not heard of this? What had happened to their paid spies, the lines of communication so carefully set up between the North and South? Damn them all to hell, Arthur had received not a single word of Morgause allying with the Picti!

Things had been quiet these past months. Last winter, and the one before that, had been hard throughout the country, particularly in the North, and then Morgause had been busy with a girl-child, and that was all he had heard, nothing more. Mithras had joined with the Picti!

Ider reached forward, grasped Arthur's wrist, his large hand gripping tight, clutching, as if he needed to cling to some tangible reality. 'We laughed, said it was only another raiding party.' Quietly he added, 'It wasn't.'

Earlier, Arthur had said he was jesting by considering the possibility of ignoring Ambrosius's plea. Eboracum had refused to pay any tribute to the Pendragon these past years, had solidly gone its own way. A sense of revenge was urging Arthur to let his uncle and those pompous men of Council drown in their own muck. But he could not do that. Not if Lot were allied to the Picti.

Who was it who said he would never resist the call to battle? Ah, Gwenhwyfar. She had said that to him, some time, some place; Arthur could not remember where or when. He turned away from Cei and Ider, walked slowly across the tent, lifted the flap, stared out across the trampled grass of the ground before his command tent. Opposite, the standards were placed in a cluster of proud brilliance. Red Turma's flag, Blue's, Green's . . . his own dragon, the tubular shape stirring slightly in a light breeze. Gwenhwyfar.

There was an ache inside him, like the throbbing, persistent moan of an unhealed wound. A raw, empty pain that would not, would not, ease. It was ten months now. Ten long months had they been parted, since Amr had drowned.

Beyond the standards stretched lines of tents, eight men to a tent. And beyond those, rising to meet the grey-blue of the afternoon sky, the great ditch and embankment Arthur had ordered built. The defined border between his land and Ambrosius's. He observed the man on watch; the unhurried surveillance of a designated quarter of one mile guard, Arthur's eyes following as the man turned, walked back along this side of the high, imposing palisade that topped the great turf bank towering over the ditch on the far side. How many had Morgause harnessed? Hundreds on the rampage? Thousands? Was the entire North about to go up in flames?

Morgause, youngest sister to his own mother, and his father's whore. Morgause, a woman who created power through the infliction of fear and pain. The only living person the Pendragon feared. For years he had borne her cruelties, enduring a childhood of hidden tears and silent-suffered hurting. And then he had discovered his true identity, and lost the man he had loved within the same knowing. Uthr had been his father, and the boy had not known it. Neither had Morgause. She had held plans of her own: to bear Uthr a son and become his queen when he defeated Vortigern. Only Vortigern had slain Uthr and Uthr already had a son. Morgause would never forgive the boy for being Uthr's cub. And Arthur could never forgive Morgause her evil.

Again the Pendragon scanned the defensive structure that sat guard over Ambrosius's territory. His uncle was an idealistic fool but no more than that. A fool with a dream. Were they not all fools where there was a dream to follow? He had cherished his own dreams when he was a boy, raw-spirited and with the world seemingly at his command. That summer when he had become Pendragon was the last he had seen of Morgause. He had been in Gwynedd with Cunedda. And Gwenhwyfar.

Gwenhwyfar.

He swung round, decision made. It was time old wounds were healed – before the bitch Morgause inflicted new ones. 'The Artoriani will ride direct to Eboracum under your command, Cei.' He crossed to a tent pole, took down his baldric and sword from where they hung, began to buckle them on. 'Though I doubt there is anything you can do for them now, save bury the dead. I'll meet up with you as soon as I can.'

Cei opened his arms, puzzled. 'Why, where are you going?'

Arthur was leaving the tent, he whistled the pup who came instantly awake and bounded, tail and rear end wagging, to his side. 'Gwynedd.'

Blustering, Cei rushed a few paces after him. 'Gwynedd? What in God's name for?'

Arthur's long, energetic strides had taken him beyond the tent, he stopped, retraced his steps, met Cei's exasperated expression. 'There are men in Gwynedd who know more of those northern hunting runs than Lot ever will.' He nodded at Ider. 'You have done well, lad. There may be a place for you within the Artoriani soon enough. We will see how you make out.' And he was gone.

Ider swelled with pride. The Artoriani! Was that possible? He thrust the suggestion aside, he would never be good enough, Arthur took only the best for his Artoriani. 'I heard,' he said to Cei, 'that Lady Gwenhwyfar's been in Gwynedd some months now.' He dropped the words casually into the ensuing silence.

Cei answered absently. 'Aye, she has.'

'I heard, too, that things are not so good between them, that they parted with harsh words.'

'Lad,' Cei snapped, striding away from the tent, 'your ears hear too much and your mouth flaps too wide.'

§ XXIV

Arthur was assisting with the final assessment of horses. Although each mount was thoroughly checked morning and evening for injury and lameness, the Pendragon insisted on extra examination before a march. He straightened from feeling the heat in a young stallion's swollen fetlock, and found Elen standing waiting patiently before him. She was an attractive young thing, dark-haired and dark-eyed. She was also his cousin, last-born daughter to Uthr's sister and Ambrosius Aurelianus's niece. Arthur's guest: a polite term for hostage.

'I understand we are leaving,' she said. 'To where do we go?'

Arthur nodded to the cavalryman holding the horse, indicating he might be led away. 'Stand him a while in the river, cold water may bring the swelling down, though he'll not be fit to work for some days.' He rested his left hand on his sword pommel, answered her with a curt, 'I go north.' He began walking in the direction of the hospital tent. There were always a few men loitering there, he needed to see how many had genuine illness or injury.

Tossing her proud little head, Elen fell into step beside him. Her fingers brushed and caught his, drawing his hand secretively into the folds of her skirt. 'And I? Where do I go?' Her voice rippled as smooth as fine, eastern silk.

Arthur saw no reason to make an answer. Elen had come into his keeping by an accidental miscalculation – a mistake he had quickly exploited. Her mother had died, she was to pass into Ambrosius's wardship until marriage – unfortunate that she had ridden through Arthur's territory to reach him. Arthur, as son to the eldest brother, was legally head of the family, not Ambrosius, had decided to exercise his rights and control the wardship himself. His uncle had been furious, but then, that was the intention.

Elen was pouting. 'You could have left private word that you are leaving on the morrow. I found out from the servants.'

'The right and proper way for you to hear.'

They were entering a narrow way between fodder storage tents, the grain kept rodent- and weatherproof in barrels raised from the ground on wooden pallets. Stepping swiftly before Arthur, Elen blocked his path, stood close, her breath sweet on his face, breasts brushing his chest. 'Until this day, you have not bothered yourself with the right and proper way of things, my Lord.' She stretched up, kissing him sensuously on the mouth, her body pressing closer. He did not respond. Pouting, she pulled away. 'Yesterday, and for all the days before, you would have kissed me back.'

Arthur placed a hand on each of her arms, attempting to move her aside. 'That was yesterday. Today I am busy.'

Elen stood firm, irritation setting on her face. 'Then shall I come to you tonight? I need more of your,' she fluttered her lashes, 'tutoring.'

Arthur persisted, tried again to move past. 'You knew enough before knowing me.'

Her hand was creeping along the inside of his thigh. She said suggestively, 'Any fool can learn to read and write, my Lord, it takes practice to do so well.'

148

Smoothing her gown, running her hand over breasts and hips, Elen drew attention to her slim figure. That would, to her discovered annoyance, soon be thickening. She dreaded the prospect. Pregnant women always looked so ungainly and ugly. So old!

'I have much to do, Elen. I'm sorry.' Arthur lifted her and swung her around, set her down on the narrow pathway behind him, and strode on.

'Not as sorry as you are going to be!'

Arthur stopped short and turned back to her. 'Are you threatening me?'

'Telling you the facts.' Her slit eyes and pinched nose corresponded with her venom, looked every inch a snake about to strike. 'Our uncle is already angered that you hold me as hostage, but he believes I have been kept safe. He will be outraged when he learns of our bedding together.'

'And is he, then, likely to learn of it?' Arthur's sarcasm gave away nothing of his anger, his voice was low and calm, eyes iron hard. He stood very still.

'When the child I bear becomes apparent, he will.'

Then the Pendragon laughed, head tossed back, his collar-length slightly curled brown hair ruffling with the movement. 'Bull of Mithras! You expect me to fall for that time-worn trick?'

Her dark eyes blazed. Childishly she stamped her foot. 'This is no trick! I carry your child, Arthur. He will be born come September.'

Elen stared, defiant, at the man before her. Arthur was in his twenty-seventh year, she, barely ten and six. These months within a military encampment could have been as a living death to a girl who loved dancing and chatter and clothes, the frivolities of a noble-born young woman's pampered life. The other women were soldiers' wives – or whores – the lower classes, beneath her accustomed quality of friendships. As the King's cousin she was offered every honour, every courtesy, but were she ever to try riding her horse unescorted through the gateway, were she to climb out and over that massive defence work . . . except, she had not, because she was in love with Arthur. Were the gates to be held wide and her manumission given, she would not leave. Not while she had Arthur.

He was a rugged, handsome man, his expression and temper strikingly fierce, with a passion for his men and horses, and for the sharing of love, that cavorted and soared with the needs of the day or night. His dark hair framed wind- and sun-tanned skin, heightening those brown, all-seeing eyes. Their loving had come about unexpectedly, unplanned, a thing that had happened as naturally as the moon follows the sun. She had been angry, confused – frightened – when the Pendragon had refused to allow her to join their uncle. She had raged, pleaded, cried, not eaten, and then Arthur himself had come into her allotted tent to speak with her. He had not intended to bed her, but she had wept on his shoulder and begged to be set free. A young girl with only a maidservant among the hostile environment of battle-hardened men and enduring women. Arthur had given in, his point had been made to Ambrosius anyway. She could go, he told her, had held her close with the intention of giving comfort, nothing more.

That had been six months past. A man who had a wife he had not seen since the last spring, who had lost her loving and care, and who grieved for his sons, needed the tender touch of gentle hands, the heat and careless breathlessness of love-making. But while Arthur used Elen to fill a need, she had loved him from that first night, and love can become possessive for a girl too young to know the difference between that and physical passion.

As a new spring approached she had begun to suspect that Arthur's mind was not as attentive as his body. He showed a restlessness of spirit that, until this morning, had puzzled her. Now she understood.

'You are going to Gwenhwyfar, aren't you?' The scorn in her voice was scalding.

Arthur had no answer. With a shock of discovery, he suddenly realised that he felt nothing for this girl. Nothing, not even pity. It was as if he had been dwelling in some timeless faerie world of unreality. Elen had been there, had not resisted, so he had taken her. It was as simple as that.

150

'I have not lied or deceived you, Elen. You know I have a wife.'

She clenched her fists and pressed then hard against her temples before holding her delicate hands imploringly out to him. 'I believed your honeyed words of endearment, believed you wanted and needed me. I thought you would think enough of me to set her aside, to take me with you as your new wife when time came for you to go.' She lunged forward, clutched at his arm. 'You must take me, Arthur, where else can I go if I am not yours?'

Arthur laughed at her absurdity, her naivety. 'How can I take you with me?' He laughed again, took her chin between his thumb and finer. '*Where* would I take you? You would not fit well with army life on the march, my bright-painted butterfly.'

Lamely, pleading, 'Then where will I go? I have nowhere unless I am with you.'

Arthur jerked one shoulder, flapped his hands as if he did not know, or care. 'To where you were originally meant to go. Ambrosius was, after all, named as your official guardian.'

'Uncle Ambrosius?' she squeaked. 'I cannot go to him, I carry your child!'

'Mine?' Arthur's tone was heavy with sarcasm.

'Our uncle assumes I am maiden pure,' she replied, defiant. 'He assumes you have treated me with all honour. He will be furious when he discovers what has happened.'

'You could persuade him that yours is the second Virgin birth,' Arthur said unkindly. 'He's holy enough to believe it.'

Arthur did not follow the faith of a Christian, Elen knew, his was the soldier's god, Mithras, the slayer of the White Bull. But even with that knowing, his blasphemy shocked her. She covered her mouth with her hand, her eyes wide with horror. Then her face crumpled into tears.

The Pendragon felt a sudden impulse to laugh, an imagined, lurid scene unfurling in his mind. The saintly uncle, so passionate for his beliefs and ideals, so devoted to his religion. Arthur could see him on his knees before an altar – with Elen, the whoring niece, lying atop of it, pleasuring any who cared to sample her wares.

His amusement invoked a hurl of abuse. 'You seduced me, lured me to your bed with false promises. What could I do to resist you, the great Pendragon?'

'I seduced you! What? With those large eyes of yours expressing a message as clear as a summer sky?' He moved suddenly and took sharp hold of her wrist, twisting it roughly. 'You knew what you were doing, Elen, you came easy to me. Too easy. Not for one moment do I suppose mine is the only bed you have burrowed into.'

'No!' she screamed, attempting to pull away. 'That is a lie, an outright lie!' She snatched her hand free of his grip and attempted to rake his face with her nails. He blocked the move, held her at arm's length, her kicking feet striking harmlessly at the air between them.

'Ah, my dear,' Arthur let her go, she stumbled backwards, fell against the tent. He began to turn away. 'If you play with a burning brand, you usually get your fingers scorched.'

Panting, her hair escaping its carefully dressed style, Elen sagged against the unsupportive leather of the tent. 'You are disowning me,' she gasped, as realisation finally became clear. 'You are denying me and your child!'

Arthur strolled away.

'I intend to tell him!' Elen shuffled to her feet, hitched her skirts and ran a few helpless paces after Arthur. 'I shall tell our uncle you raped me, he will believe me because I am his loving, innocent niece and you – you are a lying bastard!'

Arthur ignored her, strode on.

'Arthur,' she pleaded, sinking to her knees, genuine tears now falling. 'You cannot do this to me! Take me with you as your mistress, your whore. I ask nothing more. Ambrosius will disown me when he learns what we have done, when he knows about the child!'

Arthur had reached the end of the narrow way, swung left and out of sight.

§ XXV

Nightfall. The men were ready to move at first light. Never content

with the daily routine of barrack life, whether within an encampment or housed between turf and stone walls, they celebrated the
prospect of forthcoming action enthusiastically with strong ale, fine
wine, dancing and song.

A central mound of wood and furze blazed on the parade ground,
with smaller fires scattered like chicks around the mother hen.
Gathered to the blazing warmth of their fires were the nine hundred
men of Arthur's élite Artoriani; with them the spear-bearers,
smiths, leather workers, the armourers, medics, unsung recruits and
the three Centuries of permanent infantry. Men laughing, exchanging tales or boasting of conquest in battle and bed, their breath
clouding white against the chill of frost. The roasted meat had been
good. The drink even better.

Seated before the main fire with the officers, Cei was sipping his
wine. This idea of a feast when about to move on had become
tradition for the Cymry – the collective name for all these men. A
tradition he did not wholly approve of. He signalled an officer's
attention, found he needed to shout above the excited noise. 'Pass
word there are to be no sore heads on the morrow. Anyone unfit to
march remains behind.'

The Decurion acknowledged the order, and glanced unguarded at
the Pendragon, reddening as he realised Cei had noticed. Cei's lips
tightened into a compressed line. Arthur was already well into his
drink. How to keep the men sober when their commander swilled
more wine than Bacchus? Hastily, he crossed himself at the image of
that drunken, pagan god. He sighed and gestured impatiently. 'See
to the men, I shall deal with the officers.' Not that he could do
much. Might as well ask the tide not to turn as expect Arthur to
moderate his fill.

All the same, Cei hauled himself to his feet and approached his
King and cousin. Arthur glanced up at that moment and saw Cei's
sombre approach.

'Hai! Cei, come sit aside me. This will be a parting feast to
remember!'

Cei seated himself cross-legged next to Arthur as bidden. For a
while he watched the leaping flames hungrily devouring branches

and dried bracken, twisting and contorting in a leaping dance of yellow, orange and red. The woodsmoke smelt homely, a reminder of a hearth-fire and a wife nursing her children. His wife was among the women with their eight-month daughter. It would be pleasant to live beneath a solid roof again, not under the uncertain tremors of a leather tent, but ah, a soldier's life could never be settled. He would send his wife and child back to her father until his return. Arthur would escort her, for her parents' estate lay near Gwynedd. Cei smiled wistfully across the dark space between this fire and the women's, watched her talking to Elen. The girl seemed discontented, angered. Was she not happy then, at joining her uncle at last? Women were strange fanciful creatures . . . Arthur broke the reverie by nudging his shoulder.

'You intended to say something to me?'

Cei appeared startled. How had he known?

'I have been watching your serious face, my friend.' Arthur chuckled. 'Have noticed how your eyes, between watching your wife and our cousin, follow my wine from amphorae to goblet to lips!' He laughed the louder and slapped Cei's knee. 'You fuss like a doting mother!'

'Someone has to,' Cei growled. He turned his head to look directly at Arthur, expression challenging. 'Someone has to remain sober for the morrow.'

By way of answer Arthur drained the goblet and held it high for more wine. He drank, chuckled again. Laying a hand on Cei's shoulder he leant close, spoke in a whisper down his ear. 'This wine is reserved for me alone. 'Tis well watered.'

Cei frowned. Convincing, but was it true? He squinted at Arthur, trying to read him, knowing it would be useless. You could obtain more information from a stone than Arthur's close-guarded expressions. He was proficient at hiding thought and intention. Was also a proficient liar. Cei chewed his lip thoughtfully as the Pendragon answered some comment made further around the circle, and held out his goblet for Arthur's servant to fill with wine. The lad hesitated, glanced apprehensively at the King, who with a casual wave of his hand, gave assent to pour.

Taking a deep draught, Cei almost choked, spat the strong wine from his mouth, spluttering his rage. Wiping his dripping mouth, he cursed, 'Damn you and your lies, Arthur!'

Arthur crowed his amusement. 'The water's unexpectedly potent in these parts, cousin!'

About to respond with a second curse, Cei was interrupted by movement from the unmarried women. They were rising, shedding cloaks and boots, loosening bound hair. A great cheer and burst of applause cracked the frosted air, greeting them. The women were to dance!

At the last moment, Elen sprang to her feet. She kicked off her boots, tossed aside her cloak and linked hands within the forming circle. She too would dance, she would dance to please and excite the watching men and to taunt Arthur.

The rhythm began slowly, a haunting, evocative pace, its steady beat from drum and stamping feet resurrecting the ancient pagan memories, that even through the grip of Christianity would never be totally buried. The women trod their movement, slow-circling, their chant complementing the steady stamp, pause, stamp of bare feet on hard ground. One two, one two; one two three, one two three. Dip bend, dip bend; twirl and bend. The beat quickened as the pace picked up, the pattern becoming wild as the circle ascended into a whirling frenzy of lithe movement, the women's swirling skirts revealing tantalising glimpses of leg and thigh; their bodies writhing within the ecstasy of their own-made music.

The men were standing, had formed their own circle around the dancers, cheering and clapping, stamping along with the exultant rhythm. The dance reached its height, a screeched crescendo of voices as the women held for a brief moment, the trembling, pulsating circle and then slowed, winding down and down until the high, hot, emotion slid into the warm glow of throbbing pleasure. They came to a halt, and there followed a moment of silence when only the crackle of flames could be heard mixing with the gasping breath of sweat-drenched dancers. Then, a tumult of applause, a shout of approval from the men.

The women dispersed, scattering, laughing and chatting among the men, seeking that intimate, last sampling of enjoyment. Some men left their companions, went in search of their wives, others settled again to their drink. There were not enough women to partner every man. Their turn would come with the army whores. It would be a long night, this night of feasting.

Elen stood among the dwindling circle of women, her mouth open, breath heaving. She was hot and wet from sweat, and she wanted a man. Arthur's derisive words clawed at her brooding anger. She could have gone with any man, these months, had the offers, the opportunities, but she had lain only with the King, had the wanting of only him. The child she carried was his. And he had laughed at her, scorned her, implied she was no better than any of the army whores. There were many spaces around the circle now, the women pairing off with the men.

One lad, she did not recognise. He sprawled, the worse for drink, beside the nearest fire. A tall young man, bull-built with mouse-brown hair. He tweaked playfully at the fine material of her skirt as she passed, his other hand sliding beneath, to clutch at her slender ankle. Elen flared into anger and swung to berate his audacity, then checked. Here was given opportunity! Mildly scolding with her tongue, she plucked her skirt from his grasp, kicking his hand aside, her eyes signalling that this was a game; expressing she was ready for more.

Ider hesitated, uncertain, his drinking companion seeing the situation whispered the girl's name and family, gave a brief shake of his head, warning. Elen cursed under her breath. She was going to lose the fool unless she acted quickly! Contriving to trip, a little scream flying from her lips, she fell into his lap. Giving a pretence of embarrassment, she said hurriedly, 'I am yours, my lover, if you want me. Or have you not the balls to graze a noble-born's pasture?'

Ider needed no second invitation. Lad he might be, but he enjoyed his women. His hands flew to her bodice, his lips crushing against hers.

Something exploded against his head. He spun backwards, limp and dazed, a trickle of blood oozing from his scalp. In the same movement someone was wrenching at Elen's arm, hauling her upright. A hasty stir of reaction from other men, a fluttered wave of movement as hands reached for daggers, as quickly relaxed when the chief player in the stir was realised.

Arthur stood over Ider, his boot ready to kick again should he move, but the lad lay still, stunned by the initial blow. Elen struggled against the grip on her arm, shrieking her outrage, her nails clawing at Arthur's hand. 'Show yourself for what you are, slut!' he bellowed at her, 'but not by using my men to get at me!'

'Let me go!' Elen twisted, looked to the men for help, but they had returned to their own business. 'Let me go, Pendragon, or you will regret this insult!'

'You bring insult to yourself.' With a sneer Arthur added, 'and you hoped I would take you with me?' He let her go, thrusting her from him so that she stumbled to her knees. Threw at her as he walked away, 'There may be room among the whore carts for you.'

Insulted, humiliated, and frightened of what was to become of her, Elen fumbled among the folds of her skirt, found her dagger. She lunged for his departing back. Someone shouted, someone else thrust out a foot to topple her. Arthur whirled, the dagger ripping through his sleeve, tearing through material and flesh, leaving blood seeping where the blade had passed. He reacted instinctively, as the fighter he was, a gut response, unintentionally vicious. His left arm swung up, knocking the dagger aside, while in the same defensive movement, his foot lifted and thrust into her lower stomach.

Elen pitched forward, breath and fight whooshing from her. No one moved to aid her, she lay sprawled on the frost-hard ground, tears of rage and humiliation spotting her cheeks. Arthur was walking away, men were returning to their wine and song. Miserably alone, she stumbled to her feet, her hands clutching at the pain in her belly. 'I shall tell your wife who fathered my child!' she screamed, staggering a few paces. 'If I lose it I will tell her that you killed it! Killed yet another son, you murdering bastard!'

Arthur halted, his hand tightly clutched on his own dagger. He recovered himself, walked from the glare of fires out into the darkness.

Cei alone went to help Elen, offering her his arm to lean on, but

157

she swept him a haughty gaze, knocked him aside and stalked away. Did not realise her fortune. Had Arthur not growled explicit instructions as he strode off, she would now be dangling at the end of a rope. The Artoriani took unkindly to those who attacked their King.

§ XXVI

Elen could not go to her own tent where her maid would be waiting, a prim-faced matron who had never ceased lecturing morals all winter. Nor would she go to Arthur's. What was she to do on the morrow when he rode away? Go to her uncle – a devout Christian who preached louder and longer than a priest? Elen wanted dancing and laughter, a man to laugh and love with. After Arthur, who else would there be? After Arthur . . . fresh tears spilled down her face, what was there for her without Arthur!

Her stomach ached like a tightening cramp where he had kicked her. Her head too, thudded from the tears and fear. The palisade fencing was before her, looming darker against the lighter stardusted sky; steps upward beneath her feet as she climbed, not aware of where she was heading until an icy blast of cold air buffeted her at the top. Snuffling more tears, she leant against the wooden fencing, looking out, down across the ditch to the spread of night-dark land. The river was away to the left, glitter-sparkling the soft reflection of the stars. Away distant, about half of one mile off, a light flickered. The watch fires of Ambrosius's men, set to guard his boundaries. Oh, she did not want to go to her uncle!

A star fell, tumbling a silver trail down the sky, burning brightly hopeful a brief moment, then it was gone. It would be better to go with the whore wagons than go to Ambrosius, and there at least she would be near Arthur. Happen he would change his mind when the babe came?

She had been a fool to act as she had before his men – of course he had been angry with her! She would apologise, tell him what a fool

158

she had been – aye, she would tell him and he would forgive her and then they would . . . calmer, happier, she turned quickly, intent on going to him now, straightway before her courage failed. Her foot slipped. The frost had settled early, whitening the ground almost before daylight had faded. Down on the parade ground, between the fires where they had danced and where men and women walked, it had melted, but up here on the lonely walkway where only the night guard sauntered, it lay white and crisp, ice-smooth. In a flurry of movement, Elen fell, her arm coming out to grab hold of something to stop herself tumbling, her fingers brushed ice-cold wood, scraped, failed to grip. Her legs were sweeping from beneath her, and there was nothing to stop her falling, nothing to stop her from going over the edge of this high-built rampart walk, nothing save for the man who ran, flinging himself faster, diving forward onto his belly, hand outstretched, fingers clawing to catch hold of her as she fell over the side.

He caught at her arm – the material of her gown – the fine stuff slipping between his grasping fingers. Desperately he tried to catch hold firmer with his other hand, but the material ripped and she was gone, falling downwards, her scream ending abruptly with a thud, leaving a sickening quiet.

Arthur lay for what seemed a long while, his head over the edge, eyes closed, fingers clutching that ripped piece of garment. This was not what he had wanted – Mithras blood, what had he wanted?

Men were running, some coming up the steps, others gathering around the sprawled body that had a moment before been Elen, the flickering light from their burning torches casting dancing shadows, grotesque around where she lay. Someone was kneeling beside Arthur, a hand beneath his arm, helping him up, but Arthur pushed him aside, feeling the rise of vomit coming to his throat. He breathed slowly, kept the nausea down, clambered unsteadily to his feet.

It was Hueil who had been beside him, a young officer who had come from the north two winters past; eldest son to Caw, chief lord of Alclud. Someone else had inadvertently brought a wineskin with him. Hueil took it, handed it to Arthur.

159

The Pendragon swilled a mouthful, the wine was watered, he swallowed slowly.

'I saw what happened, my Lord, I was further along the walk. She fell, I will challenge any who says otherwise.' Hueil had a deep voice that carried clear, carried further when the air was sharp and listening for tales to spread.

Taking another gulp of wine, Arthur passed the skin to the next man along, then swivelled on his heel, stood facing Hueil. He could have the making of a good officer, this young cub, were it not for his arrogance. Pointedly, Arthur made reply. 'If there is any need to answer a challenge, I am capable of doing so for myself.' He took one step so that his breath, cloud-misting in the cold air, spumed over Hueil's face. 'Though I doubt any man here would have thought of anything untoward until you brought it to mind.' He turned away, descended the steps and, removing his own cloak, covered the dead girl.

What had he wanted these past months? A woman; companionship? Warmth and loving, to give as well as take. He had not wanted this, not wanted to spoil a young girl, end it for the both of them like this.

For the second time that night he walked away from Elen. He had been up on the walkway, looking out into the dark. He too had seen that star fall. Only his mind had been elsewhere, to the north-west, away up to where the mountains touched the sky in Gwynedd, to Caer Arfon where Gwenhwyfar had gone with his sons two months short of a year since.

He had not been aware of Elen, only that fluster of movement, the scrabbling for a handhold. He had run but had been too late, as he had been too late into the water to save Amr. And if he did not go to her soon, would be too late to make peace with Gwenhwyfar.

And out of all this, all this loneliness and needing, it was Gwenhwyfar he wanted.

§ XXVII

Gwenhwyfar was kneeling on a ragged square of discarded cloak, tending the small patch of garden that she had cherished in childhood. Spring had come early this year, the flowers blooming eagerly, with their bright, yellow heads nodding a welcome at the sun. Even the salt tang of the sea, that had roared and blustered through the long winter with malicious spite, smelt of the spring and a promise of warmer days to come.

As she dug, turning over the soil ready for sowing, she hummed a lilting tune to herself, the words trickling and running silent in her mind. A robin hopped bright-eyed at a discreet distance, stabbing at an easy-gathered meal brought to the surface. Gwenhwyfar tossed him a particularly fat worm, smiled as he gobbled the thing down and bobbed a sort of thank you in return. You knew where you were with birds and animals. Not with people or men. Husbands.

Her song was wistful, the words came to her lips. *When the heart yearns for love and the day burns for night. I will come to you, once again. We will love, once again.* An empty song really, so mockingly hollow.

'Hello, Cymraes.'

Gwenhwyfar gasped, her hand flying to her mouth, stifling the rise of a startled scream. With the same movement, her head jerked round, up; the outline of a man was shadowed against the bright glare of the low spring sun.

'You look well,' he said, for want of something better to say, 'But then, the mountains have always agreed with you.'

She replied with a shrug of one shoulder and raised her hand to shield her eyes. 'The mountains are my home. I am content here.'

They said nothing for a while, neither knowing what to say or how to say it.

Plucking courage from empty air, Gwenhwyfar said; 'I assume you have come to see your sons. Llacheu is with my brother Dogmail, he is teaching the boy to hunt.' Almost added, *That ought to be your responsibility*, but instead, waved her hand in a vague direction. 'I know not where Gwydre is gone, somewhere around the Caer getting underfoot I expect. Probably near the pig runs, he has taken a liking to a runt born some days past.' Nervous, she was talking over-fast, the words gushing like water spouting from a cracked fountain.

'I have seen him,' Arthur said, uncertain, his hands fiddling with his sword pommel for want of something better to do with them. 'He was at the stables. He showed me his pony. A good choice for him.' Then, quicker, more eagerly, 'Do you remember the pony you had as a child, Gwen?' He was trying to smile, finding it difficult to control this wanting to take her in his arms, to kiss and hold her, to never let her go. 'Remember that moth-eaten bear-rug on legs?'

Playful indignation. 'He was not moth-eaten!'

Arthur laughed then, the skin around his eyes wrinkling with amusement, his body relaxing the tautness. He extended both hands, offering to help his wife up from her knees. 'As I recall, that was your answer when I said those same words once before!'

Gwenhwyfar hesitated before taking his hands, placed her fingers with care against his. His palms felt cool, but the grip, as he enclosed her hands in his own, firm, with the strength of the world in them. She smiled back at him, half remembering that long-forgotten episode of childhood. 'Did I? Oh aye, I was so angry I threw a bucket of water over you.' She laughed, memories flooding.

He helped her stand, pulling her upward, and did not let her go immediately, but held on, keeping her to him. She was slim, her figure, even after child-bearing, as slender and lithe as a willow. And beautiful. To Arthur Gwenhwyfar would always be beautiful. He was not laughing with her. There was a pause. 'I loved you then Gwenhwyfar, as I love you now.'

She withdrew her hands from his, wiped them down the front of her old work clothes. Nervously licking her lips she backed away a pace, startled to realise that she was trembling. Indicating her garden, attempting to change the subject, she said, 'I have been here most of the afternoon, but seem to have got so little accomplished.'

'The flowers have bloomed early this year.'

She glanced, surprised, at him. 'You notice flowers?'

Quiet. 'I notice many things, Cymraes.' He was looking at her, noticing how the light touched the copper of her hair into gold, noticing the little lines of sadness that had etched themselves to the corners of her eyes. How unhappy those eyes seemed.

Another long silence, Gwenhwyfar shivered. Unfastening his cloak Arthur swung it around her shoulders. 'You are cold.'

'A cloud covers the sun, the shade is chilly this time of year.'

He stood so near, hands resting gently, possessive, on her shoulders. He smelt of horse and leather, the faint aroma of male sweat. Smelt as she remembered him.

His face was close to hers. Her breath was quickening, coming in little gasps, her breasts rising and falling. She ducked her head against the kiss. He ran a finger under her chin, tilting her head upward again, holding it there, fixing her gold-flecked, green eyes with his own penetrating brown stare. That touch, that one simple, thrilling touch, burnt into her skin, setting her heart leaping, her stomach knotting.

'Arthur, I . . .'

'Na, Gwenhwyfar, no words. No more hard words between us.' He eased her to him, bent his head and kissed her, a light, tender loving that barely brushed her lips. She caught her breath as he let her go briefly to move his body closer. Then he kissed her again, more insistent; long and soft, with a passion that was being held in tight check.

Confused reaction whirled in her. She wanted to pull away, to slap his face, to scream all the curses she knew at him. Why then was she responding? Kissing him back? Why was her body taking aflame for him?

A great weight hurtled at them, breaking the embrace. Cursing, Arthur staggered and attempting to keep his balance, let his wife go. With the support of his arms abruptly removed and the body of the massive hound clamouring against her side, Gwenhwyfar fell backwards. The young dog ecstatically straddled her, huge paws resting on her shoulders, whimpered delight.

Helplessly laughing, she batted him away. 'You great oaf!' she chided fending off the dog's tongue from washing her face and ears. 'Mind where you place those bear-paws!' Laughing. How long since

163

she had last laughed? 'Na, you great beast, do not nip my ears!' Laughed louder as the pup playfully chewed at her dangling ear-rings.

Arthur was far from amused. He gripped the dog's collar and hauled the squirming animal away with a severe reprimand.

'Do not scold him,' Gwenhwyfar pleaded, 'he's only a pup, he has not yet learnt manners.' Stroking the ecstatic dog's broad head, her fingers moving to scratch at a soft spot between his forelegs, she asked, 'What is his name?'

'Cabal,' Arthur growled.

A tall, muscular-built young man with short mouse-brown hair and brown-tanned skin was running up, his expression a mixture of anger and apprehension. Seeing the dog he spurted forward to grab the collar with his large hands, as Arthur had done, profuse apologies spurring from his lips. 'He broke away, Sir. Damned pup was in a frenzy to be with you!'

Arthur growled something that Gwenhwyfar did not catch above the noise of Cabal's struggling and whimpering to be free. 'It is not fair to hold him back, Arthur,' Gwenhwyfar pleaded. 'Let him greet us, then he will be satisfied.'

Scowling, Arthur jerked his head, giving this new young man permission to let the dog loose. Gratefully, Ider let go the absurd creature and Cabal again bounded against his master's leg as he brushed past in his eagerness to reach Gwenhwyfar, sitting still on the pathway.

'Curse you, dog!' Arthur bellowed. 'Will you never learn?'

Gwenhwyfar hugged the hound to her, making a fuss of him. Aye, you knew where you were with animals. With his initial enthusiasm slackening, Cabal moved away from her and nosed lovingly back at Arthur, nudging his master's hand. Grinning, Ider stepped forward to assist Gwenhwyfar to her feet. Their eyes met as she smiled up at him and held.

The eldest son of a moderately wealthy wool merchant, Ider had been expected to follow his father, to carry on the trade when the time came. But he hated those stinking, oily fleeces; he wanted to fight, to join with the Pendragon, to become one of the Artoriani.

His father had forbidden the dream. So he hated his father too. His mother, proud of her eldest son, had secretly purchased a battered sword and encouraged him to join Eboracum's militia. Both had taken a beating for that. Two winters past, she had died. There was nothing more for Ider to care for, not even his brother now. He had cared for no thing and no one – until this moment, when his grey eyes met with the green sparkle of Gwenhwyfar's.

He felt a surging leap deep inside him, something that was far stronger than the love a mother gave, something warm in the pit of his stomach. She was beautiful, Gwenhwyfar. Ider fell in love with her at that first exchange of smiling eyes.

Gwenhwyfar saw it, recognised it. She took her eyes from his, began to brush ineffectually with her hands at her dusty skirts. 'I do not know you.' Feeling flattered, flustered, she had to say something. 'Are you new to my husband's service?'

'Aye, my Lady.' Ider had learnt a long time since, to hide hurt and doubt by play-acting. By making everything seem larger than it really was the pain inside grew less. 'I am Ider, I brought word of attack upon Eboracum to the Pendragon.' A grin of pride spread across his square, firm, face.

Gwenhwyfar smiled warmly at him. She liked him, a lad probably from home for the first time. 'My husband must be impressed with you if he trusts his dog to your keeping.' She meant her words, for Arthur was very possessive of his animals. And his family, when he had the time for them.

Ider swelled with a glow of pleasure and pride at her praise. 'He's a grand dog,' he replied, still grinning. 'I've always wanted a dog, but my father wouldn't allow it.'

'You were told to keep him back,' Arthur chided, realising it was time he interrupted this exchange. 'See to it you keep my orders in future.'

Head slightly bowed, Ider mumbled an apology.

'Take the dog to the kitchens,' Arthur added, dismissing the lad. 'A bone or something will set his mind occupied on his belly.'

Ider threaded his fingers through the dog's collar, had gone a few paces when Arthur caught up with him, took hold of his shoulder.

'And I advise you, lad, if you want to stay in my service, to curb your inclination for over-friendly conversation with my wife.'

Ider saluted smartly. 'Aye, Sir.' Walked away with a jaunty stride, but not before tossing a last, broad smile at Gwenhwyfar.

'He seems a good lad,' she observed, watching him persuade Cabal to leave with him. Had Arthur seen that look of new-born devotion in his eyes?

'Raw and green,' Arthur remarked, 'but he will improve. He has guts and determination, qualities I need in my men.'

He had not seen. She relaxed, forgot Ider when Arthur said, 'Gwenhwyfar . . .'

He made to touch her, but she turned quickly away, bending to gather her gardening tools. Arthur took them from her and when she objected, asked, 'Where do they go?'

She pointed along the path to a lean-to shed built against the rear of one of the granaries. He followed her into it, placed the stuff onto a shelf.

'Have you greeted Enniaun?' she asked, ducking away from his hand when he reached towards her. 'Of course you have, you would not enter a Caer without first seeking its Lord.' She retreated into the sunlight, began walking in the direction of her brother's Hall, taking long strides and talking all the while, her hands holding the cloak folded around herself, defensive and protective. 'My brother was pleased to see you, I would wager. He has two sons now, did you know? My other brothers have their own established territories, they ride here often enough, when the hunting brings them this way – which is why Dogmail is here. It will be good to have the Hall filled this evening with men of your Artoriani. Where are you intending to make camp? There is still the remains of the Roman fortress of course, but there is also a good meadow by the river, ideal for men and horses. You are welcome to that.'

Arthur, following in her wake, lengthened his stride and caught hold of her arm, swinging her pace and speech to a halt. 'Whoa! What is this? Idle conversation to keep me at bay? Hie, it is me, Arthur.' He flapped his hand, pointing at himself. 'Tck,' he twitched the corner of his mouth, searching for words. He had hold

166

of both her shoulders. 'I did not ride all this way just to catch up on family news.'

Gwenhwyfar studied his left hand, focusing on a battered gold band with the image of a dragon imprinted on it. Uthr had given him that ring when he had been a boy. There were so many things she ought to say; good, bad, angry. Loving things. Where to begin? But she shrugged him off, walked on. 'Family news is important to the family.'

'Aye. If you are lucky enough to have a family that is worth its importance.'

A spark of tawny-gold defiance flashed in her eye, her head lifting. 'Is yours not important then?'

Arthur backed off a pace, his hands spread, held submissive. 'Not the family on my side of the shield, na. Ambrosius, my mother, neither have much love for me, nor I for them.' His hands dropped, though not his eyes. 'There are only three who mean more to me than sun, moon, sea and sky.'

Fighting pricking tears, Gwenhwyfar was relieved when they rounded the corner of the granary and the Hall came into sight. She pointed, eager. 'Look! Enniaun is ready to give formal greeting!' She walked on, faster, Arthur a pace behind, his fingers thrusting deep though the leather strap of his baldric, slung aslant across his chest.

'Is that Geraint?' she asked, seeking those she knew among the men of Arthur's escort. 'He has lost weight; have you not been feeding him? I do not see Cei. Is he not with you?'

Terse. 'Na, he is not with me.'

Glancing towards the abrupt answer, Gwenhwyfar said no more.

People of the Caer and settlement were crowding to gather outside the Hall, eager to share in the welcome of visitors, their excited voices a rising burble as the King and Gwenhwyfar approached.

Enniaun's personal guard were drawn up in two columns either side of the Hall doors, their iron-shod spears held tip downmost in the formal greeting of friendship. At the apex stood Enniaun and his royal family of Gwynedd, Teleri his wife, herself a princess from the north-west, and their two young sons, Catwalaun and Owain. Their daughter, almost the same age as Llacheu, was with Gwydre, holding his hand, ordering him to stand straight and not fidget.

Before the Hall, spears also tip down, the Artoriani wearing parade armour and standing ranked with shoulders squared behind the two standard bearers who held the fluttering Red Dragon and Blue Turma's own banner. An impression of undefeatable strength and fierce pride. Gwenhwyfar smiled at Arthur. 'How far beyond the Caer did you make halt to clean up and change?'

Arthur grinned back at her. 'A few miles. You should have seen us before, the grime was hand-span thick!'

The waiting Artoriani rustled, a hint of movement, aware of the nearing presence of their King and his Queen. Geraint barked an order; as one, they raised their spears, bringing the wooden shafts clashing once across their shields in salute.

'Gwenhwyfar. There are things we must discuss.'

'What? Now?' They were approaching Enniaun. Not here! Must she face him and the memory of these past months before all these watching eyes? They were walking close but not touching. She quickened her stride.

'Soon. When I have finished talking with your brother.' They mounted the three wooden steps.

Enniaun came forward, unaware of his sister's panic, or the vast emptiness welling inside Arthur at the line of rebuffs that he seemed to be receiving from her. The Lord of Gwynedd acknowledged his Supreme King with bended head and knee, then sprang to embrace him in friendship. 'I greet you Arthur, King, kindred and friend. Welcome to my Hall, welcome to Gwynedd.'

'Croeso! Welcome!' The shout, in a mixture of the British and Latin tongues was taken up with enthusiasm by the still increasing number of gathered onlookers. A cheering and shouting that was surely heard as far as the distant mountains and the snow-tipped Yr Wyddfa. The Artoriani answered with a wordless shout, 'Aye-eeeee', that rang throughout the Caer and was caught by the sea wind, tossed high to the clouds and the circling, shrilling gulls.

Teleri was offering the gold chalice of welcome. Arthur took it and drank deep, passed it first to Enniaun then back to Teleri and last to Gwenhwyfar. To each he spoke different words.

To Enniaun; 'May our hunting follow the same path, and be good.'

To Teleri; 'May your house prosper, and your sons and daughters bring you pride and sons and daughters of their own.'

To Gwenhwyfar; 'May the ceasing of the storm return the sun to your heart.'

Gwenhwyfar took the chalice between both hands and sipped. She was about to pass it back to her husband with a similar traditional reply, as her brother and Teleri had done, but on impulse, changed her mind. Tipping the thing, she spilt a little onto the wooden step as an offering for the old gods, and said, 'The night has been long and it will come again, but between each blackness will always come the light of day.' She smiled, a little shy, at Arthur, the greeting spreading suddenly in genuine welcome from her lips to her eyes, coming truly from her heart, as she realised how much she had missed him.

Arthur took the chalice from her, his fingers briefly brushing hers, their eyes meeting and at last holding. She did not look away, did not remove her hands from his touch. Were it not that he would grossly offend the Caer and its Lord, Arthur would have swept her to the privacy of her chamber and claimed her there and then. But he could not. Instead, he spoke for her ears alone to hear, 'Mithras, Cymraes, you are more beautiful than a summer's dawn the day after battle.' He swung away from her then, sending the chalice down to Geraint and the men, the vessel passing along the line, pausing to be refilled and drunk, a multitude of greetings and thanks flowing with that welcoming wine.

§ XXVIII

'I hear you stay only the one night. You come a long distance for such a brief visit.' Gwenhwyfar sat on the river bank, arms hugging drawn-up knees. It was a place she often came to of an evening, a quiet sanctuary away from the day-long bustle of the Caer. A peaceful place, where she could think.

Arthur stood a few yards away, tossing pebbles, skimming them over the surface of the calm river. The tide was in, the water rode high. 'I am needed in the North, Cei is already marching with the Artoriani. I wish to join them as soon as possible, if I delay, Lot's rabble may disperse homeward. Once they are scattered among those lonely hills . . .' He skimmed two stones together, stooped to pick up another handful. He need not add any more; Gwenhwyfar knew well enough the tactics of campaign. 'Lot is sure to know we are coming, I am wagering that while his men are drunk on success, they will lust after a confrontation with me.' He lobbed the last pebble, watched it sink, and seated himself on the bank, leaning back on his hands, legs stretched before him.

A three-quarter moon was rising against the blue-black evening sky, giving strength to the fading light. A flighty wind was whispering through the trees on the opposite bank and behind, the camp fires of the Artoriani winked like stars against the darkening rise of the hill. Men's voices were a distant murmur of talk and laughter. The soft settling of a spring night, with its heady scent of day-warmed new grass, damp earth and awakening blossom.

Gwenhwyfar asked, 'Has he come south to entice you into a fight?'

'Lot? I should think so. The synod was meeting there, but why else bother with Eboracum? Since the river burst its banks yet again with that high tide last year, the place has been all but dead. Too many lost their trade and business to the mud, it is a skeleton of a town, a few diehards like Ider's father stay on; for the rest, the place will soon be left to the Saex settlers. The English seem indifferent to the temperament of water levels.' He snorted a chuckle of amusement. 'The men of the Church close their eyes to the decline of the towns, but it seems their God has other plans.'

'You accept Lot's challenge then?'

Lot? Arthur thought. *Not Lot, Morgause.* He rolled onto his stomach. Plucking a stalk of grass, began chewing it, sucking the sweet spring taste from its stem. 'When have I turned down a challenge?' He cast the flattened stalk aside, rolled again to lie on his back, lacing his fingers behind his head to gaze up at the first stars. 'It would be unwise to ignore this. A few of Vortigern's Saex who stayed in the north after attacking your da's old stronghold may have joined with Lot. Kindred of Hengest.' And Winifred, who wished the Pendragon dead, was Hengest's granddaughter. Coincidental of course.

As if reading his thoughts, Gwenhwyfar asked, 'Has Winifred a hand in that?'

Arthur was counting the stars. Six. Seven. 'I thought she might, but na, I think not. Were the Church to discover it, she would lose all the ground she has so far made.'

'She intends for her son to be the next Pendragon,' How could she say that so calmly, Gwenhwyfar wondered.

Arthur sat up, sat as his wife, with arms around his knees. 'Not while Llacheu lives.' He spoke firmly, committed. 'Llacheu will be King after I am gone.' Somewhere along the opposite bank a creature dived into the water, the splash followed by the alarm of disturbed ducks. More stars. The sky was quite dark now, the river too. The last time they had been together, they had been beside a river.

Standing, Arthur walked to the edge of the bank, stood looking down at the lazy current so slow here, this close to the sea. The tide would turn soon.

He did not say that it was not Winifred's interfering that he feared, nor that the few Saex who were joined with Lot were insignificant. That it was Morgause he was after. Instead, he said into the gathering darkness, 'Caer Arfon is not the same without your da. He was a good man, a man worth listening to. He would have enjoyed returning to take back the North with me.'

'He would have liked to have seen our boys. Enniaun has given them both ponies, but Da would have enjoyed the doing.' Gwenhwyfar released a shaking breath, overfull of the sad memories of death.

Arthur stood silent a long while, nursing his own thoughts of the same theme. Then he said, 'I could not come, Cymraes, before this. I have no reason – I have been busy dealing with Ambrosius's irritations and the building of my defensive work – my own attempt at irritation – but that is only an excuse. I just could not come.'

It was her turn to remain silent. A bat fluttered past. 'I understand, but it is none the easier to bear.' Tears threatened, she choked them down, she would not cry. Could not, there had been enough tears. 'The understanding makes none of it easier.' It had not been his fault that she had left him. It had been her decision, hers alone.

Cloaked by the darkness, Arthur let go the deception, let his despair rise and break through the surface of his shield-wall. He had held it in for so long, this grief and loneliness. To the night he said, 'I would that I could change everything, change the passing of time.' His voice cracked into a desperate sob. He squatted abruptly, burying his head on arms folded across his knees. The last time he had cried like this was as a child. When his father, the man he had loved but had never known in life to be his father, had been slaughtered by Vortigern in battle.

Gwenhwyfar did not move. Once, she would have comforted him, held him close and showed warmth and love.

Muffled, he said, 'I am the all-powerful Pendragon. I can do almost anything I please except hold your love, and bring him back.'

'Who?' she asked, deliberately obtuse. 'Bring who back? Da or Amr?'

'Both.' Arthur snapped his head up, defiant, the thin moon lit the pale, silvered streak of unchecked tears. Admitted the truth: 'Amr.' He swallowed. 'He haunts me. I see him still, drowning in that water. I struggle to save him, but I can never reach his outstretched hands. I try and I try, but never can I reach him.'

'Amr is dead.' Gwenhwyfar spoke flatly, remote and hardened. 'He has been dead many months. Here among the mountains I have grieved for him.' *Grieved for so much*, she thought. *For you, and you never came.* 'The tears stop. Eventually.'

Arthur rose to his feet but made no attempt to move, feared she would flinch from him should he try to touch her. Feared the rejection. 'You ought not to have left me, Gwenhwyfar.'

'Ought I not?'

He could see her eyes flash in the dim moonlight, knew all too well, how their colours would be swirling in mixed shades of green behind flecks and sparks of tawny gold.

'Not in anger. If you had waited it would have passed; would have eased. We could have shared our grief, made it the easier for both of us.' Arthur sighed, spread his hands helplessly. 'You are still angry with me. Blame me.'

Gwenhwyfar wrapped her cloak tighter around herself, absently rubbing her arms against the rising chill of night. 'It took a long while for the grief to subside – not go, it will never go, but the hurt you give me, Arthur, will that ever subside? You wound me again and again and again. All I can do is fight you, learn how to hate where once I loved. I have to be angry because otherwise the hurting is too much, too great.'

Arthur walked a few paces along the bank, watching the pattern of moonlight dazzle on the river. A mist was rising. 'I learnt from childhood to shield my feelings, to hide my fears and grief. For all my life I have been lonely, with no one to turn to for comfort. I learnt early that anger smothers the pain. I learnt that at three summers of age, when the woman who I eventually discovered was my mother slapped my hand from her skirts, kicking me aside like a cur. Then I learnt to hate Morgause, Uthr's whore, who treated me like dog-shit and locked me in dark places as punishment. And later, there came Winifred to hate.' He was fiddling with the gold buckle of his baldric, his finger's tracing its intricate pattern.

'And for me? Has the hate now come for me also?' Gwenhwyfar asked.

With his back to her he replied. 'Amr was my son as much as he was yours.' He stared at the faint glint of gold beneath his fingers. 'I could accept you leaving, Gwenhwyfar. Although I was bleeding inside, I knew why you had to run here to Gwynedd. But did you have to take my other two sons?' He turned to face her. 'On that day I lost Amr and Llacheu and Gwydre. And you.' He bit his lip, stared a long while at the grass beneath his feet. 'What do I feel for you?' Again he looked at her, his expression pleading, painful. 'I made no attempt to stop you leaving, I told myself that I did not need you – I could find a woman to keep me warm at night without adding the daytime demands of a wife.'

He swallowed tears, his voice dropping to a choked whisper. 'After a while, I even convinced myself that I had decided right.' He crossed the space between them in three strides, squatted beside her, his hands hovering, uncertain whether to touch her. 'I seldom admit to being wrong, Gwen, in my position I cannot afford to do so, I must always seem assured – right – yet I am admitting it now. I have been wrong over this thing concerning you and me.'

He turned his head from her, wiped his face with his hand, rubbing the stubble of beard growth, clearing the fall of tears. 'Mithras help me, Cymraes, I have no idea how to put things aright between us. I can handle men, battle. But this aching inside me . . .' He spread his hands, bowed his head.

'Why did you come here?' Gwenhwyfar too was fighting tears. 'I was growing used to being without you.'

'To ask Enniaun to join with me against Lot.'

Gwenhwyfar answered sharply, 'Anyone could have done that! Cei, Geraint, a messenger. It did not need the Pendragon Lord himself to summon Enniaun to a hosting. I want the real reason!'

He answered with the same whetted hostility, on the defence, attacking her sudden anger. 'Gwynedd is my strongest ally. I have no wish to fight a few skirmishes with Lot. It is important I win the North and keep it. I needed to ensure Enniaun also shares that importance.'

Gwenhwyfar laughed, scornful. 'And I thought, for one stupid moment, that you had come to see me and your sons!' She scrabbled to her feet, spun on her heel and walked quickly away, up the slope heading for the wind-rustled trees. Her cloak snagged on a thistle, she snatched at it impatiently, hurried on.

Arthur cursed beneath his breath, made after her. Why could he never express what he wanted to say in the way he intended? Why did his words always come out with the wrong meaning! In the darkness his foot caught in a mole hill, he sprawled to his knees, a stab of pain shooting up his left arm. Cursing vividly, he climbed to his feet. The night spun, a haze of blinding red and brilliant white. He swallowed the rising wave of nausea, stumbled, cradling the intense pain stabbing from his wrist and up his forearm. Gwenhwyfar was nearing the trees, he might never catch her once she reached their shelter.

Ignoring the pain, he ran, caught up with her under the first night shadows of the dark canopy. Hearing his breathing, his running step, Gwenhwyfar too broke into a run. He pitched forward, bringing her down in a tumble of cloak and skirts, found he was fighting her.

Gwenhwyfar was deceptively strong. Her slender figure gave her an appearance of mild gentleness, but childhood years of running with a pack of brothers had developed a skill that once acquired was never lost. She fought Arthur now, with all the ability she possessed.

Lunging with her fist, she caught him square on the jaw. As he reeled, she rolled away from his grasp, rising to her feet in the same movement, but this time, she did not run. Already he was getting up. She brought the hem of her skirt between her legs, tucked it through her waist belt, forming crude bracae, freeing her for movement.

Arthur licked his lips, calmed his breathing, shut his mind to the throbbing pain spreading rapidly up his arm. That dagger wound Elen had given him was barely healed, he could do without the jagged tear ripping open. What was she going to do? Run, or fight this thing out? Gwenhwyfar's moods were as tempestuous as a summer storm. It was difficult in the dark, an opponent could usually be judged by the eyes, that brief flicker of movement preceding action. But he could not see her eyes so well in the poor light beneath the trees.

She feinted right, pretending to run. Arthur stepped swiftly into her path, grunting as she spun aside, her leg catching behind his, tripping him. He caught her as he fell, bringing her down with him, their bodies rolling down the embankment out onto the moonlit meadow.

For a moment they struggled, neither gaining a hold; then Arthur managed to pin her arms above her head. Straddling her, he knelt over her. She was breathing heavily; let her body fall limp, submissive. He relaxed. Her knee rammed into his groin, her body arching to tip him sideways. Before he hit the ground she was up, her foot slamming into his stomach.

'Mithras,' he hissed, 'if that is how you wish it.' He removed his sword and baldric, let the weapon fall to the grass, and tore the gold brooch-pin from his shoulder, freeing his cloak. Winding it around his left arm he pulled the initial fold as tight as he could to act as a support against his injured wrist and the sticky feel of welling blood from that dagger wound. Using the thing as a shield, he circled, watching her, waiting for the right moment to spring.

When he chose to move she anticipated well, darting aside beyond reach. The second time he lunged, she repeated her action, but on the third stepped forward to meet him, her hip thrusting, knocking his body, disrupting his balance. He had expected it. Arthur knew how well Gwenhwyfar could fight, knew also her tricks.

He swivelled to counteract her, his right arm encircled her waist, spun her on her own momentum, sending her sprawling into the damp grass.

'Had enough?' he panted.

She kicked with her leg making him jump aside, allowing her time to rise. Then she came at him with her dagger.

For a moment Arthur found he was in trouble. Again and again he parried her blade with his cloak shield, found he was facing a wildcat intent on doing damage. He let her fury fly, for she had to release the anger and pain. He dared not draw his own dagger. He backed steadily away, letting her drive at him, letting her do the attacking, letting her become the more winded and tired. When he was ready, judging the timing with skilled practice, he blocked her, striking upwards with his fist, hitting her jaw harder than he intended.

Gwenhwyfar crumpled and lay still.

Tossing his cloak aside, Arthur knelt beside her, desperately anxious. He patted her face, called her name. Oh Mithras blood, he had hit her too hard! Relief whooshed from his held breath as her eyelids fluttered.

As consciousness returned, Gwenhwyfar brought her hand back and swiped feebly at him, he blocked it easily enough, holding her hand tight in his own as he knelt over her. Words, some angry, some downright obscene, chased through his mind, none reached his lips, instead, he covered her mouth with his. She answered him, her mouth seeking his, her arms going around his shoulders, drawing him down, closer.

Their love-making was as fierce and intense as their fighting.

Arthur left for the North at sunrise. Enniaun, with Gwynedd's fighting men, intending to follow within the passing of a few days.

Proud on the fine-bred grey pony his uncle had given him, Llacheu rode, chatting joyfully to Geraint. Somewhere behind with the baggage mules, travelled Gwydre, Enid and Nessa. Gwenhwyfar rode beside Arthur. *As far as Caer Luel*, she had said. *I will come as far as Caer Luel. No further*.

Arthur watched her as she rode; she caught him looking, saw that boyish grin spread across his mouth. Announced curtly, 'If you say one word about last night, Pendragon, I will ensure your men know how you came to injure your wrist.'

His expression was innocent amazement. 'I was not going to say anything!'

They rode on for almost one quarter of a mile. Then, without one hint of a smile or mischievous grin, he added, 'Tonight though, I'll show you what I was thinking.'

Gwenhwyfar tried not to laugh.

April 462

§ XXIX

Winifred combed Cerdic's hair, chiding him for fidgeting.

'But you're pulling, it hurts!'

'You'll have a lot more hurts than pulled hair to endure before you grow old my lad!' his mother scolded. She tucked the comb under her arm, inspected the boy's neat cleanliness. Spitting on her finger, she wiped at a dirt mark on his cheek, then satisfied, released him with a curt, 'You'll do.'

'Why all this fuss anyway?' he asked, scuffing the floor with his sandals. To himself muttered, 'anyone would think this poxed Ambrosius was already King or something.'

Unfortunate that Winifred heard. She grabbed hold of his arm, turning him roughly to face her with a strict reprimanding shake. 'Insolent boy,' she hissed, to herself added, 'how like your bastard father you are!' She took both his arms in her hands, squatted before him so that her eyes were level with his.

'Listen to me, child, and listen well. Ambrosius Aurelianus will be riding through that gate,' she dipped her head over her left shoulder, 'at any moment. He is to be greeted and treated with full respect. Do you understand me?' She gave the boy a shake again, to emphasise her meaning.

Cerdic nodded, dutifully agreed. Better not antagonise her too much, her moods had been hard enough to endure as it was these past weeks. Like a bear with an arrow wound his mother, lately.

'Arthur, your father, has patched his differences with his uncle. They are not exactly reconciled, but have at least agreed to differ.' And that could put an end to her plans. Damn Arthur, damn him to Hell!

Cerdic shrugged, so what?

His mother caught the gesture, shook the boy harder. 'Do you not see, child? If the Pendragon is killed in this war with Lot of the North, Ambrosius will become supreme. It will be up to Ambrosius to appoint the next king!' She did not add, *It must be Cerdic, it will be my Cerdic!*

So Cerdic promised to keep himself clean and trotted away, running as soon as he was out of his mother's sight. There was a large old tree at the junction of the steading's track and the road that snaked down from Venta Bulgarium. He'd get a good view of Ambrosius and his men approaching.

The sky was slate-grey, there would be more rain soon. The track up to the farmsteading was drying out, but remained muddied enough to mark his sandals and the hem of his new white tunic. Cerdic, clinging along the lowest bough of his tree, shivered. The wind was shifting, coming in from the sea. The tide was turning, probably. Cerdic liked the sea. He wanted to go in one of the great Jute long ships one day, if ever his mother would relent and let him visit her grandfather. He had seen them, those wonderful ships, battling against a storm swell or sailing gracefully before a summer wind. Horses . . . Ambrosius was coming.

Cerdic swung down from his perch, stood with arms folded, legs straddled. He watched critically as the first riders swept past at a jogtrot, stepped forward, his hand held upright as Ambrosius's horse approached. The man commanded a halt, drew his mount to a stand. He regarded Cerdic a moment, before solemnly raising his own hand in greeting.

'Cerdic.' The boy had his father's eyes and the Pendragon nose – except there was something more behind that precocious expression. Haughtiness? Superiority? Sa, that was it. Ambrosius shifted in the saddle, an uncomfortable feeling, being regarded as an insignificant by a boy seven years of age.

Cerdic nodded assent, his lips pursing. His upraised hand had been intended as a signal to halt, not a polite greeting. 'You have come to talk with my mother. She is not happy with the written treaty you have made with my father. Neither am I.'

Ambrosius lifted his eyebrows. 'Are you not?'

Cerdic missed the adult sarcasm. 'My mother says you intend to be King after my father has gone, that you will ignore my valid claim to be the next King.'

182

Ambrosius, as with all his family, was a tall man. He sat his horse, regarding the boy, in a mind not to answer but to ride directly on. There was much for him to do and he had no time to waste with small, impudent boys. He also wished to get this coming interview with Winifred over and done with and be on his way. She would not like being told that another had been appointed as Abbess at Venta, nor would she much like having her own mind overturned. Ambrosius had no liking for the woman, in fact, bitterly regretted being so influenced by her. It galled him to admit the small truth that Winifred was manipulative and greedy for the material things of life, with the needs of God coming a distant second. Galled even more to acknowledge that Arthur the Pendragon was mayhap right in some things. About his first wife, Winifred, the child of Vortigern being one, and, it seemed, looking at this flaxen-haired, chubby boy, the ambitious intent of his son, Cerdic for another. Knowing the Pendragon as he did, and looking upon the boy's arrogance, Ambrosius realised that Arthur was justified in disliking the lad, for all that he was of his own flesh and blood. There was too much Saex greed in him.

In return, Cerdic stared at Ambrosius. He saw a man in his late thirties, with receding hair and a thin-fleshed face. He had been ill, so his mother said. Was there any family resemblance? Did Ambrosius share any feature with Arthur? Eyes, cheek-bones, chin? Cerdic did not know, for he had never seen his father. Wanted to meet him – oh aye, wanted to meet the man who detested his own son and made no secret that he wished him dead. Wanted to meet him because Cerdic fully intended to kill his father. He dreamt about it often, planned the event to the smallest detail. A death by dagger or sword, an execution for the hatred and misery the father had caused the son and the first wife. Standing looking so intently at Ambrosius Aurelianus, Cerdic decided that perhaps he, too, ought be removed. He did not like the man. Liked him even less when he at last answered.

'I have no intention of becoming a king, boy. It is a title I oppose. If death befalls your father before his son has come of age, then I will take the full legal title of Governor of All Britain. Until then, I remain Comes Britanniarum, Governor of Britannia Secunda.'

Cerdic had bristled at the reference to son. It was not himself this man referred to, but that other boy, Llacheu. Through clenched teeth he said, 'I am the Pendragon's son. I will be king after him.'

Ambrosius nudged his horse into a walk, his entourage moving off with him. All he said to the boy was, 'We shall see.'

Cerdic watched the group of men ride up the track, followed a short way, to see his mother come out the house, curtsey obedience to the British man. Inside, they would share wine and bread and meat, and talk of the future. Winifred was intent on ensuring that Ambrosius, now that he was allied to Arthur, still agreed to her position as legal and only wife to the Pendragon. Their divorce, she maintained, had not been accepted by his Holiness the Christian Pope in Rome; ergo, she was still the Pendragon's wife, Cerdic his only legitimate son.

Cerdic decided to go fishing. Having met Ambrosius, having seen that look of undisguised scorn for a Saex-born boy, he felt there would be no sympathetic help from Ambrosius Aurelianus when the time came to fight for the royal torque and the Pendragon banner.

Cerdic was only seven years old, but already he knew these things, and knew also that one day, one day, he *would* be King of Britain.

May 462

§ XXX

'Damn this rain!' Cei burst into Arthur's tent, dripping water over the hard-stamped floor. The dog, Cabal, pricked his ears at the disturbance, lifted his head, but seeing it was Cei, a friend, flopped back to sleep, stretching his belly, with a sigh of contentment, to the warmth of the brazier. Cei flung back the hood of his saturated cloak and shook himself as Cabal, were he wet, would have done.

'Do come in Cei,' Arthur drawled, without glancing up from the parchment he was reading. 'Why not make it as wet in here as it is out there?'

Cei scowled across the tent, and throwing the cloak to Arthur's skinny boy slave, strode with a half-audible growl to the central brazier, kicking Cabal aside to be nearer the warmth. He rubbed his hands before it a moment, then stood warming his buttocks, a thin wisp of steam rising from his damp clothing.

Arthur was stretched the length of his rumpled sleeping cot, boots muddied, legs gaitered, shoulders supported by a rolled saddle blanket. At his elbow was a table supporting a flagon of wine. In one hand, a half empty pewter tankard, in the other, the letter from Gwenhwyfar. It had come with the supplies. Already its edges were crumpled and bent from his reading and rereading of it.

Looking up, Arthur studied his cousin a moment. A big man, muscular, with a bull neck, deep chest and broad shoulders. His square chin jutted from an equally square, hard-lined face which carried an expression of displeasure, all too often found there these days. Inverted eyebrows drooped with the taut, disapproving mouth. Cei was angry about something. Again. When was he not? Draining the wine, Arthur replaced his tankard on the table and unravelled the parchment that had rolled up on itself. He scanned the writing, finding the passage where he had left off and continued reading. He could hear her voice as he read the words, see her laughing, smiling face. By the gods, how he missed her!

'It is well that some of us are able to idle our time,' Cei muttered crossly.

Arthur ignored him.

Irritably, Cei crossed to a second, larger table strewn as was usual with Arthur, by a multitude of maps, unread letters and parchments. He uncovered another tankard and inspected its inside for cleanliness. A distasteful sound left his lips. 'Call this clean, boy?' He thrust the thing at the slave who was holding Cei's saturated cloak before a second brazier in a valiant attempt to dry it. 'This is disgustingly filthy – like the rest of this tent. Look at the place. A midden heap!!' Emphasising his displeasure, Cei prodded the muddle on the table with his finger and then kicked at a discarded wine flagon that lay abandoned on the floor.

The boy dropped the cloak in a ragged heap and ran to take the tankard with a spate of profuse apolgies. He scurried away, out into the rain, promising to clean it immediately.

'You are over soft on him, Arthur. He needs a sound thrashing!'

Letting the parchment spring to a loose roll before starting to wind it tighter, Arthur commented, 'You are in a delightful mood this day.' He swung his legs from the cot. Sitting on the edge he stretched and yawned, sniffed loudly, then peered hopefully into the wine flagon, wrinkling his nose to discover it empty. That was the last of the best wine. He sighed. Barley-brewed ale from here on.

'The patrol was not good I assume?' he said, returning his attention to his glowering cousin.

'The patrol,' came the sharp retort, 'was a God-cursed useless waste of time.'

Eyes sparking amusement, Arthur said with annoying cheeriness, 'Bad as a wet laundry day, eh?'

In his sour mood, Cei failed to appreciate the teasing humour. Instead, the remark brought forth an upsurge of exasperation and discontent. 'For three days, Arthur,' he railed, stalking around the small confine of Arthur's tent, 'we have encamped here. Enniaun ought have joined with us by now.' He stopped before Arthur, hands gesticulating. 'Let us face facts. He is not coming. Why should he march from Gwynedd? What interest has he in the old hunting runs of his dead father?'

'He has a great interest, Cei,' Arthur answered, with quiet conviction, all humour gone. He raised an eyebrow, looked directly, almost challengingly, at his cousin. 'He will be here.'

Cei faltered, taken aback by the conviction of that bland statement. He turned away, back to the brazier. 'That is as may be,' he changed verbal direction, attacking from an alternative level, 'but for how much longer are you intending to hang your head and allow these Northern curs to harass our patrols and thieve our supplies?' His arms were whirling with grievance. 'The rain soaks through clothing and tents; the wind is bitter cold and the horses are kicking and snapping at each other with bad temper – as are most of the men. We are wasting valuable time idling our heels here – and damn it,' Cei kicked savagely at a table leg, 'all you do is sit on your backside,' he kicked a second time, harder, 'reading!'

Arthur scratched the base of his neck. How he would like a bath! His belly rumbled. 'What has happened to supper, I wonder?' He spoke the thought aloud, stretching a second time, easing the muscles along his shoulders. Pushing himself lazily to his feet, he ambled past the angry Cei towards the closed tent flap, running a finger as he passed across the muddle on top of his work table. With a scowl, he peered out into the darkening evening. Rain was falling straight down like an opaque curtain, drumming on the leather tent, spattering water-logged ground, the drops leaping and dancing. The grass, churned and muddied, had rivulets of water forming a series of channels seeking a way to lower ground. There would be flooding on the flat, the rivers would be high too. At least here among the ruins of a Roman fort there was shelter enough to light the cooking fires. The men had eaten well these past few days – one grumble they could not toss at him! Game was in plentiful supply here, north of the Wall.

Gweir was returning at a quick trot, head down, shoulders hunched against the rain, the cleaned tankard clutched tight in both hands. The lad needed a cloak.

189

Arthur stepped aside to allow the boy entrance, taking the drinking vessel from him as he did so. 'Not much point of a clean tankard,' he said, bending slightly lower so as to be nearer the boy's ear, and thrusting his nose into the lad's face, 'when I have nothing to put in it.'

The boy reddened and stumbled a horrified apology.

Good-natured, Arthur laughed and ruffled the lad's wet hair. He was ten summers, although it could be one more or one less, and not particularly proficient as a personal slave, but Arthur liked him. He had found the boy, huddled and wretched, in the darkness of what remained of the Principia building back at Vercovicium. A ragged, hungry, frightened boy, with tear stains on his grimed face, hiding among the rubble.

'What's your name?' Arthur had asked, holding the squirming child at a safe distance, mindful of the frantically kicking feet, lunging fists and things crawling in matted hair and filthy clothing.

'That be my business!' the lad had spat, struggling to be free of Arthur's restraining hold.

'Wrong.' Arthur had bundled the lad without ceremony down the hill and into the nearest water for a thorough dowsing. 'As from now, it is my business also.'

The boy's burst of outrage at being taken as slave evaporated with the discovery of who this man, callously dunking him in cold river water, was. Inside the passing of a day the boy worshipped his new master, went around – even through this pouring fall of rain – with a grin as broad as an oak trunk. When the men from the North came raiding they had slain his family and claimed the stock. Lying low until they had gone, Gweir had survived as best he could. Had he known the wonders he would discover as slave to Arthur the King, he would not have taken such fright when the soldiers rode into the fort where he was taking shelter. But then, if the boy had not put up such a spirited fight when Arthur had found him hiding, the Pendragon would never have established that first basis of liking.

Gweir whirled on his heel and disappeared into the rain once more, trotting in the direction of the stores wagons, his bare feet spattering among the puddles, kicking up spray and mud.

'He needs boots,' Arthur thought. Said aloud. 'The boy has nothing save the rags on his back. I ought have attended that afore now. Fetch my supper too!' he shouted to the departing figure. 'My belly is growling!'

Waving an acknowledging hand, Gweir ducked through the rain, jumping the gullies of running water.

Cei sounded a disparaging snort as Arthur, chuckling quietly, ambled back to the table, his hand fondling Cabal's ears as he passed the sleeping dog. 'You treat the wretch as if he were a son, Arthur. A witless, lazy good-for-nothing – you ought sell him to someone who would teach him a few harsher lessons if you have not the heart to do so.'

'To you?' Arthur queried, glancing at Cei who was seating himself on the tent's only stool.

'I would not treat him as softly as you do.'

Placing both hands on the table, the Pendragon leant forward, smiling lazily. 'What is it with you lately, Cei? You are as sour as ruined wine. Gweir is just a boy. A homeless, lost, British boy who has known nought but a life of harsh words and herding sheep. Until a few days past, he had never seen a fine-made tankard, let alone Roman wine to slop into it!'

'I will tell you what is wrong with me,' Cei stormed, stamping to his feet, angered at this unnecessary lecture. 'I am sick to death of tramping these cursed hills. Sick to death of getting wet; of waiting for your brother-by-law who is not going to come – and I am sick to the stomach of your damned good humour!'

Arthur laughed, the sound rumbling from deep in his chest, his facial skin wrinkling into creases around his eyes and mouth. Chuckling, he strode from behind the table, his arm extending to wrap across Cei's ox-muscled shoulders. 'I would have thought, my friend,' he thumped Cei's back, 'that my good mood was a thing to be welcomed! How often have you complained about the opposite?' He lightly scuffed Cei's hair, as he had the lad's. 'Enniaun will be here soon, you have my word.' He could be so certain, sound so assured, for Gwenhwyfar's letter had confirmed it. Enniaun had passed through Caer Luel riding North into the hills as he and

Arthur had planned – though her couched words had been damned difficult to decipher! Idle? Mithras, it had taken him half the day to interpret her hidden meaning! They had to be careful, take no risks, for letters could too easily fall into enemy hands, secrets must be kept safe, but blood of the Bull, Gwenhwyfar's phrasing was too cryptic! 'Then we can move north and begin the business we came here for.' He snorted another guffaw. 'I can do nothing to stop the rain, mind!' He slapped Cei's back the harder. 'Meanwhile, we stay within the limits of the terrain that we know. And wait.'

Gweir returned, cleared a space on the table and set down a bowl, uncovering it to reveal steaming stew, poured barley-beer from a jug. Hungry, Arthur began to eat, spooning thick venison gravy supplemented with herbs and root vegetables. Through a mouthful, he told the boy, 'My cousin is right. This tent is a mess.' Swallowing, added gruffly, 'Get it tidied – but do not touch my table!'

Looking about him, Gweir ran his hands through straggling, greasy hair and puffed out his cheeks. He might as well try to stop the rain as clear the wake of Arthur's scattered debris! He had already made several attempts to tidy the place, but whenever he began clearing away the muddle of strewn papers, discarded clothing and military paraphernalia, Arthur, who seemed to be forever within the tent, always bellowed at him to 'cease that infernal rustling!' Gweir bent and began sorting a muddle of muddied, damp clothing strewn in one corner, his fingers dwelling over the softness of the quality weave.

Warmer, dried, his humour improving, Cei rubbed the side of his nose, scratched behind his ear, tentatively suggested, 'Would you ride patrol tomorrow, Arthur?'

Swallowing a mouthful, Arthur spooned more meat. 'I'll consider it.'

Cei helped himself to more beer. 'Knowing your damned luck it'll stop raining by morning.'

Laughing, Arthur agreed to go, even if it still rained; noticed Gweir. 'Oh for the Bull's sake, boy, stop fiddling with that bundle of clothing and fetch more of this stew. A bowl for Cei also.'

The boy sighed. Letting his arms open, he allowed the garments to tumble to the floor in a heap. He had begun to wonder if Arthur's other slave had also had this same problem to deal with. Had he deliberately fallen down those steps at Caer Luel? The pain of a broken leg was worth enduring for a while if it meant a rest from trying to accomplish an impossibility! He paused just inside the tent opening, gloomily looking out at the pouring rain. Aye, and a good, long lie in a dry bed.

'Gweir!' The lad spun around at Arthur's sharp, commanding voice. What else could be amiss? Arthur was squatting on his heels, rummaging through the bundle that Gweir had dropped; he straightened, holding a plaid-weave cloak and tossed it casually at the boy. 'Take this as your own,' the Pendragon said, 'and after you have fetched the stew, go to Gaius and tell him to fit you a pair of boots.'

Gweir caught the cloak and stood clutching it to him with his mouth open, unbelieving. He had owned nothing save rags afore now, nothing as grand as a plaid cloak and a pair of boots! 'For me?' he managed to croak, gazing with new heights of adoration at the man before him. 'Be this for me?'

'What?' Arthur rumbled, 'is it not good enough for you? I suppose you'll be wanting a damned new tunic to go with it? Get yourself one while you're about your boots – and bracae. We will come in for some hard marching within a few days like as not, I can't have a snivelling boy whining about his cold feet and balls, trotting at my heels.'

Gweir began to stammer thanks, but Arthur cut him short. 'I am tired of having a rough-shorn tup mooning around my tent. If you're dressed in the part of a king's slave you'll start doing your duties like one!'

His face alight, Gweir nodded eagerly, and clutching the cloak to him, scuttled out into the night.

'You spoil the brat. Give it a few months, and he'll be no good to you,' Cei warned, wagging his finger.

'Given time, and then the right training,' Arthur corrected, 'he has the making of the next generation of Artoriani. I need such boys, Cei. For the boys become men.'

§ XXXI

By the early afternoon of the next day, drenching rain had eased to a pattering drizzle, then stopped altogether, leaving a dull, leaden sky pressing heavily over brooding hills and rain-sodden trees. Ground squelched beneath hooves, becoming churned into caking mud which covered horses' legs and spattered their bellies and riders' boots. The biting wind from the north-east had veered. It still blustered like some crusty, foul-tempered old gentleman, but had, at least, lost some of the jagged bite.

Arthur rode with deceptive ease in the saddle, the leather creaking with a soporific rhythm. One hand rested on his thigh, the other held Hasta's reins with the lighest touch, his body moving at ease with the horse's dancing stride; the animal, with head high and ears pricked, was as fresh as he had been at the beginning of the day, though they had covered many miles since the rain-wet dawn. Behind the Pendragon, a few men of the patrol talked quietly between themselves, their voices no more than the rustle of wind in the trees. They had seen or heard no sound, other than that of nature, all morning. There seemed nothing out of place in this narrow, peaceful valley.

Hasta snatched at a branch, stripping the leaves as he passed, letting the thing swish back as he let go. Raindrops cascading in a shower over Arthur found their way down his neck and he swore under his breath. The horse, chewing contentedly flicked his ears at his rider's voice, then halted, abrupt, alert, ears pricking, blowing nostrils scenting the wind. Alarmed, Hasta snorted and attempted to duck sideways, brought to an immediate halt by pressure from Arthur's heel, calf and tightening of reins.

Arthur flung his arm wide to signal his men to halt. Instant stillness; silence, save for the steady drip drip of several days' rain from tree and bush. A crow somewhere cawed once, a harsh, lonely call that when stilled left the place eerily quiet. Hasta snorted again and Arthur laid his hand reassuringly along the horse's neck.

Wolf? he thought, his own ears and eyes, all senses, alert. *Animal wolf or human wolf?* Ahead, the trees thickened and the deer trail they had been following curved sharply to the left around a tumble of boulders that had slid down the steep incline of the valley, piling in a straggled heap at the bottom. The landslip must have occurred years past, for vegetation had reclaimed the hillside and jumble of rocks. One or two sapling trees were pushing a determined way through gaps between the displaced terrain. Over his shoulder, Arthur caught the soft movement of bows being made ready, could almost hear the thud of hearts pumping a mixture of apprehension and excitement.

The patrol had been routine up until now, almost a pleasant day's ride. Scouts yesterday had reported no activity this side of the Roman road. There had been no sightings of the small, roaming warbands from Lot's gathered army for two days. Who was ahead?

They waited long minutes, expecting at any moment the swish and thud of an arrow, or a blood-chilling, attacking war-cry. Lips compressed in grim decision. Arthur drew his sword, the blade making a soft, menacing hiss as it eased from the sheepskin-lined scabbard. He touched his heels to Hasta's flank, and the stallion, as unnerved as the men, lifted his head and whinnied, a shrill, unexpected sound in the tense silence. Arthur's body jerked with taut surprise and jagged the iron bit. Hasta's tail swished at the sudden pain, his head tossing, ears flattening along his skull, angrily danced sideways, crab-stepping.

Hoofbeats coming at a fast gallop! Then a savage, fiercesome yelling, and from around the concealing bend came four riders with swords drawn, mouths open screaming their war-cry – Artoriani scouts!

Hasta shied violently; several of the patrol horses swung away snorting, frightened by the apparitions coming from nowhere and making such a terrible noise.

'Sweet Jesu!' The foremost scout cursed, desperately hauling his mount to a skidding halt. The animal plunged, almost went down. The three others, a neck's length behind, swerved to avoid the leader, one rider catapulted over his mount's shoulder, lay winded in the churned ground, a second grabbed hold of his horse's mane, valiantly attempting to remain seated. Two of Arthur's patrol were unhorsed. One sprang immediately to his feet, the other, face chalk pale, lay with his leg bent beneath him, the bone shattered at the thigh.

'We took you for Northern curs!' one of the four riders explained through panting breath, scrambling, embarrassed, from lying half across his mount's neck into the security of the saddle.

Arthur had steadied Hasta and was swearing profoundly, the curses riddled with explosive anger. 'Call yourself scouts?' he yelled. 'You incompetent curs, whore-son imbeciles! You deserve not the name Artoriani! Dung-midden whelps – if we had been a raiding party you would have your guts split open by now!'

The Artoriani scout before him reddened, to hide growing embarrassment said over-quickly, 'We were riding hard for camp – Lord Enniaun is a handful of miles over yonder, coming up from Caer Luel.' He twisted around in the saddle, pointing back up the heavily wooded valley. 'His men were riding easy, well in the open, making no attempt at concealment.' He frowned momentarily. 'Why have they taken so long to join us, my Lord?'

Arthur's head came up, eyes squinting keenly against the sudden burst of brilliant sunshine, his body tense with anticipated excitement. If his own men were asking questions . . . !

Lot's army, having swept south as far as Eboracum, carving a bloody trail of murder and destruction, had retreated northward again, lying nearer their own hunting runs, leaving only scattered warbands to watch for Arthur's coming. Lot knew of the Pendragon's whereabouts and his every move – Arthur had made no attempt at concealment. They were marching in easy stages into a baited trap. Lot wanted a fight with Arthur, needed to win if he were to hold the North as his own. The Pendragon had gone along with the pretence of innocence these past weeks, appeared seemingly fooled, heading blindly into waiting destruction – had deliberately delayed because he was waiting for Enniaun. And at last he had come! With his young men of Gwynedd eager to blood their new spears, and with the older men, men who, when young, had hunted as the Votadini over these same high, windswept hills and along these same deep, tree-cluttered valleys. Men who had an intimate knowledge of these northern lands where the wind swept as sharp as a dagger's blade. Land over which once, the great Lion Lord, Gwenhwyfar's father, Cunedda had ruled, before Vortigern forced him south to Gwynedd.

Enniaun's war-host had marched leisurely and conspicuously up from Caer Luel, giving Lot's scouts ample chance for a good look at their strength and numbers. Except the scouts had seen only what they were meant to see. Were unaware of a band of hand-picked men who had followed the hidden routes, travelling by night and following the wolf runs through the hills and the secretive deer trails along the wooded valleys; circling with stealth around and up into the North. Behind Lot and his waiting host.

The Pendragon, despite his air of good humour and indifference, had been growing more anxious with each nightfall, had expected Enniaun, at the latest, yester eve. If Enniaun's secretive band of men were discovered then all would be lost; Lot must not know that Arthur was aware of what lay ahead, must believe that the Pendragon was overstepping himself, was too cocksure of his past successes. 'You have spoken with my Lord Enniaun?' Arthur's question to his scout was edged with the sharpness of a new-whetted blade.

A second scout shook his head in answer. 'Na, Sir, we but saw him and his men in the distance. We showed ourselves and they signalled reply.'

Arthur nodded vague approval and swung Hasta round. He rode to the injured man, watched a moment as a comrade axed two sapling trees and stripped the branches to fashion a stretcher. 'See him comfortable, and you two,' Arthur indicated two men, 'stay here with him. We'll collect you on the way back. I ride to welcome Gwynedd.' He grinned suddenly, showing white teeth against weather-browned skin, his eyes wrinkling with delight. If his own men assumed that Gwynedd was coming up direct from the Wall, then Lot too, would, with Fortuna's blessing, assume the same. He dismounted, went to the groaning cavalryman, laid his hand, concerned, on the young man's shoulder, said, 'Easy lad, we shall not be long away.'

The Wall, with the exception of Caer Luel to the west, had long since been abandoned as a military viability – there simply was not adequate funding or men to patrol it efficiently. The wealthy towns, like Eboracum and Lindum, with their pompous Governors backed by the bigotry of the Church, refused to supplement the pay and keep of a permanent garrison of Arthur's rough-voiced and equally rough-mannered men, choosing instead, to raise their own local militia in times of threatened trouble. That had, it seemed, proved insufficient.

North of the Wall the territories had been abandoned by Vortigern for the same untenable reasons, left to rot under the shifting power surges of petty overlords, Saex, British, Scotti or Picti leaders who came and went as often as the wind changed.

The scattered common-folk, the sheep-herds, the poor farmers, the wolf and deer hunters, the few surviving traders, cared little who ruled over this desolate, uncared-for land. They scratched a living from one harsh winter to the next and prayed that whatever present warrior band was besieging Dun Pelidr, they would leave the farmsteadings alone. What did it matter to a poor man who occupied the royal place? Tithes had to be paid to whoever decided to call himself lord.

Arthur had not been surprised at Lot's rise to power. Once the father had died, it had been inevitable that the son would grope for an ambition held long in check by an old man who had advocated fealty to Rome. Would seek to become Lord over more than one poor, wind-burnt estate. These abandoned lands of the Votadini were ripe for the harvesting, waiting for a man to emerge to wield the scythe. Lot was a bull-head of a boy turned to an ox of a man, thick of muscle, and in Arthur's opinion, of sense. But with someone behind him to guide the sword arm, someone nurturing the seeds of greed into fruition, a man who could achieve much. Especially if such a man had a wife named Morgause.

Riding down the valley to meet Enniaun, Arthur found himself thinking profoundly of Morgause. Witch, he called her. Witch-Woman. The thought came, was dismissed, but came again: was it Lot he was so anxious to face and defeat, or Morgause? So many evils had she put upon him, so much of her vile scent still clung, like the lingering stench of midden-muck, even after all these long years.

As he approached Enniaun, Arthur raised his hand in salute and welcome. Spurring Hasta to gallop the last few yards, he leapt from the saddle as they came up together, Enniaun too, jumping from his horse, arms outstretched, calling a greeting. Embracing, the men held together a moment, close in kinship and affinity; pulled a little apart to exchange wide grins and a hurried, most private word.

'It is done?' Arthur asked, his eyebrow rising slightly with the anxious questioning.

Enniaun playfully cuffed the Pendragon's shoulder, beamed, 'A trap is none so dangerous when you carry a stick with which to spring it!'

§ XXXII

Concentrating, lips parted, eyes wide, Llacheu stealthily brought the two carved wooden horses from behind a stool leg. He waited an agonising moment, then letting loose a fierce, piercing yell, plunged them forward, one in each hand, stumping their legs on the stone floor, making clicking hoofbeat sounds with his tongue. 'Charge!' he screamed as he brought the horses crashing forward into his brother's lined row of crudely carved Roman soldiers.

Shouting as loud, Gwydre protested as his men were swept to each side by Llacheu's scything hands. 'You didn't give me a chance to fight back!'

'That's the point of battle,' Llacheu retorted with a knowing sneer. 'Do not give the enemy a chance to attack you first.'

'Well it's not fair!'

And they were fighting, the toys forgotten, both boys tumbling over and over, fists and feet hammering at each other, the battle game suddenly for real.

Nessa, hurrying from her sewing, tried to pull them apart and screeched as teeth sank into her arm. Enid ran to separate the boys – and Gwenhwyfar came into the room, her arms full of white cloth freshly cleaned and collected from the fullers. The fight stopped, the

199

boys backing from each other hurling accusations; Nessa was crying and scolding both at once and nursing her arm; Enid was standing, hands on hips, also scolding.

Enduring the combined noise a moment only, Gwenhwyfar shouted for quiet. It settled reluctantly, lumbering like a rock fall. Gwydre had the last mutter.

'I do not care who started it,' his mother retorted, sweeping across the room to lay the cloth on a table. 'I want to hear no more of it.'

'But he . . .'

'I was only . . .' the boys tried together to explain.

'No more!'

Llacheu hung his head. 'Na, Mother.'

Gwenhwyfar raised an eyebrow at her other son. Gwydre glowered – looking for all the world like his father – climbed down, reluctant, from his anger. 'Na, Mother.'

Showing her arm, Nessa expressed her indignation. 'Look what they did to me, the heathens!'

Inspecting the bruising, Gwenhwyfar crooked her finger at the boys, made them stand before her. 'Which one of you bit Nessa?'

'He did,' they said simultaneously, pointing at each other.

'Then you will both be punished. You will not ride this afternoon.' Turning her back on them Gwenhwyfar unrolled the cloth. There was more than she needed here but it was good cloth, worth its buying. She measured with her fingers, planning with her eye. Aye, a dragon embroidered in scarlet red, decorated with gold thread . . . it would make a fine new banner for Arthur. She sauntered to the unshuttered window, peeped out. The boys were standing gloomily, Llacheu chewing his lip, Gwydre trying not to cry. 'What a shame,' she said, 'the first afternoon it has not rained.' Again she looked out, her eyes going north to the fuzzed line of distant hills. Did the rain fall where Arthur was? Had the two armies yet met . . . was Arthur all right . . . ?

Come with me, Gwen.

No. I am not yet ready to face more dying.

Yet was it any easier to not know what was happening, up away beyond those hills? He had sent only one letter to her three. She sighed, a slight sound. That was unfair, he would not have the time to write. Too late for regrets; she wished she had gone with him. But then, life was stitched together by regrets.

'*What will you do if Morgause is there?*' she had asked Arthur, curled against him in bed the night before he rode away north. He had not answered immediately and when he did it was with uncertainty. '*Hang her? Behead her? I don't know.*'

Llacheu had come to the window, was looking where his mother watched. His hand slipped into hers, gripped tight. 'Will there be much fighting, Mam?'

'I expect so.' She forced a smile for him. 'Your da is almost as keen as you when it comes to fighting.'

Her son grinned back at her, 'And almost as good!'

She laughed. 'Aye, almost.'

§ XXXIII

The Artoriani. A brotherhood of nine hundred permanent, élite cavalry under the direct command of their King, Arthur, the Pendragon. Professional men doing a professional job.

The marching camp had swelled with the arrival of Gwynedd, the newcomers settling their weapons and personal bundles around their own fires to the western edge, billeting their horses to their own picket lines. With the gathered infantry, the local militiamen, the number of fighting men came close to three thousand. The Cymry, the Companions. Arthur was aware they might not number enough, but he held one advantage, now that Enniaun had come.

It was evening, time for the nightly gathering of officers and allied lords to discuss details of the morrow. The rain had begun again, pattering softly on the oiled leather of Arthur's command tent and a slight wind outside found holes and openings to cram through, causing cross-draughts and currents that fanned the torches and braziers, trailing the smoke in crazy spirals.

'I suppose,' one of the older Artoriani officers asked, 'it would be too much to hope that Lot will not be able to hold his men together much longer? As much as I would regret a wasted march, it would be somewhat agreeable to find they have gathered their spears and gone home to hearth and women-folk.'

But the men who, beyond the King's tent, settled themselves to sleep, rolling themselves into blankets and under cloaks, eight men to a tent would have been disappointed, had that officer's words came true. Hearts were high, even through the drizzle of fine rain, tempers good, the mood expectant, excited. They were to march in earnest come morning; no more paddling around among these mire-drenched, mist-bound hills.

Enniaun accepted beer from the boy Gweir, pointed to a parchment map spread across the table, cleared for once of Arthur's accumulated muddle. He moved a broad finger up the line representing the long sweep of the Roman road, stabbed his nail into a point slightly to the west, where crudely drawn trees were marked. 'Here,' he said, with a hint of finality, 'the hills that we now occupy drop down to the flat plain of the Great River. To the north bank, the first fringes of the Caledonian Forest stretching from here,' he ran his spread fingers a long way up the map, 'into the highlands.' He folded his arms across his chest and for emphasis, stepped one pace back from the table. 'Lot waits for us one mile north of the river, within the cover of dense woodland.'

'How many to his name, my Lord?' That was Hueil from Alclud. 'Did you see enough to estimate?'

Enniaun, a deep frown of concentration etched beneath his bush of red hair, pondered a reply. He regarded Arthur, who stood with hands resting flat against the edge of the table, steady eyes answering his hesitant gaze. The Pendragon nodded once, giving permission for him to continue.

'It is my guess,' Enniaun spoke slowly, thinking as he formed the words. His eyes flickered around the allied Lords and officers of the militia gathered men, assessing their courage. They led good men, whole-hearted loyal to Arthur, but they were not disciplined Artoriani, some held no experience of a real fight. Cattle raiding, minor squabbles, the odd skirmish – what was that to full battle? 'Close to five thousand.'

There came a series of low, unbelieving whistles. Those who had been at the back, leaning against the tent poles or squatting by the braziers, came alert to attention, stepped nearer those grouped around the table. The older and wiser among them shook their heads. That was a lot of men to fight!

'Their numbers may be many, but I doubt their hearts are as strong, or their skill as great.' Meriaun spoke plain, hands tucked beneath his armpits, legs spread wide. His father had been Cunedda's eldest-born, butchered as an example against rebellion when the North, in support of Uthr Pendragon, rose and lost to Vortigern. It was some small portion of personal pride this, the reclaiming of a land that ought, one day, to have been his own.

Taking his hands from the table, Arthur stood back, eyes and thoughts on the map spread before him. The road stretching north; high, open moorland; thick-wooded valleys. Almost reverently, he reached forward to touch a drawn line that meandered between the position of their present camp and the great mass of the Caledonian Forest. 'The Great River.' He spoke slowly, his mind working with the gift of battle genius. 'We need to cross it. We could head for the coast,' his finger stabbed at the wide estuary, 'but there it is wider, with marsh and mudflats. Also, a long ride east. The same applies if we go west, upstream, save the width will be negligible.' He paused, his hand hovering, mind tumbling with ideas, most instantly rejected. 'For a fording port we need the middle reaches, ahead of us.' He brought his finger back. 'Neither too high, nor too low, and aware that from here,' he indicated the point, 'the current is tidal.' He chewed a split fingernail. 'Which means we ford the Great River where Lot wants us to.'

Cei cleared his throat, bent to peer at the map, his bottom lip jutting out. 'They are holed up in those north-bank woods now, but will they not come down to meet us when we are at our most vulnerable?'

Many nodded, that seemed most likely.

Arthur lifted a corner of the map, retrieved a thin stick of charcoal, and carefully marked in their route northwards. 'We marched at an easy pace.' He was thinking aloud, planning. 'Coming along the Wall and crossing the hills, to here.' He circled the position of their present camp and tossed the charcoal, catching it, holding it between curled fingers. 'We made no secret of our passing, and have not hurried our pace.'

'Watched all the while.' Cei's disapproval was rancid in his throat. 'We ought to have shown them our strength afore this.'

Arthur's reply was indifferent. 'Our archers and scouts have picked off more of their men then they have ours – and with less heat than losing our tempers would achieve.'

'Aside that,' Hueil spoke, coming forward, a slight swagger of self-importance to his step, 'we needed to give my Lord of Gwynedd's chosen scouts time – and adequate diversion – to ride north and back undetected?'

'Precisely.' Arthur acknowledged the young man's observation. He had hopes for Hueil.

'You ought to have informed us of what Gwynedd was up to,' Cei remarked gruffly.

'Must all my decisions be accountable to you then?' Arthur reacted with quick anger, facing Cei broadside on.

'Na!' Cei shouted back. 'But oft-times I wonder why I am honoured with this empty title of second-in-command! Command of what? Hollow evasions and hidden secrets.' He stood square before the Pendragon, arms animated with annoyance, adding for good measure, 'What if you had been killed? What then?' He dropped his hands, raised one slowly, imploring. 'God's truth, Arthur, what is it? Do you no longer trust me?'

'I suggest,' Enniaun said, coming around the table, diffusing the rise of temper by pointing back to the map and the matter of tactics, 'that I take my men along this valley here and circle around through the trees, to come up behind Lot. With luck, he will not suspect such a move, believing us unaware of his position.'

Arthur turned his back on Cei, the slight squabble immediate forgotten, passed over as nothing serious. 'My guess is that he will attack at the river crossing, but he may lure us into the woods where our Artoriani will be at a greater disadvantage.'

Cei, although smarting, was studying the river lower down. 'What if I took two Turmae to cross here? I could circle from the right flank. With Enniaun coming from the left . . .'

'That would split us into three – four with a rearguard reserve.' Arthur rolled the suggestion uneasily around in his mind.

'It could be the end of us should Lot decide to make a full fight of it as we ford the river,' Meriaun observed.

Arthur nodded. 'That is my thought also.' He spread his hands, a grin of expectant pleasure erupting on his face. 'But that is a chance we shall have to take.'

§ XXXIV

They came down from the hills in the same easy, almost relaxed style that they had been pursuing since leaving the undulating trail of the Wall. The Cymry, a combined hosting of Artoriani, men of Gwynedd and local men, hunched against the iron bite of a salt-tanged sea wind that hustled in from the distant coast, creeping between leather and metal armour, under wool or animal-skin cloaks. As the rain that had seemed to fall continuously over these northern hills finally appeared to ease they made their last camp five miles south of the Great River.

It was all intentional deception. They had marched in closed ranks, bunched together, with the pack horses in the central baggage lines led on short rein; men tramping shoulder to shoulder, spear jostling shield. Fewer tents were pitched around wider spread fires, with men doubling up to snatch a few hours of restless sleep. Age-worn tactics to fool those watching eyes into believing there were fewer numbers than expected. Come the dawn crossing of the river, and by the blessed generosity of Fortuna, Lot might never notice that Arthur's ranks had depleted overnight.

Enniaun and Cei moved with their men after the blackness of night had settled, and were long gone come the hours before dawn when the remaining men were roused. Not knowing when they might get the chance again, they ate a sustaining meal of porridge and wheat-bread, washed down with barley-ale. Horses were muzzled and hooves muffled. Through the concealing solitude of a moonless night they moved with the stealth of hunters approaching wind-wary prey, aiming to ford the river during that mind-confusing time of pre-dawn when the new morning is neither dark nor light, night nor day. The time when long-waiting men are stiffened from the night's damp chill and are at their heaviest, with senses hazy and fallible.

Arthur drew rein where the thinning trees opened out onto the spread of the river's flood-plain, wide and flat on this southern side, steep and well wooded on the other. He sat a while, one arm leaning casually across Hasta's arched white crest, staring ahead, looking as though he saw naught but the ghost shadows of mist-shrouded bush and tree and the darker stretch where the river ran.

Through the quietness came the ripple and rush of water, the river was high with the rain, feeding down from the hills with the many gushing tributaries. The woods smelt of peated leaf-mould, of damp earth and dew-sprinkled leaves and bark. Ahead, the mist was rising, the air, fresh and sharp, as keen as a whetted blade; rich, invigorating smells driving all thoughts of half-yearned sleep from a man's early awakened mind. Arthur had planned this, surprise being a tactic he used often and used well. For good reason had stories of his Artoriani spread from hearth to hearth, into chieftains' Halls or peasant bothies alike. Tales of how Arthur and his Artoriani would appear from a swirling mist, or rain-dripping woods on the crest of a dawn much as this. Conjured from nothing, horse and man, spears and shields raised, their war-cry shrieking like the cries of risen spirits. *Seeming a thousand, thousand men,* the storytellers said with awe and a quick breath. *White horses, red; flecked blood and foam. Glinting spear and shining sword, the blue blade of death! Aieee . . . a thousand thousand they seem, though they number but the nine of a hundred!*

Arthur ran his hand down the length of Hasta's neck. The stallion's white coat glimmered in the faint light, the sparkle of dew and mist turning the tip of each hair to a silvered sheen. To the east,

206

the sky was tinged with a first, faint glimmer of the coming day. A half-smile twitched to the side of the Pendragon's lip. He reached up his hand, tightened the strap of his war-cap. Well had he encouraged the telling of those tales! Well did he use the discipline and harnessed nerve of his men, and aye, the useful shoulder of a hill or the slope of a woodland, and the eddies of a river's dawn mist!

He signalled to Gweir, standing at Hasta's head, for the muzzle to be slipped and the hoof muffles to be removed. Behind, the soft rustle of movement as other shield-bearers obeyed the same command, or men dismounted to do their own. The task finished, again Arthur nodded to the boy. 'Go now lad, back to the baggage-holding behind the rearguard. Battle is no place for a lad so green behind the ears.'

Gweir glanced to his Lord, pleading with his eyes, but Arthur shook his head, jerked his thumb over his shoulder. Reluctant, feet and heart heavy, Gweir went.

Night-dark sky was becoming tinged with slow-spreading fingers of pale, creeping light. The drifting mist hovered uncertain above and between the clumps of alder and willow trees. Arthur signalled to advance at a walk; the horses, spaced wide now to give the illusion, should anyone be able to see, of more numbers than there were, held in tight check, stride kept short; riders' breath held, stomachs taut, the expectation at any moment of a sudden harsh shout from the far bank and the mortal swish and thud of shot arrows. Down through the mist, parting its caressing whiteness like a ship's bow wave, silent shrouded hoofbeats swishing through knee-high morning-wet grass. Ahead, the black path of water, where the mist danced thicker, tighter. The two leading Turmae of horse eased into the cold swirl, one above the chosen crossing point to break the force, the other down-river to snare pony or man swept away. It had begun!

As the pink-grey strip of light along the horizon broadened, there still came no shout from the opposite bank, still no alarmed shadows moved. A few birds were rehearsing their dawn song, tuning their voices as a harper sets his instrument. A vixen yipped somewhere up-river, answered by the deeper bark of her mate. The arch of the black sky was forming the dark blue-black colour of an angry, newly acquired bruise. The foreguard of infantry, wading with steady and measured pace, crossed without incident, establishing the all important bridgehead, digging their trenches with all haste and speed, hunching their wet-clothed bodies behind the thrown-up mound of mud and earth. Behind, ranked along the far bank, mounted archers waited tense with arrows notched, bowstrings and nerves taut.

Then it came, urgent shouts from the darkness of the close-crowded trees ranged along the northern bank and the surging hiss of sudden, uprushing movement, the first sigh of enemy arrows skimming low, their deadly flight arching over and down. The cries of wounded and dying men exploded the quiet stillness and Arthur's men into a foam of action. Expected, but none the less startling, attack and defence gathered momentum with the swiftness of a single boulder tossed down a rock-strewn slope.

No matter how many precautions, how organised, the crossing of a river of this width, depth and flow would always leave men open to attack. A river left a man vulnerable, with nowhere to hide or run, the current dragging at feet and thigh, hampering movement. A place to meet death, a river crossing.

The one satisfaction, it was as Arthur had thought it would be. Lot's war-hosting swept forward in a sighing rush from the steep wooded hills, coming like an east wind from nowhere sweeping over a summer-ripe cornfield. But the dawn crossing had been right, for Arthur's men had achieved those first, few, precious minutes to throw up a defensive line. As Arthur had intended, Lot had been caught unawares.

Horses belly deep in water plunged forward, or tried to turn back, held in check by determined riders. Animals screamed in pain or fear, or anger. Some fell as arrows pierced, finding those places that maimed with a burst of maddening pain. Men fell too, the force of water sweeping them away, their hands desperately clutching for a hold that was not there. The first few were lucky, the down-river line of rope held firm by the chain of riders stretching from bank to bank caught them, bundled them spluttering and gasping ashore, but then a horse, riderless, maddened by pain and blinded by an arrow shaft deep in its eye socket, entangled with one of the stretched ropes.

The animal plunged, men swore as the line pulled taut and ripped through their hands. The rope severed, curling back with the sharp hiss of a loosed whiplash, its sodden weight adding velocity. Two men were knocked from their horses, both thanked God for the sense of extra lines securing them to their mounts, but the barricade was broken, and the enemy was swarming along the far bank now, coming down from their hiding places among the trees and shadows, fighting sword to shield with the British.

The centre of infantry, flanked by cavalry, was pushing forward, battling for each precarious step across the churning flow, the water coming at its deepest almost up to their armpits. A steady arrow-cloud hissed above their heads from their own archers, forcing Lot's men to keep low. The fore defence was swelling on the opposite bank, scrambling up the steep slopes, as more and more infantry ploughed across, fighting hand to hand. And still the enemy, some dazed, a few sleep trodden, were bursting from the woods, spears raised as high as their war song. Dawn had come and gone. The sun, a ball of red-orange was rising, chasing away the last cobwebs of white mist.

Arthur sat with his own Turma of men, watching. It would be his turn to cross soon. Was this fighting a bluff, or the real thing? Was it to be settled here at this river fording or were Lot's hounds to be called off at some moment, some time soon, to run seemingly with tails tucked low into . . . who knew what?

A Picti spear cast in a wide arc above the reddening water, thudded into a soldier's shield. The man staggered, almost lost his footing to the cling of rushing water, righted himself, plunged onwards. Arthur saw another well-cast spear knock a man from his horse, fall, go down beneath the churned water. And another, and another.

Soon it would be time for the last of his men to cross.

Were a wing of these northern wildmen to appear on this southern bank now . . . Arthur shuddered, thrust the thought aside, yet unease tightened like a clenched fist, deep inside his belly. He screwed his eyes across the stretch of water, scanning the standards of the enemy, bobbing beneath the lush greenness of foliage. Lot's emblem was the purple thistle that grew in abundance on these northern moorlands. He could not see it . . . His heart lurched, his throat clamming dry and tight. There it was! Near the centre! 'Oh God, whether you are pagan or Christian,' he breathed aloud, 'let my judgement not be wrong in this!'

If Lot did not break; if he did not soon make a run up that slope, through those woods of oak and ash and beech . . . then this campaign, all he had built, would end here, at a butchering by a river, for there was not enough room to manoeuvre on that far bank. Already the fighting was spilling over, back into the water. His cavalry were hampered by the slope, the press of trees . . . come on! Move! Make your pretence at running!

Five out of the seven of Arthur's scouts had slid easy into the marching column late yesterday. Aye, they reported, there were archers and swordsmen waiting on the far bank, sound in their ease, waiting at the ford; and aye, many more were secreted near a large clearing to the north. There was a woman there too, they said, waiting beneath a spread-winged, raven banner. Arthur's stomach had churned at that. Sa, she was here then, Morgause.

A new worry knotted in his throat. What if this was how they had been supposed to think? Could Lot know that Arthur had sent men so far ahead to watch and report back? Then, had Enniaun and Cei made their crossings safe? Were they even now working their way inwards from left and right flank, drawing the net tighter, only to find Lot, too, had silently moved his men under the cover of night to take Arthur at the fording? Where in the Bull's name, were those final two scouts? They had orders to stay and observe throughout the night hours, to return in that last essential hour before dawn. They had not come.

Could they have fallen to the same fate as the unsuspecting enemy Watch? All five of Lot's men lay wide-eyed, unmoving, with throats silently slit. The story could read as easily the same for Arthur's scouts.

Someone was shouting his name. Arthur turned Hasta, cantered fast to meet the Blue Turma Decurion, the last remaining, save for the rearguard reserve.

'We are ready to go, Sir.'

Arthur nodded. 'No sign of those last scouts?'

'None, Sir. I have seen Lot's banner over there.' The Decurion ducked his head in the direction of the far bank, pointed with his spear.

'As have I,' Arthur replied, setting himself deeper into the saddle and mustering composure into his tone. 'The man who titles himself King of the North has chosen to fight personally at the river. That is fine with me. I shall have his end the sooner. Come, it is time we joined our companions!'

Arthur whistled Cabal; the dog ceased his meticulous scratching at some irritant behind his left ear, and raising himself, ambled to stand at Hasta's near-side foreleg.

Unexpectedly, Gwenhwyfar's face flickered before Arthur's eyes. Angry, impassioned. *'Why take Cabal?'* she had chided. *'He is too young, too raw. You expect over-much of his loyalty, as you do of all who walk within your shadow.'*

Too young? His right ear was already scarred from some dogfight and two bitches had borne his pups. The dog whined, not understanding the delay. Untried he might be, but he came from a line of warrior dogs, and recognised by instinct the scent and sound of battle. Arthur unfastened a loop of rope from his belt. 'Ah,' he said, leaning from the saddle to thread it through Cabal's bronze-studded collar, 'it is hard enough to leave my woman behind. How could I leave you also, my young friend?'

The Pendragon swivelled in his saddle, cast a weather-eye over the drawn ranks of the waiting rearguard. The mist had full lifted now, the sun, shining briefly through parting cloud to show a flicker of blue-washed sky. Faces startled out at him, boys mostly, younger sons of chieftains, the shield-bearers. Boys. Among them, to Arthur's sudden rise of annoyance, Gweir. Damn the lad, what was he doing there?

He stood, clasping Arthur's third-best spear, for all the world as though he were some seasoned warrior. Little fool! A smile gathered to Arthur's mouth. Little fool. He flashed a grin at the Decurion by his side, round to the last waiting men, Blue Turma, the King's Turma of Artoriani.

Arthur urged Hasta down the muddied bank into the turbulence of water, with Cabal close at the horse's shoulder, the length of rope keeping him from being swept away. The dog was immediately swimming strongly, his head lifting high, tail floating like a rudder, air snorting through his black, scarred nose.

'Mithras,' Arthur gasped as Hasta plunged, swimming also, 'this water's bloody cold!'

§ XXXV

Somehow they were across. Somehow, Mithras in his wisdom knew how, they were pressing forward, over the open space beyond the bank and up into the trees, pushing Lot's men back, gaining ground. Under foot and hoof the earth was slippery, churned with mud and blood. No time to guide thrashing hooves away from wounded and dying men; those who could not drag themselves to safety found themselves trampled.

Arthur fought within his King's Turma, joining the right flank as they rode up out of the water in a vain hope to turn the Northmen up-river into the wide sweep of a bend. Close behind the Pendragon rode his standard bearer, clench-jawed, attempting to keep the Dragon high, but the trees came low down the slope on this side of the river, and branches snared its tubular shape and flying streamers, catching it like some snarling pack of bared-teeth animals. There were two undisputed rules of battle: obey orders, and ensure that the King and his banner did not fall.

A shout from the left of centre. The infantry had broken through the hard-held wedge of Northmen and Picti. Only briefly could Arthur afford to take in the situation, to cast a quick, experienced eye over the sway of battle, the knotted groups of men, the strew of the dead. He swung his sword two-handed, almost absently, at the neck of a Northman, his blade slicing through bone and sinew, blood spurting in a thin fountain of red stink. Others of Lot's men were falling back, heading away up the slope, ducking beneath trees, turning to run . . . a shout went up among the British militia-raised men, a lifting and swaying of uncast spears and raising of shield and sword, axe or staff. A tossed shout of triumph that scuttled through the overhang of branch and leaf. Lot's banner was seen, bobbing and weaving away up and over the slope, men, Northmen and Picti, were starting to run, dodging through the trees, bent low, heads and shoulders crouched . . . The sun was one hour high in the sky, the fighting had been brief, too brief.

Arthur breathed relief, they had guessed right then. Lot was feigning a retreat, though it did not take much of a fool to see they were not fleeing in terror, but running easy, unhurried, drawing Arthur's men forward. Not a single Northman was discarding his weapons, or scrambling, terrified for his life, to safety. They almost trotted, one or two even turning to wave their swords and shout abusive taunts. The British must not yet follow the wolf into his lair . . . despatch these last men, snatch a few short moments to gain breath and wipe bloody hands and swords, then they would dismount, leave the horses here along the bank and under the trees with the rearguard and . . . what in the Bull's name!

'Gweir,' Arthur yelled, outrage darkening his face. 'You whore-son whelp! What are you doing across here!' He spurred Hasta into a flying leap, came aside the boy thrusting like a raged bull-calf at a Picti twice his height. Arthur's sword felled the man; glared down at the lad, who stood panting, beaming up at his Lord.

'I'm followin' orders, Sir. You told the rearguard to make all haste across the water when you had them on the run!' He pointed with Arthur's third-best spear, its blade spotted with blood, up through the trees. 'And they be a-runnin' Lord! Runnin' like a scared hare afore the fox!'

'And when,' Arthur asked, 'were you authorised to become part of the rearguard? I'll have the hide off your back for this disobedience, lad!' Arthur roared the reprimand through panting breath, needing to turn attention aside from the boy, to cut down two painted men coming at them from the right. Cabal launched himself at one, teeth bared, snarling. Arthur plunged his sword into the other.

He glanced again at the centre and cursed vehemently, all thought of Gweir forgotten. His officers and men of the Artoriani were standing firm, beginning to dismount, picket the horses as ordered, but not the untried men of the militia! Curse and damn the whelps – may the Hag of the Underworld take the cur sons! He damned knew this would happen!

'Hold hard!' Arthur bellowed, casting his command after the stream of British taking to their heels after Lot's fleeing men. Hasta wheeled, his head tossing, feet dancing, foam flecking back to splotch Arthur's iron-studded leather tunic. The King turned to his Signifier who, like the standard bearer, was sheltered by a knot of soldiers whose sole function was to protect these two vulnerable men. 'Sound me the stand!' Arthur shouted. 'We must not thrust ahead in a rag-tag rabble!'

The call sounded from the trumpets, taken up further down the line, sounding again and again, 'stand hard . . . stand hard . . .' But these young British men were not drilled to instant obeyal of Arthur's commands; they were cattle-raiders, hunters, craftsmen – untried, easily excited, easily led.

A hand touched Arthur's thigh, fingers gripping a moment, jolting his attention. He sucked in his breath, raised his sword, stopped short as he recognised the blood-smeared face of one of his missing scouts. 'Where in the name of Mithras have you been?' he roared, the anger at the stupidity of the British militia spilling over at this man. 'Never mind – make your report, hurry man, 'tis urgent!' Arthur was leaning from the saddle, gripping the scout by the shoulder.

'Lord,' the man panted, his own hand resting on Hasta's shoulder, leaving a streak of other men's blood there on the white coat. 'We found ourselves pinned down by a band of Picti who chose to rut with their camp whores close where we were hidden – we could not move until dawn.' He took a breath. 'Then I had to fight my way to you! As my Lord Enniaun reported, the men here at the river are but

214

a part of the main body; t'other side o' this hill, deeper into the woods, the rest wait in ambush. If we pursue unchecked, Sir,' he glanced, nervously, uneasily, at the cheering and yelling British, 'we will be slaughtered, Sir.'

Arthur swivelled to face his Signifier. 'Do not stop sounding the stand until I give orders to the contrary! Decurion!' He kicked Hasta to move, the enemy, who moments before had been swarming thick and deadly all round were thinning fast, only a handful left, too involved in hand-to-hand combat to turn and run.

Arthur yanked Hasta to a halt beside the mounted Decurion, ordered, 'Send a rider to each chieftain – they must hold here and regroup.' He swore colourfully as he looked towards those young men, chieftains' sons, brothers, cousins. 'Forget it. Cancel that last order. It's too late.' The Pendragon lifted his hand, let it fall hopelessly, uselessly, cried, 'Damn them, damn them to hell! They're chasing like untrained pups on a false trail!'

Close to despair, Arthur ordered the re-form. As the trumpets changed their signals, the Artoriani responded without question, forming lined ranks within three beats of a heart. Those dismounted vaulted their horses, nudged into line. Eyes, all eyes on Arthur the Pendragon, their King. Discipline, instant obeyal of orders. Drill, drill and more drill; manoeuvres practised over and over and over, until man and horse could perform a given command in his sleep. The raised militiamen were almost gone, away up the hill, lost among the trees, whooping their fools' victory.

§ XXXVI

The carnage beneath the overhang of crowding trees was something those men who survived that grey, mist-dripping morning would take a long while to forget.

Chasing the retreating Northmen, the British had full forgotten, or disregarded, the danger and the warning. And the orders. Did not realise until too late, far too late, that the willow and alder trees climbing the slope on the northern side of the Great River were giving way into the denser, thicker forests of lowland oak, ash, elm and birch.

Lot had planned well, was pleased with his cunning. He ran with his warriors at an easy lope, spears and weapons carried low, heads bent, breath and muscles pumping, running north-west together as a pack. A hunting pack, luring instead of chasing along a scant-seen track where the red deer trod – and suddenly they were upon a clearing, stretching away between the patrol of trees; a natural arena, echoing a Roman amphitheatre where gladiators fought and died upon the bloodied sand. Only this was covered in an ocean of blue flowers, and the spectators lay in wait, hidden among the dappled shade of breeze-murmured leaves. Waited in held- breath silence for their comrades to come rushing through, and turn . . .

The scent was rich; a heady, potent smell as strong as last summer's fermented wine, a tranquil sea of brilliant blue, etched against the surrounding dark and pale-green, wind-teased, silvered or variegated foliage. And running behind the Northmen came the British, cheering, for they thought they had them trapped. Then with the swiftness of a swooping hawk, the calm became ragged, the bluebell flowers became trampled and squashed, and the still silence foamed into a raging shout, with the sudden uprush of the storm. White bulbs, shredded stalks, scattered leaves. Bluest blue and sweet scent, stained and gored by red and stink.

Wounded, appalled, sickened, the British tried to pull back, to seek escape, stumbling and crying, but they found no exit, for the men of Lot's host were all around, save to the rear, where their own men were still coming, heedless, mindless of the death that awaited them.

Arthur had no time to show emotion of either extreme, neither pity nor anger. They had been told, warned. Nor had he time to think or plan. His intended action was gone, in ruins. If he was going to save any of those irresponsible fools, he would need to move fast.

A barked, short command and the trumpets sounded. Two Turmae, at a gallop, swung to either side, spreading their line as they reached the thickening trees; they burst beneath the foliage, hacking up into the overhang of branch and bough, chopping at the legs and arms of concealed men tossing spears and arrows; hacking a path through undergrowth and bush, weaving in and out of sturdy oak trunks and slender birch, around obstacles as if making the steps of some grotesque mounted dance. Following in their wake, others of the Artoriani on foot, their horses left back down the hill with the rearguard as planned, marched forward, line upon line, steady marching, swords slashing, daggers piercing. Rescue and revenge.

Incredibly they were smashing through the ambush, rolling foward, driving the men of the North before them; Lot's warriors and his allies were giving ground; slow, reluctant, fighting as cornered prey, inch by painful inch, but giving ground to Arthur and his desperate men!

Those outer mounted wings kept the thing tight, contained, cramped in the clearing, with no way ahead, no escape behind. *'We must contain them,'* Arthur had insisted. *'If Lot breaks and comes up behind us in the heavy woodland, we'll be finished, every last man and horse of us. Keep close formation, press forward, leave nowhere for him to manoeuvre – let their own weight of numbers and choice of location loose on them.'* Arthur was glad that he knew in advance of that bluebell-scented clearing . . .

They needed to form a mounted wall all around; there were not enough men to make the noose, tighten the rope and fight at the same time. Where was Enniaun? Cei? Close, hand-to-hand fighting now, sword and dagger, fists, teeth, feet. Heads butting, fingers gouging, the situation desperate. The cries and screams of wounded men and ponies; the all-pervading, constant shriek and stench of death with the raised voice of war song.

Arthur could only see what was happening within his own small group of men, had no idea how things were going even a few yards beyond, save for the sway in the rise and fall of sound. It was never easy to fight effectively in the confine of small space – it was up to each individual officer to command his own men, up to each man to make instant decision, to fight and move as he saw fit. But Arthur had faith in each and every one of his prized Artoriani. Of Morgause and her raven banner, no sign – but then, in this crush and shove, neither could he see Lot's thistle. She had been here last night, was she watching from some concealed place of safety? Or had she slipped quietly away as the Painted Ones took position, to let the men do the fighting? Morgause had not trained to use the weapons of war, she had been Roman born and bred – but born as the rotten apple in the barrel.

A Picti rose up, seemingly out of the ground beside Hasta's feet. The stallion leapt sidewards, crashed into the solid trunk of a gnarled, aged oak tree, crushing Arthur's leg. With his other boot, Arthur desperately kicked the horse forward, saw Cabal leap at the yelling man, the great dog's teeth tearing into the soft, vulnerable flesh of the throat; but another was there, a dark Picti with the swirling blue tattooed patterns on his cheeks, across the nakedness of shoulders, arms and chest. Arthur saw Cabal crumple, fall, and hauled Hasta around, anger and hatred blazing. 'Ca . . . bal!' He swung his sword down at this savage who held a dagger dripping dog's blood in his hand, and the warrior moved with lithe speed, crouching low as the horse plunged, thrusting his dagger hilt-deep into the horse's chest. The world was spinning, slowly rotating. Hasta was pitching, head going down, legs collapsing, Arthur was rolling across the stallion's neck, falling towards a clump of bluebells that were somehow not yet crushed or bloodied. His leg felt heavy from where it had been slammed against the tree, his breath knocked from him by the suddenness of the crashing fall. He saw the Picti, the red-bladed dagger scoring down, felt fire sear through his shoulder and down the length of his left arm, saw so much death spangling the gay patches of bluebell blue.

§ XXXVII

Someone was above him, whirling a spear, screaming nonsense words of furious abuse. Other voices, joining, shouting. Arthur was

218

aware of these sounds mingling with the swish and sigh of what seemed one moment like an incoming tide, the next, the movement of the trees shuffled and agitated by a rising wind. And before his eyes, a blur of red on a purple-black oozing mist; he felt hands under his armpits, dragging him backwards. He wanted to say no, leave me, let me rest, I'll be all right in a moment. But the words would not come.

They put him down, his back against a trunk, covered him with a cloak. Arthur blinked sweat from his eyes. His war-cap and shield had gone but his right hand still gripped the hilt of his sword, he would not let go of it, kept its firm, reassuring comfort nestling against his finger and sweating palm. The fuzziness of blurred vision was fading, his left shoulder and arm were quite numb. When he glanced down, the ripped sleeve of his leather-padded tunic was a wet, dark mess. A boy was leaning over him, concerned, very pale, very frightened. 'I'm all right, Gweir,' Arthur croaked, 'just give me a while to gain breath.'

When he next had the strength to raise his head, open his eyes, the fighting had swept up and over him. The clearing was emptying, save for the bloodied mounds of dead men and dead horses. There were sounds coming from the trees on the far side, of men dying, and a new, braver sound of men cheering victory.

Arthur struggled to his feet, pushing himself up with his sword. His leg ached, it would be bruised from thigh to calf, but at least the bone was not fractured. He handed the weapon to Gweir, grinned at the boy, whose colour was flushing back to his cheeks as the fear of his Lord's imminent death faded. 'You still here, boy?' Arthur said, 'I've not forgotten the beating I promised you, you young whelp. Your orders were to stay with the baggage.'

Gweir grinned back at his Lord. 'As well I did not, or you'd be dead!'

Another voice, deeper, gruffer. Ider, the messenger from Eboracum. He clipped his palm around Gweir's ear. 'Hold your tongue, cub!'

Arthur swayed a little, the ground rising and falling before him, then steadied, the dizziness passing. He managed a few steps, though his leg trumpeted against it, his eyes looking straight ahead past the dead bulk of Hasta and the matted, bloodied bundle that had once been Cabal.

Ider said something. He heard the voice, did not listen to the words. The boy Gweir disappeared, returning a moment later leading a riderless black hill pony. Its ears were flattened, eyes rolling white with fear, blood was spattered on its right shoulder. Ider wiped at it with his hand, found no wound. 'It's his rider's gore,' he said, holding the animal steady while Arthur tried a second attempt to mount.

'My legs are about as useless as a babe's.' He laughed with a strange, light-headed humour. He managed, struggling, to get up on the pony's back, sat swaying, his left arm hanging useless. Ignoring the reins his right hand clutched a handful of wiry mane to stop himself from falling.

Ider led the pony into the clearing, across the straggle of crushed bluebells, stepping over or around the dead, walking to meet Artoriani emerging from the trees across the far end. They wore broad grins like battle honours on their blood-smeared, sweat-streaked faces, were laughing, raising spear and sword, proclaiming triumph.

As he came up to him, Arthur regarded the Decurion of Blue Turma who, interpreting the Pendragon's familiar questioning expression as praise, launched, delighted, into his report. 'Lot's men have burrowed their way out and have fled with tails tucked well atween their backsides.' Added, with swaggering confidence, 'We are pursuing, Sir, but hold little hope of finding many in these woods.' His grin, and that of the men gathering behind him, broadened. 'They were like rats caught in a trap my Lord Pendragon, when Enniaun and Cei swept in from the north. They threw down their weapons and ran – or tried to, for they'd nowhere to run to, save the spear tips of Gwynedd and Red Turma.'

'And your own Blue Turma was so exhilarated,' Arthur drawled, coolly, 'by the salt taste of blood, that they left their King for a whelped brat of a slave and an untried lad from Eboracum to defend?' His explosion of anger gushed, ferocious, with those last words, biting hard, deep in its contempt.

220

The Decurion's face flushed scarlet, the beam of triumph instantly gone. Several men exchanged glances or hung their heads, others shifted uncomfortably from foot to foot. 'And Lot? What have you done with him?' Arthur asked, his anger cutting harder for the sarcasm behind the question.

The Decurion faced his lord direct not bringing further shame by giving in to the pounding desire to look away, to curl up, to shrink into the ground. He stamped to attention. 'I believe men are looking for him, Sir.'

'*I believe* is not good enough Decurion!' Arthur's bark ripped across the clearing with the force of a hurled hunting spear. 'I want him alive – if he does not already lie dead.'

'Sir!' The Decurion brought his arm smartly across his chest, his fist striking the breast of his tunic in the traditional Roman salute, and turned aside, halted as Arthur said:

'Decurion, apart from that one, shall we say, oversight, I am proud of you and the men this day.' He took a slow breath, fought the pain and rising nausea, glared through squinting eyes at the boy Gweir hovering anxiously at his side. 'And you boy, will receive your manumission. After Ider has tanned your backside raw.'

§ XXXVIII

Faces floated, hovering through a feverish mist of red pain. Faces, coming and going, sometimes the same face, sometimes a different one. Once he thought he heard someone scream a long way off, another time he lay half-awake drowning in the swirl of clinging fog, listening to the sound of a woman's tears.

Arthur jeered at himself, conscious even in that half-life between dream and reality that no woman would sit crying over him. Laugh happen, aye, there was many a woman who would laugh at his death, but na, never cry. Strange, this semi-conscious existence between the real and unreal, where sense mixed with the ridiculous.

221

And beside him, whenever the dark pain-mist cleared, someone lifting his head, coaxing that bitter-tasting liquid down his throat. Next time, when he woke next time, he would tell this medical orderly how like a woman's hands his were . . . He swallowed the mixture gratefully, for it brought sleep that eased the pain. The sleep he welcomed, but not the dreams.

Why did they always drift into dreams of Gwenhwyfar? Summer days. A breeze sighing through the trees; rivers, cool and rippling. Gwenhywfar beside him laughing and teasing. Walking together; riding. Her copper hair cascading on a pillow as they made love. Gwenhwyfar . . . he opened his eyes. Had he heard a voice? Was that movement? The tent was dim, almost dark; light flared suddenly, casting a grotesque, leaping shadow as someone adjusted the lamp's wick. He was still dreaming then, a strange dream though, this one. Arthur moved, caught his breath, an audible hiss clenching sharp in his teeth. The figure turned and walked to him, her tread rustling on the rush-strewn floor.

'You are awake?' She bent over him, touched his cheek. Behind the smile, her face was taut and drawn, dark circles bruised beneath her eyes. Her hair, unbound and hanging loose, swung forward, its fragrance of summer-scented flowers sweeping away the sickly smell of fever from his nostrils. She lifted his hand into hers, seated herself on the cot.

'I'm not sure,' he answered, drowsily, slightly confused. 'Am I?'

His hair was damp from his own sweat, she smoothed it back from his forehead. Her fingers were cool on his skin. He squeezed the hand holding his. 'For a dream, you seem solid enough.' He laughed weakly. 'But you must be a dream, why else would the Lady Gwenhwyfar be sitting on my bed? She is at Caer Luel.'

She looked tired and strained, made a dismissive gesture with her hand. 'The Lady Gwenhwyfar is where she ought to be, beside her husband, who has courted death these past weeks.'

'Ah.' Arthur closed his eyes. Gods, but his arm ached! 'So my wife comes out of duty. I am a fool to have expected anything else.'

His eyes were closed. Gwenhwyfar leant forward, placed her lips on his, her kiss lingering an instant. As if embarrassed, she made to move hastily back, but Arthur twined his uninjured arm around her waist, keeping her to him.

'Did you come from duty then? Or love?' He opened his eyes, holding her gaze. Bitterly, he added, 'Or was it to witness my death, to know the exact moment of receiving your manumission from me?'

She made no attempt to answer. She was shaking, though, and her face had the paleness of a winter's moon. She had let go his hand, was toying with the ruby ring that he had given her for their marriage. There were tears on her cheeks when she looked up, looked back at him. 'Day and night I have fought to keep you from death, Arthur.'

'How long have you been here?' The heavy sarcasm in his voice had altered, changing to quiet apology.

'Enniaun himself rode hard to fetch me. We nigh on killed the horses on the ride back.' She added, staring at her hands, 'It was feared you would not live.'

With a slight sigh she flexed her aching neck and shoulder muscles. 'Your medics and officers were all frightened, preferred to place the responsibility of whether you lived or died in my lap. I have been beside you for almost two weeks. I told them that you are too stubborn to die. When they said it may be God's wish, I told them that you would never allow His wish to override your own narrow-minded views.'

Arthur managed a feeble grin. 'I think there was some sort of a compliment hidden in there somewhere.'

A smile creased Gwenhwyfar's face. 'There was.' The smile broadened, 'Except, of course, without me here you would have had to fight alone and would have lost the battle.'

'My medical staff are capable men.'

'They have many wounded also to take care of.'

'I'm glad you came.' Arthur sucked his bottom lip, his lowered eyes staring at the blanket covering his naked body. He glanced up and away to a vacant point along the tent's ceiling. 'I do not deserve you, do I?'

'No,' Gwenhwyfar said. 'No, you don't.'

July 462

§ XXXIX

Winifred was still smouldering with fury at not being appointed Abbess. It was unreasonable to suppose that Arthur had been responsible for blocking her being awarded the position – but nothing that man did would surprise her. Once a bastard, always a bastard.

Graciously, politely, she served wine to the man, a Saxon, seated beside her. As always she showed welcome to her guests, especially to those men who were of use in her political games. Only a rather tight, straight mouth betrayed her anger.

Had she become Abbess, Winifred would have achieved a respected position of authority, and her financial assets would have increased dramatically, not that she was lacking in that direction. But a woman alone – a handsome woman and a wealthy one – attracted the attention of men. Young, old, landowners, ambition-holders, sharing a common factor of an eagerness to get their hands on her wealth – and her. As an abbess, although still entitled to marry she would have legitimate reason to be protected from the more outrageous advances and propositions. She did not want another husband. Were she to commit herself to another man then Arthur would be lost to her, and she would have to admit his divorce.

She missed a man in her bed – but it was Arthur she wanted, no other. Arthur, because he was the father of her son, and because when he set her aside he had torn her pride into ruins. And she loved him still. For all the hurt and pain he had caused her, she loved him. She was not going to get him back, she suspected, but she still had to try, still had to hope that one day . . . ah, but if that were not possible she must make him acknowledge their son. Cerdic as his heir would go a long way to mending that shattered pride. And of course, as mother to a king, Winifred would again have an elevated position of authority, like the one she had enjoyed as daughter to Vortigern. A discarded wife of the Pendragon did not create the same air of importance outside her own little domain where she ruled, although she generated enough interest for the menfolk. Bees around the honeypot. Leofric, seated beside her, was one of them.

Leofric was more than a trader – a merchant adventurer, he styled himself. The British would call him a pirate. With his family connections to one of the highest ranking royal Saxon houses he was wealthy in his own right, he held a hidage of land that would put even the Pendragon to shame and owned a fleet of longships, all of which plied ambitious trade – some legitimate. He was sitting sprawled on the short grass beneath the shade of a wide-spread oak tree, drinking Winifred's best wine and trying, again, to tempt her with marriage. It was his fourth visit, his third proposal. Winifred was flattered, but refused him.

'I am not seeking a husband,' she stated, slightly amused at his persistence. A handsome man of thirty or so years, he would make a good husband, but not for Winifred, she did not want another husband. She wanted Arthur, father of her son.

'Your son needs a father.' Leofric had already realised Cerdic might be the key to success but it was the wrong thing to say, for although Winifred laughed, there was ice in her reply.

'Cedric has a father.' She offered more wine, he accepted.

'But he thinks nothing of the boy, nor, as I hear it, of his other sons.'

He sipped his wine. How much, how little, should he tell? He wanted Winifred as wife, could not afford to anger her. 'They say,' he began, tentative, 'that the Pendragon was wounded, courted death.' He noted how Winifred's eyes widened slightly, saw the tremble to her hand – this was news to her then! 'There are many,' he added, 'who would welcome such an ending to Arthur.'

Winifred made no reply, busied herself with arranging the fall of her skirt more tidily. She did not want Arthur dead. Death was too final. God love her, why did she not want him dead? There were reasons, Cerdic must be acclaimed, he was yet too young to fight for his own rights; many reasons, all convenient excuses.

The Saxon was still talking, telling of how Lot and his witch-wife were not yet beaten, that there would need be another battle. Winifred closed her eyes, only half listening. Aye, all excuses. She fought Arthur, trying to plot and scheme his downfall, his public humiliation, but beneath the bitterness that cloyed for revenge, she did not want him dead. She still loved him, wanted him back as her own, wanted him too much for the finality of death.

Leofric knew little of this British Pendragon beyond reputation and gossip. He could not see Winifred's obsession with wanting revenge. Have the whore-son killed and claim his title for the son, that is what he would do – intended to do, once he had Winifred as wife. A man who was father to a boy king could be a powerful and wealthy man.

'For all that he is a king, a man who kills his own son and murders his whores when he has finished with them does not seem worthy of being a father.' He said it with a shrug, meaning no offence, and was astounded when Winifred angrily rounded on him, defending the Pendragon.

'That is ugly rumour. I heard it that the girl fell.' Serve the silly bitch right! The pity was that his other slut, the one he called wife, did not as conveniently fall and break her neck!

Leofric lifted his hands in surrender. That was not as he understood, but why waste the breath in arguing when he had other more important matters to pursue?

§ XL

It would soon be time for harvest and the muttered, discontented grumbling was growing. The British militiamen – those few left after the decimation beneath the trees above the Great River – saw the war as ended. They had a victory under their belt, Lot was beaten and they chafed to sing about it around their own hearths, crow about it to their women. From knowledge and experience, Arthur and his men knew better.

Lot, managing to escape by the narrowest of Fortuna's intervention, must have realised how close he had come to destroying Arthur. Had it not been for the eager ferocity of Cei and Enniaun's joint attack from the rear, then it would have been Arthur fleeing through those woods, dodging death or slavery; it would have been Arthur stripped of clothing and weapons and cast without a second glance onto the mounded pyres.

With someone as hungry for power as Morgause, all could not be settled within the fighting of a single battle. Her husband had lost the advantage and was now on the defensive, he had to prove that he was worthy to be her king. And the Northmen knew they had come so close to annihilating the Pendragon's Cymry! There was many a warrior of Lot's out there who nursed a grievance of humiliation and shame or bitter regret. Emotions that did not lend themselves to a war-hosting going peaceably home to their womenfolk. That Lot and his witch-wife would rally to fight another day was more than probable; the only uncertainty, when.

For Arthur, movement was an effort. They had carried him, when the fever had gone, on a litter to the derelict old Roman fortress that had once been Trimontium, made him a bed in the only serviceable stone-built store-room and got on with urgent rebuilding. The defence walls were to be restored to full height, the outer ditch redug deeper, into a sharper V; grain and supply stores were soon erected and filled with supplies brought up from the South, and timber-framed huts rapidly replaced leather tents. The Pendragon's northern stronghold took on an air of permanency.

June's alternated days of brilliant sunshine, drizzling rain and drifting mist shuffled into a slightly warmer July, and the grumblings became more than growled talk across the night fires.

The building work was finished and they began the waiting game. Bored, restless, the British chieftains came to Arthur. He dragged himself from his bed to meet them, cajoled, argued, flattered and fawned. Tried anger and derision, but in the end, let them go. The Artoriani would fight without them. At least Enniaun and his men of Gwynedd stayed, but they were not many. Not against the forces Lot could muster.

Summer gave way to the tawny browns and gleaming golds of a sparkling autumn and the first frosts whitened the withering bracken and heather. Arthur's arm was almost healed and a cold wind, blustering in from the north-east, chivvied the last remaining leaves from the trees, stripping branches and huddling men into the warmth of their cloaks.

Winter stalked over the hills, and word came that many days' march to the north, Lot was again gathering men to his thistle banner.

December 462

§ XLI

Gwenhwyfar, her head resting on her propping hand, ran a finger down the length of the scar that snaked from Arthur's collar bone to wrist. In places the angry redness was paling to white, but the viciousness of the wound still knotted her stomach whenever she looked at it. The memory of when he had lain saturated with his own sweat and tossing in fever was not yet fully thrust aside; that awful night when the Medical Optio had stood shaking his head, convinced that the arm would have to be amputated. If Gwenhwyfar had not been there to protest, to beg for just twenty-four more hours . . . She shuddered.

'Does it still pain you?' she asked, retracing the disfigurement a second time.

'Occasionally. A soldier learns to put up with the memory of old wounds.' Arthur turned his head on the pillow and smiled at her. 'Though there are certain places where a man dreads a sword thrust more than any other.'

Gwenhwyfar fingered another faded scar which ran beneath the dark hairs covering his nipples and chest, 'Your body is not the one I knew nine years ago.'

'I've ridden many miles through those years, Cymraes.' He lay on his back, drowsing in the warm comfort that hangs between wakefulness and sleep, his right arm curled beneath his head. Outside, the wind was roaring, buffeting against the timber and wattle-daubing, swirling the first fall of light snow; its jagged breath finding a way beneath the wooden door, making the flames of the hearth-fire contort and leap.

A while ago, they had made love, her passion as fierce as his, their enjoyment leaving them breathless and damp with sweat. The touch of her fingers exploring the scars on his chest and arms was arousing him again. He guided her hand beneath the fur bed-coverings, placed it over a raised scar on his inner thigh. 'Remember this one?'

'I remember! Those weeks while you recovered at your mother's villa were happy ones. We were young and we were lovers; nothing stood between us, not even Winifred's hot breath on our necks – and she was then your taken wife.' She paused, moved her hand intimately higher. 'I should have realised then, shouldn't I?'

He regarded her with a questioning frown. 'Realised what?'

'That I am a fool to love you.' She stroked the fine, soft hairs of his belly, letting her fingers wander lower.

Arthur's breath caught, his stomach knotting with the thrill of desire, responded to her kiss as she leant over him, covering his mouth with hers. He slid his hands up her back, delighting in the smooth silk of her warm skin.

'A fool eh?' he murmured as he twined his hand in the thickness of her copper-gold hair, holding her to him. 'That you might be, but you are also the most beautiful, and I love you.' Their love-making was softer this time, not so impetuous, the giving and receiving of intimate loving.

A while after, Gwenhwyfar lay watching the dim shadows skittering across the walls. Into the semi-darkness of their small, private chamber said, 'Arthur?'

'Mmm?' He was almost asleep.

'What will you do when you eventually capture Morgause?'

His eyes snapped open but he remained still. What would he do? Have her flogged, throw her to the men for their pleasure – take her himself? Throw her to drown in the peat bogs, bury her alive . . . he had ideas of a hundred and more cruel and humiliating ways to avenge his childhood. 'Hang her,' he said simply. And he shut his eyes and went to sleep feeling for once, that he had spoken the truth. She was not worth anything more. To be hung like a common criminal was enough, he'd not waste time and energy or emotion doing more.

The fire burned low and the wind continued its buffeting of the world outside. They slept with his arm around her waist. The snow-sprinkled night wheeled slowly through the dark hours, turned to meet the coming new day.

An urgent thumping on the closed door startled Arthur awake.

'Mithras, what now?' he groaned, burrowed deeper below the bed-furs, wriggling his body closer to his wife. He shut his eyes tight, opened them again as the knocking persisted. Letting his breath slide from him in a long, low moan he rolled away from Gwenhwyfar and sat up stiffly. He yawned, rubbed his face. 'Come!' he bellowed, angry at the intrusion, 'What is it?'

Gwenhwyfar, awake also, gathered a fur to cover her breasts, Arthur swung his legs from the bed and strode naked across the circular hut towards the opening door.

Enniaun stepped inside quickly, a swirl of wind and snow leaping from the darkness, entering with him to chase the fire-shadows higher. He shut the door almost before he was through, his wolf-skin cloak was snow-spattered, his hair wind-tossed.

He was breathless, panting. The wind was rising outside, and he had hurried, run, across to the Pendragon's chamber. 'Arthur. Lot is beyond the outer defences with a Picti war-hosting at his back.'

§ XLII

Enniaun had never seen Arthur so very angry, nor had the men.

No one spoke as the Pendragon strode across the hard ground of the inner yard and took the wooden steps up to the rampart walk above the gateway two at a time. Careful not to become skylined, the Pendragon kept his body low, hidden behind the protection of the timber battlements. He peered across, out into the thick, snow-whirled darkness. Nothing, only the dance of snowflakes against the night.

Cei was there, beside the high, wooden wall of the watch tower, his hand hovering nervously above his sword. 'It is difficult to see through this swirl of snow, my Lord, but they are there. They must have come in under cover of this weather.'

Arthur glared at him, his lips and eyes threateningly narrowed. 'Obviously,' he said coldly. 'And where are the scouts who are supposed to bring warning of just such a thing as this?'

'Some rode in as dusk fell. They had seen nothing.' Cei was twisting the folds of his heavy cloak in his fingers. The leather straps of his helmet swung loose around his jaw. He had ridden many a rough ride on the crest of Arthur's temper, this one tonight was going to be roughest of all, for it was justified.

'Some?' Arthur queried in a deceptively light tone. All the while his furious eyes bore into Cei's, who looked helplessly at Enniaun for support. It was not forthcoming.

He cleared his throat. 'It was assumed the other three were sheltering from the snow.'

'*It was assumed the other three were sheltering from the snow,*' Arthur cruelly mimicked Cei's explanation, flung his arm towards the blackness beyond the falling snowflakes. 'And do you still assume that?'

Cei reddened. 'No, my Lord.' He jutted his chin, defiantly challenging Arthur's anger. Justified himself with 'We did not expect Lot to attack a fort such as this – you yourself doubted he would do so – and especially not in this weather.'

Arthur ran his tongue over the inside of his cheek, stared at the haze of whiteness. Very softly, with a menace that was chiller than the night air, said, 'Lot is allied with the Picti, and the Picti excel at fighting in any weather, Cei. I assumed you knew that.'

Someone behind coughed, Arthur turned abruptly, barked at the hovering man. 'Well?'

'Do I turn out and ready the men, Sir?'

Curt, Arthur nodded assent, adding, 'With no noise, Decurion.' He cut his hand through the air, emphasising the order. 'I want no noise. Understand? No noise, all must seem as normal. Keep the night guard at its posting, and if they have not attacked by then, sound the third watch. We must make Lot believe that we are not aware of his coming.'

He turned back to Cei, asked caustically, 'Do you think you could possibly manage to see to it that the horses are saddled and made ready quietly also? Or would that small responsibility be over-much for you?'

Cei took in a sharp, hissing breath at the ruthless sarcasm, saluted

238

and whirled on his heel, his hands bunched in tight fists at his side. Say nothing, obey orders. But by God's grace, one day . . . one day!

'That was uncalled for Arthur,' Enniaun said, with calm observation. He gestured to the watch guard behind. 'Particularly within hearing of the men.'

'When I want counsel on what to say or not to say to my commanding officers I shall ask for it,' Arthur retorted sharply.

'That too, was uncalled for.' Enniaun pushed himself away from the timbered wall against which he had been leaning, stood before the Pendragon. 'We are all taken by surprise. None could have foreseen this. You are the brilliant commander after all, and even you did not.'

Arthur swung around, his fist raised. Unafraid, Enniaun caught the arm as it swung back. 'Do we quarrel atween ourselves now then, brother-by-law? Have we the luxury to spend time on petty squabbles?'

Arthur sucked in his breath, slowly unclenched his fist, watching closely as the fingers uncurled, relaxed. Then, mood changing abruptly, he slapped Enniaun's arm in an apologetic manner. Laughed, his voice low. 'You are, of course, right.'

Enniaun, too, relaxed. 'I speak as my mind runs, Arthur. You are pushing Cei too far over his limit. You know his heart is not in this war.'

'Aye, he would rather be at his wife's hearth.' Arthur snorted contempt. 'He ought to bed an army whore or two if he so misses the pleasures of a woman.'

He spoke tactlessly, for Enniaun flared again. 'Most of us', he hissed, 'are loyal to our wives. Someone is lucky enough to have his wife with him. He also has the joy of having his children here. He has no need to sit and gaze into the fires wondering how his sons are growing.' The volatile rage in him was unusual; Enniaun was a mild-tempered man, taking each day for how it came.

For a second time Arthur swung round to face his brother-by-law. 'It was you, I recall, who fetched Gwenhwyfar north. She, who ordered our two sons to be fetched. I did not know of it. I lay close to death.'

'You have kept them here.'

Arthur tossed his hand high, fingers wide, 'So you are also bleating because I have my family with me and you do not?'

'I am not foolish enough to bring cubs and a pregnant woman into a war-zone!'

'Brother!' The two men spun on their heels as Gwenhwyfar, wrapped in a thick mantle of a wolf-skin cloak, its head-hood pulled well forward, made her way up the slippery wooden steps. 'When I foolishly let out that private information in your presence some days past, you gave me your word that it would spread no further.' Her anger, matched that of the men.

Enniaun was staring at a point on the ground near his boot, ashamed to meet his sister's gaze. He had indeed promised to hold his silence, the words had slipped out, unexpectedly, uncontrolled.

'When?' Arthur asked Gwenhwyfar curtly.

'I am barely three months carrying. I was not over-certain of my dates, that is why I have said nothing.'

Arthur did not believe her reason for silence, but let the matter rest. Most certainly, he would not have allowed her to stay this far north had he known. But she was here, and that was an end of it, so he said, 'Fetch the boys from their beds and go back to our own chamber. Stay there. I will issue orders for a guard.'

'I would rather be helping with the wounded.'

Arthur opened his mouth to make some protesting retort, swallowed it. 'You do not usually bother to ask permission to go against me,' he said with a glimmer of humour, 'Why do so this time?'

Gwenhwyfar laughed with him, and stepped forward to kiss his cheek. 'I only ask when I know you will readily agree.'

He pretended to swipe at her backside. 'You vixen! Aye, go then. You will be of much use to the men.' Then, as she began to descend the steps, 'Gwenhwyfar.'

She paused, looked up at him.

'I would have the boys near you. Find them some corner where they will not be in the way. Stay there. Whatever happens, Cymraes, stay inside.'

240

Gwenhwyfar gave the briefest nod of acquiescence. 'I will look to them, husband.' She started again down the steps. No need to add more. She knew well what Arthur meant. Better for their sons to die quickly, painlessly by her own blade, than fall into Lot's hands should things not go well.

On impulse, Arthur jumped after her, took hold of her wrist, swinging her back to him. He kissed her, once, lightly, on the lips. 'The boys are important, but so are you. Stay inside Gwenhwyfar, please.'

Their eyes met, thoughts and meaning passing unspoken between them. Flakes of snow settled on her lashes. 'Is that an order?'

Arthur dropped her wrist, shrugged one shoulder. 'Na,' he sighed, 'I ask it. If Lot defeats us . . . ' He could not finish, he could not put those numbing, terrifying thoughts into words.

Gwenhwyfar touched his hand with her fingers, a soft smile tingeing her face. He could see her eyes shining in the faint glow from the smoking torches, tawny gold against brilliant green. Her smile broadened. 'I will obey you. This once, anyway.'

Arthur smiled back at her. 'Glad I am that I have you with me, Gwenhwyfar.'

She kissed him. 'Glad I am to be here.' Then she whirled away, hurrying into the snow. There was much to prepare, and little time to do it in.

Arthur ran back up the steps. Cautiously, he moved to the fence and peered over. Nothing, save white snow against black night. Nothing to see, but there was a feel, a vibration, a knowing that there was something there . . . instinct. Enniaun came up behind him, he too peered cautiously over the top of the defences. 'There was nothing seen, nothing heard, just a blur, a hint of moving wind and rippled grass. Shadows scuttling in the night-dark. Something's out there, we do not know for certain what.' He chuckled. 'It could well be a wandering herd of cattle or horse.'

Arthur pulled back from the fence. 'Na, the gut-feeling is too strong. Lot's out there.' He sucked his lower lip between his teeth, thoughtful. He ought not to have reprimanded Cei in such a harsh manner. The man was becoming an oppressive bore of late though, with his moralistic lecturing on the Christian God and his over-cautious, unasked advice. Into the darkness he said, 'I apologise Enniaun. I am angry with you and Cei because I am angry at myself.' He turned with a grin, offering his hand in friendship. 'It's not easy to yell at yourself.'

Enniaun took the hand, clasped it firm between his own. Grinned also. 'Your disagreement with me, Arthur, I can shoulder. Your quick temper is a thing we are all used to.' He spread his hands, 'But how in the realms of all Hell I am going to obtain my sister's forgiveness for letting my tongue wag I know not!'

Arthur clapped the big man's shoulder and began to descend the steps. 'Forget it, I suspected anyway,' he chuckled. 'I notice when her woman's courses do not come, and her spewing into a bucket of a morning!' He reached the flat ground and walked with a long stride in the direction of the picket lines of horses. Tossed over his shoulder, 'I love her too much not to notice.'

§ XLIII

Attack came an hour before dawn. There was nothing of their coming at first, just a shadow behind the light swirl of snow and a swift, uprushing sigh of movement.

They ran with notched ladders that spanned the wide ditches and reached the height of the palisade walls, their spears and arrows humming through the darkness, some flaming an arc of fire that caught and spluttered. Despite the wet, the wind fanned the smouldering thatch, but the Pendragon had expected it, had men ready to form a bucket chain while others tore down the burning roofing, forking it to burn ineffectually in a piled heap. And all the while the attackers came dodging and weaving through the hail of British flights of spear and arrow – if there was any surprise that Arthur was ready for them, Lot's hosting showed no concern of it. They poured over the outer defences, laying their ladders against the walls, climbing and scrabbling swiftly; where one man fell, another took his place. Lot's men of the North fought spear to spear alongside the Picti warriors, who were semi-naked, even in this cold swirl of winter, their chests, arms and shoulders patterned by the blue dye pricked into their skin. Single-minded men who knew that this time, they must have the victory.

The Artoriani fought them off, this initial wave of attack; sent them melting back into the first-touch light of dawn. The snow had ceased, but the wind still shouted across the hills, shuffling the wet, white, bloodied stuff up against the fort's walls, into the ditches and covering over the scattered dead.

Arthur tugged loose the straps of his helemt and wiped sweat from his face, peered cautiously over the ramparts at the bodies lying in the red, snow-muddied slush, then down into the fortress below and along the walkway. His nose and mouth curled in distaste. Too many of his own men dead or wounded. Not enough of the enemy. He did not pause over-long, but hurried down the steps, two at a time, jumping the last three, calling his officers to assemble within his private quarters.

Three did not come. Two dead, one wounded.

'We have several choices.' Arthur, his arms folded, back straight, legs slight apart, came straight to the point.

They stood, or squatted around the unlit central hearth, cramped together in the confined space. The King's timber-built Hall would have been more appropriate, but the medics were busy there with the wounded.

'One,' Arthur ticked his thoughts off on his fingers, 'we stay within the fort to beat off each attack, our numbers growing weaker with each onslaught. Two,' he spread a second finger, 'we hold out as best we can till nightfall then attempt to withdraw.'

'What?' The response was instant, outraged, angry. 'Run with our tails tucked atween our legs!' Enniaun's voice was the loudest, indignant, horrified at the suggestion.

Arthur ignored the rumble of protest to what would never be his decision, tapped a third finger. 'Or three,' he paused for quiet listening to resettle, 'We go out and meet them.'

Again, voices rose as they discussed the suggestion, tossing the two choices – the second was automatically deleted – back and forth. While none were under any illusion that Arthur would, in the end, do as he saw best, they recognised that the Pendragon was willing to hear them out first; it was for that he was so loyally followed, so respected.

'We could hold out for many days,' one Decurion said, pitching his voice above the general squall of the others. 'We have more than adequate water and food.'

'For ourselves, aye,' someone else added, 'but not for the horses. We have them safely picketed along the night lines, grain-fed and well watered – fortunately – but daylight normally sees them grazing outside.'

'Then the three choices become the one,' Meriaun remarked cheerfully. He rubbed his hands together eagerly. Several men grinned at him.

'They must be expecting such a move,' Cei pointed out blandly, his pride still bruised from Arthur's tongue-lashing. But damn the man, why did he have such a knack of being so contritely apologetic without the need of saying a word? How many times had Cei vowed that Arthur's temper had flown its last in his direction? How many times had Arthur won him round? The Pendragon was bewitched, no matter how many wounds he inflicted, he always followed through with some magical salve that had Cei wagging his tail in obedient loyalty. Damn it, Cei loved him.

He happened to glance up, caught Gwenhwyfar's eye. She was sitting with her legs curled beneath her in the shadows of the fur-covered bed. It was not that Cei begrudged her being with them, it was the principle. A campaign was not the place for women. There would always be a few of the men's wives, hardened army women, and the whores of course. They appeared as surely as flies gathered around a rotting carcass. But Gwenhwyfar was no sewage-spawned baggage. Cei sighed. Was it because he always felt so uncomfortable in the presence of Arthur's Lady? She too, was caught within the Pendragon's enchanted spell that bound those who loved him tight to his side. And Arthur loved her. All his love, aside from that of a father's love for his sons, went to her. There was nothing left to give back to Cei, his cousin, his foster-brother.

Gwenhwyfar had looked away, was throwing a fur around her shoulders. It was chilly in the room, with the hearth-fire gone out.

'If they are expecting us,' Arthur said, 'we must ensure they do not have the chance to prepare a reception.' He was enjoying himself. This was his constant dream, to lead his men to fight, to outwit the other man. To win. 'And I expect we can come up with one or two little tricks that will scare the blue off their snow-white skins!'

§ XLIV

The noise, the shouting and clamour from the battlements, was rising as the second attack, coming an hour later, gained momentum. Arthur, momentarily glancing at the sway of fighting up there, swung up onto his horse and settled his thighs under the two forward pommel horns, his buttocks against the rear two. Agitated by the sounds and smells of fighting, the animal's ears were flat upon its skull, a mean look in the rolling whites of its eyes. But then, Onager was a stallion whose ears were permanently flat back, whose teeth were always bared or snapping at some unfortunate who ventured over-close.

An uneasy love-hate relationship existed between the Pendragon and the chestnut horse. He was a magnificent beast, taller than usual, measuring a little below six and ten hand-spans to the withers, and with a depth of chest and solidity of muscle that showed all too clearly his immense strength and power. Unfortunate that he had the temper of a wounded rogue boar and the kick of a wild ass. Arthur had named him Onager, calling him for the powerful Roman catapults that were renowned for their dangerous kickback after firing. He was a good horse in battle, with courage to equal his height and stamina, but unreliable with people, and his stubbornness of self-will was as unmovable as his rider's. For this, Arthur had always chosen Hasta in preference, a horse who put his heart and

245

soul into doing his best to please. Arthur had wept over the loss of his favourite horse, one night when the summer heat sweltered relentless, even through the hours of darkness. He had thought Gwenhwyfar to be asleep and the pain of his wounded arm blistering and pounding had awoken memories of that fight in the clearing, memories of loss. Had it been the pain, or the frustration at being bed-bound while his wound healed, that had caused the deep feeling of despair to wash over him?

He missed Cabal, his young fool of a hound too. Even now, his fingers would feel at his side for the brindled head that was no longer there. For Cabal too, he had shed tears. Gwenhwyfar had held him like a child while he sobbed aside the pain, cradling his sorrow, soft-stroking the loss from throbbing temples and aching throat, and her tears had fallen with his. They could share this, the sorrow of lost animals, but not the death of a son. Sometimes, the pain ran too deep.

Arthur tightened his hold on the reins as he felt Onager raise an off-hindleg and strike out. Someone behind hissed, cursed. Arthur turned his head to see Meriaun rubbing his thigh.

'God curse that damn monster of yours, Arthur!'

'Did he catch you?'

Meriaun stepped back to a safer distance. 'Na, I know better than to get over-close! My grandsire ought have had the whore-son gelded as a foal.' He studied the animal's handsome head beneath the flat ears and rolling eyes, the perfect conformation, added, 'Yet, I see why he did not.'

An officer approached, wary of the horse's stamping rear hoof, stopped a few yards short. 'All are ready, my Lord.'

Nodding, Arthur peered at Cei, standing ready, a frown of concern on his face, before the Hall, Enniaun beside him. With that familiar expression of left eyebrow raised, right eye narrowed, Arthur said, almost flippantly, 'I leave the fort to your command then, Cei.'

Cei saluted. His voice was thick, cracked slightly as he answered. 'The outcome of this day will be sung to the children of our children.'

246

Arthur returned the salute. 'Aye. Let us pray the song is one of victory not defeat.' As his heel nudged Onager forward into a walk, he said over his shoulder, 'If things go badly, do what you can to pull out, Cei. I trust you to see well to our men.'

Cei choked down a sob of despair. He liked it little that Arthur was to be riding out without him; but someone needed to remain in command on the inside, and here it was, one of those rare, embracing compliments that Arthur could so casually toss aside to breach any gap of anger or irritation.

With pride, Arthur ran his gaze over the mounted men awaiting his order to move off. They were taking a terrible risk splitting their force like this, but then, what was battle if not a risk? He raised his hand, about to signal, but someone ducked through the crush of men and horses to stand panting at Onager's shoulder. The horse snorted, flattened his ears further.

Arthur hastily checked the stallion and regarded the little man, a Christian priest. He had appeared out of the mist one autumn afternoon, striding alone across the moors, with no possessions save the clothes he wore, a staff he carried, and a small leather-bound volume of the Holy Gospels. That he was sent to them by God himself, no one doubted – including Arthur – for this gentle, quietly spoken man, dedicated to spreading the word of the Christ, had arrived two mornings after their previous Holy Father had died of dysentery.

'I thank you for the blessing you gave my men, Father,' Arthur said, shielding his irritation at the man's reckless approach so close to the horse. 'I trust your prayers will be heard and answered by your Christian God.'

'He always answers, my Lord King,' Cethrwm answered with a teasing smile. 'It is just that some of us do not listen.'

Arthur returned the smile, adding a slight chuckle. He liked this priest, an honest, pleasant man, who did not push the Word of God, ramming it day after day down your throat, until you wanted to vomit it out. Na, Cethrwm told the stories of Christ, of his time on this earth, of his healing and courage. Arthur could stomach that, and had, to his own great amusement, found himself listening once or twice.

The priest fumbled with something he held in his hand. He licked dry lips, seemed nervous, embarrassed.

Arthur had to say, impatiently, for they must begin this thing, 'Father, the men of Gwynedd and half my Artoriani are fighting for their lives and for those in this entire fortress up there on the battlements, and I am waiting to give the order to open the gates for the rest of us to do what we can. If you have something to say, then please say it quickly.'

'You are not a believer in the Christ, are you my King?'

Arthur rolled his eyes skyward, biting his temper. 'Na, I am not.' Onager crashed a hindleg towards the horse behind. Arthur cursed. 'I am sorry, this is not the time nor place to be discussing my lack of religion.'

Cethrwm extended his hand, holding out something that was in it, his eyes meeting with Arthur's pleading for him to listen, to take the thing. 'My Lord, wear this on your shoulder. It is a portrait of the Virgin, Our Mother of Christ. I believe it to be most ancient, coming from the very time that Christ walked our earth. It is the only possession of value that I own, save my Bible.' He was talking hurriedly, his voice rising in his agitation. 'It is a thing which means a lot to me. I am reluctant to part with it – none has seen it before now, I keep it hidden beneath my robe.' He licked his dry lips. 'For many years I have been guilty of sin by keeping this thing to myself. The Holy Lady came to me in a dream last night, she said I was to give her portrait to you, for you to carry into battle, so that through Her, you may realise the Truth of Her Son.' The words came in a rush as Cethrwm thrust the thing into Arthur's hand and spun away, running with his robe hitched to his knees back into the Hall, where already the wounded from this assault were being carried.

For a blind moment, Arthur stared after him, astonished, then glanced down at the oval brooch in his hand. He laughed then, a loud roar of delighted amusement, head back, mouth wide, laughed, his head shaking, tears, almost, coming to his eyes. Still chuckling he turned in his saddle and grinned at the men, holding the brooch high, though they would be hard pressed to see its fine painted detail. 'See,' he shouted above the noise, 'it is a portrait of the Lady.

The Mother rides with us!' He fastened it beside the great cloak-pin at his left shoulder, the shout of approval increasing as word rippled back through the ranks.

Arthur raised his hand, the wooden doors beneath the entrance towers swung inwards and the Artoriani, spears raised, heads back, mouths open and yelling their battle-cry plunged out into the swarm of Lot's war-hosting.

Cethrwm, so devoted to God, so immersed in the short-sighted values of Christianity, had not seen beyond his belief. Aye, the woman with dark eyes and veiled in pale blue, was indeed a mother, but she was not, as the priest thought, the Holy Virgin Mary, Mother of God. She was earlier, older than that, was the pagan Goddess, the Earth Mother.

Arthur roared his laughter as he cast his spear, seeing, with a grunt of satisfaction, it thud deep into a warrior's chest. Then he had his sword out and had no more time to reflect on how each man within this furious mêlée would look upon the Mother, be she of Christ, or the Goddess.

§ XLV

The prisoner, hands bound firm by coarse rope, stood tall, proud, before the British Pendragon. Arthur was deliberately ignoring him, paying attention to the stark gash snaking across the ribs of a bay stallion. The horse fidgeted, half-raising his off-hindleg in protest as Arthur's fingers probed the jagged wound.

'It will heal well enough,' he said to the cavalryman holding the animal's drooping head, 'though the scar will be an ugly one. It saddens my heart that his rider did not escape as lightly.' He patted the horse's flank. Too many of his men were as badly wounded, awaiting treatment within the Hall – more, like the rider of this bay, lay growing cold beneath their cloaks awaiting burial.

As if seeing the prisoner for the first time Arthur, with his head back and slightly cocked to one side, stared long and hard at him through slit, appraising eyes. They were lucky indeed to have captured him, these Eastern Picti men were as wily as wolves when it came to vanishing among the undergrowth.

Fresh blood oozed through old that had dried and crusted around the man's thigh, a deep wound, reason for his capture. The Pendragon noted the slight flicker of his eyes at the brooch pinned to Arthur's cloak. Absently, he toyed with it, watching with satisfaction as the same superstitious flicker came again. 'You,' Arthur, said, using the tongue of the Picti, 'are no doubt craving the honourable death of a warrior. I could order it so, and the same swift death for Lot's captured lowland curs.' Arthur dropped his hand ostentatiously to his sword hilt. 'Or, I may decide to order your maiming and let you go back, blinded, worthless and mutilated, to your people.'

He paused, his calculating gaze never leaving the man's guarded expression. 'There again, I could show mercy and grant you pardon, in return for some small gesture of loyalty to me, the Supreme King.'

The prisoner spat at Arthur's boots. A smile played over the Pendragon's mouth. 'Na, I thought the idea would not appeal.' He turned to the two men keeping firm hold of the prisoner's bonds. 'Have the captives blinded and gelded then throw them to the wolves. Oh, and Decurion,' he added as an afterthought, 'have Lot brought to my chamber, I would speak with the traitor before you do the same with him.' As he knew they might, the words caused the prisoner to react with cautious uncertainty.

Arthur stepped closer, saying with venom, 'Aye, I have the whelp who has dared call himself King of the North. That is my title.' He made a dismissive gesture and turned away, swinging back at an afterthought to add; 'One thing I would know. What were you promised in return for this alliance? Whatever, it would almost certainly be as hollow as a decayed oak.' Arthur fingered his brooch again, ensuring the man saw it clearly.

That flicker to the eye had come again in the Picti man, an uncertainty, a doubt. Arthur smiled, a lazy, unconcerned expression. The figure painted on that brooch, representing the Mother, the pre-eminent goddess of these pagan clans, meant much, very much.

250

Arthur laughed and began to walk away, called over his shoulder, 'Morgause is no goddess.' The man's eyes had narrowed, ah, so Arthur was riding the right track! He was several paces away now, half turned, 'I wear the image of the Mother. To me, she gave her protection and the victory, not to Morgause or her whore-son husband.' He paused. 'See that my orders are carried out, Decurion.'

And Arthur strode away, heading for his private chamber. He lay on the bed, still wearing cloak, muddied boots and battle-stained bracae. Within a few breaths, he was asleep.

§ XLVI

Rotating his aching shoulders, Arthur attempted to ease the weariness from his muscles. All he really wanted was to lie on his bed and finish the sleep that had been so necessarily short. He sighed and returned his attention to the man standing before him, bound as the Picti captive had been. Only this prisoner was clad in rich dress and had more to lose than the Picti and the other hundred or so lowland prisoners who had half an hour since been herded beyond the gates, naked of clothing and weaponry, blinded, and mutilated of their manhood. Most would not survive the night. It was the way of things.

'I am weary, and I have yet to see to the well-being of my men,' Arthur said to Lot, dispassionately, 'I will not waste breath on trivial formalities. Your instigated rising of the North has been crushed.' He waved his hand to silence Lot's denial. 'My Artoriani will soon head further north, to purge the foul stench that you and your bitch wife have created.' He sat forward on his stool, rested an elbow on his thigh, cupping his stubbled chin in his palm and threw a lie at Lot. 'The prisoner I questioned told me Morgause was the leader behind this uprising. I could not believe that. A woman such as she cannnot think beyond who next is to share her bed.'

Lot angered, but held his tongue.

'I believe it was you who rallied the North; you who arranged alliance with the Picti. Whatever it was you promised them in return, cannot now be given. You have failed, Lot.' Arthur shrugged. 'You will shortly be joining the other unfortunates beyond our defences.'

Lot licked his dry lips nervously. It was one thing facing the Pendragon with a thousand and a thousand men at your back, quite another to be herded, defeated, before him. It had all seemed so promising back in his own Hall, where he and Morgause and his warriors had talked of easy victory. With Morgause's suggestion of an alliance with the Picti the possibility of losing had never entered his head.

Arthur suddenly tired of the pointless taunting. He flapped his hand at the guard. 'Take this pathetic fool away, blind and geld him as you have the others and throw him over the battlements. Either the fall shall kill him, or the waiting wolves.'

The guard saluted and began dragging Lot from the chamber.

Lot panicked. He squirmed from the man's hands, flinging himself to his knees before Arthur. 'My Lord, let me speak! I beg you!'

'I have other matters to attend.'

'It was Morgause who sent to the Picti for alliance. The Eastern Clan need a royal woman as high priestess and queen. We offered our daughter to their king.'

Arthur controlled the quick catch of breath. So-o, that was how they did it! And the one Clan would call to the other for support . . . Speaking slowly, he countered, 'But your daughter is not even a handful of years old.'

' 'Tis old enough to become a Clan queen!' Lot replied with pride.

It took only a rapid moment for Arthur to mull over the information, to reach conclusion. He laughed cynically. 'The Picti were to have had their queen, but I doubt Morgause was intending for it to be your daughter! If victory had gone your way, Lot, you would now be dead. Conveniently killed in battle.'

Lot was shaking his head. 'No,' he mumbled, 'it was not agreed like that!'

Arthur lunged to his feet in sudden anger, crossed the small space

252

between him and Lot, his hand reaching for the sagging flesh of the man's quivering throat. 'For you, you poor, blind, used fool, it was agreed like that. The Picti would not unite and raise a war-hosting for a pathetic rebel and the bedding of a baby girl but, for Morgause, and holdng the entire North, they would!'

Lot looked wildly around the chamber, seeking the help of some sympathetic eye, but not one of Arthur's men gave him anything but a returned stare of contempt and loathing. He hung his head, swallowed hard. 'You have it wrong. She has been a good wife to me, she is loyal and faithful.' He could not believe Arthur. Would not believe him! Even though he feared, deep down, that he spoke the truth of it.

Movement at the door, footsteps beyond, the latch lifting. Enniaun strode into the room. He saluted, indicated he wished to speak privately.

Standing well aside from Lot, Arthur's cheek twitched as he listened to his brother-by-law's news, strode back to stand close before his captive.

'So you do not believe me? Your infant daughter has been escorted into my care. It seems, in the haste to flee with her Picti friends, your wife forgot to look for her safety.' Arthur hooked his thumbs through his baldric, stood rocking slightly from heel to toe, said mockingly, 'I assume she *is* your daughter?'

Lot reddened in quick, hurt anger. 'By the light, you shall pay for that insult to my wife!'

Arthur lifted his hands, let them fall in a subtle, resigned gesture. 'It is you who are about to pay for insults, Lot, not I.' To Enniaun he said, 'Have the girl killed.'

Lot's face drained from ash-grey to colourless white. He was walking a night terror from which there was no hope of waking. 'She is a child! You would not murder an innocent child!'

Returning to his stool, Arthur sat, wincing at the ache running down his arm, shuddering through his thigh. Old wounds resented new battles. 'You said yourself, she is betrothed to an enemy king. Through that marriage she could become a powerful enemy herself. By implication, she carries the death penalty. Morgause would have

253

known this well enough when she abandoned her to save her own skin.'

'Christ's blood, Pendragon, she is my daughter!'

'Despatch the child, Enniaun, but with speed and no pain.'

Enniaun nodded, drew his sword as he left. Unpleasant, but necessary. War was unpleasant.

Lot shuffled forward on his knees, tears flowing, voice breaking, begged, 'You cannot do this!' Lost, defeated, broken, his head hung, his chest heaving in sorrow, he blurted, 'What do you wish from me then, Pendragon?' He looked up, pleading. 'Ask and it shall be yours.'

Arthur wanted many things, but one wanting soared above all others. Morgause.

He felt sudden pity for this man before him, answered, with genuine sorrow, 'I cannot spare her for those reasons I have already said, and for the suspicion that she may not be your child, but a Picti-born daughter.'

Lot bit his lip, choked. There was no hope then. 'For myself,' he gulped, 'I ask nothing, do with me what you will. It is the way things must be; but for my daughter I plead a grave, do not leave her for carrion meat. She is a child, none of this her doing.'

The guards moved forward, took Lot from the chamber. It would be done immediately, his ending. Arthur heard his pleading as the door shut, begging this concession for one so small and innocent.

Arthur walked to the table, poured himself a large goblet of wine, drank it down in one gulp. The door opened again, closed, a light tread behind him, Gwenhwyfar's.

'I heard,' she said. She stood, her hands clasped across the slight bulge that was widening her waist. 'I have seen the little girl also.'

Arthur made no reply.

Suddenly angry, Gwenhwyfar snapped, 'I realise she cannot be allowed to live – but what he asks . . .'

Arthur swung around, tears were watering his eyes. 'I have sons, happen that one new in there,' he pointed at her belly, 'is my daughter. Death must come, but well do I understand the after-wards. She would have a burial, Gwenhwyfar, without the need of an asking.'

§ XLVII

Morgause was desperate – would this poor-bred hill pony not move any faster! Stupid creature, damn stupid men, why had they not found her a better horse to ride! The pony, labouring from the forced pace through this swirl of wind-crusted snow, stumbled, pitched his rider forward. Morgause shrieked as she fell, toppling over its shaggy head and neck as the animal sank to its knees in a drift of snow. It lay winded a moment before scrambling to its feet, breath coming in gasps, head lowered, snow settling along its mane and shaggy rump.

Several men ploughed their way to help Morgause up, but angrily she shrugged them aside. There were but a handful of them now; many they had left behind to die, more than half not surviving the last two nights. The wounded they had not even bothered with. They would not have lived long in this cruel weather anyway. Two miles to Din Eidyn, only two more damn miles!

Remounting the pony, Morgause kicked it onwards, the men huddling about her as they struggled through the drifting snow. They must reach the coast, could not stop, could not rest, for Arthur was not far behind. Every so often they could hear the baying of his men between the howling of the wind. The Artoriani, mounted on better horses and with the courage and elation of victory, would be upon them if they stopped – curse all the gods and these poxed Picti cowards! Did they not see that they had to get her across the firth and to safety before Arthur came!

The Pendragon could not believe they had lost her. So damned close, so close to capturing the woman and having an end to her! He stood at the water's edge, thin ice rimming the shallows where wind-patted waves ran against the snow-patterned rocks. He kicked a loose stone, sent it tumbling with a splash into the water of the Bodotria Firth, Lost her to a damned fishing boat that was pulling strong for the far shore.

The dead pony lay in a crumpled heap, fifty or so Picti men squatting, heads hung low in defeat beside it. With no more boats to take them she had left them, abandoned them to Arthur's mercy, taking only those few that could fit in safely with her. Arthur watched as the boat progressed further towards the hills of the far side, hoping a squall of wind would capsize the thing, but the men along these coasts were experienced sailors, knew how to handle a craft, even in a snow-pocked wind as strong as this.

He could not see her clearly now, for the craft was going fast before the wind, but she had been close enough for her voice to carry when first the Artoriani had arrived. Close enough to laugh and mock him, to jeer that he had lost after all.

'I warn you, Pendragon, do not try to follow me, for if you do I shall call a curse upon you that you shall for all time regret!'

'I do not fear you witch-woman!' he had called impotently from the shore.

'Oh, but you do, Arthur, you do!'

He turned away, stared with dispassion at the hunkered Picti. Defeated men. It was in his heart to let them go, poor bastards. Hard enough to know the hurt of losing without being abandoned to the horrors of a victor's mercy. They deserved better than this; although didn't they all?

Arthur walked back over the rocks, mounted Onager. His men were ready to do as they must, but he sat a moment before giving the order, watching the boat that was so small now, barely seen.

'You come after me, Pendragon, and I shall curse your sons. One has died, none shall live. I shall see to it, Pendragon. If you come after me I will have your sons!'

'I'll be back for you Morgause,' Arthur said to the grey, white-spumed waves. He was afraid of her, afraid of her mocking, threatening words, but he was more afraid of letting her stay loose. 'Come the spring, I'll be back.' He looked at the Picti men, haggard and cold, weary, pointed at two of them, the strongest looking, had them hauled to their feet.

'You two I will not slay. You will be given food and warm cloaks, allowed to go to your home.' Arthur leant forward over Onager's neck, one arm resting along the chestnut's crest. 'And you will tell them, those people of Edda, that your lord fell in battle and that Lot and his daughter were executed by my orders.' His narrowed eyes bored into the nearest man, a man with dark eyes and hair. 'Tell them that when the first buds show on the trees after the going of the snows, they will see my Artoriani in Caledonia, and their hills will run red from the blood of every man, woman and child that I find. I will do this, I will burn and I will kill – but I promise this also, in the name of the Dragon that is my banner, not one person shall be harmed if I am given Morgause. Not one warrior, not one boy-child. The life of your people, your families, for one woman.' He lifted a single finger, held it a moment before raising his eyebrows, an expression to emphasise that he meant every word. 'To show this as truth, your men here will be given honourable death. There will be no mutilation, no torture.' He smiled a lazy, superior smile. 'It is Morgause who treats brave and noble warriors with disrespect, not the Pendragon.' And then he turned Onager and rode away, south back to Trimontium. Trying to convince himself that he was not afraid of Morgause, or her threatening words.

September 463

§ XLVIII

'Lady, a young man is asking to see you.'

Gwenhwyfar was sewing the delicate gold stitching of the dragon's eye on the new banner she had been working these past, long months. It was near finished, would be ready when Arthur returned here to Caer Luel from the highlands of the north. She raised her head from the intricate work, her fingers hesitating before making the next stitch. 'A messenger? From my Lord Pendragon?'

Bad news? Good? Her heart thumped.

Nessa shook her head. 'Na, my lady, he has ridden from the south.' Added with a twinkle of excitement, 'He's a handsome lad, gives his name as Bedwyr ap Ectha.'

Hands flying to her cheeks with a gasp of surprised pleasure, the sewing quite forgotten, Gwenhwyfar leapt to her feet and ran across the chamber as a man entered through the open door. She squeaked with delight, and laughing, flung herself into his open arms. Bedwyr twirled her around as if she were a young girl again, hugged her, kissed her cheek.

'How you have gown!' she said with approval, releasing herself from his embrace, but holding, still, to his hands. 'Let me look at you!' She stepped back, smiling, assessing the young man. With a flop of dark hair, and eyes that sparked a promise of mischief, he was indeed handsome! He was not quite Arthur's tall height, nor as thickset as his elder brother, Cei, who was broad built, with a bull neck and solid, squared features. Bedwyr's chin was set as square as Cei's, his eyes as deep and dark, but he was altogether leaner, more supple. If Cei was the ox, then Bedwyr most certainly was the stag.

Taking his hand, and leading him to her own comfortable chair, Gwenhwyfar exclaimed, 'Why, I saw you last when you were, oh, two and ten winters old!' She calculated quickly in her mind, her eyes widening with disbelief. 'That is eight years past!' She shook her head at the quick passing of years, kissed him again on the cheek. 'Oh it is good to see you Bedwyr!' She withdrew her hands from his, sat back on her heels, asked Nessa to fetch wine and food.

The girl, standing by the door, remained immobile, staring. Never had she seen a man so desirable!

'Nessa!'

She visibly jumped at Gwenhwyfar's rebuke, scuttled from the room, raising her gown almost to her knees as she ran, red-faced with embarrassment. Amused, Gwenhwyfar cast a reprimanding frown at the young man. 'I trust you will not have the same effect on all my serving women!'

'What effect?' he asked innocently.

Kneeling on a wolf-skin beside him, Gwenhwyfar playfully slapped his knee. 'You have grown into a rogue Bedwyr ap Ectha! I think you most certainly do not emulate your aunt's piety!'

He hesitated a heart beat moment before laughing, a warm, rich sound, rising from deep within his chest. 'Arthur's mother had straight-faced ideals, they were never mine!' Quickly he asked her questions. 'How is Arthur? How goes the campaign in the North?' He sat forward to the edge of the chair, caught her hand again. 'Tell me, I wish to know all the details. All of them, mind!'

'All? We'll be here into next summer!' Gwenhwyfar laughed with him – oh it was so good to see him, this boy she had known during those distantly remembered days of exile in Less Britain, before she had Arthur for her own. Those had been dark, sad days of loneliness for Gwenhwyfar. The boy Bedwyr, with his spontaneous laughter and chatter had brought sunshine into the rainy days.

'The fighting is over,' she said, 'Arthur is making his way south.' Did she sound a little too impatient?

It had been a long summer, waiting here at Caer Luel. When the snows began to creep from the hills, the Artoriani had saddled their horses and ridden north, as Arthur had said. Gwenhwyfar, swelling with child, had turned south to this better protected place, Caer Luel, to wait: only to give birth to a dead-born boy, and then wait again with her grief, wait for Arthur to send word that he was returning, frightened that word would come that he was never to come back.

262

And now Bedwyr was here, and as when he was a boy, the sun seemed to have appeared from behind the storm clouds. Arthur was coming, she knew that, and the grieving and fear suddenly lifted. Tucking her feet beneath her, Gwenhwyfar settled herself comfortably. 'But what of you? We had hoped you would come to join with the Artoriani before this.'

Bedwyr went to the door, took the tray that Nessa carried, put it on a side table and began helping himself to food. He had his back to Gwenhwyfar but she did not need to see his expression, for the bitterness in his voice was potent. 'I could not come for I have been caring for a saddened, ageing woman as she neared the ending of her days.'

He swung around to her as she began to protest an answer. 'Arthur should have come, Gwenhwyfar, when I wrote three years past to tell him his mother was ill.' He nodded his head, lips set firm. 'It took her a twelve-month to die. I spent those months in and out of a stinking sick room, where a grieving woman asked every day to see her son! Not once did Arthur care to come to her, or even send word. My brother came, once, when our King could spare him, but not my cousin. Not Arthur.'

Gwenhwyfar had no words to say. She had not known.

He turned again to the food, piled bread and meat and preserves on a platter, strode to the chair and seated himself. Began to eat.

'Arthur never told me.' Gwenhwyfar stared into the glow of the brazier. The charcoal was a warm red, a comforting, comfortable colour. The news shocked her, the hearing of Ygrainne's death and that Arthur had never said. But then, they had been apart so long, so often, separated by her own grief . . . 'He has been much preoccupied these past years.' It was an excuse, she knew, but what more could she say?

His mouth full, Bedwyr made no comment.

She tried, 'He could not have come, even if . . .'

Bedwyr interrupted, said candidly, 'Even if he'd have wanted to?'

Risking an apologetic smile, Gwenhwyfar stated the truth. 'Arthur had no love for his mother, nor she for him.' Bolder, added, 'For Arthur, Ygrainne has never existed. I think,' she dropped her hands to her lap, sat examing her fingers. Her sewing needle had pricked the skin on one, leaving it rough and sore. 'I think he never forgave her for abandoning him to Morgause.'

Chewing cold chicken, Bedwyr asked a question he had never been able to answer for himself. 'Why was Morgause so cruel to him? She never harmed Cei or myself.'

'You and Cei had a father. Arthur did not.' Standing up, Gwenhwyfar went to fetch wine, poured for herself and Bedwyr. 'And Uthr loved him, a boy who was supposedly a bastard born. For that, Morgause taunted Arthur, and the taunting turned to a hating that has seethed beyond proportion.'

'Is that why she was behind this war in the North?'

'Partly.'

Bedwyr spread his hands, laughed, breaking the melancholy of serious talk. 'Well it is no more. Ygrainne is gone and so, we hope, has her sister Morgause. My father, Ectha, is well and is content seeing to Arthur's estate in Less Britain, and I have been travelling.'

'Travelling?' Curious, Gwenhwyfar settled herself once again on the wolf-skin, eager, like a child, to hear a story.

'I had a mind to see something of the Roman world before it all disappeared under the bloody swords of various barbarian pirates. With the duty to my aunt relieved from me, I have followed my fancy a while.'

Then he told of ships and strange beasts, of Italy and Rome. Of the Holy Land and Africa. Of a sun so hot it burnt your skin through your clothes and plains of sand that went on for ever. 'I have lain seasick in wallowing ships, ridden on camels that made me feel sicker and loved and laughed with women more beautiful than Venus! I have seen and heard and smelt the wonders of the world – and almost gave myself to God, when I feared I had caught the pox.'

Gwenhwyfar cast an anxious glance at him. 'Pox?'

He laughed. 'I awoke one night, my body a mass of itching sores – I was convinced I was going to die. I vowed as I lay sweating in a fever that should I survive till morning I would seek a vocation within the Church.'

Intrigued, she asked, 'What happened?'

264

Bedwyr guffawed. 'I discovered I had made my bed on some damned insects' nest, who were rightfully angry at my intrusion! I figured an act of my own stupidity did not warrant such drastic penance, and besides,' his laughter increased, 'I found a pretty maid in the next village who was obliging enough to rub a healing salve on the bites.'

Gwenhwyfar crowed with delight, reached forward to slap him playfully around the ear. 'Ah Bedwyr. I ought to berate you for not coming earlier to us!' She dropped serious. 'We have been in such sore need of laughter, Arthur and I.'

He flapped his hand, embarrassed, regretful. 'I was angry with Arthur, but it was a childish anger, given from grief. Ygrainne treated him as no mother should treat a son, but she had been good to me. I owed her a time for grief.' Then he laughed again, 'But I am here now. Travelling has lost its appeal and I have forgiven my cousin.' He winked. 'Aside from that, my purse grows empty. I had to go somewhere, and now that I have escaped the estate where I was born and grew, I realise that I do not much care for the prospect of a lifetime of harvesting grapes.'

Laughing with him, Gwenhwyfar took his hands in hers, already the feeling of hope and promise that had eluded her and Arthur these past few tormented years was returning. When Arthur came back all would get better. They would find somewhere of their own to settle, and she would have another son . . . another son to replace the two little ones who lay cold in their graves.

'So what have you a mind to do now?' She forced the brightness back. She was half teasing, expecting some jested answer for return.

But he said, unexpected in its seriousness, 'I intend to see the Wall.'

Gwenhwyfar drew a little apart from him. 'What? You arrive and then leave us again?'

'Na,' he chided. 'Not straight away, in a day or two.' He leant forward and tweaked a strand of hair coming loose from her braid. 'I need to meet your two boys first, and have a good sleep and a bath!' He rose from the chair and wandered around the small room, touching a wall hanging, scenting a bowl of picked flowers. Smiling at Nessa as she glanced up at his passing. *And Bed a woman*, he thought. Nessa smiled back, her cheeks tinged pink. She had read his thought.

'The Wall?' Gwenhwyfar queried. 'There is little to see save mile upon mile of stone, broken occasionally by a derelict fort.'

Nessa spoke, excited, eager to be included in the conversation. 'What of the Spirit, my lady? They say as how there is the spirit of some poor soldier left pacing the rampart walk in solitary patrol.'

'Nonsense, Nessa.'

Suddenly Bedwyr seized Gwenhwyfar's hand, pulled her to her feet, whirled her a few paces, his face alight with enthusiasm. 'How do we know it is nonsense till we have discovered for ourselves?' He danced her a few more turns around the chamber. 'Come with me! Let us find this spirit! Let you and me ride together.'

'I don't think . . .'

He stopped, held his arms wide. 'Oh come on! When you were no more than a girl in Less Britain we would ride on many a brave-hearted adventure together!'

'I am no longer the young maid, and I have cantered through enough adventures beside my Lord husband, without starting a new one with his irresponsible young cousin!'

He pouted, his lower lip poking from beneath the upper. Then he whirled to Nessa, hauled her to her feet, danced her a few paces. 'Nessa would come with me, wouldn't you, lass?'

Breathless, the serving girl knew not how to answer. Imploring, she gazed at her mistress. She had been given her manumission from slavery months back, but many of the decisions that came with freedom she still felt uncertain about taking.

Shaking her head, Gwenhwyfar laughed, surrendered to the tide of enthusiasm. Why not? Until Arthur returned, there was nothing else to do at Caer Luel.

§ XLIX

They had ridden easy, taking pleasure in the warmth of a late, drowsing summer that was reluctant to mature into autumn. They slept in the shelter of crumbling forts; rode side by side, pointing out birds in flight, a herd of running deer, once, a wolf sighted in the distance, watching them in turn. Laughing together; enjoying the sun and wild silence. They reached as far as they great fortress of Cilurnum, but discovering the bridge no longer spanned the wide river, decided to pass the night in its protection, then turn about and return to Caer Luel. Arthur would, after all, be expected back soon, Gwenhwyfar was missing her boys, and the weather was changing.

Late afternoon they gave the horses their heads, as blackening skies rumbled behind the first fall of rain. Blowing, sides heaving, the animals galloped up the rise towards the next mile-castle. It was a hastily made choice – ride back to the nearer, smaller turret, or hasten on to the further, yet larger mile-castle. With the wind and rain coming at their backs, there was no difficulty in the decision.

Clattering through the gateway, their escort of ten men dismounted hurriedly and ran with the animals to what little shelter was provided by the remaining timbers of the stabling. Thunder crashed overhead, moments after a vivid streak of light ripped across the black sky. Bedwyr was all for ushering Gwenhwyfar and Nessa into the nearest intact building.

'Rest in here,' he shouted, kicking the broken door aside with his foot. 'I shall help the men gather wood for a fire.'

Gwenhwyfar was indignant. 'I am as capable as you at collecting wood! Nessa, go inside, prepare what you can.' She gathered her sodden cloak tighter to her, pushed past Bedwyr and made for a store-room abutting the height of the Wall. Roofed with turves, holes here and there had been patched and mended, a recently hung animal skin covered the doorway. Gwenwyfar entered cautiously. Who had been here? Herdsman? Hunter? A trader? She ducked inside, wrinkling her nose at the mixture of fetid odours. Animal dung, mustiness, stale smoke – and something else? Something she could not place. It took some moments for her eyes to grow used to the dimness; she waited, her hand resting on the door lintel. She could see now where a hearth-fire had been built and crossed to it; the ash was quite cold. No wood, save for a few unburnt branches lying around. She gathered them and began pulling at the heap of bracken stacked in one corner. It smelt none too pleasant, but would serve well enough for bedding with a cloak thrown over it.

She was turning for the doorway when a sound in the other corner alerted her. Rats? She listened, studying the heaped pile of what appeared to be mildewed rags. Must have been rats. As she lifted the animal-skin over the doorway the sound came again, a low moan.

Shouting for Bedwyr, Gwenhwyfar dropped her gathered bundle and ran to the corner, kicking the foul heap of stuff aside. Two frightened grey eyes, set in a dirty face swamped by a tangle of black, unwashed hair, met hers.

Bedwyr darted in, sword drawn, two of the escort hard at his heel.

'Jesu,' he swore, 'where did she come from?'

Gwenhwyfar squatted, her hands held forward, palms down, showing peace and good intention. 'Put up your sword, Bedwyr, she is frightened enough without that.'

'Not until I have reason to believe she is not so frightened as to be hostile.'

Gwenhwyfar clicked her tongue. 'Do as I say. Even were she inclined to hurting us, she is in no condition for it. The lass is in heavy labour.'

The girl – Gwenhwyfar discovered later that she was barely ten and three summers of age – was curled in a ball, knees drawn up against the pain that swamped her abdomen. Her face contorted, and now that she was discovered, another whimper left her lips.

'There is bracken, make it into bedding,' Gwenhwyfar ordered Bedwyr, 'and I require a fire for light and warmth. You,' she nodded at one of the escort, 'fetch Nessa. There is a spare cloak in my baggage, tell her to bring it.'

Exchanging a shared expression of resignation, the men did as they were ordered. Gwenhwyfar persuaded the girl to let her feel her swollen body, silently counting as the contraction ceased and another followed.

'How long have you been here?' she asked.

The girl was ragged and unkempt. Gwenhwyfar wondered when she had last eaten. Judging by the harsh, protruding bones, some time since.

'Three days,' the girl gasped.

'And the pains? When did they come.'

'Las' night,' the girl groaned, between chattering teeth. 'I am so cold, Lady. I had nought more strength to light a fire with. Please,' she grabbed for Gwenhwyfar's hand, clung tight. 'Please stop this pain, I can bear no more of it!'

Reassuringly Gwenhwyfar patted her hand. 'It will not be long afore it ends.'

Nessa thrust in, her tongue clicking with disapproval. 'What in God's good name is a mere child like this doing alone out here? And in her condition!'

'Have water fetched,' Gwenhwyfar ordered, ignoring Nessa's flood of agitated concern. She was a good hand-maid, but inclined to prattle.

Bedwyr himself brought the water, placed it beside the fire that was flickering into life through black, reeking, smoke. He touched Gwenhwyfar's arm, indicated the door. 'I must speak with you.'

'Not now.'

'Now!'

About to make a sharp retort, Gwenhwyfar saw his firm, determined look. 'Quickly then.' She withdrew with him, leaving Nessa to comfort the girl.

Sheltering beneath the slight roof overhang, Bedwyr turned his back to the wet, placed a hand on the wattle wall, said, 'I appreciate the lass needs help, but it is not for us to get involved here. She is of the Picti People, you can see that by her darkness, and she wears a slave collar.' The rain fell in a straight sheet of grey that all but obliterated the entrance gate on the far side of the rectangular courtyard. Gwenhwyfar had made no response.

Irritated, Bedwyr continued, 'Where she has run from I cannot imagine.'

'Nor do I care,' Gwenhwyfar snapped. 'She's a child who is having a child, and she is very frightened.' Her fists were screwed tight, her body taut. 'You men, you take your pleasures where you will, not concerning yourselves with the consequence of nine months hence . . .'

Bedwyr held his hands in surrender. 'Whoa! I am not at fault here!'

Gwenhwyfar shuddered a release of breath, calming herself. 'I am sorry. That girl is barely on the brink of womanhood, yet some man has bedded her, got her with child.'

Bedwyr shrugged, unconcerned. 'She is a slave.'

'And that makes it all right?' When he did not answer Gwenhwyfar persisted, 'Slaves have basic rights no less than any person high- or low-born. The right to be warm and fed. The right to remain a maiden until the body is grown.'

Bedwyr placed a hand on her shoulder. 'I agree with you, but we cannot stay long here. We must move on.'

'We can go nowhere in this storm and night will soon be approaching. Are we not to camp here?' She smiled, patted his hand. 'The babe ought to be safe born come morning.'

The men ate a thin gruel of corn and wild fowl and the thunder raged, drowning the girl's screams. The horses stamped uneasily and the men made the sign against evil. Night came, with the rain settling into a steady drizzle.

An hour after full dark Bedwyr came to find Gwenhwyfar, stood talking with her again beyond the door.

'The birth is wrong, Bedwyr. I fear for babe and girl.'

His patience was ebbing. This was all getting out of control. It was one thing to ride, merry-making for a few miles along the Wall, but to be squatting here in this squalid midden-heap, exposing the Pendragon's Lady to God alone knew what . . . 'Look,' he said. 'She's an escaped slave. What manner of death faces her when she is returned to her master? Let me put a swift end to her now. She will feel no more pain and —'

270

'You disgust me.' Gwenhwyfar turned on her heel and, tossing the door-skin aside, ducked back into the hut.

At a loss, Bedwyr ran his fingers through his rain-wet hair. He had a bad feeling growing in the pit of his belly about this nonsense, was beginning to wish he had never initiated this damn fool excursion.

Why was Gwenhwyfar behaving so God-damned stubborn about a slave and her brat? This was not the Gwenhwyfar he had known as a boy in Less Britain, the practical woman who could cope calmly and reasonably with awkward situations. Slowly, shaking his head, Bedwyr retraced his steps back through the mud to the men and their fire. He supposed this uncharacteristic behaviour was to do with the loss of her own small babe – but surely she would be over that? A child's death was a common enough thing, expected almost, for babe's were frail creatures. And she still had the other two boys, still had Llacheu and Gwydre; how much loss could one small babe leave? He shrugged. Women were strange creatures. A pity though, he had always thought Gwenhwyfar different to the rest of them. He ducked into the smokey-damp warmth of the men's shelter, shook his head. They would not be leaving this wretched place this side of the morrow's morning.

§ L

Sweeping a hand through the crown of her hair, Gwenhwyfar raked the curls with her spread fingers. She felt unwashed and itchy; there was water in the burn beyond the gate, how long before she could cleanse herself of the grime from this squalid place? She sighed and hunkered down to her heels beside the babe that was once again whimpering, its knees drawn tight against its belly.

Patiently, Nessa dribbled cooled, boiled water into its mouth. Within moments it spewed it back. The hand-maid shook her head. The child would not survive long.

Gwenhwyfar glanced at the mother, sleeping fitfully, then screwed her eyes shut against threatening tears. The memories of her

271

own last child, that had been born close to death, were too new and vivid. The ragged skin draped across the door was thrown back, and Bedwyr entered, his hair and shoulders glistening wet. 'It's raining again,' he said pointlessly. 'I thought it would not hold off for long.' Resisting the impulse to cover his mouth and nose against the putrid stench that filled the place, he added, 'I know not how you stand this foul air.'

'The smell of death,' Gwenhwyfar answered despondently, without looking round. 'You grow used to it.' She lifted the baby, cradling the pathetic thing in her arms, giving it some love as its brief, pain-ridden life fluttered and surrendered to what had to be. Her tears were there, but did not come. The terrible remembrance of her own recent loss had carried her beyond the point of weeping.

She laid the dead child beside the fire, covering the little body with a rough-spun blanket. The mother stirred, her hollow eyes resting on the bundle. She had said little of who she was, where she had come from. Was not likely to say more; Gwenhwyfar did not wish to know.

'Shall I take the babe? Bury it?' Bedwyr squatted before her, concerned; she looked so tired and sad. 'We knew it would die,' he reminded her, as though he had spoken the words a thousand times. To himself he had, sitting before a smoking fire in the derelict guard room, where the men of the escort had said nought, although their uneasy thoughts showed plain enough.

When Gwenhwyfar failed to answer, he sighed, moved to gather the dead child and strode once more out into the rain. What was the use? She had been determined to stay from the outset and was hardly likely to ride away now, not until the thing was finished. He crossed himself, hoped the girl's god would hurry and take her. Preferably before mid-morning; that would give them chance to cover a few more miles.

Gwenhwyfar watched him go. Poor Bedwyr.

'You are a good woman, Lady. May Christ give you his blessing.' The girl's eyes had flickered open, she attempted a smile.

Startled, Gwenhwyfar gasped, went to her. 'You are a Christian?' The girl glanced at the fire, saw the bundle had been removed. In less than a whisper, said, 'Jesu looked on me with His love, when he sent you.'

'It was the storm that brought us to this place, not Christ.'

The girl tried to laugh. She would have been pretty, had it not been for the grime and pain-hollowed cheeks. 'He brought the storm.' Her speech was slurring through a daze of the sickly stuff Gwenhwyfar had induced her to drink. 'That one with you,' she managed, 'though he is kind, he would not have stayed. He would have waited for the anger in the skies to pass, then ridden on. After dispatching me first.'

Gwenhwyfar could not deny it.

'Why did our Lord take my babe?'

Gwenhwyfar did not know how to answer, it was a question she would ask for herself. But there was no need to think of one. The girl could ask Christ.

Tutting beneath her breath at the senseless waste of life, Nessa covered the dead girl, said, 'I'll inform Lord Bedwyr,' and scuttled from the hut, hurrying through the rain, relieved that at last they could be gone from this foul place.

Gwenhwyfar rose, her joints stiff, back aching, thinking and thinking of her own dead children, folded her arms around herself to stop the shivering. She had never forgotten plump little Amr, and now the other son, born three months past. She saw in front of her, where the dead girl's babe had lain, her own child's little crinkled face, blue tinged, his lungs unable to breathe life-giving air. She leant against the rough stonework of the Wall, which formed the rear of the room, rested her head against its cold, old dampness, closed her eyes, and wept.

Rain drummed on the turf roof, finding its way through the gaps and holes, puddling on the earth floor. Thunder was again grumbling somewhere. Gwenhwyfar left the hut, stood beyond the shelter of the sloping roof, letting the cooling rain mingle with her hot tears. She could hear the men thankfully preparing to leave, they were talking and laughing, gathering their belongings, saddling their horses. The north gate through the Wall was barred by a broken hurdle, beyond stretched the solitude of the rain-mizzled hills. Gwenhwyfar lifted the hurdle aside, intending to go only as far as the trickling burn. She did not notice the rain stinging against her skin as she splashed through the water, up the far bank and out onto the open moorland.

Walking, stumbling, not caring where her feet trod, she was unaware of all but this sudden ache of intense misery. The pain of loss eases, but never quite goes, is always there ready to return, unexpected, uninvited, at some potent reminder. The mile-castle on the Wall fell behind, hidden by the swirl of mist and rise of land, but Gwenhwyfar did not notice, did not care.

The chink of harness and thud of hooves might have been muffled by the rumbling of thunder, the rhythmical patter of rain. Whatever reason, she did not hear. From nowhere, there before her, riding out of the mist came a host of men. She stopped, bewildered and confused. Someone laughed.

'What master are you escaped from then?'

'What master would care to keep such ragged property?'

'I wager she'd look none so poor were we to strip her!'

'It's so long since I've seen a woman, any maid would look well, stripped!'

Another voice, an officer. 'What is the disturbance? Good God! Lady Pendragon!'

Gwenhwyfar crumpled to her knees.

'Gwenhwyfar?' The familiar voice floated somewhere above her in the darkness, came again. 'Gwenhwyfar?' A hand patted her cheek, rubbed at her cold fingers. Her eyes flickered. Opened. She looked up into creased, worried eyes.

'Arthur?' she croaked, not believing it was him. Her hand felt for his body, rested against the thick, rain-wet leather of his tunic. 'Arthur? Is it you?'

'Aye.' He supported her shoulders and waist, allowed her to lean against him. A multitude of questions were in his mind, hammering to be answered. 'What, in the name of Mithras, are you doing out here alone, and in this sorry state? If someone has done harm to you I shall stretch his neck as long as the Wall for this!' He was angry, she could tell, more than angry.

'I . . . it is a long story.' Gwenhwyfar scrabbled to her feet, clutching at her husband as the world whirled in a dizzying spin. When the mist cleared, she saw men of the Artoriani clustered around, their faces grimed and weary from their march, expressions concerned. She looked down at herself, her skin, her clothes; touched the tangle of soaked, matted hair. What was she doing out here? Her mind whirled in a rush of confusion, as misted as these rain-sodden hills.

Arthur caught at her arm, alarmed, pointed to her tunic. 'This is blood!' Vaguely, she looked at it. Blood? The blood of life come and gone. The blood of death. He shook her. 'What has happened, Cymraes? Tell me!'

Another voice, female, caused him to glare above Gwenhwyfar's bowed head. 'So this is your queen? Sa, I remember as a child she preferred the appearance of a midden slave.'

Gwenhwyfar's head ached, her temples throbbed, forehead pounded. Her neck felt as though it were bound by iron. It took great effort to lift her head. Who was this woman? Why was she riding with the Artoriani? Nausea bubbled in her throat, the moors misted and swayed, swirling into hazy circles. She fought the faintness and became aware again of her appearance, of where, who, she was. She stared at the woman cloaked in a hooded silver wolf-skin, and who despite the rain and hardship of riding with an army on the march, appeared as having barely a lock of her barley-corn, fair hair out of place. Gwenhwyfar turned to her husband. 'You did not hang her then.'

Morgause tossed back her head and laughed, a sound that, had it been a scent, would have smelled of sickly, sweet perfume. 'Hang me? Arthur could never hang me!'

Lips pressed together, the Pendragon removed his cloak, swung it around Gwenhwyfar's shoulders. He ignored Morgause, though her tauts and comments were becoming more difficult by the day to endure. But she was right, he could not hang her, or drown her or hack off her head . . . 'Re-form the line of march,' he barked, propelling his wife, none so gently, towards his stallion.

§ LI

Warmed with hot broth and dressed in dry clothing, Gwenhwyfar silently suffered Nessa's more than vociferous scolding. 'We had no idea where to search for you. My poor Lord Bedwyr has received such a tongue-lashing from the King as was never heard! We thought he would strike the lad!'

The comb in Nessa's hand flew from her fingers as Gwenhwyfar swung sharply around, protesting, 'Bedwyr has done no wrong in this!'

Nessa sniffed loudly. 'Lord Pendragon says the whole thing was a foolish venture. I am inclined to agree.' She began combing again, none so gently.

Gwenhwyfar squirmed around a second time, the comb lodging in a tangle. 'Shame on you! Do you think I've not noticed who you've recently curled up with?'

'Tch! Keep yourself still Lady, or I'll be ripping your hair out!' Added tartly, 'I could as easily sleep with him at Caer Luel, but oh no, he had to entice you out here to these rain-soaked hills!'

Gwenhwyfar stamped to her feet, tearing the comb from a knot of hair and throwing it to the bed. 'He did not entice me! I had as much of the decision.'

'Then you acted with as much stupidity as he.' Arthur entered the tent, flinging his sodden cloak from his shoulders as he came. The boy Gweir, as ever trotting behind, deftly retrieved it. 'By the Bull, it's wet out there!' Arthur went to the brazier, lifted one foot to rest it on a stool; stood with arms folded and that familiar half-squint to his eyes, regarding his wife.

She returned his stare, determined not to be the first to glance away, unsure of what he was thinking, or intending to say, aware she had been foolish – in all of it. But it had seemed such a lovely idea at the outset. He lifted one eyebrow higher, leant slight forward, giving question. Waiting answer.

With a slight toss to her hair. 'I was bored. A ride along the Wall suited me well.' As if that explained all!

Arthur made no comment. For a moment more he stood, rocking gently against the raised leg, then suddenly, as if dismissing the thing, crossed to the bed pallet and lay down, placing his arms behind his head.

Gweir hurried past Gwenhwyfar and began removing Arthur's muddied boots. Finished, he glanced shyly at his Lord's wife and asked, 'Can I fetch you anything, Lady?'

Answering for her, Arthur growled, 'You can fetch a draught of wine, then get out.' He shut his eyes, scratched at an itch on his nose and pointed at Nessa. 'Take her with you.'

Nessa bridled, about to make a retort. Gwenhwyfar hastily placed a hand on her arm. 'I need you no more this night, Nessa, thank you.'

'And where,' she replied sharply, 'am I supposed to go? Do I, then, sleep out in the rain, or share a blanket with one of *them*?' She tossed her pert head in the direction of the men's tents.

Arthur chuckled. 'They'd like that!'

Gweir cast nervously between master and mistress, unsure whether to speak, risked, his voice quivering, 'If you please, there is a place within Lady Morgause's tent.'

Arthur stretched, yawned. 'She has been complaining that the single hand-maid I granted her was not sufficient. You ought to be well received.'

Nessa snorted. 'I'd rather take the first offer!' Gathering her belongings she swept out after Gweir, saying unnecessarily loud 'Escort me to the stores tent, I'll make my bed there.'

'There is no need to be so angry.'

'No?' Arthur's voice was heavy with sarcasm as he answered Gwenhwyfar. In one fluid movement he rose from the bed and crossed to her, to grip her arms roughly in his hands. 'I find you wandering alone in the middle of nowhere, looking like a peasant-bred slut and you tell me not to be angry!'

Gwenhwyfar dropped her eyes to the rush matting on the floor, bit her lip. 'I meant with Nessa. None of this is her fault.'

Arthur strode across to the other side of the tent, arms waving, animated. 'What if I had been an enemy? A missed band of Lot's

277

rebels or some young, hot-headed Saex boys? There are wolf-packs aplenty roaming these hills. Blood-in-hell, Gwenhwyfar!' His raised his arms, hands spread. 'You could have been torn to pieces by either one of them!' He paced around the small confine of the tent in frustration. 'Going off by yourself was inexcusable; Bedwyr I've reprimanded severely; I'm ashamed of the both of you.'

Gwenhwyfar wiped at her eyes with the back of her hand. 'He is not to blame. I insisted on staying with the girl. He was not aware I had left the place.' She twirled her marriage ring around her finger, focusing on its flash of light as the gem caught in the dim reflection from the single lamp, trying hard not to cry.

Arthur swung to face her, 'Then he *ought* to have been aware!' He was struggling to keep his intense anger in check, the whole foolish escapade was so stupidly undertaken – so damned perilous. 'I expected to return to Caer Luel, find you there with a welcome befitting the Supreme King, not come across you looking and smelling as some putrid swine-maiden.' He put his hand to his forehead, rubbed at the ache that was pounding behind his temples. 'Mithras knows what Morgause is making of all this!'

'Oh, I see!' Gwenhwyfar's head snapped up, eyes flashing as many sparks as her ring. 'Is that what bothers you? What Morgause thinks!'

'Of course not!' Arthur bellowed, his anger intensifying.

'Am I then a prisoner of yours?' Gwenhwyfar shouted back. 'Must I stay where you send me? Am I not allowed to ride or travel where I will? I was foolish to wander away alone I admit, but for the rest, I had adequate escort and this tract of land is now free of rebels or warring Saex, as you well know, otherwise you would never have ridden so far north.' She was tired, miserable, and in the wrong. All three of which made her stamp her foot and declare, 'I am a free woman first, then your wife. If I wanted to leave this tent now, you could not stop me!'

'Go on then, leave. Go, make your bed elsewhere!' Arthur strode to the tent opening, ripped it back, gestured elaborately with his hand for her to leave. 'Go find another runaway slave to make a fool of yourself with!'

'Gods, you disgust me!' Furious, Gwenhwyfar snatched up her

cloak and flinging it around her shoulders stalked out, not looking at him, staring straight ahead at the dark crags that rose opposite beyond the wooden palisade of the marching camp.

Arthur thrust the flap from his hand and threw himself on the bed, attempted to make himself comfortable, to sleep. Finding her unexpectedly as he had, out here along the Wall, wandering and distraught, had frightened him. The fear had materialised as anger, and anger was a thing difficult to diffuse. His heart was hammering, head pounding and his hand scratched by some object, Gwenhwyfar's comb. Stamping to his feet, he returned to the opening. She was some yards outside the palisade, men hovering inside the fence, uncertain, agitated, not knowing what to do.

Arthur ran to the wooden posts, flung the comb at her retreating back. 'Take your comb, you need something to improve your present state!'

It was a good throw, striking her shoulder before it fell. Gwenhwyfar stooped for it almost as it landed, spun around and hurled it back. It fell short of the fence, lost somewhere among the long grass. 'Keep it. Give it to Morgause.' She turned her back on him, began striding away in the direction of the crags, heedless of the cold drizzle.

Arthur swore. 'Damn you Gwenhwyfar, what makes you so bloody obstinate?' He went a few steps, realised the discomfort of soaking grass on bare feet, cursed, swung back to his tent and cursed again as he searched for his boots. Pulling one on, he hopped, pulling on the other, back out the flap, through the gateway and took off after her. Finally, breathless, he caught her and grasped her arm, swinging her to a halt.

Her hand swept out, aiming to slap him. He ducked, shouted the truth of his anger. 'You ought not to have stayed with that girl!' He was yelling at her, his hands on her arms, shaking and shaking her. 'You are my wife, not some escaped slave's physician.'

'Was I to abandon her and the child then? Leave them to die unloved and afraid?'

'They died anyway!' Still holding her, refusing to let her go, shaking her, he stormed, 'You could have caught some infection from her!' Calmer, gasping for breath, he released her, stood before her, face contorted in anguish and grief. Said mutely, 'Damn it, Cymraes . . .' Again he took her arms, but more gently, tenderly and possessively. 'I could not lose you for the sake of some wretched slave girl.' He stepped forward, bent his head, kissed her. 'If you ever, ever, give me such cause for fear over your safety again, I swear I shall personally lock you in your chamber and leave you there until such time as I return to release you.'

Before she could answer, he lifted her and carried her back down the slight rise and into their tent.

§ LII

Morgause seethed, though she took great care not to show it. That whelp riding ahead would gloat were she to show discomfort – and that satisfaction, under no circumstance, would she give him. Called himself King? Ha! He was not half the man his father, Uthr, had been! There was no time that she could remember not loathing Arthur, as a boy or man. Had she realised when he was a child what the man would become . . . ah, but what use was stewing over might-have-beens? The future was the important thing, if he intended to allow her a future. That Arthur meant her to be entombed as a prisoner, or to see her hang, she had no doubt – and unless she could coil a tendril tight around the Pendragon's damn neck soon, then such a disagreeable future looked set. Had she only borne Uthr a son . . .

Her hands were bound and her horse tethered to the one being ridden in close attendence; she rode straight-backed, regally and with pride. Ah no, she would not let her anger give a public show!

There were, however, some intriguing compensations. The rumours that Arthur and Gwenhwyfar were often quarrelling were true then. And what of those other tales that had filtered north? The delibrate drowning of his own child, for instance, and the murder of his mistress, the one who had been carrying his child? She would have to discover more for these were things she could use to her own advantage.

She glanced at her escort – guard – riding beside her. Were he not one of Arthur's curs he would be a most pleasing young man to look upon. Good chin, clear eyes, skilled hands. Torso and legs not too fat, nor too skinny. She liked flesh on her men but not too much. A fat man, she had found, would wheeze and grunt in bed like an old foraging boar, but a man of all bone would have no stamina.

The morning air smelt clean and fresh after the rain, the hills and trees wearing a tinge of autumn gold. A pleasant enough day, considering her predicament. There was no hope of a rescue, those Picti turds – barbarian fools – had abandoned her to Arthur. So a few settlements had been burnt, a few women and children slaughtered – were they as important as herself! If Edda had lived . . . if Lot had not been such a coward, if those damn fool men had not wasted time in gathering the war-hosting together in the first place . . . there, the ifs and buts again!

The horse beside her stumbled and she glanced again at its rider, intending some scathing remark, but a sudden instinctive inspiration changed the scorn to flattery. 'You handle a horse well, young sir.'

'I pride myself that I am an accomplished rider.'

Morgause lowered her sweeping lashes. 'I would warrant, any mare would respond well to your, gentle, guiding hands.'

Hueil's smile was swaggering. He knew as well as she that their words were not directed at horses.

January 464

§ LIII

Morgause ran her fingernail, a thing as sharp as a wildcat's claw, down the dark hairs of Hueil's broad and muscular chest. Sweat still glimmered there, from the exertion of their love-making. She snuggled sensuously closer, appreciating the warmth and comfort of his body, for the governor's palace at Caer Luel was a chill, damp place. She had never been one to lie alone at night, and saw no reason why being a prisoner of Arthur's should alter her nocturnal requirements. Experienced in discretion – her husband, for certain, had remained unaware of her lovers – it had come easy for Hueil, as Captain of the guard, to be with her.

A fine soldier, Hueil, with ability, skill and courage. One of Arthur's most promising young officers. The son of a north-western lord, Hueil wanted to be a leader, not a follower, and such a man, a man who nursed ambition, fitted neatly into Morgause's scheming palm. Neatly enough for the fingers slowly to close around, draw in deeper and ensnare.

'I hear the Pendragon departed in a sour temper this morning,' she said, in her honey-sweet voice. 'Have he and Gwenhwyfar quarrelled again?' She wound a curl of his abundant, chest hair around her finger. Her hands were slender, smooth; the skin unroughened and unwrinkled by labour or age. She took great care of her hands, for you could tell a lot about a woman by the way she used her hands. 'Lai, lai,' she sighed, 'I really do not understand why he keeps her as wife. A woman with such a sour tongue should surely be better placed deep beneath the peat-bogs.'

Hueil took her fingers, delicately kissed each tip. There was so much he still wanted, was impatient to wait for – but this woman, this magnificent, beauteous, creature, was actually his, all his! Even the waiting for a kingdom to call his own paled into insignificance aside possessing the body of Morgause. He lightly bit her index finger, ran his hand up the smooth skin of her arm to fondle her swan's neck. The luck of Fortuna had certainly smiled on him the day Arthur had ordered him to take personal charge of the Lady Morgause. He smirked privately to himself, though by the gods, the King had not meant quite so intimately personal! 'I believe my Lady Pendragon is still disgruntled over your place of lodging. The repercussions at the King putting you here, in a comfortable room,' Morgause snorted through her nose, indignant. Comfortable? Call this apology for a hovel, comfortable? 'are even now, still rippling.' Hueil chuckled maliciously. 'It's rumoured that our King took the choice of attending this episcopal meeting at Aquae Sulis in preference to enduring her ill-humour!' He chortled louder, 'For 'tis no secret how Arthur does love those men of the Church!' He chuckled again, added, ' 'Tis the one thing I agree with him over, the pedantics of the Church!'

Morgause smoothed his chest hair, thick spread over his muscles and spreading down to his navel. Her words simultaneously smoothing his ruffled temper, which was as thick. 'Your father's devotion to the Christian God has embittered you, my lover.'

Sliding an arm around her waist, Hueil drew her delightful nakedness to him. Ah, but she felt good! 'My father has as much sense as a pack-mule. He is too tight shackled to the will of the Bishops. If he were to look beyond the walls of his stone-built church he would see that his land is disappearing under the heel of the Scotti settlers!'

'One day,' Morgause kissed his shoulder, his neck, her lips cool against his flesh, 'one day soon, he shall be gone and you shall rule in his stead.' Her lips moved to his chest. 'And then you can take the title of king yourself.'

'That day may yet be far off,' Hueil grunted miserably. 'Long-lasting health flourishes for my kin.'

Morgause bent her head, delicately kissed each of his nipples. 'For you, then,' she glanced up at him, her smile seductive, 'I am glad.' Thought to herself, *fool man, there are many ways to ensure health takes a turn for the worst!* 'Then there is Arthur,' she said. 'Would he allow you to rule as you wish, not as he commands?'

She busied herself with her attention to his chest, keeping her face averted, lest he read her thoughts too closely. She had chosen well in Hueil, but must not push too far, too soon. Subtle manipulation; implanted suggestions; words said in the right place at the right time. He had arrogance and ambition, qualities that easily overrode doubts of conscience. Hueil would not be a man to balk over trivialities such as loyalty and conscience when the eventual chance to take what he craved was offered.

'When . . . I . . . am . . . King,' he said between kisses to the crown of her head, 'none shall tell me what I can or cannot do.' He grasped her hair, forced her head up, placing his lips on hers in a prolonged kiss. 'I shall need a queen, Morgause. A woman who would inspire men to take up arms with me against any who dared dispute my authority.' He kissed her again, possessive, with supremacy. 'Any, who dare.'

Morgause's breasts brushed his skin as she shifted position. She had suckled no children, they had not lost their firm, youthful shape. 'Will you find such a queen, think you?'

With his knee he parted her thighs, wanting his pleasure. 'Have I so far to look for one?'

Morgause feigned a response to his clumsy, all too quickly finished coupling. He was a man too hurried and impatient, too full of his own self-importance, to satisfy her desires. It did not matter. The mid-morning door-guard provided those extra comforts that a woman such as she required. It would not be so easy to find someone to secure her freedom. 'You forget,' she whispered as he settled to sleep. 'I am Arthur's property now, to be disposed of as he bids. I am his prisoner. I cannot choose for myself.'

Sleep was saturating him; through a yawn he answered, 'Arthur would deny you are a prisoner.'

'He insists I am his guest, yet there are guards beyond my door and letters I write are read – as are those few I receive.' She lay beside him, her body moulding to his. 'What do we do if Arthur will not allow me to be your queen?'

Hueil's breathing began to deepen, through drowsing semi-sleep he said, 'Arthur will have no say in the matter, once I am proclaimed King of my own lands.'

Morgause smiled. For all his usefulness, this young man was an arrogant fool! Did he think it would be so easy to defy Arthur? This thing must be carefully planned; as carefully executed. She shuddered slightly. That was not a word she cared to use, executed. Her life – death – hung close to the balance of the Pendragon's whim. 'I think, my lover,' she mused aloud, though Hueil was now asleep, 'you must become a King very soon.'

She lay silent, as he slept, watching the shadows move slowly over the walls, across the floor, waiting for dawn to finger the cracks around the ill-fitting window shutters. All she need do was nurture her seedling implantation, and wait patiently for the harvesting.

§ LIV

Gwenhwyfar sat on a low wall surrounding a rectangular ornamental pool in the gardens of the Governor's palace at Caer Luel. Gardens looked so sorrowful in winter, dead heads, decaying stalks and uncleared weeds, leaves greyed or browned by the nip of frost, no flowers, no blossom. The Governor's Lady cared for the place as best she could, but even her enthusiasm did not extend into the chill bite of mid-winter. It was January, and the garden was left to fend for itself until the first delights of snowdrop and primrose should show themselves among the remnants of last year's decayed splendour. The air smelt of the sea, for the wind was from the west. It was a mild day, a brief respite from the past weeks of a cold, easterly blow that had kept everyone indoors huddled beneath their cloaks and around the smoking fires. Gwenhwyfar had chilblains on her toes that itched, sore, of an evening. She needed new boots. She sighed and cast a handful of pebbles, scooped from the pathway, into the thick, pea-broth scum of the water. She missed Arthur. She sighed again, deeper. Yet, when they were together they invariably quarrelled. He had not needed to attend this synod, could as easily have sent a representative, but na, he had wanted to swagger before the Bishops, to show how clever he had been to subdue and lay claim to the North and avenge the death and destruction of Eboracum. Showing off she had called it. Hence the quarrel. They would not be impressed by his achievement of course, but Arthur could never stay still in one place for long, not within stone-built buildings, and not with a legitimate opportunity to be moving, doing. When he would return was any god's guess.

On what had once been an immaculately terraced lawn, but now sprouted more moss and weeds than grass, her two sons were playing noisily with Llacheu's young pup, a birthday gift from Arthur. The dog was barking wildly, circling the laughing boys as they teased it to catch a dangling piece of sacking. Gwenhwyfar joined their laughter as the animal leapt, catching the thing in his teeth, and with much growling, shook his catch furiously, then took off with it at a run, the boys tumbling in squealing pursuit.

Someone added his laughter. Gwenhwyfar turned, startled, half hoping that Arthur had come home, and saw Bedwyr approaching. She stood, held her hands outstretched to him with a wide, pleased, smile of welcome.

'Bedwyr! I had not expected your early return. How went the hunting?'

'Well enough for us to enjoy an excellent feast this evening! God's Grace, but the weather is uncommonly pleasant for the time of year.' He had reached her, took her hands, kissed her on both cheeks. He screwed his eyes at the glare in the pale-washed, low-hanging winter sun. 'Though I grant the water has a film of ice on it of a morning.' He still had hold of her hands.

'Bright and sunny it might be, but I've grown cold sitting out here.' Gwenhwyfar retrieved her hands and threaded her arm through his for the benefit of warmth and friendship. 'Come, walk with me a while.' Together, they negotiated a flight of foot-worn stone steps and threaded their way along an overgrown, winding path, Bedwyr kicking aside evergreen shrubs and dead-leaved plants. They talked of minor things, Bedwyr of the day's hunting, Gwehwyfar of Llacheu's pup, of the garden, of the horses wintering in the pastures beyond the Caer walls, of friends and family. Once or twice, of Arthur. When Gwenhwyfar admitted that she regretted not riding with her husband, as he had asked of her, Bedwyr stopped short and placing both hands over his heart, pretended to stagger backwards. 'What? You would be parted from me? Ah, but I am sorely wounded.' He turned away, threw his arm against a tree, imitated sobbing. 'She wants to leave me, loves me not!'

Gwenhwyfar laughed, playfully slapped the brown hair growing thick and curled on his head. 'Fool!' He was a burst of spring sunshine on a rainy day, always laughing, always jesting or telling some amusing tale. The boys loved him. He was almost one with them, for his merriment was that of a child. She added, chuckling, 'More like the departure of my hand-maid would bring you grief, you rogue!'

Bedwyr feigned wounded innocence. 'I am as pure as a nun's white under-garments my Lady!'

Gwenhwyfar crumpled into deeper laughter, rethreaded her arm through his and walked him forward. 'And how would you be knowing of things such as a nun's private apparel?' They turned onto a second path that skirted the rear wall of the guest chambers. Bedwyr squeezed her hand, said low, almost into her ear, 'Not all nuns are as chaste as they would like us to assume.'

With a mock disapproving frown, Gwenhwyfar brushed his hand from hers. 'I say again, Bedwyr ap Ectha, you are a rogue!' They had stopped once more, were standing close, their laughter at his absurdity dancing with the dappled afternoon sunlight. Impulsive, Gwenhwyfar placed a light kiss on Bedwyr's cheek, her hands resting on his chest. 'You would cheer the dullest place, Bedwyr. Glad I am that you are here.'

Suddenly serious, an experience rare in one known for his quick laughter and constant humour, he replied, 'Glad I am to be here, my Lady,' his brown eyes casting direct into her green.

Her heart thump-thumped with a leap of mixed feelings. Alarm, excitement, flattery. They were standing so close. If he kissed her, she would respond, kiss him back . . . She caught her breath, what madness was this! Playfully, she pushed him from her, said with light

290

gaiety, 'You'd have me believing you travelled all the way back from Rome just to be near me next.'

Stunned, astonished, he replied, 'But I did! Why else would I come to a place that is normally cold enough to freeze a man's balls off?' He scooped her hand, brought it quickly to his lips. 'For you, my beloved and fairest of all women, would I travel beyond the edge of the world!' He held his arms out, let them drop with a slap to his side, added with an indifferent shrug, 'Save, I would need to return by nightfall, or else my Nessa would find some other to warm her bed.' He cavorted a few strides, then swept her a bow. 'I am away to the bath-house, assuming the water is hotter than the ice-pool it was yester eve. Till we dine, my Lady . . .'

Gwenhwyfar watched him go, walking jauntily, his arms swinging, head back, singing out of tune at the top of his voice. He disappeared around the corner. It had grown colder, the clouds were hustling the winter-blue sky, crowding in great packs of silver and gold-edged shadow-shaded grey. She gathered her cloak tighter around her shoulders, shivered, rubbed her hands together. Her fingers were quite numb.

The harsh, unmelodious call of a mobbed crow caused her to glance up and a movement at one of the small, square windows arrested her attention. Someone had been watching! Gwenhwyfar sucked in her angry breath, released it slowly. Morgause. Spying on her, her evil presence permeating even out here into the winter-straddled gardens. Arthur ought never to have lodged her in the guest chambers. The prison cells, or better still, an unmarked grave, was the more appropriate! But no, Arthur had his own plan, his own decision, and so Morgause was made comfortable. The ride back along the Wall, returning here to Caer Luel, had been tense, with an atmosphere of hostility between the two royal women. Gwenhwyfar had assumed Arthur would send Morgause to some distant place for safe holding and that they, with their boys, would ride to some comfortable place for the duration of winter. Into Gwynedd for instance, returning with Enniaun or Cei, whose wife lodged with her parents on the shores of Bala lake. But no, her husband had decided to make Caer their winter residence.

291

'Aye, you bitch,' she said, tossing her words up at the window, 'you think you can hold Arthur, tempt him with your beguiling smile. Well you try it, just you try it!' She swung away, walked with quick steps back to the main garden where she called to her sons that she was returning inside.

Morgause frightened her – Arthur was feared of her too, though he would never admit it. Gwenhwyfar's fear ran with a personal dread, for Morgause was an alluring, beautiful woman, a woman who caught the eyes and lust of men. And Arthur enjoyed beautiful women. She forced such dark thoughts aside. Rumour around the Caer was that he had gone away to escape her, his wife, but it was not true. They had exchanged worse quarrels than those hurled between them recently about Morgause – and the night together before he had left for the south was far from disagreeable! She smiled at the intimate memory of their loving. She should have gone with him – he had begged her to, but like a fool she had refused. The thought of travelling in cold, wet winter weather had not appealed, but then were things much better here at Caer Luel?

Oh she would like to know who it was who started all these vicious, spiteful rumours! The Caer had been a welcoming enough place before Morgause had come. It was she who stirred things, with her oh so seductive smile! Gwenhwyfar banged through the door into the palace, startling the Watch guard and drawing the attention of several servants. Let them gawp, they were always so eager to think the worst and go tattling, skirts hitched, to tell Morgause the latest gossip.

Arthur should have had her hung!

She slowed her wild pace as she came closer to her own chamber. Arthur should have had an end to her up in the North, not brought her here, or anywhere. She was trouble, Morgause.

§ LV

'It is good that we have patched our differences, Arthur.'

Arthur sniffed loudly, moved aside to allow a woman to squeeze

292

past, wondered whether to voice his true thoughts at Ambrosius or not. 'Let us say we have agreed to tolerate each other.'

Ambrosius waved greeting to an acquaintance, spoke briefly to another, nodding and smiling, standing as though he were some royal figure receiving acclaim. Arthur knew several people here, milling in the forecourt before the amphitheatre, but liked none of them. One or two offered ingratiating smiles, received no response for their effort. The noble residents of Aquae Sulis were a shallow lot, of Ambrosius's ilk. Pure Roman, clinging, determined, to their generations-bred life-style; Arthur held no liking for them. The Council, concluded now, had at least been passably worthwhile with some, small, public agreement reached. That was something.

He accepted wine from a serving girl, sipped; it was tolerably good stuff. The play they were waiting to see was a bastion of normality for this Roman town. Their theatre, their games, laws and rites, were unaltered Roman. Aquae Sulis had not been terrorised by sea-wolves, and trade, dignity and superiority still flourished in abundance although the decay was creeping in. Cracking walls and derelict buildings – even the famous bath-house had fallen into disrepair.

Ambrosius finished his conversation, turned again to Arthur and said entirely unexpectedly, 'Your wife is here, did you know?'

Arthur swallowed quickly, a heart-thud of surprised pleasure. Gwenhwyfar? Here after all? She had refused to come with him, though he had asked, almost pleaded; she said she had no wish to spend several weeks among pompous old fools fussing and farting over irrelevancies. He peered about him, at the throng of people, easing now as they began to enter the theatre proper to take their seats. 'Here literally or here in town?' he asked.

'In town, though possibly attending this play also, that I do not know. I am not well acquainted with the Lady Winifred's engagements.'

Expression souring, Arthur drained his goblet, handed the empty vessel to a passing slave. Winifred. Not Gwenhwyfar. He should have realised. Gwenhwyfar would have come direct to him, fool to have thought it was her. Fool, to be so disappointed.

293

'She has, I believe,' Ambrosius continued, beginning to amble towards the entrance, 'brought your son with her.'

For a heartbeat Arthur almost hit him. His fist had been clenched, begun to draw back . . . but he took a deep breath, forcibly relaxed his arm muscles, his fingers. 'Winifred', he said, with an over-politeness that screeched of his displeasure and annoyance, 'is not my wife.' He met Ambrosius's eyes, stared pointedly. 'Until you realise and accept that fact Ambrosius, there can never be, will never be, an end to this animosity that slithers so potent between us.'

Ambrosius Aurelianus was a tall man, though not as tall as Arthur. He returned the direct gaze eye to eye, unflinching. After all, Arthur's father Uthr, was his elder brother, and Uthr had glowered just as fiercely on occasion. He probed the inside of his cheek with his tongue, dropped his gaze, spread his hands in submission. 'We are here to see fine actors, a rare treat, let us enjoy ourselves this afternoon my nephew, not quarrel.' He took Arthur's elbow, guided him beneath the entrance arch. They were almost through, the tiers of filling seats rising ahead of them, when Ambrosius added, 'For what it is worth, Pendragon, I share your dislike of the woman and have no intention, should some tragedy befall yourself, of allowing her breed-less son access to a British title.'

Arthur stopped short, amazed. Had he heard aright here?

Ambrosius had walked on a few paces. He too stopped, turned and smiled at his nephew, eyes twinkling with a mixture of amusement and threat. 'You see, I do not oppose you in everything, Arthur. Some things, I agree with whole-hearted. You must accept, mind, that I may not recognise Gwenhwyfar's sons either.' He gestured for Arthur to proceed with him, indicating the crowd pressing behind. 'Though I admit your eldest, Llacheu, would, below myself, be obvious choice to take command – when he has become a man of course.'

Drily, Arthur answered, 'Of course.'

Ambrosius was threading his way along the row of seats, found his, gestured for Arthur to be seated beside him.

'And does this sudden preference,' Arthur asked, prodding his cushion into a more comfortable shape, 'extend to accepting the title of king?'

Ambrosius folded his cloak across his knees, answered with a broad grin, 'One thing at a time, Pendragon, one turnabout at a time.'

Cerdic watched little of the play, engrossed as he was in studying the man seated in the centre rows, where the important men were. So, this was his father, Arthur, the great Pendragon. He was disappointed. He had expected a large man with bulging muscles, haughty eyes, proud carriage, perhaps wearing armour, most definitely decked in jewels. The Archbishop Patricius, God rest his soul, had seemed more regal than the man sitting over there, laughing and clapping and entering the full spirit of this comic play. A king, a supreme king such as his father called himself, should surely behave moderately, with dignity and grace, not storm to his feet shouting and laughing in common with the audience? And Cerdic had expected his father to be handsome, but his nose was large, his hair in need of cutting and combing, and wanting a shave too. All the man had were a few rings, a gold torque around his throat and two ordinary cloak pins. A king ought dress like a king, behave like a king.

Cerdic would, for certain, when he became king.

February 464

§ LVI

Llacheu and Gwydre had placed themselves to the side of Caer Luel's banqueting hall, close to the back, where the flickering of hearth-fire and lamp shadow, with luck, allowed two boys to pass unnoticed. Llacheu squatted, sharing his dish of boiled eggs with his brother. Gwydre was grinning, his mouth and chin splotched with dribbed egg-yolk, his wooden spoon dipping industriously into the delicious sauce of ground pine kernels, pepper and lovage mixed with honey and vinegar. The boys cared little for the recipe, all they knew was that it tasted good.

The hall was full to bursting with invited men and women of the Caer and officers and selected men of the Artoriani. They squashed along benches, elbowing for room, hands reaching and scrabbling for food, the dishes passing the length of the trestle tables, wine and ale flowing from jug to tankard to mouth. Above it all, the ululation of voices; talking, laughing, exchanging jest or friendly disagreement. A busy enjoyment of merry-making.

Llacheu nudged his younger brother's arm, nodded at the high table, said, his mouth full, spluttering sauce, 'See the harper seated next to Da? Mam said how he is the best in all our world.'

Gwydre licked sticky fingers, said with fierce loyalty, 'Our mam sings pretty.'

Scathing, Llacheu retorted, 'Of course she does, but you need a real harper for the Warrior's Hall.'

Gwydre shrugged good natured and wiped his fingers round the bowl to scrape the last residue. 'Happen so, but Mam still sings pretty.' He looked hopefully towards the nearest over-crowded table, his eyes roaming greedily over the many dishes. The pasties looked exceptionally good.

A woman servant bustled past, her cheeks puffing red from the heat of so many packed into one room, and all the to and fro-ing.

299

From the corner of her eye she noticed the boys hunkered in their corner and stopped, retracing her steps to stand before them. They stared anxiously up at her glowering expression, Llacheu risking an impudent grin.

'What be you two doing 'ere?' she asked sharply, her face furrowing into creases of suspicion. 'Your mam know you be 'ere?'

Llacheu nodded furiously, figuring a nod was not so damning as a verbal lie.

The woman's frown cracked deeper. Gwydre's mop of chestnut hair flopped over his hazel eyes, he brushed it back, leaving a trace of kernel sauce across his forehead. Eagerly he said, 'This is a special feast for our da, we are leaving the Caer on the morrow.' His lips pouted as he glanced down at the empty bowl resting in his lap. 'We're never allowed to join in the fun.' Again he looked up, an engaging smile swamping his chubby, very dirty, face. Gwydre was an endearing boy, he had the knack of smiling so that whoever scolded found it difficult to retain their ill-temper. It worked especially well on his mother, but was not so effective on Enid. Innocently he asked, 'I'm in my seventh year now though, and my brother's two years older, so why is that, do you think?'

The woman had birthed five boys, grown now and gone to homesteadings of their own. She knew well the ways and pleasures of youngsters – and aside, did she really have the time to chase these two imps from the place? The next course was already being shouted for and those empty tankards would go clean through the table boards if they were thumped any the harder. She fought a desire to laugh at Gwydre, kept her face stern. 'Just you stay there then. Don't you dare let me catch you getting under our feet!' The boys nodded vigorously. 'You may as well have this then,' she added, placing the last meat pastie from her tray onto Gwydre's dish. 'Happen I'll bring you something else later – no promises mind.' And she was gone, chiding the men at the nearest table for being so impatient.

Arthur was in high spirits, almost content. His return a few weeks past had heralded a sudden change in what had otherwise been a mild winter. Snow had blasted down from the north-east, whirling in a blizzard that had lasted for two days, leaving the land from coast to distant hills buried under a white mantle that came up to a man's waist. With a change of wind, the weather had improved, but a cold frost had locked the snow-melt into sheets of ice that had only begun to thaw these last few days with the return of a welcome, if somewhat erratic, sunshine. And now, too, Arthur intended to leave, much to Gwenhwyfar's relief. Caer Luel had outlasted its welcome.

'Now that Ambrosius seems to be reaching sensible conclusions,' Arthur said, helping himself to slices of roast swan, 'I can take time to sort our family life.' He piled meat onto Gwenhwyfar's platter. 'We ought to search for a Caer of our own.' He stuffed meat into his mouth, chewed a moment, swallowed, adding, 'Somewhere distant enough from my uncle so as not to ride in each other's saddle, but near enough to remind him of my presence.' About to say more, he stopped as a shouted curse, carrying clear above the noise of talk and laughter, sent a flutter of unease scuttling the length of the Hall. Two men were leaping to their feet, fists bunched, voices raised.

'What now?' Arthur grumbled. 'Surely they have not over-drunk already?' He signalled to a senior officer to investigate the disturbance, but like the rush of fire among dry tinder, the argument was already escalating. More men were rising, benches were being knocked, a scuffle began. One man, arms flailing, went down and uproar burst through the Hall. Others were springing up, tables tipped, scattering dishes and food and wine. Dogs began to bark, joyfully leaping to devour the unexpected feast scattered to the tessellated floor. A servant screamed.

Arthur hurled from his seat, bellowing for peace. Angry, joined by several officers, he stormed the distance between his own table and the fight, wading into the group of excited young men pushing and shoving at each other. His hand clamped on a tunic collar and he brought Bedwyr, fists swinging, face red, to his feet. Another officer hauled at a second lad, Ider.

On the floor, glowering and attempting to stem a bloodied nose, sprawled Hueil.

'I will have no fighting in my presence!' Arthur did not shout, his wrath was obvious without the need of a raised voice. His eyes, narrowed in fierce authority, swept from one offender to the other. 'If you have a grievance then settle it in private, outside!'

'He spreads insults against my Lady Gwenhwyfar like muck over a farm field!' Ider blurted, furious, pointing an accusing finger at Hueil.

Bedwyr trod heavily on his foot. 'Hush, you fool!'

Ider reddened, but it was too late, the words were out.

Arthur released Bedwyr, his grasping fingers slowly uncurling, extended his hand low for Hueil to take, hauled the stocky young man to his feet.

In his one and twenty summers, Hueil had gathered enough grievance to his shoulders for a man twice that age. Arthur had seen his potential, a promising young officer whose strengths of determination, ability and natural empathy with a horse were all qualities needed for the Artoriani. But Hueil had soured, his ambition turning to bitterness. The Pendragon tolerated his arrogance because there was just reason behind that sourness, but he was disappointed in the lad, knew the time would soon come to find some excuse to be rid of him. For a young man, eager and capable in a fight, it must gall like ill-fitting harness to a plough team to have a father who refused to see the creeping danger of settlers encroaching his land. A Godly man, Hueil's father Caw trusted in the Lord for deliverance. Hueil, sensibly in Arthur's eye, placed his trust more to a sword's edge. It was plain evident that unless the father took to defence soon, his land would be swamped by Scotti settlers and Hueil would be left with next to naught when the time came to step into Caw's boots. Arthur remembered well the years of frustration serving under Vortigern, years of waiting for the right opportunity to take what he wanted, and because he remembered, had sympathised with this other young man. But Hueil had not the forbearance that Arthur had shown. His was a gnawing impatience, extending into manifold grievances and quick anger. Arthur wondered for how much longer the lad would wait on his father. Until an opportune excuse to forcibly take his birthright presented itself?

Experience, and a shrewd ability to judge a man's character, showed the Pendragon that one so quick to draw a blade and slow to concede defeat could now prove dangerous. Hueil's was always one of the strongest voices when swearing loyalty, his was the most savage of swords in battle. Yet for all that, and the understanding behind the reasons, Arthur mistrusted him, and this winter at Caer Luel had strengthened those minor, niggling suspicions into firm fact. Arthur knew of Hueil's bedding with Morgause. He liked it not, but was astute enough to reckon it easier to watch someone already being watched. As things stood, Hueil posed only a small threat for he had few friends. Aside, Arthur wagered, if he gave Morgause enough rope, happen she would fashion her own noose. If it were Hueil who was foolish enough to provide her with it then that was his misfortune.

That Morgause was in some way responsible for this quarrel, Arthur had no doubt – the woman was behind every disagreement, every grumble and sour word. By right, she ought not to be feasting in this hall, but as his 'guest' how could she not attend? By right, she should be dead, alongside her British husband and Picti lover! But those Eastern Picti of Caledonia were not quite as settled as Arthur liked to make out, and while they alone would not have the men for many a season to go against him again, he could not give cause for the tribal clans to unite. Hanging a priestess of the Mother Goddess might just give them cause to pitch their spears together and what Morgause and Lot had failed to accomplish he could achieve with one hanging – an achievement he would rather not aim for. Aye well, that was his excuse. He knew it went deeper than that.

'You could never execute me, Arthur,' she had said as the Picti had handed her over into his care – his care mark you, they had made it quite clear that she was not to be harmed. 'I belonged to your father, you would never willingly destroy something that he had loved.'

Arthur glanced at her, sitting three places from Gwenhwyfar, calmly eating, dressed in fine, bright-dyed silk. She was a beautiful woman, Morgause. Nearing her late thirties, still with the figure and looks of a girl. Some of it was painted beauty, those heavily lined eyes of kohl and the lead and chalk powder to the face, but Morgause would always be as a Venus, drawing men around her as moths to the flame. Batting their wings against the heat, only to fall scorched and broken. He ought to make an end of her, toss her over the battlements, leave her for the wolves or pitch her, bound hand and foot, into the peat bogs. But he could not. He could not in cold blood murder her – Arthur had a shrewd realisation that in death, Morgause would haunt him more potently than when she was alive and under his constant watch. Aside all that, it brought him some small, pleasurable revenge knowing that she feared his intentions, even if that pleasure was personal and probably most unwise. He held the leash secured tight around her pretty, swan-white neck and he could pull that noose tighter, when and where he wanted. Except he could not admit, even to himself, that to tighten that noose fully would be impossible.

'What is all this?' Arthur snapped, taking his eyes and thoughts from Morgause. 'If you have a thing to say, Hueil, then say it openly. To me.'

Hueil's frustration was running deeper than ever it had before. Frustration with what lay before his nose; at his many brothers who were as blinded as his father; and impatience with Arthur who gave him as little regard as did his father. For three long years had Hueil served the Pendragon with courage, strength and loyalty. What had been his reward? Naught. Still he was a minor officer, nor had he been awarded personal triumph. Why was he not yet Decurion? Why did Arthur not show him the respect he gave to others – to Bedwyr for instance, this new untried boy? Hueil was thrown only the picked bones, while Bedwyr received the flesh from the carcass.

'Well?' Arthur folded his arms, stood calm. Deceptively calm.

Glowering, Hueil wiped the back of his hand at the drip of blood coming from his nose, smearing it across his upper lip and cheek. Squarely he met Arthur's gaze. 'I said naught of consequence.'

Bedwyr sprang forward, fists clenched. 'Naught of consequence! By God you cur's whelp; you insult Lady Gwenhwyfar's honour and then say 'tis naught of consequence! I shall have your tongue and manhood for this!' Nostrils flared, eyes wide, he raised his dagger, ready to strike. Arthur reacted with skill and speed, knocking the blade from Bedwyr's fist, sending the lad sprawling.

'I will have no killing!' the Pendragon hissed through clamped teeth. Breathing hard through exertion and anger, he turned on his heel and asked again of Hueil, 'What causes this disturbance?'

Hueil realised, too late, that his tongue had run away with words that would have been better left unsaid. Lowering clenched fists, he made a step away from Arthur, offering submission. 'I uttered some fool remark.' He faked a laugh. 'My senses are awash with your fine wine.'

'To that I agree,' Arthur replied drily, 'yet still I wish to know what it was you said.'

Hueil lifted his head, tilting his chin into his familiar arrogant angle. 'I urge you to leave it my Lord. I spoke out of turn. Let it rest at that.' Were he a king in his own right, no man could have argued at that, no man, not even the Pendragon, would have dared give him the look Arthur was now giving him.

There followed several moments of uneasy silence. Hueil glowered, there was no getting out of this. All right then, since Arthur forced him to speak, he would say what he had to say plainly. 'I asked Bedwyr how he spends his leisure now that you are returned. Now that he can no longer visit your wife's chamber of an evening.' Silence was rapidly falling around the Hall. All heard Hueil say, 'I remarked that he had spent so much time in her private company while you were away, that he could now, surely, wield a spindle with better dexterity than his sword.'

There were a few titters of laughter from those of the Caer, not from Arthur's men. Gwenhwyfar sat silent, her heart beating fast as a stampeding herd of horse. Arthur tolerated Hueil, she did not. She disliked his arrogance, disliked more his intimate association with Morgause.

Bedwyr had scrambled to his feet, hot coals of rage burning his cheeks, knuckles white on clenched fists. His answer stung like an irate wasp. 'My friendship is no secret. I am often in the King and Lady Pendragon's shared company.'

Hueil sniggered. 'It is not your visits when my Lord Pendragon is in residence that I question, but those when he is not.'

Llacheu and Gwydre huddled deeper into their concealing shadow, the younger boy clutching at his elder brother's tunic.

Llacheu placed his arm around the boy's shoulders, drawing him close, his brotherly protection diminishing his own rapid anxiety. The voices were loud, threatening, the atmosphere that had a moment since been of congenial laughter, blasted suddenly into tense hostility.

'Will there be a fight?' Gwydre asked in hushed whisper.

Llacheu shook his head for answer. 'Da would not permit brawling.' His reassurance did not sound convincing. He was uncertain what was being said, unsure of the dark implications, but understood well enough that something unpleasant was happening. And that the unpleasantness was directed at Bedwyr and his mam.

Morgause dipped her fingers into a bowl of scented water, elegantly wiped them on the linen towel proffered by a slave. She had known, when innocently letting slip certain information, that Hueil would not be able to keep it to himself for long. How predictable the poor fool was!

Gwenhwyfar sat, hands clenched. She wanted to answer Hueil, wanted to cross the feasting Hall in quick strides and strike that suggestive leer from his sour face. She was shaking too much, her legs would not carry her the distance. She must remain seated, it was for her husband to deal with this.

Arthur was saying nothing. He stood with eyes semi-closed, head inclined. The entire Hall had fallen silent, save for the snarl of dogs fighting over scattered meat and fish.

With a brief flicker of passing uncertainty, Hueil glanced at Morgause. She nodded imperceptibly, a slight movement of her head, a slow down-sweep of her lashes. He was doing well, so long as he did not stretch the mileage. Placing spread fingers on his chest, he intoned, 'What have I said that can cause Bedwyr such concern? I only repeat that which is on every man's lips. Since he claims innocence why does he seem so hostile?'

'You dung heap!' Bedwyr lunged forward, only to be blocked a second time, more forcefully, by Arthur.

'Hold!'

'But Lord . . . !' Bedwyr dropped back, his pride hurt; hurt more when Arthur again rounded on him. 'I said hold! Obey me!' To

306

Hueil he said, 'You had best be certain of gossip, you take a chance by daring to repeat it before me.' He turned away, sickened. So the thing was to happen. The dog was turning to bite the master's hand. It was expected, but Arthur had not bargained on Gwenhwyfar's hand also being mauled.

'I would advise,' Morgause's voice was silk smooth in the silence of the Hall, 'seeking what truth lies behind this gossip.'

Arthur whirled around, strode across the tessellated flooring that showed ample evidence of once seeing better days. He put his hands to the table, opposite her, leant his weight on them, and said, his face contorted, 'When I require your advice, madam, I shall seek it. I would suggest not holding your breath for that time.' He swung away, took one step, was halted in mid-stride by her calling:

'Bedwyr's attentions to your wife are witnessed. You were away some many weeks, Arthur, a woman can grow lonely for a man's company. Were I a husband,' Morgause was saying, her words throbbing through Gwenhwyfar's swirling head, 'I would ask, if a wife were seen kissing and embracing a young man in the openness of a garden when her husband was abroad, what intimacies then, might occur in the privacy of her chamber?'

Gwenhwyfar felt the colour drain from her face, her hand went involuntarily to her mouth, she rammed the back of her hand hard against her lips to stem the cry of rage.

Bedwyr was incensed. He appealed to Arthur, 'You cannot believe this vomited filth!'

'You were seen, Bedwyr,' Morgause persisted, as calm as a tranquil river. 'Before you make open love to a married woman, particularly a woman married to a king, I suggest you ensure you are not over-watched.' She selected a honey cake and bit delicately into it.

§ LVII

Hushed murmurs, a few mutters of protest from Arthur's men were heard, but the invited guests this night were mostly from the settlement and stronghold – Councillors, dignitaries, men of trade and note – and well acquainted with Bedwyr. He had flirted with almost every woman present, tossing flattering remarks, giving looks of appraisal; drawing pink blushes to a maiden's cheek and to the elder matrons', pleased that they could still draw a young man's attention. Women – and husbands – exchanged knowing glances. Aye, the lad was one for the ladies! Gwenhwyfar felt suddenly sick with apprehension. Her stomach heaved to her throat, her body trembled. Too easy was it to read those sneering looks on people's faces, to imagine what vileness they were thinking and murmuring. People would more easily believe the excitement of lies, than accept the tedium of truth. Arthur had his back to the table, to her. With a slight turn of his head he cast a sideways glance at her, looked quickly away before their eyes should meet. She blinked aside tears. Surely he did not believe these lies? Did not doubt her faithfulness . . . surely?

He was a few yards from her. Staring ahead, not looking at her, his fists were clenched tight, the nails biting into the soft flesh of his palms, fighting the pain of uncertainty. Somehow Gwenhwyfar managed to get to her feet, though her body was shaking, her knees threatening to buckle. She walked calmly and with dignity around the table. Faces and voices faded. Nothing, no one, mattered except Arthur. She stared steadily at him as she came, people parting to make way for her. What madness was happening here this night?

'My husband, you are my only love. We have our disagreements and our sadness, as do all partners of marriage, but never would I betray you or that love. Never.'

Hueil had followed Arthur, stood eight paces to his other side. He snorted derision. 'Do you not expect her to deny it?' He was warming to this thing, the overspill of resentment frothing to the surface. 'They are lovers. Both have betrayed you as king and husband and cousin. Neither of them is openly going to admit it.'

'Ask whether she denies allowing Bedwyr to her chamber when she is alone. Whether she denies meeting with him in the garden, embracing him.' Morgause was smiling, pleasantly, almost off-handedly. The odious bitch!

Gwenhwyfar flung back a taut answer. 'I do not deny either. Bedwyr is my kin, he is as a brother to me.'

Morgause gave a low chuckle of amusement. 'Yet, he is not, technically, a brother, is he?' Her voice carried very well, even at a soft murmur.

Arthur had not moved, saying nothing. Gwenhwyfar stepped closer to him, her hand extended but not daring to touch him. 'You do not believe this nonsense! Do you?' Her hurt for a moment had flared into anger, was struck suddenly to fear when he at last met her eyes. 'You do!' she gasped. 'My god, you do!,' She bit her lip, let her imploring hand drop to her side; dared not reach out, lest he brush her aside.

Arthur bit his bottom lip. He was breathing fast, his nostrils flaring, chest heaving for air, fingers gripping the cold touch of his sword pommel. He dared not take a glance towards the walls, dared not look, for he knew they were closing in on him, surrounding him, waiting to fall and crush him. He wanted to run, reach for cool, sweet air, for the vault of unbounded, starlit sky. Nor dared he look at Gwenhwyfar, for fear that just this once she lied to him.

Their quarrels were nothing, heated words between two people with opposing wills, nothing more than sparing or sword practice, an edge against which to sharpen ideas and opinions. All right, he admitted, whores had shared his bed even when they should not, but they meant nothing more than a way to satisfy a need. And aye, she had left him for a while, and in his solitude he had turned to Elen, but Gwenhwyfar had gone because of her grief, not because of their often exchanged anger. He loved Gwenhwyfar, above all life he loved Gwenhwyfar, and it hurt deeper than any battlefield wound that others could snarl these vile accusations at her. He ought to make an end of Morgause, make an end to this incessant stirring of hatred and malice, and that hurt more, hurt that even to protect the woman he would willingly die for, he did not have it in him to kill Morgause.

Unaware of his King's surging anguish, Hueil made another step forward. 'I regret this must come into the open, but the truth ought not be hidden behind shadows. As one of your friends,' he flicked his eyes around the assembly, 'I am relieved that I found the courage to inform you of this treachery.'

Bedwyr crossed the distance between himself and Hueil in three long strides, swung him angrily around. 'Friend? Courage? Aye, it takes courage to repeat such filth!'

Hesitant at first, Gwenhwyfar reached out and rested her hand lightly on Arthur's hand, a cold hand that was clasped so tight around his sword. When he did not flinch from her touch, she said, 'It is not I who lie, my Lord. Not I who deceive you.' She lowered her eyes. 'On the life of our two sons, Arthur, I do not lie.'

Hueil laughed. With his fists bunched at his lips, head back, chest thrusting out, he bellowed laughter. 'What!' he guffawed, 'Arthur's sons? It is in my mind that the King let the one drown beacause he suspected it was not his to call son!'

A dreadful silence slammed across the room.

For Arthur, it was as though an enchantment had been broken. He spun Hueil around with his right hand, his left fist coming back and forward in a movement so fast that few saw it. Hueil staggered, fell, fresh blood streaming from his nose. He was a fighting man, a tribes-warrior and the eldest son of a chieftain. No man treated him so. Not even a king. Enraged, he was instantly on his feet. Heedless of the blood spurting down his chin and tunic, he lowered his head and butted Arthur full in the stomach, the force sending them both reeling, crashing into the table behind, where Morgause sat. She moved, calmly but quickly, left the Hall, returned to her chamber with a slight, triumphant smile. Arthur was fighting, and doubt had been sown on Gwenhwyfar's fidelity. Hueil? Arthur could not have him killed, for he was an honoured chieftain's son and the repercussions would be immense were the Pendragon to act so foolishly. But Hueil would be forced to leave Arthur's service, would become his enemy, and where would he go, save back to his father's lands? And once there, it would take small contrivance to help him take a kingship – and set her free.

Morgause inclined her head to the two guards outside her door and entered her chamber. For all her annoyance at being kept here against her will at Caer Luel, it had been a most interesting evening.

§ LVIII

No one had noticed Morgause leave. Gwenhwyfar was swept aside, almost forgotten, as the crowd formed a hurried, eager circle around the two men. There was nothing people liked better than to watch a fight. Arthur was stripping his leather jerkin, his sword belt, Bedwyr taking them from him, saying with fervour, 'Leave some of him for me to finish!' Gwenhwyfar stuffed her fingers in her mouth to stop the scream escaping.

The two men circled, eye fixed to eye, watching for that first important move, fists clenched, muscles taut. Hueil kicked, his boot missing Arthur's thigh as Arthur stepped aside, his foot in turn missing Hueil's outstretched leg by the breadth of a hair. Again they circled, sprang, hands gripping on tunic-clad arms, their wrestling evenly matched for strength, though Arthur was the taller. He brought his opponent down, both men collapsing to the floor, where they rolled several times, neither able to gain the advantage.

Arthur was on top, shifted his weight and Hueil thrust up with his knee, sending the Pendragon careering backwards into the circle of cheering onlookers. Hueil was up. Roaring he smashed his fist into Arthur's stomach; he doubled, but as he straightened, sent his own fist upwards into Hueil's chin. They traded blows, each punch finding a mark. Both were bloodied, Hueil from his still streaming nose, Arthur from a jagged gash raking from temple to eyebrow.

Suddenly they were down once more, Arthur on top with his hands gripping Hueil's hair, lifting his head, banging it again and again to the floor.

Gwenhwyfar clawed her way through the crowd who cheered, calling advice, whistling encouragement. 'Stop it!' she screamed, 'stop them!' She tugged at one man's tunic, tried another, an officer this time who, in the heat of excitement thrust her aside. Desperate, she ran to Arthur, pulling at him, pleading. He took no notice, continued pounding Hueil's head.

That grip on his arm, the slight distraction, was enough for Hueil to gather his senses and effort of strength. He shoved Arthur from him, sending him and Gwenhwyfar sprawling to the floor. Bedwyr dragged Gwenhwyfar away, holding her tight to him, cried, 'Leave them, Gwen, it is for Arthur to finish, Arthur alone and in his own way.'

She struggled. 'Kick the bastard, Arthur!' Bedwyr was shouting. 'Use your feet, man!'

Twisting free of Bedwyr's hold – he barely heeded her going – Gwenhwyfar thrust her way out through the press of rowdy spectators, one man only murmuring a brief apology on realising who she was. Women stood shoulder to shoulder with their menfolk; some shouting louder, even coarser than their husbands. They were like animals; a wolf-pack, baying for the kill at the scent of blood. Then a low moan swept around the circle as Arthur took a sharp blow, staggered and lost his balance. Hueil, grinning, took advantage, jumped, pinned his opponent down.

Gwenhwyfar did not look back. She heard the howl rising from thirsting lips, encouraging the savagery of one victim pitted against another. A bestial lust that Rome in her day had exploited with the staged deaths of the arena. Cock, bull, bear. Men, women and children. Covering her ears with her hands, she fled, ran to where there would be no people, to where she could hide, curl into a foetal ball and submit to the misery. She went to where she had always gone when seeking solitude in this place brim-full of wearisome people; to the garden.

There was no moon this night; the few lights that did emit from small windows and open colonnades casting only a dim glow. The overgrowth of winter-dead shrubs and plants, the neglected trees, cast weird and wonderful shadows against the darkness. Gwenhwyfar slumped against the wall of the fish pool, which held only weeds, no fish. She was sobbing, long shuddering breaths catching harsh in her aching chest. Nothing made sense, nothing seemed real, solid. She huddled, blind to sound, touch and feel, spiralling down into a pit of reaching, grappling hands. Vaguely aware of numbing cold and throbbing pain, she slithered to the hard frost-gripped ground. None of it mattered. None of it, for she thought, wrongly, that Arthur had listened to them. Listened to

312

their lies; believed them. Worry, hate, jealousy, subdued emotions and feelings which by accustomed habit she usually thrust aside, rose unbidden to the surface. Why had he believed them? And now Arthur was fighting. For her? No, not for her, for his own hurt pride. The confused emotions swirled through hurt and back to fear; fear for Arthur. Fighting. He delighted in battle, but was not so good when it came to wrestling. He relied on weapons, his skill with sword and shield unequalled. He could fight well enough to hold his own if evenly matched, but Hueil was accomplished with his fists.

Arthur was breathing hard, sweat trickling into his eyes, soaking into the linen of his shirt. He crouched, again circling, balancing lightly on the balls of his feet, waiting for the chance to spring and gain a firm hold. His one satisfaction Hueil was breathing as hard, the sweat standing as proud on his forehead. The intensity of anger had given way to something deeper in Arthur. This was something more between them now, more than proving a point.

Some watching, Bedwyr, Geraint and Meriaun, men who knew Arthur well, realised the mutation to this darker side. Morgause, with her eye for seizing power, would have recognised it instantly, were she there. Gwenhwyfar certainly did, which is why she had fled. This was the young stallion challenging the old. Only one could lead. Only one could win, and live. There was nothing visibly to show how the thing had shifted, how the shadow blended from a heated quarrel to the death fight; from the settling of angry words to the taking of leadership. However it happened, the watchers' intoxication subtly altered, their excited shouts beginning to fade. This thing had become serious.

Hueil, from where many would later wonder, suddenly had a dagger in his hand. Some said he had been passed it, others that he had it hidden in his boot; no matter, it was in his hand, slicing at Arthur's belly. Astonished, Arthur leapt back as he saw the blade flash, but not fast enough. It carved a streak of blood and he blocked a second slash with his arm, using it as a shield. He tried ramming his elbow hard against Hueil's chest but his foot slipped, forcing him to spring apart, eyes, ears, senses, oblivious of everything save this man

313

trying to kill him. Someone was quick-witted enough to toss a dagger to Arthur, but he missed the catch, it fell at his feet. Hueil tried to kick it aside but Arthur was quicker. He sprang, rolled, was up, the dagger in his hand in one fluid movement.

Someone said, 'Should this not be stopped?' Several agreed. None made any movement.

Llacheu sat crouched in the shadow of the wall, Gwydre's head burrowed into his tunic, the younger boy shaking with fear. Both had witnessed their mother, blinded by fear and tears, leave. Both, though not understanding the shouting, realised enough to know that something awful was passing this night. Their mam was upset. Da was fighting. No ordinary fight as the men often displayed on the training ground. No friendly wrestle to keep muscles and wits sharp. This was the real, deadly thing. He was an intelligent boy, Llacheu. He listened, watched, gained much from his observance of father and men. Saw too the women's side, the love and hurt Gwenhwyfar had for Arthur. Understood it, for as a child he loved his father beyond question but was often confused by his acid temper. Knew also that his da loved his mam. Why did they quarrel? And why had his father not ordered Hueil instantly arrested when he had spoken those terrible accusations? Llacheu recognised malicious lies when he heard them, did not his father?

He had to see for himself, had to watch! The shouting, the cheering, he had tolerated, for such noise was always at the training ground: men's good-natured jeering at a companion's ill-timed stroke of the sword or bad javelin throw; bursting laughter when someone was unhorsed; cheers, respectful praise for quick thinking. This unnerving semi-silence was altogether different. No words, only the occasional sharp breath or exclamation. What was happening?

He stood, settled his brother safe in the corner. 'Stay there,' he ordered. Gwydre, his lip caught between chattering teeth, nodded.

It was easy for Llacheu to push his way through. No one paid him heed, assumed he was some impertinent servant boy. He squirmed to the front just as Hueil first produced the dagger, bit back a startled cry as he saw his father's shirt tear and soak with blood. He watched in fascinated horror, everything seemingly slowed, drained. Sound, action. Hate and blood rising in a slow stench of time-captured movement.

His father parried a blow, thrust with his own dagger. Hueil feinted to the left. Arthur as he caught the ruse, countered, slipped again on the blood-stained floor, went down. Fell, his face pale, staring gape-mouthed as Hueil seized his chance and with dagger raised, came to make Arthur's end.

Llacheu screamed. His body moved; it seemed as if he were running through thigh-deep mud, he couldn't get there; couldn't get to his da! Bedwyr too was pounding forward as Llacheu ran. The boy was there first, leaping at Hueil, his hands thrusting the weapon aside, deflecting the blade to rip through his own tunic. Hueil staggered under the unexpected weight of fury. He cried out, dropped his weapon. Llacheu fell, tears of rage and pain mingling with the soaking blood.

All life in that room paused, became petrified for two, three heartbeats. Bedwyr stilled in mid-run; men's mouths fell open in half-shout; women, hands clamped to lips, chalk-white faces. Stilled, as if a spell had cast over them all.

As suddenly the spell was lifted. Movement, noise. Screams from women, confusion, a babble of angry shouts and jeers. The crowd surged forward. Someone, a friend, had the sense to drag Hueil aside, usher him away out through the servants and slaves gathered beyond the kitchen archway. A sword was pressed in his hand. Go they urged, take a horse, go quickly!

Gwenhwyfar was cold. She was shivering. She fought to get herself to her feet, could not, gave up the struggle. Her body ached, her head throbbed. She wished she would die, here and now, wished death could end this misery and pain. A shadow of movement, a figure ran, breathing heavily, crouching low through the garden. He ran to the far wall, flung a handful of stones at square panes of time-dusted glass.

'Morgause!' The voice was slurred, urgent with breathless fear. 'Morgause!'

She came to the window, opened it, peered out. 'Hueil? What in . . . ?'

'Quiet! Listen to me.'

'Dare you use that tone with me!'

'Silence, woman! I need to leave. I have slain Arthur's son.'

Gwenhwyfar struggled to her feet, the words slamming into her like a spear thrust. Arthur's son? My son? She staggered forward.

'You cannot leave without me, Hueil!' Morgause squealed, sudden panic rising in her.

'I must, I have no time to take you. Arthur will be after me for this, after me for my life, and I shall have no chance of survival if I am caught.' Hueil shuddered at the thought of the death Arthur would impose. Buried in sand, with the head only displayed, a blunted sword to hew at the neck . . . torn apart by horses crazed with firebrands . . .

Gwenhwyfar let go the support of the wall and crumpled to the gravel pathway. Her son. Her son was dead? Which son? Gwydre, Llacheu . . .

'I hear the hunt; they are coming.' Hueil swung aside, darted for the shadows, calling, 'I'll be back for you, Morgause. When I have taken my kingdom and Arthur dare raise no hand against me, I pledge I shall come back for you!'

§ LIX

Arthur stood at the end of Llacheu's bed, body slumped, head bowed. One of the few remaining lights was flickering, the wick burning low; a wraith of smoke spiralled upward from it. Dawn must not be far off. He rose, walked with acute stiffness to the irritating candle and snuffed it out. For a long while he stood looking at it. Empty of feeling, empty of thought. The boy slept. The injury looked worse than it really was. Within the passing of a few months, there would barely be a scar. Not on the skin; not for Llacheu. But for himself and Gwenhwyfar?

He crossed the room, opening the door with care, slipped out into the dim-lit corridor beyond. Bedwyr sprang to his feet, jumping to attention. He was dishevelled, dark beard growth shadowing his chin. One hand resting on the door catch, Arthur regarded his cousin, snorted, 'Do I appear to you as you do to me?'

Bedwyr attempted a lop-sided grin. 'At least I don't have those livid cuts and bruises.'

Closing the door, Arthur placed his arm around Bedwyr's shoulder, began walking with him. 'Remind me, next time you quarrel, lad, to let you sort it out on your own.' Arthur touched his fingers to his swollen cheek, winced. 'There must be less painful ways of settling an argument!'

'Arthur, I . . .'

'Leave it. There is no need for words.' Arthur paused, made his decision. 'I intend to leave as planned. Morgause remains here but I need someone to watch over her. I want you to be that someone.'

Bedwyr hung his head, bit his lip, found the courage to say, with trembling voice, 'Then you do not want me near you. You do not trust me.'

They had reached Arthur's chamber. He peered inside, Gwenhwyfar was asleep. They had found her, huddled and exhausted, and carried her here. Arthur himself had undressed her, held her close while he told her that their son was going to be all right.

To Bedwyr, he explained, 'I ask you to guard Morgause, lad, because, beyond my wife, you are the only other person I can, do, trust implicitly.'

The night passed quiet; Arthur had lain beside Gwenhwyfar on the bed, intending to rest for a while only, had fallen asleep almost before his eyes had closed. It was mid-morning before he awoke. As he moved, Gwenhwyfar said, 'Do you sleep fully clothed now, then?'

Arthur opened one eye. She sat propped beside him, her hair tumbling around her face, cascading down her shoulders. Her eyes were puffy, her skin pale as fresh-settled snow. He sat up, groaned as seemingly a thousand muscles roared protest. 'It saves the bother of dressing.' He swung his legs to the floor, groaned again. 'Mithras love, but I am stiff.'

'I expect your body aches too.' With a smile, Gwenhwyfar slid in the lewd jest.

Arthur shifted, slowly, to look at her. He cupped her face in his hand. 'You scared me last night, Cymraes.'

Instantly she flashed back. 'As you scared me!'

'What was I to have done? Laughed it off? Let them walk away?'

'You are the King. There are better ways of proving something a lie than fighting over it.'

Arthur could not answer that. His body told him the same, but when Gwenhwyfar quietly added, 'Or were you not sure it was a lie?' he caught his breath.

Arthur sprang round, grasped her hair, jerking her head sharply back. He was leaning very close, his breath angry on her face. 'Let me say this once, and once only. If ever I find you in a compromising situation with a man, then I would not bother fighting for you. You and he would be instantly dead. That, I shall personally see to.' The force behind his anger took her breath away, for they were not words stated for effect. He meant them.

'You love me that much?' she whispered.

'That much.'

§ LX

Two people, many miles from Caer Luel, were interested in the animosity that had overspilled into hatred between Arthur and Hueil of Alclud. One was the Lady Winifred. Her ears pricked with interest when traders from the north-western coast brought embellished gossip of the fight. A pity that the boy had not been killed after all, but he was young still, he might well not reach maturity. For Arthur she was a little more sympathetic – it would not suit her purpose to have him dead, not until those two brats of Gwenhwyfar's

318

were safely out of the way. As for Gwenhwyfar herself, well, once tales were rumoured they were hard to set aside, and Winifred had every intention of ensuring the gossip of the Queen's infidelity received much airing. Morgause she did not know, nor wanted to; Arthur was a fool not to have the woman dispatched, but then, Arthur always had been the fool where women were concerned.

It was Amlawdd, a petty lord with a smallholding of land over to the western coats beyond Aquae Sulis, who was the most interested in the spiralling gossip. Hueil's mother and his own mother were cousins, and the boy from the North had come to live in the South for several years. Amlawdd and he had run as cubs from the same pack, learning to hunt and ride and fight together. But young whelps grow to manhood, and the friendships of childhood dwindle with age, the distance between the two boys who had become men greatening when Hueil joined with Arthur.

Amlawdd was no friend of the Pendragon. A family feud, begun with Arthur's father taking the wife of Amlawdd's eldest brother as his own, had expanded through hatred and murder. The enmity separated the two as effectively as the Roman-built Wall had once separated North from South. Delight abounded at Amlawdd's marsh-bound hill-fortress when, as spring flourished into full blossom, he received personal written word from his boyhood companion, confirming the gossip. So Hueil was to go against the King? Hah! Amlawdd would be behind him in that! It was too early yet to call a war-hosting, but never was it too early to start forging swords, crafting shields and fashioning war spears!

June 464

§ LXI

It was time Arthur had a permanent base – well past time. He needed a home for his wife and his sons, a stronghold to lodge and train his cavalry, and pastures to breed and graze his horses. He needed, above all, to establish a secure and permanent base from which to rule. Until now everything was scattered, or transitory. Marching camps, temporary grazing, a small herd of mares here, youngstock there. He needed somewhere of his own. The Summer Land and Dumnonia was littered with abandoned old hill-forts that had seen their use before Rome came with her tidy ideas of building towns and legionary fortresses. Some of these he knew well, others were vaguely remembered from those days of serving as a raw youth in Vortigern's army. The place he needed would be well within his own undisputedly held land; somewhere from where any activities along the Saex borders could be dealt with quickly and efficiently. Not too far from where he could keep close watch on Ambrosius and Amlawdd – especially Amlawdd – and from where he could ride north, should, or rather when, the need to face Hueil came.

For some weeks, during the blazing heat of this early June, he had felt a prickly sensation of unease regarding this peaceful indifference that had settled on Britain like a quietly fallen mantle of contented sleep. It was welcome, this peace, most welcome, but then, was there often not a dropping of the wind or a ceasing of rain before the real storm thundered its anger? Agreed borders were too quiet; sea lanes almost empty save for the trading ships. The economy was picking up. The harvests had been good. Ambrosius, and even Winifred, were being congenial. Hengest was getting old, his son, Aesc would soon be ruling in the Cantii land so it was rumoured. Would the treaties hold? And for how long would the young men of the English – all the English, not merely the Cantii – be content with growing their crops, grazing their cattle and raising their sons to

323

be farmers, not warriors? How long before another such as Icel decided to rattle the peace into a bloody wave of excitement? There had been no movement from Hueil, no raiding, no killing. But could it, would it, all last?

Arthur doubted it, but it was best to cut the hay while the sun shone – and while the blue-skied warmth of June smiled on the world, he would take time to establish his own stronghold. A place fit for a king.

Easing the chin strap of his helmet with one finger, Arthur glanced behind at Gwenhwyfar who rode with the boys. He pointed ahead, answering her weary expression of appeal. 'If my memory serves me correct we will see the place I'm thinking of just beyond this rise.' He had to assume this was a temporary hold on war. Had to make ready for the next upsurge of wanting and greed. He was the Pendragon; was supreme.

And he intended to stay that way.

Gwenhwyfar was laughing, and again Arthur turned, his frown creasing his face. Llacheu and Gwydre had joined her delighted laughter as young Ider said something that increased their amusement. Arthur could not catch the words. Irritably he faced forward, stared hotly between his mare's ears. Ider was a boy still, for all his size and strength. He showed promise, but then, so had Hueil at first. Had placing the lad among the men of Gwenhwyfar's personal bodyguard been a wise decision? The lad took too much on himself, assumed too great a liberty between that fine line of devotion to his Lady for her protection and that other kind of devotion. Arthur clenched his teeth. Stupid, unjustified thoughts! But thoughts, for all their unwarranted beginnings, that would not, could not, leave him.

Ah, Morgause had known full well what she was doing when she had used her lover to plant seeds of doubt against Gwenhwyfar in Arthur's mind! Except that it was no longer Bedwyr who posed a threat to Gwenhwyfar's love and loyalty, but a gangling, over-sized youth who grinned and eyed her inanely, like a love-sick moon-child. Ider followed at her heel like a motherless pup, was always there.

324

Glancing over his shoulder he saw Ider riding close at Gwenhwyfar's side. Na, he was no longer a greenstick boy, he had matured since he had come all those months past from Eboracum, become a man with the rutting instinct of all young men out for first blood. And Gwenhwyfar was a beautiful woman. She had borne children, yet her figure was as slender as it had been in her youth, her hair still shone with that alluring glow of sunlight shimmering on beaten copper, and her green eyes were as alive as stars burning on a frosted winter's night. Gwenhwyfar might well, as she professed, be only fond of the boy, but it was not fondness that Ider returned. Arthur's teeth sank into his lower lip. He recognised that appreciative gaze all too well. Gods, had he himself not looked at enough women with that same lusting eye? Happen it was time he moved Ider to some other post.

Ahead, Cei had dropped out from the foreguard and wheeled his mount to drop in alongside Arthur. The Pendragon sighed. Problems. One after another whirling like scavenging ravens. Cei was daily becoming more reticent, more jealous of the favours given to other men. Some imagined bitterness was eating him as mould eats into the flesh of fruit. Arthur would have to sort it before it festered into something too cancerous to be amputated.

'Is that it?' Cei was pointing to a hill a few miles ahead.

Squinting into the brightness, Arthur thrust aside his grumbling muddle of brooding thoughts. He nodded. 'Aye, it is.'

His black mood left as suddenly as it had come. Arthur halted his mare, waited for Gwenhwyfar to draw rein next to him. Leaning from the saddle, he caught her hand, dipped his head eagerly to the shape of that hill rising above the heat-haze and clusters of scrubby trees and bushes. 'Our home, Cymraes. Caer Cadan.'

§ LXII

Gwenhwyfar stood on the highest point of the hill, knuckles resting lightly on her hips, eyes narrowed to see better across the distance.

At this height, there was a lively wind which lifted her braids and toyed with the wisps of loose hair that never could be tamed into conforming. Below, in a patchwork of colour, the Summer Land stretched rich and fertile, spreading like some elaborately embroidered tapestry. This, literally, was summer land. Come winter, the rivers and streams rose and covered the flat miles of marshland that never drained completely dry, even when elsewhere was thirsting under drought. Winter was a time of boats and fishing, of lakes and water-meadows idling around the few, scattered islands of high ground.

With the onset of evening, the day's heat-haze had eased and the view from up here, beneath a mackerel and mare's-tail sky, was beautiful. The blue was the colour of a heron's egg, sweeping down to touch the grey-misted smudge of hills that strode along the distant horizons. And there, rising from the greens and yellows and browns, alone, and shouting its existence, the unmistakable shape of Yns Witrin.

Gwenhwyfar heard a footfall in the grass. She smiled and laid her head back into his shoulder as Arthur came up behind, encircled her waist with his arms. 'When I fled Less Britain,' she said, 'after you and I had spent those months there together as lovers, I came to be at Yns Witrin. Terrible things had happened to me, things I would rather not remember. I was alone, and lost and frightened. I was carrying your child, our first-born son. I walked often on the Tor, yet, never once was I aware of this place.'

'I am told it blends with these hills behind.' Arthur said, dipping his head to the range of hills running to the south-east. 'Caer Cadan is difficult to see unless you know where to look for it.'

Wrapping her arms around herself, Gwenhwyfar enclosed his embrace. The sky, where the sun was sinking beyond the horizon, was beginning to flush with red and gold; fingers of pink and purple reaching to caress the darkening blueness, touching the underside of the evening clouds. 'You never forget,' she said, letting her weight prop against him. 'You think you have. You think the bad memories of darkness and fear have been shut safe in a box, shut away for ever, but it comes back every so often, when you least expect it.

Something rattles the lid and you find yourself face to face with the things you thought you had forgotten.'

Arthur laid his cheek against her hair, breathed in her womanly scent. She wore no perfume, but she rinsed her hair with herbal infusions, and her clothes were laid in the oak chests among layers of dried lavender and rosemary. She smelt of flowers, meadows.

Closing her eyes, Gwenhwyfar too breathed in deeply, smelt horse and leather, masculine aromas mingling with the scent of the grass and the summer breeze. The air was cool, clear, with a permeating atmosphere of promise. 'This is a good place, Arthur.' She meant it. 'The Summer Land carries the blessing of the old gods and the peace of the new Christ.' She opened her eyes, turned her head to smile at him. 'It is a fitting site for the Pendragon to build his Caer.'

He kissed her neck, nuzzling her warmth and love. 'I came here during those first few months of serving Vortigern – I cannot recall why my patrol was in this area now. Huh,' he laughed to himself, 'I decided, even then, that one day I'd have the Summer Land back as my own and make my place here.' He turned her around to face inwards over the grass enclosure, indicated a gap in the weather-worn remains of the pre-Roman defensive ridge topping the natural hill. 'We'll build a main gateway there, and another over there.' He swung her to where he was pointing. 'With banks and ditches for defence and palisade along the top. On the land down there, we will grow grain to bake bread and brew ale. We can graze our horses and watch the foals grow fine and strong.'

Gwenhwyfar laughed at his enthusiasm. 'And build a suitable King's Hall I trust! No more flapping tents.'

'My dearest love, we will have a Hall to surpass any that has ever been built!' Arthur announced with a tossed laugh. He sprang away, his arms whirling as he strode across the daisy-littered grass. 'Here,' he said coming to a halt and gesturing to right and left. 'We will build it here, so that on evenings such as this we can stand together by the open door and look with pride and pleasure over our kingdom!'

Catching his eagerness, Gwenhwyfar went to him, threaded her arm through his. 'Oh aye? Build where the bite of the wind will whistle through the walls, rattle the window shutters and blow smoke back down the smoke-holes?'

Arthur wrinkled his nose at her jesting, swiping playfully at her. 'Those passing along the road to Yns Witrin will look up and see my fortress and our Hall sitting proud beyond formidable ramparts. They shall see and say, "*That is where our King sits in justice and protection.*"'

Gwenhwyfar's happy laughter was rising. 'Unless you also build a chapel,' she mocked, 'they will be raising their fists and saying "*that is where a heathen cur-son sits in tyranny over our Christian ways,*" and they will grunt and look at your magnificent Hall and berate you for using their taxes for such improper use!'

'They would not dare!' Arthur rolled his eyes innocently skyward, contemplated a sarcastic answer, then conceded, 'Aye, they would. All right, we will have a chapel too. It can go over there.' He pointed vaguely to a far corner, added wickedly, 'near the latrine.'

Gwenhwyfar slapped him playfully, he grabbed her around the waist and began to tickle her, his fingers biting between her ribs. She fought him off and ran giggling down the slope, Arthur in pursuit. He caught her, though not as quickly as he'd expected – she always had been fleet on her feet. They fell together, laughing wildly, rolling down the slope. Stopped against somebody's legs.

Clutching Gwenhwyfar to him, Arthur looked up to Cei's sullen countenance.

'I came to inform you,' his humourless tone matched the expression, 'that the men are assembled before the priest, awaiting your presence before blessings can be offered on the camp.'

'Oh.' Arthur coughed and released Gwenhwyfar who snorted, smothering further laughter. He pushed himself to his feet, brushed ineffectually at grass stains on his tunic, offered lamely, 'We were discussing the layout of buildings.'

'So I see.'

What was it with Cei? Standing there like some pompous school tutor, nostrils flaring, breath quickening. Was a husband not allowed to romp with his own wife? Arthur offered his hand to

Gwenhwyfar, pulled her to her feet, and turning deliberately from Cei, walked with her across the expanse of grass to where the men had pitched the tents. It had become habit for Cethrwm, their priest, to say some holy words before the first cooking fires were lit and the men took their ease. A habit Arthur could well do without, but most of his men followed this Christ God; he could not deny them their belief because it was not his own. No commander had that right.

Cei had dropped behind a pace. Older only by two summers, he looked as though the gap was nearer ten. His hair had receded and his facial skin was wrinkled, hanging in loose jowls around chin and throat. An old injury to his back bothered him, though he hid the pain well. It occurred to Arthur, a thought come unexpectedly, that he ought to give Cei more praise where it was due, for too often did he bark and growl at his cousin; occurred to him also that never once had he openly said thank you. Impulsively he turned, held out his hand, intending to invite the man to walk in company beside him, watched in horror as Cei's step faltered and, hand clasping at his chest, he stumbled to his knees.

Arthur rushed to his side, Gwenhwyfar, at his shout of alarm running with him. 'Fetch a medic!' Arthur cried, urgently cradling Cei into his arms, loosening the man's tunic and belt. 'Hurry, Cymraes!'

Cei was sweating, his skin clammy, a blue tinge to his lips, but the breathing was easier. Surely, his breathing was easier? 'God's love, Cei,' Arthur panted, 'don't die. I need you too much for you to die.' Tears slipped down the Pendragon's cheeks as his cousin and foster-brother clasped his hand, held tight as though he were a man drowning, with only a single rope to bring him safe ashore. He managed a wheezing smile, croaked through choking breath, 'Na lad, you'll not be getting rid of my sour face so easily.'

The first thing to be constructed in Arthur's new stronghold was a grave for Cei.

January 465

§ LXIII

The horses' breath billowed from their nostrils in great clouds of dragon smoke, rising with the steam from their thick winter coats. The riders too, exhaled white-misted breath whenever they spoke or laughed. Several rubbed arms with stiff hands or stamped numbed feet on the frozen ground as their sweating bodies cooled. It had been a fast, energetic chase, a hard gallop over several miles. What in Christ's good name was taking the dogs so long? They had run the boar to ground in this thicket, had sent the dogs in to flush him out. Well-trained dogs that would keep their distance.

Llacheu grinned at his brother, his bright-red cheeks glowing, hair tousled and eyes still watering from the whip of the wind. Despite the biting cold it was a good hunt, one of the best – aye well, the two boys had to take the adults' word for that, neither had hunted boar before. And by all that was dear, this boar was some wonderful initiation!

He was reputed to be a monster of a beast, striking terror into the hearts of the scattered farms and steadings around the new stronghold of Caer Cadan. Many a good hunter had set out to finish the brute, too many had failed to return.

The great boar, a fearsome old man of the woods, had grunted in annoyance at the first distant baying of the dogs as they discovered his scent beneath an aged oak, where some half-hour before he had been contentedly rooting for his breakfast. With speed amazing for his huge size, he trotted further from the disagreeable sounds. Twisting and turning his way through the patches of woodland he passed into open country where peasants scratched a living, and headed for the marshland over towards Yns Witrin, into the scattered thickets of alder and willow. The boar stopped once to scratch his snout in a muddied hollow, rooting for titbits; the dogs did not unduly bother him. They were a nuisance, but he had dealt with dogs before. And men.

Arthur hefted his spear, cast a glance at his sons who had inched forward. 'Stay back,' he ordered. 'When the dogs send him out, he'll be madder than a pain-racked bull.' Then he grinned at them. 'Your mam was quite right to protest at your coming. Boars are dangerous beasts, not to be trusted.' He winked. 'But a man has to learn how to hunt.'

'A man needs to learn many things before he can call himself a man.'

Arthur spun around, startled, as did the men with him. A young woman stood beneath the willows. Dressed in green and brown she blended with the winter-clad trees, seemed almost a part of them. Several men caught their breath, for she had not been there a moment earlier. 'You come to hunt the great boar?' she asked, stepping forward from the shadows, her earth-brown cloak sweeping back, revealing a lithe, slender figure. She was not beautiful, this young woman with dark hair and even darker eyes, but there was something about her that arrested a man's attention, something about the way that she half smiled. 'The King hunts the king,' she said, her eyes shining. Mocking? 'But which king will win?'

Arthur was no raw, superstitious youth, he did not believe in demons lurking among the shadows or an old hag's love potions, but this creature startled him, made his heart bump uneasy, the hairs rise on his neck. What he did not see with his own eyes he did not believe, yet, here was a woman who had come from nowhere. . . . He managed to stammer a greeting, adding with more confidence, 'You know who I am, Lady, but I know you not. What is your name?'

She smiled again, that half-smile, as she took another step from beneath the overhang of trees. 'Oh I know you, Arthur the Pendragon. I have known you since . . .' she fluttered her hand, tossing her hair back with a slight shake of her head. Her bright eyes were watching him, looking into him. 'Since before the dawn of my time.'

A whine came from within the trees, followed by a howl, picked up by others, rising almost instantly to wild baying. 'They've found the cur-son!' someone shouted. There was a general shuffling, men adjusting their grip on their heavy boar spears, eyes excitedly, anxiously searching the edge of the trees. Waiting. When Arthur looked again, quickly, over his shoulder, the woman was gone. Nothing to show she had been there, no movement of grass or branch, no footprint on the frost-wet ground. Then an outraged pig's squeal and the pack baying the find. Snarling. Yelping. Silence. A Decurion exchanged a grim look with Arthur.

'One's gone in, he's had it.'

Arthur nodded. Damn the dog! Good hounds were hard to come by, and some of these used this day were of the best. And damn that boar. Hunting dogs were valuable animals.

'Gwydre, step back,' Llacheu called to his brother. The younger boy waved him irritably to silence. How could he see from back there? He wanted to miss nothing, see everything.

'Gwydre!' Llacheu insisted, 'step back.'

Gwydre would be seeing his eighth summer this year. A lad with the likelihood of taking after his father in height, his mother's colouring. A boy full of laughter and mischief. Who, like his da, would never do as he was asked.

The hounds were giving full tongue. Something large was crashing about in the undergrowth, coming nearer. Arthur turned at his eldest son's voice, saw Gwydre hopping from one leg to the other. He motioned with his hand, letting go his firm grip on the spear. 'Get back, boy!' he cursed, 'this is no game!'

The thicket of overgrown reeds and withies parted with a crash of splintering bark, a great blue-black creature erupted, sticks and twigs showering in all directions as he hurtled out, grunting, head low, jaws slavering. Blood of the gored hound dripped from his left tusk, covered the bristles of his snout. At sight of the men he faltered, small, pig eyes mad red, darting from crouched man to man. Movement. A swirl of bright blue, smaller, nearer than the rest.

Arthur's hands clamped with a gasp of indrawn breath on the spear. Mithras, the thing was big! For a fleeting moment he had to fight the overwhelming instinct to run.

Boars, despite their bulk, were fast creatures, unpredictable, fatally dangerous if underestimated. The hold on a boar spear must be right, the charge met and challenged with the full force of the creature's own weight, the spear driven clean through chest and heart. One hand too low down the shaft and it could be the hunter not the hunted who lay squealing with the death blood gushing.

The boar's attention diverted to Gwydre, the lad's cloak swirling as he turned to run in sudden panic at the appearance of this great, bristling monster that stank of hot breath, blood and pig. Arthur screamed at his son to be still, keep still! No time to think – he leapt in the animal's path, crouched, his spear braced against his hip. The grip wasn't right – no time to change it.

The boar saw the man and the thrusting spear. He knew all about spears. The jagged scars on his thick hide were testament to that. He swerved, meeting the blade at an angle, the pain bursting into him, piercing chest and lung; black blood spurted onto hoar-frosted grass. The shaft bent. Arthur's body took the force of the slamming weight, pain ripping up his arm as the spear drove into the boar. He hung on, dragged along as others rushed to help, spears aimed, daggers drawn. The shaft broke, snapped in a shatter of splintered wood and Arthur fell, rolled, bruised and shaken, blood, his own and the boar's, covering hands and thigh where a tusk had ripped through leather bracae and flesh. And the great boar turned to fight, his tusks thrashing, squealing defiance and rage.

Free of the man's weight, the boar charged, heedless of his injury, blinded of senses, pain-maddened by the spear blade and taste of blood in his nose and mouth. A second spear plunged into his rear quarters. He did not even feel it.

It was all happening so quickly! So much noise and confusion! Gwydre hovered, uncertain between running and standing still, frightened by the sounds and smells. The domestic farm boars were large creatures, not to be tangled with, but this creature was as big again as the biggest pig. Gwydre had never seen anything so grossly huge. He panicked, ran. Heard his father roaring, his brother screaming, vaguely saw a fluttered movement to his left, a woman running forward flapping her arms, waving her cloak, her mouth open, shouting something at him, but he could not hear over the belling of excited dogs and the incessant pig squealing that went on and on and on. Saw only the red angry eyes of the boar.

He felt nothing as the brute's tusk drove into him and shook him aside with the ease of a spirited wind blowing a fallen leaf. Felt nothing as he was flung several feet into the air; crumpled to the ground, dead.

PART TWO

The Banner Flies

April 465

§ I

Caer Cadan, Arthur's stronghold, was built on an isolated plateau of eighteen or so acres, rising two hundred and fifty feet above the vivid, fresh, spring colours of the new-growing Summer Land. Tall, unruly trees had encroached along and up the crumbling defensive works of the ditches and banks, the scrub and grass beneath their spread of foliage, scrambling thick and tangled. Abandoned after the Romans had settled Britain, the Caer, for so many centuries a proud *Dun* of the Celtic peoples, had sat nodding quiet and lonely under the summer sun, or sleeping sound beneath winter-covered mantles of snow, unused until Arthur came to awaken its spirit and revive new life into its ancient heart. Caer Cadan blossomed as the Artoriani laid aside their shields and spears and took up instead axes and carpenters tools. From the slumbering vacancy of the abandonment, the complex building rose, phoenix like, to become the pride of her King; a stronghold to dominate the south-west, a royal place from where Arthur could finally become the ruling King that he had always intended to be. Britain was his, and they had, at least for a while, a unity of peace. Prosperity rose as rapidly as the timbered walls of the King's Hall, kitchens, stabling, barns and dwelling places. Those trees had been felled, the spring cleared of choking debris and the ditches re-dug, the banks re-built. Timbered walkways trudged along the top-most, highest bank and double gateways secured entrance and exit beneath commanding watch-towers.

Some of the building, the stone facing in particular, was crudely fashioned, for already the craft of Roman ways was being lost, but there was enough memory to build strong, and the Hall, sixty-three by thirty-four feet, sighted along the axial ridge atop the central summit of the plateau, stood king-proud over stronghold and surrounding country. From here, beat the heart of the place, and

343

from here, Arthur lived and ruled as King, father and husband, enjoying with his Queen, Gwenhwyfar, this first spring-time settled in their own place, anticipating together, the expectation of contentment.

'You ride to Lindinis on the morrow then?' The King, Arthur, tossed the question at Gwenhwyfar from the table where he sat composing a letter to his ex-wife. They were in their private chamber, to the rear of the Hall, and he had written one short sentence only, had no idea what else to write. The woman had the effrontery to offer her services to act as mediator between himself and Aesc of the Cantii. Hengest was dead and the son now King, treaties would need renegotiating, the dance began again. The Pendragon felt quite capable of initiating such a meeting for himself – yet Winifred was Aesc's niece, she could be, the gods forbid, useful.

This was their private chamber, a quiet place aside from the daily bustle of family life. built, as with the Hall and most of the other buildings, of solid timber posts, wattle and daub plastered walls and a reed-thatched roof. The chamber, warm and comfortable adjoined the public place of the King's Hall. Built in the British style, there was very little that was Roman about Caer Cadan, save the luxury of interior furnishings in this private, homely, dwelling place. Gwenhwyfar had her high-backed wicker chair, Arthur, his favourite couch – and their large bed with the carved wooden head-board, rope and leather webbing, and wool stuffed mattress. The gay wall hangings were rich fashioned, the candle and lamp-stands silver and bronze. Gwenhwyfar's pride was the valued red Samian pottery that, even when her mother had been young, was becoming a rarity to own.

Arthur had allowed lavish wealth for his Hall and home. They deserved the pleasure of luxury after enduring for so long the mud-slush of marching camps and damp, cold tents.

Arthur smoothed the stylus through the last word that he had written on the soft beeswax, looked across at Gwenhwyfar, quirked a smile at her extreme expression of irritation. She never was a woman who settled comfortably to a woman's work. A memory of the past flashed into his mind, of her as a child, declaring hotly that she would rather learn to hunt than sew.

She was standing at the loom, a verticle, wooden structure, bending slightly and grumbling to herself, unpicking a knot in the weave. Then she dropped the wooden shuttle, sending the stone weights dangling at the end lengths of the warp threads as it clattered, unravelling thread, to the floor. 'Sod it,' she cursed.

Stifling his laughter, Arthur came from his desk and helped her retrieve the wool, patiently unpicked the knot for her. 'I do better at this than you,' he laughed. 'Happen you could write to Winifred for me?'

Flouncing to a stool, taking a goblet of wine from the table as she passed, Gwenhwyfar seated herself with a huff of indignation. 'I hate weaving,' she announced. 'Enid professes to enjoy it, I can't think what's wrong with the woman.'

Returning to his desk, Arthur placed a quick kiss on her forehead. 'Lindinis?' he asked again.

'Aye, I intend to leave first thing, there is much I need. It will be easier to ride to the market than summon traders here.'

Squinting at the few words he had written, Arthur said, 'You will take Llacheu?'

'Of course, he will enjoy it.'

Arthur said nothing, sat staring at the wax tablet.

He had taken Gwydre's death so hard, shouldering the blame atop that of Amr's cruel ending. Gwenhwyfar stood, crossed to him and from behind, placed her arms about him. She was hurting too, some days it seemed as if the pain would never, never ease, but she had been strong this time, able to take Arthur in her arms and help him to weep, secure in the knowledge of her love. A love that she gave without condition.

Why the strength this time, why not last? Well, she was content now, settled and at rest. They had their own home, their own Hall, and there had been no fighting between Saex or British, no quarrelling with Ambrosius or the Council and Church for many months – nothing, save those little irritations that squirmed from Winifred's rat-nest of course. When Amr had died, it had been as a last straw added to her overbalancing heap of doubts and weariness. But now her doubts were gone – almost – and a bright, burning energy replaced her weariness, an energy that made the pain of Gwydre's death easier to bear. No, it was Arthur this time who carried the weight of grief, him that she worried about.

'Llacheu will be in no danger,' she pointed out. 'We ride to our nearest town with adequate escort through our own territory.'

Reaching his arms behind his head, Arthur clasped her neck, bringing her closer to him. 'Who rides escort?'

'Red Turma.'

'Ah.' He let her go, started shuffling the several piles of unread correspondence about his desk; parchment scrolls and wax tablets, petitions and complaints. The tedious business of being a King.

Gwenhwyfar returned to her loom; the plaid was wrong, she had missed alternating the colour four rows back. Oh well. What had he meant by *ah*? Happen she ought to ask, but then, it was probably nothing, just one of his irritating ways. She looked again at the weave. When she had made his banner, the red and gold dragon that writhed across a white flag, she had stitched well, making a thing that, even to her own eyes was well crafted and exquisitely done. But then, she had wanted to make that, had wanted to create something special for Arthur, and for Llacheu when he followed . . . Impatient, she began unpicking the wrongly fashioned weave. If only the threads of life could be so easily unravelled when something went wrong!

§ II

The courtyard lay in a rough-shaped rectangle between the stables, the Hall and the kitchens. It was small but serviceable; a place where the horses could be brought up for mounting or tending, and only recently cobbled; through the winter it had squelched with churned mud. The fourth side was open, giving way to a narrow track that wound down the rise of this, the highest ground of the Caer, to the southern gateway. The north and east gates had grander, wider tracks that strode their way through the complex of buildings to the large, public doors of the King's Hall. This courtyard was a more private place, though it was often, as today, crowded with men, horses and the ever-present scrabble of dogs.

Watching as Ider helped Gwenhwyfar mount, Arthur noticed how the lad's eyes never left her face, held a look of saturated adoration. The Pendragon shrugged, dismissed the uneasy feeling of jealousy which seemed to bother him so often of late. Most of the men adored Gwenhwyfar – who could blame them! Ach, he was seeking shadows on a cloudy day. The younger lads – aye and even the older men –fell over their own feet to take a chance at serving their queen, that was as it should be. Except it always seemed to be Ider who was there first, always Ider helping her to mount, or to fetch and carry.

Gwenhwyfar was mounted, and riding with her escort towards the gateway, Llacheu on his fine grey pony, chattering away to the Decurion, the officer in charge. Always talking, that boy, as noisy as a squawking magpie! Arthur turned back to the Hall, fighting an impulse to run after them, to say he would ride with them . . . what in the name of Mithras was wrong with him? All these dark fears and churlish doubts; some days, it was like living a waking nightmare. A nightmare where water swirled and a boy's hand reached for rescue, rescue from a great boar with blood eyes and stinking breath.

Fifteen men, half a Turma, rode with his wife and son, fifteen experienced, loyal men – this was ridiculous, there was much to be done this day, best to shrug nonsense thoughts aside and get on with matters that needed attention. Yet still he looked to where the last horse trotted beneath the wooden guard tower and out through the open gateway, listened to the sounds of hooves clattering down the cobbled lane. Morgause had set these dark thoughts of foreboding, she with her high laugh and gloating eyes, Morgause who delighted in nurturing the belief of her witchcraft. *If you come after me, Pendragon, none of your sons shall live* . . .

From beneath the grey clouds that had been threatening rain since dawn, came a shrill screeching and a beating of wings. Starlings mobbed a hawk, the small against the mighty. Enduring the fury a while, the larger bird ignored the flapping wings and abuse, then tired of the game, circled higher; sailing on the wind over the flat lands spreading out to Yns Witrin, standing proud above the winter-come waters, silhouetted against the horizon of grey sky. Daily, the higher ground was pushing through the dissipating flood-waters. Summer would be come again soon.

Yns Witrin. A place of the old gods and of the new. Of sanctuary and solitude. Where lived the Lake Lady. A place where Gwenhwyfar said she had found peace.

Morgause's threats were no more than that, he knew the woman, knew the extent of her evil-minded ways. He called her witch as a derisive word – she held no power, no magic, not beyond the allure a beautiful woman had over a man keen for lust. He would have known if she had more, for he had suffered from her cruelties long enough as a child. Arthur chewed his lower lip, stood squinting across the distance at that hill. Yet she professed to be a priestess of the Goddess, had spent a while over there beneath the impressive Tor of Yns Witrin with the Ladies who lived by the Lake. The lake which even in the hottest of summers never dried. There was only one of the Ladies now, so folk said, a young woman, the last of her kind here in the Christian-dominated South. One Lady serving the Goddess, as Morgause professed also to do. Arthur thought he had seen her, this lone priestess, suspected that she and the black-haired faerie-woman who had tried so gallantly to save Gwydre from the boar were the same person. One day he would ride to Yns Witrin and find out for certain, thank her. It had been a brave thing that she had done, to run as she had, attempting to divert that great brute's attention. Arthur turned again, intending to make for the Hall, but stopped. Damn it, one day might never come! There were always so many things to be approached 'one day'.

Impulsively, he shouted for his horse to be made ready. He needed something to ease this black mood from his throbbing head. Something to make him forget Gwydre, and Amr, to cease this incessant worry about Llacheu. And the Lady would know of Morgause. Would know whether she truly held the power of life or death over his sons.

The tavern in Lindinis was crowded, these bustling market days were always welcome to those shopkeepers who needed the extra trade. Ider pushed through first, making way to the only table unoccupied. With his hand he dusted the bench, helped his Lady be seated. Llacheu scrambled beside his mother, who invited the other two men of her escort while in town to sit also. Damos and Caradog shuffled along the opposite bench as Ider, swaggering to the bar, called loudly for wine.

'Can't you see I'm busy!' the little dark-haired man behind the counter growled, pouring a tankard of ale with one hand, busily stirring a ladle round with the other. Casually Ider took the ladle from him, stirred a couple more rotations and scooped some stew from the earthenware jar embedded into the counter. He sniffed it, took a small taste. 'This good enough for my Lady?' he asked.

The bartender scowled at him. 'Good enough for a queen that stuff.'

Ider's answering grin echoed the sarcasm in his voice as he leant across the counter and said, 'It had better be, it is for the Queen and her escort that I buy it.'

For a brief moment, the tavern-keeper was tempted to match a similar scathing reply, but he glanced at the woman seated at the corner table, noticed her copper-bright hair, her rich clothing, then the golden torque around her throat. No ordinary woman wore such an item of value. She was talking to a boy fidgeting beside her.

'Aye,' Ider prompted, 'my Lady Gwenhwyfar, wife to the Pendragon, and their son.' To emphasise his point he touched the bronze dragon badge on his shoulder. He leant a little further forward, spoke directly into the man's face. 'I'm Artoriani. My Lord Pendragon takes unkindly to rat-poison being served to his Lady or his men.' The pleasant smile he gave as he carefully handed the ladle back to its owner portrayed a meaning far removed from friendship.

Within moments, clean bowls appeared and a flagon of fine wine was opened. The tavern-owner bustled from behind the counter, wiping his hands on a grubby apron tied around his middle, personally served his eminent customers, thoughts flickering faster than a racing storm wind. *As served to Queen Gwenhwyfar! I can raise my prices, advertise around the town; get a better standard of clientele coming in!* Already, in his mind, his takings box was bursting with gold, his pockets bulging with riches. Bossily he shuffled men away from Gwenhwyfar's corner, proclaiming the lady needed privacy and not crowding. Good-natured, knowing the man's gruff, grasping ways, his regular customers complied. Miltiades was always after the making of more money.

Three men standing propped on their elbows at the bar quietly finished their ale and pushed their way out through the tavern onto the street. This was a side street, bustling with people, bristling with shops and traders. Two doors along was the laundry, wafting its repugnant mixture of smells through the open doors. The tallest of the three men stopped to use the almost full urine pot outside – a slave, about to empty it, politely thanked him, waited for him to finish. Fulling was not a pleasant job, but a slave could not complain, at least this boy had the easier task of emptying the public pot, the other boy had to take the cloth from the vat inside after it had lain stiffening in the collected urine. His hands were blistered and sore, and he was shunned even by the laundry cat because of the stench that clung to his clothing, skin and hair.

The three men strolled on, heading for where they had left their horses, three men dressed in hunting gear; ordinary men, save one had a glint of excited mischief, wore the torque of a chieftain's son around his short, bull-muscled neck and a golden frog, the emblem of his father Amlawdd, on his shoulder.

§ IV

Though it was warmer than the last few weeks, the sun had not managed to shoulder through the banks of cloud, and by late afternoon a fine drizzle was falling. Riding home, Llacheu paid no mind to the weather, for rain was a part of life, as unavoidable as night. Though he had been talking briskly when first they left Lindinis, he had fallen silent. Death was a part of life, a part he saw often. His father's men, their wives and their children could be mortally wounded or fall prey to sickness and disease. But to lose a brother, a brother whom you had played with, curled asleep with, fought, laughed or cried with, had been for all its part of the everyday way of things, hard to bear.

Amr he had missed, but Amr had been young, and beyond his chubby smile and babe's needs, Llacheu had not known him. Gwydre, though, had been a constant companion, not always an amicable one, for brothers often did not agree, but their squabbling had been no more than pups in the same litter scrapping over a choice bone. As likely, when the growling ceased, they would curl together, content, before the hearth-fire.

He woke some nights, sweating and screaming, the horror of that hunt returning into his dreams. Never would that terrible scene of Gwydre's killing fully leave his memory. For a boy with so much life to embrace, grief faded quickly; beyond the occasional thorn-prick reminder, Gwydre's voice, his face were becoming an echo as faint as a half-remembered dream. But sometimes, he missed his brother painfully.

His head nodded forward, tired from the day's excitement; they would all sleep sound this night; for it had been a long, busy day. They were all tired, some of the men half dozing as they rode, hunched beneath their cloaks against the rain, hands easy on the reins, bodies swaying with the steady rhythm of their horses' pace. The ambush came unexpected.

No more than a handful of men, well armed, attacked with hunting bows and spears where the road narrowed through the encroaching shrub. Four of the escort lay dead before they could draw sword, among them the Decurion and Caradog. The Artoriani spurred their horses forward, attempting to reach and close in around their Lady and Llacheu, who, coming fully awake, was gallantly drawing his own dagger and riding close to his mother in order to protect her. Ider, torn between the decision to aid

Gwenhwyfar or the boy made a rapid choice for the boy. Leaping from his own horse, he jumped towards the lad, scooped him in his arm and tumbled to the grass, covering him with his own shield as they fell. Gwenhwyfar, seeing Llacheu with Ider, drew her own sword, trying to think calmly, to plan, all the while her mind was screaming for the boy's safety. An arrow thrummed, pierced her mare's neck, bright blood spurting down the chestnut hide from the severed jugular. The horse crumpled, falling head first into a tangle of legs, and pitching her rider off; Gwehwyfar hit the ground hard, her head catching on a rock half-hidden beneath last autumn's fall. Shapes moved around her. Voices, shouting and grunting as the attackers came up out from the bushes to fight hand to hand. Llacheu was pushed against her; he scrabbled close, arms going around her, his dagger tight in his hand, ready to stab at anyone who came too near.

The clash of sword on shield, swearing, the smell of fresh blood. Ider stood over Gwenhwyfar and the boy, his boots planted to either side, fighting for his own life and theirs. But mostly, theirs.

When not on campaign, Arthur's men drilled daily. Weapon training, marching, wrestling, running. Every day, in every weather. Drill, drill and drill again. To fight effectively a man must be fit and ready for action. They grumbled of course, complained and cursed at the officers for being fatherless sons of whore-house bitches, their profanities increasing when compelled to cover miles on route marches carrying full pack. But if man or beast could not keep up, then the Artoriani was no longer the place for them. Fit men, fit horses; disciplined, drilled, professionals.

A man leapt at Ider, screaming some wordless battle-cry, ran into the sweeping stroke of Ider's sword. Gwenhwyfar, her senses returning, but her head still spinning, pulled Llacheu, protesting, beneath her. A weight fell across her legs, something warm and wet spattered her skin. She looked up, wished she hadn't, buried her head again.

The Artoriani losses were heavy, but the remainder were skilled enough to win through, and ensure that not one of their attackers got away. Not even the young man with the golden torque who had come from the tavern in Lindinis.

Ider took three great lungfuls of air, regarded the six men standing as he was, out of breath and blood-splotched. Three horses lay dead. At a quick glance, two others would need to be destroyed. Probably more. He sheathed his sword, kicked the dead man from his Lady's legs and lifted her with ease as if she were a child. Llacheu sprang immediately to his feet, teeth bared, dagger scything. 'Whoa, little cub,' Ider chided, putting a restraining hand on the lad's head. 'The fighting is done, let us tend your mam.' Carrying her a few paces, he set Gwenhwyfar down under the spread new-leaf boughs of a tree where the grass was green and untrampled.

With gentle hands he inspected the bloodied swelling to her forehead. ' 'Tis not deep,' he said, removing his neck cloth, 'but you'll have a bruise the size of a goose egg. I'll damp this with water, it will ease the hurting, my Lady.'

Gwenhwyfar stayed him from rising, her hand going to his arm. She was pale, felt nauseous and was trembling, but still she said, 'I am all right. See to those in more need than I.' She indicated the others. Gravely Ider nodded, and handed the cloth to Llacheu, who ran to a stream trickling a few yards off to wet it. He said nothing as he quietly went to help the injured of his Turma. His friends. Forcing herself to stand, Gwenhwyfar let the world swim by a few times. She was of no use sitting idle by this tree while men needed help. She swayed, fought down a wave of sickness. Deep, even breaths to steady the dizzying swirl. Concentrate. One foot before the other. Why did the ground heave so? Llacheu came back, his face grey, concerned, silently handed her the wet cloth. She smiled and thanked him, assured him she was not seriously injured, just a bit dizzy.

Ider was kneeling beside Damos, whose cuirass was soaked, stained with a dark redness that was almost black. Gwenhwyfar knelt opposite him, shook her head at Ider's grief-stricken questioning face. There was no hope. The arrow had pierced deep into his lung, the breath coming in a spittle of rattling gasps.

Damos clung to Ider's hand, felt Gwenhwyfar's cool fingers touch his hot forehead. They had been companions from the start, these two young men, good companions, good friends. He croaked, through a hurting breath, 'We had good hunting, my friend, you and I together.'

Ider said nothing. His throat choked, words stuck.

'I would give half my pay for a cool drink of water,' Damos added with a cough. A little cough, with a soft breathing out of air.

'I'll fetch some!' Ider was half up, eager to be doing something of use, but Gwenhwyfar shook her head again. 'He has no need of it, Ider. There will be cool water in plenty where he has gone.' She folded Damos's hands across his chest. He looked no more than he was sleeping, save for the black blood.

Sinking to the stained grass, Ider dropped his head into his hands and wept like a disconsolate child.

Gwenhwyfar left him with his grief, went to tend another, Llacheu, silent, trotted at her heel, fetching water when she asked, helping to tear bandaging, rolling, holding, helping where he could.

And all the while, Gwenhwyfar was thinking, will it never end, this horror of death that surrounded her? What had happened to the sunshine and the laughter? Why was there nothing but rain and tears?

With the Decurion dead, the men left were disorientated, the suddenness of an attack in country that was not hostile leaving them stunned. They needed to be up and doing, not sitting dwelling on it, so Gwenhwyfar set them to work, tending the wounded, dispatching the horses. Searching the bodies of their attackers. 'We must know who they were, where they come from. My Lord would wish to know.' She added with a snarl of ferociousness that few had heard before, 'As do I.'

The men nodded, faces set. As did they.

Stone-faced, Ider stood beside Gwenhwyfar, allowing her to finish bandaging a wound in a man's thigh. She sat back on her heels, looking up at him, waited for him to speak. 'We have identified one of the bastards,' he said curtly. He turned on his heel, strode to where a body lay slightly apart from the others.

Before following, Gwenhwyfar smiled at the injured man. 'That will be sore for a while, but will mend.' She struggled wearily to her feet. The rain was still drizzling and light would be fading soon. Her legs felt as heavy as her throbbing head. She went to join Ider, but at sight of the body, turned away, fell forward onto her hands and knees and retched into the grass. She knew the whore-son, she knew him! The nephew of a name from the past. A name with a face she still saw, occasionally, when the mares of the night brought dreams of despair and fear. The young man's features were the same, the same colouring, the same snarling, greasy expression. For a second time she vomited. Ider knelt beside her, rubbing her back, easing the discomfort, unsure what else to do.

She sat up, managed a weak smile. Simply, she said, 'Did any get away?'

'None.'

Her eyes were seeing beyond Ider, seeing again a time and remembered faces at Vortigern's court. 'He was at Londinium, this man's uncle.' She took several breaths to calm herself.

'Who is he?' Ider asked, meaning the dead man.

For a long while she did not answer. Then on a drawn breath, 'He is Rhica, the son of Amlawdd.' Gwenhwyfar swallowed, went on to explain with dry lips and throat, 'Amlawdd had a brother, an older brother, Gorlois by name. Gorlois had a young wife, but she left her brutal husband for another, her lover. To keep her, the lover was forced to kill Gorlois, and from that sprang a war that ended with Uthr – the lover – and his woman – Ygrainne – fleeing to exile.' She lifted her hand, let it fall in a hopeless gesture. 'And so began the hatred between the Pendragon and the kindred of Gorlois: his brothers, Amlawdd and,' she had to steady her breath again before saying, 'Melwas.'

'My Lady?' Ider took her hand, was alarmed to feel it so cold. 'Are you unwell? You have turned so pale . . .' The last name meant nothing to him.

She managed a smile, attempted to reassure him, and Llacheu who had trotted over. She knelt, held her son close, said over his head to Ider, 'No matter how far buried you think it is, the past will always rise again to the surface.' She began to get to her feet, Ider helped her up. She nodded a curt order at the waiting men, 'Bring this body. My husband will wish to see it.'

355

'And these others, Lady?'

Venom was in her voice as she answered, 'Leave them. Carrion eat vermin.' The men exchanged glances. One ventured, tentatively, 'Christian people require a Christian burial, my Lady.'

Gwenhwyfar laughed caustically. 'I doubt the men of Amlawdd are bothered by the niceties of Christianity. His brother Melwas, when he ran sword in sheath with the Saex, certainly was not.' Added, 'They would not have bothered to bury us.' She watched as two men lifted Rhica and carried him to one of the waiting mounts.

To no one in particular Gwenhwyfar said, 'Gorlois was slain by Uthr and Melwas by myself. Now there is only Amlawdd. Who shall bring his death and end the thing?' It had been a rhetorical question, she was not even aware she had spoken aloud, but Ider answered with iron coldness.

'If it was he who ordered this killing, then it shall be me, Lady Gwenhwyfar. I swear I shall avenge this bloody day.'

Gwenhwyfar regarded Ider through slit eyes, much as her husband would have done. 'Let it rest. This thing has circled warily beyond the shadows of the fire for many and many a year. For now, we must see to our own, get them returned to Caer Cadan.'

§ V

Morgaine took pride in her hair, always kept it combed and clean. There was little more to do here among the solitude of these hovels that had once housed the community of the Ladies at the base of the Tor. She was alone now, for the last of the other women had died, toothless in old age. Morgaine was the only one left. The young women did not come to seek service to the Goddess any more – they went to the far side of the Tor now, down the hill a way, to the holy house of the Christian sisters who dressed in drab black, and cut their hair short, hiding what remained under a veil.

Morgaine remained beccause she had nowhere else to go, no one to go with. She had been born here. Her mother, within a few moments of clearing the birthing-blood from the tiny body and the mucus from the nose and mouth, had given the child into the service of the Goddess. The women – there had been several other Ladies then – had welcomed the offering, twittering and fussing around her mother, taking her too, as one with themselves. But Morgause had always been like that, one willing to sacrifice anything for her own gain. It had been no hardship to give her new-born daughter to the jangling, colourfully garbed women, for Morgause had not wanted the babe. Morgaine knew that. Knew it from the first days of fear and understanding. From the day when, as a child of no more than five years, she found Morgause suddenly to be gone without explanation or word of farewell. Gone, as if she had never existed – save for the bruising on the child's legs, the scalds to her hands, and the many other, inward, unseen scars.

That had been a good, most glorious day when Morgaine discovered her mother was gone. It had been the day when there had been a great excitement down among the complex of Christian buildings, for a man had come, and found his lost woman. Morgaine would have been punished, had her mother discovered that she had wandered down into the holy community; Morgause was always punishing her. For being lazy or stupid or clumsy, all excuses for the real reason, for being born a girl-child. But Morgaine had often pattered secretly down the lane to watch the gentle, kindly, sisters, or to spy on the crowds gathering to worship in the Christian church. That day, she had tiptoed closer than ever before because there seemed such an excitement in the air. The man had tossed her a coin after his marriage service to his beloved lady. She had dropped the thing and cried. And the man had stooped and picked it up and put it in her hand, smiling. No one had ever smiled at Morgaine before, or told her not to cry. For that, she had loved him, and loved him still. No matter that he was now the Pendragon and called king.

That was ten years past. Morgaine was alone now, but at least the old Ladies had taught her well. She had learnt eagerly, once Morgause had gone. She knew how to heal and to mix potions, she could chant the ritual verses of the Goddess, knew how to interpret the clouds and the direction of the wind, the names of the stars and the cycle of the moon and planets. Could understand the rustlings of nature, and could write in the Latin hand and the old language of the runes; read the written words in her mind without the need to move her lips. She knew great magic.

And so she lived alone among the ruins of what had once been a shrine to an increasingly impotent goddess, with only the birds and beasts for companions, her scrolls and wax tablets for comfort, knowing nothing of what lay beyond a mile distant from Yns Witrin. She could see, from the great, imposing height of the Tor, across that spread land of the Summer Realm, could see another world beneath the vast stretch of sky, where men and women loved and laughed, where children were born and grew. She could see across to the hills and the distant glimmer of sun-shimmered sea, all the while wanting to go, wanting to leave, knowing she would never summon the courage to disobey the command of her mother.

Morgaine looked up, disturbed by the frantic rush of beating wings. Many of the winter birds were still here, the lingering cold making them reluctant to leave for their nesting sites. She put down her comb, stood, squinting into the grey sky. No sign of a hawk, what had disturbed them from their feeding, out on the lush water-meadows? Then the geese went up, honking and calling, their clamour of wings beating shrill warning of an intruder. Someone was approaching her lake. The birds and the grazing geese always warned her. Many believed she possessed the Sight, but Morgaine knew it was simply the alarm of the birds. She hoped it would only be a peasant woman coming for a salve, or a young maid for a love-potion. More likely it was a man who wanted her body. They often came to try for that. Aye, even the Christian men.

While she lived within the solitude of the Goddess's presence she was safe enough, for she, a maiden still, was under the command of superstitious respect. Here, in the Goddess's realm of Yns Witrin she was protected from their wanting. But only while she stayed. The power of the Goddess held only here, within the brooding shadow of her Tor.

§ VI

Arthur approached Yns Witrin with unease, for it was an intimidating place. Yet he was no Christian to be in fear of, or damn, the Old Ways; even his following of the Roman soldiers' god Mithras was not a devout faith. Arthur cursed in the name of Mithras, but did not particularly believe – most certainly did not worship. In all truth, he embraced the pagan god because it irked the Christian church to be bloody minded. No one told Arthur what he could or could not do.

Rising over five hundred feet, the grass-covered Tor shadowed its reflection in the eerie stillness of surrounding floodwater, a parallel world. There were passages and caverns beneath, it was said, a way down into the Underworld kingdom of the dead. A holy place, long before the Christians claimed the area as theirs, for the presence of the Spirit – whichever name he or she went by – was strong among this cluster of evocative hills that floated within the creeping mist and floodwater marshes.

Arthur was riding alone, he had sent the three men of his escort to the Christian settlement, where they would find ale and shelter from the wind and threatening rain. He drew rein at the edge of the still lake, looking across the placid water towards the sacred hill. Two swans dibbling in the shallow water further along regarded him with hostility, the cob standing, spreading his wings in a threatening gesture of defiance. The other birds, the geese and the marsh-waders, were still agitated by his presence, circling and calling their alarm. Arthur ignored them, sat his horse, looking at a path that wound its complicated route up from the far shore-line of trees in a mazed spiral to the summit of the Tor, its terraces, time-stamped by the passage of feet from generation following generation. In the days of the old gods, the dead had been carried along its ritual way for burial in the underground chambers, or the women had danced along its miz-maze line to honour the Goddess. Few remembered the sacred track through the spiral now and the dead were buried in the Christian cemeteries. The Goddess was becoming impotent, forgotten.

While he sat, silent and still, the birds had settled again. Arthur swung his leg over one of the fore-pommel horns and dismounted, his boots squelching in the boggy ground. He knotted the reins and hobbled the mare. Leaving her to graze, he walked to the edge of the still water. Gwenhwyfar had walked often on this Tor, she had told him, while she sought to come to terms with the horrors that had come upon her. *The holy sisters were kind, but the Tor has a timeless silence that gives a special healing of its own.*

Two children. Their lives begun by him and ended by him. The shadows of Amr and Gwydre whispered and muttered constantly behind his shoulder.

Arthur stepped forward, his boots sank to the ankles in sucking water, but the ground beneath was solid. He took another step. Was this the mystery of the Tor? If you crossed these deceiving shallows, climbed to the summit, if you managed those tests, one way or another, did you fine peace? He walked another step.

'Take one more step, and you will be up to your neck in water.'

Arthur spun round, catching his breath at the voice coming from behind, a little from the left. He swung so sharply he lost his balance and footing, almost fell, one knee going into the mud.

'I have expected you. Welcome, my King,' the woman said, coming from the shadow of the alder trees. She was clad in a muffling cloak, the hood pulled well forward, hiding her face, but Arthur knew who she was. No other woman could appear so silently from nowhere. Only the Lady could do that.

'There are ways across,' she said, stepping to the right and out into what appeared to be lake. 'Paths of firm, higher ground, which will take you safe if you know them.' She began walking, the marsh-water coming no higher than her ankles. She stopped, stood a moment, watching his uncertainty, then tossed back the hood, revealing her face and unbound dark hair. She extended her hand in invitation for him to follow, said simply, 'Come.'

A sudden image of Morgause had come to Arthur's mind. Why? Because she had once been here? 'A woman I know was once priestess here,' he said, standing on the firm ground.

The Lady bowed her head in acknowledgement. 'There have been many priestesses to the Mother.'

Arthur's heart was pounding, fear streaking up and down his spine, tingling his fingers and sending dampness trickling from beneath his arms. It was almost as if he were talking to the Goddess herself through this startling, strange creature. She had a plain, solemn face with a nose too long, but when she smiled at him, the smile set free a brilliance of sun-dazzling brightness through her eyes, making the plainness almost beautiful. Again she beckoned, the blue-marked patterns of creatures twisted around and around each other writhing up her bare arm as she moved. Again, she said, 'Come.'

And Arthur followed, as she knew he would.

The men stood pensive, exchanging nervous glances. One, holding the reins of their King's horse, stroked the mare's soft muzzle as another removed the hobbles. He straightened, shrugging. 'Lord Pendragon would not have intended to leave her here all night.'

'No more would he spend the night here himself!' The third man shivered, nodded at the dark, ominous bulk of the Tor, black against the darkening evening sky, and crossed himself.

'Where is he then?'

'Over there?'

'Surely not!'

'We must find him,' the man holding the mare said. 'And soon. I've no wish to be in the shadow of the Tor come dark.'

Murmurs of agreement.

They called out, shouting the King's name. Mocking echoes came back across the black, black water. *Lord Pendragon . . . Pendragon . . . Pendragon . . .*

It was raining, a steady, chilling drizzle that spattered on their faces, dribbled into the lake, making a thousand, tiny splashing circles that ran and fussed into each other. They heard no dip of a coracle's paddle, or footsteps wading through water, but there, suddenly, out of the darkness beneath the trees stepped a man. Arthur's escort started in feared alarm, with hissing breath drew their swords. One man swore.

'How's this?' Arthur asked, moving to his mare to take the reins.

'Bellowing my name across this silence, then making ready to kill me when I appear?'

'My Lord, you startled us!'

'So I see.' Arthur mounted, settled in the saddle, surveyed the blackness of the Tor a moment before wheeling and setting for home at a canter.

§ VII

Boots muddied, cloak sodden by the rain which had deteriorated from drizzle to earnest downfall on his way back, Arthur burst into his Hall and crossed immediately to the group of men who had leapt to their feet beside the hearth-fire. 'You,' he snarled with a mixture of contempt and rage, his finger stabbing at them, 'are confined to barracks until such time as I am able to consider a more fitting reprimand for your damned incompetence!'

The men of Gwenhwyfar's escort said nothing, some hung their heads, others bit their lips, staring straight ahead.

For several seconds Arthur glared at them, his breathing heavy, jaw clamped tight. His eyes rested on Ider. 'How many dead?' he barked. Ider answered, gave also the number wounded.

'And horses lost?'

Again Ider answered, monosyllabic. For a long moment Arthur glowered at the young man, then let his furious eyes range over the others before sweeping his cloak off his shoulders and striding across the wooden floor into his own, private chamber beyond the public Hall. The men let go their breath with sighs of relief, squatted again before the heat of the fire. He would be back, of course, after seeing to the well-being of his wife and son. And then, he'd have something to say. They were not looking forward to the prospect.

Gwenhwyfar was curled before the fire, drowsing. Her head ached. She had thought of going to bed, but had not the energy or inclination to move away from the warmth of the comforting flames.

The blaze stirred as the door opened, closed. She did not look up or open her eyes, knew it must be Arthur returned from wherever it was he had been. Only Arthur would enter their private chamber without knocking. Or Llacheu, but he was abed, asleep.

Arthur crossed the room and hunkered down opposite her on the far side of the hearth, holding his spread palms to the heat. He said nothing for a long moment, watched his wife, then said at last, 'That is quite a bruise to your head.'

Eyes still closed, Gwenhwyfar answered, 'I can't let you have the honour of all the battle scars you know.' She sat up, smiled at him, her fingers reaching to touch lightly the lump to her forehead, 'Though I think I'll not take too many.'

He chuckled at her jest, added wood to the fire, watching as the log caught, a jet of blue-yellow flame hissing from an attached, withered leaf. 'What happened?' It was asked professionally, as he would of one of his officers. No criticism or reprimand, just the asking.

'We were ambushed. Three miles along the road. Amlawdd's son.'

Casually, Arthur added a second log, settled himself on his heels the more comfortably. 'Na, I know that, I mean *what* happened?'

She did not quite follow, shrugged her shoulders slightly. 'What usually happens in an ambush? We were riding home, we came to where the scrub narrows into the track and they attacked.'

Arthur stood, his hand resting automatically on his sword pommel by his side. 'So, my Artoriani, my men whom I drill and drill and drill again, were not alert? Had set no post rider? Sent no scouts ahead?'

Wearily, Gwenhwyfar shook her head. He was angry, though he was trying to hold it in check. She supposed he had every right to be. All she could answer, justify, was, 'We were three miles from the Caer, Arthur. Would you expect to be attacked so near your own stronghold?'

He let his hand drop from his sword with a brief, conceding gesture. Na, he would not. But then, neither would he expect his men, men assigned as escort, bodyguard duty, to make assumptions.

'They are answerable, Gwenhwyfar. Their lax supervision put your life and my son's in danger. I cannot do nothing about it.'

He was returning to the door, had his hand on the latch, when Gwenhwyfar twisted around to plead, 'The error has taught them – all of us – well enough. I was as much to blame.'

'It has not, and you were not. Failure to do their duty efficiently is not a mere error, Cymraes.' And he had gone, shutting the door with a firm click behind him. She knew she would hear every word he spoke to the men, for Arthur in a temper could shout very, very loud.

Ider sat hunched against the outside wall of the latrines. A safe location to sit and brood, knowing no one would come and bother you in such a disagreeable place. Across his knees was his sword. He had cleaned and cleaned it again these past few hours, but still he could not seem to polish away those smears of sticky, clinging blood. To any other eye the metal would appear to gleam, but Ider could see the stains, knowing that the blood spilt this day – na, yesterday it was now – could so easily have been his beloved Lady's. He had failed her, and had failed his Lord, and as the Pendragon had said, he was not fit to call himself Artoriani.

'*Call yourself a soldier?*' Arthur had sneered at them all, those dejected, embarrassed, worthless curs who had ridden as escort. '*Call yourself Artoriani? Blood of Mithras, my son could do a better job!*' He had not been scolding Ider alone, but the lad had taken the rebuke personally, because he felt responsible. No matter that the Turma was on latrine duty for the next month, with their pay docked and confined to the Caer, punishment could never be enough for Ider. He was unworthy of his Lady, and nothing, nothing would atone for the fact that because of him, she or her son could have died, as his friends had died.

They deserved to be avenged. The father of that bastard who had attacked them deserved his heart cut out and fed to the dogs. It ought to be done, by God! Someone ought to take revenge for a wicked day's work. I could do it! Ider thought. I could slay the whore-son's father, were I not confined to barracks. Fortunate that he had an excuse to dismiss the planted idea, shrug it aside. It was the Pendragon's place to deal with this thing, not Ider's. But it had not been Arthur who had so nearly allowed Gwenhwyfar to die.

§ VIII

Morning. Scudding grey clouds, fidgeting across a sullen sky, had blown in cold in addition to wet; and there was not much of a promise of improvement. The horses being made ready for the day's routine patrol snorted and stamped against the chill easterly wind. Gwenhwyfar was assisting to saddle them; she enjoyed being at the stables, grooming, oiling the leather of bridle or saddle, tacking up. Since those first days of early childhood she had helped with the horses, saw no reason why she should stop now.

A man, short of breath, came up behind her. 'He is not to be found, my Lady.'

Wrestling with the girth straps of the saddle, she answered irritably, 'Nonsense. Lord Pendragon has confined my escort to the Caer. Ider must be here somewhere.' She prodded the horse's blown belly, tried again with the girth.

Unwilling to disagree with the Queen, the man had no option. For over an hour he had been searching the place, asking questions, peering and prying, in, under and behind. Lady Pendragon had asked him to fetch Ider to her and he could not find him. Emphatically he stated, 'He is not within this Caer, my Lady.'

With a grunt of success, Gwenhwyfar fastened the girth buckle, stood, hands on hips, considering. Ider was no boy to act churlish from a justified rebuking, had faced harsher scorn on the drill ground. Surely he would not disobey a punishment and take himself off in a temper of sulking? Llacheu would, were Arthur to punish with his tongue in the way he had lashed Ider and the men yesterday, but then Llacheu was a child, Ider a grown man.

'Have you spoken with last night's officer of the Watch?' Gwenhwyfar queried, running her fingers down inside the now tight girth, smoothing any wrinkles from the sensitive skin beneath. 'Question him. Discreetly.'

Where was Ider? Where would he go? Did he lie sodden in drink somewhere? Gwenhwyfar had made a cursory search for him herself, first thing, intending to ask how he fared this morning, for he had taken the death of comrades hard. A difficult thing, to bear grief alone.

The man returned, panting harder for Caer Cadan was no small site. He swallowed several times, bent forward, hands on thighs to gain breath, when able to talk, gasped, 'Ider rode out at first light. Said he had urgent business to attend. Direct orders.'

The fool, the damned, idiotic fool! Gwenhwyfar knew instinctively where he had gone. And why. The horse she had been saddling was a war stallion, well muscled, sharp tempered and agitated by the needling rain. No mount for a woman, but Gwenhwyfar had handled horses nearly all her life. She hitched her skirt and clambered into the saddle, kicking him into a canter almost before she was settled, heading for the Eastern gateway.

The horse responded eagerly, Gwenhwyfar's urgency communicating as excitement. The men, those not on given duties, followed her across the Caer at a run, curious in the wake of those drumming hooves. Pulling the horse up, Gwenhwyfar slid to the ground, flinging the reins at the nearest, gape-mouthed onlookers and ran into the guard room, pausing only for her eyes to adjust to the dim light within. She ran up the two flights of wooden steps, calling for Arthur, knowing he was atop with his officers, inspecting some minor modifications to the watch tower. 'My Lord!' Her anguished cry as she burst out into the daylight brought heads snapping round.

The Pendragon walked with long strides to meet her, shouldering aside those in his way. What the hell was wrong? Had word come at the Western gate? Several thoughts flashed through his mind, the most alarming concerning Hueil. That he would soon be gathering an army was a certainty. The King's spies kept watch on trouble again flaring in the North, although Arthur did not need spies to forewarn him of Hueil's intentions. The day news had come that the old lord of Alclud had been hounded from his own land into exile was confirmation enough. Hueil had proclaimed himself Lord, and Hueil would not wait long.

Anxiously Arthur caught Gwenhwyfar in his hands, held her at arm's length, steadying her, searching her face for clues. What she gasped was very far from expectation.

'I think Ider has gone to challenge Amlawdd!' The hubbub of voices ceased, all attention fell on Gwenhwyfar.

Meriaun, Gwenhwyfar's nephew, and, since Cei's death, Arthur's second-in-command, called across from the rampant walkway, 'Ider is confined to barracks.'

Turning her head, Gwenhwyfar glanced briefly at him, urgently at Arthur, clutching fearfully at his arm. 'He was distraught at the shambles of yesterday. I fear he has gone to prove himself worthy of the Artoriani and to take revenge! I know he has! Arthur, he will be in grave danger!'

Arthur's eyes flickered, several unreasonable thoughts springing to mind. How did she know? Was she, then, so close to Ider that she knew his every move? Mentally, he shrugged the jealousy aside. Such a foolish gesture summed Ider up. A lad of brave talk and heroic ideals, believing in more than the truth, and living in a world of exaggeration and glorious triumph. Ider was still wet behind the ears; he needed a few more sobering battles to bring his young heels firmly back to an old earth.

Gwenhwyfar was plucking at her husband's sleeve, her fingers twitching desperate concern. 'You called the men worthless last night, Arthur, and worse. Ider would have been so hurt.' She moved her hand, laid her long, slim fingers on Arthur's chest, her expression willing him to understand and not be angry. 'He is a good cavalryman. In years to come he will be one of your best, but for now he is fresh from youth and angry over the death of his friends.'

Arthur had heard enough. Abruptly he tossed aside her arm. 'So, am I not angry over the death of my men? An attack on my family? Did this whore's whelp think I intended to do nothing? Expect me to let Amlawdd get away with this insult from his son?' he did not wait for an answer, was already swinging towards the steps, barking orders to make the men ready. 'It is not for a young pup to take matters into his own hands. When I give orders I expect them to be obeyed!' Gwenhwyfar bit her lip. She had not succeeded in keeping her husband's temper in check then. At the first step, he finished, 'I was intending to let Amlawdd sweat for a few days. If Ider, the fool, has gone to slay him, we could have a full bloody war on our hands.'

He did not pause as he ran down the two flights of steps and out into the grey-cloud daylight. 'Amlawdd will kill him.' He snarled over his shoulder, 'which will save me the bother of stringing him up myself.'

'Let me come with you?'

It had taken less than an hour to make ready. Three Turmae of Artoriani, ninety men and officers, were mounted and lined in rank ready to move out. The colours of their standards fluttered in the skirmishing wind beside the Dragon, Arthur's new banner that Gwenhwyfar had made. Red upon a white background, the proud battle colours of the Artoriani. The sore fingers and short tempers that had gone into the thing! It looked grand, fluttering and tossing from its wooden cross-pole, impatient to be off and doing with the men.

Arthur swung up on his stallion, ignored Gwenhwyfar, holding the horse's reins while he mounted. Again, she repeated, 'Let me come.'

'No.' His answer had sounded too sharp, too much a reprimand. Softening his tone, he explained his reason for denying her. 'I know not what we shall find, Cymraes. If Amlawdd was behind this, he is to be punished, but I cannot risk a war with him, not while Hueil threatens to run the hills tinder-dry in the North. This attack,' he gestured at the stiff body of Rhica bound across a pack mule, 'may be as much of a surprise to the father as it was to us.' He sniffed sardonically. 'Although I doubt it.' He settled himself in the saddle, tossed his cloak comfortable and gathered the reins.

'What do you intend to do?' Gwenhwyfar had not let go her hold on the reins.

Arthur shrugged his shoulders. Do? He had no idea, hoped something would come to mind before he reached Amlawdd's fortress. 'I'll talk and be polite and politic. An exercise in diplomacy. Assuming Ider hasn't buggered things up too much.'

Gwenhwyfar smiled up at him, eyes sparking triumph. 'Then, if you ride in peace, there is no reason for me not to come with you.' She put her hand on his thigh, her eyes desperately pleading. 'Ider fought well for me, Arthur, were it not for him I would now be a stiffening corpse.'

'Were it not for him, I would not be riding to stop a war before it starts. I am King, Cymraes, not Ider.' He reached out to run his finger down her cheek, under her chin. 'Or do you harbour thoughts that you would rather have him instead of me?'

She caught his hand in her own, laced her fingers with his. 'I know Ider has a love for me, but it is only a cub's raw feelings for an ideal. He will soon find a woman of his own and beyond his duties, forget all about me.' She kissed Arthur's palm, placed the hand on the stallion's reins and met her eyes to his. 'For my part, I feel a fond responsibility for the lad.'

Arthur leant forward, touched her lips briefly with his own. 'I'll be back as soon as I can.' A second kiss. He held her eyes a moment. He wanted to believe her. Had to believe her, for he could not exist without Gwenhwyfar's love. With sudden movement he raised his arm and signalled to move out.

Not stopping to watch them leave, Gwenhwyfar ran to her chamber and seized up a cloak and the sword that Arthur had ordered specially made for her. Some inches shorter than his own, a blade of thirty-six inches, this had a carved ivory grip fashioned of a size to fit her smaller woman's hand and a biting-sharp edge. She buckled on the bronze-studded leather baldric and scabbard, had no time for changing into bracae and tunic. She could always discard the hampering swirl of skirts and fight in under-tunic if necessary, or naked. She laughed cussedly as she ran for the stables. That would stir the men!

She flung a bridle and saddle on the nearest tethered stallion, and mounted. Arthur was already down the hill, riding at a steady jog westwards. His expression was black thunder as Gwenhwyfar, urging her horse at a reckless speed past the ranks, drew level with him and reined in.

369

'I said no!' he roared. He kicked his horse on, causing the bad-tempered animal to bound forwards, ears back, neck snaking.

Gwenhwyfar kept pace. 'The insult came to me also, Arthur. You cannot stop me from coming.'

His hands jerked the reins, causing his stallion's ears to flatten in protest. Snorting, Onager lashed out, his hind leg pistoning at Gwenhwyfar's black, whose teeth bared in response, front hoof striking out.

'Bull of Mithras!' Arthur bellowed, hauling his stallion aside. These were war-horses, temperamental, often savage, trained to fight. Then he laughed, ran his hand soothingly down his stallion's neck and jerking his head for Gwenhwyfar to ride beside him, moved off at a trot. 'Damn you, wife, you and your bloody independence!'

Gwenhwyfar responded to his laughter. 'Independence is it? I'm coming along to give Ider a damned piece of my mind before you take the opportunity from me!'

§ IX

Ider pushed his horse on, alternating between a steady trot and the occasional loping canter. The Artoriani war-horses were corn fed where possible, it gave them stamina and muscle, an edge, that essential turn of speed. When he had set out from Caer Cadan, hot with rage and humiliation, he had no idea what he was going to do when he reached Amlawdd's stronghold. The idea had come slowly, working into his mind and ripening as he rode. It was a good plan. Aye, a good plan!

He waited under the cloaking shadow of rain-dripping trees till dawn, dozing a fitful, dream-riddled sleep, dreaming of frogs. Several times he woke startled, afraid. He squatted then, hunkered down, afraid to sleep, mindful of the rain-wet long grass that could hide the bodies of those repulsive creatures. Waited and watched the night surrendering to the inevitability of day. He could still hear

370

them, the frogs that lived in this eternally wet estuary where the Summer Land marshes drained into the sea. Not for nothing was Amlawdd's fortress that was rising as a dark shadow against the day-bleaching sky commonly called the Mount of Frogs. Ider detested the things.

The gates were opening as he walked his horse, head low on a loose rein, up the steep, muddied track. From the vantage point of the watch tower, the keeper looked down through suspicious eyes at the approaching rider. Ider halted, tipped his head up to him, nodded good day. The keeper sniffed disdainfully, indicated the lad's sword while ostentatiously knocking an arrow into his own held bow. 'You come well armed.'

Easing his buttocks in the saddle, Ider kept his hands well sighted on the reins, away from the sword pommel. 'A lone traveller must be prepared for dangers on the road.' He smiled congenially. 'Even here, beneath the gaze of Amlawdd's imposing Caer, a man may not be safe.'

The gatekeeper sniffed again, wiped his nose on his tunic sleeve, did not lower the bow. He ducked his head backwards. 'My Lord welcomes only those guests who come with good cause.'

Ider nudged his horse into the darker shadows that stretched from the gate-tunnel entrance. Raising his hand, said mildly, pleasantly, 'Oh, I come with a bloody good cause, don't worry on that score.' He trotted through, beneath the watch tower, fought the desire to glance back, to see whether the man had lowered his bow.

The cluster of ramshackle dwelling places, as with most forts, were built in a scatter radiating from the heart of the place, the Lord's Hall. From the escape holes in the reed-thatched roofs, came curling wisps of smoke, dark and sulky against the lead-grey sky. Several women were already about their daily business, one in particular, a dark-haired woman, smiling at him as he passed, the smile beneath her eye suggesting more than that of a simple greeting to a stranger.

A gaggle of children, mostly boys, milled around Ider's horse to escort him up the steep incline to the Hall, chattering and laughing, asking questions, patting his horse, touching his sword, shield and spears. He reined in before the Hall, dismounted, handed the reins to the nearest boy. 'Take care of him.' He felt in his waist pouch, found a bent and battered bronze coin, tossed it to the boy. Coins were a rarity, the rich economy of the Romans giving way to a return to the old systems of barter and trade; minted coins were for the wealthy, and Arthur's well-paid men. Ider needed to make an impression and the boy's whoop of delighted thanks suggested he was treading the right direction. For all that, his hand slid to feel the security of his sword, needing that small reassurance as he took a breath and walked into the none too welcoming, gaping mouth of the open doorway, hoping that his story of desertion from the Pendragon's incessant foul-tempered reprimands would be accepted at least long enough to be able to get near Amlawdd. Beyond that, Ider had not planned, but then, there would not be much beyond the killing of Amlawdd. He stepped through the door. A second, fleeting hope, almost a prayer. That his own death would be quick.

§ X

Morgaine sang as she cooked her supper of gathered root herbs and a fat young partridge, a gift left by those who remembered the Goddess. Her pleasant voice rose high above the rain-shimmering trees, echoing her intensity of happiness. She ought not to sing, ought not to be so happy, for soon she would need to find a stylus and wax tablet – and the courage – to write to her mother. She dare not disobey, for Morgause had many bound spies to ensure that the words on the wind reached her hungry ears, for all that she was a prisoner of the King and shut away at Caer Luel. Morgaine would have preferred him to have killed the evil bitch. It was a terrible thing to say about your own mother, but the truth was often terrible.

She would have to write that he had come; that Arthur had come to her . . . she ceased her song, the words trailing into a silence as she sat back on her heels, her hands going tight around her drawn knees. Morgause had sent her orders, some written, passed through trusted hands, others whispered on the lips of travellers. *Arthur will come, to you,* she had said. *I pay traders to talk of you, and one day his curiosity will make him come. You must get a child from him, for such a child will be useful to me. And then you will kill this Pendragon, for me to raise his child for my own.*

A single tear slid down Morgaine's cheek, she let it trickle unheeded across her skin, let it drip. Arthur had come, and they had sat, sipping her sweet fermented wine, eating goat's cheese and fresh-baked barley bread and they had talked companionably to each other. Talked and laughed together as friends, a new and wonderful experience for Morgaine, for she had never talked for conversation's sake, or shared laughter with a friend. Nor had she ever loved with a man – nor had she still, for she could not do as Morgause had ordered, could not lie with a man with spite and hate as her reason. She loved Arthur, could not bring about their union by wickedness and greed.

He had slept, sprawled on her bed of meadow hay and sweet-smelling herbs, he had lain back and slept. And she had sat, as she sat now, beside the hearth-fire, squatting on her heels with her hands gathered around her knees, watching him sleep. Watching as the strain of tiredness eased from his deep-sleeping body.

How could she tell that hag woman, who so unexpectedly, and so menacingly had returned again into her sheltered, peaceful life, of something as precious as love?

He had woken as day began to fade into evening, his face relaxed, body eased and mind mended. She was a healer, Morgaine, a healer, not a murdering, torturing bitch like her sow-bred mother! Morgaine would not spoil her love for this man with her mother's cruel spite! Would not!

More tears slithered down her skin, the fat from her supper dripped on the flames and hissed, the partridge flesh scorching and burning, but Morgaine did not see or hear. Her head bowed to her knees and she began to cry, the great enormity of happiness gone, and in its place a void of lonely despair. She would not betray the Pendragon, not for all the fear and punishments threatened by her mother, because one day, one day, he might find it in him to come to her again, and love her.

XI

Delays lengthened the ride for Arthur, Gwenhwyfar and the men from Caer Cadan to Amlawdd's fortress. The wind had shifted round from the north-east and the clouds shed their load in a downpour that sent the puddles and muddied ruts hissing and boiling. The men tightened their cloaks around their necks, and the horses, with ears flattened, tried to turn their rumps into the needle-pointed, stinging rain. Already agitated, a horse shied violently as a nesting bird took sudden flight from beneath its hooves. It was one of those accidents that are unexpected and unavoidable. The horse squealed, ducked sharply to the left, his head dropping, back humping and the rider tumbled across his shoulder, landing awkwardly.

They stopped to assess the damage, standing drearily in the pouring rain, found a broken collar-bone. The Decurion fashioned a sling, one man was detached from the ranks to escort the injured man back to the Caer. Delay. The ground underfoot, already well marshy, sucked and squelched beneath hooves. They could travel only at a walk, any faster and the horses would flounder. More delay.

Midday. The light was little more than that of early evening. It was growing colder, the rain falling in a steady sheet, the horses' coats steaming. The view ahead was obscured by the slush of rain and the binding mist that seethed and curled from the flood levels up to join the low, menacing cloud. Then, an hour's ride west of Yns Witrin, they found the bridge down. The river had risen four hand-spans and was gushing in a mass of white foam through the fallen, twisted timbers, swept aside by the raging current.

Arthur halted, sat morosely regarding the jagged ends of wood that gaped like wolf's fangs above the fast flow of the river. He sniffed dripping rain from his nose, turned in the saddle, eyed a squalid settlement clinging miserably to the higher ground a quarter of a mile off. A haphazard clutter of decrepit wattle huts squatted between scrubby rectangular fields divided by hawthorn hedges, the plots resembling the staggered pattern of a mortared brick-built wall. The hawthorn, once cut and twisted into an efficient barrier for keeping stock in or out, was escaping from its enforced lacing, its seedlings growing up like boar's bristles, unchecked, unkempt. The outer fields were untended. Come harvest, thistles would choke what little corn grew. A despondent place for a pathetic community of people who no longer cared.

A man nursing an axe, stood watching the men ride up from the river. Ragged sacking covered his head against the rain, crude leggings and grass-stuffed boots adorned his legs. His beard was unkempt, his hair unshorn, fleas and lice shuffled and hopped about his clothing and unwashed body. As Arthur approached, he waited, holding that great, sharp-honed axe across his folded arms, the blade bright, glistening among the dark rattle of rain.

The dwellings, appearing decayed from the kindness of distance, turned out to be worse than that. Two were burnt-out remains, gutted, with only a few pathetic reminders to show that some building had once stood there. Another had only its front wall standing, nothing else, a fourth, no roof. Among it all lay the black, heat-twisted remains of bodies. Women, young children, a cow, two goats, and even a skinny, mange-furred dog. Beneath the shelter of a partially collapsed wall of the fifth a bedraggled woman squatted with three round-eyed children, huddling cold, wet, hungry and miserable.

'When, how, did this happen?' Arthur asked, appalled, as he approached and reined in. He had seen squalor, seen the ruin left behind an invading army or victorious rout. But this? The Summer Land was peaceful, relatively prosperous.

The man took his time to answer. He looked directly at Arthur, assessing him, chewed on toothless gums, spat. 'Day afore yesterday.'

The Decurion beside the Pendragon asked, 'When did the bridge go?'

The man studied him and glanced almost with a sneer at Gwenhwyfar, some paces behind. He spat again into the ankle-deep mud. 'Don't rightly know, nor care.'

The Decurion leant forward in his saddle, impatient. He spoke loudly, slowly, as if talking to an idiot moon-calf. 'Has a lone rider passed this way during the night?'

'Don't know that either.'

'Imbecile! Do you know anything?'

Arthur motioned for his officer to be silent, brought his right leg over his horse's withers, casually hooked it over one of the two front saddle horns.

He looked around at the overgrown hedges, a gate-less gap in the wall. The place had been raided and burnt, but had there been anything worth the raiding?

He indicated the poorly kept walls. 'Your village is undefended.'

'Not much worth defending.' The man was becoming irritating.

Arthur smiled, enforcing good nature, slid from his horse, his feet sinking in the ooze. 'Is it worth defending them?' He gestured at the children, the dead.

'What chance did we have against armed men?'

'Where are the rest of your menfolk?'

The man scratched behind his left earlobe, eventually tossed his head at a piled heap of timber and rubbish that had been burnt. 'They killed 'em. Tied 'em up, burnt 'em.' Arthur decided against pursuing further questions. The answers were too sickening.

'You are alive,' the Decurion observed with a snarl. The man did not rise to the bait, stared a moment, shrugged, spat, answered, 'I were not 'ere.'

Again, Arthur waved his officer quiet. They had not the time to stand bickering. 'Where do folk cross the river when the bridge is down?'

Drawling, insolent, 'Wouldn't know. Bridge has never been down afore.'

Gwenhwyfar too, had dismounted. While the men talked she made her way to the woman. She squatted before her, heedless of the mud caking her boots, noted the sunken, hollow eyes that had no more tears left to be cried, realised the filthy bundle in the woman's arms was a child. The thing whimpered, its tiny face turning outward, its face flushed scarlet.

'Is the child ill?' Gwenhwyfar asked softly, smiling, the question intended as friendly conversation, the answer was obvious. The mother drew away, wide-eyed, frightened, a half-scream on her lips, the child clutched tighter in her arms.

Sudden movement behind! Arthur screamed a warning, leapt forward, his sword coming as he moved into his hand, but he was too slow! The axe, that bright-honed axe head, was coming down, falling towards Gwenhwyfar as the peasant split the air with the full force of his arms and shoulders. She ducked, rolled aside as Arthur lunged, both their breaths hissing with the need for instant motion. The axe thudded into the sludge where a hair's breadth before, Gwenhwyfar had squatted.

Arthur's sword was at the man's throat, pricking against the skin. Breathing heavily, nostrils flared and anger great, he snarled, 'Is this how you welcome travellers?' He brought the sword up, holding it two-handed, intending to bring it down through the man's skull, but stopped, the blade raised, as, fearless, the peasant said, 'This is how your kind treat the poor.' There was no fear, only scorn and contempt.

Although her heart beat wildly, Gwenhwyfar tried to give the impression of unconcern, as if having an axe almost splitting your skull in two was an everyday occurrence. She laughed ironically to herself. As, it seemed, these past two days, it surely was! 'Leave it, Arthur,' she said, 'these people have suffered enough.' She pulled herself from the mud, crouched again before the woman. 'Can I help?'

The man bent to retrieve his axe, but Arthur's sword crashed between him and the weapon. 'My wife is generous, I am not. Another movement and I will have your arm off.'

The man returned Arthur's fierce glare. 'Your kind have done enough here. We need nothing, save for you to be gone and leave us alone.'

Arthur, tipped his head to one side, curiosity overcoming anger, lowered his sword but did not sheath it. 'Our kind?'

'Aye,' the man stared directly at him, 'your kind.' His clenched knuckles were white, jaw tense. 'Your kind. Those who find pleasure in killing the innocent. Your kind, who destroy our homes, burn and trample our meagre crops, steal or slaughter our stock.' His enraged eyes slid to the young mother cradling the child. 'Rape and butcher our womenfolk.' None too gently, he prodded Arthur's chest with a grubby finger. 'There's one law for your kind, another for mine. You take what you please, do as you please. We accept that or die.'

'That is not my law,' Arthur answered, sliding his sword into its scabbard.

'That's how it is.'

'Then it should not be.'

'What should be and what is are differing matters, my Lord Pendragon.' The man bent again, picked up his axe. Arthur made no attempt to stop him.

The Decurion, standing behind Arthur, his own sword still drawn, snorted disdain. He was cold and wet, wanted to leave this depressing place, wanted to find that young idiot Ider, string him up as punishment against desertion and go home. 'Ah, so you know who we are!' Drily he added, 'I wondered.'

The villager swung to face him. 'I know well who you are! I can see with my eyes. I recognise the Dragon.' He spat contemptuously at the banner. 'The Pendragon, defender of the land? Don't make me laugh! Where were you on the morning before last? Where were you when they came to burn and steal, kill and rape?'

'Who?' Gwenhwyfar asked the young mother. 'Who came? Sea-raiders?' She glanced at Arthur, surely not this far inland? Arthur shook his head, shrugged his shoulders, as much at a loss as she was.

The mother – she could be no more than ten and five summers –was rocking her baby, bringing what little comfort she could to the miserable child. She spoke in a timid whisper. 'Amlawdd's people.'

'And you call them my kind?' Arthur roared, his fists bunching, teeth grating. 'I assure you, my friend, the low-born whore's son who dared do such as this is not of my kind.'

Gwenhwyfar held her arms out for the baby, took it gently, the tiny thing was burning with fever. She stood, rocking the child as the mother had done, said, 'We are here to revenge ourselves on Amlawdd for wrongs his son has done to us. He is to pay for the

378

death of men of the Artoriani. So too shall he pay for that which has been done here.'

The man sneered at her, snorting disbelief. 'Today Amlawdd shall grovel before you, tomorrow his men shall come raiding again. He means to take for himself a kingdom.' He looked pointedly at Arthur. 'Your kingdom.'

Arthur's bland expression was his familiar, implacable, grim squint, right eye half shut, left eyebrow raised. He had his spies, his people, and no word had come to him of this. He spoke now with a tone as hard as iron. 'No one takes from me.'

Gwenhwyfar handed the baby back to his mother. There was nothing she could do, it was clearly dying. 'Give him love. He needs no more in this life.'

'I am the only man here now.' The peasant spoke again, his bluster and anger giving ground to the hopelessness of it all. He swept a hand at the remains of the settlement. 'When they attacked, I was not here, I had taken my daughter to wed with a good man.' He tossed his head south, wiped a dirt-encrusted hand under his nose. 'Had I not taken her that day . . .' He left the thoughts unspoken.

'We will be coming back,' Gwenhwyfar said to him, to the woman. 'We will return with your stolen cattle and some of our men will stay to help you rebuild.'

The Decurion muttered something disparaging, Gwenhwyfar was about to snap a curt reprimand, but Arthur cut in. 'These poor wretches are as much my responsibility as the Artoriani. Who can they trust if their King turns his back on them?'

Arthur grasped the peasant's hand between his own, held it a moment with genuine friendship. 'My Lady Gwenhwyfar speaks true. It shall be.'

They rode away into the rain, Gwenhwyfar looking back once at the desolate place. Too often she took warmth, food and security for granted. And her husband's protective sword. Others, too many others, had not that privilege.

XII

Evening was closing in, though the afternoon was barely spent. Relentless rain and heavy cloud surrounded the light, sent it scuttling away into the west. The gates were already closed when Pendragon reached Amlawdd's fortress.

'Open!' the Decurion roared, riding forward to hammer on the solid, iron-studded doors with the pommel of his sword. A face appeared over the wooden tower, two disgruntled eyes above a set mouth peering down at the riders below.

'My Lord has gone to his supper. There will be no admittance till the sun rises on the morrow.' The face withdrew, an open insult.

Arthur bellowed at the blank space above the defences, 'Open the gate, you dog's turd, before I order my men to batter it down!'

The gatekeeper laughed scornfully from his side of the palisade. 'And who is it who threatens my Lord's property with so few men? Be off with you!'

Arthur turned his horse, stood the stallion so he had clear view of the watch tower and the wooden fencing. 'I, Arthur the Pendragon, demand it!'

The gatekeeper hesitated, squinted at the sodden banner hanging lank on its pole.

'I, and a guard of the Artoriani.' Arthur walked his horse directly beneath the tower, looked up into the keeper's face, his expression murderous thunder, his hand beginning to draw his sword, defying the man to bar them entrance. The keeper flicked his gaze nervously across the group below, withdrew. There came a sound of footsteps clattering down wooden steps, exchanged words, running feet. The gate opened.

Arthur held the reins casually in one hand, the other resting lightly on his sword pommel, followed the track up the incline through the tangle of dwelling places, where faint lights were starting to flicker against the seeping darkness. A crash from the Hall as the doors burst open, spewing light and men, and Amlawdd himself stood silhouetted against the brightness, arms folded, legs planted wide, his Hall warriors craning their necks to see the better, crowding behind.

Arms spread as wide as his false smile, Amlawdd tramped down the steps, his welcome greeting Arthur, who was dismounting, as if he were a brother long from home. 'Pendragon! Welcome to my humble stronghold, thrice welcome! It is honoured I am to call you guest!'

Arthur returned the smile and the bear-hug, knowing both for the sham they were. As false as a carved, walrus-ivory tooth. He had never been inside Amlawdd's gates, avoided the place, until the necessity of this day, had never been nearer than a wattle hut built two miles distant beside the causeway that ran high above the marsh-levels even in the wettest of winters. He cast a quick seeking glance at the people beginning to crowd around, men and women, a few children, found her, the woman he occasionally met in that small flea-ridden hut, caught her swift-sent smile, but did not return it. He was not supposed to know Brigid of the Dark Eyes. Amlawdd would have her dead if he suspected Arthur bedded the stronghold's whore, Arthur's planted spy.

Amlawdd was nodding, laughing, creating congeniality. 'If you had sent word of your coming, I would have ensured a feast be prepared in your honour; as it is, we have just this moment started our meagre supper.' He gestured a small, helpless apology. 'We can find you something of course . . .' He bellowed for the cup of welcome to be brought. Then he saw Gwenhwyfar, coming from the darkness behind Arthur's horse, her hair tossing loose, the torch-light settling shadows leaping across her face.

There were several things Amlawdd wanted. One was Arthur's death, the second, kingship, which would come with the success of the first, and seeing Gwenhwyfar, he added a third. He wanted Arthur's power and title, why not his woman also? With a look that conveyed more than polite greeting, Amlawdd stepped forward to welcome her, to embrace her as he had Arthur, but Gwenhwyfar had no intention of being touched by this toad-spawned maggot. She stepped away from his advance, stood beside her husband, her hand, like his, resting lightly on the sword pommel at her hip.

Pretending not to notice, Amlawdd ushered Arthur into the glowing warmth of his Hall and feigning delight as he escorted the unexpected guests to the table set across the far end, made elaborate show of offering Arthur his own comfortable, cushioned seat.

'I do not see your son, Amlawdd,' Arthur said, raising his eyebrows in question at Rhica's wife as she dipped a reverence to the King.

She had to answer. 'He is hunting, my Lord. We expect him not till the morrow.'

Arthur left the matter there for now, smiling to himself at the knowledge that Rhica's body was safe with the rest of his men, camped a mile to the south. Food, good wine and ale were brought. Amlawdd lived well.

The Artoriani, hand-picked men with a steady eye and hand, sat among Amlawdd's men. They ate and listened and watched, saw that through the rising laughter and talk, they in turn were watched. As a weasel watches a young hare before striking the death-blow.

Gwenhwyfar ate little. She had no stomach for the food. The atmosphere was polite if not convivial, there seemed no anxiety over Rhica. His wife, Eigr, had obviously spoken part truth, his return not yet expected. There was no sign of Ider. She sat between Arthur and Amlawdd, sitting as close to her husband as she could. Like his two deceased brothers Gorlois and Melwas, Amlawdd was a heavily built man, but unlike them, did not run to excess weight. A giant of a man, powerful in size and strength, he had a square-framed body that was muscularly toned and hardened: an ominous opponent at arms. Easy to see he and Melwas were of the same brood. Melwas had been shorter, his corpulence accentuating the difference of height, and his was the unconcealed sadistic ruthlessness. Amlawdd was more prudent. Gwenhwyfar's insides were knotting at this enforced reminder of a man who had murdered her beloved brother, raped her, and brutally beaten Arthur. Melwas was dead, she herself had killed him, but Amlawdd was very much alive and his thigh was pressing against hers, his fingers brushing her hand, eyes lingering on the swell of her breasts beneath her gown. Mithras' blood but she wanted to slit the bastard's throat here and now!

Amlawdd's hand managed to find its way to her knee. She frantically nudged Arthur's arm, but he was involved in conversation with Rhica's wife, a quiet woman, who seemed not to have the courage to shoo away a hissing goose. Married at ten and four years, now, unknowingly, a widow at two and twenty!

Tearing the wing from a roasted chicken, Arthur bit into the tender flesh. He was enjoying himself, enjoying this deception. It was a game he excelled at. He said to Eigr, 'Your husband hunts often then. Alone or with friends?'

Eigr wished she were not seated beside the King but he had insisted and to refuse would have been to offer insult. Her husband's father had been of no help, besotted as he was by Gwenhwyfar. She glanced from him to his fat and lazy wife, seated on Amlawdd's left. She seemed oblivious to her husband's undisguised attentions towards Gwenhwyfar. Had that been Rhica . . . Eigr swallowed a mouthful of wine. Had Rhica been here, he too would be curling himself around Gwenhwyfar, for she was a beautiful woman, and Eigr was plain. Rhica preferred beautiful women. He told his wife so, often.

With lowered eyes, she toyed with her finger rings. The Pendragon's questioning was flustering her, she answered as best she could. Aye, Rhica was often away. *Thank the God.* No, not often alone, usually with friends. No, she knew not what or where he hunted. *Nor did she care.*

Arthur smiled in his most charming manner, interspersed the interrogation with trivial matters. She knew nothing, was too feared to be hiding anything of importance. Feared of her husband or Amlawdd? Both? Arthur drank his wine. Well, she had one less to fear now!

Beneath the table, Amlawdd was edging his hand higher. The prick of a dagger tip in a most personal place instantly stopped the upward movement. Gwenhwyfar smiled innocently at him, her vivid green eyes swirling with sparks of tawny gold. Smiling, sweetly smiling, she said, very quietly, so that only Amlawdd might hear, 'If you do not keep your fat fingers to yourself, I will geld you. Here. Now. My husband would be pleased to have the rest of you.'

Wisely, he left her alone.

Tugging a comb through her hair with such force that a bone tooth broke, Gwenhwyfar cursed and hurled the thing across the room. She sat cross-legged on the bed, her back to Arthur, who was whistling tunelessly. An intensely irritating sound.

'I have no doubt,' she said contemptuously, 'that were Amlawdd to walk in here at this moment and demand I strip naked for his pleasure, you would go, smiling, and leave me to him.'

'Nonsense,' Arthur grunted as he heaved off his boot, began removing his bracae.

'Nonsense is it?' Gwenhwyfar unfolded her legs, rolled to her knees and faced her husband. 'Is it nonsense that he was groping me out there, while you sat next to me pretending not to notice?'

Arthur rumpled her hair with his fingers as though he was soothing a ruffled child. 'I knew you'd soon sort him out.'

'Oh, did you!' Gwenhwyfar slapped his hand away. 'The man is a licentious, fat-bellied bastard. As was his brother. Have you forgotten what I suffered at the hands of his brother?'

'Gorlois was much the same, from what I hear.' Arthur made a crude noise through his lips. 'No match for my father though! He took Ygrainne from him with the ease of plucking ripe fruit from the tree.'

Gwenhwyfar hissed sinisterly, annoyed at Arthur's apparent unconcern and good humour, 'Happen Amlawdd plans to turn the spear!'

Arthur briefly frowned, he had not considered the possibility of a similar revenge. A lazy smile spread. He leant forward, kissed his wife's pouting lips. 'You'd not let him.'

'With no help from you!'

He kissed her again, slower, with more deliberation and force, suddenly glad that she was with him. Naked, he settled himself beneath the bed-furs, inviting Gwenhwyfar in beside him. 'While Amlawdd's senses were conveniently occupied with pawing at you . . .'

'What!'

'Oh hush, woman, while you distracted his attention. There, does that sound more tactful? I was able to ask questions.' He was unthreading the lacings to her undertunic. 'I warned that you must take your own risks by coming with me. Amlawdd's rutting is part of that risk.'

Huffily, Gwenhwyfar withdrew Arthur's hand from inside her tunic. 'Yours too, it seems.' A second time, she slapped his hand away. 'Did you learn much?'

'A little.' Arthur paid no mind to her ill temper or batting hand. 'I'll have all I want by dawn.'

§ XIII

Cramp tingling in his arm woke Arthur from a deep sleep. Carefully he withdrew it from beneath Gwenhwyfar, rubbing the painful sensation of a thousand thousand pricking arrows. He sat up, reached for his bracae lying tumbled beside the bed on the floor. Gwenhwyfar stirred, mumbled.

'I need to relieve myself,' he whispered. 'Go back to sleep.' He tucked the sleeping-fur tighter around her body, holding in the warmth where his own body had lain. Pulling a tunic over his head, and throwing a cloak over his shoulders, he picked up his boots and made for the door. Once, he glanced back at Gwenhwyfar before he slid silently out. She was a mound beneath the fur, safe asleep.

Brigid was waiting for him, curled before the night-dead embers of her fire, her head resting on cushioning arms, dark hair falling forward, covering her face. He crept into the round bothy, knelt beside her and lightly touched her shoulder. She sat up, startled, her mouth forming a soundless exclamation. Relaxing, she smiled, welcoming and well content. 'My Lord, I waited. I must have slept.'

Arthur squatted beside her, fed kindling to the low fire, the flames licking gratefully at the replenishment. 'I could not come earlier. Not with my wife in my bed.'

Brigid said nothing, thought, *why bring her?*

As if hearing, Arthur answered, 'It is difficult to say no to Gwenhwyfar.' He laughed softly, his hand reaching out for a hank of black hair. 'As it is difficult to say no to you.'

Brigid laid her hand over his, brought it slowly down inside the half-open lacing of her tunic, placed it over her round breast. But he made no response. Nor did he return the kiss she gave him. He did not want her this night. Shrugging, Brigid moved away from him, fed more wood to the fire.

'Do you know where Rhica is?' His question was not totally unexpected.

'Hunting.'

'Wolves or dragons?'

Brigid flicked a glance at him. They had lain together, three, four times in her little hut down by the causeway where the men not of the stronghold more often came to her. And each time she had answered his questions, told of all she knew concerning Amlawdd and his poxed allies and kindred. Arthur paid her well for her spying. They were taking a chance meeting here in her dwelling place within the stronghold. But then, she was a whore, they could always claim she was about her business.

The Pendragon chuckled at her hesitation. He leant across the gap between them, and kissed her in a different way from how he kissed Gwenhwyfar. Brigid was for using, his Cymraes for loving. He fumbled in his waist pouch, brought out a gold ring and a brooch, tossed them into her lap. 'I always pay, my beauty, for whatever you give me.' The jewels disappeared quickly into her fingers, away into her own pouch. 'A stranger has come here, to Amlawdd's Hall. Where is he?' Arthur's tone was urgent.

'He is not here.'

Arthur grabbed hold of her hair, held it in a tight grasp. 'You are here within Amlawdd's Caer at my command, Brigid. I pay you well. I expect satisfaction.'

Her posture was lewdly provocative. Deliberately misunderstanding, she answered, 'That I can give, were you to cease asking questions and strip yourself of tunic and bracae.'

Shrewdly, Arthur regarded her through slit eyes. She was not idly boasting, for Brigid was skilled in her crafts of loving – and listening. He did not need her, but then, why rely on rations when a banquet was offered?

Sweating, breathing hard, Arthur rolled from her and gathered his cloak against his damp body. Waited. She would tell him now, all he needed to know.

She lay beside him, her naked body glistening in the flickering firelight. 'Amlawdd does not love so well as you.'

Arthur picked at some meat that was left in the crevice of his tooth. 'Amlawdd, I would wager, does little as well as I.'

She sat up, drew her knees to her stomach. 'He came to me earlier, when first the Hall settled for the night. He does not pay so high as you.'

'And of what did he talk?'

Brigid began braiding her loose black hair, her arms raised, firming her breasts, making them seem rounder, fuller. 'Of Rhica not yet returning. He is afraid of his son you know. Rhica also wants a kingship. Amlawdd suspects him to be allied to you.' She laughed suddenly, throwing back her head in amusement, her white teeth gleaming in the light from the sparking fire. 'He once told me that someone ensures the Pendragon knows all that goes on here. He thinks it is Rhica who informs, and in return you will secure him this stronghold.' She laughed, her hand reaching out to trace one of the many scars scything across Arthur's skin. 'Rhica lies with me occasionally, but keeps his mind dark. Apart from boasting of the women he takes, he says little. He desperately seeks power for himself, he is belly-full of hatred.' Her finger stroked higher, Arthur ignored her. 'Is Amlawdd right? Does Rhica ally with you?'

Arthur shook his head. 'No. Tell me more of Amlawdd.'

She shruggled. 'He is angered at your unexpected visit. He told of what, when he makes a move against you, he will do to you.' She paused, dare she add more? 'Of what he would do with Gwenhwyfar when she becomes his.'

Arthur's eyes narrowed. None of this was news. He knew it from other sources, and by his own observations. 'He wants my royal torque and my wife.' He snorted contempt. Gwenhwyfar was safe enough. His fingers rubbed gently along the familiar curve of the gold, dragon-shaped torque at his neck. So was this.

But when Brigid said the next, he sat alert, intent. This was news! 'When Hueil of the North rides against you, Amlawdd intends to join with him. Hueil is to rule the North, Amlawdd the South. He boasts that he will be Wledig, supreme.'

Arthur sat silent, digesting her words. Hueil. He sucked his lower lip. Must he watch his back sooner than he thought?

Brigid fed more fuel to the fire, the orange glow shadowing across the curve of her breasts and hips, said, 'Rhica is impatient for power, he is raiding farmsteadings and settlements, taking his own land.'

Arthur answered casually, 'Only raiding? Nothing more?'

She waved her hand, dismissive, her nose wrinkling. 'He has only the stomach to steal the cattle and women from peasants. Amlawdd has quarrelled with him often over it, warning him not to overstep the traces. Too much would bring you to this coast.'

Arthur's eyes met hers and she saw suddenly why he was there. He nodded, once, a slight, almost imperceptible agreement to her realisation. 'Too much has brought me.'

For a while and a while, Brigid thought on the information, a stirring in her stomach that things were about to change. 'The young man, Ider?' She slid one of her rings from her finger, toyed with it. 'I wondered if he were here on your business, but he made no secret of his identity, the others who whisper your password come as traders. Amlawdd did not much like him.' He had been a fine-looking young man, worthy of Brigid's admiring scrutiny as he had ridden past her open door. A pity Amlawdd had ordered him killed before she had a chance to invite him inside.

She wriggled forward, bored with all the talk, slid her hands up Arthur's back. ' 'Tis not wise to send a boy to do a man's work, my Lord.'

Arthur's reply was gruff as he removed her hands, stood and dressed. 'Nor should a man use a whore when he has a wife to warm his bed.'

§ XIV

Gwenhwyfar was furious. She stood three paces within the door, fists clenched, eyes shooting gold-flecked arrows of fire, finding it difficult to speak, so great was her rage. 'You stand there,' she spat, 'and calmly tell me that we are leaving? Leaving without a damn thing!' Her arms flew into the air, came down and clapped against her body with a simultaneous exhalation of exasperation. 'I do not understand you, Arthur Pendragon. All these years I have at least had the comfort of knowing why you act as you do. Bull's blood, Arthur, now you take that from me!'

He stood with his back to the closed door. He had known she would react badly to his announcement, and Gwenhwyfar riled was not an easy woman to face. He spread his arms. 'I can do nothing here, Cymraes.' He walked towards her, intending to place sympathetic hands on her shoulders but she stepped away. He sighed, a battlefield was sometimes preferable to Gwenhwyfar in a temper.

He tried again to explain. 'I have come direct from Amlawdd.' A brief grin twitched. 'He was not pleased at being roused at first light, but changed his mind when he realised I was bidding him farewell.' The grin broadened. 'For some reason, Amlawdd is not too keen on having us here!' Gwenhwyfar did not return the laughter. He conceded to her grim expression, fell serious again. 'He says the raids on villages are through Rhica's youthful high spirits. It seems true – were I to punish every chieftain whose son went cattle raiding, I would need to hang every man in the country!' Her face remained stern. This was not going well. 'What has been stolen is to be returned, I have Amlawdd's assurance of that.'

'And you believe him?' she retorted, plonking herself on the bed, wincing as its hardness rattled through her body. 'Are you going soft in the head or something? Rhica tried to kill me, and your son, or have you forgotten?'

Arthur's patience was beginning to wear thin. He wanted to be gone from this place, not standing here wasting riding time, arguing with his wife. 'No I have not forgotten, Amlawdd was not involved, will not defy me until Hueil is ready to march south.' Arthur swept his fingers through his ruffled dark hair. 'It was Rhica's doing, Cymraes, the attack on you, not Amlawdd's. It may even not have been planned. A chance encounter which Rhica's swelling greed took advantage of.'

Gwenhwyfar's answer was derisive, 'And that makes it all right, does it!'

Arthur responded instantly, 'It has been kept as no secret that Rhica was hunting down towards Lindinis.' He was fastening his cloak pin, making ready to leave. 'It is reasonable to assume that Rhica saw you in Lindinis. There is only the one road for you to take – all he had to do was choose his place and wait for you.'

'And Amlawdd?'

'Has too much wagered with Hueil.' Arthur turned to the door, with his hand on the latch said, 'I'll fetch the horses up. He will not cross me until he is ready, not even when he learns of Rhica's death.'

Gwenhwyfar had not moved. Calmly, distinctly, she stated, 'And what will you do, Arthur, when he is ready? When next time he succeeds in killing me? Come talk to him again? Drink his wine, eat his food and lay his whore?'

Arthur's hand froze on the depressed latch.

'Do you think me that much a fool? You were gone too long last night, returned with the smell of woodsmoke and woman clinging to you.'

Arthur swallowed, very slowly he let go of the latch, turned to face her. 'She is in my pay, Gwenhwyfar.'

'Are not they all?'

She had misunderstood. Arthur stepped forward hurriedly, his head shaking, hands wildly gesturing. 'Na, I do not mean like that, Brigid is my informer here. I need her to keep close eye on Amlawdd.'

'Yet you bedded her.'

'Aye, I bedded her! Brigid is a two-faced bitch who could as easily tattle to Amlawdd as to me. I give her pretty jewels and pretty words and keep her belly full with my attentions and her tongue wagging in my direction.' He held up a finger, was standing before her. 'And before you say it, aye, I also enjoy it. I told you not to ride here with me, it was your choice, not mine. If the saddle's giving you a sore backside either put up with it or get off and walk!' He knew he ought not to be shouting, but admitting being in the wrong was not an easy medicine to swallow. He marched back to the door, tore it open. 'I am leaving, I have something to do. If you want to stay here that's up to you. No doubt Amlawdd will find you a bed.'

'Damn you, Arthur!' Gwenhwyfar ran to the door, shouting as his departing back. 'If that is what you want, leave me here to finish Amlawdd my way!' She pulled her sword from its scabbard, waved the blade in the vague direction of Amlawdd's Hall.

Arthur halted in mid-stride, closed his eyes and exhaled through his nose. He turned round, strode back to her, pushed her inside the chamber and slammed the door shut behind him. 'You know damned well that is not what I want.' He took her angry face between his hands, tilted his head on one side and suddenly smiled. 'Mithras but you are beautiful when you glower like that?'

'Don't try to sweet talk me, Pendragon!'

Indignant he put his hand on his heart. 'Me? Sweet talk you? You're too bad-tempered for that, my lass!' He was winning her round! He breathed a sigh of relief. Blood, that had been a close one! He placed a light kiss on her cheek, left her a moment to fetch her cloak and draped it around her shoulders. 'Brigid has told me everything we need to know, Cymraes, but she is a cunning cow, she'll only tell on her terms. And she is very jealous of you.' He spread his hands, offering peace. 'I am with Brigid, what, once a year?' A small lie would not do harm. 'She has to live with the knowing you have me all the rest of the nights.'

Swallowing her pride, Gwenhwyfar asked, 'She told you of Ider?'

Grim, Arthur nodded.

'Bad news?'

Again he nodded, but this time reached out for her and held her to him. He laid his head against hers, stroked the softness of her unruly hair. 'He was in love with you, wasn't he?' Only a slight pause before asking, 'Did you love him back?'

She half laughed, began to reply, 'Of course not, I . . .' then realised what he had said. 'Was? Arthur, you said was?' She brought her head up from his chest, searched his eyes, those usually unreadable, veiled eyes that kept his secrets to himself. But not this time; the hurt and unnecessary waste was there, plain to see. 'Amlawdd had him killed?'

For a third time, Arthur nodded. He would not trust his voice to answer. He had loved Ider too, though, for all that was dear to him, he hoped her love was the same platonic affection that they shared with all the men.

'There is nothing we can do for him, Cymraes, save go and find his body and give him burial.'

Bitter, Gwenhwyfar pushed him from her, her hands viciously thumping on his chest. 'So, you let Amlawdd attack your family and murder your men without revenge?'

He contained an angry retort, accepting her remark as justified, misguided perhaps, but justified.

'I know what I am doing, Cymraes. Trust me. Please?'

She was on the verge of shouting again, but something in his voice caught at her, a hint of intention, a self-made promise that he was not lying, but waiting. 'I do trust you,' she acknowledged, 'where men are concerned.' Her smiled widened. 'Well? Are we going?' She picked up her saddle bag, planted a cheery kiss on his cheek as she passed him on her way to the door. 'But trust you to keep your bracae on where a woman's concerned? I'd have more faith in a cockerel laying an egg!'

Arthur laughed, sauntered after her, linked his arm through hers as they strolled down the incline to the waiting horses. It was a fine day, the rain quite gone, the earth smelling rich and dark from its wetting. The sun had risen in a splendour of bright hope and Gwenhwyfar screwed her eyes against its morning-low glare. When they reached the horses, Arthur bent, took Gwenhwyfar's knee and hoisted her into the saddle. She settled herself comfortably, walked her horse beside Arthur's as they rode towards the gate-house. Asked, almost casually, 'And does Amlawdd know that Rhica will not be returning from his hunting?'

Arthur pushed into a trot, answered curtly, 'No, but he soon will.'

They found Ider where Brigid said they would, lying beside the curve of the river, half hidden by last autumn's dead bracken with the broken haft of a spear protruding at an angle from his stomach, the dried ooze of dark blood staining his tunic. Squatting beside the body, Arthur massaged his face with his hand. No matter how many deaths he witnessed, each brought that rise of bile. The fool, the damn-fool lad. What had he hoped to achieve? If it were an easy thing to be rid of that poxed bastard Amlawdd, then Arthur himself would have slit him open years past. But to die like this . . . again, he wiped his face, sat a moment, staring at the spear shaft, thinking, saying, nothing. He heard a footfall behind and leapt up, spinning around, grasped Gwenhwyfar and turned her aside in the one swift-made motion. 'You do not want to see, Cymraes.'

Her smile was weak, a brave face. 'There are many things I do not want Arthur, but I seem to get them anyway.'

He let her go, stood with her, his arm light around her waist as she too looked at the bloody mess that had once been a promising young man.

Tears were trickling down her face as Gwenhwyfar knelt beside the body. His face was bruised, one lip gashed. They had beaten him first then. Did she love him? Arthur had asked that of her, and now she asked herself. Arthur angered her so often, he was not always faithful to her. To take a lover would be one way of paying back the frequent pain Arthur caused her, but then, you did not cure a wound to the thigh by making another on the arm.

Ider? A lover? He had made her laugh when she felt like crying, made her feel safe when Arthur was not around. She had liked him, but loved him beyond the love one gave to a good friend? No, there was only one Gwenhwyfar loved, which is why she choked down the pain and kept her eyes closed. She tentatively touched the bruised swelling on Ider's cheek, drew back immediately with a squeal, leapt to her feet. 'Christ God's mercy!' she yelped, 'he's alive, Arthur!'

The Pendragon had instinctively drawn his sword at her startled exclamation. He dropped it to the grass, flung himself down beside

393

Ider, reaching to search for a beat of life. It was there! Faint, but there!

They fashioned a litter from blankets and spears for Ider, riding slowly, stopping frequently, and left Rhica's body where Ider had been found, impaled by that same broken haft of spear. Except now, it wore a dragon pennant so that Amlawdd would know when they found his son – Arthur had already insured through Brigid that he would be found – that Arthur had declared the war, and dared Amlawdd to respond.

June 465

§ XV

'My head aches.'

Gwenhwyfar glanced up from the letter she was writing at her son. He did seem rather pale. 'You have been in the sun over-long, go sit in the shade a while.'

'But the fish prefer the sun, I'll not catch anything if I move.'

Gwenhwyfar laughed, pointed at the rod and line. 'You have not caught anything anyway!'

That was true, but the boy had no intention of conceding her point. He fitted bait to the hook, cast his line and watched the worm wriggle a moment beneath the cool, green water. He sat on the bank, his feet dangling into the river; there were fish, he could see them further out sheltering in the weeds mid-stream. Once or twice he saw one rise, take a fly. He would do better with a lighter weight line and a fly for bait, worms did not seem to be favoured this day. Happen the shade would be better; he swivelled his head to study the overhanging trees up-river. Pike might lurk there, in those shadows – his mouth opened in a silent oh as a figure came from out of the shade, its finger pressed firm to lips, head shaking. Grinning, Llacheu immediately understood, entered into the jest.

His father had been gone several days, buying horses in Dumnonia. Always they needed horses. The breeding and training of a war-horse did not happen overnight, and illness or injury accounted for many a beast being put out to pasture or destroyed. Constantly, the stock had to be kept up to number. There were men Arthur had especially appointed as horse buyers, horse traders who knew their job, whom Arthur paid well, but occasionally the Pendragon liked to go out for himself, to barter and haggle, to see the bad against the good. And to be seen among the people of Britain.

He had returned to Caer Cadan to be told his wife and son were somewhere down by the river, had ridden to find them. Tethering Lamerei among the trees, Arthur had crept beneath the cool shadows, intending to leap out and startle the both of them, but Llacheu had turned his head, spotted his father. Arthur motioned him to stay quiet, grinned back at the boy as Llacheu entered the game.

Gwenhwyfar had her back propped against a tree, was bent over a wax tablet lying against her knees. The stylus was between her teeth as she thought on what to write next. So difficult, trying to be friendly yet formal. She added a few more words into the soft wax, yelped as two hands dug into her waist, the stylus scoring across the wax face, scratching through the handwriting.

'You turd!' she chided, leaping to her feet, the stylus dropping from her fingers, falling into the grass. 'You're more the child than our son!'

Arthur grinned at her, then across to Llacheu, 'I'm a better fisherman though – you'd do better in the shade, lad, it's too hot out here.'

Gwenhwyfar was standing with her hands spread on her hips. With her copper-gold hair braided and wound about her head and wearing a thin-woven, sleeveless tunic, she looked cool, summery. Her cross expression did not fool her husband, he knew she was pleased to see him. He tweaked a shoulder strap aside, kissed her shoulder, then her neck.

'Missed me?' he murmured.

'Not in the slightest,' she replied, sliding her arms about his waist and offering a more intimate kiss of greeting.

'Can I see to Lamerei?' Llacheu asked, all interest in fish disappearing now his father was home.

'Aye, lad, I've watered her but you could take her up to the Caer and rub her down.' Arthur mischievously pulled a pin from Gwenhwyfar's hair, loosening the wind of braiding so that one side slid down. She batted his hand, tried to refasten it as her husband walked with their son into the trees towards the patiently waiting mare.

Boosting his son into the saddle, Arthur handed him the reins. 'No cantering, it's too hot and she's come a long way today.'

Llacheu nodded his head. 'I'll only walk her.' He did not feel like doing more, even though this was a rare chance to ride his da's horse. His head ached, and his throat felt scratchy and dry. He headed the mare for the roadway leading up into the Caer, found he was not much enjoying the ride.

Arthur, wearing riding gear, felt hot and uncomfortable under the mail and leather. The river beckoned cool and inviting. Returning to Gwenhwyfar he began to strip, dumped his clothes in a pile beside her and plunged naked into the river, sending a spray of water across the bank and over his wife.

Gwenhwyfar squealed and called him a colourfully expressive name. He laughed and deliberately splashed her again before diving under and swimming a few yards upstream. The world below the surface was deliciously cool and green. Arthur smiled to himself as a few fish swam busily out of his way: Llacheu needed some tips in fishing it seemed! He surfaced, rolled onto his back and let the current float him back downstream, until, opposite Gwenhwyfar again, he sat in the shallows, enjoying the coolness lap around his body.

'Who do you write to?' he asked, pillowing his head on the bank, closing his eyes against the fierce glare of the sun.

'Ider. He sent word that he is healing well. I write to tell him that we are thinking of him and wish him with us.'

Silence. Arthur stirred his feet, sending rippling waves lapping at the reeds. 'If you were free of me, would you take another as huband?' He let his legs float before him, the muscles taut, keeping them straight against the flow of the river.

'I have no wish to be free of you.' Gwenhwyfar smiled adding with a jest, 'At least not most of the time. When you are in full flood with some raging anger, then I might be occasionally tempted.'

The water swirled as Arthur began climbing out and up the bank. 'Na, I am serious here. It is a good wager that I shall not live to old age. How many soldiers do you see with grey hair and wrinkled skin?'

Folding the two wooden halves of the tablet together, Gwenhwyfar secured the stylus safely and cradled her up-drawn knees, watching Arthur rub himself dry with his under-tunic.

'There's many a good soldier who has received his retirement discharge.' With a defiant tilt to her chin, she added, 'As you well know.' It was an uncomfortable subject, talking of this was tempting the Fates. The old stories came to mind, how the three Goddesses wove the threaded patterns of life. The shuttles could so easily become snared, tangled – it was never known when one of them could be listening, and to talk of something unpleasant might just amuse the Goddess to weave it onto her loom.

'Would you?'

'Would I what?'

He stood with his back to the river, bent over, drying his legs. 'Take another as husband.'

'What is this?' She took a breath, answered patiently but with finality, 'No, I would not.'

He looked up, tossed his damp tunic to dry in the sun. 'Not even Ider?'

For a moment Gwenhwyfar thought he was still teasing, realised he was not. She had to think carefully before answering. It was in her mind to storm to her feet, and slap his face and stamp off in a temper, but that would not be the right reaction. If he was deliberately goading her, then he could play this nonsense game by himself. 'I am writing to Ider for the reasons I told you. Because he is Artoriani, and lying wounded in some far-off place away from his friends, who he regards as family. Ider is a good lad, he does his duty to the best of his ability, and he makes me laugh. For all that, I would not wed with him, because I happen to love the man I already have as husband and no other could ever replace him.'

'But if I were dead . . .'

'Oh shut up!' She came quickly to her feet, covered the few yards between them her hands coming out, pushed his shoulders, sending him reeling into the water. Only he had moved as fast. His own hand caught her flailing arm, his fingers clamping around her wrist, and she fell with him, screaming laughter, the wave of water swooshing up the grass bank as he rolled her over in the shallows and made up for the few days that they had been apart.

Llacheu was worse by the coming of night. The ache in his head had become more intense; he became hot and restless, thrashing about on his pallet, calling out in his sleep. He curled with the boys at the far end of the King's Hall, companionable with the grooms and the shield bearers of the Artoriani. Arthur's young servant Gweir was near Llacheu and heard him moaning. When he put out a hand to shake the lad from what he supposed to be a bad dream and felt the heat standing out like fire from his body, he ran as if the hounds of the gods were after him to wake Gwenhwyfar.

§ XVI

For three days Llacheu's fever raged, and then a harsh, racking cough developed. Gwenhwyfar gave him what herbal medicines she could to lower his body heat and ease the pain in his chest, but nothing seemed to work, not even the infusions made from the wild garlic. The boy's hair was plastered wet to his forehead, the linen on the bed beneath him damp. Sometimes he slept, his breathing rattling in his throat, or he tossed, arms flinging wide, his tired voice moaning with the pain of the coughing and his aching limbs and tight, constricted chest. By the morning of the fourth day, Arthur could take no more of watching his last surviving son fight for life.

The daily routine in and around the complex of buildings at Caer Cadan was muted, the men and women grim-faced, their laughter absent. Eyes would turn to the chamber at the rear of the King's Hall. Father Cethrwm lodged himself on his knees within the square-crossed stone-built chapel; some of the non-Christian men sacrificed a lamb one night, down below the ramparts where their ceremony could be private, away from any possible disapproval by Christian officers.

Enid put the idea into Arthur's head. She was coming from the dim-lit chamber, carrying a bundle of bed-linen, soiled and damp, as he was approaching from outside. Arthur took a step back to allow her to pass through the door. She shook her head slowly, her face

401

blotched by weeping. ' 'Tis only the Mother who can help him now. God bless 'im.' And she shifted the bundle beneath one arm to make the sign of the holy cross.

Arthur entered the room as Llacheu eased from a bout of coughing, stood a long while within the doorway, watching Gwenhwyfar bathing the boy's face and body, her own appearance taut and bedraggled. *Only the Mother* . . . Enid had meant the Holy Mother, the Virgin Mary, Mother of God. But there was another, older Mother and she had a servant who had a reputation – aye, even among the Christian kind – as having the gift of healing.

'Cymraes, I am going to Yns Witrin.'

Gwenhwyfar looked across the room at Arthur, saw his haggard expression through the haze of her own red-tired eyes. She nodded once, said merely, 'Take care.'

She doubted the healing woman who lived there now, the Lady, would know of any different medicines, but accepted that her husband had to try for something. And mayhap the Goddess would listen, and smile her blessing on their son.

Arthur swung away from the chamber, strode down the slope towards the stabling at the far side of the Caer. He would take Onager, for the stallion was faster than his mare. Eleven miles, as the black raven could fly. Further, on horseback. For there were dykes and ditches, rivers. Marsh ground that even in the height of the hottest summer was boggy underfoot, with hollows and pits that could trap a man and a horse and claim them for a watery grave. Arthur had made forced marches on many occasions, swinging into the steady jogtrot stride of cavalry on the move, but this ride was nothing like any march that he had ever experienced. Onager had a long stride, and for all his faults of temper, a stamina and willingness that surpassed any horse Arthur had known. Where the hill of Caer Cadan levelled onto the Summer Land, he gave the animal his head and the stallion responded, ears back, tail carried banner-like, typical of his descendency from the desert-bred horses of Arabia. His legs stretched into a gallop that took him faster than the wind – and he would have gone on until he dropped had Arthur let him, but no horse could sustain such a pace over a distance. Jogtrot, drop to a walk, jogtrot again. The stride was long, comfortable, the horse balanced, head lowered, not fighting the bit. A horse corn-fed and as fit as Onager could travel for several days, thirty, forty miles a day, at such a pace. Eleven or so miles, and Arthur covered the distance in little more than an hour.

The last time he had come, he had felt the superstitious fear of this place, the quivering, skin-prickling uncertainty of the unknown. This time he simply needed to do something for his son, exactly what, he did not know. He just had to be doing something, anything. He set Onager at where Morgaine had told him to look for the path through the waters; the places where the reeds grew taller, where a stone showed here and there, one marker, a slender tree stump. As he followed it the birds took flight. She had told him of that mystery too, of how they warned of someone's approach. 'The magic', she had said, 'comes in making the natural things appear as magic.'

Would she be there on the far shore, waiting for him? Arthur called, no sign of her. He dismounted, let Onager graze, searched her hut, empty, called again.

There was an emptiness about this place that crept into the bones, surrounding the soul like invisible threads round and round, pulling tighter. An emptiness as deep and as towering as the lake and the Tor reflected in it. Arthur could feel it, stretching into a past where the Goddess had ruled, when Rome had been nothing more than a sheep-herd's hut.

He began to climb the Tor, the steep side that went up from behind Morgaine's hut. It was a breathless climb that had the backs of his legs aching and chest heaving, but he did not stop, went straight up, digging his boots into the grass, using his hands occasionally to pull himself higher.

Suddenly he was at the top. There had been no wind as he had crossed the lake and climbed, not even a breeze on this warm, sun-bright day, but as he stepped from the shelter of the high Tor, the wind hit him with the force of a shield blow, slamming into him, taking the last of panting breath. His cloak whipped around him like some magical garment taken sudden life, his hair billowed about his face, the strength of the wind stinging his eyes, slamming up his nostrils to batter at his brain. And she was there, standing with her back to him, standing, one hand laid on the granite Stone that topped the highest point of the Tor, her hair unbound, flying in the wind. She was naked, her skin bare to the raw bite of the world, looking out across the levels at the hills where Caer Cadan would be – had she seen him coming? She must have seen Onager, a chestnut horse coming fast, jumping streams and ditches. She must have seen the birds rise too, but she had not turned. Happen she did not expect others to come up here, to the Goddess's sacred place.

He said her name, the wind tore his voice and ran off with it across the levels, but he had a feeling that she knew he was there. She turned, said without surprise, 'I knew you would come to me again. It is fitting that you make it this day, for it is the Solstice, the day of life and giving.'

She was very slender, her woman-curved body sun-browned beneath the writhe of serpents and creatures tattooed across her thighs and belly, and around her breasts. The ritual-made marks of a priestess. She came up to Arthur, stood very close, and kissed him, light upon the lips. He wanted her, for no other reason than that she was a woman and he a man, but not now, not here – he could not, not while his son lay so close to death. He dared not touch her, for the feel of her skin might fan the flame of want; instead, he took a step back, noticed how his shadow in the late-afternoon sun stretched before him, lay atop hers, as close as a lover would lie.

He explained quickly in a few short words, why he had come. Morgaine listened, her head cocked slightly to one side, like a small bird hearing for worms, then she took his hand, led him with her, following a foot-worn path that dipped abruptly down from this great height to the narrower length of the hill. They were suddenly out of the wind and into a localised silence more total than Arthur had ever experienced. He could see the rippling of water on the lake, the two swans gliding across its surface, geese foraging among the shallows and Onager grazing, fancied he could hear him chewing, the jingle of his bit, the creak of leather. Hear the swish of stirred leaves among the trees that trundled in their full summer glory below, and the birds, busy about their young. Could hear the wind rushing by above, behind, up there on the height, but here, where he walked a pace behind Morgaine, nothing. Not even the grass whispered.

She stopped, turned to him, her face troubled, one hand gesturing in helplessness. 'I must do as my mother commands, for she will bring a terrible revenge on us if I do not.'

Misunderstanding, thinking she was talking of the Goddess, Arthur urgently took her hand. 'I will do anything if it will help my son.'

Morgaine sought his eye. There were tears in hers as she said, 'Would you lie with me? It is that she demands.'

He still had her hand. He turned it over, studied her palm, there was a faint scar of a burn running across the flesh, age-old. Slowly he lifted the hand, placed his lips on the pale mark. 'Was that not the Old Way?'

Shy, the tears still there, Morgaine answered, 'A maiden of the Goddess and a king would join to ensure life and fertility for the land. Before the Romans came and took away those kings, and replaced our Goddess with gods of their own doing.'

'Will it help my son?'

She had realised his misunderstanding, used it, seizing on it to do what she had to do. 'In one way, it might.' Her answer had a different meaning from the question he had asked, but for all her deliberate twisting, she believed she spoke the truth.

He thought the answer ambiguous, but accepted it. 'Then is her command so terrible? Am I so terrible?'

The sun dipped into a blaze of evening sunset as they lay cradled together, skin against skin, under the warmth of Arthur's cloak. He dozed; Morgaine, her head on his chest, lay with her eyes open, awake. She had tricked him, and felt miserable for that, but the loving he had given her was so wonderful that, by the triple guise of the Goddess, she would willingly trick him again!

It had been her mother, Morgause, she had talked of, not the Goddess. Morgause, who had sent word only two days past from

405

where she was kept prisoner that if Morgaine did not engineer some way of meeting with Arthur, then she would unleash an army from the north to come against the Pendragon. *For I will be free of him, daughter, one way or another.* Morgaine believed her, for Morgause was a woman of power, who thrust fear into the bellies of all who were beneath her command. And Morgaine would not have Arthur dead, not for want of doing as her mother ordered.

At least she had not lied to him. Morgause would be content now, now that this thing was done, and Arthur would be safe from her wickedness, for a while – and the son too, should he survive this fever, for Morgause would certainly have had the boy killed had she carried out her threat of an army.

Poor Morgaine, in her innocence, had no realistic knowledge of the world or the way her evil-hearted mother manipulated people into doing her bidding for her own ends.

Gwenhwyfar never asked what happened at Yns Witrin, or whether Arthur had found the Lady, and if he had, how she had helped, and what had been her price of payment. It was a thing best not to ask, for she knew of the old laws and customs, happen better than Arthur. And she knew too, unlike her husband, whose daughter Morgaine of the Lake was. She knew these things but did not ask, for it did not matter. Whatever the payment that Arthur had made to the Goddess, whatever the future might make of it, the price was worth it, for when Arthur returned, quiet and afraid of what he might find, Llacheu was sleeping the natural sleep of a child who had suffered an illness, but was safe through it, and set on the road to recovering.

September 465

§ XVII

Nessa ducked through the small side streets of Deva's rambling, civilian settlement, it was late afternoon, but few were about, the rain keeping them indoors. It was only servants who scurried, cloaks and hoods held close, through these cobbled, dung-strewn streets on such a wet afternoon.

When the Pendragon and family moved south to the new Caer, her request to remain with Bedwyr had been granted, they had been here at Deva a few months now, moved at Arthur's express orders. Caer Luel, he feared, held a handful too much sympathy for Hueil, who was gathering his strength with a pace the wrong side of a canter. Deva was a stronger settlement, clinging to its Roman military loyalty, still affectionately called the City of Legions, though the rows of barracks that had once housed the *Legio XX Valeria Victrix*, the Twentieth Legion, the Brave and Victorious, had stood empty for longer than a man living could remember. To reach Deva, Hueil would need to trail his men down through Rheged, giving time for Arthur to receive the alarm – and Deva ranged against Gwynedd's borders. Gwynedd would be in this thing too when Hueil marched, for his deposed father and ousted brothers had fled into the protection of Gwynedd, where Caw's eldest daughter was wedded to Dogmail, son of Cunedda, and brother to Enniaun.

Coming out from the side street onto a busier Via Castrorum, Nessa dodged around an ox cart trundling its slow way along to the west gate, and ducked into an ill-lit alleyway opposite. She stopped at the third door along, looked over her shoulder and entered. From the folds of her cloak she brought a scroll of parchment, handed it with solemnity to the house slave who came bustling to receive her.

She waited, alone in the quietness of this ante-chamber, while the slave went in search of her master. She took off her cloak, shook the worst of the wet from its folds, patted her hair into place, inspected a bronze statuette standing upon a tri-legged table, squeaked, startled, as a voice rumbled across the echoing room.

'You came for me, Madam?'

Nessa spun around, indicated the scroll held in the man's corpulent hand. 'My mistress is ill, the letter bids me bring you to her. Only you, of all the apothecaries residing in this settlement, will she see.'

The apothecary smiled, nodded self-gratification. 'I will come within the hour.' Nessa bobbed a brief, polite curtesy and let herself out once again into the rain-wet street. There were plenty others, slaves or servants, who could have run this errand to fetch the apothecary to Morgause, but she insisted Nessa go, and for the sake of peace it was not wise to cross Morgause's demands, however unreasonable they might be.

Morgause, Bedwyr had decided, had a temper like a spear-struck boar, a vocabulary as rancid as a gutter whore and was as companionable as a cloak full of fleas. Aside from that, and assuming he stayed well out of her way, preferably a long way, she was bearable.

He was seated cross-legged outside her door, cleaning his sword. It did not need the attention, but it was something to do while he waited for that odious, fat little man to leave. Morgause called him her personal physician – an exaggerated title for a back-street dispenser of herbs and potions, but, if he kept the bitch happy, who was Bedwyr to argue? She had first summoned him within a week of arriving here – stomach cramps it had been then, and an insistence that she was being deliberately poisoned. Then came headaches, a sprained ankle, female trouble. This time it was a head-cold. From the fuss she made, anyone could be forgiven for thinking she was dying from a fatal dose of the pox. Huh, if only!

Bedwyr enjoyed this position of command; life, beyond Morgause, was easy. He had wanted to join Arthur, but comparative idleness suited him just as well. He was not a lazy man, but neither was he restless as his cousin the Pendragon could be. The time to fight would come and Bedwyr was content to wait. The hunting around Deva was good and there came enough demands to keep a mind alert – and he had Nessa to warm him at night, and their new-started first babe beginning to show around her belly. He ought to consider marrying her, but Nessa always shied from the suggestion, saying a noble-born man needed a woman of the same kind as wife, that she was content to be his mistress.

Nessa was in there now, with Morgause and this wretched apothecary. Morgause forbade him to enter her room and he had need to place someone of trust there, to ensure Arthur's strict ruling. No visitors for Morgause. No letters, in or out. No communication with the world beyond the fortress of Deva's strong, defensive walls. She was to be constantly watched in health or illness, never allowed to be alone. Two guards at the door, two maids – and Nessa to stand beside the apothecary while he poked and pried at whatever ailment currently threatened Morgause.

Yet still the bloody messages got through! There was no proof of it, nothing concrete, but Arthur had sent word that things were passing down the wind. How? How the damned hell was she doing it? Bedwyr rubbed more oil lovingly into the blade of his sword, his hands busy with the familiar task, mind currying for answers. Almost, he could believe the gossip that Morgause was a witch with a knowledge of the magic arts. Could it be the birds that took her messages south and north? The black ravens that lived along the roof-tops of the watch towers? Did she have the Sight? Was it in the flame of the hearth-fire that she saw all that Arthur did? Or perhaps, as they said down in the officers' quarters, she really could talk to the wind. Questions, questions. Black-and-white questions producing a myriad of rainbow-mixed answers!

He took up his stone and began easing it in long, steady strokes down the oiled and gleaming sword, giving it an edge as sharp as a frosted winter's morning, working with a love and deliberation that flowed from his hands; and with it, a half-thought wish that he could take up this blade and slit the woman's throat, put an end to these answerless riddles.

Sounds from beyond the door, a woman coughing, the apothecary's stertorous voice, footsteps. The latch lifted, the door swinging open. Bedwyr set down his stone, rose, the sword held beneath his folded arms, stood blocking the narrow corridor from the chamber.

The apothecary was a summer-fattened weasel, with small darting eyes and the stench of rotten cabbage about him. His tunic was patched and faded, bracae bulging tight around his middle that barrelled beneath a triple chin, wobbling under red-blotched, sweating skin. His teeth were false, ivory-carved, his hair, what remained of it, greasy. How in all the god's guises, could Morgause bear his touch and foul breath! There could only be one reason, one reason alone for these constant petty illnesses, this summoning of a next-to-worthless peasants' apothecary.

With menacing slowness, Bedwyr raised his sword as the man shambled along the corridor. He stopped, his little eyes almost disappearing beneath the red-splotched flesh, the sword tip touching light against his belly.

'Open your bag,' Bedwyr ordered. 'Empty the contents to the floor.' The man took breath to protest, but Bedwyr nudged the sword. 'You can open it for me, sir, or I can kill you and then look at my leisure.' Bedwyr's smile was wicked. 'It is your choice.'

Bedwyr squatted, rifled through the spill of instruments, phials and pots. No papers, no parchments, no slate or wax tablets. Nothing. He stood, again pointed the sword. 'Now strip.'

Nessa was furious with him, taking Bedwyr's suspicions as personal insult. For three days she avoided him, choosing to sleep instead with the women, tossing her pert head whenever he came to talk with her, turning her back on him. As always, Morgause delighted in the conflict, taking pleasure in stirring sour words between lovers, however indirectly.

Her room, her prison, had all the trappings of luxurious comfort: fine-made furniture and rich wall hangings. But quality surroundings, the best food and wine, perfumes and expensive clothing, could never make up for her loss of freedom – especially at the hands of this whelp.

But muddying calm water in the course of her plotting, seeing the sweet turn sour, had always amused her. Confinement had its compensations.

October 465

§ XVIII

Winifred's steading to the south of Venta Bulgarium – or Winifred's Castre as the English were calling it – seemed prosperous enough. Arthur and his escort of a single Turma followed the track through outlying fields, all well hedged and fenced, enclosing plump, healthy stock. The hay-ricks were high stacked, sweet smelling and free from mildew. It galled like an ill-fitting saddle that Winifred's farm was thriving. Did no drought or driving rain threaten Saex crops then? Arthur's nostrils flared, as if assailed by some foul stench. It seemed even the elements did not dare confront this bloody woman!

Judging by the number of buildings, this farm was of village status. Winifred's personal dwelling, situated predominantly on a slight rise, was large, rectangular, with all the outward appearance of a queen's Hall. The smoke trails of a camp curled into the pale, washed-blue sky beyond the steading. A white horse standard, sited central to the bustling activity and scattered camp fires, fluttered in the lazy breeze. Aesc, son of Hengest, was already here then. Arthur rode easy in the saddle, unhurried.

Were all the inhabitants gathered to witness his arrival? Women stood at house-place doorways, hands raised, shielding the glare of a low autumn sun. Red-cheeked, excited children clustered at their skirts. The men were drifting in from their tithed strip fields to join their womenfolk, the murmurings and exchanged speculative talk rising as the Pendragon rode past. His fingers clenched tighter around Onager's reins as he saw Winifred come from her Hall. She stood waiting, her expression unreadable; came, poised and graceful, down the steps as he rode up and halted. Playing the dignity of a queen.

Arthur frowned as he saw a tall man emerging from the cluster of people at the doorway behind her. Ambrosius Aurelianus. They had *pax* between them, Arthur and his Uncle, but for the amiable intention, the one did still not wholly trust the other; it was an uneasy, tentative peace. Winifred could, as always, hatch a melting pot of mischief. A flutter of unease buffeted his insides – who was that man in the Christian stories, the one who entered the lion's den? Daniel? Arthur had a sudden, overwhelming empathy with Daniel.

Ten years past he had intended to have Winifred executed, when she was still his wife, but the heavy rain of that year had burst the Hafren's banks and she had escaped. He regretted, as he dismounted and subjected himself to her over-intimate embrace, failing to hang her. Had he pursued that escape and hacked her bloody head off, he would not be saddled with her, her son, or this damned Council – well that last was not true, Hengest's son ruled the Cantii Saex, they would need to meet at some time, sooner or later. Except later would have been preferable to this meeting arranged by Winifred.

She was talking as she escorted him, her arm linked possessively, through his, up the steps and into her house-place. Polite conversation, asking after his health, the journey, saying he must be hungry. 'You received my letter?' she asked as they approached Ambrosius.

Arthur nodded a stilted, though courteous, greeting to the man. 'Which one?'

Laughing, Winifred took his answer as a jest, sounding like a young girl. She looked striking too, though the close-caught veil around her head and face hid her fair Saxon-coloured hair. Her skin was clear, eyes sparkling bright. Her dark, Christian garments suited her plumper figure, bringing elegance to her stature. Her only item of jewellery, aside the keys dangling from her belt, was an ornate cross hanging between her ample breasts. At two years short of thirty, she was a handsome woman and despite the cold blood that Arthur knew to run behind this warm smile of welcome, still desirable. But then, he reflected, an adder was beautiful to look at. It was the bite you had to be wary of.

Two boys stood with the cluster of adults, both glowering. The fair one, the shorter of the two and full of his own self-importance, had to be his son, Cerdic. The other, the dark-haired tall boy with the fixed scowl, Vitolinus, Winifred's brother.

Wine was brought – though not the shared chalice. That was a British tribal tradition, surviving from heathen days, and Winifred ostentatiously professed the Christian faith. Ambrosius came to make his greeting, as irritated as Arthur that Winifred insisted on remaining fixed at her ex-husband's side. The Pendragon managed to loosen the limpet cling of her arm, extricating himself with the need to greet his uncle.

'I did not expect to see you at this Council with the English, Ambrosius,' Arthur said, adding as he nodded in the direction of the dark-haired boy, 'Nor do I recall giving permission for Vortigern's brat to be here.' They had clasped hands, a brief touch, instantly broken as they stepped back from each other, eye looking to eye, each wary of the other's intention.

'I have my reasons to be here, nephew, and Vitolinus was entrusted into my jurisdiction when you took him as hostage from Hengest. He is secure enough.'

Arthur laughed without humour. 'As long as you realise the responsibility for him lies firmly on your shoulders.' With meaning, he added, 'I do not want him going back to the Saex.'

Ambrosius inclined his head, Winifred purposefully threaded her arm through Arthur's again, and steered him further into the Hall, walking intimately close. 'I assure you, Arthur, my brother is quite safe under my personal eye.' She spoke firm, the first hint of austerity tarnishing the glitter of sunny disposition.

'Ah.' Arthur pointedly removed her arm, took a step away from her familiarity. That he believed. Winifred would allow no one to stand in the way of her own-born son – who could, given the right circumstances, be as entitled to rule the Cantii Land after Aesc as Vitolinus. And Vitolinus, for that very reason, was as good as dead, were he to tread beyond the bounds of his stipulated, monastic life. Arthur chuckled quietly to himself. Another victim for the lion's den?

Of that other boy, his son, Arthur said nothing.

He eventually managed to extricate himself and join his men as they made camp – on the furthest side of the steading, away from the Saex. There was a copse of beech, flaring with October colour, distinct against the green of the oak wood that strode across the hill beyond the boundary wall. The bracken had turned gold, and there had come a touch of frost with the dawn. The air was crisp, the smell of autumn-damp soil rich and pleasant. The men had not brought tents, a one-night halt needed no fuss. They would roll themselves in their wolf-skin cloaks before the smored fires and sleep with their heads on their saddles. Arthur tossed his own saddlebag down beside a fire that was already blazing. What suited his men would suit himself good enough, it would not be the first time he awoke with his hair frozen to the hard ground. It was a part of soldiering, along with poor food and the ache of old wounds.

The sunset blazed brief but glorious, promising another fine day on the morrow, and as the sky turned from glowing orange to velvet purple, Arthur put his cloak about his shoulders and returned, reluctantly, to Winifred's Hall, taking only two men as escort.

Once again Winifred welcomed him with a show of fondness, led him to the high table, spread with autumn-brilliant flowers, dishes of tempting fruits and pastries, jars brimming with wine. She had excelled herself for this special feasting. Ambrosius was seated with several men from the Church – the two boys were at the table also. So, Winifred was ensuring her son would be noticed? Well, let her flaunt him, he, Arthur, would not rise to her bait!

Many others were crowded into the Hall. Half the size of Arthur's Hall at Caer Cadan, but twice as opulent. The walls were part stone-built, in Arthur's place, shields and weapons would be hung, here, rich tapestries and embroideries, depicting Christian scenes decorated the pink-coloured plastered walls.

There were no rushes spread over the floor, the boards lay bare, but swept and scrubbed clean. Roof beams bore no tangle of dusty cobwebs or discarded bird's nests. Even the smoke from torches, lamps and hearth-fire seemed to obey Winifred's rule of neat tidiness, for the columns marched straight, smartly out the smoke-holes – there came, a stir from beyond the door, like an eddy of sudden gusting wind, and tall, fair-haired, bearded men were

418

striding in, proud in their armour. The man at the front wore no shirt, woollen bracae and boots only, with a red-woven cloak tossed about his shoulders. Amulets ringed his forearms and biceps, a heavy chain of worked gold lay on his chest, crossing under his jewel-encrusted baldric. So this was Aesc, the son of Hengest and brother to Winifred's mother. Aesc, who led the Jute settlers of the Cantii territory.

The Saex – there were forty of them – halted. There was no salute, no acknowledgement to Arthur. They stood in silence, Aesc's bodyguard ranked before the Pendragon and the two men of his Turma who stood at either shoulder.

Aesc stepped forward. He was a man of bulk; bull neck, heavy jowled, with eyes that were narrow but missed not the falling of a sparrow's feather. 'Arthur!' he said in his guttural Germanic tongue, 'this is well met!'

Arthur made no attempt to offer a hand of greeting. The Saex had come armed, whereas his Artoriani had entered the settlement that afternoon with spear tips down. 'You come wearing a sword and carrying shield and spear.' Arthur spoke casually, in a dialect of Aesc's own tongue. It was a scored point over the Jute, for he spoke no British or Latin. Arthur indicated his own two men, who carried no weapons. 'I understood this meeting was to be for the renewing of the treaties of peace that I made with your honoured father; not to toss insults of hostility.'

The Jute stood a hand-span taller than Arthur, his chest glistened with rubbed oil, showing the ripple of muscle. He dipped his spear towards Arthur's own sword. 'You wear a sword.'

Arthur threaded his thumbs through the leather baldric from which the sword was hung. 'I do. But then, as Supreme King of all Britain, I am entitled to.' He regarded Aesc some shrewd moments longer, judging the man, then moving with casual slowness, began to draw the weapon. Several of Aesc's men caught their breath and started forward, but Aesc turned his head, growled his displeasure at them, ordering them to remain still.

Ignoring the mistrust, Arthur held the naked sword flat across his palms, letting the flickering torchlight ripple on its faceted welding.

Crafted by the heating of iron rods twisted together like in the making of a plaited rope, then reheated white-hot before being hammered flat into a blade that held unbound strength and beauty and finally polished and honed to an edge that could slice the wind, Arthur's great sword shimmered its perfection. An awed hush fell over the Saex kind. 'This,' Arthur said, 'is the sword of Wayland, given to mortal man's keeping by the Lady.'

Aesc smiled, a lopsided half-grin beneath his braided moustache and bushed beard. He had heard the story, told him by his own father, the story of how the Pendragon came by the wondrous sword of the English gods. 'You possess it still?'

The Pendragon let the heavy blade point swing to the ground, stood holding the hilt in both hands. 'I possess it still. I took it in battle. There is no man with strength enough to take it from me.' For a moment he held Aesc's gaze, then he walked down the length of the Hall, the crowd of silent watching men and women parting before him, walked to the doorway, where solemnly he leant the beautiful sword against the plaster wall.

He turned, paced back up the Hall, stood again before Aesc. 'I rest my weapon within the sacred threshold of this Hall. Where none, save my own hand, shall risk the wrath of the God that does protect this dwelling by the touching of it.' Arthur stepped aside. It was an open challenge. Respond, or give a greater insult that would bring shame on Aesc and all his kindred's kindred. All eyes rested on the Jute leader.

Aesc stayed motionless and then suddenly he laughed, a single bark of mirth. He drew his sword, strode down the Hall and placed his weapon alongside Arthur's, the two blades touching. 'Now we show that our teeth are bared not in snarls of war, but in smiles of friendship!' He barked an order for his men similarly to stack their weapons, came before the Pendragon, extending his arms in greeting. Arthur almost felt his bones give way beneath that crushing embrace. This man needed no weapon, for he had strength enough in those oak-built arms to crush a bear.

'You live well,' Arthur observed to Winifred as the slaves brought around huge platters of boar and venison and beef. The laughter of a

420

filled feasting Hall swirled high to the rafters, as headily potent as the wine, as rich as the food.

'Well enough for a woman alone.'

Arthur sipped his wine. 'I have not hindered you to re-wed. The Englishman Leofric asks for you often enough, so I hear. You ought to accept; a man in your bed may give you other things to do aside from writing letters to me.'

Winifred, with no intention of answering his taunting, let the remark sail to the roof beams. She busied herself with selecting meat, masking the rise of heat to her face. Leofric's persistence was becoming an embarrassment. Her constant refusals were getting her nowhere, she would have to think again on how to deal with the wretched man!

Seeing her discomfort, Arthur laughed. He pointed at Ambrosius, said, his mouth full of venison, 'Why not wed with my uncle? I would need only to pay the one set of spies then!' Not surprisingly, Winifred did not share his laughter.

Cerdic, to Arthur's annoyance, was also seated at the high table a few places down, but near enough to overhear. Loudly, the boy retorted, 'My mother already has a husband. It is not I who bears the description bastard.'

Arthur selected bread, broke off a hunk. If Llacheu had spoken such an intentional insult, then regardless of company he would have been instantly thrashed. He bit into the bread, fresh baked, still warm from the ovens. 'Your crops have been good this year then, Winifred?' He was determined not to let the brat rile him, though by the Bull he was finding it difficult!

They talked of minor things, the weather, the harvest, steering a clear path around the subjects that could cause argument. Politics and marriage. The Christian Church. Arthur noted that the carvings on the roof beams and lintels bore traditional pagan designs similar to the carved heads and faces in his own Hall, put there to ward off the spirits of evil. Christianity, no matter how strong it grew, would never quite shrug aside the binding rules of man's frail superstition. He mustered courage to toss a direct statement. 'Gwenhwyfar is my legal wife, Winifred. I realise you dislike the fact, but like it or no, there it is.'

'God's laws speak against putting aside a wife,' she answered, defiant.

'I do not believe in God.'

'If one winter the snows came and did not thaw,' Winifred spoke quickly, her hand resting, light but possessive, on Arthur's arm, 'would you expect me to stay in my Hall, muffled in furs and say, "the snow is here, I must accept it and long no more for the warmth of summer"?' Her fingers caressed the smooth inner skin along his forearm. 'I cannot deny my need for the sun any more than I can relinquish my love for you.'

Arthur knew well how Winifred excelled at manipulating words to fit her need, but in this, obscurely, he believed her.

Cerdic was finding this whole situation difficult to handle. As a young child, he had clung to the belief that one day the King of all Britain would come riding on a white stallion and place his mother where she belonged, as Queen, and himself as Prince and heir. It had all been some misunderstanding, this separation between his mother and father, some political move beyond a child's reasoning. When Arthur at last came, there would be great joy and celebration. He would take his son up on his saddle before the people and show that he, Cerdic, was the cherished son of a king. Then his father would kiss his mother, hold her close and disappear into the privacy of the sleeping place, as his friend Wulfric always did with his wife after they had quarrelled.

Summer had followed summer, and Arthur had never come until now. And now it was too late. For Cerdic felt himself no longer to be a child, and he had learnt to hate Arthur, as he had assumed his mother hated him. How often had he heard Winifred spit words of animosity and contempt for the Pendragon? Heard her shrill at the injustice of his desertion? Cerdic had witnessed his mother's tears, her suffering at being a woman wronged and for that, above all, Cerdic hated his father.

The Pendragon's unexpected acceptance to attend this arranged Council had shocked everyone. Cerdic had thought his mother would tell Arthur when he arrived of their suffering and pain. Was that not why she had been so flustered all this day? Was that not why she had spoken so sharply to him during the afternoon? Why then, did she not spit out the words of contempt? What he had not bargained for was his mother's star-shine sparkle of happiness as Arthur's horse and escort came into view. She was like those silly unwed girls who giggled at the young men. Where were the rantings, the venting of hurt feeling and frustration? What had happened to those oft-repeated threats of what she would do and say to Arthur when she saw him? Where was the bold talk that had been a background noise to Cerdic's entire life? The boy could not believe, would not accept, that his mother still loved the Pendragon!

He stabbed his eating dagger into the meat, screwing the blade round, imagining how it would be to thrust the point into Arthur's heart.

Vitolinus was seated next to Cerdic. This was the first time the boys had met, cloistered as Vitolinus was in that dismal monastery, chanting his way from one monotonous day to the next. He placed his hand over Cerdic's. 'One day,' he said, 'when we have the wit and strength of a man grown, the Pendragon shall answer to our blades.'

Cerdic, eyes rounding, regarded Winifred's brother with new-found respect. In a rush of needing to understand, he blurted, 'Why does my mother fondle him so? She is like the new-married women pawing all over their taken husbands.'

Vitolinus helped himself to food; the monastery stuff was poor. He made no attempt at an answer. If his sister wanted to make the prize fool of herself by draping herself all over that bastard, then it was her concern. Personally speaking, he would rather see the Pendragon's throat slit open.

§ XIX

The Hall was rising, men and women going tired and drink-filled to their beds. Aesc departed with much noise and parade. The serious talking would come on the morrow, this night had been for feasting,

423

idle conversation and laughter. A chance to make assessments, first impressions and hasty judgements. Drink-muffled minds did not lend themselves to hard bargaining and possible disagreement. Arthur found himself releasing a breath of held tension once Aesc and his ostentatious bodyguard had departed. While he held no fear for the man, a picked quarrel at this juncture was not desirable.

Ambrosius rose from the bench, gave his good-nights to Winifred and Arthur, but the Pendragon rose with him. 'I will walk with you,' Arthur said, nodding his leaving to Winifred. At the door he retrieved his sword, slid it, with an inward sigh of relief, into his scabbard. It felt like having an arm missing, not having the sword swinging comfortably against his hip.

'I sleep within the shelter of Our Lord,' Ambrosius said as they stepped outside, indicating Winifred's chapel. 'The priest has comfortable rooms beyond.'

There was a brittle touch of frost in the air, with the stars littering the sky as if they were the uncountable camp fires of some vast army. Several man were drifting to or returning from the latrine pits.

Arthur pointed to the left, said, 'I need to check the horses, will you walk with me?'

His uncle saw no reason to refuse, the night was chill but it had been hot and fuggy within the crowded Hall. To sleep on a muzzy head would cause discomfort come morning, so he walked alongside Arthur, saying nothing, their boots scrunching on the frost-hard ground.

Several horses whinnied low calls of greeting as they approached. They looked well enough, with hay piled in the centre, water buckets filled. Arthur leant across the fencing, hand extended to stroke a soft, enquiring muzzle.

'It is some time since we talked alone,' he said cautiously.

'There has been naught for the saying.'

I am not fully forgiven yet for all my sins then, Arthur thought wearily, said cheerfully, 'Your son is well?' It was always difficult talking of Ambrosius's born son, for the lad had suffered illness as a young boy, leaving his legs twisted and weak.

As he had hoped, pride encouraged Ambrosius to answer friendly enough, 'He shows promise despite his mis-formity. Poor legs do not necessarily make a poor mind. He has much of my mother in him —and the build of her father.'

Relaxing, Arthur laughed. He really had nothing to fear from Ambrosius, they were both, when it came down to it, fighting in the same Turma. 'Without that beard I trust! Bull's blood,' he faltered briefly, aware of Ambrosius's frown at his use of the pagan oath, carried on, 'I was terrified of the man. Built as big as a giant, wide as an oak, and that great bush of hair smothering his face and chin! Mithras he was enormous!'

Ambrosius too, leaned on the fence, stretched his hand to pat a chestnut horse. 'I was not aware you knew him?'

'Aye, you all came to Less Britain one summer. I was what, three, four? You seemed so adult to me, though you are, what, only a handful of years older?'

Ambrosius was frowning, leaning on his arms along the top rail of the fence. He shook his head, lifted one hand in apology. 'I confess I do not remember you. Less Britain I do, Ygrainne, Uthr but . . .' He let the sentence trail off, embarrassed.

Arthur grunted. ' 'Tis not so surprising. You would not have noticed a boy who was thought to be the fatherless son of a serving girl.'

Ambrosius's frown had deepened, trying to recall that far distant summer. He had enjoyed himself in Less Britain, had even, for that short while, liked his elder brother, Uthr. 'Wait, I do remember! A grimed lad toddling round me like a pup at heel, always clutching a damned wooden sword! Christ's love, was that you?' He was laughing, delighted at the return of that memory of youth.

Grinning, Arthur nodded. 'Aye, that was me.'

'Christ's love!' Ambrosius repeated. 'I remember kicking you because you were becoming such a bloody nuisance!'

They were both laughing, their arms going around each other's shoulders in the mutual sharing of the past. 'I kicked you back. Received a thrashing for it too.' Arthur's laughter eased, he shook his head, occasionally guffawing. 'It took me some months to understand why I was the one thrashed when you had been the one

425

to kick first.' He shrugged. 'It falls hard on a lad to be labelled bastard-born.'

Turning so that his back leant against the wooden fence, Ambrosius said, 'Yet you have abandoned your son to be so labelled.'

Arthur chewed his lip. 'The circumstances are different.'

'No, they are not. Winifred is, for all her faults, a good woman at heart, you know.' They had somehow moved a few paces apart, the shared congeniality fading.

'She is a clever woman, I grant you that.'

Although he knew he was wasting his breath, Ambrosius pursued the subject. 'She has founded three churches and donated much financial help towards the feeding and shelter of the poor and sick.'

'Were I also to build a Christian church, would that change your opinion of me?' Arthur retorted.

'No.'

'I thought not.'

A group of men, Saex, reeled by on the return from the latrines, their singing and drunken laughter loud against the still night. They did not see the two men leaning against the fence. Arthur glanced at Ambrosius. It was as well his uncle spoke nothing of the English tongue, for the group's remarks had not been over-polite about the Christian British. He fondled the horse before him, a fine young chestnut with a good, bold eye, the Decurion's horse. Onager was tethered in the barn, Arthur could never turn him loose with others. 'Why do you still hate me, Ambrosius? What great wrong have I done you?'

Ambrosius tilted his head back, gazed up at the stars. God's wondrous creations. Did he hate Arthur? Christ Jesu said to love. No, he did not hate the Pendragon, was irritated by him, more like. Jealous even? As he had been jealous of his older, wiser and braver brother? A difficult medicine to swallow, the truth. He sighed, closed his eyes in brief prayer. What was there to answer?

'Because you have turned out to be everything that I, as a boy, had so wanted to be.'

Arthur laughed. 'What? Bloody-minded, callous, a fornicating adulterer and a heathen!' The laughter deepened. 'I think those are some of the milder descriptive terms you have publicly applied to me.'

Annoyed that Arthur had deliberately misunderstood, Ambrosius jeered, 'Do you deny them?' He dropped his eyes from the skies, his challenge direct.

Arthur shrugged, replied amiably, unoffended. 'I'm trying to give up the adultery.' He laughed again, aware even in the darkness of Ambrosius's disapproval. 'Hard to believe, but true! I have been an honest and faithful husband for some months now.' Losing the laughter, he turned the subject. 'Can you deny my achievement with the Artoriani? We have peace.' He sniffed pessimistically. He was tired, the day's ride had been long and his thigh was aching, that old wound, throbbing deep within the muscles. 'Though for how long, only your God, Hueil of the North, and the English have the knowing.'

When Ambrosius made no reply, Arthur asked, 'I need your help to keep this peace, Uncle. If you can take care of God for me, I'll deal with Hueil, and together, we can tether the English.' Still nothing from Ambrosius. Arthur swung away from the fence, striking the top bar angrily with his fist. 'You see only what you want to see, Ambrosius. The sunny days, the corn growing high in well-tended fields.' Arthur stepped towards the other man, his fist raised, clenched, nostrils flaring. 'Well rain falls too, you know. Harvests fail.'

His breathing had quickened, he took several deep breaths to regain control of the anger. He did not want to argue. Limply he said, 'Our people, British people, backed a tyrant, Vortigern, because they were belly-sick of Rome's corruption. Rome claimed our taxes, our menfolk – needed here – and gave nothing in return except hollow promises. The power that was Rome is dying, is dead. I have no wish to die with it.' Arthur expected his uncle to answer, to belch his usual claims for the Roman way, that the Emperor would be back. Nothing. Ambrosius just stood there, looking up at the stars. Arthur had thought himself too tired for an argument, but suddenly he wanted one. Suddenly wanted to shout and bellow. To kick the man who had first kicked him, and not worry about getting thrashed for it. And so he goaded him again, sneering mockery at his uncle's ideals. 'Would you like me to send a plea to the western Emperor then? I assume Severus has not yet been murdered?' His tone was thick with sarcasm. 'I doubt he could take time away from balancing on his tenuous hold of cliff-edged power to consider our plight, but if that is what you wish . . .' Arthur smacked his palm to his forehead, 'Fool I am! Happen you would prefer I implored the Emperor of the East, Leo himself. Will he have enough interest in us, a rain-sodden destitute little island, to make sail and come to our aid?'

Ambrosius at last answered. His voice was very quiet, subdued. 'We tried appealing before.'

'And were told to look to ourselves. Which is what I am doing.' Arthur slid his thumb through his sword belt, rocked forward onto the balls of his feet and back to his heels. 'Another bishop could come and teach my men to shout "alleluia" and send the enemy running in fear. It worked well once before, I believe.'

Ambrosius growled something inaudible at Arthur's ridicule, then stated, 'Bishop Germanus was a good man, a valiant soldier and a devout man of God.'

His hands held out flat, palms down, Arthur conceded, 'If my tutoring serves me well he had come with Papal blessing to see Vortigern secure as king, provided that same king could comply fully with the putting down of certain heretical notions that were abroad at the time. One of those strange quirks of fate led the bishop to be in a position to see off a small band of hostile raiders.'

Turning aside, Ambrosius laced his fingers behind his back. The stars were indeed, beautiful this night. It was true, the Christian Church had blessed Vortigern's claim to the kingdom, verifying that Britain, then as now, was very much alone.

Breaking the stiff, angry silence, Arthur said, 'Rome is finished, Ambrosius, the sooner you accept that, the sooner we can forget our quarrelling and work together for our own land, our own people.'

Ambrosius sighed, audibly loud, long. He pushed himself from the fence, turned to face Arthur, offered his hand. 'You are right. Everything you say is right. I agree.'

428

For a long moment Arthur stood there, gaping open-mouthed from Ambrosius's face to his outstretched hand, back to his face. Had he drunk more wine than he thought then? Surely he was drunk? Hesitant, half afeared that he was dreaming and to take that hand would break the dream, Arthur took his uncle's proffered grasp. Then they were laughing together, embracing, patting each other's shoulders. Stupidly, Arthur almost had the need to brush a tear from his eye.

'You will back me fully tomorrow then, when I make a new treaty with Aesc?' Arthur held his breath, not daring to hope for an answer.

'Aye.' Ambrosius raised his arms, let them drop. 'It does us no good to be at each other's throats. There are enough bastards out there trying to do that for us.'

Arthur's elation lasted a few moments longer, then faded. Suspicious, he questioned, 'What is in this for you? Why the change of heart?'

Ambrosius had the decency to appear slightly embarrassed. 'Two reasons.' He held up a finger. 'One: you are to insist that Aesc allows the church at Durovernum to be rebuilt and that a priest is permitted to reside there.'

'Canti Byrig they call it now,' Arthur corrected absently. 'Two?'

'You also become Christian.'

Arthur roared with laughter. He bent forward, his hands on his thighs, laughing, shaking his head. 'Mithras' blood, Ambrosius, are you serious?' He glanced up, still laughing. 'Gods, you are!'

Ambrosius shrugged, then smiled, the expression broadening into a grin. 'No, but it was worth a try!' He clapped Arthur's shoulder, again offered his hand, which Arthur took in new friendship and accepted partnership.

A rustle of a woman's skirts. Arthur spun around at the footfall behind him, a slave, timid, reluctant to speak. He beckoned her nearer, asked her business.

'My Lady asks you to her chamber. She wishes to talk with you.'

Arthur hesitated. He was in no mood for more of Winifred this night. He touched Ambrosius's arm, said with a chuckle, 'To you, Winifred may be a good woman; to me, she is a pain in the arse.'

To his surprise, Ambrosius answered, 'I meant she is good for the Church. Personally, she gives me constipation too.'

Reluctant, Arthur began to follow the girl back to the Hall. As an afterthought, Ambrosius called after him, 'I would ask also that you ensure the boy does not become King after you, Arthur.'

'That is three things,' Arthur answered, his laughter booming into the crisp night air.

§ XX

Cerdic tugged at the sleeve of his new-found friend, whispered, 'Vitolinus, are you asleep?'

The other boy grunted, opened one eye. 'I was. What is it?'

They were curled together beneath a shared sleeping-fur in the far corner of the Hall, a warm niche where no draughts reached, Cerdic's accustomed sleeping place. The younger boy pointed across the mounds of Winifred's men, sleeping, snoring, a few clutching their women close. His finger was shaking. 'He's gone to my mother!'

Vitolinus groaned, rolled over, pulling the fur closer about his ears. Already he was regretting becoming involved with this spoilt whelp. 'Go to sleep.'

Cerdic persisted, shaking the older boy. 'Do you not hear me? Arthur is with my mother.'

An uninterested murmur. 'So what?'

More agitated, Cerdic pulled the soft fur aside, Vitolinus sat up with a curse, his hand half raised to cuff the boy. 'You little brat I'll . . .' but Cerdic caught his wrist. 'Do you not understand? Arthur is alone with her.'

Vitolinus snatched back the fur, began tucking it around himself again. 'You were complaining that he was not her true husband were you not? Well, now he is, so shut up and go to sleep.'

Cerdic's retort hissed sinisterly into the dim light of the Hall interior. 'I am old enough to know why men lie with women. To get sons.'

Vitolinus had lain down, but the words struck home. He sat up again, squinted at the shadows hiding the door that led from the Public Hall to Winifred's private chambers. Sons. Ah. The last thing Vitolinus needed was yet another brat of Arthur's. Cerdic and Llacheu were two too many already.

He patted Cerdic's shoulders in a fond, brotherly way. 'Good point, lad. Come on.' He tossed the fur aside, began to step between the scatter of sleeping men, Cerdic following.

'Where are we going?' The boy whispered, glancing anxiously over his shoulder at the closed door of his mother's chamber.

'For a piss, where do you think?' A malevolent grin crept across Vitolinus's face. 'And while we're out there, we'll see about interrupting the adding of one to the population.'

§ XXI

Arthur seated himself on a stool before a table covered with a fine embroidered cloth. On it sat a comb, bronze mirror, an ash-wood box and a larger box of carved walrus ivory. To one side lay a leather-bound Bible. Winifred dismissed the slave, poured fresh wine into a silver goblet, handed it to him. It was good stuff, imported. She offered fruit, he declined.

She was, Arthur noted with amusement, now clad in something nearer the form of dress he was more accustomed to her wearing. Gone was the plain black weave and veil, in their place a gown of the finest flame-coloured silk, the cut fashioned to cling to the ample contours of her body. Her hair, golden-fair as her mother's had been, hung loose in rippling waves down her back. A delicate perfume of summer-scented flowers wafted behind her as she moved. A holy woman of God? Arthur coughed to conceal laughter.

Winifred seated herself on a second stool some distance from him, folded her hands into her lap. 'You look as I so well remember you,' she said. 'The years have been kind.'

'Your memory must be at fault then,' he jibed drily.

He was watching her, Winifred noted, as a man looks at a woman he wants. 'What is it Arthur, that makes women love you so?' She spoke with a soft sigh of regret and longing. 'You are a thorough bastard.'

He laughed. 'Must be my natural charm.' He swilled his wine around in the goblet, aware he had already drunk too much this night. Even so, he did not refuse when she rose to pour him more.

'Oh?' She placed her finger lightly under his chin. 'You possess charm? I never knew.'

With sudden movement, Arthur stood, seized her wrist, put his goblet on the table, took the wine jug from her and placed it there also. When he kissed her, she responded, eager. His hand was going up her back, beneath the fall of hair to her neck.

Winifred closed her eyes, let her head fall back, his touch sending sensations, all these years neglected, pulsing. Her words came on a whispered breath: 'My Lord, love with me as we have before!'

Arthur's hand was caressing her throat, and then the fingers were clasping tighter, squeezing. Her eyes snapped open, her own hands clawing at his as she tried to breathe.

'Love as we did before? I never loved you then, Winifred, have no intention starting now.' He shoved her from him, sending her reeling to the floor. Calmly, he retrieved his wine, sat, drinking it.

Winifred scrambled to her feet, lunged, knocking the goblet from his hand and struck his cheek one sharp blow with her open palm, moved quickly back beyond his reach.

'Ah, that is more the Winifred I recall.' Arthur brushed at the wine splashes on his tunic, amusement clinging obstinately to his expression. 'You had me worried for a moment, I thought Ambrosius spoke right and you really had become a good, Christian woman.' He rubbed the sting of his cheek. 'I see not.'

'You are beneath contempt, Arthur Pendragon!'

He stood, coming forward in one lithe movement, again catching hold of her.

432

'I? Whoa, Winifred! Who is it who has fluttered her eyelashes, simpered and spoken of love this evening? What!' He moved slightly away from her, without releasing her. 'You mean I have read you wrong? You were not intending to lure me into your bed?'

She hissed, like a disturbed snake, 'I would not have you in my bed were you the last man alive!'

Arthur let her go, pushing her from him. He filled his goblet again, not caring that he was becoming drunk. 'You always were a liar.' He swallowed a large mouthful of wine. 'Now we have that little game put behind us, can we move on to business?'

She was angry, he could see, by the pinch of her nostrils, the flutter of breath, but give her credit, was controlling it well. She had learnt something then, these years. For himself, despite the many misgivings which on more than one occasion had almost turned him for home on the ride here, Arthur was enjoying himself. It was probably the wine.

Leaning forward, resting his elbow on his knee, a wicked grin spread across his face. 'I have still not decided what it was that enticed me to agree to come here. But, since I am here, and your pathetic attempt at seduction has failed, what else have you in mind for me? Do you and Aesc plan to slaughter me like Hengest did the British at Council?'

'Kill you?' She was brushing at her rumpled gown, patting her hair into place. 'How I would dearly love to!' Regaining a hesitant composure, Winifred seated herself. Devil take the man, how did he manage to raise her passions so easily – temper and desire?

She forced a smile, breathed slowly and deeply. 'I will see you dead one day, Arthur, but not yet, not until the time is right. I want you to live a few summers more.'

Arthur sat back, lazily resting his arm on the table. 'Naturally. Cerdic is not old enough to contest my title.'

'His time will come. Cerdic will fight you.'

'I look forward to the encounter.' Idly, he picked up the Bible lying on the table, the gospels written on parchment and carefully stitched together within a leather cover. He opened the delicate book and peered at the finely copied writing, his eyes swimming as the multitude of tiny words blurred. By the Bull, he was tired!

Passionately Winifred exclaimed, 'There does not have to be a fight!'

Arthur shut the book. 'You actually read this? Mithras, is it worth the strain to your sight?' Answering her, 'Of course there does.'

Winifred had seated herself, sitting straight-backed, poised and elegant. 'Many of your chieftains are returning to how it was, before Rome came. They are happy to renew the old laws, divide their land between sons so that all take a share. Please,' Winifred stretched her hand out for the fragile book Arthur was toying with, 'please, treat that with care, it is of great value.'

Arthur peered at the thing he held, as if unaware how it had got there, tossed it, none too gently, back to the table. 'Unfortunately,' he drawled – the wine really was too strong for this late hour – 'the old system has its flaw of fratricide. Brothers are not always the best of friends.'

'It works well enough for Cunedda's brood in Gwynedd.'

Arthur looked at her shrewdly. 'You seem remarkably well informed of what is happening many miles beyond these boundaries. Cunedda's brood are controlled by the strongest brother, Enniaun Girt. The grandsons may not be so,' he paused, reluctant to say the word loyal, said instead, with scorn, 'brotherly.' He narrowed his eyes, 'Cerdic wishes both myself and Llacheu dead.' Cynically, he added, 'Someone must have planted and nurtured that idea for it to germinate and flourish so profusely.'

Winifred laced the chain of her crucifix through her fingers. Her head was bowed and she spoke in what was barely a whisper, as if to speak the words aloud would bring reality to them. 'It may be you or Llacheu to slay Cerdic.' She looked up, her face riddled with dread. A mother's fear for her only son.

Arthur had risen, was walking around the chamber, touching various items. Winifred's loom; sweet-smelling herbs drying in bunches; a wall-hanging. He remembered Winifred embroidering it, he had liked the thing, a vivid depiction of a boar hunt. She had, if he recalled, been making it for him. Odd how he remembered that.

He studied the scene. A boar at bay, men triumphant in their

434

chase. His thoughts went to Gwydre. The boy lying bloodied and dead. His voice choked as he said in a rare moment of letting down his guard, 'I would not willingly kill a son of mine.'

Winifred came quickly to his side, took Arthur's hand lightly in her own. Guessed, rightly, at his thoughts. 'I grieved for your sons.'

Arthur barked a disdainful laugh, retrieved his hand. 'You? Grieved over Amr and Gwydre? Damn it, do you take me for the complete fool!'

Her answer slapped unexpectedly. 'I am a mother! The death of a son, any son, brings a sharing of grief between mothers who love and fear for their children.'

Scornfully Arthur flung at her, 'Even with Gwenhwyfar?'

Compassionately Winifred replied, 'For the loss of a son, aye, even with Gwenhwyfar.' Added with a rueful smile, 'Though I admit to preferring her sons not to have been also yours.'

Arthur stood uncomfortable at this revealing honesty in Winifred. Her scheming and deceptions he could handle, this opening of her heart was becoming unnerving. And she spoke the truth, he knew that. He ambled away, his back to her. 'I did not come to this chamber for your pity.'

He spun round, head raised like an alert stag as she next said, 'You came because you fear the death of another son. What will you do, Pendragon, if Llacheu dies?'

Arthur's skin crawled. How had she known? On the few days that it took to ride here, Arthur had repeatedly questioned himself as to why he was responding to the invitation to meet Aesc on Winifred's land. It was a thing he had to do eventually, meet with Hengest's successor, but not on Winifred's steading. So why had he accepted? Curiosity? Boredom? Peace, apart from the rumblings from the North and Amlawdd's constant growling, had settled like an enchanted pollen dust over Britain. Months had passed quietly, Briton and Saex alike content to battle against the vagaries of weather rather than one another.

Winifred broke his thoughts, her hand on his arm, holding firm. 'You may one day need Cerdic,' she purred. Quicker, her breath

435

held, 'Take him with you when you return to Caer Cadan. Let your two sons grow as brothers.'

Arthur stared at her incredulously. Had he heard right? 'You would trust me with him?'

'He is your son.'

'He is of Saex blood. His grandmother was daughter to Hengest, his mother's uncle now rules the Cantii territory.' Arthur swept her hold from his arm, not liking the suggestion. Disliking more the damned bloody sense of it. 'When he is grown, Cerdic can lay claim to powerful allies. For those reasons it would suit me to have him out of the way.'

Winifred had heard all the rumours. Did not think that Arthur was capable of deliberately drowning his son. 'You would not murder one of your own.' She said emphatically, believing it.

'Do not count on that! Were there just cause, I would slice my sword through his neck.' Arthur was equally emphatic.

'Arthur,' excited, she took his hands within her own, 'instead of fighting one another our sons could fight together! Think on it! What allies they could become!'

It was tempting, too bloody tempting. The instincts of a seasoned soldier were buffeting Arthur like storm waves on the shore; he could smell danger as strong as the pungent odour of that smoking candle in the corner of the chamber. Winifred would not willingly give up her son, not into his – or, more potent – Gwenhwyfar's care.

Her next words ran chill down his spine. 'If you do not take him, Arthur, then I shall send him with Aesc. It is your choice as to who brings my son to manhood. You, or,' she laughed maliciously, 'the Saex.'

Then he saw the reason behind all this. To take the title Pendragon, Cerdic needed to be taught how to fight, how to use sword and shield – and how to lead men. He could not learn that from his mother, or even a swordmaster. He needed to be with a king – needed to be with his father. Arthur twisted a derisive, mocking grin, stepped away from her, lifted his wine and drained the goblet. He went to the far door, the one that would open out into the night air. 'Very well, Cerdic returns with me.' He saw her smiled relief, saw it fade as he added, 'I have been asked by Ambrosius to turn to this Christian God of yours. If I were to follow his advice, I would need to pay atonement for my sins. I'll build a monastery near Caer Cadan and offer my son to His service.' Her hand had gone to her throat, colour draining from her face. 'The idea serves well enough to keep Vitolinus from learning how to use his manhood. It will be the same for Cerdic.'

Before he stepped into the shrouding darkness, he finished with a threat. 'And if you send Cerdic to Aesc I personally will release Vitolinus. He has more claim to the Saex kingdom than your brat. Think on it.'

Arthur stamped directly across the horse paddock to where his men had made camp, half mindful that someone else might accost him before he had a chance to join them and sleep this night. The horses were restless, snorting, ears back, but Arthur was angry with Winifred, tired, and had drunk more than enough. That sputtering candle in Winifred's room had cast a stronger reek of smoke than he realised, for he could smell it on his cloak. He stopped abruptly, head up, scenting the frosted air. It was smoke he could smell but not from a candle . . . Mithras' love! The barn was on fire!

§ XXII

Onager was inside that barn. Mean he might be, but he was a good war-horse, and Arthur, and the men of the Artoriani relied on their horses, thought of them almost as family. Running for the nearest door Arthur was bellowing, yelling the word, 'Fire! Fire!' His own men were rousing first, being the nearest, sleeping outside, but the Hall doors were opening, the night-watch peering out at the sudden commotion.

Arthur reached the door, pulled at it, was flung back as a blast of heat and flame erupted outward, engulfing door, lintel and wall. Inside, Onager was screaming, kicking; Arthur could imagine the great beast lashing out at the wooden partitions of his stall – he was tethered, had he yet managed to break the rope? God's love, he could not lose another stallion! He raced around to the front double doors, praying to every god that was listening that they had not been barred from the inside. Belches of flame were streaming up into the sky now on the far side from where he had just come. Men were tumbling out from the Hall, some pulling on tunic and bracae, others tearing, naked, running for buckets, fetching water, forming a linking chain from well to barn, and Aesc's Saex were coming from their camp.

Arthur, with his hands on one of the huge doors, paused a heartbeat of a moment. If the flames spat out from this end of the building as they had the other, he would never get in, never get Onager out . . . He lifted the latch, the door gave, swung outwards, hens bustling and flapping, squawking as they fluttered in panic from the confine of the place, caused Arthur to take a step backwards, his arms going up to shield his face from their alarm. Black smoke billowed out, no flame this end, but the hiss and crackle rose louder, and inside, Arthur could see the red hell at the far end of the barn creeping nearer, and Onager, this end, rearing, twisting and plunging.

All the Pendragon could do was fill his lungs with breath and plunge into the choking blackness. Vaguely, he heard someone scream his name, Winifred's voice, but he ignored it, directed his full attention to the panic-stricken horse plunging and terrified four yards within the left-hand side of the barn. The flames were slithering nearer, touched another bank of stacked hay, and rocketed upwards with a great, whooshing roar, caught at the roof. Arthur was at the stall, desperately trying not to hear the rush of sound coming nearer above him, or the creaking groans from the tortured roof beams. He had to slip in beside the stallion, had to reach the tethering rope that held so damned fast. Onager was plunging, throwing himself from side to side. His hoof pistoned out, slamming into the partition wall, lashed out again, caught Arthur a blow to the thigh that made him gasp in pain – but he was past, was at his head! Gentle, calm, Arthur laid his hand along the massive horse's neck, stroking, soothing, murmuring soft, crooning words.

438

'Whoa there, my beauty, my brave lad. This is a fine old mess eh? Come now, easy my boy, let us be going from here, come lad, come.' He could not untie the rope, so tight had Onager pulled the fastening, didn't bother to try. He had his dagger out, through the rope, and his hand laid firm on the halter in a moment. He pushed the stallion backwards, one hand insistent on his chest, clicking his tongue. 'Back, step back.' Onager was frightened, blinded and choked by the acrid smoke, but for all his vicious manner, he had trust in his master and took a step backwards. 'Good lad, good boy. Again, back, back.'

The smoke was thickening, the flames darting now along floor, wall and roof. The rear wall suddenly crashed down, timbers giving way in a belch of fuming smoke and shooting flame. The heat was becoming intense, the noise deafening, but Onager was out from the stall and Arthur turned him for the open door. For a throat-gasping moment he thought the animal was not going to go forward, but Onager was a war-horse and though he was shaking and scared, he dropped his head and walked beside the only man he would let ride him, walked to the door and out through the reek of smoke into the cool darkness of a star-studded night.

Someone came to try and take the horse, but Arthur waved him aside and led the animal across the paddock, filled with men running and shouting, or standing looking stunned, speechless. The buckets had been abandoned, there came another tremendous crash and the barn roof fell in, the flames lighting the night sky in a fireball of orange and red and dense black smoke. Arthur did not see it, for he was across the paddock, leading Onager through the gate, across the cool, frost-sparkled grass into the field, where he would have been curled asleep with his men, had he been able. The other horses had fled to the furthest side, milling by the wall, feet stamping, snorting, ears going back and forth, frightened by the smells and sounds.

At last Arthur could stop. Gweir appeared, face blackened, eyes round-white. 'Master? Are you all right, Sir?'

Arthur could make no answer. His throat felt dry and sore, his lungs heavy and congested. Another man appeared, his Decurion, and took Onager's halter as Arthur passed it to him. For long, long moments, Arthur stood there, on the furthest side of the field, bent double, hands on his thighs, trying to get his breath while coughing the vileness out from him. Gweir had disappeared but within a moment came back, clutching a tankard of winter-cold water. He gave it to his master, who nodded his thanks and sipped the delicious liquid that cooled the burning that ran from tongue to belly.

They all looked up, round, as the final agony came. The walls buckled, the barn fell. It would not burn for much longer for there was nothing left for the fire to consume.

§ XXIII

The tracks were easy enough to follow, two horses, galloping. Arthur's horses, war stallions that had been painstakingly trained and taught, a bay and chestnut. Where the trees had thickened into denser woodland and the frost-rutted track divided, the horses had slowed, halted a moment, then been pushed on again, uphill, deeper into the woods. Ridden. Bolting horses did not stop to decide in which direction to run, they went fast and straight.

Dawn had been thick with the heavy reek of smoke. All the stored hay and grain was gone. The gathered grain harvest for the steading. Two men had been killed, one hit by falling beams, the other caught by flame as he bravely tried to save some of that precious grain. Gone also were two of Arthur's horses – and two boys.

By mid-morning Cerdic and Vitolinus had not been found, and then the tracks were discovered. Arthur himself, mounted on another horse – for Onager was still shivering, his coat scorched and blackened in places, his tail singed – followed the trail of hoof prints, his men, grim, silent behind. Occasionally they checked, where the ground had frozen too hard to betray a print, but Arthur was a soldier, and his men were experienced scouts and hunters. Always they found the way again, following at a jogtrot or walk, but following. Silent, angry.

A stream twisted its way between steep-sided earth banks that

440

gouged a path through the close-growing trees. The woods were silent, no sound of bird song, no mournful call of a wolf. Only Arthur and his Turma of Artoriani, the rustle of grass and fallen leaves beneath the hooves, the occasional jangle of bit and creak of leather. The tracks of two horses were plain here beneath the trees on the layers of leaf mould where the frost had not yet come. Down the steep bank, the earth was scoured and crumbled where the animals had slid into the water.

Arthur drew rein at the top of the bank. There were no tracks on the far side. He studied the double line of disturbed pebbles and floating weed beneath the sluggish water. They had gone upstream then. He pushed his horse to follow, rode on a hundred or so yards, then his horse snorted, plunged, as a boy, with dirt- and tear-smeared face, clad in a muddied, wet tunic and boots, appeared suddenly from around the bend ahead. Arthur cursed. The boy, wading down through the water, intent on re-trailing his way home, was as startled to see the men. He bit off an exclamation, stood, hands clasped into fists at his sides looking up into the cold eyes of Arthur, the Pendragon.

The man returned the look with searing contempt. The boy's skin was ash-pale beneath all the grime, that first startled horror of unexpected meeting becoming masked, steadfastly thrust aside into a show of defiance. The boy's legs were shaking and his stomach churning. He wanted to run, wanted to shout that it had not been his fault, that he was not to blame. It had been the other boy's idea, not his. He had only meant to scare the horses, not start a fire. But Vitolinus did not run, or blurt out his protests. He faced the Pendragon and lifted his arm to point upstream.

'Cerdic is hurt. He fell.'

Arthur said nothing, continued that awful, contemptuous stare, then kicked his horse into a trot, bending low beneath sweeping branches, riding past Vitolinus, ignoring him. Another rider, towards the rear of the column, lifted the boy and set him before his saddle. No one had spoken, not one single man uttered a word.

The bay stood beside a clump of alder trees, head down, hide stained with dried sweat, his near-side foreleg hanging limp. The stream narrowed here, the banks reared steep. The second horse, the chestnut, lay up against the earth bank, body half covered by water, the ugly twist of his head showing his neck to be broken. To the left, propped against a tree, lay Cerdic, his skin white as chalk dust, sweat pricking on his forehead. He saw Arthur ride around the bend of the stream, tried to move, his face contorting in pain, and fear.

Arthur reined in, slid from his horse, leaving the animal to graze, and walked past the injured boy, paying him not even a cursory glance. Approaching the bay with extended hand and soft words, he petted the miserable animal, smoothing the wrinkled coat where sweat had dried, talking all the while in low nonsense words while he moved down the shoulder past the knee to the swollen, misshapen fetlock joint. Straightening, he drew his sword, again patted the horse's neck, fondled his ears, and quickly, before the animal knew it to happen, brought the blade through the throat. The horse dropped, blood gushing, the life left within the muscles and veins twitching and jerking.

They had been good horses.

The chestnut's rider, Arthur's Decurion, a man whose father and father's father had bred horses, slipped from his borrowed mount and walked towards the grotesque body. He stood a moment looking down at the lifeless hulk and the sightless eyes, remembering the pride that had been there only yesterday. He turned quickly away, walked back to his borrowed horse and mounted with a stiff back and erect head. Their horses meant much to the Artoriani.

Many eyes swivelled from the dead chestnut to Arthur, to Cerdic, back to Arthur, wiping his bloodied sword blade on the grass. Aye, they all knew it was wrong to become attached to their mounts, knew that sentiment had no place beside a warrior's sword, but the knowing did not ease the doing. Not one man there, watching as Arthur walked towards the boy huddled against that tree, made any attempt at objection, or frowned, or even cared, as Arthur kicked out, his boot connecting savagely with Cerdic's fractured thigh. The bones grated, blood spurted. Cerdic screamed.

Vitolinus, standing uncertain at the rear where his escort had dumped him, darted forward. His hands grasped at Arthur's tunic, pleading, tears spurting down his face. 'It was not Cerdic's fault! The chestnut slipped, it was an accident. An accident!'

Arthur whirled, his hand sweeping back and down across the boy's cheek, the blow sending the boy tumbling, blood spurting from his nose. Nostril's flaring, the Pendragon hauled Vitolinus to his feet, held the boy by the collar.

'Accident? Was the bay, too, an accident? Was it an accident that set ablaze your sister's barn where my stallion was stabled? Was it accident that has destroyed the stored harvest, killed two men and two horses?'

Vitolinus cried out, as Arthur's fist again hit him. No one attempted to interfere. They watched, silent, blank, with no pity.

Cerdic, the pain intense, teeth chattering, sweat soaking into his eyes, shouted, 'Leave him be!' He attempted to rise. The world spun red and black. 'Leave him, you murdering bastard!'

The red rage that had seized Arthur at this senseless waste calmed. He flung Vitolinus from him, swung around, fists clenched, breathing hard. Cerdic flinched, expecting blows to fall on him, but Arthur stood where he was.

'Murdering bastard is it?' Arthur could barely talk for the raw, burning anger that filled his throat. 'You think that of me now, boy. Na. You have not yet seen how much of a murdering bastard I can be.'

He went to his horse, mounted, heeled it into a trot, rode away. Behind him, without a backward glance, rode his Artoriani. A lone bird glided silent on spread wings to a nearby branch, black eyes cold as death, eyeing over the pickings. The scavengers were coming, drawing closer, their harsh, excited caws breaking the silence of the woods.

Arthur kicked his mount into a canter. He had a meeting with Aesc and already the day was half wasted.

Cerdic watched him go, through a hazed blur of tears and pain, watched his father ride away and leave him there.

Vitolinus crawled to his feet, spitting blood from his mouth along with a broken tooth. He would have to walk back to the steading,

fetch help. It would be a long walk, but even so, the undamaged side
of his face formed a smile of relief.

'Jesu,' he said, 'I thought he was going to kill us!'

Cerdic made no answer, but his thought showed.. *I'll be killing him
first!*

§ XXIV

Vitolinus made his way back to Winifred's steading, stopping as he
stumbled to the edge of the oak woods, breathless, hurting, angry
and humiliated. Arthur was surveying the remains of the barn. The
blackened timbers were sticking obscenely upright; the burnt,
charred rafters, hanging, fallen, one still resting across the supports.
Smoke still drifted here and there, and the acrid, choking smell
wafted even as far as these trees. He watched Arthur step through
what had once been the huge double doors – only the doorposts
remained – watched as the Pendragon bent, picked something up. It
must have been metal, for it glinted, caught by the afternoon sun.

Summoning courage, Vitolinus took a step out from the shaded
protection of the trees into the cloud-scuttered sunlight, ready to
cross down the slope into the steading. A bird, a kestrel he thought
flew low over his head and he lifted his eyes to watch its passing, saw
the autumn blueness of the sun-glistened sky, and the majesty of the
trees, tinged with the first stirrings of colourful splendour. And
suddenly freedom seized him. He had never known what it was like
to stand entirely alone beneath the shade of an oak tree and feel the
smart slap of sun on his face. Always, when he was young, his
mother had been beside him or behind or before; his mother with her
stifling possessive loving that had swamped him, engulfed him, so
that his stomach heaved and his throat choked, clawed to be free of
her. But he was a small boy, he had not the knowledge or
understanding to run from her. Then Arthur had rescued him. Oh,
that glorious day when he realised he was no longer to remain with
his doting mother! They had been living with his grandsire, old

444

Hengest, and Arthur had beaten him in battle. Part of the price of surrender had been the handing over of the boy Vitolinus. But it had turned out to be a brief happiness, for he was put into Ambrosius Aurelianus's care, that dour-faced, God-praising bore, and from him, to the monastery. Where his sister, the so revered and oh so hypocritical, two-faced bitch could keep eye to him.

Freedom! He held his arms wide, let his head fall back, and smelt and tasted its feel. Ah, it was good! Drunk on the heady intoxication, he stepped back into the concealing shadows and waited. He saw Winifred's men hurrying up the trail into the woods, watched them returning later with a boy lying on a stretcher, his mother running in a flurry of high-carried skirts to tend him. He waited and watched as the afternoon shadows lengthened and the two leaders, the British Pendragon and the Jute Aesc, came together in Council, sitting out in the open, gathered circular around the huge-built fire, to make their peace and promises of treaty. Watched and waited for the long, cold-nip night to turn through the darkness into the pink-fringed dawn. Watched, with a sneering grin of hatred, as the Pendragon mounted and rode away. Waited for Aesc to make his way to the river where his two ships lay moored.

And then he cut himself a staff, hitched his cloak tighter around his shoulder and started eastward. He would follow the coast, would walk to Aesc's country, make his own way, in his own time and his own freedom, to return to his kindred. He could have gone down to the river, waited by the boats and begged his uncle to take him on board. But Aesc might have refused; Winifred, the old sow, might have been there, or the po-faced Ambrosius.

Na! He would make his own passage to Aesc's territory, for then he could present himself truly as free-born, and no man could mock or jeer him, or accuse him of a cowardly running away.

He would go to Aesc, and learn how to become a man. He needed to learn, for there were two things he now wanted. His freedom, and to make an end to the bastard he hated more than any person living. Arthur, the Pendragon.

§ XXV

'Mam?' Llacheu lifted his eyes from the ash-spear shaft he was rubbing smooth, the thing intended as a gift for his father when he returned. 'Why has Da gone to see Winifred? I thought he detested the disagreeable bitch.' The sun had set half an hour gone, its brief blaze of glory fading into evening. Beyond their private chamber, Caer Cadan was preparing for the night.

'It is not for you to call her so!' Gwenhwyfar reprimanded her son, not entirely masking her amusement. Llacheu had mimicked Arthur's tone and often-used expression. He was so very much like his father, even down to that familiar squinting look of one eye half closed, the other eyebrow raised. When he grew, the voice too would be similar.

The boy had muttered a response, she did not quite hear what, but did not question him. It was probably something rude about Winifred, and she had no heart to chide him for thoughts she herself harboured. Aloud he said, 'Do you think Cerdic will want Da's torque when he is grown?'

Gwenhwyfar was kneeling beside a brindled hound sitting patient by the central hearth-fire, pulling burrs and ticks from his thick coat. Her nimble fingers had caught a flea, broken it in two but at her son's question, she paused, hands hovering above the dog. She considered an answer, to tell the truth or pass it away? Llacheu was ten years of age, a child no more. She began again to search for parasites on the dog's coat, chiding the animal to cease his ridiculous squirming and lie still.

'Da said you were to be the firmer with him,' Llacheu informed her as the hound scrabbled to his feet and attempted to wash Gwenhwyfar's ears with his tongue.

Laughing, she pushed him away, wiped at her wet face. 'Da then, can have the training of him! The dog is soft in the brain!' They laughed together, mother and son, sharing the friendship of their dogs and the pleasure of each other's company.

She had not answered the question, and as their laughter faded, Llacheu repeated, 'Well, do you?'

'Do I what?'

'Cerdic.'

Gwenhwyfar sat back on her heels, her lower lip pouting as she considered an answer. The dog seized the opportunity to wriggle away and lay down next to Llacheu's dog Blaidd, yawning, his mouth a gaping chasm of white teeth and pink tongue.

She answered with the truth. 'Cerdic will want to be called Pendragon, aye. His mother is teaching him to expect it.'

Llacheu held the spear shaft before him, squinting along its length. It was a good shaft, would serve well. He nodded to himself in satisfaction, set it aside and stood up, stretching. He was not yet growing into his height, though it would come within the next few years. His child's body was slender, with firm, maturing muscles, his hair, a light brown, cascading to his collar in an unruly mop, never tidy. And his eyes were Arthur's eyes, expressive, able to reflect laughter or anger; as thick lashed, as deep and dark. He finished his stretch, enjoying the pull of cramped muscles along his neck and back. 'Then he will have to fight me for it! I am not afraid of Cerdic.' Aye, so much like Arthur!

'Then you ought to be!' Gwenhwyfar's reply was matter of fact. 'Your father fears what he may become.'

Llacheu snorted disbelief. 'A boy brought up by a woman on a farmsteading? What will he know of war and fighting?'

'A boy whose father is King of all Britain, whose uncle is Aesc of the Cantii, whose grandsire was the Saxon Hengest. Do I add to the list?' Gwenhwyfar had risen to her feet stood before her son, her hands going to his shoulders, giving them a little shake as she spoke. 'He may not stay with his mother. What if she sends him to live with his uncle? Have you thought of that?'

The boy's answer was pert, combined with a shake of his head. 'Father would never allow it.'

'Your father might not be able to stop it!'

Llacheu shrugged, and bent to retrieve the spear shaft from the floor where he had laid it. He did not fully understand this intense

447

animosity between his mother and that other woman who had once been his father's wife. He, Llacheu, was Arthur's first-born, legitimate son, so why all this fuss about poxed Cerdic? Except, he understood one thing. He wanted to follow his father and be the next Pendragon – very, very much. And if Cerdic had that same wanting, then there would indeed be a fight for possession of the Dragon. 'I will have the Artoriani behind me?' Llacheu said, half turning to look at his mother, a slight rise in his voice with the question. He wanted his father's torque and banner, but there was a hard part; he would only get them when his father was dead. And beyond anything – beyond everything – Llacheu did not want his father dead!

Gwenhwyfar must have caught the pain of his expression, for she held out her arms to the lad, a sudden fear pricking that he was, perhaps, too old now to respond to a mother's hug. But Llacheu grinned and flung his arms around her broadening waist, snuggling his head into the bulge that was the new baby growing within her.

'The Artoriani will follow Arthur's son to beyond the sea's edge,' she said, stroking his unruly hair into a semblance of order, 'but only if that son is worthy for the following. And you,' she ruffled his hair back into its customary untidiness, 'will be more than worthy.'

The lamps would need trimming, several were smoking. Darkness was thickening outside. Llacheu stretched up to place a light kiss on her cheek. 'Poor Cerdic. I almost feel sorry for him.'

The baby was uncomfortable, for all it was only four months within her, and perhaps with a little too much irritability Gwenhwyfar answered, 'Do not waste your sorrow. He is not deserving of it.'

Whistling to the dogs, who instantly came alert from sleep, Llacheu made for the door to walk them before he made for his bed. His mother was often short-tempered these days; he had asked Enid about it, and received a pert answer. *'You'd be bad-tempered if you had to carry a damn great lump about for nine months!'* He threw a quick grin at Gwenhwyfar. 'Cerdic, I think, must be as disagreeable as his bloody bitch of a mother.' He ducked out before she could make an answer.

Gwenhwyfar laughed and settled herself before the fire, her feet tucked under her skirts. She sat for a while, enjoying the comfort of this, her home, letting the warmth flush her cheeks red, letting her thoughts wander. Within the passing of a few years Llacheu would become a man. An idle, passing, thought; would he break as many hearts as had his father? Gwenhwyfar sighed. Her son ought to have brothers beside him, loyal brothers. She prayed often, to both the Virgin Christian Mary and the Old Goddess. Prayed that she carried a boy, a new brother for Llacheu.

The fire crackled, Gwenhwyfar yawned. She had a headache coming on. Too much sitting about, not enough walking, ah, but she was so tired! She ought to think about going to bed, yet she did not welcome it for the bed gave little comfort, despite its new goose-feather mattress, fine linen sheets, and covering furs. A bed was such a lonely place when your man was not there to share it. She got to her feet, winced and stamped her numbed foot as a rush of blood sent her toes tingling. Hopping to the bed, she sat on its edge, rubbing vigorously at the needle-sharp prickling.

The sound of boots approaching outside made her lift her head. Knuckles rapped on the door, a man cleared his throat nervously. Gwenhwyfar groaned. Now what? Wearily, she went to open the door.

The man who stood there held his woollen cap sheepishly in his hands, twisting it around and around, a faint, tentative smile on his face.

Uncertain, for the light was poor, she questioned, 'Ider?'

Eagerly, the young man nodded, the smile becoming bolder.

'It is Ider! You are returned! And are you well?' Pleased, Gwenhwyfar held her hands to him as she gabbled the questions, drew him inward, into the light of lamp and fire, standing him within the threshold of her chamber. He reddened, embarrassed at her enthusiasm and affectionate greeting. He had half expected to be turned away, told to go straight to barracks.

'You look splendid,' she appraised, her tiredness forgotten as she circled around him, noting he was thinner, but that his skin was sun-browned, his eyes bright-dancing. Again she took up his hands,

449

turning them over, inspecting the healthy pink colour beneath the nails, the pad of firm flesh to the palm. 'Your wounds are healed? You are allowed back to us?' The questions came in a rush. He managed to stammer answers, and then there was a slither of paws on the steps beyond the door and the swirl of the two dogs entering, seemingly a whole pack by the extent of the barking and wagging of tails. Llacheu was there and hugging his good friend Ider, asking the same questions as his mother, pulling the man further in; and the door was shut, a stool found. His cloak and the saddle-bag were taken, laid in a corner; a tankard of ale was pressed into his hand, the wild exchange of laughter and chatter tumbling in a rush of shared excitement. Enid was called, asked to fetch some more wine and bring food.

Ider drank his ale and answered the questions fired at him as best he could. Aye, his wounds were healed, and aye, the medics at Aquae Sulis had at last passed him fit, but no, he had not enjoyed his time there. 'Jesu,' he complained, 'the women are as prim as a duck's arse!' He drank thirstily, wiped ale from his upper lip with the back of his hand. 'Even the ale there tastes as bad as that muck they call healing water. It tasted more like boar's piss to me!'

The two dogs were nosing at his leather bag. Llacheu absently called them away, returned to the urgent questioning, but the dogs ignored him. Blaidd pawed at the bag, whimpering. Suddenly there was a shrill yowl and the dog leapt backward yelping, the other dog, Cadarn, began barking. Gwenhwyfar, Ider and Llacheu sprang to their feet.

'What the hell!' Ider roared, as he strode across the small chamber towards the snarling, barking dogs, Llacheu with him, shouting at the animals to be quiet.

The leather bag had tumbled to the floor, tangled with Ider's cloak. Gwenhwyfar, at Ider's other side, grabbed his arm, pointed at it. 'Mithras! The thing's moving!'

Ider grinned, lifted the bag and cloak, advised Llacheu to put the dogs through into the main Hall a while. They objected, but at the boy's firm insistence, out they went. Loosening the cords that held the bag closed, Ider put his hand inside and withdrew a ball of tabby,

450

spiky fur with two black-tipped ears flattened above frightened round eyes. The tiny creature opened its mouth, and issued a plaintive, wailing, meow.

Gwenhwyfar laughed, clapping her hands, delighted. 'Oh, the dear thing!'

Grinning, Ider handed her the kitten. He grimly surveyed the several red scratch marks along the back of his hand. 'Dear', was not a description he would have used.

Gwenhwyfar fondled the animal, admiring its softness, its perfect markings, let Llacheu have his turn at cuddling it. 'Where did it come from?' she asked. They had no cats at Caer Cadan for they used weasels to keep down the mice and rats in the granary stores.

'Two days back, I stopped a night at a farmsteading. The kitten's mother had died and the woman of the house couldn't be bothered with the litter. She'd already killed the others.' Ider shrugged, non-committal. 'It seemed a shame not to let such a tiny thing have a decent chance at life, just for the sake of dripping some milk down its throat.'

Llacheu had set the kitten on the floor. Gwenhwyfar squatted and flicked her fingers, the kitten pounced. They all laughed.

'It's not that young, it'll soon be fully independent,' Llacheu observed. He took some meat off the dishes on the table, held it to the kitten, who took it and chewed ravenously, spitting and swearing prolifically at Llacheu when he came too close. They laughed again.

'She'll make a fine hunter that one!' Ider observed.

And then they were talking again, Gwenhwyfar motioning Ider to the stool, she herself taking the comfortable chair. Llacheu was playing with the kitten, dragging a length of thin-twined rope around the floor, the cat leaping and pouncing and growling. Ider told them of his wound and his healing, of the scar that swept through his waist where the spear had pierced him, nearly ending his life. With the thirst all boys have for such things, Llacheu forgot the kitten, which instantly flopped to the floor and fell asleep, and asked to see the scar. Ider stood, removed his tunic and under-shirt to show them.

The door opened, whirling in a squall of sudden falling rain and a gusting of wind that sent the lamp and hearth-fire flames leaping in a frenzy of sparks and flared light. His cloak billowing, Arthur stepped into the room, his boots rapping on the wooden floor, hearing chatter and laughter, seeing, in that first, flurried instant of his unexpected entrance, his wife kneeling before a man who was stripped naked to the waist and who stood near enough to the bed as not to matter.

§ XXVI

Arthur was undressing, preparing for bed. He had come across his wife, seemingly in that first hasty moment, alone with a half naked man. He had leapt to a wrong conclusion, and felt foolish. That made him irritable. Gwenhwyfar was already abed, nestled under the furs. The kitten sat on top of her, batting and nibbling at her playing fingers. She had tried conversation, Arthur's only answers grunts and mumbles, and so had given up, occupied herself with the kitten instead. Hiding her hurt. He knew she was angry with him, and embarrassed at his misjudged reaction, but the thing was done, committed.

He had his tunic off, his boots, stood clad only in his leather bracae. 'All right,' he said, not quite as calm and collected as he had intended; he took a breath, tried again, 'I jumped to conclusions. I was wrong, I saw what I thought I saw, not what I was seeing. Throwing Ider out onto his arse was a stupid, arrogant and jealous act, and I shall apologise to him in the morning – but damn it, Cymraes, what was I supposed to think?' He turned to look at her, his arms spread, helpless, vulnerable. It was the only apology she was going to get, and if she didn't like it, then she could go to hell. He would not beg for her forgiveness.

'That's the point, Arthur, you did not think, you assumed.' Gwenhwyfar lifted the kitten and put it to the floor, where it scampered a few feet then squatted, puddling among the spread

452

bracken. It scratched at the dried stuff, then, leaping into the air, bounded stiff-legged and tail as vertical as a banner's shaft, sideways, like a scuttling crab, across the room.

No, he had not thought. He had acted in a blind sudden-come rage of jealousy, hurling Ider from the room by the scruff of his neck along with a torrent of abuse. Arthur sucked his lower lip, unlaced his bracae and stepped out of them. It was only after, as he had slammed the door and turned to bellow at his wife that he had seen Llacheu kneeling beside her, and Enid standing behind. He shrugged his left shoulder, lifted his hands again, his apology sincere. 'I was a bit,' he searched for a fitting word, tried a tentative grin, 'hasty?'

'You were a damn fool.' She was laughing, for all that her expression indicated cross indignation and the inflection in her voice seemed harsh. Behind the pretence, the laughter was there.

'Mithras, bloody hell!' Arthur leapt into the air, skittering a dance of pain and surprise; the kitten had jumped to his thigh and was clinging to the flesh. Wincing and cursing, Arthur picked it off, and unhooking each claw from his skin, dropped it to the floor, where it promptly sat down and scratched industriously behind its ear. 'Gods damn the little sod!'

Gwenhwyfar was laughing outright now, her arm clutching at her stomach, pointing with her other hand at Arthur's predicament. 'Oh, dear!' she exclaimed, wiping at the tears, trying to control her amusement but laughing all the louder.

Growling, Arthur crossed to the bed, aiming a kick at the cat as he passed, earning a batted paw and scratched toe for the trouble. It did nothing to ease his wife's crowing.

Beyond the chamber, the trumpets blared to signal the change of the Watch. The gates had been shut and barred – anyone still down in the tavern would be locked out for the night with a charge to face come morning. Latrine duty was the usual punishment. Few men missed the closing of those gates at the second Watch.

Gwenhwyfar snuggled into Arthur's warmth, her mind drifting into that comfortable, drowsy place that lingered between awake and asleep. He shifted his arm around her, laid his face against her hair. 'Hello, wife.'

'Hello, fool.'

Arthur grunted, hugged her body closer.

'How was the bitch Winifred then?' Gwenhwyfar asked, her eyes closed, the daze of drowsing not quite strong enough to bring full sleep. 'Haggard and shrivelled? As sour-mouthed as ever?'

'She tried to seduce me.'

It was Gwenhwyfar's turn to snort. She moved into a more comfortable position, her arm going around her husband, liking the feel of his skin, even with its patterning of various scars. 'That is one woman I do not fear competition from!'

Arthur kissed the top of her head, said, 'She is still handsome.' His wife's only response was a derogatory noise. She nestled her head into his shoulder, did not ask of Cerdic.

Distant noises from beyond the walls filtered through into the chamber; the sound of the men coming off Watch going to their beds, an owl flying low over the Caer calling to its mate. A dog barking, answered by another, and a man's gruff voice shouting at the curs to be quiet. The normal sounds of night and a place preparing to sleep.

Inside, the fire crackled as a log shifted; the timbers of the roof beams creaked as they too settled. The bracken rustled with a slight sound, a small creature scuttled from the shadows, sniffed at a dropped piece of bread that the dogs had missed. There was enough light for Arthur to watch the mouse as it squatted, nibbling at the prize held between its forepaws. The kitten too, watched, mesmerised. She stared, wide-eyed, quite still. The mouse must have scented her, for it ceased eating, froze a moment, then panicked, spinning around and whisking back into its hole with a cheeky flick of its long tail. The kitten arched its back, the fur standing up in spiky tufts, spat and then fled into the shadows running along the far walls.

Arthur slid lower into the bed, wriggling his toes into the luxury of warmth. 'Damn useful cat that one will be. It's afraid of mice.'

Gwenhwyfar laughed, and then, as the last lamp flickered out, said into the fire-glow, 'I missed you.'

Arthur kissed her, then showed how much he had missed her, expressing with his body why he had acted the jealous fool. She was his woman, and he loved her.

454

February 466

§ XXVII

Clouds, like wisping mare's tails patterned a sky that was the blue of a kingfisher's feather. A playful wind lifted Gwenhwyfar's cloak as she trudged, breathless, up the rising ground towards the Hall. The doors stood open, pushed wide back to clear the fug of hearth smoke, spilled beer and stale air but she walked along the outer daub-covered wattle wall, down to the far end and stepped through the similarly open door of the private chamber at the rear. Inside, she spread her arms wide and dropped the heavy weight of firewood. With her bulk of pregnancy, it was easier to drop the load, than add the logs one by one to the heap. Enid entered, carrying water for the cooking pot.

'You ought not carry heavy loads,' she chided, clicking her tongue in disapproval. 'You have servants to do such tasks.'

'The wood needed replenishing.' Gwenhwyfar's answer was mildly irritable as she eased the ache in her back. Only a few weeks more and the babe would be born, thank the gods!

'It's a waste, you having servants.' Enid sniffed her sarcasm. 'Might as well be rid of us.' She was a good woman, caring for Gwenhwyfar and Llacheu, but inclined to fuss. Gwenhwyfar gave her an affectionate, patient hug. Enid, for all her servant's chiding, was a woman worth her height in gold.

'I'll not carry any more wood, I promise.'

Enid nodded at the heap of logs. 'No need now, is there? You've done it all.'

Reluctant as she was to admit it, Gwenhwyfar was tired. She had slept fitfully last night, tossing beside Arthur, who had barely stirred – the wine and ale had passed around the Hall several times too many last night. She eased herself into the wicker chair, a comfortable seat with arms and goose-down-filled cushions, and closed her eyes a moment.

Enid shook her head, tutted a muttered admonishment and fetched her Lady a warming cup of herbal brew. 'Drink this, it'll be good for you and the babe.' As if she knew these things, added, 'He'll be here soon.'

Gwenhwyfar smiled, sipped at the drink. No point arguing, the birth was not due for several weeks yet. She knew her dates, her monthly flow being as regular as the moon-cycle, but it was never any point arguing with Enid once she had decided on a thing. Although, for this, Gwenhwyfar hoped her maidservant was right.

She tried to doze, but the restlessness that had been about her during the morning was reaching out to her again. There were tasks that needing seeing to; the washed laundry was spread to dry in the day's rare sun over bushes and grass, it would need gathering and folding, and she ought to finish the tidying of her establishing herb garden. The frosts were still common at night and the more delicate plants needed their protective covering of manure straw replenished. Straggle-grown bushes cutting back, tying up. Then there were the herbs already gathered and drying among the low rafters of the small chamber adjoining this one, where the jars and pots and amphorae of preserves and oil were stored.

Their harvested seed heads or petals would be dried now. Ready for using in healing remedies, for making sweet scented perfume pots, or for scattering among the floor rushes.

Noise and laughter from outside, a horse neighing, men's voices. Arthur was back from hunting then; he would come in a moment, tell her of how it had gone, after he had seen to the horses. She ambled about the room, twitching a hanging tapestry straight, setting a bowl of dried fruits to the centre of a table, fiddling unnecessarily with unimportant things. Enid had disappeared, was hopefully ensuring the slaves were folding the laundry correctly. You had to stand over slaves, an idle lot, who would do very little if they thought they could get away with it. Gwenhwyfar preferred free-born servants who had a pride in their work and loyalty. But then, could a slave be expected to have pride? Where was the pride in being a prisoner, bound to a lord's whim and command?

She walked to the door, stood in the weak afternoon sunlight slanting through the opening, the light catching her hair, turning its copper red to burning gold. Over by the stables, Arthur saw her, waved, shouted something, she could not hear what. He looked happy, he was laughing with the men and Llacheu, pointing to a fine, fat buck being carried up the hill for the women to make ready for skinning and cooking. The hide would make a new pair of boots for Llacheu. He was growing so! As she thought of him, her son waved also; from his expression, he too had enjoyed the hunt.

A dog was barking and jumping at the carcass, the clouds were thickening into billows of dark cumulus. Was snow coming? They had been lucky these past days, after the heavy snows of an early winter. Gwenhwyfar peered away down the hill, gasped as a sharp pain shot across her abdomen. She doubled, almost fell to her knees, her hands clutching at the pain that felt as though she were being ripped in two.

Arthur clicked his tongue at his horse, and with Llacheu beside him, began leading the animal into its stable. There were only a few stalls, most of the horses were kept at grass in the walled and fenced paddocks ranging around the foot of the Caer. Excited, Llacheu was reliving the hunt, his chatter retelling that first sighting of the buck and then its brave stand against the dogs. It had been a fine chase, a good run. But Arthur was only half listening. His laughter had died, a frown beginning to crease his face. He had glanced over his shoulder, his attention caught by a cry, saw Gwenhwyfar slump forward, fall. He pushed past the horse, ran across the courtyard. His boot slipping, he fell to one knee, but was up, running again, taking Gwenhwyfar in his arms as she gasped and fought the intense pain that clawed and tore at her.

Arthur shouted for help, for someone to fetch Enid, as he lifted his wife and carried her inside to the bed, but Enid would be too late for there was blood trailing on the floor, on his arms; blood and water gushing from Gwenhwyfar. Arthur tore at her skirts, fumbling, ripping the material in his haste to free her clothing. She was sobbing now, clutching at her abdomen, her knees drawn up, tears falling as her face contorted in pain.

The head was there, Arthur could see it, a mass of dark, wet hair –

where the hell was Enid? He bellowed for someone to get her, saw the doorway crowded with the curious, the concerned. In three strides he was there, slamming it shut as he yelled, 'Do something bloody useful! Fetch whatever it is a woman needs at a birthing. Move yourselves!' Then back to Gwenhwyfar, standing over her, stroking the sweat from her forehead and cheeks, clasping her hand as her fingers flailed to hold onto something. She was half sitting, pushing down, the gasping turning to panting. Her panic was easing, the pain not as intense now the head was nearly out.

'Mithras,' Arthur declared, himself almost sobbing, 'I don't know how to birth a child.'

The shoulders were out, one more push and it would be over. In the space it took for a breath, Gwenhwyfar half-laughed, 'it seems you are about to learn then, husband.' Quickly, he fetched sufficient thread from Gwenhwyfar's sewing basket, ready for the cord – his mind jumping, unexpected to the unsummoned memory of a woman with her head back, laughing. '*I will have your sons!*' He thrust the image of Morgause aside and the child was there. As he would have done with a foal, he tied and cut the cord, lifted the child and wrapped it in one of his own linen under-tunics that he had snatched up. The door swung open in a flurry of running feet and panting breath, Enid. But there was nothing she could do, nothing. The tears streaking his face, Arthur showed her the boy, a minute old, cradled in his arms. The boy he had seen born, his son. And the tears came into Enid's eyes. She put her hand to Arthur's arm, her head giving the briefest, despairing shake, and then she was gone to tend her mistress, and Arthur was pushing through the door, shouldering through the crowd and going to his horse. He mounted, rode at a canter, the bundle that would have been his son clutched tight to his aching chest, the tears falling and falling as he rode from the Caer.

§ XXVIII

The wind talked, up here on the summit of the Tor. Sometimes it whispered or crooned lovers' talk, caressing and soothing. Or it could shout and bellow, its anger blasting and pummelling, but always, incessantly, in whatever voice, the wind talked. Murmuring through the grass, slamming against the single, standing Stone or moaning as it slipped past the height to race down and along the valley.

Today, this late-winter afternoon, the wind prattled through the grass and tumbled around the solid, granite blackness of the man-high Stone against which Morgaine propped her back. She had been there since morning, huddled beneath a thick cloak, just sitting, staring out from this great height across the winter water, broken only by the drab trees and cast of muddied trackways.

On a clear day, the view was of for ever, the ripple of sun-warmed or snow-mantled hills playing faerie tricks, their distance in the shape-changing light confusing the senses of perspective and location. The sun-shimmered glimpse of sea sparkled beyond meadows that danced with a glory of flowers, the grazing land kissed by a flutter of butterfly wings and choired by the joyous glory-singing of birds. And as the shout of summer colour turned to the brilliance of autumn reds and golds, the blue and silver of the water came again, spreading and creeping up and over the river banks, to lie silent and mysterious beneath the gilded wonder of a full moon. The water-lands, ghost-shadowed by the Tor and her sister hills, wreathed by the beauty of a lowlying, white-breathed mist. The sun would rise in all his proud splendour from behind his evocative, night-dark, magical domain, to spread his warm, cupping hand of life. And the soft, gold moon would take her turn, bringing the gentle ease of sleep-silent peace. Yns Witrin, as it always had been and always would be. The centre, the heart, of the Old World, where even the ways of the new and the word of the Christ would never entirely silence the presence of the Goddess.

To the south-east lay a ramble of low hills, and when there was no wind playing over them Morgaine would sometimes see the grey fuzz of smoke against the sky. Smoke from the cooking fires, hearth-fires, the blacksmith's forge and the tavern and settlement of Caer Cadan, Arthur's stronghold. Often she would sit up here on the solitary loneliness of the Tor, with only the wind's voice and the presence of the Goddess for company, sit and watch the slow drift of that vague blur of smoke.

Eight months ago he had come, and he had not come again. It could all have been a dream, a fanciful wanting, his coming to her – but there were some things that showed beyond doubt that it had been reality.

There was no smoke this day, the sky was too grey, the wind too sprightly. The Caer itself could not be seen, though she had tried. Standing and standing, she fixed her eyes on where she knew it to be, but could not see its ditches and ramparts, its wooden-built palisade and high gate towers. The hills behind rose higher than the mound that was the Caer, enclosing its presence against their overpowering greens and browns and greys. There was nothing, from up here on the Tor, to show that across the other side of the summer meadows or winter floods, there bustled a busy place of men and horses. Nothing to be seen of the man Morgaine loved beyond living.

She had not sent word to her mother – let the hag find out from some other spiteful direction! She, Morgaine, would not betray this thing that was good and loving and beautiful to that evil bitch! The wind told her she knew, though. She could hear its persistent voice scuttling through the grasses, *Morgause knows! Morgause knows!*

Several times, Morgaine had been tempted to leave the Tor, to seek sanctuary among the Christian women, once going as far as the gate passing through the brick-built wall that encompassed their holy place. But a bell had rung from the little wattle-built chapel dedicated to the Mother of Christ, and women had come from their cloisters and buildings, and courage had failed her. She had run, tears falling, heart pumping, back up the long hill and through the secret ways across the lying water, climbing up and up, to the sanctuary height of the Tor.

462

Dark was setting now, easing like a whisper from the eastern sky, the blue fading to the purple black of evening, the land below the Tor merging with the deepening star-speckled darkness. Nothing moved, nothing showed except dark against dark, but still Morgaine sat with her back against the Stone. Lights did not show from the Caer, it was too far away to see the glimmer of torch or cooking fire. He was too far away, distanced by the miles of the summer levels and the barrier of a life that held no place, nor thought, for her. He was a king, a soldier. He had a wife, men to command. And what had she? A childhood of fear and neglect had passed into a solitary loneliness that brought its own dreaded fears. She had nothing, nothing except this great, overwhelming, stomach-tightening love for a man she had seen only in glimpses, and known intimately for just one, brief-passed sharing of time.

The cold made her move at last. Her body was stiff, bones and muscles cramped; it would be easier to follow the gentle slope, along the crest of the long hill, wind around and then drop down, but quicker to go straight down, the steep way, slithering on the wet grass. Her small, neat-kept hut was beneath this steeper side. She was cold, tired and lonely, felt suddenly the need for her own hearth, the comfort of her bed and the company of her own-made things. She took the quicker way, sliding in places, walking side-step in others, going straight down the mass of the Tor and brought herself up sharp, a small gasp escaping her parted lips. A light glimmered from her hut, a horse stood tethered outside. How had someone come? How had she missed the signs? Her heart pounded, mind whirled. The birds – love of the Goddess, the birds! She had seen them rise, seen and ignored their natural warning, so deep had she been in the wallowing suffocation of self-pity!

Cautious, she slithered the last few yards, drawing her dagger from her belt. It could be anyone who had come; a traveller wanting potions or healing, a *Myrddin* man, a Wise Man – there were still a few, the last remnants of the old Priesthood, the ones the Romans had called Druid, but she had heard of none travelling on this side of the Hafren River. Someone sent from Morgause? That, she was expecting. Her mother would not tolerate this silence from her daughter and the ignoring of sent messages. Or . . . With silent tread she inched towards the door, telling herself not to hope – but who else would ride such a well-fed, quality horse? Sounds came from within, the fire crackling, the ladle clanking against the cooking pot. The mouth-watering aroma of stew cooking. Who would have the impertinence to kindle a fire beneath her prepared supper? Quietly she lifted the greased latch, pushed open the door, dagger raised, heart hammering, throat dry, prepared to fight. She would not let a sly toad of Morgause's take her without a fight!

It was no one of Morgause's sending. Morgaine stood, numb, disbelieving, the dagger forgotten; stood staring at him as he stared, as unexpectedly surprised, back at her.

The baby, held in the crook of his arm, whimpered, jerking her senses back to reality. She stepped across the threshold into the warmth and light, closed the door, shutting out the judging mistrust of the night's eyes. He was cradling the child awkwardly, the bundle balanced across his knees as he squatted before the fire, tending the flame. As naturally as if every day she found a distraught, dishevelled man with a young child making himself at home within her hut, Morgaine took the baby from Arthur and began to fold back the linen that swaddled it. He did not watch her, busied himself instead with stirring the stew. Nor did she say anything as she saw the deformity, the misshapen spine and the cruel stump of an unformed leg. Wordless, she wrapped the boy, only a few hours old – for he still had the birth blood on him – and offered him back to Arthur.

The Pendragon remained squatting, shook his head, a single, negative movement. His voice was dry, choking grief, as he said, his eyes following the leap and flicker of hearth-flame, 'I did not know what to do, where to go. I found myself here.' And then he looked up at her, looked beyond the bulge that was her own advanced pregnancy to the pale, sunken face and large, dark eyes that had swamped with the sharing of his great sorrow. 'I could not just kill him, take a blade and slit his throat. Not my son. Not another son.' His voice broke and he turned away to hide his tears.

Morgaine touched his shoulder, resting her fingers against the taut muscles of his neck, feeling his hair where it curled against his tunic collar. She said nothing, gave only the one reassuring, understanding touch, and was gone, back out into the night, up this steepest side of the Tor that rose and rose into the darkness. When she returned, and for all her bulk of child-bearing, she was not gone long, she carried nothing. The boy was for the Goddess, in her wisdom, to take down into the Other World. It was not for mortal man to have the ending of something so new begun.

She served the stew into bowls, but, for all its goodness, neither ate of it. An owl called from away up on the Tor, and somewhere a wolf announced its presence with a drawn, mournful cry. Once, Morgaine fancied she heard the distant, pitiful wail of a child, but the wind had its own tales to tell this night, and its voice was rising as if in welcome to the pale spill of moonlight that rose serenely from behind the black-shadowed Tor.

Arthur wanted to get himself drunk, wanted to curse and shout, cry. She had poured him wine, but it was sweet stuff, not as palatable as the soldiers' fermentations that he was used to. Her brew would only bring a churning stomach and retching sickness.

She wanted to say so many things, to hold him, touch him. Love with him. Oh, for how many nights had she lain awake on her bed, dreaming and hoping of his coming again! In her imagination, had she felt his arms around her, his lips against hers, their bodies close in shared love. And now he was here, she could only sit and feel his misery. Her own heart-leap of happiness at having him here, seated aside her fire, drinking her wine, was somehow obscene, unclean.

Arthur sipped his drink, she knew he did not like it, though he was attempting to conceal the frown, the slight twist to his mouth. She had nothing else. Strong wine made her head dance, her eyes blur and her stomach heave. Only once had she become drunk, gulping mouthfuls of the heady stuff she had found in the other hut, drinking to drown the fear and enormous loneliness. That was when the last of the other women had died, the last of the old Ladies who had brought her up, taught her everything of the Goddess. She had held no love for those women, who had been as austere and hard as her mother had been – though not as cruel, no one could ever be as cruel as Morgause. Their deaths had been as nothing more than the passing of a goat or flower, a thing that happened except, when the last died, Morgaine had the facing of solitude. And even the crusty snarlings of an old woman were preferable to the nothingness of being alone. For three days she had lain ill after that wine. When the sickness finally ceased and the world stopped its crazy whirling, Morgaine had lain the last Lady in her hut, with all the amphorae and jugs and skins of wine and sent the lot to the goddess in a blaze of flame and billow of smoke. Nothing had passed her lips since, save the sweet taste of water or the lightly potent wine of her own making.

The geese were restless, their squabbling harsh voices drifting up from the night-dark lake. She offered Arthur more food, he refused.

There was a long silence, then he said, as casually as if he were enquiring the cost of wine, 'Is the child mine?' He surprised himself, as much as her, at that asking. Her babe could be any man's.

She met his eyes, nodded. 'It is yours. With you, it was my first time. There has been no one else.' *Nor will there be.* She did not add that, for she did not want to explain how someone else's touch would taint the memory of him, would defile her loving of him. How would a man understand that? A man such as she knew Arthur to be?

For his part, Arthur believed her. There seemed no reason not to. He was about to make an answer, but Morgaine raised her hand, silencing him, her head up, alert. There! Again! A sound from outside; Arthur heard it too. He was on his feet, drawing his sword, which left the sheep-skin-lined scabbard with the gentle breath of a whisper, the naked blade shimmering in the danced flicker of fire-light. The latch was lifting, slowly, the door coming open, a rattle of entering wind slithering through the gap, harrying the flames into a higher, more frenzied dance. Arthur was behind the door, breath held, sword ready, and as the person out in the night stepped into the room, he moved with the precise ease of a soldier, one arm going around the waist, the other holding the bright sharpened sword-edge at her throat. With a sneer and a snort of contempt, Arthur thrust the woman forward, away from him, slamming the door shut with the heel of his boot. The woman stumbled to her knees, his sword pricked in the small of her back.

'Well, well, what interesting visitors you have, Morgaine.' He lowered the sword, squatted before the fire.

The woman, forcing a smile, dusted down her skirts, clambered to her feet. 'Hello, Arthur, what do you here?' Her eyes flickered to Morgaine, sitting quite still on the far side of the hearth, took in her pregnancy, and said with contempt, 'I would assume you to be whoring, except it seems that that is an old tale.'

'Ah.' Arthur's half-smile, through his expression of one eyebrow raised, the other eye half shut, was sardonic. 'But then, you know all there is to know about whoring, don't you, Brigid?'

Brigid swung her cloak from her shoulders, hung it from a nail on the wall, pulled a stool from beneath the only small table and sat before the fire, holding her hands to the warmth. She seemed at ease in this place, at home, knowing where things were kept, the layout of the hut. 'We were wondering,' she said, helping herself to a bowl of stew, 'what had become of you, Morgaine.' Her eyes bore into the other, younger woman. 'Your mother is most concerned for your welfare.'

With his weight on his heels, the sword resting across his knees in the time-old way of a soldier seemingly at ease but ready for the slightest movement, Arthur regarded Brigid, the whore of Amlawdd's settlement, his paid spy. And, seemingly, someone else's.

He had not noticed before, the crow-foot wrinkles at her eyes, the taut line to her mouth. Or the hardness behind those eyes. He glanced casually at Morgaine, needed no intense studying to see she was afraid; realised, as he had not seen before, that she was not long from childhood. Realised something else simultaneously, two things that thumped into him as if an axe had split into his head, sending his senses reeling, heart racing and muscles tightening. The hair on his neck, he could feel, was rising, sweat trickled down his back beneath his linen under-tunic. Careful! Do not let the thoughts touch the face! Impassive, he shifted weight slightly, cradling the sheen of his sword into his arms. Took a wild guess. 'So you spy for Morgause then, my pretty whore.'

Thinking he meant herself, Morgaine dipped her head, her teeth biting into her lip, her hands, clasped in her lap, clenching tighter. What was she if not a whore and an evil utensil of Morgause's? He would never believe her if she were to protest, were to say she had not told her mother of . . . of what? Of how she had used her body to tempt him? How she had encouraged him to lie with her? Get her with child, as her mother had instructed her to do?

Brigid, tossing her head higher, brandishing her arrogance, knew the Pendragon was talking to her, not that snivelling wretch seated opposite. Light of the Moon, the Lady should have exposed the useless brat at birth! 'I serve myself.'

'You serve me. I pay you.' Arthur looked with slit eyes, spoke neutrally, almost flippant. Dangerously.

Contempt seethed from Brigid as she regarded him back. 'You receive your worth!'

His answer was soft spoken, menacing. 'Na, my pretty one, a whore is never valued for worth, only results.'

A slight rise of doubt wavered Brigid's poise. She had come to Yns Witrin to find what foolishness Morgaine was playing at. No messages of importance had passed through her these last few months, nothing beyond what naturally sailed on the wind. That she was hiding something had become obvious as autumn faded into winter. Morgause had sent instructions, through a much-risked route, to find out what and why. The pregnancy was an explanation, perhaps half expected, but not Arthur, here, taking his leisure at the fool child's hearth. And how much leisure had he taken? Nine months of it? 'Morgause will not be pleased that you have been tumbling her daughter.' She meant it to hurt, to be mocking, spiteful, but Arthur only laughed, hiding well the turmoil he felt at her words.

'You do not share your mistress's serving of the Goddess then? It seems I know more of her laws than you do.' It was those laws that had made him believe Morgaine when she said the child was his. The chosen Lady must give herself, for her first time, to a king. The Goddess made mortal, to bear a child for the replenishment of the earth. Morgaine was too timid, too much the innocent, to go against the rules. Only the child of a king would bring the blessing of the Goddess. The child was his, as much as Morgaine was Morgause's daughter. Inside, he was seething with anger at these damned women, and at himself for walking blind-eyed into Morgause's snare. Why had he not seen the obvious? The eyes, the face, even the voice were Morgause!

Brigid controlled her annoyance. It had shaken her to find Arthur here, to know that everything was ruined, ended. Her thoughts had been racing as to how she could warn Morgause that the networked chain of messengers and spies were severed at the most important end. But then, did it matter? Outside this one thing, they were not needed, not now. 'Your wife,' she sniped, 'will no doubt be interested to hear that for the King, the Old Ways are not finished with.'

'My wife,' Arthur answered, 'will not know of it.' A third guess, unrealised until this moment, found the reason behind the trap that he had so obligingly walked into. How Morgause would crow that he, Arthur, had sired a child by her daughter, a priestess of the Goddess. Mithras' blood, and until now he had thought the Church's view of him unreasonable? Ambrosius himself would string him up by the balls were this ever to get out!

Brigid laughed. 'Our proud King! How they will mock you in the North, when they hear how you so honour the Lady you keep prisoner! When they hear how you placed your seed in her chosen vessel! How you give them a son to become their War-Lord and King, the grandson of the Goddess on Earth!' She was jangling laughter, rocking back and forth on her stool, appreciating the jest, the irony. The laughter ceased abruptly as she felt the cold bite of a dagger on her throat.

Morgaine stood before her, her lip snarling, both hands clasped about the weapon, anger shaking the rigid hold.

'You make it sound as though my child was created for something sordid and evil! That is not the way of the Goddess. She is of understanding and love, of life and beauty. A harsh mistress at times, for where life is given it must also be taken. But she would not inflict pain for the amusement of it. Morgause is not of the Goddess, or if she is, then no longer am I.' Her eyes were wide with a madness that had suddenly come upon her, a shrieking, releasing surge of at last seeing the path that would take her away from these long years of despair. 'My bitch mother will not hear of my borne child. No one, aside myself and its father, will know.' And she drove the dagger home, pushing her weight behind the blade, thrusting it in up to the hilt, the sharpened metal spurting through sinew and blood, choking off Brigid's scream as it cut through the vocal cords, through the spine and out through her neck.

Dawn. The stirring of a new day touched the night sky behind the Tor, fingering spreading tendrils of delicate pink and pale, creeping yellow. Arthur had taken Brigid's body to the lake, pushing the black-haired woman into the soft mud at the edge, weighting the carcass with rocks. Then he had talked with Morgaine a while, conversation and idle chatter to ease the shaking reaction from her – never easy the first time of killing. She had slept for the last few hours of darkness, her body curled against him, her head on his shoulder. Arthur had sat, awake, the touch of his naked sword against his thigh, ready should anyone else come. With the dawn, he had to go. He ought not to have lingered, could not afford to stay longer. She stirred, woke, puff-eyed, blotchy-skinned, still frightened. Before leaving he kissed her, as a friend would give a parting kiss, and handed her a battered gold ring from his smallest finger. 'It was given me by my father,' he explained. 'It is most precious to me.' He paused, uncertain what more to say, whether indeed he should say more.

'If the child lives, if it is as boy –' he spoke hesitantly, reluctant – 'there may be a time when those who need to know will recognise that ring, and, through it, know him to be a son of mine.' And he was gone, out into the paling sky, through the trees, up onto his horse and away at a canter.

Morgaine watched him go, her hand resting on the bulge that was his child. He had asked, as they had talked, if she knew who had sired her. When she answered that she did not know, he had shrugged, said perhaps her mother had not known. But Morgaine had shaken her head, told him, *'She knew him. When I was a child, she would taunt me, tell me it was as well he had not known of me. I grew to know my father would be ashamed of me.'*

'How old are you, Morgaine?'

'Five and ten. My birthing day was the day of the Roman new year.'

He had not spoken for a long while after that, and then she had slept, and dawn had come, and here she was watching him ride away. The tears came to her eyes, for she knew that he would not come back.

She stepped from the hut and made her way along the hidden paths running across the lake and through the water-meadows. The birds that had risen at Arthur's going renewed the protesting at this second disturbance, but she ignored them, walked purposefully with a sudden-come strength of courage to the muddied track that led from the pagan place of Yns Witrin to the calm comfort of the Holy Sisters. She would not birth her child for the Goddess, for Morgause. This was Arthur's child, and he or she belonged in the new, Christian world. She took nothing with her, not even a cloak, for she wanted nothing from her miserable, despairing life. Arthur had given her a new hope, a new way, and she had to seize this one chance of following it. For the sake of the child, she had to.

As Arthur rode home, following the threaded ways of higher ground and the tracks through the marsh, he did not look back. He would not go again to the Tor. It held for him nothing save the memory of a misshapen child given back to from where it came, and a menacing, dark-tainted thought of a horror so great that he had at first tried to push it aside and bury it. But a thought, once sown, takes root; especially when such a thought shouts the truth.

'Five and ten,' Morgaine had said. Five and ten years past, Arthur had been a boy on the brink of manhood, a boy who thought himself to be a bastard, born of a serving girl. Five and ten years past, Uthr, the Pendragon had been slain by the old King Vortigern and Arthur had been revealed not as a serving girl's brat, but as Uthr's true and only son. Five and ten years past, Morgause had still been mistress to the great Uthr. She had not known then that he was Arthur's father.

But would have known it as she birthed a girl-child. Would have known it when she instructed that girl-child to ensure she showed herself to the new Pendragon. Knowing that once seen, the urge of lust would, eventually, lead him to his own half-sister's bed.

March 466

§ XXIX

Gweir ducked quickly through the door into his Lord's chamber. 'My Lord, there is a woman demanding to see you.'

Arthur did not answer, for he had his eyes closed while Gwenhwyfar, laughing, poured a jug of hot water over his head. He was taking a bath in the relative warmth of their own chamber; it was not suitable to build a complex bath-house here at Caer Cadan, and the weather did not lend itself to bathing naked in the winter-cold river. Most of the men went dirty, but for themselves Gwenhwyfar insisted on regular bathing. She and Llacheu had taken their turn in the round, wooden tub and now it was Arthur's. He wiped at his face with the linen towel Gwenhwyfar passed him. 'Who? What woman?' He stood, water dripping from his wet-glistening body. A dozen possibilities skittered through his mind – not one of them the name Gweir announced as he flicked an embarrassed glance at his mistress.

'She gives herself the title Lady Pendragon.'

'Love of Mithras!' 'What?' Arthur and Gwenhwyfar exclaimed together, she, wearing only a thin under-tunic, poised with a second towel, about to rub dry her hair, he, standing naked in the tub of water.

The door banged open letting in a stream of blasting cold wind and rain and a woman swathed in a wolf-skin cloak, dressed in the black garb of a Christian. 'God's death, you wretched, heathen boy! Dare you leave me standing out in the rain . . .' Winifred stopped, stood staring at the scene before her.

The silence was embarrassingly long. Arthur made the first move by draping the linen around himself and stepping from the tub. 'I normally receive guests in the public surroundings of my Hall, not unannounced in the privacy of my chamber.' He indicated a second door with his hand. 'Happen you would grant me the courtesy of waiting for me there?'

Winifred recovered herself, the red flush to her face receding, but her heart was still bumping. It had been a long time since she had seen a man naked, a long time since she had seen Arthur so. His body, despite the harsh marking of scars, was as desirable as that first time when she had slid quietly, uninvited and unexpected, into his bed.

She crossed herself against the sin of that rush of erotic thoughts, stepped with dignity past Gwenhwyfar, whose lips were pressed tight with anger, to the inner door that Gweir had run to open. On the threshold she thought again, turned back to look at Arthur. 'What I have to say is most urgent, my Lord. I have ridden personally to tell you that I have received word of Hueil. He is on the move, marching south.'

'What?' Arthur was across the room in three strides, the cloth slipping forgotten from his body. 'How do you know this?'

'We have heard nothing!' Gwenhwyfar cast a worried glance at her husband, who, slamming the door closed, was urgently drawing his first wife back into the chamber. 'Why have we not heard?'

Arthur waved her to silence, seated Winifred on a stool, began searching for his clothes and dressing, modesty irrelevant. 'Tell me, and tell me quickly, woman,' he snapped at Winifred; 'Fetch wine,' to Gweir, and Gwenhwyfar, tossing her a gown, 'Get dressed.'

Winifred, perversely refusing to hurry, unbuckled the fastening of her heavy, wet cloak, handed it to the servant boy, smoothed her gown, patted her hair straight. 'I heard because sail with a good following wind travels faster than horse.' She raised a chiding finger at Arthur. 'You ought to instruct your spies to use ships, my Lord, as I do.'

'Get on with it,' Arthur snarled.

Unruffled, Winifred answered, 'The Saxon, Leofric, brought word to me. He had been,' she paused, 'trading, in the North.' Pirating off the coast of Dalriada, but she was not going to admit that. 'He saw the war-host leaving Alclud. Hueil may be down as far as Caer Luel by now.'

Arthur swore, began searching among a tangle of linen for his sword and scabbard. Gwenhwyfar, fastening one shoulder of her gown, the brooch for the other between her teeth, grunted at him, nodded towards his riding cloak. 'Under there,' she said, removing the brooch, pinning the second fastening. Arthur kicked the garment aside, buckled his sword about his waist.

What a flurry of disorganisation – Winifred was enjoying this! She had never in her life ridden so far or so fast, thrashing her horse into a gallop for most of the way, determined to reach Arthur and alert him personally. Why? She did not know. Leofric had laughed at her panic, saying Arthur would find out for himself soon enough; the officer of her bodyguard had begged her to stay in her steading, to send servants with the message instead, but no, she had wanted to do this thing, take the urgent word to her Lord – because she had some vague hope that the Pendragon would reward her? Grant her what she desired for her son? Possibly, probably. She had not stopped to think, had ordered horses saddled and ridden, now here she was, sitting in Arthur's private chamber, and for once, happen the only time in her life, he was treating her with respect.

He was at the outer door, yelling for the officers of the Artoriani to be assembled immediately in the Hall. He swung back to lift his cloak from the floor, crossed to Gwenhwyfar and kissed her quickly on the cheek, saying, 'At last, Cymraes, the waiting is over.' He was like a young boy, the excitement and anticipation bubbling from him like winter-melt from the hillside. In his enthusiasm he crossed to Winifred, took her shoulders in his hands and kissed her cheek also, then he was heading for the inner door.

Glowing with self-pleasure, Winifred tipped her head to one side, asked, as he was about to disappear into the Hall, 'Have I, then, done well, my Lord?'

'Aye,' Arthur grinned at her, 'very well.' He was gone, his voice, shouting orders, ringing back through the closed door.

Winifred was left alone in the room with Gwenhwyfar, the first time they had met for, oh, the gods knew how many years! Gwenhwyfar was piling her hair into some order, pinning it as best she could. She looked at the other woman, her eyes narrow, suspecting. 'Whatever you have come for,' she warned venomously, 'you will not be getting it.'

Winifred folded her hands into her lap, smiled in the sickly, unpleasantly sweet way that Gwenhwyfar remembered so well, and said, 'Do you not think so? I think I nearly have it!'

§ XXX

'I was at the holy house of Yns Witrin three weeks past. I go there often to meet with the Sisters.'

Arthur continued with his writing, ignoring Winifred who sat, her feet stretched towards one of the braziers in his private chamber, having taken the room over as her own for this one night that she would be staying. Gwenhwyfar had moodily gathered a few personal belongings and huffed out into the Hall, professing that she would rather sleep among the hounds than with a sow. Even Arthur, who knew Winifred well, marvelled at the level of the woman's audacity.

He was sitting at his desk, hurriedly writing letters to be taken immediately by the messengers already saddling their horses. It was the advantage of his Artoriani, no weeks or months to assemble a war-hosting, no time wasted preparing war gear and supplies. They were ready, eager to march. Would leave at dawn for the North.

'A young woman was there, heavy with child she was, dark-haired. Much agitated.'

Arthur snorted. 'So what is that to me?'

Standing, Winifred walked elegantly behind the desk, stood at Arthur's shoulder, leaning slightly forward to read what he was writing, and to who. 'Winta of the Humbrenses?' she said with genuine interest. 'Will he go north to fight with you?'

Arthur did not answer, merely grunted a response.

'Oh, of course.' Winifred smiled, more of a smirk, 'did you not agree a betrothal between his daughter and your Llacheu some months back? You are allied kin now, are you not?'

A second grunt. Was there anything this damned woman did not know?

She idled her fingers up his arm, rested them on the back of his neck, bending closer, her breath warm on his cheek. 'I helped birth the child when it came. It was a male, lusty, well formed.' She moved her hand to stroke his hair at the nape of his neck. 'The mother has called him Medraut.'

Damn her to her Christian hell! Arthur slammed the wooden tablet to Winta shut, angrily sealed it. His ally would have men marching north within a day of receiving the message, they would meet at Pengwern. He selected a third tablet, began a similar urgent message for Enniaun of Gwynedd. The first, to Ambrosius, was already on its way.

'One of the Sisters,' Winifred continued in her wheedling tone, 'said the woman, the young woman, was the one they call the Lady.'

Arthur's stylus hovered over the wax, his fingers going tighter around the wood.

'I thought that strange,' Winifred added, 'seeing as the rumours announce that she is dead.' She ran her hand down his back, remembering him standing naked before her earlier. 'You must have heard those same rumours.'

He had, but he said nothing, continued writing. The gossip had passed quickly, scandal travelled faster than a diving falcon! The Lady was no longer living by her lake, they said, and then, after a heavy rainstorm, the body of a dark-haired woman had been found, water-bloated, throat cut. The Lady, they added, with a sorry shake of their heads and signing the mark of protection, was no more. Only Arthur knew the fast-running tales to be wrong, the body was Brigid, not the Lady.

Winifred was reading what he had written. She pointed to a word. 'That is spelt wrongly.'

Irritably, Arthur corrected it.

Going back to the stool, Winifred settled herself comfortably, arranging her skirts, her veil. 'I thought it strange that this woman, this young woman who might or might not have once called herself the Lady, should wear around her neck, dangling from a rope of plaited hair, a battered, old, gold ring.'

Arthur looked up sharply. Winifred smiled. Ah, her guessing was right then! She held her hands to the flames, waited a moment before adding, 'I would regret having to tell your wife that her son has yet another brother he may need to fight for the title Pendragon.'

Coming slowly to his feet Arthur hissed, 'You bitch!'

'There again,' she said, admiring the spark of a ruby ring on her left hand, 'I may decide to keep the information to myself.' She looked round, up at him as he stood over her. 'For a price.'

'Which is?'

Her laugh had never been a pleasant sound to Arthur's ears. 'Oh, husband!' She looked at him. 'You know my price.'

Arthur stood glaring at her a moment, considering all the ways he could kill her, here and now, but then he turned on his heel, stalked to his desk and selected a small piece of unused parchment. He wrote quickly, a few words only, affixed his seal and flung it across the room at her. Swarming to his feet, he took up the letter to Enniaun that he had not yet finished, and the stylus, and stormed towards the door. He flung it wide after snarling, 'Go back on your word, bitch, and I will personally hang you and your brat.' Half-way through the door he added, 'Don't bother to read it, the spelling is in order.'

Alone, Winifred held the scroll a moment between her hands at her breast. She was shaking. Had it been that easy, after all these years, that easy? Reverently, she read what Arthur had put.

I acknowledge Cerdic, the child of Winifred, as my second-born son. And then his name, simply written, *Arthur, Pendragon.*

§ XXXI

Hueil swept down through the bracken-covered hills above Caer Luel. The impoverished town, with no stomach for a fight, threw the gates wide and welcomed him inside, granting the respect due a warrior prince of Dalriada.

In return, Hueil magnanimously forgave the town its misguided support to the Pendragon, and made no mention that his Lady, Queen Morgause, had been held a prisoner there. That was the

480

Pendragon's doing, not the town's, it was Arthur and his kind who would repay the insult. Hueil wooed and won them with glowing words and a brimming smile. The Caer needed protection? From whom – the Picti? Na, they had been Morgause's people, they would not attack her friends. Dalriada? But were not Dalriada, Caer Luel and the proud people of the North all brothers? Hueil had come to free them, not fight them! And they cheered him, carried the young Lord high on their shoulders. No one contradicted that Morgause was now nothing to the Picti, no one mentioned that Hueil's true blood brothers had been forced to flee from his sword into the safety of Gwynedd. No one referred to the fact that Hueil had overthrown his own father. What did the North get from the Pendragon? Poverty and starving bellies, that's what! Arthur took their gold and their grain to feed and pay his own, and laughed at these western Northmen for their cowardice. No more, Hueil had cried, no more will we bow and scrape to a Southerner who cares not a poxed whore for us!

Hueil resumed his march south, the entire British North with him; the men who had backed Lot, who resented Arthur's arrogance and the loss of face; Rheged, the fierce men of the high hills that swept through the wild country to either side of the Wall; his own men of Dalriada. An army swollen by young, eager men bound by the common factor of the North, their North. How easily they forget! A few years before they were fighting each other – those very same men who now walked side by side had vied for the supremacy of kingship. But the warrior kind were fickle. All they needed was a balanced spear, a sharpened sword and a leader to follow. The reason mattered little, as did who it was they fought. The blood-warming lure of a battle song paid small heed to detail.

They followed the old Roman roads, marching at a steady pace through high, wooded country to Deva. The elders of a few farmsteadings tucked safe in sheltered valleys listened as they passed with little concern, the young men took up their hunting spears and warm, wolf-skin cloaks and climbed the bleak hills to the high roadway to join them. It was a chance that Hueil took, seeking a fight so close behind the winter snows, but the North was used to the snarl of bad weather, and he planned not to linger at the City of Legions. He wanted Morgause free, Arthur dead and the North as his own. He had the land and its people, now, with the months of careful planning set into motion, he would have the other two.

§ XXXII

Under forced pace, Arthur reached Pengwern, *The Alder Grove Between the Three Rivers*, within five days. He made camp on the defensive ridge above the crags, overlooking the marsh and its clusters of winter-shabby alder trees. One thing his damned first wife had not known, had not told him, was that Amlawdd was coming behind, along the march of the Hafren. Ahead, Hueil was settled on the high, sandy ground that lay behind the two great estuaries to either side of Deva. The Artoriani were caught between the two. The Pendragon could not turn to face Hueil knowing that whoreson from the south was at his back; but Hueil had the more men, could do a damn lot of damage were he to set them hunting off the leash. And where was Hueil headed – south to meet with Arthur, Deva to rescue Morgause or into Gwynedd? His father and brothers were there – a cowardly lot of god-mumbling nanny-goats admitted, but it was possible Hueil still counted them a threat. Help for the Artoriani was coming. Winta was on his way to the meeting place, but where was Gwynedd?

Gwenhwyfar had been watching Arthur as he listened, grim-lipped, brows frowning, as his scouts made their report about Amlawdd, their sweat-grimed faces reflecting the sparks and flare of the mounded fire. The glow shed enough light into the darkness of this moonless night to see men's faces clearly, read their expressions, their slipped thoughts. She needed no light to recognise her husband's biting anger, felt it with him.

Arthur had made no objection when she had calmly announced that she was riding with him to this war. The marching would be hard, the fighting too, but Gwenhwyfar had never been a cosseted woman, she had marched with him before and would, no doubt, do so again in the future. The short time the Artoriani needed to prepare was enough for her also to make ready. Now that they had a Caer of their own she could accompany Arthur, now that Llacheu was older, now that she had no small children. For Gwenhwyfar it was as if she had never borne that last child. There was nothing, except an ache in the back of her mind to remind her of another dead-born son. Arthur had not told her the truth, and she had no cause to think differently. And a war-trail allowed little time for thinking, which is why she had come, why Arthur had agreed.

'I'll ride into Gwynedd, see what delays my brothers coming.' She smiled, quite calm, as the men seated around Arthur's fire turned to look at her. One or two protested, others murmured agreement. 'I can stir the fire in their winter-fat bellies.' It was something practical she could do, that would leave the men free for the fighting that would soon come. Gwynedd should already have been with Arthur, should have been waiting. His messengers used only the best horses. Gwynedd should already have sewn these Hafren marches so tight that Amlawdd would be caught in the rear with nowhere to go, save home. But no one had seen sign nor word of Gwynedd.

As she got to her feet, Arthur caught at her hand, holding her, half risen, her face level with his. 'Leave Llacheu with me?' He asked it as a question, unsure whether he was making the right choice, but she smiled, nodded. 'I ride fast, husband, and take only a small escort. For all the dangers, he will be safer with you.' She was about to turn away from the heat and light of the fire, but he caught her tighter, twisting himself around to add, 'Take Ider and . . .' He glanced at his officers seated circular around the fire, good men, all of them trustworthy and capable in a fight. Geraint, old Mabon wearing his beloved wolf-skin and who had served under Uthr, Gwenwynwyn, Peredur; others who had affectionate names, men such as 'Iron-Fist' and 'Boar's Beard'. Arthur's eye fell on Meriaun, Gwenhwyfar's cousin. They had once quarrelled, Meriaun and his uncle, Enniaun of Gwynedd, and the anger between them had never healed. Arthur had to make a decision, the right decision, who to send with Gwenhwyfar across the marshes of these three rivers and up into Gwynedd, because word, brought quietly in the night to Arthur's ears, was that Gwynedd was too tied with her own problems to enter this war. He might need Meriaun if he had to meet Amlawdd or Hueil within the next few days, but then, so might his Cymraes. 'Go with her, Meriaun, you also know the ways through the mountains.'

Meriaun had anticipated the order, was straight to his feet, saluting and turning on his heel to go select men and horses, Gwenhwyfar leaving with him to say farewell to Llacheu, to fetch her warmest cloak.

Arthur waited by the makeshift gateway, a sturdy tree, cut and hefted across the gap in the crumbling old earthworks that had once served as his stronghold's defences. He stepped out from the shadows as they rode up, his wife, Meriaun and the guard of thirty well-armed, best-trained men, put his hand to her horse's neck as she halted, the animal side-stepping, tossing its head at the exciting prospect of a night ride.

'Take care,' he said simply to her. 'Take care.'

Gwenhwyfar leaned down from her horse and kissed him, once, lightly, as so many times he had kissed her before riding out. 'I have Meriaun and Ider to protect me, and I go into the mountains where I was born.' She touched his face, stubbled with the growth of an unshaven beard. 'You also take care.' And she was gone, heeling her horse into a trot as the men hauled the trunk from across the gap, gone where the black space of night hovered beyond the slope that dropped down with alarming steepness into the dark, bog-bound levels of marsh and deep-shadowed alder. Arthur saw only the swish of her horse's tail and her hand, raised in parting.

At dawn, Hueil left his secure ridge, and swung down towards Deva, and Morgause. And Amlawdd, with his following of baggage carts and army whores, broke their night camp and marched for Viroconium.

§ XXXIII

Gwenhwyfar and the men rode as far as practical in the darkness, making slow passage through the marshes and across the river. They stopped to rest and graze the horses and to snatch a brief few hours sleep before entering the heavily wooded valley that would take them up into Gwynedd.

The winter snows had come and turned to rain, although the heights of Moel Siabod and Yr Wyddfa were still decked in white blankets. Gwenhwyfar had known winters when even the tough hill sheep had perished beneath snows that lay impenetrable for weeks. This had been a wet, cold winter, though there was even now time for the snows to come again. It was the first week into March, but there were not many early flowers or green buds on the trees. Spring would be late this year.

They were watched as they entered the valley. There was nothing seen or heard, only a feeling of eyes on their backs and the tell-tale sign of their horses' ears twitching back and forth, listening. And then, as the sun rose, eight mounted men appeared from out of the dawn mist, Gwynedd men, weapons drawn but not raised, politely offering escort.

They were taken along the valley to Enniaun, who waited for them beneath the ancient stronghold called the Place of Ravens, a hill fort of old magic, rich in stories, wraithed in superstition. Gwenhwyfar's father, the great Lion Lord Cunedda, had been laid to rest up there. Enniaun's horses were still saddled, traces of wet mud and sweat clinging to their coats. His boots, too, were muddy and he looked tired, drawn and dishevelled. The mist had settled lower, drifting down the mountains, the grey breath masking the quiet hills and wooded slopes, making them quieter still. Gwenhwyfar's sense of distinct unease sprang into full alarm. She jumped from her mare, ran to her eldest brother crying, 'What is wrong?'

Enniaun retained his tired smile of greeting, hugged his sister to him, indicated the fire his men had set. Hares were roasting, and a brace of duck. 'Sit near the fire, sister, food will be ready soon.' He

485

took her elbow, guided her towards the warmth while calling for drink to be brought. Rebellious, Gwenhwyfar shook him off, stamped her foot. A childish action, but one that seemed fitting. 'I don't want warmth or food or drink. I want to know why you are not riding to aid my husband, and what is happening here in Gwynedd!'

Enniaun persisted, tried again to seat her before the fire; his sister's sudden-flared tempers had not dampened with the years, then! With a sigh and gesture of submission, he seated himself, accepted wine. 'It is some while since I last had chance to fill my belly, I intend to eat, even if you do not.' He began on a portion of hare, added with exasperation, 'For God's sake sit down, woman – aye and you, nephew.' Enniaun nodded at Meriaun, who stood near the horses wearing a frosted frown. 'Let me eat, then we can talk.'

Meriaun, not as easily riled as Gwenhwyfar, sat cross-legged to the opposite side of the fire, regarding his uncle through critical eyes. He had noticed some of the things Gwenhwyfar had not. The men were dropping with fatigue, several with bandages covering wounds. The horses went ungroomed, also wounded, some of them. He helped himself to meat, offered some to Gwenhwyfar, who reluctantly flounced to the grass beside him.

Enniaun took only one mouthful, then launched into explanation. 'We cannot help Arthur. Powys is grumbling along our borders again and the sea-wolves are also at our throats. Môn, it seems is no longer enough for them. Ships are lying off our coast as far down as Ceredigion.' Enniaun paused as riders approached, coming at a hard canter, their horses slithering to a halt. Two men leapt from the saddles, strode with quick, long paces towards the fire, wasted no time with formality or greeting. Enniaun finished what he had been saying. 'There have been a few skirmishes, nothing serious, but . . .'

Abloyc, their brother, stripping his gloves from his hands, completed the sentence. 'But if we pull our men out to aid the Pendragon, Powys and the sea-wolves will be like bees swarming to spilt honey.' Briefly, he and the other man, Dogmail, embraced their sister before flopping down before the fire, expressions as grim as Enniaun's.

486

Caught between Gwynedd's need and that of her husband, Gwenhwyfar pleaded, 'Help us now, and when Hueil is finished Arthur will bring the Artoriani to flush every sea-pirate from Gwynedd and Ceredigion. Powys will not dare go against the Pendragon! Arthur will help you, as soon as he can!'

Enniaun was shaking his head, sadly, slowly. Dogmail shifted himself to a more comfortable position, and Abloyc's fingers were fiddling with his dagger. None was willing to answer the truth. Someone had to, had to spit it out. Surprisingly, the someone was Meriaun, who thought of himself no longer of Gwynedd but of the Artoriani.

'Arthur may not be able to help, Gwen. Gwynedd does not have the knowing of how long this bad blood with Hueil may last.' Reluctantly he returned Gwenhwyfar's direct challenging gaze. 'Nor can Gwynedd rely on Arthur having the victory of this thing.'

She was on her feet, defensive anger and frustration spilling over the boil. 'Were Gwynedd to help, victory would be a certainty! We have only the Artoriani and a handful of Winta's men. The militias this side of the Wall have refused to march out lest Hueil attacks their settlements. We are but a few against the many!'

The men made no answer, they sat cross-legged around the fire, expressions embarrassed, knowing she had the right of it, but the right was on the wrong side of a damned impossible situation. Dogmail, sitting, studying his hands, not raising the courage to look at her, spoke: 'When Gwynedd went north with you before, it was to settle our hearts against a land which was our father's and his father's before him. Also, Gwynedd was not in the danger that she is in now.'

Gwenhwyfar ignored him, swung on her heel, the metal of her scabbard clanking as she spun. She was wasting her time here; Arthur needed every sword, and she had thirty of them here in Gwynedd.

Enniaun climbed wearily to his feet, but made no attempt to follow her. 'The sea-wolves were not roving in so full a pack then, and Lot fought with only a half-sharpened blade, he had no real stomach for a fight. Hueil has higher ambition and has been trained to fight by the best war-lord this land has ever known.' He raised his eyebrow as Gwenhwyfar halted, half turned, reluctant, to face him, dipped his head in a slight nod. 'Hueil was of the Artoriani, sister, he fights like Arthur, with his head.' Slowly Enniaun raised his arms, let them drop in a gesture of expressed frustration. 'Why do you think the raiders have set sail, at this time of year, in such numbers? Who do you think has lured them from their crumbling settlements to a promised land of gold?' His eyebrows creased lower. 'Why has Powys suddenly developed a greed to extend her borders? Hueil buys his diversionary tacts, my sister. He can afford to pay a high price to those who wish, for whatever reason, to help him.'

It was true, Gwenhwyfar knew, all true.

Enniaun swept his hand towards where some trees had been felled, to where the beginnings of a building had started. 'I had you brought here to this place for a second reason sister, beyond our meeting. I thought you would like to see, I build a holy place here,' he snorted, 'least, I had intended to. When the fighting eases, I will try again.' He leant across, took her hand in his. 'I build for our father's memory this church, and I will give this valley to the men and women of God who will come here. It will be a valley of God, of the Cross of Christ, and of peace.' He squeezed her hand, said with a choke to his voice. 'I want you to accept what I must do, sister. Arthur will.' He was no longer talking of his church of the Valle Crucis.

Meriaun was rising to his feet, brushing damp from his tunic. He held his hand out to his dead father's brother. 'We have our quarrels, my uncle, and even in this, though I see your reason, I am not certain I would follow the track you take, but,' and he shrugged, 'you are mounted and have set off on the ride. I trust God to be with you.'

Enniaun took the proffered hand, accepted what was intended as an offering of peace between them. 'Good hunting, my nephew, cast your spear well.'

Meriaun nodded, smiled, followed after Gwenhwyfar who was already calling for the men and horses.

The valley with its green hills and calm river returned to its peaceful sleeping as the riders departed their separate ways. The spirit of Cunedda, had it been watching from its sentinal post on the top of Dinas Bran, could have looked westward into the high mountains of Gwynedd, to Moel Siabod and Yr Wyddfa, or east, across the lesser hills, towards Deva. Happen, given the death that was about to strike that proud town, it was best that the old Lord rested, instead, in the sanctuary of the Other World.

§ XXXIV

Peace. The chance to sit idle by a river and cast a line for fish, to see your children grow and raise children of their own. Peace? Huh, a foolish dream that had no place in the world of men. The sickly smell of greed, Arthur thought, had a lot to answer for. He ran his hand along the arch of his stallion's neck. Onager's ears were back, as always.

When Lot had tried for the North – by the Bull, it seemed a long time ago – none had challenged the necessity of the Artoriani to fight. It was expected, begged for, and Arthur had responded. But even in these few passing years, the North had changed, aye because of that brief, flurried war, which had left it poorer than before and aside from its own kind, friendless. This time, the rich lands of the south were speaking against the need to fight in the North. Let Hueil have it, the loudest mouths said. Of what use is it to us? Caer Luel is a grinding quern dangling at our necks, Eboracum an abandoned town, left to the ravens and the poor, who care little where they dwell, and the Saex. There is nothing in the North save the smell of poverty and inhospitable, mist-shrouded hills, they said. Let Hueil have it!

Arthur's messengers, bearing their scrolls of parchment and wax tablets, had returned swiftly, bringing, time and time again, negative answers, a refusal to fight. There would be no Cymry this time, only Artoriani.

Arthur called ahead to the officer. 'Order the men to dismount. We will walk, rest the horses.' They were marching for Deva, had been riding through sparse woodland, a variety of trees and open clearings, the ground free of undergrowth. This was wet ground, low-lying, mostly marsh, scattered with treacherous bogs that sucked man and beast into hidden pits. Difficult for fast riding, perilous for fighting; Arthur wanted to be away from it. Let Amlawdd follow. He would have as hard a time of getting through this stuff as the Artoriani. And Arthur was enough ahead to choose the ground if he had to turn and make a fight of it. Deva was a handful of miles off, but horses, no matter how well fed, could not be pushed beyond endurance if they were to be needed for another day.

Only Ambrosius had sent an encouraging answer. '*Leave the groaning South to me, Pendragon,*' he had written. '*A belly-full of wind needs a strong, unpleasant-tasting purge. I wish you all the speed and success of the apothecary's vile potions, nephew!*' Dismounting, the men took their horses' reins and began walking, Arthur among them, grinning slightly as he thought on his uncle's brief communication. He had not decided whether Ambrosius had been referring to Hueil or the Southerners – but then, bellyache affected the rich as commonly as the poor. The difference was in who treated it. The fat physician with an air of self-importance or the old, toothless healing woman who lived in the tumbledown shack on the edge of the settlement? Both, Arthur thought wryly, probably prescribed the same medicines, one would be in a fancy glass phial, the other as it came, a root or leaves of a plant, wrapped in a piece of old rag to be infused over your own hearth-fire.

Ambrosius had changed his cloak for the better, and Arthur was glad, though whether there was a reasoning behind it, he was still undecided. His uncle intended to take command if anything happened to the Pendragon, that was a certainty. To do it, Ambrosius would need the backing of the men, Arthur's men, the Artoriani – Ambrosiani? Did it have the same ring? By seeking friendship with Arthur, was Ambrosius looking to his own interest? Aye well, it was something worth considering, when the time for idling by that river allowed a chance for thinking of other things besides fighting.

Arthur did not want to enter Deva; it was safer, but restricted.

That camp up on the heights of Pengwern was the last time he could chance being within a confined space. He needed freedom of movement to fight as his mounted men were trained to fight. Hueil would surely fight before turning attention to Morgause? But then, he did not have the cavalry that Arthur had. His men were the sons of farmsteaders, warrior men, the militia of Caer Luel – infantry. Infantry were no match for the Artoriani, unless they were led well, by someone who understood horses. And Hueil, once an officer of the Artoriani, did.

Casually, Arthur laid his arm over his stallion's neck, leaning his weight on the horse's shoulder. Onager's ears flattened further back, but he did not move away or kick. Arthur smiled to himself, the old bugger liked it really, this fuss and attention, only he was too mean-minded to show it. Unexpectedly, his thoughts wandered to the memory of Morgaine. Almost, almost, he could have loved her, in another life, another place. The subtle smells of her dwelling place, woodsmoke, drying herbs, clung in his nostrils, evoking her fresh, childish innocence. She was Morgause's daughter, but nothing like the mother. The one harsh and corrupt, the other timid, wanting only to please. Ah, but then, that was it, was it not? How much had the daughter wanted to please the mother? Of how much had Morgaine informed Morgause? Some? None? All of it? She had insisted, as Arthur had taken her pregnancy-swollen body and held her close, that she had sent no word concerning him to her mother. Arthur had almost believed her, almost. But even if she had not, what had Brigid been passing along the wind? He had made a mistake there, trusting that lying, two-tongued whore. At least she would lie no more, and she had not known of the child.

Checking Onager's over-enthusiastic stride, Arthur forced his mind back to the matter of Hueil. Ambition was as dangerous as greed. What was his intention? Arthur knew what he would do in Hueil's position. When he had had the choice of the woman he loved or pursuing the chance to become king, he had chosen a kingdom, reasoning the first would come when he had the second. As it had, but then, Gwenhwyfar, for all her strengths and ability, was no Morgause. With that woman at his side Hueil could obtain much. Too much. But he had to take it first, if he could. Which is why, latterly, Arthur had kept the bitch alive, why he had moved her to Deva, a more defendable fortress, and not as faint-hearted as Caer Luel. He had kept her as bait, because he knew Hueil's first move would be to secure her freedom.

Except that Arthur had not planned on Amlawdd coming up, unchecked by Gwynedd, behind him, nor Hueil moving at this time of year. Damn him, which was why the bastard was doing it! Arthur removed his helmet, wiped sweat from his forehead, closed his eyes. Hueil was ex-Artoriani, he would not blindly fall into a lure, even if the lure was the witch-woman herself. Arthur ran his fingers through damp hair, his head ached. Morgause would not sit silent and wait on hope. Messages had passed between them, gone north and south. How, damn it, how? Arthur halted, issued the order to remount. Another thought nagged persistently at the back of his mind. Had Morgaine been the pivot of all those secret sent words, or Brigid? And who else? Who else.

They saw the smoke, thick, black clouds of it rising into the low, grey winter cloud. Hueil? Arthur sent the command for his out-riders to advance, watched them gallop ahead, held the Artoriani back in closed order. The excitement of anticipation was rippling through the men and horses, the prospect of an imminent fight adding that edge to an already sharpened blade. He drew Onager to one side, letting the marching column ride past, waiting for the baggage mules to come alongside, intending to speak briefly with Llacheu riding there with Gweir and other boys of a similar age, officers' grooms most of them or, like Gweir, servants. The boys were armed, well enough to defend the baggage were an attack to come, but were nominally non-fighting youngsters who stayed well behind the lines when it came to battle. It had been a hard decision whether to bring Llacheu or leave him at Caer Cadan. But one day he would be a King and kings had to learn about war, not stay safe-tucked at home.

For one quarter of a mile Arthur rode beside his son, mounted on a fine bay horse – Llacheu rode well enough now to handle a larger, stronger animal, though it was a gelding. *A stallion is a man's ride, boy.* The lad was excited, full of questions and anticipation.

'We will be fighting, Da?'

'We?' Arthur raised an eyebrow in his son's direction. '*We* will, aye. *You* will not.'

Llacheu's face became so crestfallen that Arthur laughed. He reached across to tousle the boy's hair. 'I need you here with the other lads. We lose our baggage and we'll have no tents to sleep in, no spare war gear and no cooking pots.' Arthur nodded at the other boys, all of them sporting grins as wide as half-moons, they were important, for they fetched and carried, tended the fires and the needs of the men, and aye, the wounded.

Riders were coming fast down the line, heeling their horses into a gallop. Absently, Arthur completed what he was saying to Llacheu. 'I for one, will be wanting a comfortable bed and supper in my belly this night, so mind you do a good job.' He kicked Onager forward to meet the men: a group of senior officers, a scout and a soldier he did not know.

Sweat-streaked, breathless, the stranger urged his horse ahead of the others, hauled it to a halt as he came up to the Pendragon. Barely pausing to salute he gasped his report. 'Deva Auxiliary-man, Lucious Marcus Antonious, my Lord!' Wasted no more on formalities. 'Deva has fallen to the Dalriads.'

Arthur sat stunned, his fingers clenched around Onager's reins, the horse tossing his head and fidgeting with the bit pulling tight at his mouth. The column moved past, the men silent as they rode, the joviality of a few moments before turned to sudden, grim shock as word spread rapidly from mouth to mouth.

The Decurions brought their horses to a standstill, their faces questioning, disbelieving. One asked, 'How can this be?' Another, 'Has Hueil so great an army he can attack a fortress and gain entry within such a short passage of time?'

Lucious Marcus Antonious answered, 'It takes but a few men to take the strongest defence when someone opens the gates for them.'

A short, heart-beat moment of silence as his words were digested, then Arthur cursed, his choice of words colourful, even by his standards. *Who else helps Morgause?*

493

They rode the last few miles to Deva as though the hounds of death were baying at their heels.

§ XXXV

The sun spread a bright glow against a pale, frosted blue sky as the Artoriani approached the slight drop down to the bridge spanning the river. The tide was recently out, and the mudflats along either bank glistened under the residue of salt water. Trading ships, moved alongside the riverside warehouses, were burning fiercely, beyond salvation. Pockets of fires raged within the settlement that straggled between the fortress walls and the sluggish river. Arthur held his stallion to a tight walk as he rode, his escort following onto the bridge. Searing smoke drifting on the wind, the nauseating smell of burning caught in their throats and nostrils. Onager faltered. Trained to avoid stepping on a fallen body, his ears flicked, uncertain, awaiting command from his rider's leg, for the bridge was littered with dead and dying, the people of Deva, cut down as they ran. Ears flat, nostrils flaring, the stallion edged forward, balked again at the approach road leading up to the gateway. So many dead! Civilians; women clutching their children, tradesmen, old men, young boys. Men of Deva and Arthur's own garrisoned Artoriani. A soldier, dressed in the blue uniform of Deva's guard, staggered from the watch-house doorway, his bloodied fingers reaching for Onager's reins as he stumbled. The stallion, already wildly unnerved, attempted to side-step, but Arthur rammed his boot against the horse's flank, held him steady.

The Pendragon's eyes met with those sunken hollows of horror that were the soldier's; he tried to speak but the blood of death spilt from his mouth instead of words. Arthur leapt from the saddle, knelt beside him, cradling the dying man, uncaring who saw the grief on his face. To die in such a way; this should not have been! The fortress gateway leered open like the gaping jaws of some monstrous, bloodied beast.

Arthur laid the dead man down, stood slowly and turned his back on Deva, stared towards the distant, cloud-misted mountains of Gwynedd – where he had sent Gwenhwyfar. He closed his eyes, tightly shutting out the scenes of so much bloodshed. Where he had sent Gwenhwyfar! The Pendragon groaned, brought his hand over the beard-stubble of his mouth and chin, a discreet cough at his shoulder jolting him back from those mountains, where the gods alone knew what was happening.

The Decurion, his voice sober, constricted. 'Do we ride in, my Lord?'

'Aye, you and the escort.' He mounted Onager. It did not seem right for the day to be so bright and dazzling, not when so many innocents had done so much dying.

Were there enough hours of daylight left to head north after Hueil? Or should he plunge west to head off Amlawdd's scum? Did Gwenhwyfar need help? Arthur fought the worry aside. She was safe in Gwynedd, Hueil had gone the other way and Amlawdd was still a day to the south. He told himself again she was safe. So why this pricking along his spine, this constant need to look again at those mist-floating mountains?

Riding through the gateway, Arthur noted with a gloat of satisfaction that the scatter of corpses here were not all Deva's dead. The guard had fought well, killing as many of the Northerners as they could before the numbers became overwhelming. The gates had been opened: the scatter of the dead, the position of the main area of fighting, pointed to the obvious. It needed only one person to lift the two bars, pull back the iron bolts; one devious person who could have got past the suspicion of the guards. . . . Arthur snapped his head around, hauling Onager to one side and was out of the saddle, dropping to one knee beside a tumbled pile of Deva's slain. A woman lay with them, her throat cut. Women were lying along the streets, across the bridge, in the gateway, the Northmen slaying as they entered, caring only for the killing – but a woman lying beneath the bodies of the guard? And this woman? Here? Arthur covered her familiar face with a fold of her cloak, and remounted. Questions, the whys and the hows, ran through his mind. An answer was forming, grim, repulsive. Whoever had opened that gate had to be someone the Watch-guard would never have suspected of treachery.

At the head of his small escort, Arthur rode along the Via Praetoria making for the headquarters building, ignoring as best he could the bodies and the mess. This should have been a busy place, the main street. Should have been alive with the hectic bustle of a town's daily business.

The living were beginning to crawl from their places of concealed safety. A woman moaned over the body of her man. A shopkeeper stood staring, blank-eyed at the smoking ruin of what had been his trade. A boy, no older than ten summers, lay hunched beside the walls of a tavern, his arms locked around the limp body of a black dog. Arthur kept his eyes and concentration directed up the straight-running street, at the building ahead, choked back a half-sob at the thought that kicked him like an ox-hoof. He hoped the boy and the dog had died quickly, one sword slash, one stab of spear or dagger. He could have looked, the wounds would have told, but he did not want to see, wanted to believe they had died well.

There was an eerie half-silence hanging over the smoking roof-timbers of the old Principia building, the headquarters complex, and behind it, where once the Legion Commander would have lived in splendid grandeur, the Praetorium. An odd stillness here. The crackle of dying flames, scorched and blackened timbers settling or falling. In the distance, a dog howling, the women wailing their songs of death. Overhead, the harsh 'craa . . . aak' of a raven. Arthur shuddered. The Morrigan, the Goddess of war come in her disguise to collect the dead. It was like riding into the Underworld. He peered briefly over his shoulder to reassure himself that his men were there, behind. Their faces were grey, as his must be, their hands making the sign of protection, pagan and Christian.

They rode on through, into a courtyard that would once have boasted a fountain, green plants, been neat and ordered, but was now a place of the wounded. Even here there was only minimal noise: a man groaning, another coughing, the shuffle of feet; bloodied, dazed men. A few turned to watch the Artoriani ride in, their gaze uninterested, barely comprehending, as Arthur halted and swung down from the saddle. Bedwyr would have been here, somewhere here. Arthur forced himself to walk with controlled dignity, his hand casual on his sword pommel, between the mess of wounded men, up the steps and into the house-place, telling himself again and again not to run, not to take to his heels and scream Bedwyr's name.

Blood seemed to be everywhere, spattered across the walls, puddling on the cracked mosaic tiles, smeared on doorways. The blood of Arthur's loyal, brave men, slaughtered as they attempted to bar entrance to whoever had done this awful killing. That this house-place had been the ultimate target was beyond doubt. Arthur had no need to question as to where Morgause had been held, he only had to follow the trail of destruction, leading as pointed as any arrow along the corridor, up the stairs. He did run, then, for this upper corridor was narrow, leading to one room, where the door leaned wide open and a body lay sprawled across a bed covered with blood-slimed linen sheets. Arthur ran because that stained, tousled hair belonged to only one man, he ran and cradled the body to him, yelled with fear and alarm as the body moved, groaned, sat up. Arthur's heart was pounding, his throat had rasped dry, his breath coming in great gasps. He put his hand to his chest. 'Mithras, Bedwyr, you scared the shit out of me!'

Easing his legs over the side of the bed, Bedwyr sat cradling the side of his head. There seemed to be a lot of blood oozing through his fingers and soaking his clothing. Arthur explored the lad's arms, legs, his torso, frowned, puzzled. 'Damn it Bedwyr, you've a gash as wide as the Hafren on your head, but surely, in the gods' names, this blood is not all yours?'

Managing a feeble grin, Bedwyr patted the Pendragon's exploring hands aside. 'It's not mine. Hueil made one mistake, he did not realise I know how to use a sword. Some of this is his.'

For a hopeful moment, Arthur thought perhaps Hueil lay dead, but Bedwyr shook his head, groaned as the dizziness returned. 'Na, he is stronger than I am. I gave a good fight, but,' he touched his head, 'that bitch hit me with something. I went down like a snuffed light.' It was his turn to express a question, Arthur's to shake his head.

'Na, he's not among the dead. You might have wounded him, but Hueil's aim was to get in by treachery and out again as soon as he had Morgause. They didn't even stop to loot or rape.' He would get the men to search as they buried the dead and tended the wounded, but they would not find Hueil. Not here, anyway.

Apart from the spillage of blood near the door, and Bedwyr's on the bed sheets, the room was ordered, left as though its resident intended to be gone only a moment. On a table, phials, combs, a gold-backed bronze mirror, beside the bed, a half-drunk goblet of wine. Arthur finished it in one gulp, and searched quickly, opening chests and cupboards. Under-garments, folded, freshened with a scatter of dried lavender, clothing; the paraphernalia of a woman's face-paint. No winter fur cloak. No heavy wool garments. No boots, only soft, leather house shoes. She had known then, been prepared.

'You entrusted her care to me, Arthur. I have failed you.'

The flagon of wine beside the goblet was almost full, Arthur poured himself another drink, drained the goblet, refilled it and passed it to Bedwyr.

There was not much Arthur could answer with. It was not Bedwyr's fault, this damned mess. If anyone should take blame, it must be himself, for keeping the bitch alive when he should have slit her throat. As Gwenhwyfar had argued. He lightly shrugged one shoulder, offered more wine. 'You are a man, Bedwyr, not a god. Only He, so I am told, is infallible.'

Bedwyr accepted the second drink. 'There was no warning.' He had to talk, suddenly, let the bad taste spew from his mouth. 'They were just,' he spread his shaking hands, 'there. At dawn. They came from nowhere, appeared beyond the walls, and then . . .' He cradled his head again, the gash was not deep, despite all the blood, but his head pounded as if a thousand hooves were galloping there. He took a breath, 'Then they were just in, like that.' He glanced up at Arthur. 'Someone let them in?'

Arthur had seated himself in a chair. He nodded, suddenly too weary to answer.

His eyes narrowing, similar to his cousin's familiar expression, Bedwyr regarded Arthur across the room. 'You know who opened it don't you? Who it was passing the letters and messages in and out beneath my nose.'

Again Arthur nodded, still did not answer.

Bedwyr sighed, pushed himself from the bed, rocked a moment as the blinding headache swirled across his forehead. He bent for his sword, lying bloodied on the floor, had to put out a hand to steady himself. Straightening, he looked again, directly at Arthur. 'I had my suspicions of the apothecary. I stripped him naked, but unless he'd shoved a parchment somewhere I'd rather not look, he had nothing on him.' Their eyes met, Arthur's sad, Bedwyr's resigned. 'I began to fear it was her, but turned my back to it, hoping I was wrong.'

'If it is any comfort,' Arthur offered, standing and heading for the door, 'we all should have realised. Nessa came originally from Daliada, from the North.'

§ XXXVI

Amlawdd had set out from his west-country fortress full of enthusiasm and expectation, meeting with several petty lords and chieftains who were against Arthur. What a sight they were! Close on two hundred warriors – with the shield-bearers, women and followers of a hosting, double that number! They progressed north slowly, hugging the course of the river, laughing and chattering, foraging and hunting as they marched; camped early, for although the nights were drawing out, who wanted to march in the dark? The baggage wagons were laden with skins and amphorae of barley-brew, strong ale to keep the cold away at night and the men cheerful. Oh the carousing! The jocularity, the high spirits! A fine thing to be one with a war-hosting! They did not hurry, took time to break camp of a morning, taking longer as each night passed, for the heads of the men were becoming thicker from a night's drinking, their keenness, by the seventh morning, almost evaporated, dwindled even more when word came that the Artoriani were ahead of them.

That was not to have been; Amlawdd was supposed to meet up with Hueil near Deva where they would wait for Arthur and have a decisive end to the arrogant bastard. But Amlawdd had not bargained on the time it took to manhandle the wagons through mud and marsh, or how quickly enthusiasm ebbed once sore feet, aching shoulders and drunkenness set in. He had miscalculated how fast Arthur could move with his mounted men, who used mules for pack animals, not carts and wagons. The men were grumbling and Amlawdd himself was becoming sick of the whole thing.

A toad-faced messenger from Hueil added insult. Were it not that they had come so far, Amlawdd would have hacked the insolent braggart's head from his shoulders and gone home. Who in the gods' names did Hueil think he was? Issuing orders, sending curt, insulting commands: do this, do that. Were it not for the promise of gold and that other prize . . . There were still a few hours of daylight left, they could march for a few more miles, but this place they had come to was a good spot, Deva was ten and five miles away, they would be there on the morrow. Let Hueil wait!

The messenger Amlawdd sent off tied, riding facing his pony's tail and stripped of his clothing. It cheered the men slightly to see their Lord deal so with the upstart. 'Tell Hueil of the North that I will come when I am ready and not before!' Amlawdd shouted at the unfortunate man, as they whipped his mount into a gallop, sent it northward, leaving behind a gust of laughter. Arthur could not risk fighting Hueil knowing a hosting was behind him, of that, Amlawdd was certain. They had until tomorrow; the men needed one more night, one night of celebration and laughter before the business of battle came to hand.

The day had been bright, crisp, a day that heralded the coming of spring. Amlawdd stood at the edge of the made camp, looking across at the mountains a few miles to the west. Gwynedd, swathed in patterns of mist. Gwynedd from where the woman he wanted as his own had come. When this was over, Hueil had promised she could be his. They only needed to be rid of the Pendragon.

Clouds were striding up from the south as the afternoon descended to evening. Was that movement among those trees? This

500

was lonely, inhospitable country, either pocked with marsh and bog or clustered with striding, dense woodland. They ought to have marched the quicker, not ambled at a leisurely pace, spent so long encamped. Arthur and Hueil were professionals, soldiering born into their blood. Amlawdd was the youngest son of a man who had preferred his own hearth to that of a hosting camp fire, for all that his elder two brothers had enjoyed the rigours of warfare. Melwas had even run with the Saex kind! Ah, but where had it got them, and Gorlois? Both were dead, Gorlois slain by Arthur Pendragon and Melwas? Amlawdd knew not how he had died, or where, except rumour tattled that this Pendragon had been involved.

God's mercy! What in all hell . . . ! Amlawdd was running, drawing his sword and running, shouting, using the flat of his blade to get men moving off their backsides, screaming for someone to sound the alarm!

Gwenhwyfar had taken only thirty men with her into Gwynedd. She was hurting and anxious as she rode back to join her husband, knowing there would be no men coming to his aid from the mountains. There should not be delight in killing, but as she thundered from the shadowed concealment of the trees, with the war-cry of the Artoriani bursting from her open mouth, a satisfying sense of justice flooded her. Happen Gwynedd could not help Arthur, but neither would Amlawdd be helping Hueil.

Two hundred men, most already drunk, were unaware of what had hit them. Taken by surprise, without arms or armour to hand, badly led, poorly organised, they had no chance even against only thirty horsemen of the Artoriani.

There was not much killing, Hueil's allies surrendering before the Artoriani had chance to draw breath for a second change, throwing their spears and axes to the ground, holding their hands high, fear and horror paling their faces, disbelief hammering their minds. Amlawdd had placed himself before the hosting's standards, he and a few of his loyal men. Dry-mouthed, horrified, he offered up his sword to the woman mounted on a red-coated stallion, her own sword tip hovering too close to his male equipment for comfort. Was this the woman he had wanted for his own? The woman who had

501

seemed so perfect, so desirable? Gods, he would never be able to sleep at night for fear of what she might do with that blade! He swallowed hard, tried an affable smile, which she ignored.

Meriaun was supervising rounding up the men and women, herding them into the centre of the camp, the Artoriani helping themselves to weapons, armour, anything that looked worth the taking, including the women.

For a long moment, Gwenhwyfar sat on her horse, staring at Amlawdd, considering what to do with him. The attack, the whole event had been instinct, reaction. Arthur would probably yell at her, say she had behaved foolishly, taken an unacceptable risk, but the chance had been too great to miss! As always in hostile territory – and peaceful too after that attack near Lindinis – Artoriani scouts had ridden ahead, had reported the camp, the slovenly lack of care, no out-guards, few men on watch. It was like landing a pike with a bent brooch pin!

She had two choices now, run the bastard through or send him home, humiliated, mutilated. Na, three! A slow smile spreading across her cheeks, Gwenhwyfar brought the sword across her lap. 'I can kill you, Amlawdd, which I would like to do, or cut off your hands and take out your eyes, which I am capable of doing. A waste though, both of these, when my husband, your Lord Pendragon, needs men to fight behind his dragon banner.' Her smile increased and she put away her sword, swung her legs from the saddle and dismounted.

Gwenhwyfar walked up close to Amlawdd, savouring his stench of fear that stood proud with the sweat and darting eyes. 'We could form an alliance Amlawdd, you and I, for Arthur.' She circled him, noting how his anxious eyes swivelled to follow her.

He swallowed, hard. 'Alliance?'

'Aye, your men and your spears fighting for the Pendragon, not against him.'

Now that the possibility of a painful death seemed to be receding, Amlawdd's bravado began to return. 'Hueil paid me, promised me much for my services.'

The smile quirked around Gwenhwyfar's mouth. Services? She

had to stretch up slightly to whisper in his ear. 'Ineptitude, Amlawdd, is a more fitting word.' She stood again before him, looking him up and down, assessing him, then took a long, dramatic step backwards, flourished her arm in a southerly direction.

'You can go, Amlawdd. Take this pathetic rabble of imbeciles with you. The people of Britain will hear of how I, Gwenhywyfar, wife to the Pendragon, with thirty of my men, thought your blood unworthy of my sword.' Her green eyes, swirling with a sparkle of tawny-golden flecks, met his. 'Or . . . we can come to agreement, Amlawdd.'

And when she told of her terms, Amlawdd's fear evaporated, his disbelief altering to that of amazed wonder. So Hueil was offering the Pendragon's wife when victory was claimed? God's wondrous truth, if he had known Gwenhwyfar's terms before this, he would have been licking Arthur's boots without comment!

§ XXXVII

Morgause stood with the wind streaming her hair, holding her raven banner, proclaiming her freedom and triumph, her presence, up there on those cragged heights mocking and challenging.

The valley rose steep, awkward to negotiate, up in front of Arthur and his men. The Pendragon squinted up at the rocks and crags, deep shadowed or golden bright beneath the new-rising sun. The sky was cloudless, a perfect spring morning, though the air was crisp. Birds were twittering, busy at the first stirrings of nest making, flowers were poking their winter-sleepy heads through the greening grass. A perfect-looking day on which to die. He would not waste a wager on guessing Hueil had placed Dalriadian archers up among those rocks. He beckoned his own banner forward, took the shaft pole in his hand and walked Onager to stand alone, clearly seen, before his men.

Morgause saw, for her arm came out, her head back. Arthur could not hear, not from this distance, but knew she was laughing. He raised the banner, holding it high above his head for the bitch-woman to see. Gwenhwyfar had worked him this banner, the red dragon, proud on a white background. His banner, the Pendragon's banner.

A horse came up, halted a few paces behind. Arthur turned his head to inspect the returning scout's expression. The answering, brief, shake of his head, made Arthur's frown sink deeper.

'Nothing? No sign?'

'Nothing, my Lord. We scouted the few miles you asked of us. There is no movement, no riders coming from Gwynedd.' The scout shrugged. 'Neither is there anything of Amlawdd. They could be anywhere, the woods are dense behind us.' He gestured helplessly in the direction he meant. Only the road to Deva ran clear, a swathe of open land, empty sky. 'Were I to have more men, we could scout a wider arc . . .'

Waving his hand dismissively, Arthur shifted more comfortably in the saddle. He could not spare more men. Could not spare any men. He handed his banner back to its bearer. 'I can no longer spare you either. Form a flank watch – I need to know as soon as either of them approaches.' The Pendragon sounded calm, in command of the situation, the unknown. Where were Gwenhwyfar and her brothers? To where had Amlawdd disappeared? And how in the Bull's bloody name, were they going to fight Hueil in this damned impossible ground? Only by the smile of Fortuna would they win this one.

Wheeling Onager about, Arthur cantered back into the cover of the trees, crowding close to the rising ground of Hueil's chosen place. The baggage mules were secured half a mile back, the men waiting, spread out under the shadow of the bare-branched canopy, seeing to their war gear, their horses, putting an extra edge to dagger or sword. Several called cheerily to Arthur as he trotted by; they were to fight within the hour, when the Pendragon was ready. Nothing had been said, no orders passed; it was a thing known, a soldier's born instinct, an awareness that set the brotherhood of the Artoriani apart.

Gweir came immediately to his Lord as Arthur dismounted,

Llacheu at the servant's heels, both boys grinning as broad as an oak tree's spread. Both were wearing leather fighting gear and brandishing spears.

Arthur wanted to laugh at sight of them. He loosened Onager's girth, refastened a flapping strap on the bridle and handed the horse to his groom. 'And just where,' he said turning to face the two boys, his fists settling at his waist, his voice deepening to sound the more serious, 'do you think you two might be going, dressed like that?'

Llacheu had more nerve than Gweir, he was Arthur's son, could get away with more than a serving lad. 'We thought it would be an idea to help guard the mules, Da. We can do a better job properly dressed and armed.'

'I have men to do the work of men.'

'Which is why you need the boys to see to the pack mules.'

Arthur did laugh at that, caught neatly in his own trap! He ruffled Llacheu's hair, on sudden impulse, squatted down and clasped the boy to him, felt Llacheu's arms go around his shoulders with the same fierce need. The lad buried his face into Arthur's neck, held back an urge to cry, *Be careful, father, I love you!* The words would not come, stayed caught in the boy's dry throat. But Arthur knew he thought them, for he squeezed the boy tighter, a brief acknowledgement of words and feelings that were too precious to put into speech.

'Stay with the animals, son, and wait for your mam.' Arthur unclasped the boy's hands, moved his own grip to Llacheu's shoulders; held him at arm's length, eye meeting eye, searching deep to emphasise the importance of what he said next. 'I need you to look after her, Llacheu, for beyond you, Gwenhwyfar is all I have in this world to love and trust.'

The boy licked his dry lips, again unable to speak, aware that were he to talk, the words would come in a rush of tears and thudding fear. The moment's spell was broken as Arthur winked, stood, turned to his men, the officers gathered in a semicircle awaiting orders. With one last grip on the boy's shoulder Arthur laughed, said, so that as many as were near could hear, 'Enough of this idling, my lads! Let us be up and doing – when we are finished, we can laze on our backsides.' He fastened the straps of his helmet. 'Supper tonight will be venison stew I believe.' He grinned as the men of his Artoriani cheered. They all knew that many of them would be having no need of their supper come dark.

Llacheu watched his father walk away, the men following, filtering their way through the trees. He had Blaidd with him, his dog, and Cadarn, his mother's. They lay together, a few yards away, indifferent to the coming and going of the men, Cadarn, resigned to his mistress being away, lying asleep, head stretched out on his paws. Blaidd yawned noisily, his brown eyes fixed on Llacheu. The lad clicked his fingers and the dog ambled to his side, groaned in ecstasy as the boy rubbed that certain delectable place behind his ears.

Now that the movement of men was gone, the horses could be heard chewing grass, shaking their heads, stamping their feet. The woods were full of them, tethered to the set picket ropes or hobbled. For although the Artoriani were cavalry, fought on horseback, were unbeaten on horseback, no mounted man could ride and fight his way up that steep-sided valley. They went on foot, feeling naked without the reassurance of their mounts between their knees. As Hueil intended.

The Pendragon allowed himself one final look at that woodland as he set foot on the incline. If he were Amlawdd, he would approach soon, come up out of his sheltered hiding among the trees and take the horses before smashing into the Artoriani rear, catching them like rats in a trap. Arthur had left enough good men down there to ensure that did not happen, but that meant not so many of them were about to lay assault to the problem ahead. Where was Gwynedd, damn it!

As expected, the faces of archers appeared from behind the few scrub-stunted trees, boulders, rock overhangs, their skin showing white against the darker, natural colours of rock or winter-dull scrub. His own archers were skilled, loosing their arrows as soon as targets were seen, making every aim count; this was precision work, unlike the approach of two armies on a battlefield where arrow or spear was launched as a mass, to inflict as much damage as possible amongst ranked men. These were individual targets and Hueil had the advantage, for Arthur's men were climbing, exposed, shields covering their heads. Not easy to scrabble up and over rocks one-handed. The thud and jolt of arrows striking his own raised shield made Arthur's wrist and shoulder ache, the shields of men around him bristled with shafts, like grotesque hedgehogs, but not many arrows were making their intended targets. There was the occasional cry as one pierced thigh or leg, but the cavalry shields were larger than an infantry man's, made particularly so to give extra protection across a horse's shoulder or flank.

They were on the steepest part of the rise, climbing higher; not much noise, save the grunt and pant of men's breath, the whine and thud of arrow or spear, an occasional scream or sworn oath. Half-way up it became hand-to-hand fighting: a desperate struggle to keep a secure foothold; cover with shield, thrust with sword or dagger and remain balanced on a slope that threatened to slide from beneath your feet. Arthur was fighting instinctively, not thinking or planning, body, arms, legs, hands, just doing. Part of his mind was back there, way down the slope in those woods where the horses were, and his son. Where his wife should be.

He risked a glance, was surprised to see the glinting sparkle of blue, blue sea stretching behind the brown march of trees. The hills of Gwynedd seemed so near from up here.

A dagger sliced through the thick padding of his sleeve, blood oozing through the torn and split material. He twisted away, swung back, used his sword; another man before him, plunging a double-headed axe downwards, sending it thudding into Arthur's raised shield, splintering the wood, a jarred wave of pain quivering up Arthur's wrist and arm. His foot slipped on loose shale, his legs slithering from beneath him. He tried to steady himself with his sword arm, dared not drop his shield, as again the axe fell, shattering the wood. But the axe blade was caught! Arthur, on his knees, dropped the remainder of the useless shield and brought his sword up, two-handed, thrusting the blade into the man's belly, pushing all his weight behind it, watched the man crumple, topple forward and tumble down the slope.

No time to draw breath, another axe, and he had no shield now. The Pendragon's fingers were becoming sticky with sweat and the trickle of blood that came down his arm. His vision was blurring, sweat pouring into his eyes, the feel of blood pounding. Fighting uphill, every inch higher, another inch won. But how slow the progress, how much blood, how many dead or dying? They would never make the ridge, there were just too many of Hueil's men, too many, and too impossible to fight on, uphill!

Sounds came from behind, an odd cadence that jarred against the battle rhythm, that swept forward and up. Hooves on rock, neighing, the war-shout from men lower down the slope renewed, rising. It took a while to notice it, to be aware of it above the tunnel vision of fighting that which was in front of you. There came a creeping awareness that Artoriani and Northman alike were moving aside, a ripple in the danced movement of traded blows, a faltering hesitation.

And the horses were there, running free, unsaddled, no bridles, ears flat, teeth bared as they were driven upwards. Arthur shouted as Onager came past, the big horse's eyes rolling white, scared, as he scrambled riderless into the confusion and rising panic. With his left hand, Arthur reached out, grabbed the animal's mane and was carried forward, dragged almost, onward, up. Onager was blowing, snorting breath steaming from his widened nostrils. Others of the Artoriani, men whooping and shouting victory, were doing the same, using the brute strength of their horses to barge a wedge straight through Hueil's men, who were scattering or falling beneath hooves that struck against rock and bone, pounded into soft flesh.

A Dalriad swung at Arthur, but he took hold tighter of Onager's mane, his fingers gripping into the neck muscles of the crest, kicked out with his boot, connecting with the man's jaw, sending him backwards, out into the nothingness. He did not see the man fall, for the last few yards were ahead! Onager heaved his shoulders, thrust with his powerful hindquarters and was up, over the top, over the ridge, and galloping. It was easy to mount, to alter the grip on the mane and leap, bend forward over the stretched neck and feel the exhilaration of speed as the horse moved, fast, through the Northmen, who were running, fleeing from these animals with bared teeth, whose riders slashed with their long cavalry swords at heads and shoulders and backs, the horses responsive to the pressure of leg and thigh. They were used to this, the sound and smell of battle, of obeying leg commands only, for no man could use reins while manipulating shield and spear or sword. The panic was easing, the horses settling under control of a rider.

The wind was keening its own battle cry over the flat grass moorland, through scattered trees, as the men of the North fled, a dark shadow of heads bobbing, arms pumping. Among them, the banners of Hueil and Morgause. Somewhere, she must also be running – but Arthur had no time to look, no time to search, for some of the Dalriads, braver men, older, wiser, were regrouping, turning to fight. Men who not so long ago had fought beside Arthur against that same woman who was running for her life, somewhere ahead.

It was finished easily, quickly and without mercy. Those who had run got away; the horses and men were too tired to pursue. Weary, Arthur called the command to stand down and dropped from Onager's back, feeling his legs quivering from the unaccustomed effort of gripping a horse bare back. He led him by the forelock through the litter of dead, dying or wounded, back to the lip of the ridge where men were coming, making an end to the Northern stragglers, many men, not of the Artoriani. And a woman. She clawed her way over the lip of the ridge, her sword red, streaks of blood and sweat on her face, her copper-gold hair blowing free, its braiding long since come unbound, her smile broad, as she saw Arthur walking towards her, his own clothing and face and sword as grimed and stained as hers.

'And whose idea was it,' he said, stepping up to her, taking her hand to help her, 'to let the horses loose?'

Gwenhwyfar grinned. 'I would like to take the credit, but . . .'

She was interrupted as a man clambered up from the slope, his breath coming in gasps, as much blood and dirt on him as everyone else.

'It was my idea to send the horses up. I thought it might create a diversion,' Amlawdd said coming forward, grinning from one ear to the other, his sword outstretched, hilt first, in a gesture of peace.

'Your woman persuaded me that it would be the better option to ally with you.'

Arthur did not know what to say. He leant his weight against Onager, looked from one to the other, could not find enough energy to ask one, damned, single question.

Through the blood and dust spattering her face, Gwenhwyfar was smiling sweetly. A warning sign that she was about to do or say something Arthur was most definitely not going to like.

'In exchange for alliance,' she said, with her eyes sparkling – she was most definitely up to some mischief – 'the Pendragon will agree to give an equal share in whatever Amlawdd desires to ask for.'

Wiping his face with his hand, Arthur did little to improve his appearance, succeeded in spreading the grime around further. All he really wanted to do was go back down that hill to their made camp, find his tent and go to sleep for the next few days. Na, make that months. And here he was, standing at the edge of a battlefield playing damned silly games!

Amlawdd had sheathed his sword, was standing arms folded, legs spread. 'Do you agree, Pendragon?'

He was going to regret this. Arthur nodded, too weary to think the thing through. Stood, too stunned even to draw his sword as Amlawdd immediately replied with:

'Then I claim your wife.'

§ XXXVIII

Several thoughts galloped through Arthur's mind almost simultaneously: he had not heard right; Gwenhwyfar was mad to have planted the idea in this turd's addled brain; and, most explicit, he would slit Amlawdd's throat before ever agreeing! The day had been long, tiring and the touch of death had been a little too close down his neck for comfort, components that did not make for an easy temper or humorous mood. Arthur took several steps towards Amlawdd and prodded him, none too gently, in the chest with the tip of one finger. 'You ally with me, frog feet, or I kill you. Those are *my* terms.' He turned on his heel and stormed away, muttering dangerously beneath his breath. Several men, intending to approach him for further orders, scuttled off to find their Decurions instead.

The sun that had shone so hopefully all morning had been outmanoeuvred by banks of cloud hurtling in from the east, herded before a wind that threatened worse to come than this grey, overcast afternoon. The wounded were many, not as many dead as expected, though the numbers would rise through the night and the next few days. Of the horses, a few were lame, nothing worse. It had taken a while, and much cursing, to round them up. War mounts were trained to stand when their riders were tipped off, the reins falling loose, but running free in a mass of galloping excitement was another matter. Arthur took Onager out for an hour or two, persuaded a few of the more rebellious horses back. They could not pursue Hueil without the horses. Not that Hueil was going to get far, for Arthur had set his best scouts on following the Northern bastard's trail. Na, he would not get far. Nor would she.

Then there had been the men to see to, as Arthur always did, going around the wounded, laughing, encouraging, a gentle word for those badly hurt. His own wound was tended late in the afternoon, when the medical orderlies had finished with the more serious needs, and then he had to inspect the wounded horses . . . the list went on.

The smells of supper cooking were becoming more enticing, but things had to be done before a man could fill his belly. Arthur clenched his teeth and gripped his sword pommel for self-support. This other thing would have to be outfaced at some point. The Decurions and officers would be waiting for him by now to discuss this day's course and plan the morrow's; no surprise to find Amlawdd sitting with them, wearing that same inane grin. Gwenhwyfar also, sitting among the circle of waiting men, Llacheu beside her. Arthur glanced at her. She looked beautiful, had taken time to braid her hair, wear her jewels, a fine gown. Her eyes were dappled with that swirl of familiar tawny gold, and her smile, as he entered the circle

511

and took his place next to her, was more radiant than any sunburst after a summer storm. The Pendragon raised one eyebrow, squinted through the other eye at her. What was she up to?

Amlawdd was full of intention to speak, but Arthur was determined not to let him, not yet. There were important, more pressing matters to deal with first, like what they were going to do about Hueil.

One of the scouts had returned, keeping constant information flowing. Hueil's scum had not run far, had come together to lick each other's wounds and rejoin their strength when they realised the Artoriani were not pursuing. Rarely was an issue settled in one fight, but Arthur had no intention of letting this one drag on.

'I want Hueil dead. If not on the morrow, then the next day.' He glowered around the circle, watching his officers, judging their feelings. Was satisfied to read the same objective. He altered the mood slightly, lightening to humour. 'A peaceful life at Caer Cadan is more preferable than farting around in these miserable hills.' Several officers chuckled. 'I have a mind to return south as soon as we can – now let us plan how that can be achieved.'

The light was fading, the days still short, nights long, spring not yet strong enough to chase the darkness. Two Turmae were sent off to ensure Hueil's rabble stayed where they were, the lesser officers sent about their business. Only the Decurions, Meriaun and Llacheu remained with Arthur, and those few officers were curious about a wild-fire spreading rumour concerning Gwenhwyfar and Amlawdd. Arthur's stomach was growling. The bowl of cold porridge he had eaten at dawn this morning had emptied from his belly long since.

'I have no intention of agreeing,' he stated. He was sitting cross-legged, his sword across his lap, folded his arms to emphasise his point. 'My wife will not become Amlawdd's whore.'

Gwenhwyfar briefly touched his arm, her eyes sparking annoyance. She put two fingers across Arthur's lips, silencing his rising anger, mouthed so that Amlawdd would not see, 'Trust me!' Turned her dazzling smile on the other man. 'Do you agree to share me as wife?'

Amlawdd shouted, 'Aye!'

512

Arthur glared, growled a fierce, 'Na, I do not.'

'Then there will always be fighting between you.' Gwenhwyfar spoke matter-of-factly, almost indifferent to Arthur's rising hurt and anger. 'You must accept this, Arthur, or Amlawdd will take the men he has brought you and return south.' She looked him square in the eye. 'And I will go with him.' That came as a shock – to both men. 'I will not stay with a husband who shames me by going back on my sworn word.'

Arthur began to bluster a protest, but Gwenhwyfar silenced him. 'This is what I say. I shall be wife to both of you, for half and half a year's turn. I shall be with one while there are leaves, showing full-green upon trees and with the other when there are none to be seen. To this you must both agree, and then one must make his choice.'

Both men sat silent, although there was a small ripple of interest around the men sitting in the circle. Amlawdd chewed his lip, considering the proposal, Arthur's glower deepened. It was almost dark, but the trees, their silhouetted branches leafless against the clouded sky, were clear enough to see. Oak, ash, alder, elm: the woodland trees, winter dormant. 'I agree,' Amlawdd announced, with a confirming nod of his head.

'Arthur?'

'Huh.'

'Then choose, Amlawdd!' As she spoke, Gwenhwyfar came to her feet, stood before the flames of the hearth-fire, the winter darkness gathering around her like a cloak.

For Amlawdd the choice was easy. He would have her for his own, have her and then forget to return her! When there were no leaves on the trees the nights were longer, the bed-place sought earlier, kept later. 'I will have you now, my lovely one. Now, when there are no leaves upon the trees.' He jumped up, intending to take Gwenhwyfar in an embrace, stopped short as Arthur barked laughter that rose into deeper gurgles and then uncontrolled crowing. Anger puffed Amlawdd's face as Gwenhwyfar began laughing too, her arms going about Arthur, clinging to him. And then the others were all laughing, all of them seeing the jest. Damned if he could!

Arthur himself put him out of his misery, pointing, through streaming tears, at a group of small, barely noticeable green-leafed holly trees. Amlawdd looked, looked again, stamped over to the nearest, a smaller bush, and wrenched the thing up by the roots, casting it with a yell of fury onto the fire, to the delight of everyone else who laughed even louder.

§ XXXIX

The day after battle. Time to feel the hurting of wounds, the loss of death; to watch the sun rise and appreciate how good it was to be still alive. So much to be done on such a day.

Hueil was held among the meandering rivers and waterways that drained into the estuary, effectively secured among the marsh leas so tightly by the posted Artoriani that he could not even pass wind without Arthur knowing about it. Tomorrow, or the day after, they would have to fight again, but on the Pendragon's terms, when he chose to call the fall of the dice.

Arthur was making his way to the smith, where old Gareth could put an edge on a blade that would slice the wind. 'Hie, Pendragon!' For a moment, Arthur considered pretending he had not seen or heard, hesitated over-long.

'Still here, Amlawdd? I received the impression last night that you were going back on your sworn oath of loyalty, were to be leaving us this morning.'

'I declared my oath, but that was before your she-vixen tricked me,' Amlawdd growled, a sound to match the creased scowl on his face. Last night, he had held every intention of pulling out. Last night, he had drunk too much barley-ale. What in the gods' good name was it brewed with? He stopped beside the King, rubbed at his temples, easing the throbbing drums pounding in his head. Managed a reluctant grin. 'How, by the Bull, do you tolerate that woman as a wife? She's more devious than a whore-son cattle thief!'

Laughing, Arthur began walking again in the direction of the smith and, uninvited, Amlawdd kept pace. 'I made her my wife because I discovered it was the only way to keep an eye on her.'

'She's a damn fine woman.'

Aye, that Gwenhwyfar was. Arthur knew he was lucky to have her, but was blowed if he would admit that to this petty upstart. When Amlawdd stepped in his path suddenly, holding his hand out in friendship, Arthur was momentarily surprised. Last night, Amlawdd had stormed off in a foul temper, threatening all the reprisals and vengeances possible; half expected to find him and his men long gone by dawn. Not that they would have got far. The Artoriani had orders to kill anyone moving about these woods without the Pendragon's personal authorisation. Arthur stared at the outstretched hand, did not take it. Shifted his intent gaze to Amlawdd's face. Few men could out-stare Arthur's scrutiny.

Amlawdd was not one of those few. He shuffled uncomfortably, held the hand obstinately for Arthur to take. 'Damn it, man!' Amlawdd finally exploded. 'I'm trying to apologise for past mistakes. I'm a bloody fool who thought I knew more, and aye, I admit, thought I was better than you.' He lowered the hand. 'Well, I'm not.'

Himself tall, Arthur had to lift his head to keep his eyes fixed on this man's. That offered hand had been large, strong, could fell a man in a single blow without the need of axe or cudgel. Did he want Amlawdd's friendship? Was it genuine? Even if it was not, for a while at least, he needed it. More than he did the opposite.

Again, misreading Arthur's thought, Amlawdd tried: 'My brothers were always the heroic types.' He waved Arthur's contemptuous snort aside. 'All right, so they fought on what you consider the wrong side. The point is, they fought, were soldiers, were capable of planning a raid, a battle.' He shrugged, let the rest of his words tail off. Amlawdd was none of these things, just a medium-ability warrior with a medium interest in war, set within a giant-sized body that gave a wrong impression. He attempted a smile. 'It has taken your wife to make me think, Pendragon.' Arthur grunted at that. Think? Probably for the first time in his entire life – the family had the thinking capability of a mouldering porridge pot!

Raising his hands in an almost imploring gesture, Amlawdd met with Arthur's stone-set, blank expression. 'You want the truth from me, Pendragon? I hated my brothers, evil toad-spawned buggers, the pair of them. I was against you because everybody expected it of me, it took your damned beautiful wife to make me wonder just who the "everybody" was!' Still no response. Jesu, did the bastard want him to beg on his knees! All right, if that is what it took to show he was serious in this . . .

'Whoa! Whoa, get up.' Hastily, embarrassed, Arthur stopped the large man in the act of kneeling, thrust his hands under Amlawdd's elbows, bringing him back to his feet. He had to ask, 'What of Rhica, your son?'

Amlawdd had to answer, he acknowledged Arthur's direct searching gaze, regarded him straight back with no flicker of eye muscle or twitched concealment of lying. He spoke plain truth. 'Rhica was a deceitful, greedy bastard: I'm pleased to be rid of him.'

Arthur raised an eyebrow. 'So what do you want from me, Amlawdd? You've lost chance at my wife.'

The other man laughed, his hands on his broad waist, head back, a genuine, amused-from-the-belly laugh. 'Not if you're killed, Pendragon! I want to be around the day someone slits your throat open to comfort the lady in her distress! Next in line, as husband, so to speak.'

Resuming his intention to seek out the smith, Arthur made his way again, this time waving Amlawdd to fall in step. Gwenhwyfar would have a different view of the matter of course – and Amlawdd obviously did not realise that virtually half the entire Artoriani were here for the same reason. He chuckled, stuck out his own hand for Amlawdd to grasp.

The answering clasp was firm, sincere. 'Your Lady aside, Pendragon. I want to go home with an honour, a victory.' Unembarrassed, he added, 'Something to swank about.'

Gripping Amlawdd's shoulder Arthur promised, 'I think I can do that for you.'

Satisfied, pleased with himself, Amlawdd took his leave, Arthur watching amused, as the big man swaggered away across the encampment, filled twice his size with this sudden new-found self-pride.

At the smith's field workshop, the boy slave worked the bellows to heat a bent and twisted sword-blade in the fire. Llacheu was squatting before the heat, fascinated. Arthur rumpled the lad's hair, handed his own sword to the smith who ran his thumb along the blade, frowning at a slight nick to the edge, and grunted. No one had ever seen the old man smile, not many heard him speak beyond the few words that made up his entire vocabulary. He pointed to the blade that needed strengthening, set Arthur's aside with others. 'An hour.'

§ XL

Two hours into full dark. The wind was clamouring harder and another squall of wind-driven rain slammed the side of the tent, battering it as mercilessly as a door ram. Llacheu looked up from his bowl of oatmeal, licked the mess off his fingers, noticed his mother's frown of disapproval and grinned.

'It tastes better from fingers.'

'A spoon would keep you cleaner – ah, boy bach, look at you!' She leant forward, dabbing at a large porridge stain down his tunic, shaking her head. But her eyes were laughing, her son noted.

Arthur was seated on a stool at the only small table, attempting to write beneath the dull light of a pale, flickering lamp. Without glancing up he grunted, 'I was unaware that slop could taste any better however it's eaten.' He pinched his nose between fingers, wrote two final words, laid down his stylus and folded the two halves of the wooden tablet, carefully sealing it with wax and setting the thing aside. 'How people survive on the stuff I'll never understand.'

Llacheu scooped the last mouthful from his bowl. 'The barley-brew that washes it down helps.'

Arthur laughed, 'You have it right there!'

Finished, Llacheu turned his bowl upside down. 'When I'm King. I'll ban porridge.'

Another gust of wind. The tent shook, the leather creaking and groaning under its ropes. Arthur left his table and as he passed his son ruffled the lad's hair, saying affably, 'Do that, boy, and you'll be sentencing many a poor family to their death.' He stretched, feeling the relief of aching shoulder muscles. He gave Gwenhwyfar a quick kiss as he passed her. 'What I would give for a dish of roasted beef!'

Her eyes bright, she countered with, 'young lamb, seasoned with herbs!' Llacheu adding, 'the crisp edge of pork!' Managed to say together, their laughter rising, 'anything but porridge!'

A sudden shouting from outside stilled Arthur's chuckling. Now what? The two dogs leapt up barking and he cursed them into silence, walked towards the entrance flap, was beaten there by Llacheu. The boy peered out, ducked back, his face and hair wet from rain, eyes alight with excitement. 'A tent's near on torn loose!'

Arthur did not share the lad's excitement. He cursed again, more explicitly, and snatching up his cloak, left the bright comfort of the tent. Signalling the dogs, Llacheu followed. Rain came in great spurts, driven needle-sharp by the gusting wind, the noise was terrific, alarming but exhilarating. The trees tossing and swaying, clattering against each other, the wind itself moaning through the branches. Men calling and shouting.

Several of the men were struggling to keep hold of the flapping tent that was tossing and leaping, its dangling, flailing ropes reminding Llacheu, watching from a safe distance, of that Greek story about the woman whose hair was formed of writhing snakes. He shuddered, instinctively ducked as with a cracking roar, the strain ripped out another tent peg and the last holding rope whipped loose. It caught a man's face, cutting through his cheek and lip as efficiently as a dagger blade. The man screamed, clutched at the ripped and torn flesh that spurted blood. Three men held the wild, bucking tent briefly, others, including Arthur, scrabbling to help, but the leather was wet and slippery and their breath already sobbing from the struggle. They let go. The thing billowed up and away, a huge released bird of prey, flapping and twisting, making a desperate

518

bid for freedom. It snagged against the branches of the trees, was caught, dangled, writhing like a fish stabbed through by a spear.

Llacheu heard his father swear, a particular word he had never heard before. Grinning, the boy stored it in his memory. A good one to use before the other boys at some future date!

Arthur's arms were waving, his hands gesturing angrily, his loud, abusive words snatched by the wind. The men whose tent it was stood taking his berating, breath panting from the exertion of trying to save the thing, shoulders heaving, heads drooping. They were certain it had been pegged properly and securely; one tried to explain that someone going to the latrine ditch must have tripped over the ropes. 'We felt it jolt, Sir,' he offered, 'then the whole thing came loose.' Found the Pendragon did not seem impressed by the excuse.

Llacheu crept away, aware it was not a good idea to stay in his father's shadow when he was angry with the men. He wondered whether it might be best to return to the comfort of a dry tent, but what matter? He was wet now anyway. By walking low, head bent, back crouched and with his fingers firmly hooked through both dogs' collars he made his way past the line of tents, the blacksmith's erected bothy, and out to the horse lines. The Watch-guard, sheltering behind a large old oak, challenged his approach, nodded greeting as Llacheu identified himself.

The horses were uneasy, standing with their rumps to the rain-sharp wind, heads down, ears back. Llacheu released the dogs and went along the line, touching a muzzle here and there, stroking another horse's neck, a forehead, pulling at an ear. Onager would not be tethered here with the others. He approached his own horse, which whickered a welcome as the boy fondled its head, the lad's fingers toying with the rain-matted forelock. Beside him, Blaidd growled, and Cadarn's head came up, scenting the blustering wind, pricked ears listening to the rough darkness. Absorbed with his mount Llacheu did not notice.

Blaidd growled again and a horse squealed further down the line, the ripple of distinct unease spreading rapidly. One horse reared and several stamped, tossed their heads. Ears were back, eyes rolling. A shape, dark, crouched, disappeared into the trees. Frightened,

Llacheu shouted for the Watch, but the wind tore away his words. The boy ran, caught the man's tunic sleeve, pointed. 'There's something prowling round the horses!' he gasped, saw the man raise his spear, watched him walk forward, then Llacheu ran on, with the two dogs barking madly. He'd fetch his da!

Several times the wind almost lifted him off his feet, twice he tripped, sprawling headlong into muddied ground. Arthur had not finished his tongue-lashing of the men. 'I'll not inconvenience other men,' he was roaring, 'you'll damn well sleep in the open for your stupidity – rain or no rain!'

'Da! Da!' Llacheu was pulling at his father's arm, pointing back at the horse lines. Breathless, told him what he had seen. Alarmed, Arthur was running, men with him, swords drawn, shouting for others to follow, the lost tent quite forgotten. Each had the same thought: Hueil had sent someone to loose the horses, panic them in this wind, drive them away.

There was nothing. The tethering ropes were all knotted as they should be, the horses had quietened, even the dogs' hackles had flattened. Nothing behind the trees, up the trees, beneath. Nothing, no one. They searched for half an hour. Arthur doubled the guard, called a halt. Whoever had been creeping around the horses had gone. Then Llacheu saw the print, new made in the soft mud. He had caught it by chance, beneath the glimmer of the few wind-flared lanterns. Solemnly he pointed to it. Arthur squatted down, touched the shape with his fingers, tracing its size, glancing warily into the darkness beneath the trees. Slowly, Arthur straightened, lifting the boy into his arms as he did so, calling precise orders to the men. 'The maker of this is near by, find him and deal with it. No fuss, no noise.' He tried not to sound fearful, masking his unease from the boy, but Llacheu caught the worry all the same. 'Will we be all right, Da?' He was ten years of age, too old to be carried by his father, but he made no protest as Arthur bore him across the camp in the direction of their tent.

'You'll be fine as long as you stay in the tent with your mam.'

Gwenhwyfar was snuggling into bed. The day had been long, tiring, and she welcomed the end of it. For several nights she had found little or no sleep. Last night they had been late abed, even later sleeping, after their shared loving. There seemed a lot of noise and bustle going on outside, presumably to do with the loose tent. Something brushed against the side of the leather, the wind? Again. One of the dogs. 'Llacheu!' she called, wriggling lower beneath the sleeping furs, 'come in now, it's time for bed!' The tent flap moved, shook . . . and Gwenhwyfar screamed.

They heard the scream from the tents opposite, for it went on and on, louder, terrified. Ider was up and running for his Lady's tent before that first scream swarmed into the next. Sword drawn, with no thought of what might be beyond, he plunged through the opening.

Arthur heard it too. Hefting Llacheu into the nearest tree, shouting at the boy to stay there until told otherwise, he ran, sword in hand, running as if the hounds of the hunt were at his heels. The screaming went on, stopped abruptly.

Mithras protect her! Arthur pleaded as he ran, his breathing sobbing in his throat. His legs would not move fast enough, his breath not come quick enough! Rare for a bear to wander so close to men, but when one did, it was usually for a reason. They were wounded or hungry. Both. And wounded, hungry bears were dangerous.

Later Ider admitted his sword stroke had been nothing but desperation and luck. The bear had its back to the tent flap, was reared up. Ider had no time to think of what to do, or of his own safety. His sword was in his hand, he used it. Fortuna helped him plunge it straight through the bear's heart, Mithras himself lent the strength to push the blade in up to the hilt. Never mind that the iron buckled, snapped and broke. The bear dropped like a stone, dead. Ider scrabbled over the twitching carcass, clasped Gwenhwyfar to him and held her so tight, so close, his own body shaking as much as hers, his eyes shut tight against that horrible body lying, teeth bared, claws gleaming, inches from her. Shut tight against what would have happened had he not got here in time.

Ider became aware that someone else was in the tent. Heavy, gasping breathing, movement. He opened his eyes, met with Arthur standing there, on the other side of the brute, became aware also

that he was sitting on Gwenhwyfar's bed, holding her. Oh Christ
Jesu, the Pendragon would hack him to pieces for this! He could not
let go of her though, for her arms were about him, her face buried
against his shoulder, her body heaving as she cried. Ider licked his
dry lips, tried to express the predicament in his eyes.

Others were crowding the tent opening, peering in, whistling
surprise, concern. Curt, Arthur ordered them to remove the bear,
for someone to fetch Llacheu out of the tree, and to stop those
bloody dogs from barking! They were alone, Arthur, Ider and
Gwenhwyfar. Ider took her hands, unwound her grip, moved away
from her, his eyes not leaving his King.

The fright was passing. Gwenhwyfar became aware of the uneasy
silence, began brushing at her cheeks with the back of her hand. She
was trembling but becoming calmer. Something had to be said to
break the tension. 'Bugger that thing, it bloody scared me!' It was
the right thing. Arthur let his sword drop, wiped the sweat from his
face, answered her with his face straight, a laugh in his voice.

'Bull's balls, Cymraes, I'd suggest bed-furs are more practical
when dead.' And then he was grinning, allowing the immense relief
to show. He came to Ider, took the lad's hand in his own, pumping
the arm up and down. 'Well done, Duplicarius, well done.'

Ider said nothing, his voice struck dumb. Duplicarius? Second-in-
command of a Turma? Jesu be blessed, promotion! Arthur was
walking him towards the tent flap, ducking through with him,
calling to the men that they had a new hero to jest at. Said quiet,
under his breath for Ider alone to hear, 'I thank you, but if ever I
catch you in a similar position in my wife's tent again, you'll find
yourself promoted into the next world. Understand me?'

Ider held back the pleased grin. 'A bear's not an alibi you can use
too often is it, Sir?'

Arthur laughed, 'Na, I think a husband might just see through
that one!' He turned away, ducked back inside the tent, laughing
louder.

522

§ XLI

Once Winifred had made up her mind on something, she went ahead with the decision. Several things had become apparent these last months, some things she would rather not have had occur, but the Fates enjoyed weaving knotted snags into the warp and weft of mortal life. Some had been gradual changes, others abrupt. A few difficult to swallow, but when there was a shortage of food, even porridge was preferable to starvation. When there were choices of the future, Cerdic's future, the deciding came even harder. But now, having won the thing she desired, Arthur's written acknowledgement of Cerdic as his son, she was determined to waste no time. Cerdic had to learn how to fight, how to lead. How to become a man.

She poured her best quality wine for the man sitting opposite, taking his ease on her comfortable, newly refurbished couch. Leofric was a good man, nearing mid-age and with wealth enough to attract any woman of high ambition. The wealth did not sway Winifred, she had that for her own. Neither did the land he owned, for her own estate was not small, was well profitable. His age was suitable, and his character? Anyone, after surviving Arthur's tempers, would seem docile.

Winifred handed him the wine with a warm smile, fetched her stool, sat, with her hands demurely folded on her lap. His one useful, asset, he could fight and he could teach Cerdic what the boy needed to know.

'I have decided to accept you as husband, Leofric. But there will be conditions.'

Leofric wiped wine residue from his gold-fair moustache, nodded acquiescence. He had expected it so. No man, no matter how rich, could expect Winifred, first wife to the British Pendragon, Princess, daughter of Vortigern, granddaughter of Hengest, child of Woden, to accept marriage without terms. How many months had he waited for this? All this time of courtship; his gifts, letters, honey-tongued messengers! Thor's hammer, how much had getting this woman to accept him cost! How much more to keep her? 'I have offered already to take your son into education of arms. He will be as a son of my own.'

Winifred inclined her head, smiled. *Ah*, thought she, *because you have no son to call your own, and to embrace the one born of a king is more than adequate compensation!* Leofric understood that she had guessed his motives, did it matter that she knew? He had no one to follow his name, even after the taking of three wives. At least Winifred was proven not to be barren. He would be content to adopt a son who might be king of the British one day, and if there could be other sons born . . .

'I am happy to comply with any other desires, my dear one. Tell me your conditions.'

Keeping her hands folded, Winifred answered, 'I agree to be your wife, but I will on no account leave this estate. My son you may take with you when you have need to visit your own places across the sea. He will need to know them, and your people, for my other condition is that all that is yours becomes his upon your death.'

To his credit Leofric did not waver his relaxed smile. 'This is asking much.'

'Not so much. You are marrying the royal, and divine, blood. Your sons, should there be any, can call upon Woden as their ancestor.' And Leofric wanted that, for he was a man who held great pride and self-importance.

He spread his hands, indicating confusion. 'But if you are not to leave this estate, how do I beget my sons?'

Winifred stood, clapped her hands for the slaves to come, remove the debris of their shared meal. The interview was ended. 'I will wed with you, Leofric Golden-Hair, within the passing of this month. You may place your feet at my hearth for six months of a year, the other six I will not expect you to remain here. As for my bed, I shall invite you there when it suits me. There will be enough chance for a son to be made.' She inclined her head, offered him her hand to touch briefly, and for the first time since their knowing, placed a kiss on his cheek. Then she left the room, went to the privacy of her own chamber, her heart beat thumping in her chest. Mother of the gods! That was a more difficult thing to handle than arguing with Arthur!

She unpinned her hair, removed her gown, sat in her under-tunic before the polished bronze mirror, gazing at her distorted reflection. Leofric was not the first to ask marriage of her, nor would he be the last. She had accepted this thing because Cerdic needed the teaching. He needed to know how to manage and control an estate, to oversee the planting and harvesting, to know the accounts, needed to know how to wield an axe and a sword, a spear and a shield. He needed to become a man who could one day rule not just as a thegn over an estate, but as a king over a country. Leofric could teach him all this, as could any of the men who had sought to wed her these past few years, but with any of those other men, there had always been the risk of her having another son. And already there were too many sons stepping before and behind on Cerdic's path. She removed her under-tunic, slid naked into her bed, running her hand over the silk-softness of her body, from breasts to the curl of hair between her legs. She had not lain with any man except Arthur. Did not want this Leofric touching her, being intimate with her, soiling the memory of the man she still loved, but for Cerdic she would do it. Knowing there would at least be no sons.

She leant from the bed, extinguished the lamp on the side table, her smile satisfied that the choice had been a right one. Leofric was indeed a good man, but proud men were so quick to put blame on their women! Three wives, numerous mistresses? Ah, Winifred knew of them, had paid well to know of them. Not one had carried his child.

Ja, if she had to take a husband to secure manhood for her son, and to strengthen him for when he challenged his father or that Gwynedd bitch's brat then one who was empty of seed would be the more preferable.

Two scouts arrived within the hour of each other, from the North, where Hueil was becoming restless, and from the South where an army with the banner of the Chi Rho was approaching. Arthur posted an extra Turma of men to keep high-profile watch on Hueil and decided to deal with the South himself. Only one man could be following a banner of Christ.

Although early morning was well established, Gwenhwyfar was taking a rare chance at lazing abed. Both messages had come direct to the King's tent. After the delivering of the second, Arthur raised an eyebrow at his wife, who was lying with her arms behind her head, staring at a vague spot along the ridge-pole. 'Pity you're not dressed,' he said, feigning disapproval, 'we could have arranged a reception committee.' She was up and dressing before he finished. Chuckling, Arthur ducked out and ordered the horses made ready and returned inside. He could not resist taking hold his wife, wearing only her under-garments. Half serious, Gwenhwyfar batted him aside, complaining that he had asked her to hurry.

'It'll take a while to saddle Onager, you know how tetchy he is.' He began unlacing her breast band.

'How long is "a while"?'

Arthur had the band off, his hands taking its place over her breasts, his face nuzzling against her neck. 'Long enough,' he murmured.

They waited where the Roman road crested a slight rise, sat their jiggling horses, watching the column, half a mile distant, swing nearer, seeing the men raise their heads, the occasional pointing hand. They had been seen, then, recognised. Arthur glanced up at his banner, tossing proud in the wind that had calmed with the sunrise but was spirited enough still to bring Gwenhwyfar's beautiful dragon to life. How impressive it must be from a distance! The brilliant red and flashing gold leaping and darting against the billowing white. He allowed himself a self-congratulatory smile, leaned across the space between them and took Gwenhwyfar's hand, squeezed her fingers.

'You ought not to look so smug,' she said, her own expression as proud and delighted as his. 'I would almost think you were gloating.'

Arthur pretended shocked horror. 'Me? Never!'

Her lips pursed, a chastising shake of her head. 'Don't you try to convince me you had all this planned, Pendragon.'

He squeezed her hand again, 'I knew Ambrosius would see sense and join with me one day.'

'Liar.' They were laughing as a man detached himself from the column, spurred his horse forward, the smiles still on their faces as he approached nearer, reined to a trot, walk and halt, made formal salute.

'I was wondering,' Ambrosius said casually, almost as if they had unexpectedly met while on an afternoon's exercise, 'whether you could find use for a few extra men?'

Arthur surveyed the column, counted the number of infantry in the first quarter, made a mental calculation. Ambrosius would march in strict Roman formation. 'Mithras, Uncle, have you brought me a Legion?' he jested.

'I wish I could have, Nephew, but, as you are so fond of telling me, the days of those numbers of available men have gone.' Extending his hand in less formal greeting he added with a twinkle of laughter, 'You will needs be content with five Centuries. I have gathered all the Militia men along the way. Shaming them into coming, those who refused your first call to arm.'

Arthur took his hand, eyes alert, mind already planning how to deploy them. 'I think I can find some small use for four hundred men.'

To Gwenhwyfar's surprise, Ambrosius offered his greeting to her, his smile warm and genuinely friendly, Uncharitably, the thought *what is he gaining from this?* came to her. Did it matter? He was here, with all these men. She blushed then, as red as the dragon fluttering beside Arthur, for, drawing their horses aside to salute the column as they marched past, Ambrosius candidly announced the reason.

'I came because I have limited military experience, Pendragon. If I am to lead when you are gone, I will need more than book learning to be effective.' He held his hand palm outward to acknowledge the standard of the first Century pass by. 'You will teach me, Pendragon.'

Arthur saw Gwenhwyfar opening her mouth to make sharp retort, surreptitiously signalled her to silence. He couched his own answer politely. 'I was hoping this campaign would be a short one, Uncle!'

Ambrosius formed a stern expression, then saw what Arthur meant and relaxed into another smile. 'No, lad, I did not intend to sound so pompous!' And to Gwenhwyfar, on Arthur's far side, he offered, 'I trust, in all sincerity, my Lady, that it is your son who follows our Lord King. I merely plan for possibilities.'

She inclined her head, wanting to believe him. But not quite achieving it.

§ XLIII

Arthur's men moved up from the south during the afternoon. Artoriani, the élite cavalry, Ambrosiani, the infantry, Amlawdd and the men of Deva. The cohorts swaggered up the Roman road taking an easy pace, wedging Hueil against those already outflanking him to north and east. He had nowhere to run. To the west lay the estuary and the marsh, clustered with birds, facing with plumage puffed into the cold eye of the venomous wind: pied oyster catchers, lapwings with their call, *kee-wi kee-wi*, plovers, curlews, and always the geese, floating in grunting groups or grazing at the marsh-grass.

Bedwyr rode beside Arthur. Directly behind them were the men of Deva who had the brown stains of blood on their tunics and the new wounds to their bodies. Men who needed to rid themselves of those memories of treachery, thirsty for the work that needed to be done.

Hueil had manoeuvred as far eastward as Arthur's hovering Turmae allowed, siting his men on the firmer ground inland, reluctant to be pushed to where the winter-high rivers meandered and split into the broken places of the sea-strand. They were impatient, his men, some angered, more, bitter and grumbling. Hueil had promised them an easy victory, glory and riches for all, but all they had was this wind-tagged, desolate marsh wading beneath a grey-clouded, sullen sky. In comparison, the woods to the north seemed friendly, alluring. Beyond those trees tarried the hills and tracks and roads that led homeward. Some had attempted to go, murmuring plans between themselves, slipping away under the night cloak that hid moving shadows. A few, the lucky ones, blundered into the bogs, their water-blown bodies found drifting on the next tide. Of the rest, the Artoriani allowed no one through. The deserters were butchered and hung from the march of trees that formed a border between the marsh and the forests that ran north into the high hills.

Arthur played a war of nerve, a softening of courage. When the one day passed, and then the next, Hueil guessed the Pendragon was playing with them, as a cat would dab and pat at a mouse, let it run, capture it again. Morgause wanted to be gone, wanted to be tucked safe in the far, far North. She urged they take their chance and charge the northern patrols, declaring that even the fastest horse could not do much against a solid body of men, but Hueil argued her down. Once in those woods, he would not keep his army of frightened men together. Short of heart, they would melt into the trees and simply go home. There would not be another fight. Without a victory, no matter how small, Hueil would never again be able to bring all these men of the North together. So they stayed out on the edge of the marshes, where the rivers that descended from the hills of the north and east and south split into channels and runnels before rippling into the sea. Stayed and waited for Arthur to come, and told the men that they had a chance, a good chance, of winning.

The night hearth-fires spread across the darkness of the sea-tinged marshes, and the sound of Hueil's men talking or singing drifted in the calm, salt-damp air. The wind finally eased, then ceased, blustering out to sea at dusk with the ebb tide, giving way at dawn, to a white-pawed mist that shrouded the marsh with a cobweb cloak of wraithing shadow. Hueil raised his banner high and brought his army into the square formation that could, as long as they stood firm, resist any cavalry charge. Morgause he put at the centre with the banners and standards, ordered her sit her horse and give courage to the men. They sore needed their blood warmed, and the Goddess on Earth so vividly among them might grant enough heat to outpace the strength of the Artoriani.

Arthur would have preferred better ground than this, but to have let Hueil run further north would have brought a longer campaign, and these open, flat lands were preferable to the confine of the trees. For the both of them this was a gamble. To either side could the roll of the dice fall.

Gwenhwyfar retained her smile until the last man rode from camp, the lines and lines of cavalry; Amlawdd's men untried, untrained; the infantry militia, Ambrosius's men. The jangle of bits and harness, the chink of metal, creak of leather. The smell of horse sweat and dung, the excitement, the overshadowing anxiety. The clench of fear knotting her stomach as she watched them, watched him, go. She stood with Llacheu in front of her, hands on his shoulders, she with a smile for the men, he, laughing and waving. Both wishing them well, wishing them, all, keep safe.

Arthur had set camp on higher ground along the last edges of the trees, a hand-span of miles from where the grass-land river marsh began. The sounds began to drift across the reeds and wind-hissing grass, distorted by the distance and echo of the great vault of open sky. Indistinct sounds of horses and men screaming, the clash of sword and spear on shield, a moulded, jumbled mulch of noise.

The army women stood, some arm threaded through arm. Others sat, squatted, hunkered on their heels, in groups or alone. Waiting, their heads raised, senses alert, listening and imagining. Knowing what was happening among that vague, mist-shrouded blur of movement that was their menfolk, surviving or dying.

The boys, the grooms, the smith's lad, youngsters not yet old enough for shield-bearing or the rearguard, employed their time sharpening their own crude weapons, fashioning spear shafts, sharpening arrow blades and daggers, mending harness or tents.

They too waited and listened, but they were the men of the morrow, they could not show their fear naked, like the women. They hid their worries beneath a frenzy of tasks and errands. Kept hand and mind busy. But they listened, all the same, to the distant rise and fall of the battle song.

The mist cleared into a mid-day haze over the sand bars and mudflats of low tide, where the birds gathered in their hundreds, anxious about their search for food before the water should come again, oblivious to the matter of men a few hundred yards away. Hueil was aware that he had a chance of winning. Again and again, Arthur's cavalry had come in to the charge, the arrows of both sides coming first in a hissing wind of bright-tipped malevolence, and then the spears, their sound deeper, more haunting, the blades shrieking as they hurled towards the bringing of death or wounding. Again and again, the horses veered aside as Hueil's close-packed lines stayed firm held.

Hueil's men stood, feet planted, determination set, their fire fuelled by the screaming encouragement of their Lord's golden-haired woman. Where one man fell another stepped in his place – and they were moving forward, gaining ground. The river marsh was dropping behind, receding with the lifting mist. Hueil paused, briefly loosened his helmet straps, wiped the sweat from his forehead, took a breath. He could win this! He could!

The Pendragon too, was acutely aware that Hueil was close to victory. Not for ever could he keep throwing his horses in, trying and trying to break that solid wedge of unyielding men. He must get them to run, to break the mass. Together, Hueil's formation could stand all night and all the next day. Broken, the cavalry could finish them as easily as scything barley-corn.

He watched a heron trail slowly across the grey-dusted, cloudy sky. For all their corn feeding, the horses were lathered, breathing hard, many wounded from arrows and spears. The men too had suffered, but men could go on fighting when urged, not horses, only so much would they take before beginning to balk. There could only be one more charge. Only one.

He sent his messengers to call in Ambrosius, Meriaun, Amlawdd and Bedwyr. A hasty conference: the men and horses would appreciate the respite, the chance to draw breath, bandage wounds, adjust armour and weapons. But so too would Hueil. Time to change the balance. The birds were already beginning to circle in from the sand and mud-flats, the geese crying mournfully as they passed overhead, back to the grasslands from the shallows that were deepening with the flood-tide. Once the water came in, Hueil would be safe from rear attack, the horses useless. This one last try, to get Hueil's men to break.

§ XLIV

As the mist cleared, the women could see; indistinctly, but enough to watch what was happening, for their camp was pitched on ground higher than the flat river plain. The view spread in a panoramic scene, the great arch of sky, the mist-hazed, incoming sea, acres of marsh grass and reeds, dotted with only the occasional wind-bent tree. And beyond, the dark, smudged line that was the beginning of the northern forests. Gwenhwyfar did not sit with the women, she stayed by the ringed protective fence of staves of the camp palisade, stood watching, one step beyond the palings, her position setting her that one step nearer the war-game. Her fingers were curled tight around the pommel of her sword, clutching tighter until the knuckles turned white, her eyes never leaving that blur of movement spread across that wide, wide expanse of grassland, where moved, like a played board game, the battle pieces. The banners, the standards; bright coloured, glinting in the diffused light of reflected sea dazzle. The great squared formation that was Hueil, his banners ranged tight in the centre. Ambrosius's Chi Rho to the western boundary, Meriaun's at the east, Bedwyr north, and the Dragon, bold, emblazoned, proclaiming its lord to the south. Mixed with them, the colours and emblems of the individual Turmae. Red, Blue, Yellow. Their effigies silver gold in the occasional glimpse of sun. A boar, a bear. The Sea-Goat, the Ram . . .

Ider was watching also, standing on the opposite side of the unshuttered gateway, standing, much as Gwenhwyfar, watching the sway and shift of battle. His was the command of the camp, this rag-tag of boys and women, a command he had accepted reluctantly, half angered, mumbling and muttering against it. Until Arthur himself had told him the reason for it. *'I need someone to see to my son and my woman.'* Ider accepted the reason, but resented it. To stand and watch, helpless, while his comrades fought and died, to be down there, to be using his shield and his spears. . . . Gwenhwyfar's scream cut across his thoughts, he saw her pointing, saw her sword coming into her hand, and watched horrified as she began running, hair and cloak flying, screaming something, some wordless sound of brutal anguish.

Ider stood, his throat clamped, body frozen. 'My God!' The words repeating over and over, *'My God, My God!'*

That last charge, the horses had not veered away, but had pressed closer, the men fighting their way through the spears and swords and axes of Hueil's men, and then Arthur was down! They saw, watching from this slight hill, his banner waver as his men crowded close to where their Lord should be – and then suddenly, inexplicably, they were running, galloping, fleeing the battlefield. The Artoriani, Meriaun, Bedwyr, all of them, streaming away southward, with Ambrosius plunging from the west, his men thigh deep in swirling incoming tide. 'My God,' Ider gasped again, 'we're defeated!'

A boy dashed past, carrying sword and shield, legs pounding as he raced after the figure of his mother slithering down the slight incline. Sense returned to the stunned Ider with a startling thump. He yelled orders for his men, those few men of the Turma left as guard, and plunged after Gwenhwyfar and Llacheu, leaping at the running woman as he closed on her, bringing her down in a rough tumble of cloak, legs and hair, his arms tight around her as they rolled, she spitting and lashing out, cursing him, calling him all the names she knew. Llacheu was on him, astride his back, beating with his fist, the flat of his sword. 'Leave my mother be! Leave her!'

Ider shrugged him off, pinned Gwenhwyfar beneath him, holding her hands, knees on her legs. 'What can you do? You can't help, you can't save him! One woman, one child? Where is your sense?'

Tears were streaming down her face as she tried to push him from her, then surrendered, his sense at last reaching her. He released her, helped her to her feet, embarrassed at his action. She put her hand to his chest, leant against him, only a moment, her eyes shut, controlling the tears and the fear.

'If we are to help, we must do so clear-headed,' Ider explained, his arm around her, holding her close, his chin against her hair. How many, many times had he wanted to hold her against him, feel her body beneath his hands – but not like this, not like this! He let her go, moving her gently from him, turned her around to take a look again at their men fleeing the battlefield. The Artoriani defeated, running.

'We need to prepare for when Hueil's rabble come this way.' Ider stated it as fact, for they would come. The Northern army would come looking for the woman, the provisions, weapons. They would not find Gwenhwyfar or the boy. For that also was Ider's orders, given personally by Arthur. *Were I to lose, Ider, make them safe. Either way, make them safe.*

Unconsciously, as they barred the gate and began issuing orders to those who could to arm themselves, Ider touched his dagger. The blade was sharper than a winter's midnight frost. *Either way, make them safe!* The Pendragon had not said specifically, had no need, for Ider had understood his meaning, had bowed his head and accepted the orders to stay with Gwenhwyfar and the boy. With nowhere to run, a quick, sharp blade wielded by one who cared could be the only assurity of safety. Ider watched Gwenhwyfar organising the women, bit his lips as he fingered that dagger. Could he do it though? Could he take her life? He took a large breath, set himself to placing the boys, armed with whatever they could find along the palisade. Aye, he could do that for her.

The marshlands were emptying, abandoned to the birds and the litter of corpses and wounded. The Artoriani were going to the south, fleeing for the narrow stretch of shallow ford across the river, horses and men bunching, desperate to reach safety. Hueil's army was closing, their screams of rabid triumph drowning the cries of the gulls. At least they had passed by the camp, drawing the mob away. But they would be back when the killing at the river's crossing was ended.

It was just visible, that crossing, just. Gwenhwyfar paused, isolating her panic, to watch the inevitable ending, her brows drawing into a depression of concentration, of quick, rapid thinking. Gwenhwyfar knew the tactics of war as well as any officer, probably better than some, for she had the unique privilege of an insight into the thoughts and ideas of a war-lord gifted in the achievement of fighting. She had shared Arthur's dreams, his plans, victories and losses. Gwenhwyfar alone knew what lay behind the austere blank expression that Arthur wore as a mask. Her sudden smile startled Ider who had come up beside her, intending to offer comfort. She spun around, clapping her hands, realised he was there, flung her arms about him, kissed him, a resounding smack on his lips, was whirling away, laughing.

Astonished, Ider looked to where she had been watching, shook his head. Some madness of grief? She laughed louder at his intense puzzlement, pointed to the ford, spelling out for him what was happening.

'See? There's Onager, to the left, a way from the banner, I'd recognise that brute even from several miles distant.' Pointed to the right. 'And there's Meriaun, his flaxen-maned chestnut is as distinctive as Onager. They are not withdrawing, Ider! They are luring Hueil into a trap. See,' she swept her hand to the far side of the river, 'they are not crossing the river!'

Ider studied the spread of land. Saw indeed, that the Artoriani were drawing into ranks, lining along the banks to this side of the river. Hueil's men were plunging forward, unaware, expecting to finish the massacre while their enemy struggled to cross the narrow confine of the fording place. 'Jesu's love!' he exclaimed, 'Ambrosius has taken a wider track west – has come behind Hueil's men, the Northern bastards are trapped, they'll be slaughtered like pigs come the autumn feast!' And then he yelled a screech of battle triumph, taking Gwenhwyfar's hands and dancing her round, the both of them laughing, wide-mouthed, victorious, hugging and kissing.

Llacheu's shout of alarm broke the euphoria. He lifted his sword, indicated the knot of men heading up the rise direct for them, led by a horse whose rider carried a banner that cracked and belched in the wind of their passing. The raven banner, and behind it a woman whose gold-sun hair tossed and streamed, whose mouth was open screaming encouragement.

'Get to the horses,' Gwenhwyfar bellowed at her Turma of personal guards, running herself for her saddled stallion, Ider fast at her side. 'You,' she pointed towards a group of bewildered women, 'open enough of the gate to let us out – replace it as soon as we are through.' She swung around to others. 'For the rest, you must look to your own defence.'

The fear that had already been skittering through the camp, wreaking its stagnant breath, had staggered a moment with the swift charge of hope, flung itself back in all its triumph now that actual horror was rapidly approaching. One woman lunged forward, her face contorted, a weeping girl-child clinging to her ragged skirt. 'We do not know how to fight!'

Gwenhwyfar shook herself free of the clawing fingers. 'Every woman knows how to fight. You have your own weapons, your nails and teeth and knees and feet. Use what you have if you cannot use a billet of wood or the flat of a spade.'

Taking up a light war spear and mounting her horse, she swung towards the gate, where women and some of the boys were hauling down the hastily erected barricades. Llacheu was suddenly beside her, mounted on the horse his father had given him. He stared hard at his mother, challenging her to send him back. Her heart, the mothering part of her, had the words on her lips, *Stay!* The warrior part, that recess of her that had come down through the women of the tribe, the spirits of the past who had fought and died alongside their men, parried her natural fears, took them square on the boss of the shield and thrust them aside.

The word stay came, but not as Llacheu had expected. 'Stay with Ider. Whatever happens, Llacheu, stay near Ider.' Smiling her pride at him, Gwenhwyfar handed her son the spear she carried, drew for herself, her sword, a lighter weapon than a man's, more suited to a woman's hand, but none the less, as deadly. And they were cantering for the gateway, not yet quite cleared, jumping their horses over the last of the logs and branches, turning sharp on landing, heading down the rise of ground. A turma of Artoriani, galloping to meet the hurl of Northmen who thought they had the victory of battle safe on their backs.

Thirty men, one woman and a boy against eighty, a hundred? Eighty or so men who had eagerly anticipated the reward of first pickings, who had believed the words of the witch-woman riding among them – that there would be plenty of value to be found in Arthur's camp. Men who floundered to a ragged halt as horses thundered down from the palisade fence ahead, necks stretched, teeth bared, their riders screaming the war-cry of the Pendragon. Men who would rather have turned tail to flee, but found they had no choice but to fight. Forgotten, their hope of finding women, riches and food. And as enemy spears thudded into shield or flesh, and hooves trampled their fallen, forgot also, Morgause, the woman who had encouraged them here.

She found herself alone, no shield, sword or spear to protect her. Alarmed, she drew her horse aside to a distance of safety, the idiot animal was excited at the sounds and smells. Snorting and prancing it refused to stand still, tried to turn and bolt. Sawing at its mouth to keep it under control, Morgause watched with fascinated horor the ferocity of this counter-attack. Her breath quickened, eyes and mouth widened, enjoying this gluttony of blood-spilling, this exciting, macabre dance of kill or be killed.

They were so few, Gwenhwyfar and her small army of Arthur's men, but desperation and experience leant them strength – and these Northern whelps were frightened, unwilling to fight. Only a few of her men were down after the first rush, fallen among the many of the enemy. Her sword blade was bloodied, her horse lathered and panting from the burst of exertion, she hauled the stallion around, ready to kill again, chanced a quick glance towards where Ider rode beside her son, felt the swell of pride as the boy cast his spear, begin,

537

almost in the same movement, to draw his sword. But her smile faltered, draining to a silent scream as she saw Llacheu pitch from his horse, the bay gushing blood as its body buckled, a spear thrust deep into its chest. Ider was leaping from his own horse, was running to help the boy, who was falling, tumbling arms flailing, as the dying horse slithered a few yards on its knees, its rear hooves scrabbling for a foothold. Llacheu sprawled, unprotected, undefended, on the ground tried to move, twist away as an axe, double-bladed and red-stained, came scything downward. He saw only the Northman's muddied boots standing over him, heard Ider's sobbing shout, and the man's grunt of effort with the death-song of the blade . . . felt, extraordinarily, very little. Kill or be killed. That was always how it had been.

A raw, naked, mother's scream, high and long and never-ending, cut through the air, echoed by another exultant, high pitched laugh, a cackling of triumph.

She was no fighting woman, Morgause, she persuaded others to do the killing for her. Her talents lay with malevolent plotting and scheming, the deliberate twisting of a mind to do her will, her satisfaction swelling with the gaining of each achievement. '*I will see your sons dead, Pendragon!*' Morgause threw back her head and laughed. An idle boast, hurled as an anger-bound curse that she had held small hope of fulfilling. Her laugh shrilled across the noise of fighting, her eyes raised to the grey skies as she gloried in her unexpected success, failed to see the woman with unbound, copper-coloured hair riding with grief-snarled fury from the mêlée of fighting.

Morgause's delight faltered as she saw the sword, held firm in a grasp between both hands, saw that other woman's anger-distorted, tear-streamed face; even saw the honed perfection of that gleaming blade as it swung into its arc of death. Thought, incongruously, before it spat through her neck, that Gwenhwyfar was more beautiful than she had realised.

Gwenhwyfar's horse, guided by leg-aids alone, as were all Arthur's war horses during battle, thundered past, ears flattened back, breath hot. Morgause's animal, the cruel hold on its mouth suddenly gone,

538

reared and bolted as the spatter of blood cascaded down its shoulders. And a woman's head bounced and rolled, leaving a crazy, bloodied trail across the spring-green hill grass.

On the marshes, the birds returned. The waders and the geese, settling to the salt-tanged, wind whispering grass, waiting patient for the tide to turn and expose the mud flats and sand bars. With them, the ravens came, circling and fluttering, to begin their gruesome feeding.

A curlew stalked ponderously from the tall reed-grass, then took sudden flight out over the flooding, returning water. Its wild cry, broken voiced, and so unbearably sad.

§ JUNE

Some evenings, the sunsets were beautiful. The western skies blazed
with a glory of red and gold that burst in brilliance against the clear,
purple blueness of the fading day. Gwenhwyfar stood, with Arthur
behind her, watching the yellow-gold turn to a vivid, burning red of
blazing spendour. Caer Cadan was home, was peace. Arthur
threaded his arms about her waist stood companionably, sharing this
celebration of nature with her, his cheek resting on her soft hair.
The summer air smelt of flowers and ripening corn, sun-warmed
earth, and a lazy welcome of the cool night that was to come at the
end of this day's heat.

A screech of swifts tumbled by, one bird skimming almost above
Arthur's head as it darted and twisted. He heard the swish of its
passing wings, felt the faint waft of moved air. Laughed at its
wondrous performance.

'It's strange,' Gwenhwyfar said. 'I don't mind so much, not now.'

For Arthur, there was a moment of disorientated confusion as he
tried to understand to what she was referring. He gave up, asked
with a bewildered shake of his head, a slight frown, 'What don't you
mind?'

In her turn, Gwenhwyfar did not answer immediate, instead, she
nestled herself closer into him, pulling his arms tighter, protectively
around the swelling of the child growing within her. 'Llacheu,
Gwydre and Amr. Almost,' she took a breath, scalding back the
tears, 'almost, I feel relieved. For the thing that had to happen has
been done. For them, I have no more need to fear.' *Except for you,*
she thought, *except I still fear for you, the one I love, even more than my
dead sons and this coming child.* She twisted her head around, smiled
up at him, a man strong, confident. Not easy, to think that Arthur
would one day also be gone. One day. The future, tomorrow.

The sun, a huge red ball, sank behind a bank of dark night clouds, the golden rays shooting from behind like spear shafts marking the way to eternity. Who knew what the rising of tomorrow would bring? Laughter, pain, sorrow or happiness? Life and death. The way of the world as it was, as it is, as it will be.

Gwenhwyfar cupped Arthur's face in her hand and kissed him, then laughed, and pulled away. It was time for gathering in the King's Hall, the smell of cooking meat was becoming richer, reaching her hungry stomach. Taking his arm, threading hers through his, she walked with him up the slight rise towards the open Hall doors, glanced as they passed, at the banner fluttering occasionally as the wind caught at the cloth. It was not so white as it had once been, when first she had taken it from the loom. The Pendragon's banner was becoming ragged at the edges, and a dried, brown stain of blood spilt between the raised claws of the Dragon. Yet, for all its spoiling, it was still something good and proud and beautiful.

Gwenhwyfar smiled up at Arthur, who, with his other hand, took hers and squeezed her fingers as they walked towards the evening noise and bustle of the Caer's busy Hall. Life too, became grimed at the edges and stained, and was sometimes torn beyond repair. In the old days, before the coming of the Christ God, people believed that the pattern of things was created by three goddesses, whose task it was to weave the thread of fate on the loom of life.

Gwenhwyfar hoped this child she carried would be born a girl. She could not watch another son grow towards his death. And Arthur too, though he said nothing, had prayed silently to whatever God was listening, that he should have next, a daughter. For there were already two other sons who would one day be waiting with sword and shield to fight for what could be theirs. At least some of the fears were gone: Morgause and her boasted curse. Arthur had feared her, but what was she now? A mouldering corpse, left for the ravens and the wind and the rain. For Arthur, there was now only Morgaine and Winifred, and Gwenhwyfar. One, with her infant son Medraut, he had almost loved; one, with the boy Cerdic, he had never loved, and the other? He squeezed Gwenhwyfar's hand. Gwenhwyfar. Whatever great fears and hopes lay ahead for tomorrow and tomorrow, Gwenhwyfar, he would always love. Beyond that, only the Goddesses, the Three would know what patterns were to be woven upon the great loom of life for child, mother, and king.

Author's Note

Arthur Pendragon, to those people who study him, is a very personal and passionately viewed character. We all have our own ideas, insist ours is the correct one, and argue like mad with anyone who disagrees! I have tried, to the best of my ability, to be as accurate as possible over background details, but the why, when, how and where of Arthur himself is individual. I am not expecting anyone necessarily to agree with my telling, but then, this is only an imaginative story. A new retelling of an old, familiar tale.

Arthur, the chivalric king of the Medieval story, is not the same Arthur who appears in some of the tales that we have of him. In these, we hear of his anger at a woman who was trying to seduce one of his men, and the consequent attack on her; he is often portrayed as someone who steals from the Church. Almost, it seems, this Arthur was condemned by the Christian priests, not revered as the man who, in the stories of five hundred or so years later, initiates the finding of the Holy Grail and who carried the portrait of the Virgin on his shoulder or shield. For that particular episode, I am satisfied that my explanation is reasonable. There are many instances of the old, pagan beliefs becoming intertwined with the new, embryonic Christianity. The Mother Goddess most certainly metamorphosised into the Virgin Mary.

The people of the Middle Ages created Arthur in their own image, dressed him in Medieval armour, set him in a turreted castle and made him fight for the holy cause. This was the age of the crusades and knights in armour, and when women were regarded as little more than chattels and the bearers of sons. I do not see my Arthur or Gwenhwyfar in this setting. Arthur is a soldier, a strong dedicated leader. Gwenhwyfar is no subservient, blushing maiden. There is no Lancelot for her in my stories; she remains loyal to her Lord.

545

Hueil is fact – stories tell of a feud with Arthur. Those of Ider relate how the young man sets out to prove himself by slaying the three giants of Brent Knoll; in some stories he kills the giants but dies himself, in others, he survives. My version is a deviation, but is based on these early tales. Arthur's jealousy against Ider is also part of that old telling, as are the episodes of the bear in Gwenhwyfar's tent and Arthur questioning her about whom she would marry after his death.

Amlawdd was probably a factual character, but through the passing of time we have lost his real identity. I have used his name and existence to fit with my story but admit my usage may not be accurate. So very little of this long-past, dark age of our history is known to us as fact. A novelist's dream, for we have a free rein of imaginative invention!

Legend has it that the King's and Queen's Crags near Hadrian's Wall are so called because Arthur and Gwenhwyfar quarrelled there – even the throwing of the comb is part of that story. Apparently, you can see the mark on a rock where it fell! There are so many hills and stones named after Arthur, and I have used those few that seemed appropriate, those that tied in with my ideas.

Vercovicium is only a suggested name for Houseteads, we do not know its definite Roman name, and I confess that *Winifred Castre* for Winchester is total fabrication on my part – my only defence is that there is no agreed explanation for this city's name! *Caer Cadan* is also my own. I needed something to reflect the Camelot of legend with the actual hill fort of Cadbury Castle, Somerset. Strictly speaking the 'c' of Cadan should, in today's Welsh, mutate to a 'g' (Gadan). However, I have been advised that mutations did not influence the language until well after Arthur's time, and I therefore ask Welsh-speaking readers to forgive my liberty with their language. The building of the Valle Crucis Abbey come a long time after my story – but who knows what stood there first!

The Wandsdyke was built after the Romans but before the Saxons, as a defence from the North. The English did not know of it before they conquered this area, hence its name, 'Woden's dyke'. It seems strange that if it was built to keep the Saxons out, why did they not know of it? The answer can only be because it was built *long* before they were in that area, and must therefore have been erected by British against British. It has often been attributed to Ambrosius, but as there is no proof of this, I have given its building to Arthur.

The Medieval Norman stories – created when only the first-born, legitimate male inherited – make much of Arthur having no son. Earlier references contradict this. Nennius writing his *Historia Brittonum* in the ninth century, mentions Amr who was 'slain by his father, Arthur the soldier' and who was buried beneath the ancient stones in what is now Hereford. Llacheu, Arthur's son, was killed in battle and in the *Mabinogion*, we find the story of Gwydre, son of Arthur, killed by the boar Twrch Trwyth. . . .

Nennius is also a source of Arthur's battles. He describes twelve, the locations of which are heatedly debated. My conclusions are a general hotchpotch of theory and guesswork. For those who know about Arthur, and are asking. 'But what about the battle of Badon?' you will have to wait for Book Three.

The distances and speed of Arthur's horses are not far fetched. It is quite possible to average thirty or forty (modern) miles a day without overtaxing horses if they have adequate feeding, a moderated pace and the occasional day's rest. In 207 BC the Consul Nero covered three hundred miles in a seven-day forced march with no ill effect, save the horses lost weight.

The story of Gwenhwyfar's offer to be shared between Arthur and Amlawdd is borrowed from a most ancient tale. Correctly, the other man involved should have been Melwas, who appeared briefly in *The Kingmaking*, but Gwenhwyfar's trickery did not fit neatly into that particular story and so I have used it against Amlawdd in this. The same story is also credited to *Tristan and Isolde*. Perhaps those early Tellers of Tales felt justified in re-using a good plot to fit their heroine's needs. I feel equally justified in blatantly borrowing it for myself!